ALFRED HITCHCOCK'S
MYSTERY MAGAZINE PRESENTS
FIFTY YEARS OF
CRIME AND SUSPENSE

■

ALFRED HITCHCOCK'S
MYSTERY MAGAZINE PRESENTS

FIFTY YEARS
OF CRIME
AND
SUSPENSE

EDITED BY LINDA LANDRIGAN

PEGASUS BOOKS
NEW YORK

Alfred Hitchcock's Mystery Magazine Presents
Fifty Years of Crime and Suspense

Pegasus Books LLC
45 Wall Street, Suite 1021
New York, NY 10005

First Pegasus Books edition 2006

ISBN: 1-933648-03-1

Printed in the United States of America
Distributed by Consortium

CONTENTS

ACKNOWLEDGMENTS

Grateful acknowledgment is made to the following for their permission to use their copyrighted material. Every reasonable effort has been made to trace the ownership of all copyrighted material included in this volume. Any errors which may have occurred are inadvertent and will be corrected in subsequent editions, provided proper notification is sent to the publisher.

All stories previously appeared in *Alfred Hitchcock's Mystery Magazine*.

"Final Rites" by Doug Allyn, copyright © 1985 by Davis Publications, Inc., reprinted by permission of the author; "Making A Killing With Mama Cass" by William Bankier, copyright © 1980 by Davis Publications, Inc., reprinted by permission of Curtis Brown, Ltd; "A Candle for the Bag Lady" by Lawrence Block, copyright © 1977 by Davis Publications, Inc., reprinted by permission of the author; "Voodoo" by Rhys Bowen, copyright © 2004 by Rhys Bowen, reprinted by permission of the Jane Rotrosen Agency; "Historical Errors" by William Brittain, copyright © 1976 by H.S.D. Publications, Inc., reprinted by permission of the author; "The Muse" by Jan Burke, copyright © 1995 by Jan Burke, reprinted by permission of the author; "Sinkhole" by Carol Cail, copyright © 1995 by Carol Cail, reprinted by permission of the author; "Priests" by George Chesbro, copyright © 1991 by Davis Publications, Inc., reprinted by permission of the author; "The Cost of Kent Castwell" by Avram Davidson, copyright © 1961 by Grania Davis, proprietor, Avram Davidson Estate; "Saturday Night at the Mikado Massage" by Loren D. Estleman, copyright © 1996 by Loren D. Estleman, reprinted by permission of the author; "Lord of Obstacles" by Gregory Fallis, copyright © 1996 by Gregory

Fallis, reprinted by permission of the author; "**The Long Way Down**" by Edward D. Hoch copyright © 1965 by H.S.D. Publications, Inc., reprinted by permission of the author; "**Erie's Last Day**" by Steve Hockensmith, copyright © 2000 by Steve Hockensmith, reprinted by permission of the author; "**Recipe for Murder**" by James Holding, Jr., copyright © 1973 by H.S.D. Publications, Inc., reprinted by permission of Barry N. Malzberg; "**Hawks**" by Connie Holt, copyright © 1989 by Davis Publications, Inc., reprinted by permission of the author; "**Not a Laughing Matter**" by Evan Hunter, copyright © 1958 by H.S.D. Publications, Inc., reprinted by permission of Gelfman Schneider Literary Agents; "**My Brother's Wife**" by Rob Kantner, copyright © 1985 by Davis Publications, Inc., © renewed 1989, reprinted by permission of the author; "**The 'Method' Sheriff**" by Ed Lacy, copyright © 1967 by H.S.D. Publications, Inc; "**Tabloid Press**" by Janice Law, copyright © 1999 by Janice Law, reprinted by permission of the author; "**Pusan Nights**" by Martin Limón, copyright © 1991 by Davis Publications, Inc., reprinted by permission of the author; "**Leaving Nairobi**" by Ed McBain, copyright © 2003 by Evan Hunter, reprinted by permission of Gelfman Schneider Literary Agents; "**The Takamoku Joseki**" by Sara Paretsky, copyright © 1984 by Davis Publications, Inc., © renewed 1996, reprinted by permission of Dominick Abel Literary Agency, Inc; "**The O–Bon Cat**" by I. J. Parker, copyright © 2002 by I. J. Parker, reprinted by permission of the author; "**New Neighbor**" by Talmage Powell, copyright © 1975 by H.S.D. Publications, Inc., reprinted by permission of Barry N. Malzberg; "**Death of a Nobody**" by Bill Pronzini, copyright © 1970 by H.S.D. Publications, Inc., reprinted by permission of the author; "**#8**" by Jack Ritchie, copyright © 1958 by H.S.D. Publications, Inc., reprinted by permission of The Sternig & Byrne Literary Agency; "**Body English**" by S. J. Rozan, copyright © 1992 by S. J. Rozan, reprinted by permission of The Axelrod Agency, Inc; "**Unbearable Temptations**" by Jeffry Scott, copyright © 1990 by Davis Publications, Inc., reprinted by permission of the author; "**The Day of the Execution**" by Henry Slesar, copyright © 1957 by H.S.D. Publications, Inc., reprinted by permission of the author's estate; "**The Frightening Frammis**" by Jim Thompson, copyright © 1957 by H.S.D. Publications, Inc., © renewed 1984,

Fallis, reprinted by permission of the author; **"The Long Way Down"** by Edward D. Hoch copyright © 1965 by H.S.D. Publications, Inc., reprinted by permission of the author; **"Erie's Last Day"** by Steve Hockensmith, copyright © 2000 by Steve Hockensmith, reprinted by permission of the author; **"Recipe for Murder"** by James Holding, Jr., copyright © 1973 by H.S.D. Publications, Inc., reprinted by permission of Barry N. Malzberg; **"Hawks"** by Connie Holt, copyright © 1989 by Davis Publications, Inc., reprinted by permission of the author; **"Not a Laughing Matter"** by Evan Hunter, copyright © 1958 by H.S.D. Publications, Inc., reprinted by permission of Gelfman Schneider Literary Agents; **"My Brother's Wife"** by Rob Kantner, copyright © 1985 by Davis Publications, Inc., © renewed 1989, reprinted by permission of the author; **"The 'Method' Sheriff"** by Ed Lacy, copyright © 1967 by H.S.D. Publications, Inc; **"Tabloid Press"** by Janice Law, copyright © 1999 by Janice Law, reprinted by permission of the author; **"Pusan Nights"** by Martin Limón, copyright © 1991 by Davis Publications, Inc., reprinted by permission of the author; **"Leaving Nairobi"** by Ed McBain, copyright © 2003 by Evan Hunter, reprinted by permission of Gelfman Schneider Literary Agents; **"The Takamoku Joseki"** by Sara Paretsky, copyright © 1984 by Davis Publications, Inc., © renewed 1996, reprinted by permission of Dominick Abel Literary Agency, Inc; **"The O–Bon Cat"** by I. J. Parker, copyright © 2002 by I. J. Parker, reprinted by permission of the author; **"New Neighbor"** by Talmage Powell, copyright © 1975 by H.S.D. Publications, Inc., reprinted by permission of Barry N. Malzberg; **"Death of a Nobody"** by Bill Pronzini, copyright © 1970 by H.S.D. Publications, Inc., reprinted by permission of the author; **"#8"** by Jack Ritchie, copyright © 1958 by H.S.D. Publications, Inc., reprinted by permission of The Sternig & Byrne Literary Agency; **"Body English"** by S. J. Rozan, copyright © 1992 by S. J. Rozan, reprinted by permission of The Axelrod Agency, Inc; **"Unbearable Temptations"** by Jeffry Scott, copyright © 1990 by Davis Publications, Inc., reprinted by permission of the author; **"The Day of the Execution"** by Henry Slesar, copyright © 1957 by H.S.D. Publications, Inc., reprinted by permission of the author's estate; **"The Frightening Frammis"** by Jim Thompson, copyright © 1957 by H.S.D. Publications, Inc., © renewed 1984,

CONTENTS

ACKNOWLEDGMENTS

Grateful acknowledgment is made to the following for their permission to use their copyrighted material. Every reasonable effort has been made to trace the ownership of all copyrighted material included in this volume. Any errors which may have occurred are inadvertent and will be corrected in subsequent editions, provided proper notification is sent to the publisher.

All stories previously appeared in *Alfred Hitchcock's Mystery Magazine*.

"Final Rites" by Doug Allyn, copyright © 1985 by Davis Publications, Inc., reprinted by permission of the author; "Making A Killing With Mama Cass" by William Bankier, copyright © 1980 by Davis Publications, Inc., reprinted by permission of Curtis Brown, Ltd; "A Candle for the Bag Lady" by Lawrence Block, copyright © 1977 by Davis Publications, Inc., reprinted by permission of the author; "Voodoo" by Rhys Bowen, copyright © 2004 by Rhys Bowen, reprinted by permission of the Jane Rotrosen Agency; "Historical Errors" by William Brittain, copyright © 1976 by H.S.D. Publications, Inc., reprinted by permission of the author; "The Muse" by Jan Burke, copyright © 1995 by Jan Burke, reprinted by permission of the author; "Sinkhole" by Carol Cail, copyright © 1995 by Carol reprinted by permission of the author; "Priests" by George Chesbro, copyright © 1991 by Davis Publications, Inc., reprinted by permission of the author; "The Cost of Kent Castwell" by Avram Davidson, copyright © 1961 by Grania Davis, property of Avram Davidson Estate; "Saturday Night at the Mikado Massage" by Loren D. Estleman, copyright © 1996 by Loren D. Estleman, reprinted by permission of the author; "Lord of Obstacles" by Gregory Fallis, copyright © 1996 by reprinted by permission of Richard Curtis Associates; "**Black Spartacus**" by James Lincoln Warren, copyright © 1999 by James Lincoln Warren, reprinted by permission of the author; "**The Search for Olga Bateau**" by Stephen Wasylyk, copyright © 1987 by Davis Publications, Inc., reprinted by permission of the author's estate; "**Good Night! Good Night!**" By Donald E. Westlake, copyright © renewed 1988 by Davis Publications, Inc., reprinted by permission of the author; "**A Genuine Alectryomancer**" by Charles Willeford, copyright © 1959 by H.S.D. Publications, Inc., reprinted by permission of JET Literary Associates, Inc.

INTRODUCTION

Fifty years is a lot of stories.

When I first started to think about assembling an anthology to commemorate the fiftieth anniversary of *Alfred Hitchcock's Mystery Magazine,* I looked across my desk at the wall that holds all the issues of the magazine since December 1956 and thought, *Oh, brother.* I decided to get some help in determining which stories represented the best of the magazine's illustrious history.

I appealed to our readers in a notice in the magazine, asking them to write in and tell us their favorite stories. The response was wonderful. Some correspondents named a single story that had lingered in their minds for years. Some named a favorite author ("Anything by Stephen Wasylyk"). Others sent us on a series of treasure hunts with the words, "I don't remember the title or author, but . . ." Often these correspondents could describe a story in such detail that we were actually able to identify it.

These letters were yet further proof to us that *AHMM* is blessed with faithful readers who have continued to subscribe to the magazine for years, or even generations; in many ways they feel the magazine "belongs" to them. The letters also reminded us of the power of the short story. These stories may have been published in a small monthly magazine, but they are much more than ephemeral entertainment. Their plots and characters, their ironies and emotional impact possess an enduring resonance. They stay with us for years, often long after the issue of the magazine has disappeared.

There is no doubt the early popularity of the magazine was aided by its clear association with Alfred Hitchcock. The magazine was founded in the mid-fifties by Richard E. Decker and H.S.D.

Publications, at the time, the publishers of *Manhunt*. They made the agreement with the famous director to lend his name to the magazine.

Soon the producers of the popular half-hour television program *Alfred Hitchcock Presents* (1955–61) were mining the young magazine for published stories that they could turn into teleplays. Borden Deal's "A Bottle of Wine," from the very first issue of *AHMM*, was quickly selected for the show. Subsequently, stories by *AHMM* authors Henry Slesar, Talmage Powell, James Holding, Jack Ritchie, Ed Lacy, and Robert Bloch, to name a few, were turned into teleplays and filmed for *Alfred Hitchcock Presents* or its later incarnation, *The Alfred Hitchcock Hour* (1962–65).

Since the early days, the magazine has welcomed both seasoned pros as well as young writers still carving a niche for themselves in the mystery world. During the 1960s, *AHMM* published early stories by writers who today are Grand Masters of the field, including Donald E. Westlake and Hillary Waugh.

In 1975 *Alfred Hitchcock's Mystery Magazine* was purchased by Davis Publications, which also published *Ellery Queen's Mystery Magazine*. While other fiction digests were disappearing, *AHMM* became even more solidly established in the seventies under the stewardship of editor Eleanor Sullivan, who regularly published such talented writers as Lawrence Block and Bill Pronzini.

Cathleen Jordan came on board as editor in 1981 and quickly broadened the magazine's appeal to reach thousands of short story readers across the country. She also continued *AHMM*'s tradition of being receptive to unpublished or unknown writers. Doug Allyn, Rob Kantner, Martin Limón, and I. J. Parker are a handful of the many writers who got their start in the pages of *AHMM*.

With the help of our readers, I have chosen a representative sampling of *AHMM* stories from the past five decades. They are all engaging, finely crafted stories, and they exemplify the range and variety *AHMM* has offered over the years. Whether you are coming to them for the first time or reading them again, you can be assured of entertainment. If you are a student of writing, the stories are worth studying for their craftsmanship. As a collection, the stories show the stylistic evolution of the popular short story. In this collection you will find writers you recognize and writers that deserve more attention.

Even though fifty years may not seem like that much time, American culture has evolved in ways both subtle and dramatic, and those shifts are reflected in the stories. The Civil Rights movement, the sexual revolution and women's rights, the Vietnam war, the fall of the Berlin Wall, and the increasingly multicultural nature of our society are just some of the changes that inform these stories, giving them a relevance beyond their primary mandate, to entertain.

For their part in making this anthology come to fruition, I would like to thank Pegasus Books founder and editor, Claiborne Hancock; Dell Magazines marketing and subrights manager, Abby Browning; my assistants Nicole K. Sia and Jonas Eno-Van Fleet; and all of the readers who submitted their superb suggestions.

Linda Landrigan
April 2006, New York

JIM THOMPSON
THE FRIGHTENING FRAMMIS

February 1957

NOW RECOGNIZED as one of the great masters of noir, Jim
Thompson supported himself with a variety of jobs ranging from
oil worker and professional gambler to journalist. He published
twenty-six novels, including *The Killer Inside Me, After Dark, My
Sweet,* and *The Grifters.* Thompson appeared in the very first issue
of *AHMM,* and in that story he introduced hustler Mitch Allison,
who returns in this story as well.

■

For perhaps the hundredth time that day, Mitch Allison squared
his shoulders, wreathed his face with an engaging grin, and
swung his thumb in a gesture as old as hitchhiking. And for
perhaps the hundredth time his appeal was rudely ignored. The
oncoming car roared down on him and past him, wiping the
forced grin from his face with the nauseous blast of its
exhausts.

Mitch cursed it hideously as he continued walking, damning
the car's manufacturer, its owner, and finally, and most fulsomely,
himself.

"Just couldn't be satisfied, could you?" he grumbled bitterly.
"Sitting right up on top of the world, and it wasn't good enough

for you. Well, how do you like *this,* you stupid dull-witted moronic blankety-blank-blank!"

Mitch Allison was not the crying kind. He had grown up in a world where tears were more apt to inspire annoyance than sympathy, and a sob was likely to get you a punch in the throat. Still, he was very close to weeping now. If there had been any tears in him, he would have bawled with sheer shame and self-exasperation.

Less than a day ago, he had possessed almost twenty thousand dollars, the proceeds from robbing his wife, swindling the madam of a parlor house and pulling an intricate double double-cross on several "business" associates. Moreover, since it had been imperative for him to clear out of Los Angeles, his home town, he had had a deluxe stateroom on the eastbound Super Chief. Then . . .

Well, there was this elderly couple. Retired farmers, ostensibly, who had just sold their orange grove for a five-figure sum. So Mitch had tied into them, as the con man's saying is, suggesting a friendly little card game. What happened then was figuratively murder.

The nice old couple had taken him like Grant took Richmond. Their apparently palsied hands had made the cards perform in a manner which even Mitch, with all his years of suckering chumps, would have declared impossible. He couldn't believe his own eyes, his own senses. His twenty grand was gone and the supposed suckers were giving him the merry ha-ha in a matter of two hours.

Mitch had threatened to beat them into hamburger if they didn't return his dough. And that, of course, was a mistake, the compounding of one serious error with another. For the elderly couple—far more practiced in the con than he—had impeccable references and identification, while Mitch's were both scanty and lousy.

He couldn't establish legitimate ownership to twenty cents, let alone twenty grand. Certainly, he was in no position to explain how he had come by that twenty grand. His attempts to do so, when the old couple summoned the conductor, had led him into one palpable lie after another. In the end, he had had to jump the train, sans baggage and ceremony, to avoid arrest.

So now, here he was. Broke, disgusted, footsore, hungry, hitch-hiking his way back to Los Angeles, where he probably would get killed as soon as he was spotted. Even if no one else cared to murder him, his wife, Bette, would be itching to do so. Still, a guy had to go some place, didn't he? And having softened up Bette before, perhaps he could do it again. It was a chance—his only chance.

A hustling man needs a good front. Right now, Mitch looked like the king of the tramps.

Brushing the sweat from his eyes, he paused to stare at a sign attached to a roadside tree: *Los Angeles—125 Miles.* He looked past the sign, into the inviting shade of the trees beyond it. The ocean would be over there somewhere, not too far from the highway. If he could wash up a little, rinse out his shirt and underwear . . .

He sighed, shook his head, and walked on. It wasn't worth the trouble, he decided. It wasn't safe. The way his luck was running, he'd probably wade into a school of sharks.

In the distance, he heard another car approaching. Wearily, knowing he had to try, Mitch turned and swung his thumb.

It was a Cadillac, a big black convertible. As it began to slow down, Mitch had a feeling that no woman had ever given him such a going over and seemed to like so well what she saw as the one sitting next to the Cad's driver.

The car came on, slower and slower. It came even with him, and the woman asked, "How far to El Ciudad?"

"El Ciudad?—" the car was creeping past him; Mitch had to trot along at its side to answer the question. "You mean, the resort? About fifty miles, I think."

"I see." The woman stared at him searchingly. "Would you like a ride?" she asked.

"Would I!"

She winked at Mitch, spoke over her shoulder to the man behind the wheel. "All right, stupid. Stop. We're giving this guy a ride."

The man grunted a dispirited curse. The car stopped, then spurted forward savagely as Mitch clambered into the back seat.

"What a jerk!" The woman stared disgustedly at her companion. "Can't even give a guy a ride without trying to break his neck!"

"Dry up," the man said wearily. "Drop dead."

"So damned tight you squeak! If I'd only known what you were like before I married you!"

"Ditto. Double you in spades."

The woman took a pint of whiskey from the glove compartment, drank from it, and casually handed it back to Mitch. He took a long, thirsty drink and started to pass the bottle back. But she had turned away again, become engrossed in nagging at her husband.

Mitch was just a little embarrassed by the quarrel, but only a little. Mitch Allison was not a guy to be easily or seriously embarrassed. He took another drink, then another. Gratefully, he settled down into the deeply upholstered seat, listening disinterestedly to the woman's brittle voice and her husband's retorts.

"Jerk! Stingy! Selfish . . . ," she was saying.

"Aw, Babe, lay off, will you? It's our honeymoon, and I'm taking you to one of the nicest places in the country."

"Oh, sure! Taking me there during the off-season! Because you're just too cheap and jealous to live it up a little. Because you don't want anyone to see me!"

"Now, that isn't so, Babe. I just want to be alone with you, that's all."

"Well, I don't want to be alone with you! One week in a lifetime is enough for me . . ."

Mitch wondered what kind of chump he could be to take that sort of guff from a dame. In his own case, if Bette had ever talked that way to him—*pow!* She'd be spitting out teeth for the next year.

The woman's voice grew louder, sharper. The slump to her husband's shoulders became more pronounced. Incuriously, Mitch tried to determine what he looked like without those outsize sunglasses and the pulled-low motoring cap. But he didn't figure long. The guy straightened suddenly, swerved the car off into a grass-grown trail, and slammed on the brakes.

Mitch was almost thrown from the seat. The husband leapt from the car and went stomping off into the trees. She called after him angrily—profanely. Without turning, he disappeared from view.

The woman shrugged and looked humorously at Mitch. "Some fun, huh, mister? Guess I rode hubby a little too hard."

"Yeah," said Mitch. "Seems that you did."

"Well, he'll be back in a few minutes. Just has to sulk a little first."

She was red-haired, beautiful in a somewhat hard-faced way. But there was nothing hard-looking about her figure. She had the kind of shape a guy dreams about, but seldom sees.

Mitch's eyes lingered on her. She noticed his gaze.

"Like me, mister?" she said softly. "Like to stay with me?"

"Huh?" Mitch licked his lips. "Now, look, lady—"

"Like to have this car? Like to have half of fifty thousand dollars?"

Mitch always had been a fast guy on the uptake, but this babe was pitching right past him.

"Now, look," he repeated shakily. "I—I—"

"You look," she said. "Take a *good* look."

There was a briefcase on the front seat. She opened it and handed it back to Mitch. And Mitch looked. He reached inside, took out a handful of its contents.

The briefcase was filled, or at least half filled, with traveler's checks of one-hundred-dollar denominations. Filled, practically speaking, with one hundred dollar bills. They would have to be countersigned, of course, but that was—

"—a cinch," the woman said intently. "Look at the signature. No curlycues, no fancy stuff. All you have to do is sign the name, Martin Lonsdale—just sign it plain and simple—and we're in."

"But—" Mitch shook his head. "But I'm not—"

"But you could be Martin Lonsdale—you *could* be my husband. If you were dressed up, if you had his identification." Her voice faded at the look Mitch gave her, then resumed again, sulkily.

"Why not, anyway? I've got a few rights, haven't I? He promised me the world with a ring around it if I'd marry him, and now I can't get a nickel out of him. I can't even tap his wallet, because he keeps all of his dough out of my hands with tricks like this."

"Tough," said Mitch. "That's really tough, that is."

He returned the checks to the briefcase, snapped the lock on it, and tossed it back into the front seat. "How could I use his identification unless he was dead? Think he'd just go to sleep somewhere until I cashed the checks and made a getaway?"

The girl flounced around in the seat. Then she shrugged and got out. "Well," she said, "as long as that's the way you feel . . ."

"We'll get hubby, right?" Mitch also got out of the car. "Sure, we will—you and me together. We'll see that he gets back safe and sound, won't we?"

She whirled angrily and stomped off ahead of him. Grinning, Mitch followed her through the trees and underbrush. There was an enticing roll to her hips—a deliberately exaggerated roll. She drew her skirt up a little, on the pretext of quickening her stride, and her long perfectly shaped legs gleamed alluringly in the shade-dappled sunlight. Mitch admired the display dispassionately. Admired it, without being in the least tempted by it.

She was throwing everything she had at him, and what she had was plenty. And he, Mitch Allison, would be the first guy to admit that she had it. Still, she was a bum, a hundred and ten pounds of pure poison. Mitch grimaced distastefully. He wished she would back-talk him a little, give him some reason to put the slug on her, and he knew she was too smart to do it.

They emerged from the trees, came out on the face of a cliff overlooking the ocean. The man's trail clearly led here, but he was nowhere in sight. Mitch shot an inquiring glance at the girl. She shrugged, but her face had paled. Mitch stepped cautiously to the edge of the cliff and looked down.

Far below—a good one hundred feet at least—was the ocean, roiled, oily looking, surging thunderously with the great foam-flecked waves of the incoming tide. It was an almost straight up-and-down drop to the water. About halfway down, snagged on a bush that sprouted from the cliff face, was a man's motoring cap.

Mitch's stomach turned sickishly. Then he jumped and whirled as a wild scream rent the air.

It was the girl. She was kneeling, sobbing hysterically, at the base of a tree. Her husband's coat was there, suspended from a broken-off branch, and she was holding a slip of paper in her hands.

"I didn't mean it!" she wept. "I wouldn't have done it! I was just sore, and—"

Mitch told her curtly to shut up. He took the note from her and read it, his lips pursed with a mixture of disdain and regret.

It was too bad, certainly. Death was always regrettable, whether brought on by one's own hand or another's. Still, a guy who would end his life over a dame like this one—well, the world hadn't lost much by the action and neither had he.

Mitch wadded the note and tossed it over the cliff. He frisked the coat and tossed it after the note. Then, briskly, he examined the wallet and personal papers of the late Martin Lonsdale.

There was a telegram, confirming reservations at El Ciudad hotel and Country Club. There was a registration certificate—proof of ownership—on the Cadillac. There was a driver's license and a photostat of Martin Lonsdale's discharge from the army. Mitch examined the last two items with particular care.

Brown hair, gray eyes—yep, that was all right; that matched the description of his own eyes and hair. Weight one hundred and eighty—right on the nose again. Complexion fair—okay, also. Height six feet one inch . . .

Mitch frowned slightly. Lonsdale hadn't looked to be over five eight or nine, so—So? So nothing. Lonsdale's shoulders had been slumped; he, Mitch, had only seen the man on his feet for a few seconds. At any rate, the height on the papers matched his own and that was all that mattered.

The girl was still on her knees, weeping. Mitch told her to knock it off, for God's sake, and when she persisted he kicked her lightly in the stomach. That stopped the tears, but it pulled the stopper on some of the dirtiest language he had ever heard.

Mitch listened to it for a moment, then gave her a stinging slap on the jaw. "You've just passed the first plateau," he advised her pleasantly. "From now on, you won't get less than a handful of knuckles. Like to try for it, or will you settle for what you have?"

"You dirty, lousy, two-bit tinhorn." She glared at him, "I just lost my husband, and—"

"Which was just what you wanted," Mitch nodded, "so cut the fake sob stuff. You wanted him dead. Okay, you got your wish, and with no help from me. So now let's see if we can't do a little business together."

"Why the hell should I do business with you? I'm his widow. I've got a legal claim on the car and dough."

"Uh-huh," Mitch nodded judiciously. "And maybe you can collect, too, if you care to wait long enough—and if there aren't any other claims against the estate. And if, of course, you're still alive."

"Alive? What do you—?"

"I mean you might be executed. For murder, you know. A certain tall and handsome young man might tell the cops you pushed Martin off of that cliff."

He grinned at her. The girl's eyes blazed, then dulled in surrender.

"All right," she mumbled. "All right. But do you have to be so—so nasty, so cold-blooded? Can't you act like—uh—"

Mitch hesitated. He had less than no use for her, and it was difficult to conceal the fact. Still, when you had to do business with a person, it was best to maintain the appearance of friendliness.

"We'll get along all right, Babe." He smiled boyishly, giving her a wink. "This El Ciudad place. Is Martin known there?"

"He was never even in California before."

"Swell. That strengthens my identification. Gives us a high-class base of operations while we're cashing the checks. There's one more thing, though"—Mitch looked down at the telegram. "This only confirms a reservation for Martin Lonsdale."

"Well? It wouldn't necessarily have to mention his wife, would it? They have plenty of room at this time of the year."

Mitch nodded. "Now, about the clothes. Maybe I'm wrong, but Marty looked quite a bit smaller than—"

"They'll fit you," the girl said firmly. "Marty bought his clothes a little large. Thought they wore longer that way, you know."

She proved to be right. Except for his shoes, the dead man's clothes fitted Mitch perfectly.

Mitch retained only his own shoes and socks and threw his other clothes into the ocean. Redressed in clean underwear, an expensive white shirt and tie, and a conservative-looking blue serge suit, he climbed behind the wheel of the car. The girl, Babe, snuggled close to him. He backed out onto the highway and headed for El Ciudad.

"Mmmm . . ." Babe laid her head against his shoulder. "This is nice, isn't it, honey? And it's going to be a lot nicer, isn't it, when we get to the hotel?"

She shivered deliciously. Mitch suppressed a shudder.

"We'll cash the checks," she murmured, "and split the dough. And we'll sell the car, and split on that. We'll divide everything, even-stephen, won't we, honey? . . . Well, won't we?"

"Oh, sure. Naturally," Mitch said hastily. "You just bet we will!"

And he added silently: *Like hell!*

2.

EL CIUDAD IS just a few miles beyond the outer outskirts of Los Angeles. A truly magnificent establishment during the tourist season, it was now, in mid-summer, anything but. The great lawns were brown, tinder-dry. The long rows of palm trees were as unappetizing as banana stalks. The tennis courts were half hidden by weeds. Emptied of water, and drifted almost full of dried leaves and rubble, the swimming pool looked like some mammoth compost pit. The only spots of brightness were the red-and-white mailbox at the head of the driveway and a green telephone booth at the first tee of the golf course.

Briefly, the exterior of the place was a depressing mess, and inside it was even less prepossessing. The furniture was draped with dust covers. Painter's drop cloths, lumber, and sacks of plaster were strewn about the marble floor. Scaffolds reared toward the ceiling, and ladders were propped along the walls.

There was only a skeleton staff on duty; they were as dejected-looking as the establishment itself. The manager, also doubling as clerk, was unshaven and obviously suffering from a hang-over. He apologized curtly for the disarray, explaining that the workmen who were refurbishing the place had gone on strike.

"Not that it makes much difference," he added. "Of course, we regret the inconvenience to you"—he didn't appear to regret it—"but you're our only guests."

He cashed one of the hundred-dollar checks for Mitch, his fingers lingering hungrily over the money. A bellboy in a baggy uniform showed "Mr. and Mrs. Lonsdale" to their suite. It consisted of two rooms and a connecting bath. Mitch looked it over, dismissed the bellboy with a dollar tip, and dropped into a chair in front of the air-conditioning vent.

"You know," he told Babe, "I'm beginning to understand your irritation with Marty. If this is a sample of his behavior, going to a winter resort in the middle of summer—"

"A double-distilled jerk," Babe agreed. "Scared to death that someone might make a play for me."

"Mmm-hmm," Mitch frowned thoughtfully. "You're sure that was his only reason? No matter how scared he was of competition, this deal just doesn't seem to make sense."

"Well—" the girl hesitated. "Of course, he probably didn't know it would be this bad."

The kitchens and dining room of El Ciudad were not in operation, but the bellboy made and served them soggy sand-wiches and muddy coffee. He also supplied them with a bottle of whiskey at double the retail price. They had a few drinks and ate. Then, with another drink before him, Mitch sat down at the desk and began practicing the signature of Martin Lonsdale.

For the one check—the one cashed by the manager—he had done all right. There was only a hundred dollars involved, and the manager had no reason to suspect the signature. But it would be a different story tomorrow when he began hitting the banks. Then he would be cashing the checks in wholesale lots, cashing them with people whose business it was to be suspicious. His forgeries would have to be perfect, or else.

So he practiced and continued to practice, pausing occasionally to massage his hand or to exchange a word with the girl. When, finally, he achieved perfection, he started to work on the checks. Babe stopped him, immediately wary and alarmed.

"Why are you doing that? Aren't they supposed to be countersigned where they're cashed?"

Mitch shrugged. "Not necessarily. I can write my name in front of the person who does the cashing. Just establish, you know, that my signature is the same as the one on the checks."

"Yes, but why—"

"To save time, dammit! This is a forgery job, remember? We hold all the cards, but it *is* forgery. Which means we have to hit and get—cash in and disappear. Because sooner or later, there's going to be a rumble. Now, if you're afraid I'm going to lam out with these things—"

"Oh, now, of course I'm not, honey." But she stuck right with him until he had finished countersigning the checks. She was quite prepared, in fact, to spend the rest of the night. Mitch didn't want that. He shoved the checks back into the briefcase, locked it, and thrust it into her hands.

"Keep it," he said. "Put it under your pillow. And now get out of here so I can get some sleep."

He began to undress. The girl looked at him, poutingly.

"But, honey. I thought we were going to—uh—"

"We're both worn out," Mitch pointed out, "and there's another night coming."

He climbed into bed and turned on his side. Babe left, reluctantly. She took the briefcase with her, and she locked the connecting door on her side of the bathroom.

Mitch rolled over on his back. Wide-eyed, staring up into the darkness, he pondered the problem of giving Babe a well-deserved rooking. It was simple enough in a way—that is, the preliminary steps were simple enough. After—and *if*—he successfully cashed the checks tomorrow, he had only to catch her off guard and put her on ice for the night. Bind and gag her, and lock her up in one of the clothes closets. From that point on, however, he wasn't sure what to do. Or, rather, he knew what to do, but he didn't know how the hell he was going to do it.

He couldn't scram in the Cad. A wagon like that would leave a trail a blind man could follow. For similar reasons, he couldn't zoom away in a taxi—if, that is, it was possible to get taxi service this far from the city.

How was he going to do it, then? Equally important, where would he hide out if he was able to do it? For he would sure as hell have to hide out fast after this caper. Babe would squawk bloody murder. It wouldn't make her anything, but she'd sure squawk. Her body was soft and lush, but one look at that cast-iron mug of hers, and you knew she would.

So . . . ?

Mitch scowled in the darkness. Now, Bette, his wife, had a nondescript car. She could get him away from here, and she could hide him out indefinitely. She could—but it was preposterous to think that she would. Not after that last stunt he'd pulled on her.

Yes, he'd planned on pleading for forgiveness before his meeting with Martin and Babe Lonsdale. But the situation had been different then. There wasn't any fifty grand at stake. There wasn't the risk of a long prison stretch. If he appealed to Bette, he'd have to give her the full pitch on this deal. Which meant, naturally, that he'd be completely at her mercy. And if she wasn't feeling merciful, if he couldn't fast-talk her into giving him a break, well, that would be the end of the sleigh ride.

Enter the cops. Exit Mitch Allison and fifty grand.

I'm going to have to stop crooking everyone, Mitch thought. *From now on I'm going to be honest, with at least one person.*

He fell asleep on this pious thought. Almost immediately, it seemed, it was morning and Babe was shaking him awake.

They headed into Los Angeles, stopping at a roadside diner for breakfast. As they ate, Mitch consulted the classified telephone directory, organizing an itinerary for the day's operations. Because of the time factor, his targets—the banks—had to be in the same general area. On the other hand, they had to be separated by a discreet distance, lest he be spotted in going from one to another. Needless to say, it was also essential that he tackle only independent banks. The branch banks, with their central refer system, would nail a paper pusher on his second try.

Babe watched Mitch work, admiration in her eyes—and increasing caution. *Here is one sharp cookie,* she thought. As sharp as he was tough. A lot sharper than she'd ever be. Being the kind of dame she was, she'd contemplated throwing a curve to win. Now she knew that wouldn't do it; she'd have to put the blocks to him before he could do it to her.

She was lingering in the background when he approached the teller's cage at the first bank. She was never more than a few feet away from him throughout the day, one of the most nerve-wracking in Mitch Allison's career.

He began by pushing ten of the traveler's checks, a thousand bucks, at a time. A lead-pipe cinch was his appearance and identification. Usually a teller would do it on his own, or, if not, an executive's okay was a mere formality. Unfortunately, as Mitch soon realized, these thousand-dollar strikes couldn't get the job done. He was too short on time. He'd run out of banks before he ran out of checks. So he upped the ante to two grand, and finally to three, and things really tightened up.

Tellers automatically referred him to executives. The executives passed him up the line to their superiors. He was questioned, quizzed, studied narrowly. Again and again, his credentials were examined—the description on them checked off, item by item, with his own appearance. By ten minutes of three, when he disposed of the last check, his nerves were in knots.

He and Babe drove to a nearby bar, where he tossed down a few quick ones. Considerably calmer then, he headed the car toward El Ciudad.

"Look, honey," Babe turned suddenly in the seat and faced him. "Why are we going back to that joint, anyway? We've got the dough. Why not just dump this car for a price and beat it?"

"Just go off and leave our baggage? Start a lot of inquiries?" Mitch shook his head firmly.

"Well, no, I guess that wouldn't be so good, would it? But you said we ought to disappear fast. When are we going to do it?"

Mitch slanted a glance at her, deliberating over his reply. "I can get a guy here in LA to shoot me a come-quick telegram. It'll give us a legitimate excuse for pulling out tomorrow morning."

Babe nodded dubiously. She suggested that Mitch phone his friend now, instead of calling through El Ciudad's switchboard. Mitch said that he couldn't.

"The guy works late, see? He wouldn't be home yet. I'll call him from that phone booth out on the golf course. That'll keep anyone from listening in."

"I see," Babe repeated. "You think of everything, don't you, darling?"

They had dinner at a highway drive-in. Around dusk, Mitch brought the car to a stop on El Ciudad's parking lot. Babe reached hesitantly for the briefcase. Mitch told her to go right ahead and take it with her.

"Just don't forget, sweetheart. I can see both entrances to the joint, and I've got the keys to this buggy."

"Now, don't you worry one bit," Babe smiled at him brightly. "I'll be right inside waiting for you."

She headed for the hotel, waving to him gayly as she passed through the entrance. Mitch sauntered out to the phone booth and placed a call to Bette. Rather, since she hung up on him the first two times, he placed three calls.

At last she stayed on the wire and he was able to give her the pitch. The result was anything but reassuring. She said she'd be seeing him—she'd be out just as fast as she could make it. And he could depend on it. But there was an ominous quality to her voice, a distinctly unwifely tone. Before he could say anything more, she slammed the receiver for the third and last time.

Considerably disturbed, Mitch walked back across the dead and dying grass and entered the hotel. The manager-clerk's eyes shied away from him. The elevator-bellboy was similarly furtive. Absorbed in his worry over Bette, Mitch didn't notice. He got off at his floor and started down the hall, ducking around scaffolding, wending his way through a littered jungle of paint cans, plaster, and wallpaper.

He came to the door of his room. He turned the knob and entered.

And something crashed down on his head.

3.

IT WAS DARK when Mitch regained consciousness. He sat up, massaging his aching head, staring dizzily at the shattered glass on the floor—remains of a broken whiskey bottle. Then he remembered; realization came to him. Ripping out a curse, he ran to the window.

The Cad was still there on the parking lot. Yes, and the keys were still in his pocket. Mitch whirled, ran through the bath, and kicked open the door to the other room.

It was empty, in immaculate order, sans Babe and sans baggage. There was nothing to indicate that it ever had been tenanted. Mitch tottered back into his own room, and there was a knock on the door and he flung it open.

A man walked in and closed it behind him. He looked at Mitch. He looked down at the broken bottle. He shook his head in mild disapproval.

"So you are supposedly a sick man, Marty," he said gutturally. "So you have a great deal of money—my money. So drunk you should not get."

"H-huh? W-what?" Mitch said. "Who the hell are you?"

"So I am The Pig," the man said. "Who else?"

The name suited him. Place a pecan on top of a hen's egg and you've got a good idea of his appearance. He was perhaps five feet tall, and he probably weighed three hundred pounds. His arms were short almost to the point of deformity. He had a size six head and a size sixty waistline.

Mitch stared at him blankly, silently. The Pig apparently misunderstood his attitude.

"So you are not sure of me," he said. "So I will take it from the top and give you proof. So you are The Man's good and faithful servant through all his difficulties. So The Man passes the word that you are to pay me fifty thousand dollars for services rendered. So you are a very sick man anyway and have little to lose if detected while on the errand—"

"Wait a minute!" Mitch said. "I—I'm not—"

"So you are to transport the money in small traveler's checks. So you cannot be robbed. So they can be easily cashed without attracting unwanted attention. So you have had a day to cash them. So"—the Pig concluded firmly—"you will give me the fifty thousand."

Mitch's mouth was very dry. Slowly, the various pieces of a puzzle were beginning to add up. And what they added up to was curtains—for him. He'd really stepped into something this time: a Grade-A jam, an honest-to-Hannah, double-distilled frammis. The Pig's next words were proof of the fact.

"So you know how I earned the fifty G's, Marty. So you would not like me to give you a demonstration. It is better to die a natural death."

"N-now—now, listen!" Mitch stammered. "You've got the wrong guy, I'm not Martin Lonsdale. I'm—I'm . . . Look, I'll show you." He started to reach for his wallet. And groaned silently, remembering. He had thrown it away. There was a risk of being caught with two sets of identification, so—

"So?" The Pigs said.

"I—Look! Call this Man, whoever he is. Let me talk to him. He can tell you I'm not—"

"So," The Pig grunted, "who can call Alcatraz? So—" he added, "I will have the money, Marty."

"I don't have it! My wife—I mean the dame I registered in with—has it. She had the room next to mine, and—"

"So, but no. So I checked the registry myself. So there has been no woman with you."

"I tell you there was! These people here—they're hungry as hell, see, and she had plenty of dough to bribe them . . ." He broke off, realizing how true his words were. He resumed again, desperately: "Let me give you the whole pitch, tell you just what happened right from the beginning! I was trying to thumb a ride, see, and this big Cadillac stopped for me. And . . ."

Mitch told him the tale.

The Pig was completely unimpressed.

"So that is a fifty-grand story? So a better one I could buy for a nickel."

"But it's true! Would I make up a yarn like that? Would I come here, knowing that you'd show up to collect?"

"So people do stupid things." The Pig shrugged. "So, also, I am a day early."

"But, dammit!—" There was a discreet rap on the door. Then, it opened and Bette came in.

This Bette was a honey, a little skimpy in the chin department, perhaps, but she had plenty everywhere else. A burlesque house stripteaser, her mannerisms and dress sometimes caused her to be mistaken for a member of a far older profession.

Mitch greeted her with almost hysterical gladness. "Tell this guy, honey! For God's sake, tell him who I am!"

"Tell him . . . ?" Bette hesitated, her eyes flickering. "Why, you're Martin Lonsdale, I guess. If this is your room. Didn't you send for me to—"

"N-*nno!*" Mitch burbled. "Don't do this to me, honey! Tell him who I really am. Please!—"

One of The Pig's fat arms moved casually. The fist at the end of it smashed into Mitch's face. It was like being slugged with a brick. Mitch stumbled and fell flat across the bed. Dully, as from a distance, he heard a murmur of conversation . . .

". . . had a date with him, a hundred-dollar date. And I came all the way out here from Los Angeles . . ."

"So Marty has another date. So I will pay the hundred dollars myself . . ."

There was a crisp rustle, then a dulcet, "Oh, aren't you nice!" Then the door opened and closed, and Bette was gone. And The Pig slowly approached the bed. He had a hand in his pocket. There was a much bigger bulge in his pocket than a hand should make.

Mitch feigned unconsciousness until The Pig's hand started coming out of his pocket. Then Mitch's legs whipped up in a blur of motion. He went over backwards in a full somersault, landed on the other side of the bed, gripped and jerked it upward.

Speed simply wasn't The Pig's forte. He just wasn't built for it. He tried to get out of the way and succeeded only in tripping over his own feet. The bed came down on him, pinning him to the floor. Mitch sent him to sleep with a vicious kick in the head.

Mitch realized he had been moving in a blur. But now his mind was crystal clear, sharper than it ever had been.

Where was Babe? Simple. Since she couldn't have ridden away from the place, she must have walked. And Mitch was positive he knew where she had walked to.

What to do with The Pig? Also simple. The materials for taking care of him were readily at hand.

Mitch turned on the water in the bathtub. He went out into the hall and returned with two sacks full of quick-drying plaster . . .

He left The Pig very well taken care of, sitting in plaster up to his chin. Then, guessing that it would be faster, he ran down the stairs and out to the Cadillac. Wheels spinning, he whipped it down the horseshoe driveway and out onto the highway.

He slowed down after a mile or two, peering off to his right at the weed-grown fields that lay opposite the ocean. Suddenly, he jerked the car onto the shoulder and braked it to a stop. He got out; his eyes narrowed with grim satisfaction.

He was approximately parallel now with the place where he had assumed the identity of Martin Lonsdale. The place where Martin Lonsdale had supposedly committed suicide. And out there in this fallow field was an abandoned produce shed.

From the highway, it appeared to be utterly dark, deserted. But as Mitch leaped the ditch and approached it, he caught a faint flicker of light. He came up on the building silently. He peered through a crack in the sagging door.

There was a small stack of groceries in one corner of the room, also a large desert-type water bag. Blankets were spread out in another corner. Well back from the door, a can of beans was warming over a Sterno stove. A man stood over it, looking impatiently down at the food.

Mitch knew who he was, even without the sunglasses and cap. He also knew who he was *not*—for this man was bald and well under six feet tall.

Mitch kicked open the door and went in. The guy let out a startled "Gah!" as he flung himself forward, swinging.

He shouldn't have done it, of course. Mitch was sore enough at him, as it was. A full uppercut, and the guy soared toward the roof. He came down, horizontal, landing amidst the groceries.

Mitch snatched him to his feet and slapped him back into consciousness. "All right. Let's have the story. All of it and straight, get me? And don't ask me what story or I'll—"

"I w-won't—I mean, I'll tell you!" the man babbled frantically.

"We—tied into Lonsdale at a motor court. Figured he was carrying heavy, so Babe pulled the tears for a ride. We was just going to hold him up, you know. Honest to Gawd, that's all! But—but—"

"But he put up a fight and you had to bump him."

"*Naw!* No!" the man protested. "He dropped dead on us! I swear he did! I'd just pulled a knife on him—hadn't touched him at all—when he keeled over! Went out like a light. I guess maybe he must have had a bad ticker or something, but anyway . . ."

Mitch nodded judiciously. The Pig had indicated that Lonsdale was in bad health. "So okay. Keep singing."

"W-well, he didn't have hardly any dough in cash like we thought he would. Just that mess of checks. But we'd pumped him for a lot of info, and we figured if we could find the right kind of chump—excuse me, Mister—I mean, a guy that could pass for Lonsdale—"

"So you did a little riding up and down the highway until you found him. And you just damned near got him killed!"

He gave the guy an irritated shake. The man whimpered apologetically. "We didn't mean to, Mister. We really figured we was doing you a favor. Giving you a chance to make a piece of change."

"I'll bet. But skip it. Where's Babe?"

"At the hotel."

"Nuts!" Mitch slapped him. "You were going to hole up here until the heat was off! Now, where the hell is she?"

The man began to babble again. Babe hadn't known how soon she could scram. There'd been no set time for joining him here. She had to be at the hotel. If she wasn't, he didn't know where she was.

"Maybe run out on me," he added bitterly. "Never could trust her around the corner. I don't see how she could get away, but—"

Mitch jerked a fist swiftly upward.

When the guy came to, he was naked and the room had been stripped of its food, water, and other supplies. His clothes and everything else were bundled into one of the blankets, which Mitch was just lugging out the door.

"Wait!" The man looked at him, fearfully. "What are you going to do?"

"The question," said Mitch, "is what are *you* going to do."

He departed. A mile or so back up the road, he threw the stuff into the ditch. He arrived at the hotel, parked, and indulged in some very deep thinking.

Babe had to be inside the joint. This money-hungry outfit was hiding her for a price. But exactly where she might be—in which of its numerous rooms, the countless nooks and crannies, cellars and sub-cellars that a place like this had—there was no way of telling. Or finding out. The employees would know nothing. They'd simply hide themselves if they saw him coming. And naturally he couldn't search the place from top to bottom. It would take too long. Delivery men—possibly other guests—would be showing up. And there was The Pig to contend with. Someone must have driven him out here, and he would not have planned to stay later than morning. So someone would be calling for him, and—

Well, never mind. He had to find Babe. He had to do it fast. And since he had no way of learning her hiding place, there was only one thing to do. Force her out of it.

Leaving the hotel, Mitch walked around to the rear and located a rubbish pile. With no great difficulty, he found a five-gallon lard can and a quantity of rags. He returned to the parking lot. He shoved the can under the car's gas tank and opened the petcock. While it was filling, he knotted the rags into a rope. Then, having shut off the flow of gasoline, he went to the telephone booth and called the hotel's switchboard.

The clerk-manager answered. He advised Mitch to beat it before he called the cops. "I know you're not Lonsdale, understand? I know you're a crook. And if you're not gone from the premises in five minutes—"

"Look who's talking!" Mitch jeered. "Go ahead and call the cops! I'd like to see you do it, you liver-lipped, yellow-bellied—"

The manager hung up on him. Mitch called him back.

"Now, get this," he said harshly. "You said I was a crook. All right, I am one and I'm dangerous. I'm a crib man, an explosives expert. I've got plenty of stuff to work with. So send that dame out here and do it fast, or I'll blow your damned shack apart!"

"Really? My, my!" The man laughed sneeringly, but somewhat shakily. "Just think of that!"

"I'm telling you," Mitch said, "And this is the last time I'll tell you. Get that dame out of the woodwork, or there won't be any left."

"You wouldn't dare! If you think you can bluff—"

"In exactly five minutes," Mitch cut in, "the first charge will be set off, outside. If the dame doesn't come out, your building goes up."

He replaced the receiver, went back to the car. He picked up the rags and gasoline, moved down the walk to the red-and-white mailbox. It stood in the deep shadows of the porte cochere and he was not observed. Also, the hotel employees apparently were keeping far back from the entrance.

Mitch soaked the rag rope in the gasoline and tucked a length of it down inside the mailbox. Then he lifted the can and trickled its entire contents through the letter slot. It practically filled the box to the brim. The fluid oozed through its seams and dripped down upon the ground.

Mitch carefully scrubbed his hands with his handkerchief. Then he ignited a book of matches, dropped them on the end of the rope. And ran.

His flight was unnecessary, as it turned out. Virtually unnecessary. For the "bomb" was an almost embarrassing failure. There was a weak rumble, a kind of growl—a hungry man's stomach, Mitch thought bitterly, would make a louder one. A few blasts of smoke, and the box jiggled a bit on its moorings. But that was the size of it. That was the "explosion." It wouldn't have startled a nervous baby. As for scaring those rats inside the joint, hell, they were probably laughing themselves sick.

Oh, sure, the box burned; it practically melted. And that would give them some trouble. But that didn't help Mitch Allison any.

From far down the lawn, he looked dejectedly at the dying flames, wondering what to do now; he gasped, his eyes widening suddenly as two women burst through the entrance of El Ciudad.

One—the one in front—was Babe, barelegged, barefooted; dressed only in her bra and panties. She screamed as she ran, slapping and clawing wildly at her posterior. And it was easy to see why. For the woman chasing her was Bette, and Bette was clutching a blazing blow-torch.

She was holding it in front of her, its long blue flame aimed straight at the brassy blonde's flanks. Babe increased her speed. But Bette stayed right with her.

They came racing down the lawn toward him. Then Bette tripped and stumbled, the torch flying from her hands. And at practically the same instant, Babe collided head-on with the steel flagpole. The impact knocked her senseless. Leaving her to listen to the birdies. Mitch sat down by Bette and drew her onto his lap. Bette threw her arms around him, hugging him frantically.

"You're all right, honey? I was so worried about you! You didn't really think I meant the way I acted, did you?"

"I wouldn't have blamed you if you had," Mitch said.

"Well, I didn't. Of course, I was awfully mad at you, but you *are* my husband. I feel like murdering you myself lots of times, but I'm certainly not going to let anyone else do it!"

"That's my girl." Mitch kissed her fondly. "But—"

"I thought it was the best thing to do, honey. Just play dumb, and then go get some help. Well—"

"Just a minute," Mitch interrupted. "Where's your car?"

"Over by the ocean." Bette pointed, continued. "Like I was saying, I found *her* listening out in the hall. I mean, she ducked away real fast, but I knew she had been listening. So I figured you'd probably be all right for a little while, and I'd better see about her."

"Right," Mitch nodded. "You did exactly right, honey."

"Well, she had a room just a few doors away, Mitch. I guess they had to move her nearby because they didn't have much time. Anyway, she went in and I went right in with her . . ."

She had asked Babe the score. Babe had told her to go jump, and Bette had gone to work on her, ripping off her clothes in the process. Babe had spilled, after a time. Bette had learned, consequently, that there would be no help for Mitch unless she provided it.

"So I locked her in and went back to your room. But you were gone, and I guessed you must be all right from the looks of things. That guy in the bathtub, I mean." Bette burst into giggles, remembering. "He looked so funny, Mitch! How in the world do you ever think of those stunts?"

"Just comes natural, I guess," Mitch murmured modestly. "Go on, precious."

"Well, I went back to her room, and the clerk called and said you were threatening to blow up the place. But she wouldn't go for it. She said she was going to stay right there, no matter what, and anyway you were just bluffing. Well, I was pretty sure you were, too, but I knew you wanted to get her outside. So I went out in the hall again and dug up that big cigar lighter—"

Mitch chuckled, and kissed her again. "You did fine, baby. I'm really proud of you. You gave her a good frisk, I suppose? Searched her baggage?"

Bette nodded, biting her lip. "Yes, Mitch. She doesn't have the money."

"Don't look so down about it—" he gave her a little pat. "I didn't figure she'd keep it with her. She's ditched it outside somewhere."

"But, Mitch, you don't understand. I talked to her, and—"

"I know. She's a very stubborn girl." Mitch got to his feet. "But I'll fix that."

"But, Mitch—she told me where she put the money. When I was chasing her with the torch."

"Told you! Why didn't you say so? Where is it, for Pete's sake?"

"It isn't," Bette said miserably. "But it was." She pointed toward the hotel. "It was up there."

"Huh? What are you talking about?"

"She . . . she mailed it to herself."

4.

SICK WITH SELF-DISGUST, Mitch climbed behind the wheel of Bette's car and turned it onto the highway. Bette studied his dark face. She patted him comfortingly on the knee.

"Now, don't take it so hard, honey. It wasn't your fault."

"Whose was it, then? How a guy can be so stupid and live so long! Fifty grand, and I do myself out of it! To do it to myself, that's what kills me!"

"But you can't expect to be perfect, Mitch. No one can be smart all the time."

"Nuts!" Mitch grunted bitterly. "When was I ever smart?"

Bette declared stoutly that he had been smart lots of times. Lots and lots of times. "You know you have, honey! Just look at all the capers you've pulled! Just think of all the people who are trying to find you! I guess they wouldn't be, would they, if you hadn't outsmarted them."

"Well . . ." Mitch's shoulders straightened a little.

Bette increased her praise.

"Why, I'll bet you're the best hustler that ever was! I'll bet you could steal the socks off a guy with sore feet, without taking off his shoes!"

"You—uh—you really mean that, honey?"

"I most certainly do!" Bette nodded vigorously. "They just don't make 'em any sneakier than my Mitch. Why—why, I'll bet you're the biggest heel in the world!"

Mitch sighed on a note of contentment. Bette snuggled close to him. They rode on through the night, moving, inappropriately enough, toward the City of Angels.

HENRY SLESAR

THE DAY OF THE EXECUTION

June 1957

A PROLIFIC WRITER of short stories and television screenplays, Henry Slesar was a mainstay of the early years of *AHMM*. He was also one of a limited number of writers who moved between the magazine and the television show *Alfred Hitchcock Presents*. This story was actually adapted for *Alfred Hitchcock Presents*, where it aired as "Night of the Execution." Slesar wrote more than five hundred short stories in his career, including the popular Inspector Cross series; he also won the Edgar Award for Best First Novel in 1960 for *The Gray Flannel Shroud*.

■

When the jury foreman stood up and read the verdict, Warren Selvey, the prosecuting attorney, listened to the pronouncement of guilt as if the words were a personal citation of merit. He heard in the foreman's somber tones, not a condemnation of the accused man who shriveled like a burnt match on the courtroom chair, but a tribute to Selvey's own brilliance. *"Guilty as charged . . ."* No, Warren Selvey thought triumphantly, guilty as I've proved . . .

For a moment, the judge's melancholy eye caught Selvey's and the old man on the bench showed shock at the light of rejoicing that he saw there. But Selvey couldn't conceal his flush of happiness, his satisfaction with his own efforts, with his first major conviction.

He gathered up his documents briskly, fighting to keep his mouth appropriately grim, though it ached to smile all over his thin, brown face. He put his briefcase beneath his arm, and when he turned, faced the buzzing spectators. "Excuse me," he said soberly, and pushed his way through to the exit doors, thinking now only of Doreen.

He tried to visualize her face, tried to see the red mouth that could be hard or meltingly soft, depending on which one of her many moods happened to be dominant. He tried to imagine how she would look when she heard his good news, how her warm body would feel against his, how her arms would encompass him.

But this imagined foretaste of Doreen's delights was interrupted. There were men's eyes seeking his now, and men's hands reaching toward him to grip his hand in congratulation. Garson, the district attorney, smiling heavily and nodding his lion's head in approval of his cub's behavior. Vance, the assistant DA, grinning with half a mouth, not altogether pleased to see his junior in the spotlight. Reporters, too, and photographers, asking for statements, requesting poses.

Once, all this would have been enough for Warren Selvey. This moment, and these admiring men. But now there was Doreen, too, and the thought of her made him eager to leave the arena of his victory for a quieter, more satisfying reward.

But he didn't make good his escape. Garson caught his arm and steered him into the gray car that waited at the curb.

"How's it feel?" Garson grinned, thumping Selvey's knee as they drove off.

"Feels pretty good," Selvey said mildly, trying for the appearance of modesty. "But, hell, I can't take all the glory, Gar. Your boys made the conviction."

"You don't really mean that." Garson's eyes twinkled. "I watched you through the trial, Warren. You were tasting blood. You were an avenging sword. You put him on the waiting list for the chair, not me."

"Don't say that!" Selvey said sharply. "He was guilty as sin, and you know it. Why, the evidence was clear-cut. The jury did the only thing it could."

"That's right. The way you handled things, they did the only thing they could. But let's face it, Warren. With another prosecutor, maybe they would have done something else. Credit where credit's due, Warren."

Selvey couldn't hold back the smile any longer. It illumined his long, sharp-chinned face, and he felt the relief of having it relax his features. He leaned back against the thick cushion of the car.

"Maybe so," he said. "But I thought he was guilty, and I tried to convince everybody else. It's not just A-B-C evidence that counts, Gar. That's law school sophistry, you know that. Sometimes you just *feel* . . ."

"Sure." The DA looked out of the window. "How's the bride, Warren?"

"Oh, Doreen's fine."

"Glad to hear it. Lovely woman, Doreen."

SHE WAS LYING on the couch when he entered the apartment. He hadn't imagined this detail of his triumphant homecoming.

He came over to her and shifted slightly on the couch to let his arms surround her.

He said: "Did you hear, Doreen? Did you hear what happened?"

"I heard it on the radio."

"Well? Don't you know what it means? I've got my conviction. My first conviction, and a big one. I'm no junior anymore, Doreen."

"What will they do to that man?"

He blinked at her, tried to determine what her mood might be. "I asked for the death penalty," he said. "He killed his wife in cold blood. Why should he get anything else?"

"I just asked, Warren." She put her cheek against his shoulder.

"Death is part of the job," he said. "You know that as well as I do, Doreen. You're not holding that against me?"

She pushed him away for a moment, appeared to be deciding whether to be angry or not. Then she drew him quickly to her, her breath hot and rapid in his ear.

They embarked on a week of celebration. Quiet, intimate celebration, in dim supper clubs and with close acquaintances.

It wouldn't do for Selvey to appear publicly gay under the circumstances.

On the evening of the day the convicted Murray Rodman was sentenced to death, they stayed at home and drank hand-warmed brandy from big glasses. Doreen got drunk and playfully passionate, and Selvey thought he could never be happier. He had parlayed a mediocre law school record and an appointment as a third-class member of the state legal department into a position of importance and respect. He had married a beautiful, pampered woman and could make her whimper in his arms. He was proud of himself. He was grateful for the opportunity Murray Rodman had given him.

It was on the day of Rodman's scheduled execution that Selvey was approached by the stooped, gray-haired man with the grease-spotted hat.

He stepped out of the doorway of a drug store, his hands shoved into the pockets of his dirty tweed overcoat, his hat low over his eyes. He had white stubble on his face.

"Please," he said, "Can I talk to you a minute?"

Selvey looked him over and put a hand in his pocket for change.

"No," the man said quickly. "I don't want a handout. I just want to talk to you, Mr. Selvey."

"You know who I am?"

"Yeah, sure, Mr. Selvey. I read all about you."

Selvey's hard glance softened. "Well, I'm kind of rushed right now. Got an appointment."

"This is important, Mr. Selvey. Honest to God. Can't we go someplace? Have coffee maybe? Five minutes is all."

"Why don't you drop me a letter, or come down to the office? We're on Chambers Street—"

"It's about that man, Mr. Selvey. The one they're executing tonight."

The attorney examined the man's eyes. He saw how intent and penetrating they were.

"All right," he said. "There's a coffee shop down the street. But only five minutes, mind you."

It was almost two-thirty; the lunchtime rush at the coffee shop was over. They found a booth in the rear and sat silently while a waiter cleared the remnants of a hasty meal from the table.

Finally, the old man leaned forward and said: "My name's Arlington, Phil Arlington. I've been out of town, in Florida, else I wouldn't have let things go this far. I didn't see a paper, hear a radio, nothing like that."

"I don't get you, Mr. Arlington. Are you talking about the Rodman trial?"

"Yeah, the Rodman business. When I came back and heard what happened, I didn't know what to do. You can see that, can't you? It hurt me, hurt me bad to read what was happening to that poor man. But I was afraid. You can understand that. I was afraid."

"Afraid of what?"

The man talked to his coffee. "I had an awful time with myself, trying to decide what to do. But then I figured—hell, this Rodman is a young man. What is he, thirty-eight? I'm sixty-four, Mr. Selvey. Which is better?"

"Better for what?" Selvey was getting annoyed; he shot a look at his watch. "Talk sense, Mr. Arlington. I'm a busy man."

"I thought I'd ask your advice." The gray-haired man licked his lips. "I was afraid to go to the police right off, I thought I should ask you. Should I tell them what I did, Mr. Selvey? Should I tell them I killed that woman? Tell me. Should I?"

The world suddenly shifted on its axis. Warren Selvey's hands grew cold around the coffee cup. He stared at the man across from him.

"What are you talking about?" he said. "Rodman killed his wife. We proved that."

"No, no, that's the point. I was hitchhiking east. I got a lift into Wilford. I was walking around town, trying to figure out where to get food, a job, anything. I knocked on this door. This nice lady answered. She didn't have no job, but she gave me a sandwich. It was a ham sandwich."

"What house? How do you know it was Mrs. Rodman's house?"

"I know it was. I seen her picture, in the newspapers. She was a nice lady. If she hadn't walked into that kitchen after, it would have been okay."

"What, what?" Selvey snapped.

"I shouldn't have done it. I mean, she was real nice to me, but I was so broke. I was looking around the jars in the cupboard. You know how women are; they're always hiding dough in the jars, house money they call it. She caught me at it and got mad. She didn't yell or anything, but I could see she meant trouble. That's when I did it, Mr. Selvey. I went off my head."

"I don't believe you," Selvey said. "Nobody saw any—anybody in the neighborhood. Rodman and his wife quarreled all the time—"

The gray-haired man shrugged. "I wouldn't know anything about that, Mr. Selvey. I don't know anything about those people. But that's what happened, and that's why I want your advice." He rubbed his forehead. "I mean, if I confess now, what would they do to me?"

"Burn you," Selvey said coldly. "Burn you instead of Rodman. Is that what you want?"

Arlington paled. "No. Prison, okay. But not that."

"Then just forget about it. Understand me, Mr. Arlington? I think you dreamed the whole thing, don't you? Just think of it that way. A bad dream. Now get back on the road and forget it."

"But that man. They're killing him tonight—"

"Because he's guilty." Selvey's palm hit the table. "I *proved* him guilty. Understand?"

The man's lip trembled.

"Yes sir," he said.

Selvey got up and tossed a five on the table.

"Pay the bill," he said curtly. "Keep the change."

THAT NIGHT, DOREEN asked him the hour for the fourth time.

"Eleven," he said sullenly.

"Just another hour." She sank deep into the sofa cushions. "I wonder how he feels right now . . ."

"Cut it out!"

"My, we're jumpy tonight."

"My part's done with, Doreen. I told you that again and again. Now the state's doing its job."

She held the tip of her pink tongue between her teeth, thought-fully. "But you put him where he is, Warren. You can't deny that."

"The jury put him there!"

"You don't have to shout at *me,* attorney."

"Oh, Doreen . . ." He leaned across to make some apologetic gesture, but the telephone rang.

He picked it up angrily.

"Mr. Selvey? This is Arlington."

All over Selvey's body, a pulse throbbed.

"What do you want?"

"Mr. Selvey, I been thinking it over. What you told me today. Only I don't think it would be right, just forgetting about it. I mean—"

"Arlington, listen to me. I'd like to see you at my apartment. I'd like to see you right now."

From the sofa, Doreen said: "Hey!"

"Did you hear me, Arlington? Before you do anything rash, I want to talk to you, tell you where you stand legally. I think you owe that to yourself."

There was a pause at the other end.

"Guess maybe you're right, Mr. Selvey. Only I'm way down-town, and by the time I get there—"

"You can make it. Take the IRT subway, it's quickest. Get off at 86th Street."

When he hung up, Doreen was standing.

"Doreen, wait. I'm sorry about this. This man is—an impor-tant witness in a case I'm handling. The only time I can see him is now."

"Have fun," she said airily and went to the bedroom.

"Doreen—"

The door closed behind her. For a moment, there was silence. Then she clicked the lock.

Selvey cursed his wife's moods beneath his breath and stalked over to the bar.

By the time Arlington sounded the door chimes, Selvey had downed six inches of bourbon.

Arlington's grease-spotted hat and dirty coat looked worse than ever in the plush apartment. He took them off and looked around timidly.

"We've only got three-quarters of an hour," he said. "I've just got to do something, Mr. Selvey."

"I know what you can do," the attorney smiled. "You can have a drink and talk things over."

"I don't think I should—" But the man's eyes were already fixed on the bottle in Selvey's hands. The lawyer's smile widened.

By eleven-thirty, Arlington's voice was thick and blurred, his eyes no longer so intense, his concern over Rodman no longer so compelling.

Selvey kept his visitor's glass filled.

The old man began to mutter. He muttered about his child-hood, about some past respectability, and inveighed a string of strangers who had done him dirt. After a while, his shaggy head began to roll on his shoulders, and his heavy-lidded eyes began to close.

He was jarred out of his doze by the mantel clock's chiming.

"Whazzat?"

"Only the clock," Selvey grinned.

"Clock? What time? What time?"

"Twelve, Mr. Arlington. Your worries are over. Mr. Rodman's already paid for his crime."

"No!" The old man stood up, circling wildly. "No, that's not true. I killed that woman. Not him! They can't kill him for something he—"

"Relax, Mr. Arlington. Nothing you can do about it now."

"Yes, yes! Must tell them—the police—"

"But why? Rodman's been executed. As soon as that clock struck, he was dead. What good can you do him now?"

"Have to!" the old man sobbed. "Don't you see? Couldn't live with myself, Mr. Selvey. Please—"

He tottered over to the telephone. Swiftly, the attorney put his hand on the receiver.

"Don't," he said.

Their hands fought for the instrument, and the younger man's won easily.

"You won't stop me, Mr. Selvey. I'll go down there myself. I'll tell them all about it. And I'll tell them about you—"

He staggered toward the door. Selvey's arm went out and spun him around.

"You crazy old tramp! You're just asking for trouble. Rodman's dead—"

"I don't care!"

Selvey's arm lashed out and his hand cracked across the sagging, white-whiskered face. The old man sobbed at the blow, but persisted in his attempt to reach the door. Selvey's anger increased and he struck out again, and after the blow, his hands dropped to the old man's scrawny neck. The next idea came naturally. There wasn't much life throbbing in the old throat. A little pressure, and Selvey could stop the frantic breathing, the hoarse, scratchy voice, the damning words . . .

Selvey squeezed, harder and harder.

And then his hands let him go. The old man swayed and slid against Selvey's body to the floor.

In the doorway, rigid, icy-eyed: Doreen.

"Doreen, listen—"

"You choked him," she said.

"Self-defense!" Selvey shouted. "He broke in here, tried to rob the apartment."

She slammed the door shut, twisted the inside lock. Selvey raced across the carpet and pounded desperately on the door. He rattled the knob and called her name, but there was no answer. Then he heard the sound of a spinning telephone dial.

IT WAS BAD enough, without having Vance in the crowd that jammed the apartment. Vance, the assistant DA, who hated his guts anyway. Vance, who was smart enough to break down his burglar story without any trouble, who had learned that Selvey's visitor had been expected. Vance, who would delight in his predicament.

But Vance didn't seem delighted. He looked puzzled. He stared down at the dead body on the floor of Selvey's apartment and said: "I don't get it, Warren. I just don't get it. What did you want to kill a harmless old guy like that for?"

"Harmless? *Harmless?*"

"Sure. Harmless. That's old Arlington, I'd know him any place."

"You know him?" Selvey was stunned.

"Sure, I met up with him when I was working out of Bellaire County. Crazy old guy goes around confessing to murders. But why kill him, Warren? What for?"

JACK RITCHIE

#8

June 1958

WHEN *AHMM* invited readers to nominate their favorites for inclusion in this anthology, Jack Ritchie's "#8" was one of the stories most frequently named. Another mainstay of the early years of the magazine, Ritchie wrote more than a hundred stories for *AHMM* (sometimes under the name Steve O'Connell). His stories are notable for their economy and concision, as well as their often offbeat humor. A native of Milwaukee, Ritchie maintained that he became addicted to mysteries while serving in the Pacific during World War II. He was also one of the few writers to have his stories adapted for *Alfred Hitchcock Presents*.

■

I was doing about eighty, but the long flat road made it feel only that fast.

The redheaded kid's eyes were bright and a little wild as he listened to the car radio. When the news bulletin was over, he turned down the volume.

He wiped the side of his mouth with his hand. "So far they found seven of his victims."

I nodded. "I was listening." I took one hand off the wheel and rubbed the back of my neck, trying to work out some of the tightness.

He watched me and his grin was half sly. "You nervous about something?"

My eyes flicked in his direction. "No. Why should I be?"

The kid kept smiling. "The police got all the roads blocked for fifty miles around Edmonton."

"I heard that too."

The kid almost giggled. "He's too smart for them."

I glanced at the zipper bag he held on his lap. "Going far?"

He shrugged. "I don't know."

The kid was a little shorter than average and he had a slight build. He looked about seventeen, but he was the baby-face type and could have been five years older.

He rubbed his palms on his slacks. "Did you ever wonder what made him do it?"

I kept my eyes on the road. "No."

He licked his lips. "Maybe he got pushed too far. All his life somebody always pushed him. Somebody was always there to tell him what to do and what not to do. He got pushed once too often."

The kid stared ahead. "He exploded. A guy can take just so much. Then something's got to give."

I eased my foot on the accelerator.

He looked at me. "What are you slowing down for?"

"Low on gas," I said. "The station ahead is the first I've seen in the last forty miles. It might be another forty before I see another."

I turned off the road and pulled to a stop next to the three pumps. An elderly man came around to the driver's side of the car.

"Fill the tank," I said. "And check the oil."

The kid studied the gas station. It was a small building, the only structure in the ocean of wheat fields. The windows were grimy with dust.

I could just make out a wall phone inside.

The kid jiggled one foot. "That old man takes a long time, I don't like waiting." He watched him lift the hood to check the oil. "Why does anybody that old want to live? He'd be better off dead."

I lit a cigarette. "He wouldn't agree with you."

The kid's eyes went back to the filling station. He grinned. "There's a phone in there. You want to call anybody?"

I exhaled a puff of cigarette smoke. "No."

When the old man came back with my change, the kid leaned toward the window. "You got a radio, mister?"

The old man shook his head. "No, I like things quiet."

The kid grinned. "You got the right idea, mister. When things are quiet you live longer."

Out on the road, I brought the speed back up to eighty.

The kid was quiet for a while, and then he said, "It took guts to kill seven people. Did you ever hold a gun in your hand?"

"I guess almost everybody has."

His teeth showed through twitching lips. "Did you ever point it at anybody?"

I glanced at him.

His eyes were bright. "It's good to have people afraid of you," he said. "You're not short anymore when you got a gun."

"No," I said. "You're not a runt anymore."

He flushed slightly.

"You're the tallest man in the world," I said. "As long as nobody else has a gun too."

"It takes a lot of guts to kill," the kid said again. "Most people don't know that."

"One of those killed was a boy of five," I said. "You got anything to say about that?"

He licked his lips. "It could have been an accident."

I shook my head. "Nobody's going to think that."

His eyes seemed uncertain for a moment. "Why do you think he'd kill a kid?"

I shrugged. "That would be hard to say. He killed one person and then another and then another. Maybe after a while it didn't make any difference to him what they were. Men, women, or children. They were all the same."

The kid nodded. "You can develop a taste for killing. It's not too hard. After the first few, it doesn't matter. You get to like it."

He was silent for another five minutes. "They'll never get him. He's too smart for that."

I took my eyes off the road for a few moments. "How do you figure that? The whole country's looking for him. Everybody knows what he looks like."

The kid lifted both his thin shoulders. "Maybe he doesn't care. He did what he had to do. People will know he's a big man now."

We covered a mile without a word and then he shifted in his seat. "You heard his description over the radio?"

"Sure," I said. "For the last week."

He looked at me curiously. "And you weren't afraid to pick me up?"

"No."

His smile was still sly. "You got nerves of steel?"

I shook my head. "No. I can be scared when I have to, all right."

He kept his eyes on me. "I fit the description perfectly."

"That's right."

The road stretched ahead of us and on both sides there was nothing but the flat plain. Not a house. Not a tree.

The kid giggled. "I look just just like the killer. Everybody's scared of me. I like that."

"I hope you had fun," I said.

"I been picked up by the cops three times on this road in the last two days. I get as much publicity as the killer."

"I know," I said, "And I think you'll get more. I thought I'd find you somewhere on this highway."

I slowed down the car. "How about me? Don't I fit the description too?"

The kid almost sneered. "No. You got brown hair. His is red. Like mine."

I smiled. "But I could have dyed it."

The kid's eyes got wide when he knew what was going to happen.

He was going to be number eight.

EVAN HUNTER
NOT A LAUGHING MATTER

August 1958

PERHAPS BEST known under his pseudonym Ed McBain, Evan Hunter published such novels as *The Blackboard Jungle* under the Hunter name. And under both names, he wrote for *AHMM* throughout his long and distinguished career. He is also famous for another Hitchcock connection as the author of the screenplay for *The Birds*. A former schoolteacher and literary agent, Evan Hunter was named a Grand Master by the Mystery Writers of America in 1985. He died in 2005.

■

He hated the manager most.

Last night he had come to that realization. This morning, as he entered the department store with the Luger tucked into the waistband of his trousers, he allowed his hatred for the manager to swell up blackly until it smothered all the other hatreds he felt. The manager knew; of that he was certain. And it was his knowledge, this smirking, sneering, patronizing, knowledge that fed the hatred, nurtured it, caused it to rise like dark yeast, bubbling, boiling.

The Luger was a firm metal reassurance against his belly.

The gun had been given to him in the good days, in Vienna, by an admirer. In the good days, there had been many admirers, and many gifts. He could remember the good days. The good days would sometimes come back to him with fiercely sweet nostalgia, engulfing him in waves and waves of painful memories. He could remember the lights, and the applause, and . . .

"Good morning, Nick."

The voice, the hated voice.

He stopped abruptly. "Good morning, Mr. Atkins," he said.

Atkins was smiling. The smile was a thin curl on his narrow face, a thin bloodless curl beneath the ridiculously tenuous mustache on the cleaving edge of the hatchet face. The manager's hair was black, artfully combed to conceal a balding patch. He wore a gray pinstripe suit. Like a caricature of all store managers everywhere, he wore a carnation in his buttonhole. He continued smiling. The smile was infuriating.

"Ready for the last act?" he asked.

"Yes, Mr. Atkins."

"It *is* the last act, isn't it, Nick?" Atkins asked, smiling. "Final curtain comes down today, doesn't it? All over after today. Everything reverts back to normal after today."

"Yes, Mr. Atkins," he said. "Today is the last act."

"But no curtain calls, eh, Nick?"

His name was not Nick. His name was Randolph Blair, a name that had blazed across the theatre marquees of four continents. Atkins knew this, and had probably known it the day he'd hired him. He knew it, and so the "Nick" was an additional barb, a reminder of his current status, a sledgehammer subtlety that shouted, "Lo, how the mighty have fallen!"

"My name is not Nick," he said flatly.

Atkins snapped his fingers. "That's right, isn't it? I keep forgetting. What is it again? Randolph Something? Clair? Flair? Shmair? What *is* your name, Nick?"

"My name is Randolph Blair," he said. He fancied he said it with great dignity. He fancied he said it the way Hamlet would have announced that he was Prince of Denmark. He could remember the good days when the name Randolph Blair was the magic key to a thousand cities. He could remember hotel clerks with fluttering hands, maitre d's hovering, young girls pulling at his clothing, even telephone operators suddenly growing respectful when they heard the name. Randolph Blair. In his mind, the name was spelled in lights. Randolph Blair. The lights suddenly flickered, and then dimmed. He felt the steel outline of the Luger against his belly. He smiled thinly.

"You know my name, don't you, Mr. Atkins?"

"Yes," Atkins said. "I know your name. I hear it sometimes."

His interest was suddenly piqued. "Do you?" he asked.

"Yes. I hear people ask, every now and then, 'Say, whatever happened to Randolph Blair?' I know your name."

He felt Atkins's dart pierce his throat, felt the poison spread into his bloodstream. *Whatever happened to Randolph Blair?* A comedian had used the line on television not two weeks before, bringing down the house. Randolph Blair, the ever-popular Randolph Blair. A nothing now, a nobody, a joke for a television comic. A forgotten name, a forgotten face. But Atkins would remember. For eternity he would remember Randolph Blair's name and the face and terrible power.

"Don't . . ." he started, and then stopped abruptly.

"Don't what?"

"Don't . . . don't push me too far, Mr. Atkins."

"*Push* you, Nick?" Atkins asked innocently.

"Stop that 'Nick' business!"

"Excuse *me*, Mr. Blair," Atkins said. "Excuse *me*. I forgot who I was talking to. I thought I was talking to an old drunk who'd managed to land himself a temporary job . . ."

"Stop it!"

". . . for a few weeks. I forgot I was talking to Randolph Blair, *the* Randolph Blair, *the* biggest lush in . . ."

"I'm not a drunk!" he shouted.

"You're a drunk, all right," Atkins said. "Don't tell me about drunks. My father was one. A falling-down drunk. A screaming, hysterical drunk. I grew up with it, Nick. I watched the old man fight his imaginary monsters, killing my mother inch by inch. So don't tell me about drunks. Even if the newspapers hadn't announced your drunkenness to the world, I'd have spotted you as being a lush."

"Why'd you hire me?" he asked.

"There was a job to be filled, and I thought you could fill it."

"You hired me so you could needle me."

"Don't be ridiculous," Atkins said.

"You made a mistake. You're needling the wrong person."

"Am I?" Atkins asked blandly. "Are you one of these tough drunks? Aggressive? My father was a tough drunk in the beginning. He could lick any man in the house. The only thing he couldn't lick was the bottle. When things began crawling out of the walls, he wasn't so tough. He was a screaming, crying baby then, running to my mother's arms. Are you a tough drunk, Nick? Are you?"

"I'm not a drunk!" he said. "I haven't touched a drop since I got this job. You know that!"

"Why? Afraid it would hurt your performance?" Atkins laughed harshly. "That never seemed to bother you in the old days."

"Things are different," he said. "I want . . . I want to make a comeback. I . . . I took this job because . . . I wanted the feel again, the feel of working. You shouldn't needle me. You don't know what you're doing."

"Me? Needle you? Now, Nick, Nick, don't be silly. *I* gave you the job, didn't I? Out of all the other applicants, I chose you. So why should I needle you? That's silly, Nick."

"I've done a good job," he said, hoping Atkins would say the right thing, the right word, wanting him to say the words that would crush the hatred. "You know I've done a good job."

"Have you?" Atkins asked. "I think you've done a lousy job, Nick. As a matter of fact, I think you *always* did a lousy job. I think you were one of the worst actors who ever crossed a stage."

And in that moment, Atkins signed his own death warrant.

ALL THAT DAY, as he listened to stupid requests and questions, as he sat in his chair and the countless faces pressed toward him, he thought of killing Atkins. He did his job automatically, presenting his smiling face to the public, but his mind was concerned only with the mechanics of killing Atkins.

It was something like learning a part.

Over and over again, he rehearsed each step in his mind. The store would close at five tonight. The employees would be anxious to get home to their families. This had been a trying, harrowing few weeks, and tonight it would be over, and the employees would rush into the streets and into the subways and home to waiting loved ones. A desperate wave of rushing self-pity flooded over him. *Who are my loved ones?* he asked silently. *Who is waiting for me tonight?*

Someone was talking to him. He looked down, nodding.

"Yes, yes," he said mechanically. "And what else?"

The person kept talking. He half listened, nodding all the while, smiling, smiling.

There had been many loved ones in the good days. Women, more women than he could count. Rich women, and young women, and jaded women, and fresh young girls. Where had he been ten years ago at this time? California? Yes, of course, the picture deal. How strange it had seemed to be in a land of sunshine at that time of the year. And he had blown the picture. He had not wanted to, he had not wanted to at all. But he'd been hopelessly drunk for . . . how many days? And you can't shoot a picture when the star doesn't come to the set.

The star.

Randolph Blair.

Tonight, he would be a star again. Tonight, he would accomplish the murder of Atkins with style and grace. When they closed the doors of the store, when the shoppers left, when the endless questions, the endless requests stopped, he would go to Atkins's office. He would not even change his clothes. He would go straight to Atkins's office and he would collect his pay envelope and he would shoot him. He would run into the streets then. In the streets he would be safe. In the streets Randolph Blair—the man whose face was once known to millions—would be anonymously safe. The concept was ironical. It appealed to a vestige of humor somewhere deep within him. Randolph Blair would tonight play the most important role of his career, and he would play it anonymously.

Smiling, chuckling, he listened to the requests.

The crowd began thinning out at about four thirty. He was exhausted by that time. The only thing that kept him going was the knowledge that he would soon kill Mr. Atkins.

At four forty-five, he answered his last request. Sitting alone then, a corpulent unsmiling man, he watched the clock on the wall. Four fifty. Four fifty-two, fifty-seven. Four fifty-nine.

He got off the chair and waddled to the elevator banks. The other employees were tallying the cash register receipts, anxious to get out of the store. He buzzed for the elevator and waited.

The doors slid open. The elevator operator smiled automatically.

"All over, huh?" he asked.

"Yes, it's all over," Blair said.

"Going to pick up your envelope? Cashier's office?"

"Mr. Atkins pays me personally," he said.

"Yeah? How come?"

"He wanted it that way," he answered.

"Maybe he's hoping you'll be good to him, huh?" the operator said, and he burst out laughing.

He did not laugh with the operator. He knew very well why Atkins paid him personally. He did it so that he would have the pleasure each week of handing Randolph Blair—a man who had once earned five thousand dollars in a single week—a pay envelope containing forty-nine dollars and thirty-two cents.

"Ground floor then?" the operator asked.

"Yes. Ground floor."

When the elevator stopped, he got out of it quickly. He walked directly to Atkins's office. The secretary-receptionist was already gone. He smiled grimly, went to Atkins's door, and knocked on it.

"Who is it?" Atkins asked.

"Me," he said. "Blair."

"Oh, Nick. Come in, come in," Atkins said.

He opened the door and entered the office.

"Come for your pay?" Atkins asked.

"Yes."

He wanted to pull the Luger now and begin firing. He waited. Tensely, he waited.

"Little drink first, Nick?" Atkins asked.

"No," he said.

"Come on, come on. Little drink never hurt anybody."

"I don't drink," he said.

"My father used to say that."

"I'm not your father."

"I know," Atkins said. "Come on, have a drink. It won't hurt you. Your job's over now. Your *performance* is over." He underlined the word smirkingly. "You can have a drink. Everyone'll be taking a little drink tonight."

"No."

"Why not? I'm trying to be friendly. I'm trying to . . ."

Atkins stopped. His eyes widened slightly. The Luger had come out from beneath Blair's coat with considerable ease. He stared at the gun. "Wh . . . what's that?" he said.

"It's a gun," Blair answered coldly. "Give me my pay."

Atkins opened the drawer quickly. "Certainly. Certainly. You didn't think I was . . . was going to cheat you, did you? You . . ."

"Give me my pay."

Atkins put the envelope on the desk. Blair picked it up.

"And here's yours," he said, and he fired three times, watching Atkins collapse on the desk.

The enormity of the act rattled him. The door. The door. He had to get to it. The wastepaper basket tripped him up, sent him lunging forward, but his flailing arms gave him a measure of balance and kept him from going down.

He checked his flight before he had gone very far into the store. Poise, he told himself. Control. Remember you're Randolph Blair.

The counters were already protectively concealed by dust sheets.

They reminded him of a body, covered, dead. Atkins.

Though he bolted again, he had enough presence of mind this time to duck into a restroom.

He was unaware of how long he had remained there, but when he emerged it was evident he had completely collected himself. His walk suggested the regal, or the confident calm of an actor sure of his part. And as he walked, he upbraided himself for having behaved like a juvenile suddenly overwhelmed by stage fright.

Randolph Blair pushed through the revolving doors. There was a sharp bite to the air, the promise of snow. He took a deep breath, calmly surveyed the people hurrying along, their arms loaded with packages.

And suddenly he heard laughter, a child's thin, piercing laugh. It cut into him like a knife. He turned and saw the laughing boy, tethered by one hand to the woman beside him, the boy's pale face, his arm and forefinger pointing upward, pointing derisively.

More laughter arose. The laughter of men, of women. A festive carousel, in the show window to one side of him, started up. Its music blared. It joined in the laughter, underscoring, counterpointing the laughter.

Blair felt caught in a punishing whirlpool. There seemed no way he could stop the sound, movement, everything that conspired to batter him.

Then the sight of policemen coming out of the store was completely unnerving. They appeared to be advancing toward him. And as he pulled the Luger on them, and even as he was overpowered and disarmed, a part of his mind felt that this was all unreal, all part of a dramatic role that he was playing.

But it was not a proper part for one wearing the red coat and trousers, the black belt and boots of a department store Santa Claus, the same clothes three thousand other men in the city were wearing. To blend into their anonymity, he lacked only a white beard, and he had lost his in the frantic exit he had made from Atkins's office.

And of course to a child—and even to some adults—a Santa Claus minus a beard might be a laughing matter.

CHARLES WILLEFORD

A GENUINE ALECTRYOMANCER

February 1959

AT *AHMM* we like to think of Charles Willeford as one of our own—he actually worked as an associate editor for the magazine for a few years in the 1960s. Though he wrote and published widely, he is perhaps best remembered for his Hoke Moseley mysteries published in the 1980s, most notably *Miami Blues,* which was also made into a movie. His untimely death in 1988 put an end to a remarkable career. Here's a story from early in his association with *AHMM.*

■

On the surface, the situation is quite mad, and yet there appears to be an irrefutable logic in the chain of incidents leading to my predicament. There it floats, bobbing, just beyond my grasp, and I have to believe that if I don't snag it with my fingers this time, I certainly shall on the next or the next stroke . . . and I *must* keep swimming, keep trying. There isn't much else I can do!

Where did the old alectryomancer come from in the first place? I didn't see or hear him approach on the soft sand. I looked up from the sea and there he was, waiting patiently for me to recognize him. The blue denim rags covering his thin hips and shanks were clean. His dusky skin was the shade of wet No. 2 sandpaper, and he held a shredded-brimmed straw hat in his right hand. Once he had my attention, he nodded his head amiably and smiled, exposing toothless gums the color of a rotten mango.

"What do you want?" I said rudely. One of my chief reasons for renting a cottage on the island of Bequia was the private beach.

"Please excuse my intrusion, Mr. Waxman," the native said politely, "but when I heard that the author of *Cockfighting in the Zone of Interior* had rented a cottage on Princess Margaret Beach, I wanted to congratulate him in person."

I was mollified, and at the same time, taken aback. Of course, I had written *Cockfighting in the Zone of Interior,* but it was a thin pamphlet, privately printed, issued in a limited edition of five hundred copies. The pamphlet had been written at the request of two well-to-do Florida cockfighters who hoped to gain support for the sport from an eastern syndicate, and I had been well paid. But it certainly wasn't the type of booklet to wind up in the hands of a Bequian native in the British West Indies.

"Where did you get a copy of that?" I said, getting to my feet and brushing the damp sand off my swimming trunks.

"Gamecocks are my source of livelihood," he replied simply. "And I read everything I can concerning gamefowl. Your pamphlet, sir, was excellent."

"Thank you, but my information was excellent. I didn't know you fought gamecocks on Bequia, however. According to an English mandate passed in 1857, cockfighting was forbidden throughout the empire."

"I don't fight gamecocks, Mr. Waxman." He smiled again and held up a hand. "My interest in gamefowl lies in a parallel art: alectryomancy."

I laughed, but I was interested. I had gone to Bequia because it was a peaceful little island in the Grenadines, and I had hoped to finish a novel. But in three months time I hadn't written a line. Bored, and with little to do but stare sullenly at the sea, I found myself enjoying this curious encounter.

"That's a parallel art," I agreed, "but I didn't know there were any practitioners of alectryomancy left in the Atomic Age."

"My rooster has made some fascinating predictions concerning the atom, Mr. Waxman," the alectryomancer confided. "If you would care to visit me sometime, we could discuss his findings. Or possibly, you might be more interested in obtaining a personal reading—"

"I don't need a gamecock to make predictions for me," I said truthfully. "If I don't get some work done on my book soon, I'll run out of money and be forced to return to the States and look for work."

"Isn't your writing going well?"

"It isn't going at all."

"Then there must be a reason. And only through alectryomancy—"

I cut the interview short and returned to my cottage. After fixing a cup of coffee and thinking about the odd meeting for a few minutes, I came to the conclusion that there might possibly be an article in it. Three or four thousand words on the old fellow's occupation might conceivably find a market in the U.S., and I wasn't getting anywhere with my novel. Of course, alectryomancy is usually considered as a false science, on a par with astrology. A circle is described on the bare ground; the alphabet is then written around the outer edge of the circle, and a grain of corn is placed on each letter. A rooster is tethered to a stake in the center by his left leg, and then as he pecks a grain of corn from the various letters, the letters are written down, in order, and a message of—the science is crazy, really! For one thing, before there could be any validity to the message, the rooster would have to be able to understand a language. And a chicken's brain is about the size of a BB. Still, an article about a practicing alectryomancer would be of interest to a great many people, and I needed the money.

I didn't look the alectryomancer up immediately; things are not done so speedily in the West Indies. I prepared myself for the impending interview by thinking about it for a couple of days, and then made my way to the seer's shack on Mt. Pleasant. Bequia is a small island, and it wasn't difficult to learn where he lived.

"Where," I asked my maid, "does the old man with the rooster live?"

It is to the woman's credit that she knew to whom I referred, because every resident on the island owns a few chickens and at least one rooster. She gave directions I could understand, and even went so far as to draw a crude map with her finger on the sandy beach in front of the cottage.

Mt. Pleasant isn't a high mountain, but the path was crooked and steep and the walk of forty minutes had winded me by the time I reached the old man's shack at the peak. He greeted me warmly and invited me to enjoy the loveliness of his view. Nine miles away, the volcanic, verdant mass of St. Vincent loomed above the sea, and behind us toward the southwest, the smaller islands of the Grenadines glimmered like emeralds.

"Your view is beautiful," I said, when I was breathing normally again.

"We like it," the old native nodded his head.

"We?"

"My rooster and me."

"Oh, yes," I said casually, snapping my fingers. "I'd like to take a look at him."

A low whistle from the alectryomancer and the rooster marched sedately out of the shack he shared with his master and joined us in the clearing. He was a large whitish bird of about six pounds, with brown and red feathers splashing his wings and chest. His comb was unclipped, and his dark red wattles dangled almost to his breast. He eyed me suspiciously for a moment, cocking his head alertly to one side, and crowed deep in his throat before turning away to scratch listlessly in the dirt.

"Looks like a Whitehackle cross."

"Correct, Mr. Waxman," the alectryomancer said respectfully. "His mother was a purebred Wild Jungle Fowl."

"I suspected as much. Only purebred gamecocks can be utilized in alectryomancy, as you must know," I added pedantically.

"Of course."

For a few moments we sat quietly on the ground watching the rooster, and then I cleared my throat. "As long as I'm here, I may as well have a reading."

"I'll change my clothes." The old man smiled, exposing his raw gums for my inspection, before hobbling painfully into his shack. The shack itself was an unusual structure, built of five-gallon oil tins, smashed flat, and topped by a mauve-colored fifty-gallon oil drum, which held, I presumed, rain water. Forming an even square around the clearing were several dozen additional five-gallon tins, each containing a potted arrowroot plant. I don't suppose an alectryomancer does too much business on a small island, and the arrowroot plants probably supplemented the old man's income.

I was unprepared for the change in attire and started slightly when the alectryomancer reappeared. A dirty white cotton turban had been wrapped around his bald head, and he wore a long-sleeved blue work shirt buttoned to the neck. Tiny red felt hearts, clubs, spades, and diamonds had been sewn in thick profusion on the shirt, and larger hearts, clubs, spades, and diamonds had been sewn on the pair of faded khaki trousers he now wore instead of the ragged blue denim shorts. His feet were still bare, however, which rather spoiled the effect.

"That's a unique costume, Mr.—?"

"Wainscoting. Two Moons Wainscoting. Thank you, sir."

"Is Two Moons your given name, Mr. Wainscoting?"

"You might say that. It was given to me when I was a small boy. My father took me across the channel to St. Vincent when I was eleven years old. When I returned, my friends asked me what I had seen over there. 'St. Vincent has a moon, too,' I told them. And I've been called Two Moons ever since."

"It's a perfect name for an alectryomancer."

"I've always regarded it highly. And now . . ." Two Moons tethered the Whitehackle cross to a stake in the clearing with a piece of brown twine, and proceeded to draw a large circle around him with a pointed stick.

"The ancient Greeks," I said, to reveal to the man that I knew a few things about alectryomancy, "always described the circle on the ground *prior* to tethering the gamecock in the center."

"Yes," he agreed. "But that isn't the way we do it in the West Indies. Every island race has its own peculiarities. Of course, I can see some merit in describing the circle first, but on the other hand, it is possible that a portion of the circle will be rubbed out inadvertently when reentering it to tether the cock. I have tried both methods, and in all probability I shall use the Greek method again some time in the future. But the system employed doesn't affect the reading, or so I have learned through experience."

"You could get into an argument on that statement."

"You can have an argument on anything pertaining to alectryomancy," Two Moons said cheerfully, and he began to draw the letters of the alphabet in a clockwise direction about the outer perimeter of the circle. He apparently took considerable pride in his work, drawing large capital letters with a pointed stick, rubbing them out again when they didn't come up to his high standards, and doing them over again. He measured the distances between each letter, using his stick as a ruler, and found it necessary to redraw the s and t because they were too close together.

"Now," he said when he was finished, "the hard part is over. What is your birth date, Mr. Waxman?"

"January 2, 1919."

"You'll have to speak a trifle louder, Mr. Waxman," Two Moons said apologetically. "My old rooster's getting deaf, and I don't believe he heard you."

I repeated my birthday loudly, enunciating carefully for the rooster's benefit.

Two Moons walked counterclockwise about the circle, dropping a grain of corn in the exact center of each letter, and then sat down beside me. He signaled the gamecock with his pointed stick, and the bird crowed, wheeled about, and pecked up the grain of corn on the letter M. Two Moons wrote M on the ground, and followed it with the O, R, and T as the chicken pecked up each grain. After eating the fourth grain of corn, the rooster returned to the center of the circle, leaned wearily against the stake, and hung his head down to the ground. We waited, but it was evident from the apathy of the chicken that he was through.

"Maybe he isn't hungry?"

"We'll soon find out." Two Moons Wainscoting untied the cord from the rooster's left leg and carried him out of the circle. He scattered a few grains of corn, released the cock, and the bird scratched and gobbled down the food as if it were famished.

"He was hungry, all right, Mr. Waxman. Your reading is complete. M.O.R.T." Two Moons muttered, savoring each letter with half-closed eyes. "Mort. Is your middle name Mort, by any chance?"

"Harry Waxman, only. I dropped my middle name when I became a writer, but it wasn't Mort."

"Any relatives named Mort?"

"No." I thought carefully. "No, none at all."

"That's too bad." Two Moons shook his head. "I had hoped—"

"Hoped what?"

"That Mort didn't mean what I knew in my heart it meant." He thumped his breast with a closed fist. "*Mort* is a French word meaning death, Mr. Waxman."

"So? How does it apply to me? I'm not a Frenchman; I'm an American. If the rooster's predicting anything for me, he should do so in English."

"He doesn't know any English," Two Moons explained patiently. "I bought the chicken in Martinique, after my last rooster died. All he knows is French. On difficult readings I often have to consult a French-English dictionary—"

"Maybe he was going to write 'MORTGAGE'?" I broke in.

"I sympathize with you, Mr. Waxman." Two Moons shook his head, dislodging his dirty turban. "But in alectryomancy we can go only by what the gamecock does write, not by what he does not."

"Let's try another reading."

"Another time, perhaps. It's a great strain on my chicken, making predictions, and I only allow him to make one a day."

"Tomorrow, then," I said, getting to my feet.

"Perhaps tomorrow." He agreed reluctantly.

I took my wallet out of my hip pocket. "What do I owe you?"

"Nothing." The alectryomancer spread his arms wide, palms up, and shrugged. "I would appreciate it, however, if you autographed my copy of your pamphlet, *Cockfighting in the Zone of Interior.*"

I tapped my shirt pocket. "When I come up tomorrow. I didn't bring my fountain pen with me today—"

"If you don't mind, Mr. Waxman," Two Moons said reasonably. "In view of the prediction, I would prefer to have the autograph today. If you'll wait a minute, I have a ballpoint pen inside the house . . ."

I SLEPT FITFULLY that night, but I had slept fitfully every night of the three months I had been on Bequia. No one had informed me of the fierceness of the sand flies and mosquitoes on Princess Margaret Beach, and I had neglected to purchase a mosquito bar before departing Trinidad. But between waking and sleeping, the prediction of the Whitehackle cross gave me something to think about. I was far from satisfied with Two Moon's interpretation of the word "mort."

It was too pat. And yet, no other meaning suggested itself to me. Toward two A.M. I was reduced to considering M.O.R.T. as initials standing for something else. During the war I used to get letters from a girl in California with S.W.A.K. written across the back of the envelope. This meant "Sealed With A Kiss." When this piece of tripe crossed my mind, I cursed myself for a fool, downed three quick tumblers of Mount Gay rum, and slept soundly until dawn.

By eight-thirty A.M. I was on the mountain trail to Two Moon's metal residence. Halfway up the mountain I stopped for breath and a slow cigarette, and almost changed my mind about obtaining a second reading. Curiosity got the better of my judgment and I climbed on. When I topped the last rise to the clearing, Two Moons was sitting cross-legged in the sunlight before his shack, humming happily, and plaiting a basket out of green palm leaves. He dropped his lower jaw the moment he saw me, and his yellow eyes popped in their sockets.

"Why, it's Mr. Waxman!" He said with genuine astonishment. "I didn't expect you this morning!"

"You needn't act so surprised. I said I'd be back this morning."

"I apologize for my astonishment. But your case was remarkably similar to a reading I gave a student at Oxford, and I—"

"You attended Oxford?" It was my turn to be surprised.

"For a year and a half only," Two Moons admitted modestly. "I was putting myself through Oxford by practicing alectryomancy in the West End. I had a poor but steady clientele, actors, actresses, producers, and two or three dozen playwrights."

"I fail to see how an Oxford man could end up on Bequia," I said, looking at the alectryomancer with new respect.

"An English Dom did it," Two Moons said sorrowfully.

"Got mixed up with a woman?"

"No, sir. Not a woman, a Dom. A truly beautiful gamefowl, the English Dom. Pure white, with a yellow bill and feet. I bought the rooster in Sussex, and before utilizing his services for my clients, I had him make a practice prediction for me. Without hesitating the Dom pecked out BEQUIA. I ate the fowl for supper, packed my belongings, and left on the next ship leaving England for Barbados. I've been on Bequia ever since, thirty-two years in October."

"At any rate," I said, moved by the simple story, "one of your predictions came true."

"They all come true."

"We'll see. How about my second reading?"

"Yes, sir." Two Moons held out his right hand. "That will be ten dollars, in advance."

"Very well." I parted with a brown BWI ten-dollar bill. "Bring on your French-pecking rooster."

The rigmarole was unchanged from the day before. Two Moons Wainscoting changed from ragged blue denim shorts into his home-made costume and turban, tethered the gamecock, and drew the circle and block-letter alphabet as carefully as he had done for my first reading. He signaled with the pointed stick, and the idiotic rooster pecked M, O, R, T and stopped. After crowing half-heartedly, the bird leaned against the stake and hung his head down, bill touching the ground. I was unable to understand how the mere pecking up of four lousy grains of corn could make the chicken so tired.

"Let's wait a bit, Two Moons." I cleared my dry throat. "Maybe he'll continue."

"As you wish, Mr. Waxman."

The minutes ticked away. The sun was hot. The back of my neck stung with prickly heat. Mango flies and tiny gnats buzzed and feinted about my perspiring face, but I waited. Five minutes, ten minutes, fifteen minutes, and the stupid rooster still remained immobilized in the center of the circle.

"*Mort* comes to us all, in time," Two Moons said pityingly.

"A truth that can't be denied," I agreed, getting to my feet and stretching. "Well, thanks for the prediction, Mr. Wainscoting. But it's a hot day and I'm going for a swim." I started down the trail, my hands balled into fists inside the pockets of my khaki shorts.

"Watch out for barracuda!" Two Moons shouted after me. "And dangerous crosscurrents."

"Thanks!" I called back drily.

I didn't go swimming. I didn't do anything. I brooded, sitting in the tiny living room of my screenless cottage, staring out the window at the bright blue, cheerful waters of the bay. The first *mort* wasn't so bad, but when it came to two *morts* I was forced to do a little quiet thinking. Like all Americans, I laugh at superstition. Ha, ha! The pinch of salt, tossed carelessly over the left shoulder. A needless precaution, but I did it all the time. Did I ever place a hat upon a bed? Never. Why not? Well, just because, that's why. Did I ever walk under a ladder? No, of course not. A can of paint might cover one from above; that was prudence, not superstition. I wasn't really superstitious. Not really. But that gamecock had been so positive . . . !

Three days later I fired my maid. The woman refused to taste my food, claiming falsely that she didn't like canned pork-and-beans. I issued an ultimatum, and when she still flatly refused to eat a bite, and prevent me from being poisoned, I gave her the sack and tossed the beans into the bay.

My life became more complicated without anyone else around, but I preferred to be alone. I now had to make up the list of foodstuffs to send to St. Vincent, and I had to meet the MV *Madinina* when it steamed into the harbor on Friday to get them. But I didn't mind the activity. I wasn't hungry either, and the little I did eat was better prepared by myself. I worried, however. A bad tin of corned beef, a can of sour condensed milk, and pouf! *Mort.* I drank a lot of Mount Gay rum and a little water.

Three weeks following my second reading, I paid my third visit to Two Moons Wainscoting. I was unable to stand the fear and suspense any longer. I hadn't shaved for several days. Suppose I had cut myself with a rusty razor blade? Where could I get a tetanus shot on Bequia? My sleep was no longer fitful; I couldn't sleep at all. Three full inches had disappeared from my waistline.

"Two Moons," I said anxiously, as soon as I entered his clearing, "I've got to have another reading."

"I've been expecting you, Mr. Waxman," Two Moons said soothingly. "That is, I've been expecting word concerning you, but I must turn down your request for a third reading. This is not an arbitrary decision. The life of an alectryomancer on Bequia isn't an easy one, and I would welcome another ten-dollar bill, but I am not totally lacking in compassion, so I must refuse."

"I'll give you twenty dollars—"

Two Moons held up a hand to silence me. "Please, Mr. Waxman. This isn't a question of money! Let me summarize: you have had now two flat predictions, both of them identical. *Mort!* An ugly word, whether in French or English, but *mort* all the same. Suppose, on a third prediction, my gamecock were to peck out W.E.D.S. or a simple F.R.I.? Do you see the implication? You're a writer, Mr. Waxman, and do not lack imagination. A gamecock is incapable of telling a falsehood, and if my rooster pecked an F.R.I.—which he could do in all innocence—this is the abbreviation for Friday. Today is Tuesday. How would you feel tomorrow, on Wednesday? And then Thursday? The next day would be Friday, and Friday would be the day for what? *Mort!*" He pointed his finger at my chest and shook his head.

I shuddered as the pit of my stomach chilled. "But—"

"Please, Mr. Waxman. I cannot risk another reading. An alectryomancer has a conscience, just like everyone else, and I would suffer along with you. I must refuse your request for a third reading. I cannot; I will not do it!"

"I'm a young man," I croaked hoarsely, "and I'm not ready to die. I won't even be forty until my next birthday."

"There's an alternative." Two Moons pursed his lips and peered at me intently. "But I hesitate to mention it to a man with so little faith."

"Mention it," I said sharply. "By all means, mention it."

"You are cognizant of the West Indian *obeah?*"

"I think so. It's a spell or charm of some kind, isn't it?"

"In a way, yes. There are all kinds of *obeahs;* they can be made for good or evil, in the same manner African ju-jus are made for good or evil. Unfortunately, many West Indians have a vindictive character and often cast about for a means of vengeance for a very small grievance. This deplorable character trait, I am happy to state, is not a universal West Indian—"

"I'm not interested in the character traits of the average West Indian. I have problems of my own."

"To be sure. To shorten the rather interesting story, I possess an *obeah* that will ward off *mort* for an indefinite period."

"Let me take a look at it."

"Not so fast. Like every spell or charm or ju-ju, an *obeah* has a condition attached."

"What are the conditions?"

"Condition." He held up a long forefinger. "Singular, Mr. Waxman. A simple condition, but a condition nevertheless. Belief. Blind, unquestioning belief. So long as you believe in the *obeah* you shall have life. Not everlasting life, as promised by your optimistic Christian *obeahs,* but life for a reasonable period. The Grenadian who fashioned this *obeah* lived to be one hundred and ten."

"That's a long time."

"A very long time."

"I believe," I said desperately. "Give me the *obeah!*"

"You're an impulsive young man, Mr. Waxman. This is a valuable *obeah,* and before I can give it to you, I must test your belief. The *obeah* has a price of seventy-five dollars."

I passed the test. Happier than I had been in days, I ran lightly down the mountain trail, a small leather sack tied around my neck. The sack was securely fastened with a square knot in the rawhide thong at the back of my neck, and from time to time I fingered the knot to make certain it wouldn't slip.

Night fell. I sat in my tiny living room. The pale light of my kerosene lamp—there isn't any electricity on Bequia—made my shadow dance on the wall like a boxer. The wind was responsible for my flickering shadow, but I felt like a boxer, fighting the deadly logic of the gamecock's prediction. I clutched the sack at my neck, feeling the strange objects inside it through the leather, wondering what in the devil they were. Two Moons had warned me not to look inside—"Never look a gift horse in the mouth"—were his exact words, but I was curious all the same. If I stopped believing in the *obeah, mort* could strike suddenly at any moment. The wisdom of Two Moons Wainscoting, in denying me a third prediction, was the only bright spot in my thinking. But even with the *obeah* in my possession I couldn't live forever . . .

Not that I had any particular reason to go on living. I wasn't happy, and never had been. I was single, no dependents, no real purpose in life—really, except for writing an occasional novel or short story. But I wanted to hang on, if for no other reason than to see what would happen next. I had lost all desire to write an article on alectryomancy . . .

I felt the objects inside the *obeah* with my fingers. What were they? I jerked my hand away quickly. What if my fingers recognized one or more of the objects inside the leather sack? How could I go on believing in the efficacy of the *obeah* if I once found out what the sack contained? A nasty situation to be in, all the way around.

In the daytime, life wasn't so bad. The bright sunlight chased away the problems of the night. But everything I did, which wasn't much, was done judiciously. I still swam every day, but never ventured more than a few yards from the shore, fearing the riptides and crosscurrents. I continued to take daily hikes, but I walked slowly, like an old man with brittle bones. And I carried a cane. Most of the time I sat quietly on the narrow front porch of my cottage drinking rum-and-water. Sometimes, I wished that *mort* would come to me in the night, in my sleep, so that it would be all over and done with.

After a few lonely evenings I began to go to the hotel at night, picking my way along the beach path, playing my flashlight on every shadow before taking another step. There wasn't any electricity at the hotel either, but the porch was lighted by Coleman lanterns, and they didn't cast shadows . . .

Just a few short hours ago I was sitting at a table on the hotel verandah, staring glumly into my glass, when Bob Corbett sat down across from me. One quick glance at his red, serious face and orange moustache, and I shook my head.

"No nattering tonight, Bob," I said firmly. "I'm not up to it."

Bob Corbett is a British civil servant who makes periodic trips to the various islands, looking for fungus or something, but the government maintains a house for him on Bequia. Like many of the bored civil servants posted to the Windward Islands for three years, Bob has become addicted to the game of nattering. Nattering is a game where two persons hurl insults at each other until one of them gets angry enough to fight. During the early years of my writing career, I had served time as a desk clerk at a New York hotel for almost two years, and as a consequence, I had bested Bob Corbett in every nattering session he started. In the last session

we played, Bob had taken a swing at me with an empty Black &
White bottle.

"No nattering," Bob agreed readily, signaling the barmaid to
refill our glasses. "I really came over to make amends. I've been
standing at the bar for almost an hour without a sign of recognition from you, and if you want an apology you can have it. But
I really didn't hit you with that bottle—"

"I'm sorry, Bob. I didn't cut you; I just didn't see you," I
apologized. All at once, I felt an overwhelming desire to confide
in Bob Corbett, and I yielded impulsively to the desire. The dark
thoughts had been bottled up inside me too long. "Listen, Bob,"
I began, "did you ever hear of alectryomancy?" And I unfolded
the whole story.

"Ho-ho-ho!" Bob laughed, when I had finished. "You've been
had, old man!"

"What are you talking about?"

"Had! Taken! Bilked! And you're a New Yorker, too. That's
what makes it so funny!" Another string of bubbling ho-ho-hos
followed, and I drummed my fingers on the table impatiently.

"Old Two Moons is a notorious character in the islands," Bob
said at last, wiping his streaming eyes with the back of a freckled
hand. "This old faker and his trained rooster have caused I don't
know how many complaints to the administrator on St. Vincent
from irate tourists. His rooster, you see, is trained to peck out the
word '*mort*'! And the convincing mumbo-jumbo that Two
Moons puts with it has sucked you in."

"I don't believe it. I'd like to but I can't."

"I'll prove it to you," Bob said earnestly, leaning across the
table. "After the rooster pecked the four grains of corn, ostensibly
spelling 'mort,' he hung his head down. Right?"

"Right."

"Following this, didn't Two Moons remove the chicken from
the circle and feed him some more corn? And didn't the rooster
scratch it up and eat it?"

"Of course. That's what made the reading so effective."

"No. It proves only that the rooster is trained. Think a bit,
man. To train animals of any kind, you must always reward
them after they do their trick. And the only reward an animal
recognizes is food! A trained rooster isn't any different from a

trained bear that's been given a bottle of beer for doing a dance. A bloke I knew in Newfoundland had a bloody wolf chained in his garage, and one—"

I left the table abruptly, not waiting to find out about the bloody wolf in Newfoundland, and flashing my torch before me, ran all the way home along the beach path. As soon as my kerosene lamp was lighted, I untied the thong at the back of my neck and dumped the contents of the leather sack on the dining table. Inventory: one plastic toothpick (red); one small, round obsidian pebble; two withered jackfish eyes; one dried chameleon tail, approximately three inches long; one red checker; three battered and badly bent Coca-Cola caps; one chicken feather (yellow); assorted, unidentifiable small dried bones, and one brass disc entitling the bearer to a ten-cent beer at Freddy Ming's Cafe, Port-of-Spain, Trinidad.

A blind red film burning my eyes, I stared stupidly at the contents of the *obeah* and cursed Two Moons Wainscoting aloud for five minutes. Then I quickly scooped the objects into the leather sack, went outside, and tossed the thing into the sea. The buoyant sack floated on the surface, bobbing up and down, drifting away from shore on the outgoing tide. A great idea struck me. I would recover the *obeah* from the sea, pay a return visit to Two Moon's establishment, and feed him each object in the leather bag, one at a time.

This idea delighted me so much, I kicked off my sandals, on impulse, and dived into the sea. I soon found, with mounting apprehension, that in spite of all the strokes I was taking, I wasn't making any headway. It wasn't until then that I recalled that the natives, skilled as they are with small sailboats, never venture out in fishing boats after dark, nor will they swim after dark, not even in the bay. I was trapped in a riptide. Though I panicked, I did remember someone saying that the only way to get out of such a situation was to head for shore at a diagonal.

I've tried the diagonal business, but it hasn't worked. And so like a drowning man—which I am—clutching at a straw, I've continued swimming out to sea, trying to get my hands on that *obeah*. It's my only hope. But the currents keep carrying it just beyond my grasp. My strokes are getting much weaker now, it seems, and I'm no closer to getting my fingers on the *obeah* than I was in the beginning. The night is so black I don't even know where land is anymore. The tiny, scattered lights of Bequia have been extinguished for some time, and the night is so dark I can't even make out the mass of St. Vincent. There are barracuda out here in the deep water, and didn't Two Moons tell me to watch out for barracuda?

   "Obeah! I believe in you! I believe, I believe, I believe! I—"

DONALD E. WESTLAKE

GOOD NIGHT! GOOD NIGHT!

December 1960

NOW ONE of mystery's most popular writers, Westlake is known as a master of both the comic caper and (in his books written as Richard Stark) the violent hard-boiled novel. Westlake was a major presence in *AHMM* during the 1960s under both names, and indeed, he is known for the variety of his pseudonyms, each with its distinctive style. Westlake was named a Grand Master by the Mystery Writers of America in 1993. He not only won an Edgar Award, but was also nominated for an Oscar, for his screenplay adaptation of Jim Thompson's *The Grifters*.

■

Pain.

Pain in his chest, and in his stomach, and in his leg. And a girl was singing to him, her voice too loud. And it was dark, with shifting blue-gray forms in the distance.

I'm Don Denton, he thought. I've hurt myself.

How? How have I hurt myself? But the girl was singing too loudly, and it was impossible to think, and figure it out. And his terrific visual memory—so great a help to him as an actor—was of no help to him now. He felt himself falling away again, blacking out again, and with sudden terror he knew he wasn't fading into sleep, he was fading into death.

He *had* to wake up. Open the eyes, force the eyes open, *make* the eyes open. Listen to that damn loud girl, *listen* to her, concentrate on the words of the song, force the mind to work.

"Good night, good night.
We turn out every light;
The party's done, the night's begun,
Good night, my love, good night."

It was dark, blue-gray dark, and his eyelids were terribly heavy. He forced them up, wanting to see, wondering why the singing girl and the blue-gray dark.

It was the television set. All the lights in the room were off, and the shades were drawn against the night-glow of the city. Only the television lit the room, with shifting blues.

As he watched, the girl stopped singing and bowed to thunderous applause. And then he saw *himself,* striding across the stage, smiling and clapping his hands together, and memory came flooding back.

He was Don Denton, and this was Wednesday night, between the hours of eight and nine, and on the television screen he was watching *The Don Denton Variety Show,* taped that afternoon.

The Don Denton Variety Show was, in television jargon, live. The show that he was watching now was not a kinescope of a previous show, nor was it filmed, employing the cutting and editing techniques of film. Since it was neither, since it had been run through just as though it actually were going on the air at the time it had been performed, it was a live show, even though it had been recorded, via videotape, two hours before airtime. Due to various union requirements, it was much cheaper to do the show between five and six than between eight and nine. At the end of the show, at nine o'clock, an announcer would rapidly mumble the information that the show had been prerecorded and that the audience reaction had been technically augmented—a euphemism for canned laughter and canned applause—and so honesty and integrity would be maintained.

Denton watched all his own shows, not because he was an egotist—though he was—but out of a professional need to study his own product, to be sure that it at least did not deteriorate and, if possible, to see how it could be improved.

Tonight, after finishing the show, he had had dinner at the Athens Room and then had come home, where he now was, to watch the show. He was alone in the apartment, of course; he never permitted anyone else to be in the place while he was watching one of his shows. He had come home, changed into slacks and sport shirt and slippers, made himself a drink, flicked on the television set, and settled himself in the chair with the specially-built right arm. The arm of this chair was a miniature desk, with two small drawers in the side and a flat wooden workspace on top, where he rested his notebook.

Across the room, the eight o'clock commercials had flickered across the television screen, and then the opening credits of *The Don Denton Variety Show* had come on. He had watched and listened in approval as his name was mentioned by the announcer and appeared on the screen three times each, and then the fanfare had blared forth, the camera had been trained on the empty curtain-faced stage, and through a part in the curtain had come the tiny image of himself, in response to a thunderous burst of applause from the tape recorder in the control booth.

He had frowned. Too much applause? He didn't want the technical augmentation of the audience reaction to become too obvious. He had made a note of it.

The image of himself on the television screen had smiled and spoken and cracked a joke. Sitting in his chair at home, Don Denton had nodded approvingly. Then the image had introduced a girl singer, and Denton had turned over the pad to doodle awhile on its back. And then—

Then that memory came back, too, and he understood at last how he had been hurt. For the apartment door, off to his right, had suddenly opened, he remembered that now, and he . . .

HE TURNED ANNOYED. The show was on, damn it, he was not to be disturbed. They all knew that, knew better than to come here between eight and nine on a Wednesday night.

The only light came from the hall, behind the intruder, so that he—or she—was silhouetted, features blacked out. It was January outside, and the intruder was encased in a bulky overcoat, so Denton couldn't even tell whether it was a man or a woman.

Denton half-rose from the chair, frowning in anger. "What the hell do you—?"

Then there was a yellow-white flash from the center of the silhouetted figure, and the beginning of a thunderclap, and silence.

Until he heard the girl again, singing too loud.

HE WAS SHOT! Someone—*who?*—had come in here and shot him!

He sat slumped in the chair, trying to figure out where in his body the bullet might be and the extent of the damage. His legs ached, with a throbbing numbness. There was a clammy weight in his stomach, pressing him down, nauseating him. But the bullet wasn't there, nor in his legs. Higher, it was higher, higher . . .

There! Inside the chest, high on the right side, a burning core, a tiny center of heat and pain radiating out to the rest of his body. There it was, still within him, and he knew it was a bad wound, a terribly bad wound . . .

A crowd applauded, and he was startled. He focused his eyes again, saw himself again on the television screen, stepping back and to the side as the comic came out—"It's a funny thing about these new cars . . ."—and just to the right of the television set was the telephone on its stand.

He had to get help. The bullet was still in his chest, it was a terribly bad wound, he had to get help. He had to stand; he had to walk across the room to the telephone; he had to call for help.

He moved his right arm, and the arm seemed far away, the hand a million miles away, pushing through thick water. He tried to lean forward, and the pain buffeted him, slapping him back. He gripped the chair arms with hands that were still a million miles away; he slowly pulled himself forward, grimacing against the pain.

But his legs wouldn't work. He was paralyzed below the waist, nothing but his arms and his head were still working. He was dying, good God, he was dying, death was creeping slowly through his body. He had to get help before death reached his heart.

He tugged himself forward, and the pain lashed him, and his mouth stretched open in what should have been a scream. But no sound at all came out, only the strained rush of air. He couldn't make a sound.

The television set laughed with a thousand voices.

He looked again at the screen, the comic leering there. "Please," he whispered.

"'That's all right,' she says," the comic answered. "'I got an extra engine in the trunk.'"

The television set roared with merriment.

Bowing, bowing, on the screen, the comic winked at the dying man, laughed and waved and ran away.

Then the unwounded image of himself came back, tiny and colorless, but whole and sound, breathing and laughing, alive and sure. "That was great, Andy, great!" The image grinned up at him from the screen, asked him, "Wasn't it?"

"Please," he whispered.

"Who do you suppose we have next?" the image asked him, twinkling. "Who?"

Who? Who had done this? He had to know who had done this, who had shot him, who had tried to murder him.

He couldn't think. A busy spider scurried across his brain, trailing gray threads of fuzzy silk, webbing him in, slurring his thoughts.

No! He had to know *who!*

A key. There was a clear thought. A key, it had to be someone with a key. Remembering, thinking back, he seemed to hear again the tiny click of a key, just before the door had swung open.

They had to have a key; he had locked the door; he remembered that. The door was always locked, this was New York, Manhattan, one always locked doors.

There were only four people in the world who had keys to this apartment, aside from Denton himself, only four people in the world.

Nancy, his wife, from whom he was separated but not divorced.

Herb Martin, the chief writer for *The Don Denton Variety Show.*

Morry Stoneman, Denton's business manager.

Eddie Blake, the stooge-straight-man-second comic of the show.

It had to be one of the four. All four of them knew that he would be here, alone, watching the show at this hour. And they were the ones who had keys.

One of those four. He let the remembered faces and names of the four circle in his mind—Nancy and Herb and Morry and Eddie—while he tried to figure out which one of them would have tried to kill him.

And then he closed his eyes and almost gave himself up to death. Because it could have been any one of them. All four of them hated his guts, and so it could have been any one of them who had come here tonight to kill him.

Bitter, bitter, that was the most bitter moment of his life, to know that all four of the people closest to him hated him enough to want to see him dead.

His own voice said, "Oh, come now, Professor."

He opened his eyes, terrified. He'd almost faded away there, he'd almost passed out, and to pass out was surely to die. He could no longer feel anything in his legs, below the knee, and his fingers were no longer really parts of him. Death, death creeping in from his extremities.

No. He had to stay alive. He had to fool them, all four of them. He had to somehow stay alive. Keep thinking, keep the mind active, fight away the darkness.

Think about the four of them. Which one of them had done this?

"*Gott im Himmel,*" cried a gruff voice, and the canned laughter on the TV set followed dutifully.

Denton strained to see the television screen. Eddie Blake was there now, doing that miserable Professor routine of his. Denton watched, and wondered. Could it have been him?

EDDIE BLAKE STOOD in the doorway of the dressing room. "You wanted to see me, Don?"

Denton, sitting before the bulb-flanked mirror, removing his makeup, didn't bother to look away from his own reflection. "Come on in, Eddie," he said softly. "Close the door."

"Right," said Eddie. He stepped inside, shut the door, and stood there awkwardly, a tow-headed, hook-nosed, wide-mouthed little comic with a long thin frame and enough nervous mannerisms for twenty people.

Denton made him wait while he removed the rest of his makeup. It was a little after six, and the show had just been taped. Denton wasn't happy with the way the show had gone, and the more he thought about it, the more irritated he got. He finally turned and studied Eddie with a discontented frown. Eddie was still in the Professor costume, still in makeup, his left hand fidgeting at his side. Once, years ago, he'd been in an automobile accident, and his right arm was now weak and nearly useless.

"You were lousy tonight, Eddie," Denton said calmly. "I can't remember when you've been worse."

Eddie flushed, and his face worked, trying to hide the quick anger. He didn't say a word.

Denton lit a cigarette, more slowly than necessary, and finally said, "You back on the sauce again, Eddie?"

"You know better than that, Don," Eddie said indignantly.

"Maybe you just weren't thinking about the show tonight," Denton suggested. "Maybe you were saving yourself for that Boston date."

"I did my best, Don," Eddie insisted. "I worked my tail off."

"This show comes first, Eddie," Denton told him. He studied the comic coldly. "You ought to know that," he said. "Where would you be without this show, Eddie?"

Eddie didn't answer. He didn't have to; they both knew. Though Eddie was only a straight man, *The Don Denton Variety Show* had been his big break.

Still, Denton occasionally let him do a routine of his own, like the Professor bit tonight, and the television exposure had made it possible for Eddie to pick up a weekend nightclub job every once in a while, like the one he had in Boston that coming weekend.

"This show comes first, Eddie," Denton repeated. "You don't do anything else anywhere until you're doing your job on this show."

"Don, I—"

"Now, in your contract, you know, I've got to approve any outside booking you take on."

"Don, you aren't going to—"

"I've been pretty lax about that," Denton went on, smoothly overriding Eddie's protests. "But now I see what the result is. You start doing second-rate work here, saving yourself for your other jobs."

"Don, listen—"

"I think," Denton said, "that you'd better cut out all other jobs until you get up to form here." He nodded. "Okay, Eddie, that's all. See you at rehearsal Friday morning." He turned back to the mirror, started unbuttoning his shirt.

Behind him, Eddie fidgeted, ashen-faced. "Don," he said. "Listen, Don, you don't mean it."

Denton didn't bother answering.

"Don, look, you don't have to do this, all you have to do is tell me—"

"I just told you," said Denton.

"Don—listen, listen, what about Boston?"

"What about Boston?"

"I've got a date there this weekend, I—"

"No, you haven't."

"Don, for God's sake—"

"You'll be rehearsing all weekend. You won't have time to go to Boston."

"Don, the booking's already been made!"

"So what?"

Eddie's left hand darted and fidgeted, playing the buttons of his shirt like a clarinet. His eyes were wide and hopeless. "Don't do this, Don," he begged. "For God's sake, don't do this."

"You've done it to yourself."

"You dirty louse, *you're* the one who was way off tonight! Just because *you* can't get a laugh that doesn't come off tape—"

"Stop right there." Denton had risen now and stood glaring at the furious ineffectual comic. "Don't you forget the contract, Eddie," he said. "Don't you ever forget it. It's still got four and a half years to run. And I can always throw you off the show, cut off your pay, and still hold you to the contract. I can keep you from making a nickel, Eddie boy, and don't you forget it. Unless you'd like to wash dishes for your dough."

Eddie retreated to the door, obviously not trusting himself to stay in the dressing room any longer. "Don't push it, Don," he said, his voice trembling. "Don't push it too far."

"X plus y," said the heavily-accented voice on the television set, "iz somezing unprrro*noun*ceable!"

Denton blinked, trying to keep his eyes in focus. His sight kept blurring. He stared at the grinning figure on the screen. Eddie Blake? Could it have been Eddie Blake?

He could see the way Eddie might figure it. With Denton out of the way, the contract between them was no longer a problem. And who would be the most likely immediate replacement for

Denton on the show? Why, Eddie Blake, of course, who already knew the show. Denton's death, in Eddie's eyes, might be the stepping-stone to top banana.

But Eddie Blake? That weak, ineffectual, fidgety little nothing?

There were new voices coming from the TV now. He stared, trying to make out the picture, and finally saw it was the commercial. A husband and wife, a happy and devoted couple, and the secret of their successful marriage was—of course—their brand of toilet paper.

Successful marriage. He thought of Nancy. And of the writer, Herb Martin.

"I want a divorce, Don."

He paused in his eating. "No."

The three of them were at the table together in the Athens Room, Denton and Nancy and Herb. Nancy had said, this afternoon, that she wanted to talk to him about something important, and he had told her it would have to wait until after the show. He didn't want to be made upset by any domestic scenes just before airtime.

Herb now said, "I don't see what good it does you, Don. You obviously don't love Nancy, and she just as obviously doesn't love you. You aren't living together. So what's the sense of it?"

Denton glared sourly at Herb and pointed his fork at Nancy. "She's mine," he said. "No matter what, she's mine. It'll take a better man than you, buddy, to take anything of mine away from me."

"I can get a divorce without your consent," Nancy said. She was a lovely girl, oval face framed by long blonde hair. "I can go to Nevada—"

"Let's put it this way, sweetheart," Denton interrupted. "If there's any divorce—which there won't be—I'll be the plaintiff. And I won't even have to leave the state. Adultery will do very nicely. And the correspondent, just incidentally, used to be a Commie."

"How long do you think you can use that threat?" Herb demanded angrily.

"For as long as there's a blacklist, baby," Denton told him.

"Nineteen thirty-eight—"

"Baby, it doesn't matter *when* you were a Commie, you know that. Now, basically, I like you, Herb; I think you write some fine material. I'd hate to see you thrown out of the industry—"

"Why won't you let us *alone?*" wailed Nancy, and diners at nearby tables looked curiously around.

Denton patted his lips with the napkin and got to his feet. "You've asked your question," he said, "and I've given you the answer. I don't see any point in discussing it any more than that, do you? Oh, and I know you won't mind paying for your own dinners."

"Do me a favor," said Herb. "On your way home, get run over by a cab."

"Oh, don't joke with him, Herb," said Nancy, her voice shrill. She was—as usual—on the verge of hysterical tears.

"Who's joking?" said Herb grimly.

"All joking aside, friends," his voice said, "Dan and Ann are one of the finest dance teams in the country."

Slumped in the chair, Denton stared desperately at himself on the screen. That little self there on the screen, he could talk, he could move around, he could laugh and clap his palms together. He was alive, and content, not hurt.

Who? Who? Who? Herb or Nancy, or both of them together? He tried to think back, tried to visualize that silhouetted figure again, tried to see in memory whether it had been a man or a woman. But he couldn't tell; it had been only a bulky shape inside an overcoat, only a black shape outlined against the hall light. Inside the overcoat, it could have been as thin as Eddie, as shapely as Nancy, as muscular as Herb, as fat as Morry Stoneman.

Morry Stoneman?

Dan and Ann, one of the poorest dance teams in the country, were stumbling through their act before the cameras. Backstage, fat Morry Stoneman was dabbing at his forehead with a handkerchief and saying, "They looked good, Don, honest to God they did. They got all kinds of rave notices on the coast—"

"They're stumblebums," Denton told him coldly. He glanced out at Dan and Ann. "And I do mean stumble."

"You approved the act, Don. You gave it the okay."

"On your say-so, Morry. Or is it *my* fault?"

Morry hesitated, dabbing his face with the handkerchief, looking everywhere but at Denton. "No, Don," he said finally. "It isn't your fault."

"How much of a kickback, Morry?"

Morry's face was a white round O of injured innocence. "Don, you don't think—"

"How much are they giving you, Morry?"

The white round O collapsed, mumbled, "Five."

"Okay, Morry. We'll take that off your percentage."

"They got rave notices on the coast, Don. I swear to God they did. I can show you the clips."

Denton brushed that aside, said, "By the way, the five hundred doesn't come off the IOUs, you know that."

"Don," cried Morry, "what the hell *difference* does it make? This television business is lousy with money. What difference does it make if I try to promote a couple extra bills for myself?"

"You saw what happened to the quiz shows, you idiot. And to the guys who took money for plugs. And to the guys who took payola."

"I'm not as dumb as those clowns, Don, I couldn't be." Morry's left hand held the handkerchief, dab-dab-dabbing at his forehead. His right hand clutched Don Denton's sleeve. "All I'm trying to do," he said urgently, "is promote some extra cash so I can start paying back those IOUs. You want that money back, don't you?"

"So you can thumb your nose and walk out on me? That'll be the day, Morry."

"Listen, would I walk out on you? Don, I—"

"You aren't as bright as that chimpanzee, that monkey we had on last week," Denton snapped. "Don't you think I know you've been trying to get next to that Carlyle dame?"

Injured innocence again. "Who told you a dumb thing like that, Don? I wouldn't—"

"You won't," Denton interrupted him. "The minute you quit me, those IOUs become payable. So you can just forget Karen Carlyle."

Canned applause. It was time to go back and give Dan and Ann a big round of applause. Denton jabbed a thumb at the bowing, smiling dancers onstage. "Get them out of here," he said. "I don't want them around for the final bow." Then he trotted onstage, ignoring Morry's glare behind him.

He found the right camera and beamed at it. "For our last act tonight."

THE IMAGE ON the screen told his dying likeness, "We have that wonderful new singer—she's going to have her own show starting in March, you know—Karen *Carlyle!*"

Denton watched his black-and-white self, teeth gleaming, hands beating together. "She wants Morry," he whispered at that unhearing image. "And Morry wants her."

Morry? Was it Morry who'd shot him?

Who was it?

The space between himself and the television set seemed to blur and mist, as though a dim fog were rising there. He blinked, blinked, blinked, afraid it was death.

And in the fog, he seemed to see the four who could have done this. Herb and Nancy, directly in front of him, arms around each other, studying him in somber triumph. Eddie Blake, off to the right, his left hand playing his shirt buttons with jittery fingers as he stared at Denton with tentative defiance. And Morry, behind the others and off to the left, stood stocky and unmoving, glaring with frustration and hate.

"Which one of you?" Denton whispered. Fighting back the pain in his chest, he strained forward at them, demanding, willing them to speak, having to know.

And they spoke. "When you are dead," said Nancy, "I can marry Herb."

"When you are dead," said Eddie, "it will be *The Eddie Blake Variety Show.*"

"When you are dead," said Herb, "so is that blacklist threat."

"When you are dead," said Morry, "so are those IOUs. I can make a mint with Karen Carlyle."

"Which one of you? Which one of you?"

The fog shifted and swam; the figures faded. Straining, he could once more see that other figure, the black silhouette framed by the doorway, lit only from behind.

He stared at the silhouette, needing to know, demanding to know which one it had been.

He searched the bulky, shapeless outline, looking for something that would tell him. The remembered outline of the head, the ears, the neck, then the collar of the coat, the—

The ears. He squinted, trying to see, trying to remember, and yes, the ears were outlined plainly, and the four possibilities had just been reduced to three. For Nancy had long blonde hair, curling around her face, covering her ears. It hadn't been Nancy.

Three. It was one of three now, Herb or Eddie or Morry. But which one?

Height. That would help, if he could visualize the figure well enough, if he could see it in relation to the doorframe, the height—Eddie and Herb were both tall; Morry was short. Probably Eddie even seemed taller than he was because he was so thin. But really he was—

Denton pulled himself back. His mind was beginning to wander, and he recognized that as a danger sign. He couldn't lose consciousness, he couldn't lose awareness, not until he *knew.*

He stared at the outlined figure in the fog, and slowly he forced himself to visualize the door frame around it again, and slowly he saw it, and the figure was tall.

Eddie or Herb. Eddie or Herb.

It had to be one or the other, but that was as close as he could get. He tried to superimpose the figures of Eddie and Herb on the figure of the silhouette and got nowhere. The bulky coat ruined that; it was impossible.

Death was creeping closer, across his shoulders and down among his ribs, up from his legs to touch his stomach with icy fingers. He had to know soon, he had to know soon.

He visualized what had happened again, in the fog between himself and the television set, seeing it like a run-through for the show, seeing every step. The door opening, the black figure standing there, the bright flash—

From the figure's *right* side!

"*Herb!*" he shouted. Eddie was left-handed, and his impaired right hand would never have been able to lift the gun or squeeze the trigger, it had been Herb.

With his shout, the fog faded completely away, the outlined figure was gone. Sight and sound returned, and he heard Karen Carlyle singing her song. It was the last number of the show. It must be almost nine o'clock; he'd been sitting here wounded now for almost an hour.

Karen Carlyle stopped at last, and there was thunderous canned applause and he saw himself come striding into camera range. He saw that whole and walking, strong and smiling self come out and wave at the imaginary audience, wave at Don Denton dying in his chair.

He stared at that tiny image of himself. That was *him!* Him, at six o'clock, with two hours left, and that self could somehow change this, could somehow keep what had and was happening from happening.

Dream and reality, desire and fact, need and truth, shifted and mingled confusedly in his mind. He was barely real himself. He was dying faster now, becoming less and less real, and the image on the television screen was almost all that was left of him.

And so Denton felt the need to warn the image. "It's Herb!" he called, whispering, at that tiny blue-gray self across the room. Reality was going, like the lights of a city flicking out one by one, and darkness was spreading in. "Be careful! It's Herb!"

"That's about all the show there is, folks," answered his image.

The lights flicked out, and Denton's mind broke. "Don't go home!" he shrieked. "It's Herb!"

"I certainly hope you've enjoyed yourself," said the image, smiling at him.

"Stay away!" screamed Denton.

The image waved a careless hand, as though to tell Denton not to be silly, there was nothing wrong in the world, nothing at all. "We'll be seeing you!"

He had to get away, he had to live, he had to warn himself not to come here tonight. There was that image, the *real* Don Denton, in the television set, and right beside him was the telephone.

"Help me!" shrieked Denton all at once. "Call! Call! Help me!" And it seemed to him as though it should be the easiest thing in the world, for that real image of himself to reach over and pick up the telephone and call for help.

But, instead, that image merely waved and cried, "Good night!" The blind and stupid image of himself, blowing a kiss at the dying man in the chair.

"Help me!" Denton screamed, but the words were buried by a bubbling-up of blood, filling his throat.

The image receded, down and down, growing smaller and ever smaller as the boom camera was raised toward the ceiling. "Love you! Love you!" cried the tiny doomed image to the dead man in the chair. "Good night! Good night!"

AVRAM DAVIDSON

THE COST OF KENT CASTWELL

July 1961

AVRAM DAVIDSON is well known not only to readers of mysteries but also to readers of science fiction and fantasy. Indeed, he served as editor of *The Magazine of Fantasy and Science Fiction* for several years, and he was a winner of the Hugo Award and the World Fantasy Award (three times), in addition to the Edgar Award. And this story, in fact, was cited in *AHMM*'s own story contest.

■

Clem Goodhue met the train with his taxi. If old Mrs. Merriman were aboard, he would be sure of at least one passenger. Furthermore, old Mrs. Merriman had somehow gotten the idea that the minimum fare was a dollar. It was really seventy-five cents, but Clem had never been able to see a reason for telling her that. However, she was not aboard that morning. Sam Wells was. He was coming back from the city—been to put in a claim to have his pension increased—but Sam Wells wouldn't pay five cents to ride any distance under five miles. Clem disregarded him.

After old Sam a thin, brown-haired kid got off the train. Next came a girl, also thin and also brown-haired, who Clem thought was maybe the kid's teenage sister. Actually, it was the kid's mother.

After *that* came Kent Castwell.

Clem had seen him before, early in the summer. Strangers were not numerous in Ashby, particularly strangers who got ugly and caused commotions in bars. So Clem wouldn't forget him in a hurry. Big, husky fellow. Always seemed to be sneering at something. But the girl and the kid hadn't been with him then.

"Taxi?" Clem called.

Castwell ignored him, began to take down luggage from the train. But the young girl holding the kid by the hand turned and said, "Yes—just a minute."

"Where to?" Clem asked, when the luggage was in the taxi.

"The old Peabody place," the girl said. "You know where that is?"

"Yes. But nobody lives there anymore."

"Somebody does now. Us." The big man swore as he fiddled with the handle of the right-hand door. It was tied with ropes. "Why don't you fix this thing or get a new one?"

"Costs money," Clem said. Then, "Peabody place? Have to charge you three dollars for that."

"Let's go dammit, let's go!"

After they'd started off, Castwell said, "I'm giving you two bucks. Probably twice what it's worth, anyway."

Half-turning his head, Clem protested. "I told you, mister, it was three."

"And I'm telling you, mister," Castwell mimicked the driver's New England accent, "that I'm giving you two."

Clem argued that the Peabody Place was far out. He mentioned the price of gas, the bad condition of the road, the wear on the tires. The big man yawned. Then he used a word that Clem rarely used himself, and never in the presence of women and children. But this young woman and child didn't seem to notice.

"Stop off at Nickerson's real estate office," Castwell said.

Levi P. Nickerson, who was also the county tax assessor, said, "Mr. Castwell. I assume this is Mrs. Castwell?"

"If that's your assumption, go right ahead," said Kent. And laughed.

It wasn't a pleasant laugh. The woman smiled faintly, so L. P. Nickerson allowed himself an economical chuckle. Then he cleared his throat. City people had odd ideas of what was funny. Meanwhile, though—

"Now, Mr. Castwell. About this place you're renting. I didn't realize—you didn't mention—that you had this little one, here."

Kent said, "What if I didn't mention it? It's my own business. I haven't got all *day*—"

Nickerson pointed out that the Peabody place stood all alone, isolated, with no other house for at least a mile and no other children in the neighborhood. Mrs. Castwell (if, indeed, she *was*) said that this wouldn't matter much, because Kathie would be in school most of the day.

"School. Well, that's it, you see. The school bus, in the first place, will have to go three miles off what's been its regular route, to pick up your little girl. And that means the road will have to be plowed regular—snow gets real deep up in these parts, you know. Up till now, with nobody living in the old Peabody place, we never had to bother with the road. Now, this means," and he began to count off on his fingers, "first, it'll cost Ed Westlake, he drives the school bus, more than he figured on when he bid for the contract; second, it'll cost the county to keep your road open. That's besides the cost of the girl's schooling, which is third."

Kent Castwell said that was tough, wasn't it? "Let's have the keys, Nick," he said.

A flicker of distaste at the familiarity crossed the real estate man's face. "You don't seem to realize that all this extra expense to the county isn't covered by the tax assessment on the Peabody place," he pointed out. "Now, it just so happens that there's a house right on the outskirts of town become available this week. Miss Sarah Beech passed on, and her sister, Miss Lavinia, moved in with their married sister, Mrs. Calvin Adams. 'Twon't cost *you* any more, and it would save *us* considerable."

Castwell, sneering, got up. "What! Me live where some old-maid landlady can be on my neck all the time about messing up her pretty things? Thanks a lot. No thanks." He held out his hand. "The keys, kid. Gimme the keys." Mr. Nickerson gave him the keys. Afterwards he was to say, and to say often, that he wished he'd thrown them into Lake Amastanquit instead.

THE INCOME of the Castwell menage was not large and consisted of a monthly check and a monthly money order. The check came on the fifteenth, from a city trust company and was assumed by some to be inherited income. Others argued in favor of its being a remittance paid by Castwell's family to keep him away. The money order was made out to Louise Cane and signed by an army sergeant in Alaska. The young woman said this was alimony and that Sergeant Burndall was her former husband. Tom Talley, at the grocery store, had her sign the endorsement twice, as Louise Cane and as Louise Castwell. Tom was a cautious man.

Castwell gave Louise a hard time, there was no doubt about that. If she so much as walked in between the sofa, on which he spent most of his time, and the television, he'd leap up and belt her. More than once both she and the kid had to run out of the house to get away from him. He wouldn't follow, as a rule, because he was barefooted, as a rule, and it was too much trouble to put his shoes on.

Lie on the sofa and drink beer and watch television all afternoon, and hitch into town and drink bar whiskey and watch television all evening—that was Kent Castwell's daily schedule. He got to know who drove along the road regularly, at what time, and in which direction, and he'd be there, waiting. There was more than one who could have dispensed with the pleasure of his company, but he'd get out in the road and wave his arms and not move until the car he got in front of stopped.

What could you do about it? Put him in jail?

Sure you could.

He hadn't been living there a week before he got into a fight at the Ashby Bar.

"Disturbing the peace, using profane and abusive language, and resisting arrest—that will be ten dollars or ten days on each of the charges," said Judge Paltiel Bradford. "And count yourself lucky it's not more. Pay the clerk."

But Castwell, his ugly leer in no way improved by the dirt and bruises on his face, said, "I'll take jail."

Judge Bradford's long jaw set, then loosened. "Look here, Mr. Castwell, that was just legal language on my part. The jail is closed up. Hasn't been anybody in there since July." It was then November. "It would have to be heated, and illuminated, and the water turned on, and a guard hired. To say nothing of feeding you. Now, I don't see why the county should be put to all that expense on your account. You pay the clerk thirty dollars. You haven't got it on you, take till tomorrow. Well?"

"I'll take the jail."

"It's most inconvenient—"

"That's too bad, Your Honor."

The judge glared at him. Gamaliel Coolidge, the district attorney, stood up. "Perhaps the court would care to suspend sentence," he suggested. "Seeing it is the defendant's first offense."

The court did care. But the next week Kent was back again, on the same charge. Altogether, the sentence now came to sixty dollars, or sixty days. And again Castwell chose jail.

"I don't generally do this," the judge said, fuming. "But I'll let you pay your fine off in installments. Considering you have a wife and child."

"Uh-uh. I'll take jail."

"You won't like the food!" warned His Honor.

Castwell said he guessed the food would be up to the legal requirements. If it wasn't, he said, the State Board of Prison Inspectors would hear about it.

Some pains were taken to see that the food served Kent during his stay in jail was beyond the legal requirements—if not much beyond. The last time the state board had inspected the county jail it had cost the taxpayers two hundred dollars in repairs. It was costing them quite enough to incarcerate Kent Castwell, as it was, although the judge had reduced the cost by ordering the sentences to run concurrently.

All in all, Kent spent over a month in jail that winter, at various times. It seemed to some that whenever his money ran out, he let the county support him and let the woman and child fend for themselves. Tom Talley gave them a little credit at the store. Not much.

ED WESTLAKE, WHEN he bid again for the school bus contract, added the cost of going three miles out of his way to pick up Kathie. The county had no choice but to meet the extra charge. It was considered very thoughtless of Louise to wait till *after* the contract was signed before leaving Castwell and going back to the city with her child. The side road to the Peabody place didn't have to be plowed so often, but it still had to be plowed *some*. That extra cost, just for one man! It was maddening.

It almost seemed—no, it *did* seem—as if Kent Castwell were deliberately setting himself in the face of New England respectability and thrift. The sacred words, "Eat it up, wear it out, make it do, or do without," didn't mean a thing to him. He wasn't just indifferent. He was hostile.

Ashby was not a thriving place. It had no industries. It was not a resort town, being far from sea and mountains alike, with only the shallow, muddy waters of Lake Amastanquit for a pleasure spot. Its thin-soiled farms and meager woodlots produced a scanty return for the hard labor exacted. The young people continued to leave. Kent Castwell, unfortunately, showed no signs of leaving.

All things considered, it was not surprising that Ashby had no artists' colony. It *was* rather surprising, then, that Clem Goodhue, meeting the train with his taxi, recognized Bob Laurel at once as an artist. When asked afterwards how he had known, Clem looked smug and said that he had once been to Provincetown.

The conversation, as Clem recalled it afterwards, began with Bob Laurel's asking where he could find a house that offered low rent, peace and quiet, and a place to paint.

"So I recommended Kent Castwell," Clem said. He was talking to Sheriff Erastus Nickerson (Levi P.'s cousin) at the time.

"'Peace and *quiet?*'" the sheriff repeated. "I know Laurel's a city fellow, and an artist, but, still and all—"

They were seated in the bar of the Ashby House, drinking their weekly small glass of beer. "I looked at it this way, Erastus," the taxi man said. "Sure, there's empty houses all around that he could rent. Suppose *he*—this artist fellow—suppose *he* picks one off on a side road with nobody else living on it? Suppose *he* comes up with a wife out of somewhere, and suppose *she* has a school-age child?"

"You're right, Clem."

"'Course I'm right. Bad enough for the county to be put to all that cost for *one* house, let alone two."

"You're right, Clem. But will he stay with Castwell?"

Clem shrugged. "That I can't say. But I did my best."

Laurel stayed with Castwell. He really had no choice. The big man agreed to take him in as lodger and to give over the front room for a studio. And, holding out offers of insulating the house, putting in another window, and who knows what else, Kent Castwell persuaded the unwary artist to pay several months' rent in advance. Needless to say, he drank up the money and did nothing at all in the way of the promised improvements.

Neither District Attorney Gamaliel Coolidge nor Sheriff Nickerson, nor, for that matter, anyone else, showed Laurel much sympathy. He had grounds for a civil suit, they said; nothing else. It should be a lesson to him not to throw his money around in the future, they said.

So the unhappy artist stayed on at the old Peabody place, buying his own food and cutting his own wood, and painting, painting, painting. And all the time he knew full well that his leering landlord only waited for him to go into town in order to help himself to both food and wood.

Laurel invited Clem to have a glass of beer with him more than once, just to have someone to tell his troubles to. Besides stealing his food and fuel, Kent Castwell, it seemed, played the TV at full blast when Laurel wanted to sleep; if it was too late for TV, he set the radio to roaring. At moments when the artist was intent on delicate brushwork, Castwell would decide to bring in stove wood and drop it on the floor so that the whole house shook.

"He talks to himself in that loud, rough voice of his," Bob Laurel complained. "He has a filthy mouth. He makes fun of my painting. He—"

"I tell you what it is," Clem said. "Kent Castwell has no consideration for others. That's what it is. Yep."

Bets were taken in town, of a ten-cent cigar per bet, on how long Laurel would stand for it. Levi Nickerson, the county tax assessor, thought he'd leave as soon as his rent was up. Clem's opinion was that he'd leave sooner. "Money don't mean that much to city people," he pointed out.

Clem won.

When he came into Nickerson's house, Levi, who was sitting close to the small fire in the kitchen stove, wordlessly handed over the cigar. Clem nodded, put it in his pocket. Mrs. Abby

Nickerson sat next to her husband, wearing a man's sweater. It had belonged to her late father, whose heart had failed to survive the first reelection of Franklin D. Roosevelt, and it still had a lot of wear left in it. Abby was unraveling old socks and winding the wool into a ball. "Waste not, want not," was her motto—as well as that of every other old-time local resident.

On the stove a kettle steamed thinly. Two piles of used envelopes were on the table. They had all been addressed to the tax assessor's office of the county and had been carefully opened so as not to mutilate them. While Clem watched, Levi Nickerson removed one of the envelopes from its place on top of the uncovered kettle. The mucilage on its flaps loosened by steam, it opened out easily to Nickerson's touch. He proceeded to refold it and then reseal it so that the used outside was now inside; then he added it to the other pile.

"Saved the county eleven dollars this way last year," he observed. "Shouldn't wonder but what I don't make it twelve this year, maybe twelve-fifty." Clem gave a small appreciative grunt. "Where is he?" the tax assessor asked.

"Laurel? In the Ashby Bar. He's all packed. I told him to stay put. I told them to keep an eye on him, phone me here if he made a move to leave."

He took a sheet of paper out of his pocket and put it on the table. Levi looked at it, but made no move to pick it up. To his wife he said, "I'm expecting Erastus and Gam Coolidge over, Mrs. Nickerson. County business. I expect you can find something to do in the front of the house while we talk."

Mrs. Nickerson nodded. Even words were not wasted.

A car drove up to the house.

"That's Erastus," said his cousin. "Gam should be along—he *is* along. Might've known he wouldn't waste gasoline; came with Erastus."

The two men came into the kitchen. Mrs. Abby Nickerson arose and departed.

"Hope we can get this over with before nightfall," the sheriff said. "I don't like to drive after dark if I can help it. One of my headlights is getting dim, and they cost so darned much to replace."

Clem cleared his throat. "Well, here 'tis," he said, gesturing to the paper on the table. "Laurel's confession. 'Tell the sheriff and the DA that I'm ready to give myself up,' he says. 'I wrote it all down here,' he says. Happened about two o'clock this afternoon, I guess. Straw that broke the camel's back. Kent Castwell, he was acting up as usual. Stomping and swearing out there at the Peabody place. Words were exchanged. Laurel left to go out back," Clem said, delicately, not needing to further comment on the Peabody place's lack of indoor plumbing. "When he come back, Castwell had taken the biggest brush he could find and smeared paint over all the pictures Laurel had been working on. Ruined them completely."

There was a moment's silence. "Castwell had no call to do that," the sheriff said. "Destroying another man's property. They tell me some of those artists get as much as a hundred dollars for a painting . . . What'd he do then? Laurel, I mean."

"Picked up a piece of stove wood and hit him with it. Hit him hard."

"No doubt about his being dead, I suppose?" the sheriff asked.

Clem shook his head. "There was no blood or anything on the wood," he added. "Just another piece of stove wood . . . But he's dead, all right."

After a moment Levi Nickerson said, "His wife will have to be notified. No reason why the county should have to pay burial expenses. Hmm. I expect she won't have any money, though. Best get in touch with those trustees who sent Castwell his money every month. *They'll* pay."

Gamaliel Coolidge asked if anyone else knew. Clem said no. Bob Laurel hadn't told anyone else. He didn't seem to want to talk.

This time there was a longer silence.

"Do you realize how much Kent Castwell cost this county, one way or the other?" Nickerson asked.

Clem said he supposed hundreds of dollars. "Hundreds and *hundreds* of dollars," Nickerson said.

"*And,*" the tax assessor went on, "do you know what it will cost us to try this fellow—for murder in any degree or manslaughter?"

The district attorney said it would cost thousands. "Thousands and *thousands* . . . and that's just the trial," he elaborated. "Suppose he's found guilty and appeals? We'd be obliged to fight the appeal. More thousands. And suppose he gets a new trial? We'd have it to pay all over again."

Levi P. Nickerson opened his mouth as though it hurt him to do so. "What it would do to the county tax rate . . ." he groaned. "Kent Castwell," he said, his voice becoming crisp and definite, "is not worth it. He is just not *worth* it."

Clem took out the ten-cent cigar he'd won, sniffed it. "My opinion," he said, "it would have been much better if this fellow Laurel had just packed up and left. Anybody finding Castwell's body would assume he'd fallen and hit his head. But this confession, now—"

Sheriff Erastus Nickerson said reflectively, "I haven't read any confession. You, Gam? You, Levi? No. What you've told us, Clem, is just hearsay. Can't act on hearsay. Totally contrary to all principals of American law . . . Hmm. Mighty nice sunset." He arose and walked over to the window. His cousin followed him. So did District Attorney Coolidge. While they were looking at the sunset, Clem Goodhue, after a single glance at their backs, took the sheet of paper from the kitchen table and thrust it into the kitchen stove. There was a flare of light. It quickly died down. Clem carefully reached his hand into the stove, took out the small corner of the paper remaining, and lit his cigar with it.

The three men turned from the window.

Levi P. Nickerson was first to speak. "Can't ask any of you to stay to supper," he said. "Just a few leftovers is all we're having. I expect you'll want to be going on your way."

The two other county officials nodded.

The taxi man said, "I believe I'll stop by the Ashby Bar. Might be someone there wanting to catch the evening train. Night, Levi. Don't turn on the yard light for us."

"Wasn't going to," said Levi. "Turning them on and off, that's what burns them out. Night Clem, Gam, Erastus." He closed the door after them. "Mrs. Nickerson," he called to his wife, "you can come and start supper now. We finished our business."

EDWARD D. HOCH

THE LONG WAY DOWN

February 1965

SURELY ONE of the great practitioners of the short story form, Ed Hoch holds one of the most remarkable records in mystery: he has published an original story in every issue of *Ellery Queen's Mystery Magazine* since May 1973. Fortunately, our sister publication has been happy to share him with *AHMM* over the years, and his tightly plotted, fair-play mysteries are always favorites with readers. This story, as it happens, was subsequently adapted as an episode of the television series *McMillan and Wife*. He has also written under a number of pseudonyms, and he has developed over the years a stable of twenty-four recurring series detectives. Another *AHMM* Hoch story, "Winter Run," was the basis for the last new episode produced for *The Alfred Hitchcock Hour*.

■

Many men have disappeared under unusual circumstances, but perhaps none more unusual than those that befell Billy Calm.

The day began in a routine way for McLove. He left his apartment in midtown Manhattan and walked through the foggy March morning, just as he did on every working day of the year. When he was still several blocks away, he could make out the bottom floors of the great glass slab that was the home office of the Jupiter Steel & Brass Corporation. But above the tenth floor the fog had taken over, shrouding everything in a dense coat of moisture that could have been the roof of the world.

Underfoot, the going was slushy. The same warm air mass that had caused the fog was making short work of the previous day's two-inch snowfall. McLove, who didn't really mind Manhattan winters, was thankful that spring was only days away. Finally he turned into the massive marble lobby of the Jupiter Steel building, thinking for the hundredth time that only the garish little newsstand in one corner kept it from being an exact replica of the interior of an Egyptian tomb. Anyway, it was dry inside, without slush underfoot.

McLove's office on the twenty-first floor had been a point of creeping controversy from the very beginning. It was the executive floor, bulging with the vice presidents and others who formed the inner core of Billy Calm's little family. The very idea of sharing this exclu-sive office space with the firm's security chief had repelled many of them, but when Billy Calm spoke there were few who openly dared challenge his mandates.

McLove had moved to the executive floor soon after the forty-year-old boy genius of Wall Street had seized control of Jupiter Steel in a proxy battle that had split stockholders into armed camps. On the day Billy Calm first walked through the marble lobby to take command of his newest acquisition, a disgruntled shareholder named Raimey had shot his hat off, and actually managed to get off a second shot before being over-powered. From that day on, Billy Calm used the private elevator at the rear of the building, and McLove supervised security from the twenty-first floor.

It was a thankless task that amounted to little more than being a sometime bodyguard for Calm. His duties, in the main, consisted of keeping Calm's private elevator in working order, attending directors' meetings with the air of a reluctant outsider, supervising the security forces at the far-flung Jupiter mills, and helping with arrangements for Calm's numerous public appearances. For this he was paid fifteen thousand dollars a year, which was the principal reason he did it.

On the twenty-first floor, this morning, Margaret Mason was already at her desk outside the directors' room. She looked up as McLove stepped into the office and flashed him their private smile. "How are you, McLove?"

"Morning, Margaret. Billy in yet?"

"Mr. Calm? Not yet. He's flying in from Pittsburgh. Should be here any time now."

McLove glanced at his watch. He knew the directors' meeting was scheduled for ten, and that was only twenty minutes away. "Heard anything?" he asked, knowing that Margaret Mason was the best source of information on the entire floor. She knew everything and would tell you most of it, provided it didn't concern herself.

Now she nodded and bent forward a bit across the desk. "Mr. Calm phoned from his plane and talked with Jason Greene. The merger is going through. He'll announce it officially at the meeting this morning."

"That'll make some people around here mighty sad." McLove was thinking of W. T. Knox and Sam Hamilton, two directors who had opposed the merger talk from the very beginning. Only twenty-four hours earlier, before Billy Calm's rush flight to Pittsburgh in his private plane, it had appeared that their efforts would be successful.

"They should know better than to buck Mr. Calm," Margaret said.

"I suppose so." McLove glanced at his watch again. For some reason he was getting nervous. "Say, how about lunch, if we get out of the meeting in time?"

"Fine." She gave him the small smile again. "You're the only one I feel safe drinking with at noon."

"Be back in a few minutes."

"I'll buzz you if Mr. Calm gets in."

He glanced at the closed doors of the private elevator and nodded. Then he walked down the hall to his own office once more. He got a pack of cigarettes from his desk and went across the hall to W. T. Knox's office.

"Morning, W. T. What's new?"

The tall man looked up from a file folder he'd been studying. Thirty-seven, a man who had retained most of his youthful good looks and all of his charm, Knox was popular with the girls on twenty-one. He'd probably have been more popular if he hadn't had a pregnant wife and five children of varying ages.

"McLove, look at this weather!" He gestured toward the window, where a curtain of fog still hung. "Every winter I say

I'll move to Florida, and every winter the wife talks me into staying."

Jason Greene, balding and ultra-efficient, joined them with a sheaf of reports. "Billy should be in at any moment. He phoned me to say the merger had gone through."

Knox dropped his eyes. "I heard."

"When the word gets outs, Jupiter stock will jump another ten points."

McLove could almost feel the tension between the two men; one gloating, and the other bitter. He walked to the window and stared out at the fog, trying to see the invisible building across the street. Below, he could not even make out the setback of their own building, though it was only two floors lower. Fog . . . well, at least it meant that spring was on the way.

Then there was a third voice behind him, and he knew without turning that it belonged to Shirley Taggert, the president's personal secretary. "It's almost time for the board meeting," she said, with that hint of a southern drawl that either attracted or repelled but left no middle ground. "You people ready?"

Shirley was grim-faced but far from ugly. She was a bit younger than Margaret Mason's mid-thirties, a bit sharper of dress and mind. But she paid the penalty for being Billy Calm's secretary every time she walked down the halls. Conversations ceased, suspicious glances followed her, and there was always a half-hidden air of tension at her arrival. She ate lunch alone, and one or two fellows who had been brave enough to ask her for a date hadn't bothered to ask a second time.

"We're ready," Jason Greene told her. "Is he here yet?"

She shook her head and glanced at the clock. "He should be in any minute."

McLove left them grouped around Knox's desk and walked back down the hall. Sam Hamilton, the joker, passed him on the way and stopped to tell him a quick gag. He, at least, didn't seem awfully upset about the impending merger, even though he had opposed it. McLove liked Sam better than any of the other directors, probably because at the age of fifty he was still a big kid at heart. You could meet him on even ground and, at times, feel he was letting you outdo him.

"Anything yet?" McLove asked Margaret, returning to her desk outside the directors' room.

"No sign of Mr. Calm, but he shouldn't be long now. It's just about ten."

McLove glanced at the closed door of Billy Calm's office, next to the directors' room, and then entered the latter. The room was quite plain, with only the one door through which he had entered, and unbroken walls of dull oak paneling on either wall. The far end of the room, with two wide windows looking out at the fog, was only twenty feet away, and the conference table that was the room's only piece of furniture had just the eight necessary chairs grouped around it. Some had been heard to complain that the room lacked the stature of Jupiter Steel, but Billy Calm contended he liked the forced intimacy of it.

Now, as McLove stood looking out the windows, the whole place seemed to reflect the cold mechanization of the modern office building. The windows could not be opened. Even their cleaning had to be done from the outside, on a gondola-like platform that climbed up and down the sheer glass walls. There were no windowsills, and McLove's fingers ran unconsciously along the bottom of the window frame as he stood staring out. The fog might be lifting a little, but he couldn't be certain.

McLove went out to Margaret Mason's desk, saw that she was gathering together her copy books and pencils for the meeting, and decided to take a glance into Billy Calm's office. It was the same size as the directors' room and almost as plain in its furnishings. Only the desk, cluttered with the trivia of a businessman's lifetime, gave proof of human occupancy. On the left wall still hung the faded portrait of the firm's founder, and on the right, a more recent photograph of Israel Black, former president of Jupiter, and still a director though he never came to the meetings. This was Billy Calm's domain. From here he ruled a vast empire of holdings, and a word from him could send men to their financial ruin.

McLove straightened suddenly on hearing a man's muffled voice at Margaret's desk outside. He heard her ask, "What's the matter?" and then heard the door of the directors' room open. Hurrying back to her desk, he was just in time to see the door closing again.

"Is he finally here?"

Margaret, unaccountably white-faced, opened her mouth to answer, just as there came the tinkling crash of a breaking window from the inner room. They both heard it clearly, and she dropped the cigarette she'd been in the act of lighting. "Billy!" she screamed out. "No, Billy!"

They were at the door together after only an instant's hesitation, pushing it open before them, hurrying into the directors' room. "No," McLove said softly, staring straight ahead at the empty room and the long table and the shattered window in the opposite wall. "He jumped." Already the fog seemed to be filling the room with its damp mists as they hurried to the window and peered out at nothing.

"Billy jumped," Margaret said dully, as if unable to comprehend the fact. "He killed himself."

McLove turned and saw Knox standing in the doorway. Behind him, Greene and Hamilton and Shirley Taggert were coming up fast. "Billy Calm just jumped out of the window," McLove told them.

"No," Margaret Mason said, turning from the window. "No, no, no, no . . ." Then, suddenly overcome with the shock of it, she tumbled to the floor in a dead faint.

"Take care of her," McLove shouted to the others. "I've got to get downstairs."

Knox bent to lift the girl in his arms, while Sam Hamilton hurried to the telephone. Shirley had settled into one of the padded directors' chairs, her face devoid of all expression. And Jason Greene, loyal to the end, actually seemed to be crying.

In the hallway, McLove pushed the button of Billy Calm's private elevator and waited for it to rise from the depths of the building. The little man would have no further use for it now. He rode it down alone, leaning against its padded walls, listening to, but hardly hearing, the dreary hum of its descent. In another two minutes he was on the street, looking for the crowd that would surely be gathered, listening for the sounds of rising sirens.

But there was nothing. Nothing but the usual mid-morning traffic. Nothing but hurrying pedestrians and a gang of workmen drilling at the concrete and a policeman dully directing traffic.

There was no body.

McLove hurried over to the police officer. "A man just jumped out of the Jupiter Steel building," he said. "What happened to him?"

The policeman wrinkled his brow. "Jumped? From where?"

"Twenty-first floor. Right above us."

They both gazed upward into the gradually lifting fog. The police officer shrugged his shoulders. "Mister, I been standing in this very spot for more than an hour. Nobody jumped from up there."

"But . . ." McLove continued staring into the fog. "But he *did* jump. I practically saw him do it. And if he's not down here, where *is* he?"

Back on twenty-one, McLove found the place in a state somewhere between sheer shock and calm confusion. People were hurrying without purpose in every direction, bent on their own little useless errands. Sam Hamilton was on the phone to his broker's, trying to get the latest quotation on Jupiter stock. "The bottom'll drop out of it when this news hits," he confided to McLove. "With Billy gone, the merger won't go through."

McLove lit a cigarette. "Billy Calm is gone, all right, but he's not down there. He vanished somewhere between the twenty-first floor and the street."

"*What?*"

W. T. Knox joined them, helping a pale but steady Margaret Mason by the arm. "She'll be all right," he said. "It was the shock."

McLove reached out his hand to her. "Tell us exactly what happened. Every word of it."

"Well . . ." She hesitated and then sat down. Behind her, Hamilton and Shirley Taggert were deep in animated conversation, and Jason Greene had appeared from somewhere with a policeman in tow.

"You were at the desk," McLove began, helping her. "And I came out of the directors' room and went into Billy's office. Then what?"

"Well, Mr. Calm came in, and as he passed my desk he mumbled something. I didn't catch it, and I asked him what was the matter. He seemed awfully upset about something. Anyway, he passed my desk and went into the directors' room. He was just closing the door when you came out, and you know the rest."

McLove nodded. He knew the rest, which was nothing but the shattered window and the vanished man. "Well, the body's not down there," he told them again. "It's not anywhere. Billy Calm dived through that window and flew away."

Shirley passed Hamilton a telephone she had just answered. "Yes?" He listened a moment and then hung up. "The news about Billy went out over the stock ticker. Jupiter Steel is selling off fast. It's already down three points."

"Goodbye merger," Knox said, and though his face was grim, his voice was not.

A detective arrived on the scene to join the police officer. Quickly summoned workmen were tacking cardboard over the smashed window, carefully removing some of the jagged splinters of glass from the bottom of the frame. Things were settling down a little, and the police were starting to ask questions.

"Mr. McLove, you're in charge of security for the company?"

"That's right."

"Why was it necessary to have a security man sit in on directors' meetings?"

"Some nut tried to kill Billy Calm awhile back. He was still nervous. Private elevator and all."

"What was the nut's name?"

"Raimey, I think. Something like that. Don't know where he is now."

"And who was usually present at these meetings? I see eight chairs in there."

"Calm, and three vice presidents; Greene, Knox, and Hamilton. Also Calm's secretary, Miss Taggert, and Miss Mason, who kept the minutes of the meeting. The seventh chair is mine, and the eighth one is kept for Mr. Black, who never comes down for the meetings anymore."

"There was resentment between Calm and Black?"

"A bit. You trying to make a mystery out of this?"

The detective shrugged. "Looks like pretty much of a mystery already."

And McLove had to admit that it did.

He spent an hour with the police, both upstairs and down in the street. When they finally left just before noon, he went looking for Margaret Mason. She was back at her desk, surprisingly, looking as if nothing in the world had happened.

"How about lunch?" he said. "Maybe a martini would calm your nerves."

"I'm all right now, thanks. The offer sounds good, but you've got a date." She passed him an interoffice memo. It was signed by William T. Knox, and it requested McLove's presence in his office at noon.

"I suppose I have to tell them what I know."

"Which is?"

"Nothing. Absolutely nothing. All I know is a dozen different things that couldn't have happened to Calm. I'll try to get out of there is soon as I can. Will you wait for me? Till one, anyway?" he asked.

"Sure. Good luck."

He returned her smile, then went down the long hallway to Knox's office. It wasn't surprising to find Hamilton and Greene already there, and he settled down in the remaining chair feeling himself the center of attraction.

"Well?" Knox asked. "Where is he?"

"Gentlemen, I haven't the faintest idea."

"He's dead, of course," Jason Greene spoke up.

"Probably," McLove agreed. "But where's the body?"

Hamilton rubbed his fingers together in a nervous gesture. "That's what we have to find out. My phone has been ringing for an hour. The brokers are going wild, to say nothing of Pittsburgh!"

McLove nodded. "I gather the merger stands or falls on Billy Calm."

"Right! If he's dead, it's dead."

Jason Greene spoke again. "Billy Calm was a great man, and I'd be the last person in the world to try to sink the merger for which he worked so hard. But he's dead, all right. And there's just one place the body could have gone."

"Where's that?" Knox asked.

"It landed on a passing truck or something like that, of course."

Hamilton's eyes widened. "Sure!" he remarked sarcastically.

But McLove reluctantly shook his head. "That was the first thought the police had. We checked it out and it couldn't have happened. This building is set back from the street; it has to be, on account of this sheer glass wall. I doubt if a falling body could hit the street, and even if it did, the traffic lane on this side is torn up for repairs. And there's been a policeman on duty there all morning. The body didn't land on the sidewalk or the street, and no truck or car passed anywhere near enough."

W. T. Knox blinked and ran a hand through his thinning, but still wavy, hair. "If he didn't go down, where did he go? Up?"

"Maybe he never jumped," Hamilton suggested. "Maybe Margaret made the whole thing up."

McLove wondered at his words, wondered if Margaret had been objecting to some of his jokes again. "You forget that I was out there with her. I saw her face when that window smashed. The best actress in the world couldn't have faked that expression. Besides, I saw him go in—or at least I saw the door closing after him. It couldn't close by itself."

"And the room was empty when you two entered it a moment later," Knox said. "Therefore Billy must have gone through the window. We have to face the fact. He couldn't have been hiding under the table."

"If he didn't go down," Sam Hamilton said, "he went up! By a rope to the roof or another window."

But once more McLove shook his head. "You're forgetting that none of the windows can be opened. And it's a long way up to the roof. The police checked it though. They found nothing but an unmarked sea of melting snow and slush. Not a footprint, just a few pigeon tracks."

Jason Greene frowned across the desk. "But he didn't go down, up, or sideways, and he didn't stay in the room."

McLove wondered if he should tell them his idea, or wait until later. He decided now was as good a time as any. "Suppose he did jump, and something caught him on the way down. Suppose he's hanging there now, hidden by the fog."

"A flagpole? Something like that?"

"But there aren't any," Knox protested. "There's nothing but a smooth glass wall."

"There's one thing," McLove reminded them, looking around desk at their expectant faces. "The thing they use to wash the windows."

Jason Greene walked to the window. "We can find out easily enough. The sun has just about burned the fog away."

They couldn't see from that side of the building, so they rode down in the elevator to the street. As quickly as it had come, the fog seemed to have vanished, leaving a clear and sparkling sky with a brilliant sun seeking out the last remnants of the previous day's snow. The four of them stood in the street, in the midst of digging equipment abandoned for the lunch hour, and stared up at the great glass side of the Jupiter Steel building.

There was nothing to see. No body dangling in space, no window-washing scaffold. Nothing.

"Maybe he took it back up to the roof," Knox suggested.

"No footprints, remember?" McLove tried to cover his disappointment. "It was a long shot, anyway. The police checked the tenants for several floors beneath the broken window, and none of them saw anything. If Calm had landed on a scaffold, someone would have noticed it."

For a while longer they continued staring up at the building, each of them drawn to the tiny speck on the twenty-first floor where cardboard temporarily covered the shattered glass. "Why," Jason Greene asked suddenly, "didn't the cop down here see the falling glass when it hit? Was the window broken from the outside?"

McLove smiled. "No, the glass all went out, and down. It was the drilling again; the sound covered the glass hitting. And that section of sidewalk was blocked off. The policeman didn't hear it hit, but we were able to find pieces of it. You can see where they were swept up."

W. T. Knox sighed deeply. "I don't know. I guess I'll go to lunch. Maybe we can all think better on a full stomach."

They separated a few moments after that, and McLove went back up to twenty-one for Margaret Mason. He found her in Billy Calm's office with Shirley Taggert. They were on their knees, running their hands over the oak-paneled wall.

"What's all this?" he asked.

"Just playing detective," Margaret said. "It was Shirley's idea. She mentioned about how Mr. Calm always wanted the office left exactly as it was, and with the directors' room right next door, even though both rooms were really too small. She thought of a secret panel of some sort."

"Margaret!" Shirley got reluctantly to her feet. "You make it sound like something out of a dime novel. Really, though, it was a possibility. It would explain how he left the room without jumping from the window."

"Don't keep me in suspense," McLove said. "Did you find anything?"

"Nothing. And we've been over both sides of the wall."

"They don't build them like they used to in merry old England. Let's forget it and have lunch."

Shirley Taggert smoothed the wrinkles from her skirt. "You two go ahead. You don't want me along."

She was gone before they could protest, and McLove wasn't about to protest too loudly anyway. He didn't mind Shirley as a coworker, but like everyone else, he was acutely conscious of her position in the office scheme of things. Even now, with Billy Calm vanished into the blue, she was still a dangerous force not to be shared at social hours.

He went downstairs with Margaret, and they found an empty booth at the basement restaurant across the street. It was a place they often went after work for a drink, though lately he'd seen less of her outside of office hours. Thinking back to the first time he'd become aware of Margaret, he had only fuzzy memories of the tricks Sam Hamilton used to play. He loved to walk up behind the secretaries and tickle them—or occasionally even unzip their dresses—and he had quickly discovered that Margaret Mason was a likely candidate for his attentions. She always rewarded his efforts with a lively scream, without ever really getting upset.

It had been a rainy autumn evening some months back that McLove's path crossed hers most violently, linking them with a secret that made them drinking companions if nothing more. He'd been at loose ends that evening, and wandered into a little restaurant over by the East River. Surprisingly enough, Margaret Mason had been there, defending her honor in a back booth against a very drunk escort. McLove had moved in, flattened him with one punch, and they left him collapsed against a booth.

After that, on different drinking occasions, she had poured out the sort of lonely story he might have expected. And he'd listened and lingered, and sometimes fruitlessly imagined that he might become one of the men in her life. He knew there was no one for a long time after the bar incident, just as he knew now, by her infrequent free evenings, that there was someone again. Their drinking dates were more often being confined to lunch hours, when even two martinis were risky, and she never talked about being lonely or bored.

This day, over the first drink, she said, "It was terrible, really terrible."

"I know. It's going to get worse, I'm afraid. He's got to turn up somewhere."

"Dead or alive?"

"I wish I knew."

She lit a cigarette. "Will you be blamed for it?"

"I couldn't be expected to guard him from himself. Besides, I wasn't hired as a personal bodyguard. I'm chief of security, and that's all. I'm not a bodyguard or a detective. I don't know the first thing about fingerprints or clues. All I know about is people."

"What do you know about the Jupiter people?"

McLove finished his drink before answering. "Very little, really. Except for you, Hamilton and Knox and Greene and the rest of them are nothing more than names and faces. I've never even had a drink with any of them. I sit around at those meetings, and, frankly, I'm bored stiff. If anybody tries to blame me for this thing, they'll be looking for a new security chief."

Margaret's glass was empty, too, and he signaled the waiter for two more. It was that sort of a day. When they came, he noticed that her usually relaxed face was a bit tense, and the familiar sparkle of her blue eyes was no longer in evidence. She'd been through a lot that morning, and even the drinks were failing to relax her.

"Maybe I'll quit with you," she said.

"It's been a long time since we've talked. How have things been?"

"All right." She said it with a little shrug.

"The new boyfriend?"

"Don't call him that, please."

"I hope he's an improvement over the last one."

"So do I. At my age you get involved with some strange ones."

"Do you love him?"

She thought a moment and then answered, "I guess I do."

He lit another cigarette. "When Billy Calm passed your desk this morning, did he seem . . . ?" The sentence stopped in the middle, cut short by a sudden scream from the street. McLove stood up and looked toward the door, where a waiter was already running outside to see what had happened.

"What is it?" Margaret asked.

"I don't know, but there seems to be a crowd gathering. Come on!"

Outside, they crossed the busy street and joined the crowd on the sidewalk of the Jupiter Steel building. "What happened?" Margaret asked somebody.

"Guy jumped, I guess."

They fought their way through now, and McLove's heart was pounding with the anticipation of what they would see. It was Billy Calm, all right, crushed and dead and looking very small. But there was no doubt it was him.

A policeman arrived from somewhere with a blanket and threw it over the thing on the sidewalk. McLove saw Sam Hamilton fighting his way through the crowd to their side. "Who is it?" Hamilton asked, but he too must have known.

"Billy," McLove told him. "It's Billy Calm."

Hamilton stared at the blanket for a moment and then looked at his watch. "Three hours and forty-five minutes since he jumped. I guess he must have taken the long way down."

W. T. KNOX was pacing the floor like a caged animal, and Shirley Taggert was sobbing silently in a corner chair. It was over. Billy Calm had been found. The reaction was only beginning to set in. The worst, they all realized, was still ahead.

Jason Greene glared at Hamilton as he came into the office. "Well, the market's closed. Maybe you can stay off that phone for a while now."

Sam Hamilton didn't lose his grim smile. "Right now the price of Jupiter stock happens to be something that's important to all of us. You may be interested to know that it fell fourteen more points before they had to suspend trading in it for the rest of the session. They still don't have a closing price on it."

Knox held up both hands. "All right, all right! Let's everybody calm down and try to think. What do the police say, McLove?"

Feeling as if he were only a messenger boy between the two camps, McLove replied, "Billy was killed by the fall, and he'd been dead only a few minutes when they examined him. Body injuries' would indicate that he fell from this height."

"But where was he for nearly four hours?" Greene wanted to know. "Hanging there, invisible, outside the window?"

Shirley Taggert collected herself enough to join in the conversation. "He got out of that room somehow, and then came and jumped later," she said. "That's how it must have been."

But McLove shook his head. "I hate to throw cold water on logical explanations, but that's how it *couldn't* have been. Remember, the windows in this building can't be opened. No other window has been broken, and the one on this floor is still covered by cardboard."

"The roof!" Knox suggested.

"No. There still aren't any footprints on the roof. We checked."

"Didn't anybody see him falling?"

"Apparently not till just before he hit."

"The thing's impossible," Knox said.

"No."

They were all looking at McLove. "Then what happened?" Greene asked.

"I don't know what happened, except for one thing. Billy Calm didn't hang in space for four hours. He didn't fall off the roof, or out of any other window, which means he could only have fallen from the window in the directors' room."

"But the cardboard . . ."

"Somebody replaced it afterwards. And that means . . ."

"It means Billy was murdered," Knox breathed. "It means he didn't commit suicide."

McLove nodded. "He was murdered, and by somebody on this floor. Probably by somebody in this room." He glanced around.

NIGHT SETTLED cautiously over the city, with a scarlet sunset to the west that clung inordinately long to its reign over the skies.

The police had returned, and the questioning went on, concurrently with long distance calls to Pittsburgh and five other cities where Jupiter had mills. There was confusion, somehow more so with the coming of darkness to the outer world. Secretaries and workers from the other floors gradually drifted home, but on twenty-one life went on.

"All right," Knox breathed finally, as it was nearing eight o'clock. "We'll call a director's meeting for Monday morning, to elect a new president. That should give the market time to settle down and let us know just how bad things really are. At the same time we'll issue a statement about the proposed merger. I gather we're in agreement that it's a dead issue for the time being."

Sam Hamilton nodded, and Jason Greene reluctantly shrugged his assent. Shirley Taggert looked up from her pad. "What about old Israel Black? With Mr. Calm dead, he'll be back in the picture."

Jason Greene shrugged. "Let him come. We can keep him in line. I never thought the old guy was so bad anyway, not really."

It went on like this, the talk, the bickering, the occasional flare of temper, until nearly midnight. Finally, McLove felt he could excuse himself and head for home. In the outer office, Margaret was straightening her desk, and he was surprised to realize that she was still around. He hadn't seen her in the past few hours.

"I thought you went home," he said.

"They might have needed me."

"They'll be going all night at this rate. How about a drink?"

"I should get home."

"All right. Let me take you, then. The subways aren't safe at this hour."

She turned her face up to smile at him. "Thanks, McLove. I can use someone like you tonight."

They went down together in the elevator and out into a night turned decidedly coolish. He skipped the subway and hailed a cab. Settled on the red leather seat, he asked, "Do you want to tell me about it, Margaret?"

He couldn't see her face in the dark, but after a moment she asked, "Tell you what?"

"What really happened. I've got part of it doped out already, so you might as well tell me the whole thing."

"I don't know what you mean, McLove. Really," she protested.

"All right," he said, and was silent for twenty blocks. Then, as they stopped for a traffic light, he added, "This is murder, you know. This isn't a kid's game or a simple love affair."

"There are some things you can't talk over with anyone. I'm sorry. Here's my place. You can drop me at the corner."

He got out with her and paid the cab driver. "I think I'd like to come up," he said quietly.

"I'm sorry, McLove. I'm awfully tired."

"Want me to wait for him down here?"

She sighed and led the way inside, keeping silent until they were in the little three-room apartment he'd visited only once before. Then she shrugged off her raincoat and asked, "How much do you know?"

"I know he'll come here tonight, of all nights."

"What was it? What told you?"

"A lot of things. The elevator, for one."

She sat down. "What about the elevator?"

"Right after Billy Calm's supposed arrival, and suicide, I ran to his private elevator. It wasn't on twenty-one. It had to come up from below. He never rode any other elevator. When I finally remembered it, I realized he hadn't come up on that one, or it would still have been there."

Margaret sat frozen in the chair, her head cocked a little to one side as if listening. "What does it matter to you? You told me just this noon that none of them meant anything to you."

"They didn't, they don't. But I guess you do, Margaret. I can see what he's doing to you, and I've got to stop it before you get in too deep."

"I'm in about as deep as I can ever be, right now."

"Maybe not."

"You said you believed me. You told them all that I couldn't have been acting when I screamed out his name."

He closed his eyes for a moment, thinking that he'd heard something in the hallway. Then he said, "I did believe you. But then after the elevator bit, I realized that you never called Calm by his first name. It was always Mr. Calm, not Billy, and it would have been the same even in a moment of panic. Because he was still the president of the company. The elevator and the name—I put them together, and I knew it wasn't Billy Calm who had walked into that directors' room."

There was a noise at the door, the sound of a familiar key turning in the lock. "No," she whispered, almost to herself. "No, no, no . . ."

"And that should be our murderer now," McLove said, leaping to his feet.

"Billy!" she screamed. "Billy run! It's a trap!"

But McLove was already to the door, yanking it open, staring into the startled, frightened face of W. T. Knox.

SOMETIMES IT ENDS with a flourish, and sometimes only with the dull thud of a collapsing dream. For Knox, the whole thing had been only an extension of some sixteen hours in his life span. The fantastic plot, which had been set in motion by his attempt at suicide that morning at the Jupiter Steel building, came to an end when he succeeded in leaping to his death from the bathroom window of Margaret's apartment, while they sat waiting for the police to come.

The following morning, with only two hours' sleep behind him, McLove found himself facing Greene and Hamilton and Shirley Taggert once more, telling them the story of how it had been. There was an empty chair in the office, too, and he wondered vaguely whether it had been meant for Knox or Margaret.

"He was just a poor guy at the end of his rope," McLove told them. "He was deeply involved in an affair with Margaret Mason, and he'd sunk all his money into a desperate gamble that the merger wouldn't go through. He sold a lot of Jupiter stock short, figuring that when the merger talks collapsed, the price would fall sharply. Only Billy Calm called from his plane yesterday morning and said the merger was on. Knox thought about it for an hour or so and did some figuring. When he realized he'd be wiped out, he went into the directors' room to commit suicide."

"Why?" Shirley Taggert interrupted. "Why couldn't he jump out his own window?"

"Because there's a setback two stories down on his side. He couldn't have cleared it. He wanted a smooth drop to the sidewalk. Billy Calm could hardly have taken a running jump through the window. It was far off the floor even for a tall man, and Billy was short. And remember the slivers of glass at the bottom of the pane? When I remembered them, and remembered the height of the bottom sill from the floor, I knew that no one— especially a short man—could have gone through that window without knocking them out. No, Knox passed Margaret's desk, muttered some sort of farewell, and entered the room just as I came out of Calm's office. He smashed the window with a chair so he wouldn't have to try a dive through the thick glass, head first. And then he got ready to jump."

"Why didn't he?"

"Because he heard Margaret shout his name from the outer office. And with the shouted word *Billy*, a sudden plan came to him in that split second. He recrossed the small office quickly, and stood behind the door as we entered, knowing that I would think it was Billy Calm who had jumped. As soon as we were in the room, he simply stepped out and stood there. I thought he had arrived with the rest of you, and you, of course, thought he had entered the room with Margaret and me. I never gave it a second thought, because I was looking for Calm. But Margaret fainted when she saw he was still alive."

"But she said it was Billy Calm who entered the office," Greene protested.

"Not until later. She was starting to deny it, in fact, when she saw Knox and fainted. Remember, he carried her into the next room, and he was alone with her when she came to. He told her his money would be safe if only people thought Calm dead for a few hours. So she went along with her lover; I needn't remind you he was a handsome fellow, even though he was married. She went along with what we all thought happened, not realizing it would lead to murder."

Sam Hamilton lit a cigar. "The stock did go down."

"But not enough. And Knox knew Calm's arrival would reactivate the merger and ruin everything. I don't think he planned to kill Calm in the beginning, but as the morning wore on, it became the only way out. He waited in the private elevator when he knew Billy was due to arrive, slugged him, carried his small body to that window while we were all out to lunch, and threw him out, replacing the cardboard afterwards."

"And the stock went down some more," Hamilton said.

"That's right."

"She called him Billy," Shirley reminded them.

"It was his name. We all called him W. T., but he signed his memo to me *William T. Knox*. I suppose the two of them thought it was a great joke, her calling him Billy when they were together."

"Where is she now?" someone asked.

"The police are still questioning her. I'm going down there now, to be with her. She's been through a lot." He thought probably this would be his final day at Jupiter Steel. Somehow *he* was tired of these faces and their questions.

But as he got to his feet, Sam Hamilton asked, "Why wasn't Billy here for the meeting at ten? Where was he for those missing hours? And how did Knox know when he would really arrive?"

"Knox knew because Billy phoned him, as he had earlier in the morning."

"Phoned him? From where?"

McLove turned to stare out the window, at the clear blue of the morning sky. "From his private plane. Billy Calm was circling the city for nearly three hours. He couldn't land because of the fog."

THE "METHOD" SHERIFF

September 1967

LEN ZINBERG BEGAN his career publishing mainstream novels under his own name, but he achieved far greater success with his hard-boiled crime novels published under the name Ed Lacy. As Lacy, he published some thirty novels and nearly a hundred short stories. Sadly, however, most of his work is today unavailable. In addition to his prolific output, Lacy made another important contribution to the genre: he pioneered the use of an African American detective in his Edgar-winning novel *Room to Swing*. Much of his work reflected an engagement with social and racial issues, though our story here is more in the nature of an amusing caper.

■

The bank was a small, modernistic building, a branch of a big city bank many miles away. It was built on a recently landscaped field on the outskirts of a sleepy village, facing a turn-off connecting the highway with a new bridge.

Sheriff Banes was much like the village: old, squat, and shabby. Now, as he rushed into the bank, panting, the thin teller raced over to him and screamed, "Uncle Hank, we were robbed! Robbed!" Her face was pale with hysteria, eyes big with fright.

"A h-holdup?" The sheriff's shoulders sagged and his eyes seemed bewildered with shock. He shook himself, patted the teller's trembling shoulder with one hand, loosened the gun in his holster with his other hand. "Emma, you take it easy. Tell me what happened."

"Oh, Uncle, a—" Emma began to cry.

"Emma, call me Sheriff Banes, this is official business. It's important you get a grip on yourself, tell me exactly what happened." Walking the weeping teller to a chair, he turned to the only other man in the bank, the manager. "Okay, Tom, what happened? Make it fast, the first minutes after a crime are the most important."

"We opened as usual at nine A.M., a half hour ago. These two men came in. I was busy at my desk, opening the morning mail. The men were strangers, but they didn't look suspicious. Emma had her window open, and Helen was in the vault. After a few minutes they walked out and then Emma screamed. They'd handed her a note, telling her to fill a big paper bag with bills or they'd kill us all. I heard a car drive off, but with so much traffic passing, I can't say in which direction they went. Anyway, I ran to the door, then I called you."

Sheriff Banes felt of his windbreaker pockets for his notebook, finally grabbed a pencil and paper from the manager's desk. "Okay, what was the exact time of the robbery, Tom?"

"I'd say . . . nine thirty-two A.M."

Nodding, wetting the pencil with his lips, Sheriff Banes wrote that down. "How much did they get?"

"I haven't checked, but around twenty-six thousand dollars, all in small bills." The manager sat down, holding his head in slim hands. "Hank, we only opened this branch three months ago and a holdup already. I'll be fired!"

"Stop moaning! Can you describe them pretty well, Tom?"

"Well, I only glanced at them, you understand. They both seemed about . . . thirty, of average build. Wore dark suits and . . . yes, the heavier one carried a shopping bag. He was the one without a hat and had black hair, neatly combed. The other one had a folded newspaper and wore a hat . . . I don't remember what color his hair was."

"I had a good look at them, Hank," Helen Smith said, coming out of the vault behind the tellers' partition. She was a middle-aged, dumpy woman with faded blonde hair. "The hatless one had very dark hair and a sharp face, a foreign-looking fellow, with one of those thin moustaches. The one wearing the hunting cap, I do believe he was bald and—"

"What color hunting cap, Helen?" The sheriff asked, pencil posed in his pudgy hand.

"Why, sort of a brown cap."

Emma sat up in her chair. "No, no! It was a kind of orange hat! He was the one who gave me the note, rested his folded newspaper on the counter."

"Did he talk with an accent?"

"Uncle, none of them talked, just gave me the note. It was typed and read:

> Fill this bag with money, or everybody will be killed. There's a sawed-off shotgun in the newspaper. Wait ten minutes before giving any alarm. We have a man with a submachine gun outside.

"I was so scared, I just shoved all the cash I had in my drawer into this big paper bag and nearly fainted! They were blocking my window, so I couldn't signal to Tom or—"

"Where's the note?" Sheriff Banes cut in.

"The note? Why, they took it, with the money."

Banes groaned. "Think carefully, Emma. Did you notice anything special about the shopping bag?"

"Yes! Now that I think of it, the shopping bag had A&P printed on it!"

The sheriff pushed his hat back and scratched his wild gray hair. "Damn, must be a dozen of those supermarkets within a fifty-mile radius of here. Well . . ." He turned to the desk and picked up the phone. "I'd best call the state trooper barracks. Anybody notice the make of their getaway car?"

The two women and the manager shook their heads. Emma said, "I think, but I'm not sure now, I saw an old gray sedan parked outside, through the window."

Shaking his head, the sheriff put the phone down. "Anybody else in the bank?"

Tom said, "No, sir, we'd just opened."

"How come you had so much cash on hand?" Banes asked.

"Now, Hank—Sheriff Banes, you know one of the reasons they built this branch is, with the bridge open, we handle the payrolls for those two factories on the other side of the river, nineteen thousand, five hundred sixty-eight dollars every Wednesday morning. We make the payroll Tuesday nights. Then there's always five or six thousand in cash in Emma's drawer, at the start of a day."

Helen shook her head. "Don't know what the world's coming to. We never had a holdup before in the village, as you know, Hank. We—"

The sheriff suddenly walked over to the teller's counter, said, voice full of excitement, "Prints! Did any of you touch this counter?"

Emma shrieked, "I forgot! They both wore pigskin gloves!"

Sheriff Banes shook his head sadly. "Dammit, nothing breaking for us." He crossed to the window and moved the shade, stared out at the night. "Might get some rain," he announced.

After a moment he turned and sat on the desk, tore up the paper with his notes. "Okay, that wasn't bad. Emma, you got to keep up your crying act more, especially when the state troopers come. Aunt Helen, you were fine with that description, acted like a real confused hick. Tom, you were good, too, but you have to seem more upset. You know, like it's the end of the world. We'll have a last rehearsal tomorrow, Tuesday night, and I'll take the twenty-six grand with me. I've fixed up a nice hiding place under the floor boards in the jail. Wednesday, you phone me as soon as the bank opens and there's no customers. That's about all. Except keep in mind, we don't talk about this to anybody. We'll wait six or seven months before splitting the money. By then we all came into a little inheritance. Tom, how did I do?"

"You acted the part of a hick cop perfectly, Dad."

DEATH OF A NOBODY

February 1970

BOTH A PRACTITIONER of and an enthusiastic advocate for the noir tradition, Bill Pronzini is probably best known to readers for his Nameless Detective series. But in addition to those taut and thrilling works, redolent of the fog-enshrouded San Francisco Bay area, Pronzini has also written numerous other works, some in collaboration with his wife, Marcia Muller. Pronzini and Muller also coauthored the classic reference work *1001 Midnights*. Pronzini's great character, the Nameless Detective, makes one of his earliest appearances in this story.

■

His name was Nello. Whether this was his given name, or his surname, or simply a sorbiquet he had picked up sometime during the span of his fifty-odd years, I never found out. I doubt even Nello himself knew any longer.

He was what sociologists call "an addictive drinker who has lost all semblance of faith in God, humanity, or himself," or what the average citizen dismisses unconcernedly as "a skid row wino."

He came into my office just before ten o'clock on one of San Francisco's bitter cold autumn mornings. He had been a lawyer once, in a small town in Northern California, and there were still signs of intelligence, of manners and education, in his gaunt face. I had first encountered him more than twelve years ago, when Police Lieutenant Eberhardt and I had been rookie patrolmen. I didn't know, and had never asked, what private hell had led him from small town respectability to the oblivion of our Skid Row.

He stood just inside the door, his small hands nervously rolling and unrolling the brim of a shapeless brown fedora. His thin, almost emaciated body was encased in a pair of once-brown slacks and a tweed jacket that had worn through at both elbows, and his faded blue eyes had that tangible filminess about them that comes from too many bottles of cheap sweet wine. This morning he was sober—cold and painfully sober.

I said, "It's been a long time, Nello."

"A long time," he agreed vaguely.

"Some coffee?"

"No. No, thanks."

I poured myself a cup from the pot I keep on an old two-burner on top of one of my filing cabinets and set it down on the desk blotter. "What can I do for you?"

He cleared his throat, his lips moving as if he were tasting something by memory. Then he seemed to change his mind and took a step toward the door. "Maybe I shouldn't have come," he said to the floor. "Maybe I'd better go."

"Wait, now. What is it, Nello?"

"Chaucer," he said. "It's Chaucer."

I frowned a little. Chaucer was another habitué of the Row, like Nello an educated man who had lost part of himself sometime, somewhere, somehow; he had once taught English literature at a high school in Kansas or Nebraska, and that was where he'd got his nickname. He and Nello had been companions for a long time.

I said, "What about Chaucer?"

"He's dead," Nello said tonelessly. "I heard it on the grapevine just a little while ago. The police found him in an alley on Hubbell Street, near the railroad yards, early this morning. He was beaten to death."

"Do they know who did it?"

Nello shook his head. "But I think I might know why he was killed."

"Have you gone to the police?"

"No."

I didn't need to ask why not; noninvolvement with the law was a code by which the Row people lived, even when one of their own died violently. I said, "If you have some information that might help find Chaucer's killer, you'd better take it to them, Nello."

His lips curved into a sad, fleeting smile. "What good would it do?" he asked. "They don't care about a man like Chaucer— a wino, a bum, a nobody. Why should they bother when one of us dies?"

"Do you really believe that?"

"Yes, I believe it."

"Well, you're wrong," I said. "When someone is murdered, no matter who he is, the police do everything in their power to find the party or parties responsible. I know that for a fact, Nello; I was a cop once, remember?"

"I remember."

"Then why did you come to me?" I asked quietly. "In a way, I'm still a cop. If you don't believe the police will care, what made you think *I* would?"

"I don't know," he said. "You were always fair and decent to me, you and your friend. I thought . . . Look, maybe I just better go."

"It's up to you."

He hesitated. There was a struggle going on inside him between an almost forgotten sense of duty and the unwritten decree of the Row. Finally, he moved forward in a ponderous way and sat in the chair across from me. He put the fedora on his knee and looked at the veined backs of his hands.

I said, "Do you want to tell me about it now?"

"I can't pay you anything, you know."

"Never mind that," I said. "About the only thing I can do is take whatever you give me to the police and see that it gets into the proper hands. Communication with me isn't privileged; that's the law."

"I know the law," Nello said. "Or I knew it once."

"Okay, then."

He took a long breath, coughed, and wiped at his mouth with the palm of one hand. When he began talking, his voice was low, almost monotonous. "About three weeks ago Chaucer and I were sharing a bottle of muskie in a doorway on Sixth. It was after midnight, and the streets were empty. Old Jenny—she was one of us, a nice old lady—was standing on the corner across the street, waiting for the light to change. When it did, she started across the intersection. There were headlights approaching along Sixth, coming very fast, but I thought the car would stop at the red light. Only it didn't. It came straight on through. There was no time for Chaucer or me to call out a warning. The car hit Old Jenny, slowed for a moment, then kept on going and disappeared around the corner. Chaucer and I ran over to where Old Jenny was lying in the street, but there was nothing we could do for her; she was dead. We left, then, before the police came."

Again, the code of noninvolvement. Nello passed a hand over his face, as if the length of his explanation had left him momentarily drained. I waited silently, and after a moment he went on, "Last weekend Chaucer was panhandling in Union Square. He saw the hit-and-run car parked on the street near there. It had been repaired, he said, and had a fresh coat of paint."

"How did he know it was the same car?" I put in.

"He had gotten the license number that night on the Sixth."

"Did he tell you what it was?"

"No," Nello said. "I think he found out the name of the car's owner on Union Square, from the registration, but he didn't tell me who it was. I saw him yesterday afternoon, around three, and he was in high spirits. He said he had to take care of some business, and that if it panned out he was going to be in the chips for the first time in a long while."

I began to get it then. "You think he went out to see the owner of this car and tried to shake him down, is that it? And got himself killed for the effort."

"Yes."

"Is there anything else you can tell me? Anything that might lead to the owner?"

He moved his head from side to side.

"Chaucer didn't mention the make and model?"

"No."

"Or where the owner lived?"

"No, nothing at all."

I lighted a cigarette and thought over in my mind what he had told me. After a time I said, "All right, Nello. I'll see what I can do. As soon as anything turns up, I'll let you know."

He nodded listlessly and got to his feet. I had the feeling, watching him shuffle toward the door, that he didn't really believe anything would turn up at all.

Eberhardt had some people in his office when I got down to the Hall of Justice a half hour later, and I had to wait in the detectives' squad room until he finished his business with them. I smoked a couple of cigarettes and discussed the political situation with Inspector Branislaus, whom I knew slightly. After half an hour three men in business suits came out of Eberhardt's cubicle and marched out of the squad room in single-file cadence, like army recruits on a parade field.

I sat there for another five minutes, and then the intercom on Branislaus's desk sounded and Eberhardt's voice said it was all right for me to come in. He was cleaning out the bowl of his pipe with a penknife when I entered, and said, without looking up, "So what the hell do *you* want?"

"How about a kind word?"

"Did you see those three men who just left?"

"I saw them, sure."

"They're with the state attorney general's office," Eberhardt said, "and they've been giving me a hard time for a week on a certain matter. As a result, I haven't seen my wife in two days, and I haven't eaten since eleven o'clock yesterday morning. On top of all that, I think I've got an abscessed tooth. So whatever it is you've come for, the answer is no. Call me Sunday afternoon, and if I've made it home by then, we'll have a beer together."

I said, "Okay, Eb. But it has to do with the murder last night of a Skid Row character named Chaucer."

He frowned. "What do you know about that?"

"I can tell it to whichever homicide team is handling it, if you want."

"You can tell it to me," Eberhardt said. "Sit down."

I took his hat off a chair and put it on a corner of his desk, then sat down and lighted another cigarette.

Eberhardt said, "You smoke too much, you know that?"

"Sure," I said. "Do you remember a guy named Nello? A companion of Chaucer's? They were both on the Row when we were patrolmen."

"I remember him."

"He came to see me this morning," I said, and outlined for him what Nello had told me.

Eberhardt put the cold pipe between his teeth, took it out again, scowled at it, and set it in the ashtray on his desk. "There might be a connection," he said. "Why didn't Nello come down himself with this?"

"You know the answer to that."

"Yeah, I guess I do." He sighed softly, tiredly. "Well, I was reading the preliminary report a little while ago, before those state clowns came in; I recognized Chaucer's name. There's not much in it."

"Nello said he was beaten to death."

"Not exactly. There were some marks on him, but that wasn't the cause of death."

"What was?"

"Brain hemorrhage," Eberhardt said. "Caused by a sharp blow. The investigating officers found blood on the wall of one of the buildings in the alley, and the way it looks, his head was batted against the wall."

"What about the time of death?"

"The medical examiner fixes it at between midnight and two A.M."

"Was there anything in the alley?"

"You mean like fingerprints or shoe prints or missing buttons?"

"Like that."

"No," Eberhardt said. "And nobody saw or heard anything, of course; that area around the railroad yards is like a mausoleum after midnight."

"You really don't have much, do you?"

He shook his head. "There is one other thing, though. Chaucer had thirty-eight dollars and some change in his pockets when he was found."

"That's a lot of money for one of the Row people to be carrying around. They're usually broke."

"Uh-huh."

"It sort of substantiates Nello's story, wouldn't you say?"

"Maybe. But if this hit-and-run guy killed Chaucer, why would he give him the money first?"

"It could be that Chaucer asked for a lot more than what he had in his pockets," I said. "The guy could have given him that as a down payment and then arranged to meet him last night with the rest."

"And killed him instead," Eberhardt said. "Well, it could have happened like that."

"Look, Eb, I'd like to poke into this thing myself if I've got your permission."

"I was wondering when you'd get around to that. What's your big interest in Chaucer's death?"

"I told you, Nello came to see me this morning."

"But not to hire you."

"No," I admitted.

"Then who's going to pay your fee?"

"Maybe I'll do it gratis. I'm not doing anything else right now."

"You doing charity work these days?"

"Come on, Eb, knock it off."

"You feel sorry for Nello, is that it?"

"In a way, yes. You know what he thinks? He thinks the cops don't give a damn about finding Chaucer's killer. He's sold on that."

"Why would he think that?"

"Chaucer was a nobody, just another wino. 'Who cares,' Nello said, 'if some wino is murdered?'"

"Yeah, well, that's a crock."

"Sure, it's a crock," I said. "But Nello believes it. I wouldn't be surprised if the whole Row believes it."

Eberhardt got wearily to his feet. "I think I can spare a couple of minutes," he said. "You want to come with me down to Traffic? We'll see what hit-and-run has on Old Jenny."

"All right."

We rode the elevator down to the Traffic Bureau on the main floor and went into the office of Inspector Aldrich, who was in charge of the hit-and-run detail. He was a big, red-haired guy with a lot of freckles on his face and hands. Eberhardt told him what we wanted, and Aldrich dug around in one of his file cabinets and came up with a thin cardboard folder. He spread it open on his desk, squinted at the contents, then said at length, "Woman named Jenny Einers, sixty-three years old, hit-and-run at the intersection of Sixth and Howard Streets three weeks ago. That the one?"

"That's the one," Eberhardt said.

"We've got very little on it," Aldrich told him. "It happened at approximately twelve fifty A.M., and there were no witnesses around."

"There was one witness," I said. "Two, actually." I filled him in on what Nello had told me. When I was finished, he said, "Well, that's more than we were able to come up with."

Eberhardt asked, "Any broken glass on the scene?"

"Several shards of it, yes. One of the headlights. Nothing identifiable, though."

"What about paint scrapings?"

"Uh-huh. Forest green. General Motors color, 1966 to 1969."

"Were you able to identify the make and model?"

"No," Aldrich said. "It could have come off any one of several GM cars."

"Was there any fender or grille dirt?"

Aldrich nodded. "We put it though chemical analysis, of course. Common ground dirt, a little sand, and some gravel chips. Nothing unusual that we could work with."

"Anything else?"

"One thing. I don't know what it means, if anything."

"Yes?"

"Sawdust," Aldrich said. "We found several particles of it on the street near the point of impact."

"What kind of wood?"

"White pine."

Eberhardt's forehead wrinkled. "What do you make of it?" he asked me.

I shook my head. "I don't know."

Aldrich said, "We sent out word to all the body shops in the Bay Area the morning after. That's standard procedure. There were a couple of late-model GMs with forest green paint jobs brought in for body work, but one was a rear-ender and the other had the right front door banged up. We checked the accident reports on both, and they were clear. There was nothing else."

"Dead end," Eberhardt said.

He thanked Aldrich for his time and we went out to the elevator bank. Eberhardt pushed the *Up* button, then said, "I just can't take any more time on this right now, so you can poke around if you want. But make sure you call me if you turn up anything."

"You know I will."

"Sure," he said. "But it doesn't hurt to remind you."

The elevator doors slid open. Eberhardt got in and I crossed the lobby and went outside. Fog banks sat off to the west in great folding billows, like cotton candy. The wind was up, carrying the first trailing vapors over the city. I walked rapidly to my car.

I sat inside it for a time, with the windows rolled up and the heater on, wondering where I would go from there. Nello had said he had last seen Chaucer around three the previous afternoon, apparently just before he left the Row; and Eberhardt had said that the medical examiner had fixed the time of death at between midnight and two A.M. That left approximately nine to eleven hours of Chaucer's time unaccounted for. Assuming that Chaucer had had the money that had been found on him prior to his death, and knowing the type of individual he had been, it seemed logical that he would have circulated along the Row— even though Nello hadn't encountered him. If that were the case, then somebody there had to have seen him or spoken with him or possibly even spent some time with him.

I drove over to Seventh and began to canvass the Row. During the next two and a half hours, I walked streets littered with debris, windswept papers, and empty wine bottles, even though the city sanitation department works the area every morning. I talked to stoic bartenders with flat eyes in cheerless saloons; to dowdy waitresses with faces the color of yeast in cafes that sold hash and onions for thirty-five cents; to tired, aging hookers with names like Hey Hattie and Annie Orphan and Miss Lucinda; to liquor store clerks who counted each nickel and each dime with open contempt before serving their customers; to knots of men huddled together in doorways or on street corners, panhandling indifferent passersby and drinking from paper-wrapped bottles with only the neck showing—men called Monkey-face and Zingo and Yahoo and Bud-Bud and dozens of other names.

I learned nothing.

My feet had begun to ache, but I decided to try the area around South Park before giving up. I went into a place called Packy's. One of the men sitting at the bar was a study in varying shades of gray—iron-gray hair, washed gray eyes, red-veined gray skin, gray pinstripe suit, gray-white undershirt. He was Freddy the Dreamer, an old-timer on the Row. I went up to him and told him why I was there and asked my questions again for the hundredth time.

He said in the dreamy voice that had given him his nickname, "Sure, I seen Chaucer yesterday. Hell of a thing, what happened to him."

"What time, Freddy?"

"Around six," he answered. "He was just getting off a bus up on Mission."

"Which line?"

He shrugged. "Who knows?"

"Did you talk to him?"

"Sure," Freddy said. "We had us a party. Scotch whiskey, can you believe? Old Freddy with his very own jug of aged Scotch whiskey."

"Chaucer paid for it?"

"He was carrying a roll like you never seen. We got a flop down by the Embarcadero and went to work on that Scotch."

"Where did he get the roll, Freddy?"

"Chaucer was a kidder, you know? Him with his fancy education, a great kidder. I asked him where he picked it up, who did he mug, and he just laughed kind of secretive. 'Robin Hood,' he says. 'I got it from Robin Hood.'"

"Robin Hood?"

"That's it."

"Are you sure?"

"Yeah, I'm sure."

"Okay. What time did Chaucer leave this flop last night?"

"Who knows?" Freddy said dreamily. "With a jug of real Scotch whiskey, who knows?"

"Do you have any idea where he went when he left?"

"To see Robin Hood."

"Is that what he said?"

"He was a kidder, you know?" Freddy said. "A great kidder."

"Yeah."

"Listen, I hope you find whoever done it to him. I sure hope you do. I can still taste that Scotch whiskey."

I got out of there. *Robin Hood,* I thought as I walked to where I had left my car. It could have meant something—or nothing—

the same way the sawdust Aldrich had mentioned could have meant something or nothing.

I decided to go back and talk to Eberhardt again, but when I got there, he was out on something. One of the cops in the squad room said that he was expected back around four thirty. The clock on the wall read just a little after three, and I didn't feel much like waiting there for him.

I drove to a restaurant and had something to eat; the food, through no fault of the management, was tasteless. I felt a little depressed, the way I used to feel when I was working the Row as a patrolman. My office seemed as good a place as any to go right then, so I paid my tab and went over there.

A single piece of mail had been shoved through the slot in the door, and I picked it up off the floor and put it on the desk. As usual, it was very cold in there. I turned on the valve on the steam radiator, then sat down and opened the letter.

It was a bill from a magazine readership club. In a weak moment sometime back, I had succumbed to the sales pitch of a doe-eyed college girl. I folded the bill and the envelope and put them into my wastebasket. Then I sat there and lighted a cigarette and looked at the wall and listened to the ringing knock of the radiator as it warmed up.

Robin Hood, I thought. *Sawdust.*

I stood up after a time and picked up the coffeepot, still half full with my morning coffee. There was a thin sheen of oil on the surface, but I replaced it on the two-burner anyway to heat.

I returned to the desk, sat down, and looked at the top for a while. There was nothing much on it save for the telephone and a desk calendar and an empty wire basket. I lighted another cigarette.

Sawdust, Robin Hood. To hell with it, I thought. Let Eberhardt handle it; maybe he could make a connection. I looked at my watch. It was twenty past four. When four-thirty came, I would call him and put it in his lap. I had done all I could for Nello.

The coffee began to boil. I poured some of the black liquid into a cup and carried it to the window behind my desk. The city of San Francisco looked cold and lonely and hoary-old through the ebbing steel-wool banks of fog. I glanced down at Taylor Street three floors below; rush hour was fast approaching, and there were a lot of cars jammed up down there. A small flatbed truck was blocking two lanes of traffic, trying to back into a narrow alley across the way. It was carrying a wide load of plywood sheeting, and the driver was having difficulty jockeying the truck into the mall's slender mouth.

I watched him for a time, listening to the angry horn blasts of the blocked cars drift up from the street, and then the answer came drifting up, too, and hit me square in the face. I spilled some of the coffee getting the cup down on the desk. I picked up the San Francisco telephone directory and got it open to the Yellow Pages. Half a minute later, my finger came to rest on a boxed, single-column advertisement at the bottom of one of the pages under *Lumber—Retail*. Freddy the Dreamer had been right; Chaucer, the former teacher of English literature, had been a great kidder.

I caught up the telephone and dialed the Hall of Justice. It was four-thirty now, and maybe Eberhardt had come back. He had.

"Sherwood," I said when they got him on the line. "Sherwood Forest Products."

"I*t was the* owner's son, Ted Sherwood," Eberhardt said. "We saw the car—one of those pickups, actually a jazzed-up 1968 model with mag wheels and chrome exhausts and the like—parked in the company lot in Daly City when we drove up. I checked the registration and found out it belonged to the Sherwood kid. He was still there, he and his old man, supervising the unloading of a shipment of pine boards. We put it to him the first thing, and he lost his head and tried to run for it. He should have known better."

I nodded and drank a little of my beer. We were sitting in a small tavern near the Hall of Justice. It was after eight o'clock, and Eberhardt had just come off duty.

I said, "Did he confess?"

"Not right away," Eberhardt said. "The old man insisted he have his lawyer present, so we took him down to the Hall. When the lawyer showed, he and the old man went into a huddle. When they came out, the lawyer advised the kid to tell it straight."

"Did he?"

"He did," Eberhardt said. "He'd been out joyriding with his girlfriend and a case of beer that night three weeks ago. He'd just taken the girl home, out on Potrero Hill. I guess he must have been pretty tanked up, though he won't admit it; he says he thought the light was green at the intersection. Anyway, when he hit the old lady, he panicked and kept right on going."

"The impact must have jarred those particles of sawdust loose from the bed of the pickup," I said.

"Apparently," Eberhardt agreed. "The kid told us he made small deliveries—plywood sections, mostly—from time to time."

"How did he get the dents ironed out?"

"Some friend of his works in a body shop, and the two of them did the job at night; that's why hit-and-run didn't get a report from any of the garages. With the new paint job, and the fact that nothing had happened for three weeks, he figured he was home free."

"And then Chaucer showed up," I said.

Eberhardt inclined his head. "He wanted five hundred dollars to keep what he'd seen quiet, the crazy fool. The Sherwood kid put him off with fifty, and arranged to meet him down on the Embarcadero last night with the rest. He picked Chaucer up there and took him out to that alley on Hubbell Street. Sherwood swears he didn't mean to kill him, though; all he was going to do, he said, was rough Chaucer up a little to get him to lay off. But he's a pretty big kid, and he waded in a little too heavily. Chaucer hit his head on the building wall, and when Sherwood saw that he was dead, he panicked and beat it out of there."

"Which explains why Chaucer still had the rest of the fifty dollars on him when he was discovered."

"Yeah."

I finished the last of my beer. Eberhardt said, "One thing. How did you finally make the connection?"

"I'd seen this Sherwood Forest Products place once, when I was in Daly City on a skip-trace," I said. "Watching that truck, loaded with plywood, maneuver on Taylor Street brought it back to mind."

We sat there for a time, and then Eberhardt said, "Listen, I called my wife before I left the Hall and told her to put on some steaks. You want to come out for supper?"

"Rain check," I said. "I've got something to do."

"What's that?"

"Look up Nello. I promised him I'd let him know if anything turned up."

"Uh-huh."

"Maybe it'll restore some of his faith in humanity. Or at least in the minions of the law."

"After fifteen years on the Row?" Eberhardt said. "I doubt it."

"So do I. But there's always the chance."

Eberhardt nodded, staring into his beer glass. "So long, social worker," he said.

"So long, cop."

I went out into the cold, damp night.

JAMES HOLDING

RECIPE FOR MURDER

December 1973

BOTH UNDER his own name and as Clark Carlisle, James Holding was a frequent presence in the pages of *AHMM* from the 1960s through the 1980s. Holding enjoyed a successful career in advertising before he turned to mysteries. Holding wrote stories in three series—one a series of Ellery Queen pastiches; one about a photographer who is also an assassin; and one about a detective turned "library cop"—and he wrote numerous stand-alones as well. It was difficult to pick one story from the many that appeared in *AHMM*, but this one should certainly appeal to readers of taste.

■

The first inkling André DuBois had that his niece and her husband intended to rob him was when he found his file box of recipe cards missing from his kitchen shelf.

Before, he had vaguely suspected that they might try to borrow money from him to help finance a gourmet restaurant in Paris. However, when he returned from his expedition to the village grocer and saw that his recipe file was gone—that's when he first seriously entertained the idea that they meant to steal his greatest treasure—and even, if it should prove necessary in the end, to kill him.

André DuBois was a slender, shaggy-browed man of middle height but well past middle age, and now almost bald. His baldness, he often explained jokingly, was the result of wearing his hat indoors for so many years. His chef's cap, he meant. For he had been a world-famous chef before he withdrew from Paris to spend his declining years growing flowers and garden vegetables on the outskirts of the Italian village of Lucignano.

As he stared at the empty place on the kitchen shelf where his box of recipe cards had been, his emotions were varied, to say the least. Surprise was his first reaction. Surprise was rapidly followed by disbelief, which, in turn, gave way to incipient anger. Finally, with greater impact than any of these, he was struck by pity and shame for his niece, Yvonne, the only relative he had left in the world, the daughter of his dead brother, and now married to the man Gustav. Or *was* she married to him? Perhaps not, in these days of the sexual revolution; but here she was, at all events, in Lucignano with Gustav.

They had arrived from Arezzo driving a rented car in which they had been taking, they said, a leisurely trip about Italy, visiting Venice, Milan, Bologna, Florence, and Rome. Since Arezzo was so very close to Lucignano, Yvonne explained, they had decided on impulse to seek out her Uncle André, whom she had not seen for thirteen years, introduce him to her husband, Gustav, and thus strengthen, she hoped, the fragile thread of family relationship that had, alas, worn thin over the years for both of them.

André DuBois had made them welcome, of course. He was delighted to see his niece again, glad to meet her husband, especially pleased to have their company for a time in his retirement retreat, since he was a lonely man at best.

Yvonne had grown into a vivacious, voluptuous woman from the leggy youngster he remembered. Her hazel eyes and blonde hair (if it were genuinely blonde, which he doubted) gave her the patrician look of a northern Italian—a far cry indeed from the dark Latin mien of a Frenchwoman from Provence, which she really was. When she spoke, André noted with approval, her voice was soft and provocative, as a woman's voice should be.

As for the husband, Gustav, he was another kettle of fish entirely. A great lout of a man, bearlike and shambling, speaking with a rough Scandinavian accent that went with his name, Gustav would never win any prizes either for good looks or good manners, André decided indulgently. He felt inclined to indulgence as he looked at his handsome niece with avuncular understanding. If Gustav were Yvonne's choice, Gustav was good enough for André, too. Although—and André noticed this the moment they met—Gustav's small unblinking eyes, the color of muddy water, were set rather too close together, and the man carried with him a strong odor of perspiration.

André insisted that they stay with him for a while, eagerly offering them his own bedroom, the only one the ancient farmhouse contained. He would sleep on the sofa on the small porch where he usually ate his meals in nice weather.

Yvonne and Gustav accepted his invitation with alacrity, transferred their cheap suitcases from the rented car to André's bedroom at once, and proceeded to make themselves at home.

"Uncle André," said Yvonne, "it is so nice to see you again after all these years. And in Italy, of all places! It is so quiet here, so unspoiled and fresh, so different from smelly old France!"

"And I'm glad to see you, Yvonne," André responded warmly, "and to meet your husband, too." He was somewhat at a loss as to what to say to Gustav. "I find this place very relaxing indeed after so many years in your 'smelly old France,' as you call it." He smiled at her, his bushy eyebrows tilting upward at their outer edges in a very droll manner.

Gustav was looking about him. The room in which they sat was untidy and cluttered, a typical farmer's retreat. Its most remarkable feature was a source of metal plaques, framed certificates, and engraved medallions that almost entirely covered the wall space of the cramped room. Gustav waved a hand at them and asked, "What are all those things?"

Before André could reply, Yvonne said with a hint of laughter in her soft voice, "Gustav! Read them! They are awards for cooking, won by Uncle André from all the gourmet societies of the world!"

Gustav jumped up from his chair for a closer look at the awards. "You were a chef?" he rumbled at André. "A chef?" He paused deliberately, then said, "Not *Le Grand* André? Of *Chez Marie Antoinette* in Paris? *That* André?"

Somehow Gustav didn't sound as surprised as his words suggested. Nevertheless, André nodded and replied modestly, "That André, yes. But no longer. Now I am only a farmer, Gustav, as you see. A decrepit raiser of flowers and bland vegetables."

Yvonne laughed aloud. "You see, Gustav," she crowed, "I've been saving Uncle André as a surprise for you! The greatest chef of the century is also our own dear Uncle André!"

Gustav gave a grimace that might have been meant for a smile. "Surprise, indeed!" he said, shaking his massive head. "*Le Grand* André! In my own family!"

Yvonne jumped up, seized Gustav's hand, and danced around in a circle. To André, Gustav's heavy, awkward movements seemed more than ever like those of an ill-trained bear.

After a few turns, Yvonne dropped her husband's hand, turned to André, and cried, "You see, Uncle, the great joke is that Gustav is a chef, also! Can you believe it? Two chefs in the same family!" In her ebullience, she took hold of André's arms and would have danced him around, too, except that he protested, with a laugh, "Yvonne, no. I am too old for these childish tricks."

He glanced at Gustav's face, again expressionless around his close-set eyes, and said, "Where do you work, Gustav? Is your restaurant in Paris? Do I know it?"

"At present," Gustav said, "I am unemployed."

"Oh, bad luck. Where was your last job?"

"*Le Logis du Loup Sauvage.* In Aix."

"A fine restaurant. Famous in my own youth, if memory serves, for its *soufflé d'escargots.* And they let you go?" Small wonder, André mused. How could they expect food prepared by this great clod to be anything but unsavory, heavy, indigestible; as totally lacking in subtlety and balance as the chef himself? Aloud, he said, "Such are the hazards of our profession, Gustav. But not fatal, thankfully. Let us hope your unemployment will be only temporary, eh? Have you anything in view?"

Yvonne answered with a rush. "Oh, yes, Uncle! We have applied at all the good restaurants along the Côte d'Azur. And now in Italy, too. That is the true purpose of our trip, you see. Gustav has had interviews at *La Taverna Fenice, Martini, Savini, Pappagallo, Oliviero, Sabatini, Alfredo,* and *Hostaria dell'Orso.*"

"First-class kitchens, every one," André said.

"And failing a job at any of these," Yvonne rushed on, "we thought maybe we could find somebody to back us in establishing a restaurant of our own somewhere." She gave André a meaningful look.

Knowing the answer beforehand, André asked, "What were the results of your interviews, Gustav?"

"Uniformly negative," grumbled Gustav with an injured expression. He looked at Yvonne, a quick, furtive, sliding glance that merely flicked her for an instant before his small eyes turned back to André. "I need a specialty, of course," he said. "They all told me that."

To get rid of you, probably, André thought. Aloud he said, "That is understandable, Gustav. A chef with a good specialty will draw customers more speedily to a restaurant than topless waitresses, even." André tilted his eyebrows again.

"True," Gustav said, "as you should know better than anyone, Uncle, since your own reputation was so firmly founded on your famous specialty. Even in Copenhagen, where I received my training, the name of your *Potage François Premier* was better known among the apprentice cooks than that of Queen Elizabeth the Second."

"Thank you," André murmured, pleased despite himself at this heavy-handed compliment. "It was just a soup, after all."

"Just a soup!" Yvonne exclaimed. "You insult your genius, Uncle André! *Potage François Premier* was pure nectar! And only you in all the world knew how to make it. My father told me about it many times, boasting of your skill. And finally, when I was fifteen, he brought me to Paris and took me to *Chez Marie Antoinette* for dinner and let me taste your divine soup for myself! Do you remember?"

"I remember. You were a charming child."

"Eating that soup of yours was almost like falling in love, Uncle, did you know that? The same sudden disregard for everything else in the world except your beloved; the same headlong plunge into a willing slavery to your emotions." She looked meltingly at her husband. "Oh, Gustav," she said. Her lips parted slightly in remembered ecstasy. "There was never *anything* like Uncle André's *Potage François Premier!*"

Gustav said, "I believe you, Yvonne. Although I have never had the pleasure of tasting Uncle André's soup, every chef who ever boiled an egg knows it was superb."

André considered this statement rather fulsome, but took it in good part. He began to feel faint stirrings of sympathy for poor unemployed Gustav. He said, on a sudden impulse, "I will tell you something about *Potage François Premier.* I have never told this to anyone before, not even your father, Yvonne, although he was my dear brother. I did not create that great soup of mine. I inherited the recipe and claimed the discovery for my own."

They stared at him, shocked. "You *inherited* the recipe? From whom, is one allowed to ask?" inquired Gustav, a new shine in his unblinking eyes.

"From my father, who, in turn, inherited the recipe from *his* father. The recipe has passed in total secrecy from father to oldest son in our family for almost five hundred years now . . . ever since the first André DuBois created the soup for Lorenzo de' Medici in Florence. He called it *Zuppa Il Magnifico* in the Duke's honor."

André found himself enjoying this confession of a long-guarded secret. He warmed to his subject. "So you see," he said, smiling with his eyebrows, "the original *Potage François Premier* was not French at all. It was an Italian soup, created by an Italian chef, for an Italian duke!"

Yvonne twisted a strand of her long hair about her finger. "An Italian chef named André DuBois?" She laughed.

"Andrea dei Boschi was his name, Yvonne. He Frenchified it when he emigrated to France."

"Emigrated to France? Why?" Gustav asked. "Was he out of work, like me?" His grimace appeared again.

"Not likely . . . the greatest chef of his era. But Leonardo da Vinci tasted his *Zuppa Il Magnifico* at a Medici banquet and was so entranced at the exquisite balance of its taste factors that when he went to work for the Sforza family in Milan, he told the Duke Moro about it, and Moro offered Andrea dei Boschi a princely salary to come to Milan and be the ducal chef. Andrea yielded. And later, when Leonardo went to France to live, at the invitation of its new king, Francis the First, history repeated itself. Leonardo sang the praises of *Zuppa Il Magnifico* to King Francis, and Andrea dei Boschi was inveigled into coming to France as the king's chef. That is when *Zuppa Il Magnifico* became *Potage François Premier,* you see. And since Andrea was a compulsive gambler who invariably lost, his recipe for the soup was the only thing of value he had to leave to his son."

"Have all the oldest sons of our family been famous chefs ever since then, Uncle?" Yvonne asked, smiling.

"None," André answered. "None. Until me."

"Why not?" Gustav asked. "With a specialty like *Potage François Premier,* any dolt could become a famous chef."

André said evenly, "Very few members of our family have been dolts, Gustav. But I suppose most of my ancestors lacked the patience to capitalize on the recipe. It takes five days to make the soup."

Gustav was impressed at last. "Five days!" he echoed. "No wonder it made you famous!" He paused and his eyes flicked again to Yvonne briefly. "May I ask you something, Uncle, without impertinence?"

"Ask," said André, knowing already what was coming.

"What was your salary at *Chez Marie Antoinette?*"

"Three hundred thousand francs."

Gustav shook his bearlike head as though in pain. "And all because of a single soup recipe!"

"Not so," André said with dignity. "The cuisine at *Chez Marie* was not composed solely of a single soup, may I point out." He nodded at the awards on the walls around him. "As these citations testify, I was not known as a distinguished chef for my soup alone."

"Of course not," Yvonne said hastily.

Trying to keep the eagerness from his voice, Gustav asked, "What will become of your recipe now? You have neither a son nor a daughter. Only a niece. Does Yvonne inherit this recipe now?"

André shook his head. "I am sorry, Yvonne, but no. In my will, I have left the recipe to the *Société Gastronomique Internationale* as a historical treasure to be published and enjoyed by every amateur cook who wants it after my death. And I have sworn that no one shall have it until I die." He shrugged, a completely Gallic shrug, although by his own admission his blood was at least fractionally Italian. In implied apology he went on, "I did not know, of course, that my niece would marry a chef when I made these arrangements."

"You know it now," Gustav said gravely. "Can you not reconsider?"

"My word is given," André said simply.

"With the recipe for *Potage François Premier,*" Gustav pleaded urgently, "any restaurant of *haute cuisine* in France would happily employ me as master chef, from *La Tour d'Argent* to *La Bonne Auberge.*"

"I am sorry," André repeated. "It is impossible."

They left it then, but André slept uneasily that night on his sofa. Once, when he awoke during the night, he heard the murmur of voices from his bedroom.

At breakfast, he treated his guests to *Omelet Raspail,* served with thick unsweetened coffee and wafer-thin leaves of toasted bread. *Omelet Raspail* had been almost as famous at *Chez Marie Antoinette* as *Potage François Premier.* Gustav ate his portion with a kind of reluctant awe, smacking his thick lips in appreciation.

André said, "Gustav, my dear boy, I have been thinking. You say you badly need a specialty to win employment. I can suggest a dozen for you." He rose from the breakfast table, went to the kitchen and lifted his metal file box of recipes from the shelf over the sink. "How would you like to offer prospective employers *Mousse de Mélongeène Rousseau* as your specialty?"

"It is commonplace," Gustav said ungraciously. "Ten thousand chefs can make it."

"Only four can make it right," murmured André, but selected another card from his file. "What about *Paté de Barbotine Enceinte?* That would be unique with you and draw discriminating diners like flies. Chef Henri Courbet, who invented it, has been dead for forty years, and only two other chefs besides myself have ever been able to duplicate it. I have the recipe here in the file."

Gustav shook his head decidedly, "No good, Uncle. With this rage for slimming, paté is passé."

André sighed. "*Eh bien,* I can teach you how to prepare saddle of veal with a shallot sauce so daring and imaginative that it is irresistibly challenging to the eater. It could make your name famous in six months."

"No," Gustav said positively. "These are specialties that have seen their day, Uncle. Any chef worthy of the name can at least make a stab at preparing them, including myself." He hesitated and then came out with it baldly. "Teach me to make *Potage François Premier* and I shall conquer the world!" He did not seem to realize how silly such rodomontade sounded. "Let me but see your recipe card for *Potage François Premier,* and Yvonne and I will be in your debt forever!"

André snapped shut his box of recipe cards. "I am sorry," he said a third time, "that is impossible. There is no card in this file for my soup. The only record of that recipe, aside from the will in my avocat's hands, is here," and he tapped his forehead. Then he replaced the recipe file on the kitchen shelf and departed rather abruptly on a shopping trip to the village, intent on laying in supplies for the entertainment of his guests.

When he returned, he stepped into his kitchen for a glass of water. The summer sun was extremely hot, and he had walked four miles in its embrace. It was then that he saw his recipe file was missing.

Curiously, besides anger, he felt an inclination to weep. Perhaps because he was growing old and emotional? Or because it saddened him to find his niece involved with a lazy, parasitical, graceless clown like Gustav, who had the nerve to call himself a chef? No matter. Anger soon overcame dolor, and he went out quietly into the summer sunshine again and began a cautious reconnaissance of his property.

As expected, he soon located his two guests. They were sprawled at ease under a linden tree at the far end of his flower garden. He stood unnoticed behind a head-high stack of cut logs and regarded them.

Gustav had André's recipe box open upon his lap and was leafing through it carefully, giving each card a concentrated glare from his muddy-water eyes. André heard him say to Yvonne, who was leaning against the bole of the tree, facing her husband, "It's got to be in this file someplace, Yvonne. It's got to be! All his other recipes are here—hundreds of them."

Yvonne laughed with flat lack of merriment. "Didn't you believe him, darling, when he handed us all that *blague* about the *Société Gastronomique Internationale?*"

Gustav snorted. "The old goat was lying in his teeth, obviously. Can *you* see a world-famous chef giving up a recipe worth three hundred thousand francs a year to a stupid gourmet society? For nothing? No, he intends to sell his damned recipe to the highest bidder, believe me. Or leave it, perhaps, to his mistress, if he has one in this godforsaken place."

Yvonne laughed again. "You flatter Uncle André. If he's too old to cook soup any longer, he's also too old for love!"

That was enough for André. The anger in him was now burningly alive. He considered telephoning the police in Arezzo that he was being robbed, but he realized that the police could do nothing in these peculiar circumstances. How could you arrest a man for trying to steal a recipe that did not exist except in André's head?

In the end, André went quietly back into his house and set about preparing luncheon for his guests, after first visiting the tumbledown shack he used as toolhouse and feed shed for his fowl. He rooted about on its shelves until he found a small cardboard box, which he carried with him into the kitchen.

Yvonne and Gustav returned to the house an hour later. André greeted them cheerfully. All through the excellent luncheon—a delicate *ragoût d'agneau* served with a dry white wine of the region—he chattered away with animation. He did not succeed, however, in drawing his guests into more than laconic answers to his sallies. They seemed distraught.

Drinking the last of his wine, André said to Gustav, "Where did you go this morning while I was in the village?"

"For a walk," Gustav answered shortly.

"I can see you got very warm," said André, eyeing the perspiration stains on Gustav's dark-blue shirt and trying to ignore the offensive odor of the man.

"This Italian sun is as hot as the hinges of hell," Gustav complained.

André nodded. "Hot enough to kill you if you exercise too violently. So I hope you took a long and exhausting walk."

Gustav's lips tightened. "What do you mean by that?"

"Nothing, Gustav," Yvonne said quickly. "He was joking. Weren't you, Uncle André?"

"No," André said.

"I didn't think so." Gustav set down his wine glass, rose from his chair, and started ponderously around the table toward André.

"Wait," André said. "You want to know my recipe for *Potage François Premier,* don't you?"

Gustav said nothing, but he stopped moving toward André.

"You and Yvonne stole my recipe box this morning to search for the recipe. True?"

"Your recipe box is on the kitchen shelf," Yvonne said.

"You replaced it when you returned from your 'walk,' but only after you failed to find my recipe in it."

Gustav interposed. "We were curious about the other recipes you mentioned . . . the ones you suggested as possible specialties for me. You told us yourself last night that the recipe for *Potage François Premier* was not in the file box."

"But you didn't quite believe me, did you?"

Gustav growled. "I am tired of beating about the bush. I want your recipe for *Potage François Premier*, yes."

André laughed. "And you are prepared to steal it from me if necessary?"

"I am prepared to kill you to get it," Gustav replied.

André's eyes widened in genuine surprise. Suddenly he knew fear, yet he said quite calmly, "If you kill me, nephew, you destroy your chance of owning my recipe, do you not?"

"I didn't say I'd kill you all at once. Let me show you what I mean . . ." Gustav took two steps and stood beside André's chair. He drew back his maul-like fist. "Here is a small sample," he said, and as André attempted to stand, the fist took him on the right temple with dreadful force. Blackness descended upon him.

It was late afternoon when he came to his senses. He was lying on his own bed in his own bedroom. He tried to move his arms but found he could not. He was tightly secured by wrists and ankles to the bedposts, trussed up like a chicken. He could, however, turn his head, which was aching rather badly. When he did so, he saw his niece sitting in his old rocking chair beside the bed, smoking a cigarette and regarding his awakening with unsympathetic eyes. Beyond her, he saw that his telephone had been torn out by the roots and tossed into a corner of the room.

"Yvonne!" he said. His voice scratched, the single word came out as a croak.

Blowing smoke, she said, "Hi, Uncle. I'm sorry Gustav hurt you, but he had to, you know. You are so stubborn." She hesitated, then went on. "I advise you to cooperate fully with Gustav, because he means to have your recipe, one way or another. It is, after all, a legacy in *my* family, too. I am your brother's daughter."

"No longer," whispered André. "You are a stranger to me."

She waved a hand airily, the hand with the cigarette in it. "I guess I can afford to lose an uncle if I gain a priceless recipe," she said. "Although you must understand that your attitude wounds me deeply. Such selfishness!"

André was silent. Gustav came shambling into the room. "Awake, are you, Uncle?" he inquired. "Good. I give you three minutes to collect your senses and prod your memory. Then I want you to dictate the recipe for *Potage François Premier* to Yvonne. Or else, as the Americans say."

"Or else what?" Fear clutched André again. He shook it off impatiently.

"I'll bring you another small taste of death," Gustav said. "This time considerably more painful, however."

"I see. And if I give you my recipe, how will you be sure it is genuine?"

"I shall prepare your soup myself, here in this house, before I accept the recipe as true. Believe me, I am chef enough to recognize it. And Yvonne has tasted the original, remember. Like falling in love, I believe she said."

André saw that Yvonne now had a pad of paper on her lap and held a ball-point pen poised above it. With difficulty he summoned a shaky laugh. "I cannot believe you are serious, Gustav."

"I am very serious. Dictate."

"No," André said, testing them for the last time.

Yvonne handed Gustav her cigarette. "Here," she purred in her soft voice. "Show him, darling."

Gustav placed the burning cigarette end under André's left eye and pressed it against the flesh with disdainful carelessness. André bellowed with pain and squirmed on the bed like a maddened eel.

"You see?" Gustav said, lifting the glowing coal at last and handing the cigarette back to his wife. Yvonne took an unconcerned puff upon the stub before tamping it under her heel.

"I am ready for you to begin," she said, smiling at her uncle and gesturing with her ball-point pen.

André clenched his teeth against the pain in his cheek and thought sadly, *So it is true then. They really* would *torture me to get my recipe . . . and perhaps kill me afterward to safeguard themselves.* He felt only contempt for the man Gustav, but a corrosive sense of sorrow for his niece. He said in a low voice, "You begin with chicken stock . . ."

Gustav's pig-eyes glinted and Yvonne's pen began to race across her pad.

". . . made with lightly salted water, simmered for exactly five hours, strained, reheated, and allowed to cool four separate times. Carefully skim off the solidified fat after each cooling. Add half a cup of salted water to the kettle before each reheating, and each reheating should simmer for thirty-eight minutes."

He paused until Yvonne's pen caught up with him, then resumed. "Use five cups of the chicken stock thus obtained to boil the leanest parts of three ducklings for five hours at a slow simmer, again straining, reheating, and cooling four times, and skimming fat as before, adding four more tablespoons of the pure stock, lightly salted, to the mix before each reheating."

Gustav hung over Yvonne's shoulder, watching the words take shape upon her pad. He scarcely breathed, he was so intent.

André continued. "After straining the mixed poultry stock for the last time, use three cups of it to form a marinade in which you soak thinly cut cucumber slices for eight hours, after which you add the juice extracted from three small carrots before combining the cucumber-carrot liquor with the remaining poultry stock. You continue to reheat this stock and salt lightly until the vegetable taste factor of cucumber-carrot begins to dominate the poultry taste factor in the broth." He paused for breath and went on. "Taste frequently to ascertain the exact point of balance."

André's voice droned on, reciting a complicated formula consisting of ingredients that he knew were readily available either on his own farm or in the village grocery store. From chicken stock to the final bacon crumbs, there were twenty-six ingredients. When he finished, he said, "And that's my recipe, in its entirety. Now release me."

Gustav ignored him. He said to his wife, "Catch three of the chickens your uncle keeps in the yard behind his vegetable garden, kill them, pluck them, and bring them to me." His tone was urgent, his excitement quite genuine. Turning to André, he asked anxiously, "Do you keep ducks here?"

"A few. Beside the stream that bounds my farm on the south."

"Good! Yvonne, three ducklings, also! And hurry!"

André said, "What about me?" He strained against his bonds.

Gustav struck him a negligent backhanded blow on the cheek that was already inflamed from the cigarette burn. "Shut up," he grunted, "until I have tested your recipe."

"But that will be five days!" André was plaintive.

Gustav shrugged and left him. André could hear him rummaging the shelves of the refrigerator in the kitchen, exploring his food closet, his spice rack, his canisters, rattling the copper saucepans and kettles that André kept under his sink.

It was very late before exhaustion at last overcame the pain of André's wounds and he fell asleep. To his surprise, he slept soundly until the sun was high the next morning. He awoke to find himself stiff and sore in every muscle, and to find that his bonds had been severed during the night while he slept. He stretched, groaned, rolled over, and stood up. Two steps across the tiny bedroom showed him that the door was solidly secured. His niece and her husband had locked him in when they cut him loose. At least the primitive bathroom opening off his bedroom was available to him. The whole house was redolent of boiling chicken.

He called through the door, "Let me out!"

"Good morning, Uncle." Yvonne's voice came through the stout door between them. "You slept well, I hope?"

"You know I did not. Where's Gustav?"

"In the village, buying the ingredients you don't have here."

"I smell chicken, don't I?"

"Of course. We're almost through with the chicken stock. We worked all night."

"Do I get any breakfast?"

"Not until Gustav gets back. I'm awfully sorry, Uncle André." However, her cheerful, carefree tone told him plainly that she was not.

On the second day, he awoke to continued sounds of activity in the kitchen and could smell the distinctive odor of the soup stock formed by combining chicken and duckling liquor. He nodded to himself and did not even ask for breakfast. They brought him some rolls and coffee at noon, when Gustav reported triumphantly that they were ready to marinate the cucumbers.

André didn't sleep at all that night. He was waiting.

At three in the morning, a key turned in his locked door, and Yvonne burst into his room. "Uncle!" she cried, "Help me, please! Gustav is sick!"

André rolled over on his bed to look at her. "Gustav is sick?" he echoed, and kept his face expressionless, his emotions suppressed.

"Terribly! All of a sudden he got these awful cramps! I'm afraid he's dying! For the love of mercy, won't you please help us?"

André rose and put on an old dressing gown with calculated deliberation. Then he accompanied his niece to the kitchen. She was now almost hysterical with worry, but pathetically humble and contrite.

Gustav was lying on the kitchen floor, moaning and clutching his middle. His face, in the light of the kitchen bulbs, was the color of parchment and was drenched with sweat. He turned popping, panic-stricken eyes on André when he came into the room.

André glanced at the stove. A saucepan bubbled gently on a front burner. André was sure its contents could only be the soup stock after the marinated cucumber liquor had been added to it.

Ignoring Gustav, he looked at his niece. Her face was pinched, her eyes wild. She was weeping, he noted with surprise. Tears rolled down her cheeks and dripped unheeded onto her bosom. Her hard flippancy, her indifference, her callous manner were gone.

So she really loved that incredible lout, André concluded, with sudden compassion for his niece. He felt his resolve soften.

He said to her, "Has Gustav been tasting the soup stock?"

"Yes, of course. Ever since we added the cucumber liquor. To tell when the vegetable taste factor approached the poultry taste, just as you said."

"Often?"

She nodded silently and bent over Gustav. Then she knelt and cradled his head in her arms. "Help him, Uncle André!" she pleaded. "He's dying, isn't he?"

André took Gustav's pain-wracked body under the arms and dragged it toward the steps that led from the farmhouse porch to the lane.

"Where are you taking him?" Yvonne demanded.

"You must drive him to the hospital in Arezzo. A stomach pump may save him if you are quick enough."

"Stomach pump!" Yvonne helped to bundle Gustav, still moaning, into the backseat of their car.

"Yes," André said. "I poisoned him."

She climbed under the wheel of the car and switched on the headlights.

"You couldn't have!" she said. "You were locked in your room!" There was nothing soft or ladylike about her strident tones now.

André said, "I mixed arsenic with the salt in the kitchen, my dear, before Gustav started on the recipe. Just in case, you understand."

Yvonne started the engine, raced it for a moment to warm it, and as she slipped the car into gear, cast a worried glance over her shoulder at her husband, sprawled in the rear seat. She gulped down her sobs. "Poor Gustav!" she wailed. "He only wanted a little specialty to advance his career!"

André put a finger to the burn under his left eye. "He has one now, Yvonne. *Potage de Volaille Gustav.*"

As the car scattered dust in a headlong flight down the lane, André chuckled. "Which is to say: fresh poultry soup, lightly salted with rat poison."

TALMAGE POWELL

NEW NEIGHBOR

October 1975

A PROLIFIC WRITER of stories, Talmage Powell got his start writing for the pulps. When *AHMM* launched, he was a regular contributor under his own name and a variety of pseudonyms. Powell is also remembered for his "Ed Rivers" novels, considered to be some of the best P.I. stories of the late 1950s. In addition, he wrote for television and films, and he was the ghostwriter for several Ellery Queen novels.

■

Each of us lives in one world only," Mrs. Cappelli said, "the singular world within the skull. No two are alike. Who can possibly imagine some of the dark phantasms within the worlds other than one's own?"

Isadora, old, gray, spindly, gnarled, more friend and companion than servant, drifted to Mrs. Cappelli's side. The two women were of an age, in the autumn of their lives, with a close bond between them. The years had touched Mrs. Cappelli with the gentler brush. She was still trim; her face had not entirely surrendered its youthful lines; her once-black hair was braided in a coil atop her head, a silver tiara.

The two stood at the window of Mrs. Cappelli's slightly disarrayed and comfortably lived-in bedroom and looked from the second-story window at the youth in the backyard of the house next door.

"A strange one," Isadora agreed.

He was lounging on a plastic-webbing chaise, indolent, loose, relaxed, calmly pumping a pellet rifle. In scruffy jeans and T-shirt, he was long, tanned, and lean, slightly bony. Even in repose he was a suggestion of quick, whip-like agility and power. His face was cleanly cut, even attractive; his forehead, ears, and neck feathered with very dark hair. Idly, his gaze was roving the bushes and trees, the pines at the corners of the yard, the avocado tree, the two tall, unkempt palmettos.

He lifted the gun with a casual motion and squeezed the trigger. A bird toppled from the topmost reaches of the taller pine tree, the small body bouncing from limb to limb, showering a few needles, hanging briefly on a lower limb before it struck and was swallowed by the uncut grass along the rear of the yard.

The youth showed no sign of interest, once again pumping the gun and stirring only his eyes in a renewed search of the trees.

Mrs. Cappelli's thin figure flinched, and her eyes were held by the spot where the bird had fallen.

Isadora touched her arm. "At least it wasn't a cardinal, Maria."

"Thank you, Isadora. From this distance the details weren't clear. My eyes just aren't what they used to be."

Isadora glanced at the face that had once been the distillation of all beauty in Old Sicily. "I think we could use some tea, Maria."

Mrs. Cappelli seemed unaware when Isadora faded from her side. She remained at the window, as hushed as the hot Florida stillness outside, looking carefully at the young man on the chaise.

Mrs. Cappelli had been delighted when the house next door was rented at last. It had stood vacant for months, a casualty of Florida overbuild. Dated by its Spanish styling, it was nevertheless a sound and comfortable house in a substantial and quiet older neighborhood where urban decay had never gained the slightest foothold.

Mrs. Cappelli had expected a family. Instead there were only the mother and son arriving in a noisy old car in the wake of a van that had disgorged flimsy, worn, time-payment furniture. Mrs. Ruth Morrow and Greg. A lot of house for two people, but Mrs. Cappelli supposed, correctly, that the age of the house and its long vacancy had finally caused the desperate owner to offer it as a cut-rate bargain on the sagging rental market.

After a settling-in day or two, Mrs. Cappelli saw Mrs. Morrow pruning the dying poinsettia near the front corner of the house and went over to say hello.

It was a sultry afternoon and Mrs. Morrow looked wan and tired, with hardly enough remaining strength to snap the shears. Mrs. Cappelli wondered why Greg wasn't handling the pruning tool. He was at home. Who could doubt it? He was in there torturing a high-amplification guitar with amateurish violence. His discordant efforts were audible a block away.

"I'm Maria Cappelli," Mrs. Cappelli said pleasantly, "It's very nice to have new neighbors."

Mrs. Morrow accepted the greeting with hesitant and stand-offish self-consciousness. Her glance slipped toward the house, a silent wish that her son would turn down his guitar. She was a thin, almost frail woman. She needs, Mrs. Cappelli thought, mounds of pasta and huge bowls of steaming, mouth-watering *stufato*.

Mrs. Morrow remembered her manners with a tired smile. "Ruth Morrow," she said. She glanced about the yard. "So much to do here. Inside, the place was all dust and cobwebs." Her gaze moved to Mrs. Cappelli's comfortable abode of stucco and red tile. "You have a lovely place."

"My husband built it years before his death. We used to come here for winter vacations. To me, it was home, rather than New York. I love Florida, even the heat of the summers. My son was born in the house, right up there in that corner bedroom." Mrs. Cappelli laughed. "Shortest labor on record. Such a bambino! When he decided to make his entrance, he wouldn't even take time for a ride to the hospital."

Mrs. Cappelli's unconscious delight in her son brought Ruth Morrow's fatigued and hollow eyes to Mrs. Cappelli's face. Mrs. Cappelli was caught, held, and slightly embarrassed. Such aching eyes! So many regrets, frustrations, and bewilderments harbored in their depths . . . They were too large and dark for the thin, heavily made-up face that at one time must have been quite pretty.

"My son is named Greg," Mrs. Morrow murmured.

"Mine is named John. He's much older than your son. He has a wife and five children—such scamps!—and he comes to see me now and then when he can take the time. He is a contractor up north, always on the go."

"He must be a fine man."

Mrs. Cappelli was urged to say something comforting to the wearied mother before her. "Oh, John sowed an oat. I guess they all do before they settle down. Nowadays John is always after me to sell the old antique, as he calls the house. Come and live with him, he nags. I tell him to peddle his own papers. This is not the old country where three or four generations must brawl under one small roof."

Mrs. Morrow nodded. "It's been real nice of you to say hello, Mrs. Cappelli. I do have to run now. I work, you see. At the Serena Lounge on the beach, from six in the evening until two o'clock each morning. I always have a good bit to do to get ready for work."

"The Serena is an excellent place. John took Isadora and me there the last time he was down."

Ruth Morrow punched the tip of the pruning shears at a small brown twig. "Being a cocktail waitress isn't the height of my ambition, but without professional training, it pays more money than I'd ever hoped to make. And God knows there is never quite enough money."

It might ease the situation, Mrs. Cappelli mused, if her boy dirtied his hands with some honest toil. She said, "The honor of a job is in its execution, and I'm certain you're the best of cocktail waitresses."

The sincerity of Mrs. Cappelli's tone brought the first touch of animation to the tired face with its layered icing of makeup and framing of short, dark brown hair. Before Mrs. Morrow could respond, the front door of the house slammed, and Greg was standing in the shadow of the small portico. Both women looked toward him.

"Greg," Mrs. Morrow called, "this is Mrs. Cappelli, our next-door neighbor."

"Hi," he said, bored. He gave Mrs. Cappelli a single glance of dismissal, dropped to the walk with a single smooth stride and headed around the house.

"Greg," Ruth Morrow called, "where are you going?"

"Out," he said, without looking back.

"When will you be home?"

"When I'm damned good and ready!" He rounded the corner of the house and was out of sight.

Mrs. Morrow's face came creeping in Mrs. Cappelli's direction, but her eyes sidled away. "It's just his way of talking, Mrs. Cappelli."

Mrs. Cappelli nodded, but she didn't understand. How could Mrs. Morrow accept it? Parental respect was normal in a child, be he six or sixty.

A car engine was stabbed to roaring life and Greg raced down the driveway. He cornered the car into the street with tires screaming.

"I really have to go now, Mrs. Cappelli."

"It was a privilege to meet you," Mrs. Cappelli said.

"Well?" Isadora asked as soon as Mrs. Cappelli stepped into the house.

"She is a poor woman in the worst of all states," Mrs. Cappelli said, "a mother with a cruel and unloving son."

Isadora crossed herself.

"He is killing his mother," Mrs. Cappelli said.

Greg was an immediate neighborhood blight, a disease, an invasion. The Ransoms' playful puppy bounded into the Morrow yard, and Greg broke its leg with a kick, claiming that the flop-eared trusting mutt was charging him. He hunted chords on the thunderous guitar at one o'clock in the morning, if the mood suited him. Many evenings he was out, usually returning about three A.M. with screaming tires and unmuffled engine. Frequently he filled the Morrow house with hordes of hippies for beer and rock parties.

Neighbors grumbled and swapped irate opinions of Greg among themselves over backyard fences and coffee klatches. Lack of leadership was a stultifying, inertial force, and nothing was done about Greg until about two, one morning, when the biggest blast yet hit the peak of its frenzy in the Morrow house.

Mr. Sigmon (the white colonial across the street) decided he just couldn't stand it any longer. He threw back the cover, sat up in bed, turned on the bedside lamp, and dialed Information on his extension phone. Yes, Information informed, a phone had been installed at the Morrow address. Mr. Sigmon got the number, hesitated for a single minute, then dialed it.

The Morrow phone rang six or seven times before anyone noticed. Then a girl answered, giggling drunkenly. "If this isn't an obscene call, forget it."

"Let me speak to Greg," Mr. Sigmon said, the phone feeling sweaty in his hand.

The girl screeched for Greg, and he was on.

"Have a heart," Mr. Sigmon pleaded. "Can't you tone things down just a little?"

"Who's this?" Greg asked.

"I . . . uh . . . Mr. Sigmon, across the street."

"How'd you like a fat lip, Mr. Sigmon-across-the-street?"

"Now look, Greg . . ." Mr. Sigmon gathered his courage. "All I'm asking is that you be reasonable."

"Go cram it!"

A burst of anger burned the edges from Mr. Sigmon's timidity. "Now look here, you young pup, you quiet down over there or I'll call the police."

For a moment there was only the noise of the party on the line, the wild laughter, the shouted talk, the overpowering background of hard-rock rhythm. Then Greg said, "Well, OK, pops. You don't have to get so sore about it. We're just having some fun."

The party cooled and Mr. Sigmon stretched beside his wide-awake wife with a feeling of being an inch taller for having put a tether on Greg.

Two days later Mrs. Sigmon got out of her station wagon with a bag of groceries, crossed to the front stoop, and dropped the groceries with a thud and clatter. She put her knuckles to her mouth and screamed. Against the front door lay her cat, stiff and lifeless, its head twisted so that its muzzle pointed upward away from the shoulders.

That night Greg hosted another party, the loudest one yet.

To Mrs. Cappelli it was as if a dark presence had come among them. It wasn't the same warmly quiet old street. It was like a sinister urban street where the aura urged the hapless pedestrian to hurry along after dark with ears keened for the slightest sound.

"Perhaps the Morrows will move on," Mrs. Cappelli said at breakfast.

"Yes," Isadora agreed. "They are gypsies. But when? That's the question. Next month? A year from now? Before the youth does something even more dreadful?"

"That poor mother." Mrs. Cappelli flipped an egg in the pan. "If she moved around the world, she would not have room for her problem."

Later in the day Mrs. Cappelli carried her afternoon tea up to her bedroom. She put the steaming cup on a small table and crossed to the side window. Outside, on a level with the sill, was a small wooden ledge. Two sparrows were hopping about on it, pecking bits of food from cracks.

"Hello there," Mrs. Cappelli said, "you're early for dinner. You must be hungry, going for those leftovers."

She turned to the bureau and picked up a canister. The sparrows fluttered away as she opened the canister and reached out to spread a feast of seeds and crumbs on the ledge feeder.

The sparrows had returned by the time Mrs. Cappelli fetched her tea and settled in the wooden rocking chair near the window. Other birds arrived, more sparrows, a robin, a thrush, a tiny wren. They were a delight of movement, color; they were so naturally happy, so easy to please.

The daily bird feeding and watching was silly, perhaps—the whim of an old woman—but the birds rewarded Mrs. Cappelli with a quiet pleasure in a sometimes endless day. Therefore, she inquired of herself, isn't it a most important thing?

She wondered if the Prince would come; and then he did. Gorgeous. Regal. The most beautiful cardinal since Audubon. He had been a daily visitor a long time now. He always came to rest on the edge of the feeder, proud head lifted and tilted as he looked in at Mrs. Cappelli.

She leaned forward slightly. "Hello there," she said softly. "Is the food up to your kingly taste today?"

She couldn't quite delight in the words or in the sight of Prince and his friends. No, not anymore. She sat back, fingers curled on the arms of the chair. Today, more than yesterday or the day before, she was aware of depleted joy. She'd tried not to admit the awareness, but now, in the ritual of the birds, was a hint of anxiety, even fear in her heart. She couldn't entirely free her mind of the memory of the youth next door with his pellet gun. Pump, pump, pump . . . His strong hand working the lever while his eyes roamed the trees for an innocent, unsuspecting, and helpless target, and a feathered body twisting and turning as it plunged headlong to the ground.

Perhaps, Mrs. Cappelli thought, she should stop feeding the birds while the air gun is over there threatening them . . .

As the thought crossed her mind, she saw a sudden puff of red feathers on the cardinal's breast. The bird was gone. That quickly. That completely. The other birds scattered in sudden flight.

Mrs. Cappelli sat with a hot dryness blinding her eyes, then she snapped from the chair and hurried down through the house. With late sun searing through the cold film on her flesh, she searched along the driveway and through the shrubbery growing against the house. The cardinal's body was not to be seen, and she was sure that Greg had run over and picked up the evidence before she'd got out of the house.

She thought of him watching the ledge, seeing her birds, hearing the sound of her, perhaps, drifting from her open window as she'd chatted at the cardinal. A dark instinct had risen in him, a hunger, and his devious mind with its unknown depths had schemed. He'd waited, like a beast savoring the anticipation of the kill. Then he'd felt the thrill of pulling the trigger at last and seeing the cardinal fall.

Mrs. Cappelli turned slowly, and he was there, standing near the front walk of the Morrow house, the air gun in the crook of his arm. Tall. Lean. Young. Challenging her. Baiting her. His lips lifting in a smile that sent an icy shard through her.

She turned on stiff legs and went into her house.

The policeman's name was Longstreet, Sergeant Harley Longstreet. He was tall, strapping, with a pleasantly big-featured face and lank brown hair.

With the drapery pulled aside in the living room, Mrs. Cappelli watched him come from the Morrow house. He stood a moment, looking over his shoulder, a loose-leaf pocket notebook in his hand. Then he came across to the Cappelli front door.

Mrs. Cappelli opened the door while he was still a few feet away and stood aside for him to enter. With a glance at his face, she suspected that he hadn't been very successful with Greg Morrow. He was a nice young policeman. He'd responded quickly to her phone call. He'd heard everything she'd had to say. He hadn't thought a bird's death unimportant—not when it was coupled with the circumstances. He'd attached considerable meaning and importance to it. He had gone over to the Morrow place almost an hour ago. Now he was back.

Mrs. Cappelli stood with her fingers on the edge of the opened door. "I think I understand, Mr. Longstreet," she said with no accusation or rancor.

"He simply denies killing the bird, ma'am. Did you actually see him kill it?"

"I didn't see him pull the trigger."

"Well, you see, Mrs. Cappelli, the law is black print on white paper. Mrs. Morrow isn't home. No one else is out and about the houses close by. Without a witness or some tangible evidence I've done about all I can."

"I appreciate that, Mr. Longstreet."

He hesitated, tapping his notebook on his thumb. "He says you are a crotchety old lady who doesn't want young people in the neighborhood."

"He's a liar, Mr. Longstreet. I delight in reasonably normal young people. Do you believe him?"

"Not for a moment, Mrs. Cappelli. Not one word." He flipped his notebook open. "I checked the records briefly when I got your call, to see if he was in any of the official files. We have computers nowadays, you know. I can push a button and tell whether or not he'd been recorded in any city or county agency."

She closed the door finally and stood leaning the back of her shoulders against it. "And what did your computer tell you?"

His sharp eyes flicked between her and the notebook. "He spent two years, our Greg Morrow, in a correctional institution for maladjusted teen-agers. Committed when he was sixteen. Released on his eighteenth birthday, which was eighteen months ago. Prior to the action that put him away, he had a record of classroom disruption, of vandalism in his schools, of shaking down smaller classmates for their pocket money. He was finally put away after he assaulted a school principal."

"The principal should have given him a sound thrashing with a hickory switch," Mrs. Cappelli said. "But in that event it would have been the principal who went to jail."

"It's possible," Longstreet agreed. He tucked his notebook in his hip pocket. "We've had complaints about Greg almost from the day he was let out, in various neighborhoods where the Morrows have lived. But other than a suspended sentence for trespassing, after a house was vandalized, nothing has stood against him in court."

Mrs. Cappelli moved slowly to a large chair and sank on its edge, hands clasped on her drawn-together knees. "Mr. Longstreet, Greg Morrow is not merely a mischievous boy. He is the kind of force and fact from which those fantastic and gory newspaper headlines are too often drawn."

"That's very possible."

His tone caused her to glance up, and she caught the bitterness in his eyes. Her sympathy went out to him for the hardness of his job.

"Don't feel badly, Mr. Longstreet. I thank you for coming out and talking to him. Perhaps it will frighten him for a little while and help that much."

"We simply can't lock them up without evidence of the commission of a crime. Sometimes, then, it's too late."

"After the commission of a crime, Mr. Longstreet, it is always too late." She rose to her feet to see him out.

He stood looking down on her, the small sturdiness of her. "I'll have the police cruiser in this area increase its patrols along your street, Mrs. Cappelli. I'll do everything I possibly can."

"I'm sure of that."

"Good day, Mrs. Cappelli."

"Good day, Mr. Longstreet."

She watched him stride down the front walk and get into the unmarked police car parked against the street curbing. He sat there for a brief time after he started the engine, looking at the Morrow house; then he drove away.

As she turned, Mrs. Cappelli saw Greg. He was standing in the Morrow yard, thumbs hooked in his belt, watching the police car move toward the intersection and turn out of sight.

Mrs. Cappelli started to close the door. Then, with a sudden impulse, she went outside and walked across to the driveway that separated the two properties.

"Greg . . . may I speak to you?"

He moved only his head, turning it to stare at her. "Why should I talk to an old bitch who sics the fuzz on me?"

She whitened, but held back the swift heat of anger. "I thought we might have a civilized talk. After all, Greg, we do have to live as neighbors."

"Who says? Somebody around here could die. Old biddies are always popping off, you know."

She drew a difficult breath. "A bit of reasonableness, Greg. That's all I'm asking. I was happy when you moved into the neighborhood, so young and vigorous. I looked forward to some youthful activity next door."

"Old creep. You called the fuzz."

"You know why, Greg. Somehow I must impress on you that there are limits. Why can't we discuss them? Observe them? Live and let live?"

He looked at her with studied insolence. "You made a bad mistake calling Longstreet, old lady. I don't like it. I don't like it at all. I won't forget it, either."

Her voice rang with the first hint of anger. "Are you threatening me, Greg?"

"Who says? Can you prove to Longstreet that I am? Just your word against mine. I know how the law works. I know my rights."

"I don't think this is getting us anywhere, Greg. I regret having come out and spoken to you."

He drifted a few steps toward her. The dying sunlight marked his cheekbones sharply. His body was tense, as if coiled inside. "You got a lot more regrets in the future, old lady. You better believe it. Think about it. You won't know when, how, or where. But I don't like people trying to throw me to the fuzz."

"I hope this is just talk, Greg."

He laughed suddenly. "That school principal—the one who got me sent up. Know what happened? About a year after I got out, a hit-and-run driver marked up the punk principal's daughter, that's what. She'll be a short-legged creep the rest of her life. Sure, the fuzz questioned me—but they couldn't prove a thing."

She could bear it no longer. She turned and started toward her front door with quick steps.

"Don't forget to think about it, old lady," he called after her. "And remember—nobody ever proves a thing on Greg Morrow."

Three passing days brought Mrs. Cappelli the faint hope that Greg had thought twice and again. Perhaps his insults and threat had sufficed his ego. Usually, such fellows were mostly talk. Usually.

The fourth night Mrs. Cappelli stirred in her always-light sleep, dreaming that she smelled smoke. She murmured in her half-conscious state; and then she had the sudden, clear, icy knowledge that she was not asleep.

She flung back the sheet, a small cry in her throat, and stumbled upright, a ghostly pale figure in her ankle-length white nightgown.

"Isadora!" she cried out as she hurried into the hallway. "Isadora, lazy-head, wake up! The house is on fire!"

Isadora's bedroom door flung open and Isadora appeared, gowned like her mistress, her iron gray hair hanging in two limp braids across her shoulders.

"What is it? What's happening?" Isadora chattered, her eyes bulging. She glimpsed the faint reddish glow in the stairwell and began crossing herself again and again. "Oh, heaven be merciful! Mercy from heaven!"

Together the two women stumbled in haste down the stairway. The fiery reflection was stronger in the dining room.

"Quickly, Isadora! The kitchen!"

They ran across the dining room, wavering to a halt inside the kitchen. Mrs. Cappelli's quick glance divined the situation. The curtains over the glass portion of the outside door had caught fire first. They were now remaining bits of falling ash and embers. The flames had spread easily to the window curtains along the rear of the kitchen and were now gnawing at the cabinetwork, fouling the air with the stench of burning varnish.

Isadora dashed into the pantry, knocking pots helter-skelter as she grabbed two of the larger ones. Mrs. Cappelli was more direct. She pulled the sink squirter hose out to its full extension, turned the cold water on hard, and fought the flames back until she had drenched out the last flicker.

With wisps of smoke still seeping from the cabinetwork, Mrs. Cappelli groped for a kitchen chair and sank into it weakly. She matched long breaths with the gulps Isadora was taking, and strength began to return.

"How horrible it might have been," Isadora said through chattering teeth, "if you hadn't awakened."

"Yes," Mrs. Cappelli said.

Isadora gripped the kitchen table to help herself out of her chair. "We must call the fire department to make sure everything is out."

"Yes."

"And the police."

"No!"

Isadora looked at Mrs. Cappelli, wondering at the sharpness of her tone. "Maria . . . we know who did this. We know he has been planning, waiting, thinking, and deciding what to do."

"Yes, and tonight he made his move." Mrs. Cappelli's gaze examined the fire-blackened kitchen door and paused at its base. She got up, crossed to the door, and knelt down. She touched the ashes at the base of the door. "And so simply he did it," she said. "Not all these ashes are from burned fabric. Some of them feel very much like brittle burned paper. So easily, without breaking in or leaving marks on the kitchen door, he simply slid strips of paper underneath the door until he had a sufficient pile inside. Then it remains for him but to light the tail end of the final strip and watch the tiny flame creep along the paper under the door and ignite the pile inside. Soon the hungry flames reach up to touch the curtains . . ."

The two women were an immobile tableau—Isadora, standing beside the table, Mrs. Cappelli kneeling at the door, looking at each other.

"Yes, I see," Isadora said. "It's all very clear. It would be clear to the police. But they cannot make the youth confess. They are not permitted. And he will have an alibi, someone to swear that he was far away from this street tonight."

A small sob caught in Mrs. Cappelli's throat. "How much can we endure, Isadora? Call the firemen quickly. Then I want the phone. Late as it is, I want to hear the sound of John's voice."

At ten o'clock the following evening an airport taxicab deposited John in front of the Cappelli house.

"It's he!" Isadora said, watching him pay off the taxi and get out his single piece of luggage.

Beside Isadora, the giddy center of a little vortex of excitement, Mrs. Cappelli nudged hard with her elbow. "Quickly, Isadora! The table . . . the dinner candles."

Isadora darted from the front door, leaving Mrs. Cappelli there alone to watch the approach of her son.

He wouldn't have eaten on the plane, she knew. Mama always had one of his favorite meals waiting, whatever his hour of arrival. Tonight Mrs. Cappelli had centered the dinner on *arosto di agnello,* and already she could imagine him filling his mouth with the succulent lamb and blowing her a kiss of approval from his fingertips.

"Ah, John, John!" Her wide-flung arms enfolded his dark, towering, masculine strength, and, as always, she wept joyously.

He picked her up, almost as if he would tuck her under his arm, and kissed her on both cheeks.

"What is that I smell? Not roast lamb as only *mia madre* can make?"

"But yes, John! How was the flight? Isadora, wherever are you? Quickly, Isadora! The most handsome boy on earth is famished!"

Arm linked with her son's, Mrs. Cappelli strolled into the dining room, questions tumbling about her daughter-in-law, her precious grandchildren.

All was well up north, John assured her. All was going beautifully.

He sat down at the head of the old hand-carved walnut table, an inviting array before him, snowy linens, bone china, crystal and sterling, tall candles in beaten silver holders, fine food in covered dishes.

Isadora and Mrs. Cappelli were content to sit on either side, near the head of the table, watching him eat and anticipating his every wish from the serving dishes.

Then at last he could eat no more, and he rewarded his mother with a loving wink and appreciative little belch.

He laid his napkin on the table, pushed back his chair, and lifted one of the candles to light a thin black cigar.

Mrs. Cappelli was at his side as he walked to the windows in the side of the room and stood there looking at the lights of the Morrow house.

"Now, Mama," he said quietly, "what's this trouble?"

She told him every detail from the moment Greg Morrow had moved next door. She acquainted John with Greg's every habit, the identity of Greg's closest friends, the make, model, and license number of the Morrow car. It took her several minutes; she had accumulated a great deal of information during the time Greg had been a neighbor.

When Mrs. Cappelli finished speaking, John slipped his arm about her shoulders. "Don't worry, Mama," he said quietly. "It will be taken care of. The young animal will stop killing his mother. He will kill and maim no more animals. He will hit-run no more children. He will light no more arsonist fires. It will all be taken care of very soon, when the first proper moment arrives."

Looking up at him, Mrs. Cappelli knew it would be so. In her, regrettably, Greg Morrow had made the biggest mistake of his life.

She thought of John's grandfather and his father and of Cappelli men from Sicily to San Francisco. In all the Mafia—and it had been so for generations—there were no better soldiers than Cappelli men. They enforced Mafioso law without fear or regard—and none was more stalwart than the loving fullness of her heart, her John.

WILLIAM BRITTAIN

HISTORICAL ERRORS

February 1976

A RETIRED high school teacher, Brittain makes an educator the central character of this tale of historical accuracy and authenticity—written at a time when the United States was very interested in its own history. Brittain wrote a series of stories featuring another educator, high school science teacher Mr. Stang, as the detective. He also wrote a series of tales that are frequently termed the "Man Who Read" stories. Each features a character who is a devoted fan of a particular mystery writer and who ends up solving a mystery in the characteristic style of his literary hero.

■

Norman Kaner lifted his head from the pillow, slowly opened his eyes, and immediately regretted having done so. As the light reached his brain, the mining and blasting operation within his head began full tilt. He wet his lips with his tongue, vaguely considering whether a muskrat or some other furry creature had died inside his mouth sometime the previous night. A hangover of these sublime proportions should, he thought, be enshrined somewhere as an example and warning for future generations. He wondered if the Smithsonian Institution would be at all interested.

To drink so much, especially when driving strange roads, was unforgivable. Nevertheless, Norman managed to forgive himself. There were, after all, mitigating circumstances. Just yesterday he'd taught his final class in the pre-Revolutionary colonial period, and now he and Betty had the whole summer free for the tour of

New England for which they'd been planning and saving since he was a mere instructor at Hadley College. That in itself was cause for celebration.

The celebration had included four martinis at dinner in that tiny restaurant in southern Connecticut.

Furthermore, Betty's mother, Vera, had insisted on coming along on the vacation. No cause for rejoicing, this, but an excellent excuse for drowning one's sorrows.

Vera Blumenthal was a tiny old shrew of a woman with a mouth exceeded in size by nothing on earth except the Mississippi River and possibly the Amazon. From the time they'd left yesterday noon, she'd had a disapproving comment for each revolution of the station wagon's wheels. The back seat was too narrow, Norman was driving too fast, her arthritis was acting up, they should have taken another route to avoid traffic . . . Yakkety, yakkety, yak! Whenever Norman had attempted to talk to her, to calm her or at least shut her up, she'd resorted to her favorite catch phrase: "A pox on you, Norman. And on all your brood, too."

A pox on you, Vera, thought Norman, pressing the heels of his hands against his eye sockets and tasting once again the dregs of the drinks he'd had. Somehow he'd reeled back to the car and managed to find the road. His memory from that point on wasn't too clear. He'd stopped for a traffic light out in the middle of nowhere, and then the car door had opened and a man said something about his being under arrest. Who'd expect a cop to be waiting right there . . .

Suddenly Norman sat bolt upright on the bed. He looked about at the stout oak walls of the room and the tiny window with the hand-wrought bars. The palms of his hands pressed against the mattress, feeling not springs but a crackling something that could have been wheat straw or corn shucks.

The man had been leading a horse. Not only that, but he'd been dressed in baggy pants, gathered at the knees. His shirt had been white, with full sleeves, and his hair had been pulled back and tied behind his head. The picture was one Norman had seen hundreds of times in his own history books.

"What do you know about that?" he said wonderingly. "I've been busted by Paul Revere."

As if the words were a signal, there was the sound of a bolt being thrown outside the stout door. It creaked open ponderously. Bright sunlight streamed into the tiny cell, and Norman peeped through squinted eyes at the figure in the opening.

Ethan Allen, maybe? Or John Adams? The man was dressed in similar fashion to the policeman of the night before, with the addition of a wide-brimmed hat atop hair that hung almost to his shoulders. The 1700s? Norman shook his head. No, almost a century earlier. It was hard to believe that outside that door somewhere there was a land of jet planes and superhighways, smokestacks polluting the air and raw sewage turning clear water into poison—modern America.

The guard jangled a ring of heavy wrought-iron keys in his hand. "Come to your senses have you, neighbor?" he said. "Your brain was more than a little fuddled by strong spirits when Constable Wainright towed your strange machine into town last night."

"My wife . . . her mother," mumbled Norman thickly. "Where are they? Are they all right?"

The guard nodded. "Since our gaol makes no provision for women, Dame Pellow was kind enough to put them up for the night. Just now, I suspect, they're enjoying a bowl of her flummery to break their fast. But come, put yourself in order. It won't do to keep Justice Sawyer waiting."

"Justice . . . Oh, yeah. The drunk-driving charge." Norman patted his hip pocket. The thick wad of traveler's checks was still there.

He stood up, and his face turned white as the miners inside his skull let loose a three-megaton blast. With the palm of his hand he tried to smooth down his tousled hair.

"Tell me," he said, giving up the hair as a bad job and making ineffectual passes at the wrinkles in his pants, "what's this thing with the costumes? And the policeman on horseback? Do you folks always carry on like this, or is something special going on?"

"Illium—our little village—was one of the first settlements in New England. We have a long and proud heritage that we try to keep alive."

"Oh, yeah." Norman tapped his head with an index finger. "The Bicentennial thing. Y'know, I clean forgot this was the year for it . . ."

The guard shook his head. "We predate the Revolution by more than a century. Some ten years ago the people of Illium decided we should not let the old ways and customs die. So for one month each year we do our best to relive the early days, exactly as they were, as a reminder of the stock from which we sprang."

Norman considered the oddly dressed figure. "Not bad. Not bad at all. Just one or two little things out of place, though."

"Out of place?" The guard looked as if he'd been slapped.

"Yeah. Historical errors from the wrong time. Anachronisms. Your shoes, for example."

"What about my shoes?"

"They're cut for right and left feet. Now, most of the shoes of the 1600s were made from a single last. The right and left ones were exactly the same."

"Interesting. I'll make a note of that for the village board. We try to keep everything as authentic as possible."

"Another thing. The cop last night—Wainright, I think you said his name was—he had clubbed hair."

"Clubbed?"

Norman nodded. "Tied at the back. Not really the style in Puritan days. It usually hung loose, like yours."

"Peter Wainright won't like to hear that. He's very proud of his hair. But I'm sure he'll go along in the interests of accuracy. How is it that you know all these things?"

"I'm a professor of American history. Did my doctorate on the Pilgrim and Puritan social systems."

"Ah, a man of learning. Be sure to mention it to Justice Sawyer. He puts great store by exact knowledge. Come now. We must not keep the good justice waiting."

As he marched across the village green accompanied by the key-jingling guard, Norman was amazed at how closely Illium resembled the woodcuts he'd seen of early New England villages. Windows, porches, and in some cases entire store fronts had been altered; here a home, seemingly constructed of hand-hewn timbers. Only the closest scrutiny showed they were really commercial products. There, the blacksmith shop, complete with spreading chestnut tree; the grease rack behind the facade was barely visible through the half-open door. The tiny church on the hillside, surrounded by maple trees, might actually have been built decades before the American Revolution; amazing attention to detail.

Court was held in Justice Jonathan Sawyer's low-ceilinged living room. The furniture had been pulled back against the walls, and the justice's desk placed by the room's single window— a homey yet oddly formal setting for a trial.

Betty and Vera were waiting for him when he arrived. In his hungover condition, Norman was scarcely up to the combined onslaught of the two women.

"Norman!" chattered his wife. "This will put us at least a day behind schedule, if not more. I told you not to have so much to—"

"Sheer tomfoolery," chimed in Vera. "A pox on you, Norman. And on all your brood, too."

"We have no brood, Vera," Norman groaned. "There's just Betty and me, a condition I can hardly ignore since you—"

"Oyez, oyez!" intoned the guard. "The court of the village and town of Illium is now in session, Justice Jonathan Sawyer presiding. Those who have business before this court, approach and ye shall be heard. All rise, please."

When Justice Sawyer entered from the kitchen, it was all Norman could do to keep from laughing out loud. A short, fat man in a black cloak, he resembled nothing so much as a large globe draped for mourning, surmounted by a wig of indeterminate shape, which insisted on drooping down over one eye.

"The charge?" chanted Sawyer in a sepulchral voice.

"Public drunk and disorderly," said the guard.

"He wasn't that at all," screeched Betty. "I—I mean he was drunk, all right. But he wasn't disorderly. Mother and I both—"

Justice Sawyer's hand slammed down on the desk. "You are here on my sufferance as observers. Nothing more. Now let's get on with it."

"But she was just trying to tell you there was nothing public about Norman's being drunk," Vera carped.

"Enough, madams." Justice Sawyer's face was livid. "By my faith, I'll have order in this court! This feminine caterwauling will cease immediately."

Momentarily cowed, the two women sank back onto their chairs.

"Now then, sir," Sawyer continued, looking at Norman, "how do you plead?"

"Guilty . . . your Honor . . . sir," mumbled Norman. "But I would like to offer an explanation of why it happened."

Sawyer conferred with the guard in a hushed voice. "The court will deign to hear you out," he said finally.

"Well, it was the first day of our vacation. A half day, really, because I'd had my classes at the college all morning. There's, well, a letdown at the end of the school year, your Honor. You know how it is. I felt the need of a pick-me-up and . . . well, I guess I picked myself up too far."

"You are aware, neighbor, that under the present laws of this state I could revoke your license."

"Yes, but—"

"In addition, I could sentence you to up to sixty days in gaol and a whacking good fine?"

"Please, your Honor, it's our vacation. It won't happen again, I promise."

"However," Sawyer went on, "this court is inclined to be lenient. You seem to have enough troubles of your own without my adding to them unnecessarily." The withering glance he directed at Betty and Vera could have etched glass.

"Therefore, in keeping with the . . . eh . . . changed character of our village during this month, I sentence you to one day of confinement in the stocks."

"I beg your pardon, sir."

"The stocks. You know." Sawyer was suddenly like a child with a new toy. He swiveled about in his chair, extending hands and feet outward rigidly. "We have the stocks out there on the green, but so far nobody's been in them. It would add a great deal to the realism of our annual celebration. Otherwise . . ." Sawyer's bushy eyebrows drooped across his eyes like half-drawn blinds, ". . . the full extent of the law."

"No!" cried Betty. "I forbid it. Sitting out there with your hands and feet clamped in those boards. I'd be embarrassed to—"

"Betty, shut up!" roared Norman. "This way, we'll only be a day behind schedule." He turned back to Sawyer. "Okay, I'll go along with your sentence. Purely in the interest of historical accuracy, of course."

"Not fair." Vera again. "You could have fined him ten dollars or so, and we could have been out of this madhouse by now."

The guard took Norman by the arm and led him toward the door. Behind him, Vera and Betty were both expostulating with Justice Sawyer. As he left, Vera's inevitable rejoinder rang out in the small room: "A pox on you, Sawyer! And on all your brood, too!"

The three boards that made up the stocks were fitted into slotted timbers set deep in the clay soil. As Norman sat down on the hard wooden bench, the guard slid the two top planks upward, leaving a gap of about nine inches. Norman extended his legs and laid his ankles in the two worn semicircles cut into the wood. The guard lowered the center board, pinning the ankles in place.

"Now the wrists, neighbor."

Norman had to stretch forward, like an oarsman at the beginning of his stroke. The top section was lowered, clamping his wrists securely. From his pocket the guard took a pair of padlocks, clicking them into hasps at the top of the stocks.

Finally he stepped back. "There we are, sir. How do you feel?"

"Completely ridiculous," replied Norman. "Absolutely helpless. And slightly uncomfortable."

"The discomfort will get worse, I'm afraid. Still, it's not like it used to be. In the old days the townspeople would sometimes throw offal at a man in the stocks. I don't think any of the present villagers would try that."

"I imagine Justice Sawyer would be delighted if they would," said Norman. "Just to make things completely authentic. Say, how long have I got to stay in this thing?"

"Just until sundown. And I feel you should know, you've made Justice Sawyer very happy. He's always wanted to sentence someone to the stocks. For realism, you know. But none of the local people would agree to it."

"Speaking of realism, those padlocks are modern. In colonial days, wooden pins were used to hold the boards in place."

"Thank you. I'll mention that to Justice Sawyer. He's interested in keeping everything as accurate as possible. Oh, there is one other thing. I hope you won't mind."

From his pocket the guard drew a large sheet of foolscap paper and unfolded it. On it was printed in ornate letters a single word: *DRUNKARD*. The guard set it in place on the far side of the stocks.

"Thumbtacks," chided Norman. "No fair."

"Yes, I'll have to find some other way."

The guard strode off.

Norman sighed and wriggled unseen fingers. He glanced up at the sun and estimated it to be about ten o'clock—and the sun wouldn't set until nearly eight. It was going to be a long day, he decided. He hoped that not too many of the townspeople would laugh at him.

Within the hour there was a decided crick in Norman's back, and the sun was beating down fiercely on his bare head. A single bead of sweat dribbled down to his chin and hung there. At the same time, his nose began to itch.

A second hour passed. Norman made ineffectual passes at his shoulder with his nose, but the itching spot was just out of reach. He'd often spoken about the stocks to his classes, but until now he'd never realized the exquisite torture of actually being confined in them.

About him, the village had stirred to life. A clanging was coming from the blacksmith shop, and a girl passed by with a yoke on her shoulders from which hung two water buckets. Seeing Norman in the stocks, she tittered gleefully and then offered him a drink. At his request, she even scratched his nose. He accepted gratefully, too thirsty to be embarrassed at his helpless condition.

It was shortly after one o'clock, and fiery lances of pain were darting up Norman's back when he heard the voice behind him. "Hurts, doesn't it? Maybe this'll make you feel better."

Then hands started kneading at the aching muscles. Norman wriggled under the pressure of the fingers, moaning his pleasure at the wonderful relief.

The massage stopped, and the man walked around the stocks to face Norman. He was dressed much like the others but wore a belted greatcoat, odd for such a warm day. On the opposite side of the village green, two young men were carrying a huge timber at least ten feet long in the direction of the church.

"I'm Reverend Dabney," said the man. "Thomas Dabney. Hope I made you feel better. That's my job, and there's my factory." He jerked a thumb in the direction of the church.

"Oh, yes. You are truly a lifesaver, Mr. Dabney. When I get out of here, I'm going to buy you the biggest drink—"

"Better not. I understand that's what started this whole thing. Besides, the grog they serve at the inn tastes like dishwater. I can't wait until this month is over and I can mix myself a decent cocktail."

"You mean you can't even—"

Dabney shook his head. "'The colonial ways are our ways,' as Jonathan Sawyer's fond of saying. That's how we live for a month out of each year."

"But isn't it kind of silly to carry it too far?"

"No, I think it's worthwhile to live as our ancestors did and accept their values. And I must say, it ups attendance at church when the law says everybody has to attend."

"But to go to such extremes seems . . ."

"You mean the stocks? It seems to me that Sawyer could have been a lot harsher. Sixty days in jail would about ruin your vacation, wouldn't it? And I daresay when you get out of there you'll think twice about drinking and driving at the same time."

"I only meant that—"

"Look, if a thing like this colonial business is worth doing, it's worth going all the way. The clothing and these stocks are only a small part of it. It's the traditions that count. Living exactly as our forebears did for a full month makes us appreciate the other eleven months even more. But you've got to do it right, everything just as it was. It's a little like climbing a mountain. What challenge would there be to that if the climber knew he had a safety net under him all the time? The experience has got to be totally real to have any meaning."

"I must say, you do try hard. I pointed out a few errors to the guard, and he acted as if I were proclaiming Holy Writ."

"Yes, I heard about that. Justice Sawyer will have them corrected by next year, never fear. Maybe you'd like to come back and visit us then, and see the improvement."

"I don't know if I'll be able to stand up in a year when I get released from this thing."

Dabney chuckled and turned to watch three men pass by. They had crude racks on their backs, piled high with pieces of firewood.

They greeted Dabney cheerfully and paid no attention at all to Norman.

Then, from behind Norman, there came a sound like a stifled scream of pain and outrage. Vainly he turned his head. Finally he caught sight of a figure running toward him, a woman in a bright pink dress of modern styling—Betty.

Yet not the Betty he knew. The figure seemed to be grasping and clawing at something on her head and at the same time emitting strange, muffled groans and cries.

She rounded the stocks and looked grotesquely down at Norman. Her head was encased in a tight cage of rigid flat strips of iron. To the base of these strips was riveted a metal collar, now closed and padlocked securely around her neck, making it impossible to remove the apparatus. From one of the strips that ran down across her lips, a knobby tang of metal extended deep into her mouth, preventing coherent speech. With bloodied hands, Betty Kaner tore in vain at the thing that caged her skull.

"Gunhh . . . Og . . . Hurrr . . . Og . . ."

"That's a brank!" Norman yanked to free his hands but only succeeded in rubbing his wrists raw in the stocks.

Dabney nodded. "Gossip's bridle, they called it in the colonies. I understand Justice Sawyer warned her several times about shouting out in his courtroom before having it put on her."

"But it—it's inhuman."

"Fiddlesticks. If she'd just calm down, she'd be fine. She can breathe well enough. It's just talking that's impossible. And she has the run of the town. It's not as if she'd been shut up somewhere."

"But that—that thing on her head!"

"Og hurrr! Og hurrr!"

"Of course it hurts," said Dabney. "Stop pulling at it, and you'll be fine."

"Dabney, can't you see she's almost out of her mind with fright and shock?"

"All the better for you, old man. I guarantee when that comes off, she won't be nearly the shrew she was when it was put on."

With a moan of pure misery, Betty sank onto the dusty earth, wrapping her arms tightly about Norman's extended leg in pleading.

"Dabney, I've had enough of this. To blazes with our vacation. I intend to see the authorities about these . . . these outrages."

"Nonsense. Look at it this way. Think of the added value to your history classes. Now you can speak to them from firsthand experience about colonial punishments." Dabney rubbed his chin thoughtfully. "You know, that brank's been in our museum for about two hundred years. I didn't think we'd ever actually get to use it."

"It's monstrous!"

"No, Mr. Kaner, it's not. It's simply the way we were, more than two hundred years ago. Oh, we're not perfect in our re-creation of the past. But we're getting there."

Dabney turned to look across the village green, where a group of villagers were heading for the church, uttering loud shouts.

"I must go," he said. "I have other business."

"How can you see two fellow humans being tortured and then tell me you have other business? Don't you find that odd for a man in your line of work?"

"Not torture, Mr. Kaner. Punishment. Punishment for acts against the general welfare of the commonwealth. Punishment that is just. The punishment of our forefathers."

Something nakedly evil gleamed behind Dabney's eyes, like a snake lying in wait.

"It may interest you to know," he said, "that just before noon our local physician visited the Sawyer household. The justice had begun feeling poorly, as did his wife and both sons."

"So?"

"Measles. The doctor said he'd never before seen the disease take a whole family so suddenly."

"What's that got to do with my wife and me?"

"Not you, Mr. Kaner. And not your wife."

"Then who . . ."

"Think on it, Mr. Kaner. Think on it."

Dabney shouted at the crowd of villagers and then trotted off to join them.

Madness; the whole village was mad with their lust for historic accuracy. Betty looked up at him, her eyes pleading behind the iron cage. A slight moan came from her throat.

Moments later, from the churchyard behind the maple trees, a faint cheering came to their ears. A pall of black, greasy smoke streaked the blue sky, and then, hanging in the air like a palpable thing, was heard a single shrill scream, torn from the throat of someone tortured beyond endurance.

Norman knew then who had screamed, and in his mind the same voice came to him, snapping harshly at a little fat man in a black robe and an oversized wig: "A pox on you, Sawyer! And on all your brood, too!"

Measles!

Even as his stomach heaved at the thought of what was happening up there on the hill, a single irrelevant thought came to Norman's mind—another historical error.

In the colonies, hanging or pressing to death with great rocks were the punishments.

In the entire history of New England, there was not a single recorded case of a witch being executed by burning.

LAWRENCE BLOCK

A CANDLE FOR THE BAG LADY

November 1977

LAWRENCE BLOCK is one of the most honored writers in mystery, and with good reason. A winner of multiple Edgar awards, he has been named a Grand Master by the Mystery Writers of America. Block writes in a wide variety of styles, from espionage thrillers to hard-boileds to humorous caper stories, but among his most popular creations is the alcoholic ex-cop turned unofficial private eye Matthew Scudder. Here is a tale from the early days of Scudder's career.

■

He was a thin young man in a blue pinstripe suit. His shirt was white with a button-down collar. His glasses had oval lenses in a brown tortoiseshell frame. His hair was a dark brown, short but not severely so, neatly combed, parted on the right. I saw him come in and watched him ask a question at the bar. Billie was working afternoons that week. I watched as he nodded at the young man, then swung his sleepy eyes over in my direction. I lowered my own eyes and looked at a cup of coffee laced with bourbon while the fellow walked over to my table.

"Matthew Scudder?" I looked up at him, nodded. "I'm Aaron Creighton. I looked for you at your hotel. The fellow on the desk told me I might find you here."

Here was Armstrong's, a Ninth Avenue saloon around the corner from my Fifty-seventh Street hotel. The lunch crowd was gone except for a couple of stragglers in front whose voices were starting to thicken with alcohol. The streets outside were full of

May sunshine. The winter had been cold and deep and long. I couldn't recall a more welcome spring.

"I called you a couple of times last week, Mr. Scudder. I guess you didn't get my messages."

I'd gotten two of them and ignored them, not knowing who he was or what he wanted and unwilling to spend a dime for the answer. But I went along with the fiction. "It's a cheap hotel," I said, "They're not always too good about messages."

"I can imagine. Uh—is there someplace we can talk?"

"How about right here?"

He looked around. I don't suppose he was used to conducting his business in bars, but he evidently decided it would be all right to make an exception. He set his briefcase on the floor and seated himself across the table from me. Angela, the new day-shift waitress, hurried over to get his order. He glanced at my cup and said he'd have coffee, too.

"I'm an attorney," he said. My first thought was that he didn't look like a lawyer, but then I realized he probably dealt with civil cases. My experience as a cop had given me a lot of experience with criminal lawyers. The breed runs to several types, none of them his.

I waited for him to tell me why he wanted to hire me. But he crossed me up.

"I'm handling an estate," he said, and paused, and gave what seemed a calculated if well-intentioned smile. "It's my pleasant duty to tell you you've come into a small legacy, Mr. Scudder."

"Someone's left me money?"

"Twelve hundred dollars."

Who could have died? I'd lost touch long since with any of my relatives. My parents went years ago, and we'd never been close with the rest of the family.

I said, "Who—?"

"Mary Alice Redfield."

I repeated the name aloud. It was not entirely unfamiliar, but I had no idea who Mary Alice Redfield might be. I looked at Aaron Creighton. I couldn't make out his eyes behind the glasses but there was a smile's ghost on his thin lips, as if my reaction was not unexpected.

"She's dead?"

"Almost three months ago."

"I didn't know her."

"She knew you. You probably did know her, Mr. Scudder. Perhaps you didn't know her by name." His smile deepened. Angela had brought his coffee. He stirred milk and sugar into it, took a careful sip, nodded his approval. "Miss Redfield was murdered." He said this as if he'd had practice uttering a phrase that did not come naturally to him. "She was killed quite brutally in late February for no apparent reason, another innocent victim of street crime."

"She lived in New York?"

"Oh, yes. In this neighborhood."

"And she was killed around here?"

"On West Fifty-fifth Street between Ninth and Tenth Avenues. Her body was found in an alleyway. She'd been stabbed repeatedly and strangled with the scarf she had been wearing."

Late February. Mary Alice Redfield. West Fifty-fifth between Ninth and Tenth. Murder most foul. Stabbed and strangled, a dead woman in an alleyway. I usually kept track of murders, perhaps out of a vestige of professionalism, perhaps because I couldn't cease to be fascinated by man's inhumanity to man. Mary Alice Redfield had willed me twelve hundred dollars. And someone had knifed and strangled her, and—

"Oh, Jesus," I said. "The shopping bag lady."

Aaron Creighton nodded.

NEW YORK IS full of them. East Side, West Side, each neighborhood has its own supply of bag women. Some of them are alcoholic, but most of them have gone mad without any help from drink. They walk the streets, huddle on stoops or in doorways. They find sermons in stones and treasures in trash cans. They talk to themselves, to passers-by, to God. Sometimes they mumble. Now and then they shriek.

They carry things around with them. The shopping bags supply their generic name and their chief common denominator. Most of them seem to be paranoid, and their madness convinces them that their possessions are very valuable, that their enemies covet them. So their shopping bags are never out of their sight.

There used to be a colony of these ladies who lived in Grand Central Station. They would sit up all night in the waiting room, taking turns waddling off to the lavatory from time to time. They rarely talked to each other, but some herd instinct made them comfortable with one another. But they were not comfortable enough to trust their precious bags to one another's safekeeping, and each sad crazy lady always toted her shopping bags to and from the ladies' room.

Mary Alice Redfield had been a shopping bag lady. I don't know when she set up shop in the neighborhood. I'd been living in the same hotel ever since I resigned from the NYPD and separated from my wife and sons, and that was getting to be quite a few years now. Had Miss Redfield been on the scene that long ago? I couldn't remember her first appearance. Like so many of the neighborhood fixtures, she had been part of the scenery. Had her death not been violent and abrupt, I might never have noticed she was gone.

I'd never known her name. But she had evidently known mine, and had felt something for me that prompted her to leave money to me. How had she come to have money to leave?

She'd had a business of sorts. She would sit on a wooden soft-drink case, surrounded by three or four shopping bags, and she would sell newspapers. There's an all-night newsstand at the corner of Fifty-seventh and Eighth, and she would buy a few dozen papers there, carry them a block west to the corner of Ninth, and set up shop in a doorway. She sold the papers at retail, though I suppose some people tipped her a few cents. I could remember a few occasions when I'd bought a paper and waved away change from a dollar bill. Bread upon the waters, perhaps, if that was what had moved her to leave me the money.

I closed my eyes, brought her image into focus. A thick-set woman, stocky rather than fat. Five-three or four. Dressed usually in shapeless clothing, colorless gray and black garments, layers of clothing that varied with the season. I remembered that she sometimes wore a hat, an old straw affair with paper and plastic flowers poked into it. And I remembered her eyes—large, guileless blue eyes that were many years younger than the rest of her.

Mary Alice Redfield.

"FAMILY MONEY," Aaron Creighton was saying. "She wasn't wealthy but she had come from a family that was comfortably fixed. A bank in Baltimore handled her funds. That's where she was from originally, Baltimore, though she'd lived in New York for as long as anyone can remember. The bank sent her a check every month. Not very much, a couple of hundred dollars, but she hardly spent anything. She paid her rent—"

"I thought she lived on the street."

"No, she had a furnished room a few doors down the street from where she was killed. She lived in another rooming house on Tenth Avenue before that but moved when the building was sold. That was six or seven years ago and she lived on Fifty-fifth Street from then until her death. Her room cost her eighty dollars a month. She spent a few dollars on food. I don't know what she did with the rest. The only money in her room was a coffee can full of pennies. I've been checking the banks, and there's no record of a savings account. I suppose she may have spent it or lost it or given it away. She wasn't very firmly grounded in reality."

He sipped at his coffee. "She probably belonged in an institution," he said. "But she got along in the outside world, she functioned well enough. I don't know if she kept herself clean, and I don't know anything about how her mind worked, but I think she must have been happier than she would have been in an institution. Don't you think?"

"Probably."

"Of course she wasn't safe, not as it turned out, but anybody can get killed on the streets of New York." He frowned briefly, caught up in a private thought. Then he said, "She came to our office ten years ago. That was before my time." He told me the name of his firm, a string of Anglo-Saxon surnames. "She wanted to draw a will. The original will was a very simple document leaving everything to her sister. Then over the years she would come in from time to time to add codicils leaving specific sums to various persons. She had made a total of thirty-two bequests by the time she died. One was for twenty dollars—that was to a man named John Johnson, whom we haven't been able to locate. The remainder all ranged from five hundred to two thousand dollars." He smiled. "I've been given the task of running down the heirs."

"When did she put me into her will?"

"Two years ago in April."

I tried to think what I might have done for her then, how I might have brushed her life with mine. Nothing.

"Of course the will could be contested, Mr. Scudder. It would be easy to challenge Miss Redfield's competence, and any relative could almost certainly get it set aside. But no one wishes to challenge it. The total amount involved is slightly in excess of a quarter of a million dollars—"

"That much."

"Yes. Miss Redfield received substantially less than the income that her holdings drew over the years, so the principal kept growing during her lifetime. Now the specific bequests she made total thirty-eight thousand dollars, give or take a few hundred, and the residue goes to Miss Redfield's sister. The sister, her name is Mrs. Palmer, is a widow with grown children. She's hospitalized with cancer and heart trouble and I believe diabetic complications, and she hasn't long to live. Her children would like to see the estate settled before their mother dies, and they have enough local prominence to hurry the will through probate. So I'm authorized to tender checks for the full amount of the specific bequests on the condition that the legatees sign quitclaims acknowledging that this payment discharges in full the estate's indebtedness to them."

There was more legalese of less importance. Then he gave me papers to sign, and the whole procedure ended with a check on the table. It was payable to me and in the amount of twelve hundred dollars and no cents.

I told Creighton I'd pay for his coffee.

I HAD TIME to buy myself another drink and still get to my bank before the windows closed. I put a little of Mary Alice Redfield's legacy in my savings account, took some in cash, and sent a money order to Anita and the boys. I stopped at my hotel to check for messages. There weren't any. I had a drink at McGovern's and crossed the street to have another at Polly's Cage. It wasn't five o'clock yet, but the bar was doing good business already.

It turned into a funny night. I had dinner at the Greek place and read the *Post*, spent a little time at Joey Farrell's on Fifty-eighth

Street, then wound up getting to Armstrong's around ten thirty or thereabouts. I spent part of the evening alone at my usual table and part of it in conversation at the bar. I made a point of stretching my drinks, mixing my bourbon with coffee, making a cup last awhile, taking a glass of plain water from time to time.

But that never really works. If you're going to get drunk, you'll manage it somehow. The obstacles I placed in my path just kept me up later. By two thirty I'd done what I had set out to do. I'd made my load, and I could go home and sleep it off.

I woke around ten with less of a hangover than I'd earned and no memory of anything after I'd left Armstrong's. I was in my own bed in my own hotel room. And my clothes were hung neatly in the closet, always a good sign on a morning after. So I must have been in fairly good shape. But a certain amount of time was lost to memory, blacked out, gone.

When that first started happening I tended to worry about it. But it's the sort of thing you can get used to.

IT WAS THE money, the twelve hundred bucks. I couldn't understand the money. I had done nothing to deserve it. It had been left to me by a poor little rich woman whose name I'd not even known.

It had never occurred to me to refuse the dough. Very early in my career as a cop I'd learned an important precept. When someone put money in your hand, you closed your fingers around it and put it in your pocket. I learned that lesson well and never had cause to regret its application. I didn't walk around with my hand out, and I never took drug or homicide money, but I grabbed all the clean graft that came my way and a certain amount that wouldn't have stood a white-glove inspection. If Mary Alice thought I merited twelve hundred dollars, who was I to argue?

Ah, but it didn't quite work that way. Because somehow the money gnawed at me.

After breakfast I went to St. Paul's, but there was a service going on, a priest saying Mass, so I didn't stay. I walked down to St. Benedict the Moor's on Fifty-third Street and sat for a few minutes in a pew at the rear. I go to churches to try to think, and I gave it a shot, but my mind didn't know where to go.

I slipped six twenties into the poor box. I tithe. It's a habit I got into after I left the department, and I still don't know why I do it. God knows. Or maybe He's as mystified as I am. This time, though, there was a certain balance in the act. Mary Alice Redfield had given me twelve hundred dollars for no reason I could comprehend. I was passing on a ten percent commission to the church for no better reason.

I stopped on the way out and lit a couple of candles for various people who weren't alive anymore. One of them was for the bag lady. I didn't see how it could do her any good, but I couldn't imagine how it could harm her either.

I HAD READ some press coverage of the killing when it happened. I generally keep up with crime stories. Part of me evidently never stopped being a policeman. Now I went down to the Forty-second Street library to refresh my memory.

The *Times* had run a pair of brief back-page items, the first a report of the killing of an unidentified female derelict, the second a follow-up giving her name and age. She'd been forty-seven, I learned. This surprised me, and then I realized that any specific number would have come as a surprise. Bums and bag ladies are ageless. Mary Alice Redfield could have been thirty or sixty or anywhere in between.

The *News* had run a more extended article than the *Times,* enumerating the stab wounds—twenty-six of them—and describing the scarf wound about her throat—blue and white, a designer print, but tattered at its edges and evidently somebody's castoff. It was this article that I remembered having read.

But the *Post* had really played the story. It had appeared shortly after the new Australian owner took over the paper, and the editors were going all-out for human interest, which always translates out as sex and violence. The brutal killing of a woman touches both of those bases, and this had the added kick that she was a character. If they'd ever learned she was an heiress, it would have been page three material, but even without that knowledge they did all right by her.

The first story they ran was straight news reporting, albeit embellished with reports on the blood, the clothes she was wearing, the litter in the alley where she was found, and all that sort of thing. The next day a reporter pushed the pathos button and tapped out a story featuring capsule interviews with people in the neighborhood. Only a few of them were identified by name, and I came away with the feeling that he'd made up some peachy quotes and attributed them to unnamed nonexistent hangers-on. As a sidebar to that story, another reporter speculated on the possibility of a whole string of bag lady murders, a speculation that happily had turned out to be off the mark. The clown had presumably gone around the West Side asking shopping bag ladies if they were afraid of being the killer's next victim. I hope he faked the piece and let the ladies alone.

And that was about it. When the killer failed to strike again, the newspapers hung up on the story. Good news is no news.

I WALKED BACK from the library. It was fine weather. The winds had blown all the crap out of the sky, and there was nothing but blue overhead. The air actually had some air in it for a change. I walked west on Forty-second Street and north on Broadway, and I started noticing the number of street people, the drunks and the crazies and the unclassifiable derelicts. By the time I got within a few blocks of Fifty-seventh Street I was recognizing a large percentage of them. Each mini-neighborhood has its own human flotsam and jetsam, and they're a lot more noticeable come springtime. Winter sends some of them south and others to shelter, and there's a certain percentage who die of exposure, but when the sun warms the pavement, it brings most of them out again.

When I stopped for a paper at the corner of Eighth Avenue, I got the bag lady into the conversation. The newsie clucked his tongue and shook his head. "The damnedest thing. Just the damnedest thing."

"Murder never makes much sense."

"The hell with murder. You know what she did? You know Eddie, works for me midnight to eight? Guy with the one droopy eyelid? Now he wasn't the guy used to sell her the stack of papers. Matter of fact that was usually me. She'd come by during the late morning or early afternoon, and she'd take fifteen or twenty papers and pay me for 'em, then she'd sit on her crate down the next corner and she'd sell as many as she could, and then she'd bring 'em back, and I'd give her a refund on what she didn't sell."

"What did she pay for them?"

"Full price. And that's what she sold 'em for. The hell, I can't discount on papers. You know the margin we get. I'm not even supposed to take 'em back, but what difference does it make? It gave the poor woman something to do is my theory. She was important, she was a businesswoman. Sits there charging a quarter for something she just paid a quarter for, it's no way to get rich, but you know something? She had money. She lived like a pig, but she had money."

"So I understand."

"She left Eddie seven-twenty. You believe that? Seven hundred and twenty dollars; she willed it to him, there was this lawyer come around three weeks ago with a check. Eddie Halloran. Pay to the order of. You believe that? She never had dealings with him. I sold her the papers, I bought 'em back from her. Not that I'm complaining, not that I want the woman's money, but why Eddie? He don't know her. He can't believe she knows his name. He tells this lawyer, he says maybe she's got some other Eddie Halloran in mind. It's a common Irish name and the neighborhood's full of the Irish. I'm thinking to myself, Eddie, schmuck, take the money and shut up, but it's him all right, because in the will it says Eddie Halloran the Newsdealer. That's him, right? But why Eddie?"

Why me? "Maybe she liked the way he smiled."

"Yeah, maybe. Or the way he combed his hair. Listen, it's money in his pocket. I worried he'd go on a toot, drink it up, but he says money's no temptation. He says he's always got the price of a drink in his jeans, and there's a bar on every block but he can walk right past 'em, so why worry about a few hundred dollars? You know something? That crazy woman, I'll tell you something, I miss her. She'd come, crazy hat on her head, spacy look in her eyes, she'd buy her stack of papers and waddle off all businesslike, then she'd bring the leftovers and cash 'em in, and I'd make a joke about her when she was out of earshot, but I miss her."

"I know what you mean."

"She never hurt nobody," he said. "She never hurt a soul."

"MARY ALICE REDFIELD. Yeah, the multiple stabbing and stran-gulation." He shifted a cud-sized wad of gum from one side of his mouth to the other, pushed a lock of hair off his forehead, and yawned. "What have you got, some new information?"

"Nothing. I wanted to find out what you had."

"Yeah, right."

He worked on the chewing gum. He was a patrolman named Andersen who worked out of the Eighteenth. Another cop, a detective named Guzik, had learned that Andersen had caught the Redfield case and had taken the trouble to intro-duce the two of us. I hadn't known Andersen when I was on the force. He was younger than me, but then most people are nowadays.

He said, "Thing is, Scudder, we more or less put that one out of the way. It's in an open file. You know how it works. If we get new information, fine, but in the meantime I don't sit up nights thinking about it."

"I just wanted to see what you had."

"Well, I'm kind of tight for time, if you know what I mean. My own personal time, I set a certain store by my own time."

"I can understand that."

"You probably got some relative of the deceased for a client, wants to find out who'd do such a terrible thing to poor old Cousin Mary. Naturally you're interested because it's a chance to make a buck and a man's gotta make a living. Whether a man's a cop or a civilian, he's gotta make a buck, right?"

Uh-huh. I seem to remember that we were subtler in my day, but perhaps that's just age talking. I thought of telling him that I didn't have a client, but why should he believe me? He didn't know me. If there was nothing in it for him, why should he bother?

So I said, "You know, we're just a couple of weeks away from Memorial Day."

"Yeah, I'll buy a poppy from a Legionnaire. So what else is new?"

"Memorial Day's when women start wearing white shoes and men put straw hats on their heads. You got a new hat for the summer season, Andersen? You could use one."

"A man can always use a new hat," he said.

A *hat* is cop talk for twenty-five dollars. By the time I left the precinct house, Andersen had two tens and a five of Mary Alice Redfield's bequest to me, and I had all the data that had turned up to date.

I think Andersen won that one. I now knew that the murder weapon had been a kitchen knife with a blade approximately seven and a half inches long. That one of the stab wounds had found the heart and had probably caused death instantaneously. That it was impossible to determine whether strangulation had taken place before or after death. That *should* have been possible to determine—maybe the medical examiner hadn't wasted too much time checking her out, or maybe he'd been reluctant to commit himself. She'd been dead a few hours when they found her—the estimate was that she'd died around midnight and the body wasn't reported until half-past five. That wouldn't have ripened her all that much, not in winter weather, but most likely her personal hygiene was nothing to boast about, and she was just a shopping bag lady and you couldn't bring her back to life, so why knock yourself out running tests on her malodorous corpse?

I learned a few other things. The landlady's name. The name of the off-duty bartender heading home after a nightcap at the neighborhood after-hours joint who'd happened on the body and had been drunk enough or sober enough to take the trouble to report it. And I learned the sort of negative facts that turn up in a police report when the case is headed for an open file—the handful of non-leads that led nowhere, the witnesses who had nothing to contribute, the routine matters routinely handled. They hadn't knocked themselves out, Andersen and his partner, but would I have handled it any differently? Why knock yourself out chasing a murderer you didn't stand much chance of catching?

IN THE THEATER, SRO is good news. It means a sellout performance, Standing Room Only. But once you get out of the theater district it means Single Room Occupancy, and the designation is invariably applied to a hotel or apartment house that has seen better days.

Mary Alice Redfield's home for the last six or seven years of her life had started out as an old Rent Law tenement, built around the turn of the century, six stories tall, faced in red-brown brick, with four apartments to the floor. Now all of those little apartments had been carved into single rooms as if they were election districts gerrymandered by a maniac. There was a communal bathroom on each floor, and you didn't need a map to find it.

The manager was a Mrs. Larkin. Her blue eyes had lost most of their color, and half her hair had gone from black to gray, but she was still pert. If she's reincarnated as a bird, she'll be a house wren.

She said, "Oh, poor Mary. We're none of us safe, are we, with the streets full of monsters? I was born in this neighborhood and I'll die in it, but please, God, that'll be of natural causes. Poor Mary. There's some said she should have been locked up, but Jesus, she got along. She lived her life. And she had her check coming in every month and paid her rent on time. She had her own money, you know. She wasn't living off the public like some I could name but won't."

"I know."

"Do you want to see her room? I rented it twice since then. The first one was a young man and he didn't stay. He looked all right, but when he left I was just as glad. He said he was a sailor off a ship, and when he left he said he'd got on with another ship and was on his way to Hong Kong or some such place, but I've had no end of sailors and he didn't walk like a sailor, so I don't know what he was after doing. Then I could have rented it twelve times but didn't, because I won't rent to colored or Spanish. I've nothing against them, but I won't have them in the house. The owner says to me, 'Mrs. Larkin,' he says, 'my instructions are to rent to anybody regardless of race or creed or color, but if you was to use your own judgment, I wouldn't have to know about it.' In other words, he don't want them either, but he's after covering himself."

"I suppose he has to."

"Oh, with all the laws, but I've had no trouble." She laid a forefinger alongside her nose. It's a gesture you don't see too much these days. "Then I rented poor Mary's room two weeks ago to a very nice woman, a widow. She likes her beer, she does, but why shouldn't she have it? I keep my eye on her and she's making no trouble, and if she wants an old jar now and then, whose business is it but her own?" She fixed her blue-gray eyes on me. "You like your drink," she said.

"Is it on my breath?"

"No, but I can see it in your face. Larkin liked his drink, and there's some say it killed him, but he liked it and a man has a right to live what life he wants. And he was never a hard man when he drank, never cursed or fought or beat a woman as some I could name but won't. Mrs. Shepard's out now. That's the one took poor Mary's room, and I'll show it to you if you want."

So I saw the room. It was kept neat.

"She keeps it tidier than poor Mary," Mrs. Larkin said. "Mary wasn't dirty, you understand, but she had all her belongings—her shopping bags and other things that she kept in her room. She made a mare's nest of the place, and all the years she lived here it wasn't tidy. I would keep her bed made, but she didn't want me touching her things, and so I left the rest cluttered. She paid her rent on time and made no trouble otherwise. She had money, you know."

"Yes, I know."

"She left some to a woman on the fourth floor. A much younger woman, she'd only moved here three months before Mary was killed. If she exchanged a word with Mary I couldn't swear to it, but Mary left her almost a thousand dollars. Now Mrs. Klein across the hall lived here since before Mary ever moved in, and the two old things always had a good word for each other—all Mrs. Klein has is the welfare, and she could have made good use of a couple of dollars, but Mary left her money to Miss Strom instead." She raised her eyebrows to show her bewilderment. "Now Mrs. Klein said nothing, and I don't even know if she's had the thought that Mary might have mentioned her in her will, but Miss Strom said she didn't know what to make of it. She just couldn't understand it at all, and what I told her was you can't figure out a woman like poor Mary, who never had both her feet on the pavement. Troubled as she was, daft as she was, who's to say what she might have had on her mind?"

"Could I see Miss Strom?"

"That would be for her to say, but she's not home from work yet. She works part-time in the afternoons. She's a close one, not that she hasn't the right to be, and she's never said what it is that she does. But she's a decent sort. This is a decent house."

"I'm sure it is."

"It's single rooms and they don't cost much, so you know you're not at the Ritz Hotel, but there's decent people here and I keep it as clean as a person can. When there's not but one toilet on the floor it's a struggle. But it's decent."

"Yes."

"Poor Mary. Why'd anyone kill her? Was it sex, do you know? Not that you could imagine anyone wanting her, the old thing, but try to figure out a madman and you'll go mad your own self. Was she molested?"

"No."

"Just killed, then. Oh, God save us all. I gave her a home for almost seven years. Which it was no more than my job to do, not making it out to be charity on my part. But I had her here all that time, and of course I never knew her, you couldn't get to know a poor old soul like that, but I got used to her. Do you know what I mean?"

"I think so."

"I got used to having her about. I might say hello and good morning and not get a look in reply, but even on those days she was someone familiar, and she's gone now and we're all of us older, aren't we?"

"We are."

"The poor old thing. How could anyone do it, will you tell me that? How could anyone murder her?"

I don't think she expected an answer. It's just as well. I didn't have one.

AFTER DINNER I returned for a few minutes of conversation with Genevieve Strom. She had no idea why Miss Redfield had left her the money. She'd received $880, and she was glad to get it because she could use it, but the whole thing puzzled her. "I hardly knew her," she said more than once. "I keep thinking I ought to do something special with the money, but what?"

I made the bars that night, but drinking didn't have the urgency it had possessed the night before. I was able to keep it in proportion and to know that I'd wake up the next morning with my memory intact. In the course of things, I dropped over to the newsstand a little past midnight and talked with Eddie Halloran. He was looking good and I said as much. I remembered him when he'd gone to work for Sid three years ago. He'd been drawn then, and shaky, and his eyes always moved off to the side of whatever he was looking at. Now there was confidence in his stance and he looked years younger, though it hadn't all come back to him and maybe some of it was lost forever. I guess the booze had him pretty good before he got it kicked once and for all.

We talked about the bag lady. He said, "Know what I think it is? Somebody's sweeping the streets."

"I don't follow you."

"A clean-up campaign. A few years back, Matt, there was this gang of kids found a new way to amuse theirselves. Pick up a can of gasoline, find some bum down on the Bowery, pour the gas on him, and throw a lit match at him. You remember?"

"Yeah, I remember."

"Those kids thought they were patriots. They thought they deserved a medal. They were cleaning up the neighborhood, getting drunken bums off the streets. You know, Matt, people don't like to look at a derelict. That building up the block, the Towers? There's this grating there where the heating system's vented. You remember how the guys would sleep there in the winter. It was warm, it was comfortable, it was free, and two or three guys would be there every night catching some z's and getting warm. Remember?"

"Uh-huh. Then they fenced it."

"Right. Because the tenants complained. It didn't hurt them any, it was just the local bums sleeping it off, but the tenants pay a lot of rent and they don't like to look at bums on their way in or out of their building. The bums were outside and not bothering anybody, but it was the sight of them, you know, so the owners went to the expense of putting up cyclone fencing around where they used to sleep. It looks ugly as hell, and all it does is keep the bums out, but that's all it's supposed to do."

"That's human beings for you."

He nodded, then turned aside to sell somebody a *Daily News* and a *Racing Form*. Then he said, "I don't know what it is exactly. I was a bum, Matt. I got pretty far down. You probably don't know how far. I got as far as the Bowery. I panhandled and slept in my clothes on a bench or in a doorway. You look at men like that and you think they're just waiting to die, and they are, but some of them come back. And you can't tell for sure who's gonna come back and who's not. Somebody coulda poured gas on me, set me on fire. Sweet Jesus."

"The shopping bag lady—"

"You'll look at a bum and you'll say to yourself, Maybe I could get like that and I don't wanta think about it. Or you'll look at somebody like the shopping bag lady and say, I could go nutsy like her, so get her out of my sight. And you get people who think like Nazis—you know, take all the cripples and the lunatics and the retarded kids and give 'em an injection and Goodbye, Charlie."

"You think that's what happened to her?"

"What else?"

"But whoever did it stopped at one, Eddie."

He frowned. "Don't make sense," he said. "Unless he did the one job and the next day he got run down by a Ninth Avenue bus, and it couldn't happen to a nicer guy. Or he got scared. All that blood and it was more than he figured on. Or he left town. Could be anything like that."

"Could be."

"There's no other reason, is there? She musta been killed because she was a bag lady, right?"

"I don't know."

"Well, Jesus Christ, Matt. What other reason would anybody have for killing her?"

THE LAW FIRM where Aaron Creighton worked had offices on the seventh floor of the Flatiron Building. In addition to the four partners, eleven other lawyers had their names painted on the frosted glass door. Aaron Creighton's came second from the bottom. Well, he was young.

He was surprised to see me, and when I told him what I wanted, he said it was irregular.

"It's a matter of public record, isn't it?"

"Well, yes," he said. "That means you can find the information. It doesn't mean we're obliged to furnish it to you."

For an instant I thought I was back at the Eighteenth Precinct and a cop was trying to hustle me for the price of a new hat.

But Creighton's reservations were ethical. I wanted a list of Mary Alice Redfield's beneficiaries, including the amounts they'd received and the dates they'd been added to her will. He wasn't sure where his duty lay.

"I'd like to be helpful," he said. "Perhaps you could tell me just what your interest is."

"I'm not sure."

"I beg your pardon?"

"I don't know why I'm playing with this one. I used to be a cop, Mr. Creighton. Now I'm a sort of unofficial detective. I don't carry a license, but I do things for people and I wind up making enough that way to keep a roof overhead."

His eyes were wary. I guess he was trying to guess how I intended to earn myself a fee out of this.

"I got twelve hundred dollars out of the blue. It was left to me by a woman I didn't really know and who didn't really know me. I can't seem to slough off the feeling that I got the money for a reason. That I've been paid in advance."

"Paid for what?"

"To try and find out who killed her."

"Oh," he said. *"Oh."*

"I don't want to get the heirs together to challenge the will, if that was what was bothering you. And I can't quite make myself suspect that one of her beneficiaries killed her for the money she was leaving him. For one thing, she doesn't seem to have told people they were named in her will. She never said anything to me or to the two people I've spoken with thus far. For another, it wasn't the sort of murder that gets committed for gain. It was deliberately brutal."

"Then why do you want to know who the other beneficiaries are?"

"I don't know. Part of it's cop training. When you've got any specific leads, any hard facts, you run them down before you cast a wider net. That's only part of it. I suppose I want to get more of a sense of the woman. That's probably all I can realistically hope to get, anyway. I don't stand much chance of tracking her killer."

"The police don't seem to have gotten very far."

I nodded. "I don't think they tried too hard. And I don't think they knew she had an estate. I talked to one of the cops on the case, and if he had known that, he'd have mentioned it to me. There was nothing in her file. My guess is that they waited for her killer to run a string of murders so they'd have something more concrete to work with. It's the kind of senseless crime that usually gets repeated." I closed my eyes for a moment, reaching for an errant thought. "But he didn't repeat," I said. "So they put it on a back burner, and then they took it off the stove altogether."

"I don't know much about police work. I'm involved largely with estates and trusts." He tried a smile. "Most of my clients die of natural causes. Murder's an exception."

"It generally is. I'll probably never find him. I certainly don't expect to find him. Hell, it was all those months ago. He could have been a sailor off a ship, got tanked up and went nuts and he's in Macao or Port-au-Prince by now. No witnesses and no clues and no suspects and the trail's three months cold by now, and it's a fair bet the killer doesn't remember what he did. So many murders take place in blackout."

"Blackout?" He frowned. "You don't mean in the dark?"

"Alcoholic blackout. The prisons are full of men who got drunk and shot their wives or their best friends. Now they're serving twenty-to-life for something they don't recollect at all."

The idea unsettled him, and he looked especially young now. "That's terrifying," he said.

"Yes."

"I originally gave some thought to criminal law. My uncle Jack talked me out of it. He said you either starve or you spend your time helping professional criminals beat the system. He said that was the only way you made good money out of a criminal practice, and what you wound up doing was unpleasant and basically immoral. Of course, there are a couple of superstar criminal lawyers, the hotshots everybody knows, but the other ninety-nine percent fit what Uncle Jack said."

"I would think so, yes."

"I guess I made the right decision." He took his glasses off, inspected them, decided they were clean, put them back on again. "Sometimes I'm not so sure," he said. "Sometimes I wonder. I'll get that list for you. I should probably check with someone to make sure it's all right, but I'm not going to bother. You know lawyers. If you ask them whether it's all right to do something, they'll automatically say no. Because inaction is always safer than action, and they can't get in trouble for giving you bad advice if they tell you to sit on your hands and do nothing. I'm going overboard. Most of the time I like what I do and I'm proud of my profession. This'll take me a few minutes. Do you want some coffee in the meantime?"

I let him have his girl bring me a cup, black, no sugar. By the time I was done with the coffee, he had the list ready.

"If there's anything else I can do—"

I told him I'd let him know. He walked out to the elevator with me, waited for the cage to come wheezing up, and shook my hand. I watched him turn and head back to his office, and I had the feeling he'd have preferred to come along with me. In a day or so he'd change his mind, but right now he didn't seem too crazy about his job.

THE NEXT WEEK I worked my way through the list Aaron Creighton had given me, knowing what I was doing was essentially purposeless but compulsive about doing it all the same.

There were thirty-two names on the list. I checked off my own and Eddie Halloran and Genevieve Strom. I put additional check marks next to six people who lived outside of New York. Then I had a go at the remaining twenty-three names. Creighton had done most of the spadework for me, finding addresses to match most of the names. He'd included the date each of the thirty-two codicils had been drawn, and that enabled me to attack the list in reverse chronological order, starting with those persons who'd been made beneficiaries most recently. If this was a method, there was madness to it; it was based on the notion that a person added recently to the will would be more likely to commit homicide for gain, and I'd already decided this wasn't that kind of a killing to begin with.

Well, it gave me something to do. And it led to some interesting conversations. If the people Mary Alice Redfield had chosen to remember ran to any type, my mind wasn't subtle enough to discern it. They ranged in age, in ethnic background, in gender and sexual orientation, in economic status. Most of them were as mystified as Eddie and Genevieve and me about the bag lady's

largesse, but once in a while I'd encounter someone who attributed it to some act of kindness he'd performed, and there was
a young man named Jerry Forgash who was in no doubt whatever. He was some form of Jesus freak, and he'd given poor
Mary a couple of tracts and a Get Smart—Get Saved button,
presumably a twin to the one he wore on the breast pocket of
his chambray shirt. I suppose she put his gifts in one of her
shopping bags.

"I told her Jesus loved her," he said, "and I suppose it won her
soul for Christ. So of course she was grateful. Cast your bread
upon the waters, Brother Matthew. You know there was a disciple
of Christ named Matthew."

"I know."

He told me Jesus loved me and that I should get smart and get
saved. I managed not to get a button, but I had to take a couple
of tracts from him. I didn't have a shopping bag, so I stuck them
in my pocket.

I didn't run the whole list. People were hard to find and I wasn't
in any big rush to find them. It wasn't that kind of a case. It wasn't
a case at all, really, merely an obsession, and there was surely no
need to race the clock. Or the calendar. If anything, I was probably reluctant to finish up the names on the list. Once I ran out
of them, I'd have to find some other way to approach the woman's
murder, and I was damned if I knew where to start.

In the meantime, an odd thing happened. The word got
around that I was investigating the murder, and the whole neighborhood became very much aware of Mary Alice Redfield.
People began to seek me out. Ostensibly they had information to
give me or theories to advance, but neither the information nor
the theories ever seemed to amount to anything substantial, and
I came to see that they were merely a prelude to conversation.
Someone would start off by saying he'd seen Mary selling the *New
York Post* the afternoon before she was killed, and that would
serve as the opening wedge of a discussion of the bag woman, or
bag women in general, or various qualities of the neighborhood,
or violence in American life, or whatever.

A lot of people started off talking about the bag lady and
wound up talking about themselves. I guess most conversations
work out that way.

A nurse from Roosevelt said she never saw a shopping bag lady without hearing an inner voice say, "There but for the grace of God." She was not the only woman who confessed she worried about ending up that way. I guess it's a specter that haunts women who live alone, just as the vision of the Bowery derelict clouds the peripheral vision of hard-drinking men.

Genevieve Strom turned up at Armstrong's one night. We talked briefly about the bag lady. Two nights later she came back again, and we took turns spending our inheritances on rounds of drinks. The drinks hit her with some force, and a little past midnight she decided it was time to go. I said I'd see her home. At the corner of Fifty-seventh Street she stopped in her tracks and said, "No men in the room. That's one of Mrs. Larkin's rules."

"Old-fashioned, isn't she?"

"She runs a daycent establishment." Her mock-Irish accent was heavier than the landlady's. Her eyes, hard to read in the lamplight, raised to meet mine. "Take me someplace."

I took her to my hotel, a less decent establishment than Mrs. Larkin's. We did each other little good but no harm, and it beat being alone.

ANOTHER NIGHT I ran into Barry Mosedale at Polly's Cage. He told me there was a singer at Kid Gloves who was doing a number about the bag lady. "I can find out how you can reach him," he offered.

"Is he there now?"

He nodded and checked his watch. "He goes on in fifteen minutes. But you don't want to *go* there, do you?"

"Why not?"

"Hardly your sort of crowd, Matt."

"Cops go anywhere."

"They do, and they're welcome wherever they go, aren't they? Just let me drink this and I'll accompany you, if that's all right. You need someone to lend you immoral support."

Kid Gloves is a gay bar on Fifty-sixth west of Ninth. The decor is just a little aggressively gay lib. There's a small raised stage, a scattering of tables, a piano, and a loud jukebox. Barry Mosedale and I stood at the bar. I'd been there before and knew better than to order their coffee. I had straight bourbon. Barry had his on ice with a splash of soda.

Halfway through the drink Gordon Lurie was introduced. He wore tight jeans and a flowered shirt, sat on stage on a folding chair, sang ballads he'd written himself with his own guitar for accompaniment. I don't know if he was any good or not. It sounded to me as though all the songs had the same melody, but that may just have been a similarity of style. I don't have much of an ear.

After a song about a summer romance in Amsterdam, Gordon Lurie announced that the next number was dedicated to the memory of Mary Alice Redfield. Then he sang:

She's a shopping bag lady who lives on the sidewalks of
    Broadway,
Wearing all of her clothes and her years on her back,
Toting dead dreams in an old paper sack,
Searching the trash cans for something she lost here on
    Broadway—
Shopping bag lady.

You'd never know but she once was an actress on
    Broadway,
Speaking the words that they stuffed in her head,
Reciting the lines of the life that she led,
Thrilling her fans and her friends and her lovers on
    Broadway—
Shopping bag lady.

There are demons who lurk in the corners of minds and of
    Broadway
And after the omens and portents and signs
Came the day she forgot to remember her lines,
Put her life on a leash and took it out walking on
    Broadway—
Shopping bag lady.

There were a couple more verses, and the shopping bag lady in the song wound up murdered in a doorway, dying in defense of the

"tattered old treasures she mined in the trash cans of Broadway."
The song went over well and got a bigger hand than any of the
ones that had preceded it.

I asked Barry who Gordon Lurie was.

"You know very nearly as much as me," he said. "He started
here Tuesday. I find him whelming, personally. Neither overwhelming nor underwhelming but somewhere in the middle."

"Mary Alice never spent much time on Broadway. I never saw
her more than a block from Ninth Avenue."

"Poetic license, I'm sure. The song would lack a certain something if you substituted Ninth Avenue for Broadway. As it stands
it sounds a little like *Rhinestone Cowboy*."

"Does Lurie live around here?"

"I don't know where he lives. I have the feeling he's Canadian.
So many people are nowadays. It used to be that no one was
Canadian, and now simply everybody is. I'm sure it must be a
virus."

We listened to the rest of Gordon Lurie's act. Then Barry leaned
forward and chatted with the bartender to find out how I could
get backstage. I found my way to what passed for a dressing
room at Kid Gloves. It must have been a ladies' lavatory in a
prior incarnation.

I went in thinking I'd made a breakthrough, that Lurie had
killed her and now he was dealing with his guilt by singing about
her. I don't think I really believed this, but it supplied me with
direction and momentum. I told him my name and that I was
interested in his act. He wanted to know if I was from a record
company. "Am I on the threshold of a great opportunity? Am I
about to become an overnight success after years of travail?"

We got out of the tiny room and left the club through a side
door. Three doors down the block we sat in a cramped booth at
a coffee shop. He ordered a Greek salad and we both had coffee.

I told him I was interested in his song about the bag lady.

He brightened. "Oh, do you like it? Personally I think it's the
best thing I've written. I just wrote it a couple of days ago. I
opened next door Tuesday night. I got to New York three weeks
ago, and I had a two-week booking in the West Village, a place
called David's Table. Do you know it?"

"I don't think so."

"Another stop on the K-Y circuit. Either there aren't any straight people in New York or they don't go to nightclubs. But I was there two weeks, and then I opened at Kid Gloves. Afterward I was sitting and drinking with some people, and somebody was talking about the shopping bag lady, and I'd had enough Amaretto to be maudlin on the subject. I woke up Wednesday morning with the first verse of the song buzzing in my splitting head, and immediately wrote it down. As I was writing one verse, the next would come bubbling to the surface, and before I knew it I had all six verses." He took a cigarette, then paused in the act of lighting it to fix his eyes on me. "You told me your name," he said, "but I don't remember it."

"Matthew Scudder."

"Yes. You're the person investigating her murder."

"I'm not sure that's the right word. I've been talking to people, seeing what I can come up with. Did you know her before she was killed?"

He shook his head. "I was never even in this neighborhood before. *Oh.* I'm not a suspect, am I? Because I haven't been in New York since the fall. I haven't bothered to figure out where I was when she was killed, but I was in California at Christmas time, and I'd only gotten as far east as Chicago in early March, so I do have a fairly solid alibi."

"I never really suspected you. I think I just wanted to hear your song." I sipped some coffee. "Where did you get the facts of her life? Was she an actress?"

"I don't think so. Was she? It wasn't really *about* her, you know. It was inspired by her story, but I didn't know her or anything about her. The past few days I've been paying a lot of attention to bag ladies though. And other street people."

"I know what you mean."

"Are there more of them in New York, or is it just that they're so much more visible here? In California everybody drives, you don't see people on the street. I'm from Canada, rural Ontario, and the first city I ever spent much time in was Toronto, and there are crazy people on the streets there, but it's nothing like New York. Does the city drive them crazy, or does it just tend to draw crazy people?"

"I don't know."

"Maybe they're not crazy. Maybe they just hear a different drummer. I wonder who killed her."

"We'll probably never know."

"What I really wonder is *why* she was killed. In my song I made up the reason that somebody wanted what was in her bags. I think that works in the song, but I don't think there's much chance it happened like that."

"I don't know."

"They say she left people money—people she hardly knew. Is that the truth?" I nodded. "And she left me a song. I don't even feel that I wrote it. I woke up with it. I never set eyes on her and she touched my life. That's strange, isn't it?"

EVERYTHING WAS strange. The strangest part of all was the way it ended.

It was a Monday night. The Mets were at Shea, and I'd taken my sons to a game. The Dodgers were in for a three-game series that they eventually swept as they'd been sweeping everything lately. The boys and I got to watch them knock Jon Matlack out of the box and go on to shell his several replacements. The final count was something like 13 to 4. We stayed in our seats until the last out. Then I saw them home and caught a train back to the city.

So it was past midnight when I reached Armstrong's. Trina brought me a large double and a mug of coffee without being asked. I knocked back half of the bourbon and was dumping the rest into my coffee when she told me somebody'd been looking for me earlier. "He was in three times in the past two hours," she said. "A wiry guy, high forehead, bushy eyebrows, sort of a bulldog jaw. I guess the word for it is underslung."

"Perfectly good word."

"I said you'd probably get here sooner or later."

"I always do. Sooner or later."

"Uh-huh. Are you OK, Matt?"

"The Mets lost a close one."

"I heard it was thirteen to four."

"That's close for them these days. Did he say what it was about?"

He hadn't, but within the half hour he came in again and I was there to be found. I recognized him from Trina's description as soon as he came through the door. He looked faintly familiar, but he was nobody I knew. I suppose I'd seen him around the neighborhood.

Evidently he knew me by sight, because he found his way to my table without asking directions and took a chair without being invited to sit. He didn't say anything for a while and neither did I. I had a fresh bourbon and coffee in front of me, and I took a sip and looked him over.

He was under thirty. His cheeks were hollow, and the flesh of his face was stretched over his skull like leather that had shrunk upon drying. He wore a forest-green work shirt and a pair of khaki pants. He needed a shave.

Finally he pointed at my cup and asked me what I was drinking. When I told him, he said all he drank was beer.

"They have beer here," I said.

"Maybe I'll have what you're drinking." He turned in his chair and waved for Trina. When she came over he said he'd have bourbon and coffee, the same as I was having. He didn't say anything more until she brought the drink. Then, after he had spent quite some time stirring it, he took a sip. "Well," he said, "that's not so bad. That's OK."

"Glad you like it."

"I don't know if I'd order it again, but at least now I know what it's like."

"That's something."

"I seen you around. Matt Scudder. Used to be a cop, private eye now, blah blah blah. Right?"

"Close enough."

"My name's Floyd. I never liked it, but I'm stuck with it, right? I could change it, but who'm I kidding? Right?"

"If you say so."

"If I don't somebody else will. Floyd Karp, that's the full name. I didn't tell you my last name, did I? That's it, Floyd Karp."

"OK."

"OK, OK, OK." He pursed his lips, blew out air in a silent whistle. "What do we do now, Matt, huh? That's what I want to know."

"I'm not sure what you mean, Floyd."

"Oh, you know what I'm getting at, driving at, getting at. You know, don't you?"

By this time I suppose I did.

"I killed that old lady. I took her life, stabbed her with my knife." He flashed the saddest smile. "Steee-rangled her with her skeeee-arf. Hoist her with her own whatchacallit, petard. What's a petard?"

"I don't know, Floyd. Why'd you kill her?"

He looked at me, he looked at his coffee, he looked at me again. He said, "Had to."

"Why?"

"Same as the bourbon and coffee. Had to see. Had to taste it and find out what it was like." His eyes met mine. His were very large, hollow, empty. I fancied I could see right through them to the blackness at the back of his skull. "I couldn't get my mind away from murder," he said. His voice was more sober now, the mocking playful quality gone from it. "I tried. I just couldn't do it. It was on my mind all the time, and I was afraid of what I might do. I couldn't function, I couldn't think, I just saw blood and death all the time. I was afraid to close my eyes for fear of what I might see. I would just stay up, days it seemed, and then I'd be tired enough to pass out the minute I closed my eyes. I stopped eating. I used to be fairly heavy, and the weight just fell off of me."

"When did all this happen?"

"I don't know. All winter. And I thought if I went and did it once, I would know if I was a man or a monster or what. So I got this knife, and I went out a couple nights but lost my nerve. Then one night—almost couldn't do it, but I couldn't *not* do it, and then I was doing it and it went on forever. It was horrible."

"Why didn't you stop?"

"I don't know. I think I was afraid to stop. That doesn't make any sense, does it? I just don't know. It was insane, like being in a movie and being in the audience at the same time. Watching myself."

"No one saw you do it?"

"No. I went home. I threw the knife down a sewer. I put all my clothes in the incinerator, the ones I was wearing. I kept throwing up. All that night I would throw up, even when my stomach was empty. Dry heaves, Department of Dry Heaves. And then I guess I fell asleep, I don't know when or how, but I did, and the next day I woke up and thought I dreamed it. But I didn't."

"No."

"No. But it was over. I did it and I knew I'd never want to do it again. It was something crazy that happened and I could forget about it."

"Did you forget about it?"

A nod. "For a while. But now everybody's talking about her. Mary Alice Redfield, I killed her without knowing her name. Nobody knew her name, and now everybody knows it and it's all back in my mind. And I heard you were looking for me, and I guess, I guess. . . ." He frowned, chasing a thought around in his mind like a dog trying to capture his tail. Then he gave it up and looked at me. "So here I am," he said. "So here I am."

"Yes."

"Now what happens?"

"I think you'd better tell the police about it, Floyd."

"Why?"

"I suppose for the same reason you told me."

He thought about it. After a long time he nodded. "All right," he said. "I can accept that. I'd never kill anybody again. I know that. But—you're right, I have to tell them."

"I'll go with you if you want."

"Yeah. I want you to."

"I'll have a drink and then we'll go. You want another?"

"No. I'm not much of a drinker."

I had it without the coffee this time. After Trina brought it, I asked him how he'd picked his victim. Why the bag lady?

He started to cry. No sobs, just tears spilling from his deep-set eyes. After a while he wiped them on his sleeve.

"Because she didn't count," he said. "That's what I thought. She was nobody. Who cared if she died? Who'd miss her?" He closed his eyes tight. "Everybody misses her," he said. "Everybody."

So I took him in. I don't know what they'll do with him. It's not my problem.

It wasn't really a case, and I didn't really solve it. As far as I can see, I didn't do anything. It was the talk that drove Floyd Karp from cover, and no doubt I helped some of the talk get started, but much of it would have gotten around without me. All those legacies of Mary Alice Redfield's had made her a nine-day wonder in the neighborhood. They ran to no form known to anyone but the bag lady herself, and they had in no way led to her death, but maybe they led to its resolution, since it was one of the legacies that got me involved.

So maybe she caught her own killer. Or maybe he caught himself, as everyone does. Maybe no man's an island, and maybe everybody is.

All I know is I lit a candle for the woman, and I suspect I'm not the only one who did.

WILLIAM BANKIER

MAKING A KILLING WITH MAMA CASS

January 30, 1980

CANADIAN SHORT STORY specialist William Bankier frequently draws on his interest in music for his stories—as he does here. "Making a Killing with Mama Cass" is an excellent example of Bankier's ability to work numerous characters and plot twists into the limited space of a short story, without sacrificing clarity or character-ization. The story is a gem of compression, suggestion, and irony.

■

"**Why weren't you** at the airport?" Gary Prime said to his wife, Anitra, as she let herself into the apartment. "The car would have made sense. Instead I was stuck with an eight-dollar taxi." This was about as much anger as Gary ever expressed.

"I got your wire, but Lee had important clients in the screening room. I had to be there." Anitra glanced at herself in a mirror, wondering if her adventure had made any visible difference. Gary back a day early was all she needed. She could have used more time to compose herself, to decide where they were all going from here—herself and Gary and Lee Cosford.

"Busy while I was away?" Gary asked.

"As usual. How was London?"

"I enjoyed it." This was not the whole truth. Gary was a good mixer—his job demanded it. As a salesman for a Montreal engraving house, calling on the production departments of ad agencies, he got on well with the men who could discuss the advantages of offset reproduction versus letterpress. But throw him in with the clever boys from the creative department and it wasn't the same.

He was grateful for his free trip to England, even though he knew he'd been asked only because somebody dropped out at the last minute. His engravings were the backbone of the prize-winning campaign, therefore some Samaritan had suggested filling the vacant seat with good old Gary. He had asked Anitra to come along but she refused, pleading too much going on at Lee Cosford Productions.

"I enjoyed London," Gary repeated, "except for some of the brilliant conversation. My idea of hell is to be locked up for twenty-four hours with two copywriters, an art director, and an unlimited supply of booze. The drunker they get, the more they laugh. Only I can't see the joke half the time." Gary suspected that sometimes they derived their amusement from him. Not that he was a clod: his suit cost two hundred dollars, his shoes were shined, and he kept his hair trimmed. Maybe it was the haircut. The creative types either let their heads go altogether or had it styled and sprayed so they looked like Glen Campbell.

"Pay no attention to them," Anitra said. She was pouring herself some coffee from the pot Gary had made when he came in. She looked good against the counter in slim denims made stylish by a gold belt. "Agency guys are all the same. They think they're some kind of elite."

"Elite. That's the word. Everything is a put-down. You don't dare tell them you enjoyed a movie—they'll say it was commercial and leave you feeling stupid. To hear them, the girls going by are all dogs or hustlers, the food in the restaurant contains the 'permissible level' of rodent hairs, and the wine is sulphuric acid."

"Kill-joys."

"That's the word for them. Kill-joys. If you have a sincere feeling, you have to hide it or they'll make it into a joke."

"So you had a lousy time. At least it was free." Anitra studied her husband. Something was on his mind. He could never conceal enthusiasm—it shone from the large square face, the jaw set firm, the thick black hair neatly combed and gleaming with Vitalis.

"It was only two days, and apart from the meals, I was usually on my own." He was getting ready to tell her. "But there was a thing happened—I'm excited about it. It's as if . . ."

When Gary finished talking, Anitra could not understand what he was so worked up about. He had been watching late-night television in his hotel room and had turned on a talk show. The guest was the English actress Donna Dean, the sex symbol from the sixties, who was still pretty today but hugely overweight.

Anitra said, "And your idea is what? You want to ask her to be in a film about Mama Cass?"

"Not me. I can't ask her. A film producer has to ask her. But she'd be perfect—if you saw her you'd know what I mean. She's blonde, of course, so she'd need a dark wig. But she has the same baby face as Mama Cass and that majestic build. She was even wearing one of those big tent dresses Cass used to wear—"

Anitra found it difficult to become interested. Years ago, she had enjoyed listening to The Mamas and The Papas, and she had agreed with Gary in those days that the bell-like voice of Cass Elliott had a lot to do with the group's success. More recently, she had heard something about the young woman's untimely death, but nothing much about it had registered. "OK, there could be a film in it," Anitra said. "What's it got to do with you?"

"I'm the one to make it happen. I've got to do it."

After watching the Donna Dean interview, Gary had left the hotel and gone for a walk along Bayswater Avenue. It was midnight. Hyde Park was on his right, substantial white Edwardian buildings on his left. Ahead loomed Marble Arch and Park Lane with its lineup of hotels far posher than the one he was inhabiting. Noisy little cars, square black taxis, and an occasional red double-decker bus kept up a continuous roar beside him, but Gary hardly heard the traffic.

His mind was filled with music from the cassettes he used to play till they nearly fell apart, the songs of dreams and of young girls coming to the canyon.

According to the newspapers, Cass Elliott had died in a hotel somewhere near there. They said she choked to death on a sandwich alone in her room.

"I have to get the film going," Gary told his wife. "And now. Something tells me it's important."

"If you say so."

"Your boss said once that a feature film will never happen unless somebody puts all his energy behind it. There are too many other ideas competing for the funds and the facilities."

"Lee should know."

"Right. So I thought you might lay it on him tomorrow."

"Me? It's your idea." The last two days at Lee's place had given Anitra a shaking up. Some change in the relationship had been coming for a long time. But now she felt uncertain about her future, and the sensation was distasteful to her. From the time eight years ago when she organized her marriage to Gary, Anitra had kept uncertainties to a minimum. The false pregnancy was a cheat, but it got her out of a dismal situation at home. And it had done Gary no harm; he was forever testifying that the unexpected marriage had stabilized his life.

Now, for the sake of some excitement, she had gone with Lee Cosford. The event was satisfying enough as it was happening, but when they parted, there had been a distant look in Lee's pale eyes and Anitra was no fool.

"You'd better describe the idea to Lee yourself," she said. "I wouldn't do it justice." It would kill her to approach him with this loony request, as if she thought he owed her something.

"Just mention it. Set it up for me."

"You're a big boy, Gary. You know his number. Call him and tell him you've got a business proposition. Lee Cosford would rather talk business than anything."

LEE COSFORD, rotund and dynamic, rolled out into the waiting room and took Gary by the arm. "Stranger," he said, laughing, eyeing Prime anxiously, "where've you been keeping yourself? Come in and sit down. Stephie, make us a couple of coffees, will you?"

The idea sounded even better to Gary as he described it in Lee Cosford's panelled office, taking pulls at a huge mug of coffee, squinting against sunlight streaming through the window past the spire of a church on lower Mountain Street. Cosford lay back in his leather recliner, boots on the glass desk, eyes closed like a man in a barber chair. As Gary finished, the bells in the tower across the street began to peal. He thought it was a good omen.

Cosford opened one eye. "Is that it?"

"That's it, Lee."

The film producer sat up. "I think it's a sensational idea."

"Really?"

"Fabulous. And you've probably heard Anitra mention I want to get into feature films. You can't know how soul-destroying it is producing thirty-second pieces of film to sell detergent or sausages. Or maybe you *do* know. You have the same assignment in print."

"I know what you mean." Actually, Gary was proud of the engravings his firm produced.

"The trouble is," Cosford said, "there are too many good film ideas chasing too little money. You just can't get the financing."

"I thought there was this Canadian Film Development Council. Don't they put up money?"

"That's right." Cosford put his knees under the desk and folded his arms precisely on the cold glass. This square individual in the over-pressed suit had managed to brief himself. "The CFDC will, on occasion, back a good idea."

"And this is more than a good idea, Lee. It's a great idea."

"Right." Cosford's mind was working fast. He was more than ready to see the last of Gary Prime. "But there's only one way to approach the council. They have to see a treatment."

"Treatment?"

"Right." Cosford picked up his telephone, consulted a page of names and numbers, and began to dial. "A scenario—an outline of what the film is going to be about."

"Can't we just put the idea down in a letter?"

"No, it has to be professionally done. And I've got just the man to do it." Cosford straightened up and smiled into the phone. "Hello, Lucas? Did I wake you? Lee Cosford. Fine, how are you? Luke, facing me across my desk is a bright-eyed, bushy-tailed fellow named Gary Prime, who happens to have a sensational idea for a feature film. The idea is so good, the only person to do the treatment is Lucas Pennington."

After Gary Prime went away with an appointment to see Pennington at his apartment that afternoon, Lee Cosford wandered through a maze of corridors till he came to a small room where his film editor was seated at a Steenbeck machine with Anitra Prime at his shoulder. They were peering into the frosted glass screen at the image of a child holding a doll. The editor spun the film backward, then forward again so that the child kissed the doll while Anitra clicked her stopwatch.

"I just had your husband in. Thanks for not warning me."

"I would have guessed next week. He's quick off the mark all of a sudden."

"Never mind. I got rid of him."

"He's sincere about the idea.

"I have twenty-five sincere ideas for feature films. Nine of them are my own." Cosford opened a window and spat out into a laneway three floors below. He watched the spittle float down to disappear on gray pavement. "I sent him to Lucas Pennington to get a treatment done."

The bald-headed man at the editing machine laughed.

"Who's Lucas Pennington?" Anitra asked.

"Before your era. Once a good copywriter, now a professional drunk. He's a freelance with loads of free time. Which is another way of saying the agencies are tired of Pennington missing deadlines."

Anitra said, "It sounds like a dirty trick, Lee." She frowned at her stopwatch; she was having no end of trouble making the product shot time out properly.

"It's dirty but effective. It gets Gary off my back while he and poor old Luke use up a year pretending they're writing a movie."

IT WAS HALF past two when Gary showed up at Lucas Pennington's place on Bleury Street. The apartment was located up a flight of uncarpeted stairs above a tavern and a shop that sold sneezing powder and rubber excrement. When he heard the knock, Pennington put the gin bottle and his glass out of sight—not because he was an inhospitable man, but because there was barely enough for himself. He left magazines, newspapers, open books, soiled clothing, empty food tins, and soft-drink bottles where they were and went to the door.

With his guest inside and seated, Pennington performed a humanitarian act; he opened a window.

Gary looked at the man who was supposed to write his Mama Cass treatment. To recommend this one, Lee Cosford had to be crazy. Pennington managed to be gaunt and sloppy at the same time. He seemed somewhere in his fifties—large head, patchy gray hair on a scalp that was scabby in places, apologetic eyes, and a smile that was choreographed to cover bad teeth. He had shaved a couple of days ago and had cut himself doing it.

"OK. All right now. Right." He was rummaging around the room, not looking at Gary, sounding like a nervous infielder at the start of his final season. "Tell me about this picture of yours."

As Gary described his visit to London, his television glimpse of Donna Dean, and the flash of inspiration that led him to cast her in the role of his favorite singer, Pennington, who had discovered a notebook and a pen, lay on the floor with his head and shoulders against the baseboard, his eyes closed.

"So if Dean would agree to do it, and if we could get the right to use the original recordings for her to mime, the way the singers all do on TV these days," Gary concluded, "I think we could have a good film."

Pennington rolled sideways onto his elbow, cupping his cheek in one hand. He bit the cover off the felt-tipped pen he was holding, spat it away, and began flipping the pages of the notebook to find a clean one. They were all filled with indecipherable scrawl. At last he settled for half of the inside back cover. "Brilliant. Solid gold," he said as he tried to make marks with the pen. "Put me in, coach. Let me work on this one."

"You mean it?"

The writer turned his eyes up to Gary and they looked different—they looked angry and hungry, the apologetic wetness all gone. Pennington was feeling an old, almost-forgotten sensation, the one he used to experience in his first agency job when the new assignments came in and he couldn't wait to dazzle the copy chief and the account supervisor and the client with another brilliant idea. Quite often he would deliver a winner. Then it was cover the table with beer and how about a little more money for young Luke before Y&R lures him away with shares.

"I mean it all right," Pennington said. "You're onto a sure thing, my son. Mama Cass—that voice, the way she used to raise her hand and give that little half-salute as the song began to swing . . . I want to weep." The pen refused to write, and after tearing holes in the cover, he threw pen and notebook against the wall, struggling to his feet like a crippled, pregnant camel.

"The tragedy of her death." Pennington was pulling magazines and files from a buried tabletop, uncovering a typewriter. He used an ankle to drag a wooden chair into place, sat down, and cranked a crumpled letter around the roller, using two fingers to begin typing

on the back of the paper. "What a career she had. Cass Elliott—
there *has* to be a movie about her. And I know what you mean
about the English broad to play the role. She's almost Cass's double. And she'll do a hell of a good job—never mind the silly parts
they gave her in the sixties. She's a pro, a trained actress."

Pennington's typing was erratic. The keys kept sticking together
in bunches, and he cursed as he clawed them away from the
paper. He squinted at what he had done. "This ribbon is dead.
It's a ghost. Can you read that?"

Gary leaned over his shoulder, holding his breath. "Just barely."

"Never mind, it's coming, old son, the words are coming and
I'll hammer the bastards down. Cosford knows my situation.
He'll make a dark photostat of this and enlarge it three times."
Pennington managed to hit several keys without an overlap and
he laughed out loud. "The old rhythm," he said. "Once you've
got it, you never lose it."

"Can I do anything to help?" Gary asked, delighted with this
crazy old writer's reaction to his idea.

"Yes. Get out of here and let me work."

TWO DAYS LATER, Lucas Pennington showed up in the reception
room of Lee Cosford Productions. The girl behind the board blinked
at the sight of the very tall man in his dusty suit. It was a three-piece
blue serge—not this year's model, not this decade's. At the top of it,
above the frayed gray collar and badly knotted tie, was a wet, crimson face looking as if the man had just shaved it with a broken bottle.
At the bottom, stepping forward awkwardly across the deep-pile
carpet, were astonishing leather thong sandals over patterned socks.

Lee Cosford came out to claim his visitor. In the office he
offered gin and Pennington accepted, saying, "First since day
before yesterday. How about that, temperance fans?"

Cosford knew this had to be about the Gary Prime project. He
believed he had heard the end of it, but now here was the top writer
from a generation ago looking as if he had just seen a vision on the
road to Saint Anne de Beaupré. Cosford reached out and took the
glass away from his guest and said, "Tell me, Luke. Before you dive
back into the sauce. Is there a feature film in this Mama Cass thing?"

"Academy Awards. Cannes Festival. The idea is solid gold, my
dear. I've been working for two days on the treatment without

anything to drink but coffee and grapefruit juice. It's in this brown envelope, Lee old buddy, and what you had better do is line up tons of money and hire your cast and your director, because *somewhere* there's a lucky man who is going to make the film of the year from this here scenario of mine."

Cosford handed back the drink. "I just wanted to hear you say it." He took the envelope and went to sit behind his desk. To himself he said, *Always trust a sober Pennington.* He drew a thick sheaf of typewritten pages from the envelope. "Wow, what did you do, write a shooting script?"

"Almost. I had to force myself not to. I even went out and invested in a ribbon and a box of paper." Pennington drew on the drink, then set it aside and looked out of the window at the church spire.

Cosford studied the title page. It said, *"Blues for Mama Cass—* a film drama with interpolated music. A Lee Cosford Production written by Lucas Pennington."* The script had weight in Cosford's hands; it felt crisp and substantial—he knew the heft of valuable work. He flicked the title page over and saw the beginning of the treatment. The writing flowed. It was vintage Pennington.

The producer glanced up, wondering whether he should mention the fact that Gary Prime's name did not appear on the script. He decided to let it go for the moment.

"Do you want up-front money, Luke," he asked, "or would you rather take a share of the gross?"

Pennington made growling noises in his throat as he rubbed his hands together. "Some of each, please," he said, and out in the reception area, Stephie heard through the wall the deep, nasty sounds of her boss and his visitor laughing.

GARY TOLD ANITRA how his project was going. He enthused over the meeting with Lucas Pennington, describing what a washout the man seemed to be, then how he came alight when the idea was explained. Aware of Pennington's bad reputation, knowing it was all a ploy to fob Gary off with a loser, Anitra was tempted to warn her husband not to expect too much. But why come on as a pessimist? Let the man have his dream for a while longer. Besides, you never could tell—something *might* come of it.

It was only by accident that she discovered a few weeks later that something was indeed coming of the Mama Cass project.

Anitra encountered Stephie at the photocopy machine and happened to see that she was running off several copies of what looked like a shooting script. A glance at the title page and Anitra was off to see Lee Cosford almost at a run.

Then she slowed down, thinking, and stopped. The film business ground on at a steady pace at the best of times. No mad rush. She would wait and see what was going to happen next.

What happened was that Lee announced he was flying to London on business at the beginning of the week. He asked Stephie to book a couple of seats on the Air Canada flight for Sunday evening. If the other seat was for Gary, Anitra told herself, her husband would have been crowing before now. If it was for her, Lee would have said something. Instead, he was keeping his head down these days, acting as if he had done a sloppy job of picking her pocket and hoped she wouldn't mention it.

Anitra decided to bring up the subject as she sat in the front seat of Lee's car driving back from the Eastern Townships, where they had been filming a butter commercial. She was never so grateful for a safety belt as when she drove with Lee Cosford. The highway was fairly clear and he kept pushing the accelerator. The needle edged past eighty-five, ninety.

Suddenly the steering wheel began to shudder in Lee's hands. He straightened his arms, reducing speed. "Second time it's done that." He swore a couple of times but his eyes were bright. He was enjoying himself. "Something is wrong with this car, my dear. Anything over ninety and she tries to run away from me."

Anitra stopped bracing her feet against the floor and tried to relax, her heart still racing. "Lee," she said, "what the hell are you up to?"

"I like to drive fast," he said.

"I mean with Gary's idea. I saw the treatment Pennington wrote. You're getting ready to run with it."

"Luke says it has potential. He may be a lush, but Pennington has judgment."

"But why isn't Gary's name on the front page? Why doesn't he even know you're going ahead?"

"He will, he will—don't worry about it. As soon as I get my financing organized I'll write Gary a nice check."

"Thanks very much. Good thing I brought it up."

Cosford glanced at her and back at the road. The speedometer crept upward and a feathery vibration in the steering-wheel tickled his fingers. "Anitra, you know the film business. Let's face it, your husband is just an engraver's rep. What does he know from films? This is a Lee Cosford Production. It has to be if it's going to work." He glanced over again, and this time he encountered her eyes staring straight at him. It was a frightening sight. "Come on! Gary fluked on an idea that happens to have possibilities. OK, we're going to pay him for it. But the business of making it into a film is for me and Luke Pennington. And for you—you can be part of this, too."

They drove a mile or two in silence.

Then he said breezily, "Want to come to London? Lucas and I are flying out on Sunday night to see the agent of this actress. Come along if you want. We could have some fun." He took a hand from the wheel and reached for hers.

Anitra drew her hand away and busied herself finding her lipstick and a small mirror in her purse. She concentrated on touching up her mouth. "I don't think so, Lee." She drew neat outlines with a tiny brush. "And don't pretend you'll miss me. Shacking up was fun, wasn't it? But I guess once was enough." She snapped her purse shut and turned to look at him coldly. "Right?"

He drew his shoulders up like a man in a hailstorm. "Whatever you say," he said patiently.

GARY CAME HOME that night in a mellow frame of mind. One of the agencies had been saying good-bye to a retiring account supervisor, and good old Smitty had invited the representative of his favorite engraving house to stay for a drink. Gary let himself in at seven o'clock and was genuinely surprised to find Anitra in the living room with an empty salad plate beside her, a wineglass in her hand, and a news analysis program on television with the sound turned off. "Hello," he said. "No editing tonight? No answer-prints? No emergency at the lab?" He said this without malice.

"You sound happy."

"We just put Elgar Smith out to pasture. They made nice advertising men in those days."

"There's a salad plate for you in the fridge."

"Thanks." His smile was that of a man who's been told his lottery ticket is a winner for the third consecutive week. He came back from the kitchen with his plate and a wineglass. Anitra poured Riesling for him as he peeled off the cling-film. "Hey, you made tuna with onions." He began eating hungrily.

Anitra reached forward and switched off the TV picture. "What's the word on your film idea?' she asked.

"Early days. I suppose Pennington's working on the treatment."

She set her glass down dead center on a coaster on the broad arm of the sofa. "Luke Pennington has delivered a thirty-page outline to Lee Cosford. They're very excited about it. They have an appointment with an agent in London for next Monday."

Gary beamed and raised his glass. "Fabulous. Thanks for telling me."

"You might well thank me. I don't think Lee was going to mention it." When her husband went on eating, she said, "I saw the script. Your name isn't on it."

"So?"

"So Lee Cosford is running away with your idea, Gary. He fobbed you off on Pennington to get rid of you, and now that Luke says the idea's solid gold, Lee has adopted it."

"That's what I wanted."

"I don't believe this. Lee told me he's going to write you a check once the financing is arranged."

"All donations gratefully received." Gary looked closely at his wife and for the first time saw the extent of her rage. "It's what I wanted," he repeated. "A film about Mama Cass—something to really do her justice. The idea hit me in London when I was walking at night, as if she were still there, her spirit . . . I know that sounds stupid. But an idea is something from your soul, isn't it? That's all it is, and who knows what makes the idea spring into your mind?"

"Gary, come down to earth."

"The film is all that matters. If it's going to be done, I'm delighted. No big deal if my name isn't connected with it."

"But it's *your* concept, damn it! You've *got* to be credited! Call a lawyer tomorrow and explain what's happening. Have a stop put on Lee before he goes any further." Her husband's satisfied face enraged her. "At least get mad! They're ripping you off, they're treating you like a retarded child."

"I can't get mad. I'm too happy."

Anitra picked up the wine bottle, but her hands were shaking so hard she could not pour. Her empty glass toppled over. She left it rolling on the carpet. Gary was staring at her now, one cheek full. "Then maybe you'll get mad at this," she said. "While you were over in London falling in love with the ghost of Cass Elliott, I was back here in bed with Lee Cosford. Yes, that's right." She got up and said over her shoulder as she left the room, "Now will you come back into *this* world, Gary?"

ANITRA FOUND IT easy to make her decision the next day. Her mind was influenced by the way the men around her seemed determined to conduct business as usual. Gary did his typical early-morning flit to work, leaving one of his screwy notes on the kitchen counter. Years ago he had played with the idea of being a cartoonist; now the talent had mostly evaporated, leaving a residue of doodled heads and neat printing. Today's note referred only obliquely to last night in a speech balloon that said, "Don't blame yourself. We'll talk."

At the studio, Cosford scurried around in his characterization as Laughing Lee the benign executive. He had everybody around the place grinning, but the best Anitra could give him was a sour, knowing smile. His only direct communication with her was when he whipped into her office and said, "Do me a favor, will you, Anitra? Stephie is away sick or I'd ask her. Drive the car around to the garage and have them check the steering. Tell him about the shudder around ninety. And I'll need it by Sunday."

"I'll call and see if they can do it now," Anitra said curtly. She picked up the phone and dialed for an outside line. But when Lee left the office she set the phone down again without making the call. The suggestion in her mind was unthinkable, but she had to consider it. She did so and came to the conclusion that Cosford had something coming. Not that an accident would happen. But if it did, there would be justice in it.

Later, Cosford had to go to a luncheon meeting at the Queen Elizabeth Hotel, so he took a taxi. He telephoned from there to say that he was accepting a lift with his dairy client down to the farm in the Eastern Townships. He would be there for the weekend, returning Sunday at midday to get the car and the film scenario from his office and then to drive Luke Pennington to the airport.

Would Anitra be able to come in for an hour on Sunday to discuss taking over the reins during his absence?

"Of course." She pursued her curt manner, words at a premium. "They kept the car at the garage but promised the steering will be fixed by Saturday afternoon. I'll see that it's here."

"You're a gem." Lee was expansive after his lunch. "I'll bring you back something nice from Bond Street."

ON SUNDAY MORNING as Anitra was leaving for the studio, Gary came out of the guest room, where he had been sleeping for a couple of nights. "Have you got a minute to talk?" he said.

"I'm in a hurry."

"I've decided you're right. I'm going to see a lawyer next week. As long as the film is being made, I might as well get some credit."

He was not looking directly at her, so she was able to observe the veiled look on his face. "You still aren't mad, Gary. You're just saying what you think I want to hear."

His voice became petulant. "Well, how the hell am I supposed to please you?"

"Nobody's asking you for that. Just grow up. When somebody walks all over you, be a man—get mad."

He followed her to the door. "Are you going to see Lee?"

"I'm going to the studio. There's work to be done before he leaves for London."

When she was gone, Gary went into the living room and pressed the palms of his hands together. He looked around. Nothing like Sunday-morning light to show the dust on everything. Anitra liked to go about with a spray can and a cloth, making everything shine and smell of lemon. Lately there had been other things on her mind.

He took down the most-played cassette in his collection and slipped it into the tape deck. He turned on the amplifier, pressed START, heard a moment's silence and then the familiar harmony flowing from the speakers on the top shelf on either side of the fireplace—Mama Cass's huge, pure voice soaring over the others like a silver-belled horn.

At last he understood why Anitra was angry with him. It was a matter of expressing himself as unself-consciously as the beautiful, natural woman he was listening to. Gary knew how he felt; he had to tell Lee Cosford how he felt.

BY ONE O'CLOCK, Anitra had made two big drinks each for Cosford and Pennington. She had poured on the whisky for her boss and stinted the ginger. He was rolling with self-importance. She was glad when he looked at his watch.

"Time to hit the road," he said. "Where's the car, Anitra?"

"Around back." She had moved it there herself on Saturday. "The guy from the garage couldn't find anyplace else to park."

"Then we're off. Come on, young Lucas—Daddy is going to show you the world. So long, Mrs. Prime."

When the door closed behind them, Anitra poured herself a small drink and took it to Lee's desk, where she sat down and rummaged till she found a copy of the Mama Cass scenario. Then she began to sip and read. As she turned the pages, the realization dawned on her that this *would* make a great film. Gary was dead right. If things worked out, she and he would take it to another producer and have a go themselves.

LEE COSFORD drove aggressively to the corner and stamped on the brake pedal, throwing Pennington forward so that he had to catch himself against the padded dashboard.

"Ride 'em, cowboy," Lucas said.

"Haven't lost a passenger in years." Cosford craned his neck. "Isn't that Gary Prime?"

"It sure looks like him."

"Roll your window down. Call him over."

"Are you sure? We don't need him at the moment."

"It's Sunday—I'm feeling Christian. Call him."

Gary saw the face at the car window, wandered over, and bent himself to look inside. "Hello, Lucas. Hello, Lee. I was coming to see you."

"I'm glad. I've been meaning to talk to you about your film. We're just off to the airport. Can you drive out with us and have a drink in the lounge? Don't hesitate, my boy—it's to your benefit. Get in."

As Gary went to open the back door, Lee whispered quickly to Pennington, "Let's give the guy a small credit and one or two percent. It's little enough and may save us litigation later on."

BY TWO THIRTY, Anitra had read the script twice and finished a second drink. When the telephone rang, she jumped. It was a police officer. There had been a crash on the highway near Dorval Airport. A car left the road and ran at top speed into a concrete abutment. The license number had been put through the computer, which printed out Lee Cosford Productions as owner of the car.

"That was my boss," Anitra said, sounding disturbed. "He was on his way to catch a plane. Is there any—"

"I'm sorry. He must have been going ninety. We haven't been able to get into the car yet, but there can't be anybody alive."

Anitra telephoned home, but Gary was either out or not answering. She drove from downtown in twenty minutes, thinking about the accident she had programmed. If it wasn't murder, it was certainly manslaughter. Not that Lee or Pennington were any great loss to the world, but she had better not let on to Gary that she had sent her boss out with two doubles on an empty stomach and faulty steering. Gary lacked the imagination to do anything but call the police.

The apartment was empty. Anitra checked the TV guide and saw that the Expos were on channel six in a doubleheader against the Phillies. That meant Gary would be down at the Mount Royal in the television lounge, drinking beer and eating peanuts. No supper required tonight. But perhaps they could have that talk he'd suggested this morning. No need for lawyers now—no bitterness, but a fresh start with an exciting project they could share.

The reaction set in as Anitra made tea. She was trembling so much as she carried it into the living room that she arrived with a brimming saucer. She set it down with both hands, went to turn on the radio, and noticed a cassette inside the deck. She pressed the proper switches and out came the voice Gary had been raving about for the past few weeks, the cause of all the excitement and the maneuvering and of her deadly intervention.

Now, as never before, she could understand what turned her husband on when this woman sang. Mama Cass was solo on this track, so vibrant and alive she might have been here in the room.

Anitra listened to the entire cassette—both sides—before she realized she was feeling impatient for Gary's return. She began willing him to abandon his precious baseball telecast and get in touch with her. And so when the telephone rang she ran to answer it eagerly.

THE TAKAMOKU JOSEKI

January 1984

SARA PARETSKY has helped to transform the mystery genre within the past couple of decades. She pioneered the female hard-boiled P.I. with her popular character V. I. Warshawski, and she supported the work of other women mystery writers by founding the Sisters in Crime organizations. Paretsky's novels are distinguished by gritty realism, the loving evocation of Chicago, and engagement with larger social issues. Warshawski debuted in Paretsky's first novel, and this story appeared shortly thereafter.

■

Mr. and Mrs. Takamoku were a quiet, hardworking couple. Although they had lived in Chicago since the 1940s, when they were relocated from an Arizona detention camp, they spoke only halting English. Occasionally I ran into Mrs. Takamoku in the foyer of the old three-flat we both lived in on Belmont, or at the corner grocery store. We would exchange a few stilted sentences. She knew I lived alone in my third-floor apartment, and she worried about it, although her manners were too perfect for her to come right out and tell me to get myself a husband.

As time passed, I learned about her son, Akira, and her daughter, Yoshio, both professionals living on the West Coast. I always inquired after them, which pleased her.

With great difficulty I got her to understand that I was a private detective. This troubled her; she often wanted to know if I were doing something dangerous and would shake her head and frown as she asked. I didn't see Mr. Takamoku often. He worked for a printer and usually left long before me in the morning.

Unlike the De Paul students who form an ever-changing collage on the second floor, the Takamokus did little entertaining, or at least little noisy entertaining. Every Sunday afternoon a procession of Orientals came to their apartment, spent a quiet afternoon, and left. One or more Occidentals would join them, incongruous by their height and color. After a while, I recognized the regulars, a tall, bearded white man and six or seven Japanese and Koreans.

One Sunday evening in late November I was eating sushi and drinking sake in a storefront restaurant on Halsted. The Takamokus came in as I was finishing my first little pot of sake. I smiled and waved at them and watched with idle amusement as they conferred earnestly, darting glances at me. While they argued, a waitress brought them bowls of noodles and a plate of sushi; they were clearly regular customers with regular tastes.

At last, Mr. Takamoku came over to my table. I invited him and his wife to join me.

"Thank you, thank you," he said in an agony of embarrassment. "We only have question for you, not to disturb you."

"You're not disturbing me. What do you want to know?"

"You are familiar with American customs." That was a statement, not a question. I nodded, wondering what was coming.

"When a guest behaves badly in the house, what does an American do?"

I gave him my full attention. I had no idea what he was asking, but he would never have brought it up just to be frivolous.

"It depends," I said carefully. "Did they break up your sofa or spill tea?"

Mr. Takamoku looked at me steadily, fishing for a cigarette. Then he shook his head, slowly. "Not as much as breaking furniture. Not as little as tea on sofa. In between."

"I'd give him a second chance."

A slight crease erased itself from Mr. Takamoku's forehead. "A second chance. A very good idea. A second chance."

He went back to his wife and ate his noodles with the noisy appreciation that showed good Japanese manners. I had another pot of sake and finished about the same time as the Takamokus; we left the restaurant together. I topped them by a good five inches, so I slowed my pace to a crawl to keep step with them.

Mrs. Takamoku smiled. "You are familiar with Go?" she asked, giggling nervously.

"I'm not sure," I said cautiously, wondering if they wanted me to conjugate an intransitive irregular verb.

"It's a game. You have time to stop and see?"

"Sure," I agreed, just as Mr. Takamoku broke in with vigorous objections.

I couldn't tell whether he didn't want to inconvenience me or didn't want me intruding. However, Mrs. Takamoku insisted, so I stopped at the first floor and went into the apartment with her.

The living room was almost bare. The lack of furniture drew the eye to a beautiful Japanese doll on a stand in one corner with a bowl of dried flowers in front of her. The only other furnishing was a row of six little tables. They were quite thick and stood low on carved wooden legs. Their tops, about eighteen inches square, were crisscrossed with black lines that formed dozens of little squares. Two covered wooden bowls stood on each table.

"Go-ban," Mrs. Takamoku said, pointing to one of the tables.

I shook my head in incomprehension.

Mr. Takamoku picked up a covered bowl. It was filled with smooth white disks, the size of nickels but much thicker. I held one up and saw beautiful shades and shadows in it.

"Clam shell," Mr. Takamoku said. "They cut, then polish." He picked up a second bowl, filled with black disks. "Shale."

He knelt on a cushion in front of one of the tables and rapidly placed black and white disks on intersections of the lines. A pattern emerged.

"This is Go. Black plays, then white, then black, then white. Each tries to make territory, to make eyes." He showed me an "eye"—a clear space surrounded by black stones. "White cannot play here. Black is safe. Now white must play someplace else."

"I see." I didn't really, but I didn't think it mattered.

"This afternoon, someone knock stones from table, turn upside down, and scrape with knife."

"This table?" I asked, tapping the one he was playing on.

"Yes." He swept the stones off swiftly but carefully and put them in their little pots. He turned the board over. In the middle was a hole, carved and sanded. The wood was very thick—I suppose the hole gave it resonance.

I knelt beside him and looked. I was probably thirty years younger, but I couldn't tuck my knees under me with his grace and ease: I sat cross-legged. A faint scratch marred the sanded bottom.

"Was he American?"

Mr. and Mrs. Takamoku exchanged a look. "Japanese, but born in America," she said. "Like Akira and Yoshio."

I shook my head. "I don't understand. It's not an American custom." I climbed awkwardly back to my feet. Mr. Takamoku stood with one easy movement. He and Mrs. Takamoku thanked me profusely. I assured them it was nothing and went to bed.

THE NEXT SUNDAY was a cold, gray day with a hint of snow. I sat in my living room in front of the television, drinking coffee, dividing my attention between November's income and watching the Bears. Both were equally feeble. I was trying to decide on something friendlier to do when a knock sounded on my door. The outside buzzer hadn't rung. I got up, stacking loose papers on one arm of the chair and balancing the coffee cup on the other.

Through the peephole I could see Mrs. Takamoku. I opened the door. Her wrinkled ivory face was agitated, her eyes dilated. "Oh, good, good, you are here. You must come." She tugged at my hand.

I pulled her gently into the apartment. "What's wrong? Let me get you a drink."

"No, no." She wrung her hands in agitation, repeating that I must come, I must come.

I collected my keys and went down the worn, uncarpeted stairs with her. Her living room was filled with cigarette smoke and a crowd of anxious men. Mr. Takamoku detached himself from the group and hurried over to his wife and me. He clasped my hand and pumped it up and down.

"Good. Good you came. You are a detective, yes? You will see the police do not arrest Naoe and me."

"What's wrong, Mr. Takamoku?"

"He's dead. He's killed. Naoe and I were in camp during World War. They will arrest us."

"Who's dead?"

He shrugged helplessly. "I don't know name."

I pushed through the group. A white man lay sprawled on the floor. It was hard, given his position, to guess his age. His fair hair was thick and unmarked with gray; he must have been relatively young.

A small dribble of vomit trailed from his clenched teeth. I sniffed at it cautiously. Probably hydrocyanic acid. Not far from his body lay a teacup, a Japanese cup without handles. The contents sprayed out from it like a Rorschach. Without touching it, I sniffed again. The fumes were still discernible.

I got up. "Has anyone left since this happened?"

The tall, bearded Caucasian I'd noticed on previous Sundays looked around and said "no" in an authoritative voice.

"And have you called the police?"

Mrs. Takamoku gave an agitated cry. "No police. No. You are detective. You find murderer yourself."

I shook my head and took her gently by the hand. "If we don't call the police, they will put us all in jail for concealing a murder. You must tell them."

The bearded man said, "I'll do that."

"Who are you?"

"I'm Charles Welland. I'm a physicist at the University of Chicago, but on Sundays I'm a Go player."

"I see . . . I'm V. I. Warshawski. I live upstairs: I'm a private investigator. The police look very dimly on all citizens who don't report murders, but especially on P.I.'s."

Welland went into the dining room, where the Takamokus kept their phone. I told the Takamokus and their guests that no one could leave before the police gave them permission, then followed Welland to make sure he didn't call anyone besides the police, or take the opportunity to get rid of a vial of poison.

The Go players seemed resigned, albeit very nervous. All of them smoked ferociously; the thick air grew bluer. They split into small groups, five Japanese together, four Koreans in another clump. A lone Chinese fiddled with the stones on one of the Go-bans.

None of them spoke English well enough to give a clear account of how the young man died. When Welland came back, I asked him for a detailed report.

The physicist claimed not to know his name. The dead man had only been coming to the Go club the last month or two.

"Did someone bring him? Or did he just show up one day?"

Welland shrugged. "He just showed up. Word gets around among Go players. I'm sure he told me his name—it just didn't stick. I think he worked for Hansen Electronic, the big computer firm."

I asked if everyone there were regular players. Welland knew all of them by sight, if not by name. They didn't all come every Sunday, but none of the others was a newcomer.

"I see. Okay. What happened today?"

Welland scratched his beard. He had bushy, arched eyebrows that jumped up to punctuate his stronger statements. I thought that was pretty sexy. I pulled my mind back to what he was saying.

"I got here around one thirty. I think three games were in progress. This guy"—he jerked his thumb toward the dead man—"arrived a bit later. He and I played a game. Then Mr. Hito arrived and the two of them had a game. Dr. Han showed up, and he and I were playing when the whole thing happened. Mrs. Takamoku sets out tea and snacks. We all wander around and help ourselves. About four, this guy took a swallow of tea, gave a terrible cry, and died."

"Is there anything important about the game they were playing?"

Welland looked at the board. A handful of black and white stones stood on the corner points. He shook his head. "They'd just started. It looks like our dead friend was trying the Takamoku joseki. That's a complicated one—I've never seen it used in actual play before."

"What's that? Anything to do with Mr. Takamoku?"

"The joseki are the beginning moves in the corners. Takamoku is this one"—he pointed at the far side—"where black plays on the five-four point—the point where the fourth and fifth lines intersect. It wasn't named for our host. That's just coincidence."

SERGEANT McGONNIGAL didn't find out much more than I had. A thickset young detective, he has had a lot of experience and treated his frightened audience gently. He was a little less kind to me, demanding roughly why I was there, what my connection with the dead man was, who my client was. It didn't cheer him up any to hear that I was working for the Takamokus, but he let me stay with them while he questioned them. He sent for a young Korean officer to interrogate the Koreans in the group. Welland, who spoke fluent Japanese, translated the Japanese interviews. Dr. Han, the lone Chinese, struggled along on his own.

McGonnigal learned that the dead man's name was Peter Folger. He learned that people were milling around all the time watching one another play. He also learned that no one paid attention to anything but the game they were playing, or watching.

"The Japanese say the Go player forgets his father's funeral," Welland explained. "It's a game of tremendous concentration."

No one admitted knowing Folger outside the Go club. No one knew how he found out that the Takamokus hosted Go every Sunday.

My clients hovered tensely in the background, convinced that McGonnigal would arrest them at any minute. But they could add nothing to the story. Anyone who wanted to play was welcome at their apartment on Sunday afternoon. Why should he show a credential? If he knew how to play, that was the proof.

McGonnigal pounced on that. Was Folger a good player? Everyone looked around and nodded. Yes, not the best—that was clearly Dr. Han or Mr. Kim, one of the Koreans—but quite good enough. Perhaps first *kyu*, whatever that was.

After two hours of this, McGonnigal decided he was getting nowhere. Someone in the room must have had a connection with Folger, but we weren't going to find it by questioning the group. We'd have to dig into their backgrounds.

A uniformed man started collecting addresses while McGonnigal went to his car to radio for plainclothes reinforcements. He wanted everyone in the room tailed and wanted to call from a private phone. A useless precaution, I thought: the innocent wouldn't know they were being followed and the guilty would expect it.

McGonnigal returned shortly, his face angry. He had a bland-faced, square-jawed man in tow, Derek Hatfield of the FBI. He did computer fraud for them. Our paths had crossed a few times on white-collar crime. I'd found him smart and knowledgeable, but also humorless and overbearing.

"Hello, Derek," I said, without getting up from the cushion I was sitting on. "What brings you here?"

"He had the place under surveillance," McGonnigal said, biting off the words. "He won't tell me who he was looking for."

Derek walked over to Folger's body, covered now with a sheet, which he pulled back. He looked at Folger's face and nodded. "I'm going to have to phone my office for instructions."

"Just a minute," McGonnigal said. "You know the guy, right? You tell me what you were watching him for."

Derek raised his eyebrows haughtily. "I'll have to make a call first."

"Don't be an ass, Hatfield," I said. "You think you're impressing us with how mysterious the FBI is, but you're not, really. You know your boss will tell you to cooperate with the city if it's murder. And we might be able to clear this thing up right now, glory for everyone. We knew Folger worked for Hansen Electronic. He wasn't one of your guys working undercover, was he?"

Hatfield glared at me. "I can't answer that."

"Look," I said reasonably. "Either he worked for you and was investigating problems at Hansen, or he worked for them and you suspected he was involved in some kind of fraud. I know there's a lot of talk about Hansen's new Series J computer—was he passing secrets?"

Hatfield put his hands in his pockets and scowled in thought. At last he said to McGonnigal, "Is there someplace we can talk?"

I asked Mrs. Takamoku if we could use her kitchen for a few minutes. Her lips moved nervously, but she took Hatfield and me down the hall. Her apartment was laid out like mine, and the kitchens were similar, at least in appliances. Hers was spotless; mine has that lived-in look.

McGonnigal told the uniformed man not to let anyone leave or make any phone calls and followed us.

Hatfield leaned against the back door. I perched on a bar stool next to a high wooden table. McGonnigal stood in the doorway leading down the hall.

"You got someone here named Miyake?" Hatfield asked.

McGonnigal looked through the sheaf of notes in his hand and shook his head.

"Anyone here work for Kawamoto?"

Kawamoto is a big Japanese electronics firm, one of Mitsubishi's peers and a strong rival of Hansen in the mega-computer market.

"Hatfield. Are you trying to tell us that Folger was passing Series J secrets to someone from Kawamoto over the Go boards here?"

Hatfield shifted uncomfortably. "We only got onto it three weeks ago. Folger was just a go-between. We offered him immunity if he would finger the guy from Kawamoto. He couldn't describe him well enough for us to make a pickup. He was going to shake hands with him or touch him in some way as they left the building."

"The Judas trick," I remarked.

"Huh?" Hatfield looked puzzled.

McGonnigal smiled for the first time that afternoon. "The man I kiss is the one you want. You should've gone to Catholic school, Hatfield."

"Yeah. Anyway, Folger must've told this guy Miyake we were closing in." Hatfield shook his head disgustedly. "Miyake must be part of that group out there, just using an assumed name. We got a tail put on all of them." He straightened up and started back toward the hall.

"How was Folger passing the information?" I asked.

"It was on microdots."

"Stay where you are. I might be able to tell you which one is Miyake without leaving the building."

Of course, both Hatfield and McGonnigal started yelling at me at once. Why was I suppressing evidence, what did I know, they'd have me arrested. "Calm down, boys," I said. "I don't have any evidence. But now that I know the crime, I think I know how the information was passed. I just need to talk to my clients."

Mr. and Mrs. Takamoku looked at me anxiously when I came back to the living room. I got them to follow me into the hall. "They're not going to arrest you," I assured them. "But I need to know who turned over the Go board last week. Is he here today?"

They talked briefly in Japanese, then Mr. Takamoku said, "We should not betray guest. But murder is much worse. Man in orange shirt, named Hamai."

Hamai, or Miyake, as Hatfield called him, resisted valiantly. When the police started to put handcuffs on him, he popped another gelatin capsule into his mouth. He was dead almost before they realized what he had done.

Hatfield, impersonal as always, searched his body for the microdot. Hamai had stuck it to his upper lip, where it looked like a mole against his dark skin.

"How did you know?" McGonnigal grumbled, after the bodies had been carted off, and the Takamokus' efforts to turn their life savings over to me successfully averted.

"He turned over a Go board here last week. That troubled my clients enough that they asked me about it. Once I knew we were looking for the transfer of information, it was obvious that Folger had stuck the dot in the hole under the board. Hamai couldn't get at it, so he had to turn the whole board over. Today, Folger must have put it in a more accessible spot."

Hatfield left to make his top-secret report. McGonnigal followed his uniformed men out of the apartment. Welland held the door for me.

"Was his name Hamai or Miyake?" he asked.

"Oh, I think his real name was Hamai—that's what all his identification said. He must have used a false name with Folger. After all, he knew you guys never pay attention to each other's names—you probably wouldn't even notice what Folger called him. If you could figure out who Folger was."

Welland smiled; his bushy eyebrows danced. "How about a drink? I'd like to salute a lady clever enough to solve the Takamoku joseki unaided."

I looked at my watch. Three hours ago I'd been trying to think of something friendlier to do than watch the Bears get pummeled. This sounded like a good bet. I slipped my hand through his arm and went outside with him.

ROB KANTNER
MY BROTHER'S WIFE

February 1985

ROB KANTNER made his fiction debut in the pages of *AHMM* in 1982 with the first of his popular stories featuring Detroit blue-collar P.I. Ben Perkins. Kantner went on to publish *The Back-Door Man* in 1986 followed by eight other Perkins novels and numerous short stories, for which he has won four Shamus Awards from the Private Eye Writers of America. This story is vintage Perkins.

■

Don't blame me for not spotting Marybeth sooner. The bar was crowded, I was on a case, and most people, private detectives included, don't notice people in places where they don't expect to see them.

The case was one of those generally dreary prospective-employee background things. I was with a woman named Angie in a bar called Rushing the Growler, a rompin' stompin' burger and beer joint in the city of Frederick, Michigan. Angie was an ex-squeeze of the investigatee. They'd broken up bad, she was eager to talk, and she was a lady who liked her drinks, so I asked her what she'd have.

"Three-Hole Punch," she said to the bartender.

I lighted a cigar and stared into Angie's dark eyes. "What in heaven's name is that?"

She smiled. "The latest thing, Ben. A shot of 151 Bacardi, a shot of dry gin, and a splash of Golden Grain, shaken with pineapple-grapefruit juice over rocks in a tall glass with a maraschino cherry on top."

The bartender set it before her. I swear I saw the cubes smoking. No problem loosening *her* tongue, I thought. I ordered a beer, turned to Angie to begin the casual questioning, and in the far corner of the bar, just visible around the edge of the high back of a booth, I saw Marybeth.

She sat across from a broad-shouldered young man with short, smooth black hair. They were alone, and they were talking, and they didn't see me.

I watched them as I absentmindedly probed Angie for information about my subject, information that, under the terrifying momentum of Three-Hole Punch, she seemed glad to provide.

As we talked, I considered how perfect Rushing the Growler was for illicit meetings. Loud, crowded, smoky, big booths, lots of little alcoves. I was, after all, here on a somewhat illicit mission myself. The fact that it led to something more personal with Angie—albeit brief—is not important. I could do that. I wasn't married. Marybeth was. To my brother.

SINCE I GOT the information I needed from Angie that night, turned in my report the next day, and (not incidentally) got paid, there was no reason for me to go all the way back out to Frederick the next night. But I did anyhow. Marybeth showed up about seven, with her young man in tow. They sat at a secluded corner booth and talked and drank for nearly two hours. She didn't notice me. I wondered what she'd have done if she had.

And I wondered what I was going to do about it. For the next couple of days, I made a brave, determined attempt to do exactly nothing. None of your business, Ben. Stay out of it, Ben. Don't you have enough trouble of your own to handle, Ben? That routine.

But one thing I've never been able to do for very long is kid myself. I know my own cons too well. I'm a nosy bastard is the point. Which is, probably, why I'm a detective. I wondered how other detectives dealt with this kind of situation. Have to bring it up at the next meeting of the Greater Detroit Nosy Bastard Club, private detective division.

A few nights later, I rolled over to the Ford assembly plant in Wayne. A big lazy moon hung high in the hot, black summer sky as I parked three spaces down from a gleaming, sky blue Ford Econoline van. I nervously smoked a cigar as I waited, leaning against the hood of my Mustang. A bell shrieked from the distant plant, signaling shift-end, and men poured out, fired up their cars, and got the hell out of there. After a couple of minutes my brother, Bill Perkins, came strolling down the lane toward his van. I raised a hand and he nodded and continued toward me, black lunchbox hanging from one hand.

Bill's eight years older than me. We don't look much alike. He's short, stocky, almost totally bald now, with a narrow face and big nose and squinting eyes. He's placid of face, calm of voice, a man of slow, totally predictable movements. He wore a green shortsleeved dress shirt, snug slacks, highly polished black loafers. "Hey, Ben," he said as he reached me.

"Bill," I nodded. "Buy you a beer?"

"Why sure." I pulled a cold six of Stroh's off the front seat, snapped two loose, handed him one, and popped mine. Bill set his lunchbox on the hood of the Mustang and opened his beer as I leaned an elbow on the ragtop and took a gulp. "What brings you out this way?" Bill asked.

Impossible to answer truthfully because I didn't know myself. I mean, I knew, but I wasn't going to blab about having seen Marybeth twice in a saloon with a stranger. I was, so to speak, sounding him out. I didn't know what I expected to get done here, which is a dangerous way to do business. Carole Somers, a trial lawyer acquaintance of mine, says that the cardinal rule of examination is: Don't ask a question unless you already know the answer.

"Haven't seen you in a while," was my lame answer.

"Ee-yeah. Couple-three months. We doing Stapfer on the Fourth again, right?"

"Sure." This was about the only tradition my family had left. When we were boys, our daddy and Uncle Dan always took us fishing on Stapfer Lake on the Fourth of July, which was a couple of days off now. Bill and I continued the tradition even though Daddy died back in '63 and Uncle Dan was permanently disabled and living in a rest home (I mean, retirement community). "Uncle Dan coming along?" I asked.

"Talked to him yesterday," Bill answered. "Said he'd try." Uncle Dan hadn't come with us—had been physically unable to—for fifteen years. But we always invited him, and he always said he'd try.

I dropped my cigar on the dirty pavement and crushed it out with my boot. Over the rim of my beer can, I eyed my brother as I tipped beer into my mouth. His face was shrouded in shadow; his bald head gleamed in the moonlight. He leaned silent, placid, solid as a bridge abutment. I groped for words, for the angle that, in my investigating work, usually came easily, and could think of nothing. Bill was my brother, but as adults we were strangers. The few conversations we had over the course of a year fell into well-worn, predictable patterns. Cars and tools and baseball and the old neighborhood, none of which could help me find out what I wanted (not necessarily needed) to know.

The parking lot was silent now, afternoon men on their fast ride home through the dark, midnight men beginning their shift on the thumping, screaming, hot assembly line inside. Bill broke the silence. "Saw baby sister the other day."

He let the unasked question hang in the air. I hadn't seen Libby in two years, not since our Uncle Andrew died.

With just the slightest shrug, Bill sipped his beer and went on. "Took off a lot of weight. Looking damn good now. She got her a job counseling in one of those weight-loss places. Doin' good."

I set my empty beer can on the ragtop, fetched myself a fresh one and, as I popped it, asked casually, "How's Marybeth?"

"Fine, thanks."

"Still working that job out there?"

"City of Frederick police. Right. Just a typist, but the pay's good. You know them civil service jobs."

"Pretty long drive, though."

"Oh well, I-94 straight out, not too bad." Bill drained his beer. "She's staying out at her sister's in Jackson for a few days. Having a little visit, drive to work's a lot shorter from there."

Bill absently drummed his empty beer can with his thick fingers. I asked, "'Nother one?"

"Naw, better roll, Ben. Thanks." He handed me his empty, picked up his lunchbox, and headed toward the Econoline with that slow, rolling walk that reminded me so much of Daddy. Over his shoulder he called, "The landing at Stapfer. The Fourth, six A.M. sharp. Got it?"

"Yeah, bro." I gathered up the empties, tossed them into the back of the Mustang, and got out of there.

Driving through the hot night, I thought about Marybeth staying at her sister's in Jackson. A visit? Or had she left Bill? Or had he thrown her out? And what about the guy she was meeting at Rushing the Growler? What the hell gives here, anyhow?

It was none of my business, but it didn't feel right. I'd have to look into it, keep an eye out, and if something needed fixing, I'd sure God have to fix it.

IT WASN'T LIKE I was between jobs and had nothing better to do. My big corporate client had six more job applicants who needed checking out, at five hundred per, cash money. Carole Somers had called that morning about a client in Wayne County jail, charged with murder, thought maybe I could help. The outdoor maintenance work at Norwegian Wood was getting pretty intense, this being the height of the summer, lot of work to schedule and ass to kick. But I did as little as I could get away with the next day, drove like hell to Frederick during the supper hour, and by dusk, about the time Marybeth arrived with her Mister Wonderful, I was ready.

My battered old Canon, loaded with a fresh roll of twelve-hundred-speed print, worked great. I shot up all ten frames, getting virtually every angle except from directly overhead, as Marybeth and the man leaned close together over the table, talking, laughing, drinking drinks, absorbed in each other. Then I strolled out of there, unobserved by both.

I WAS BACK the next night, cameraless. I grabbed a stool at one corner of the bar and watched Marybeth and her swain as they went through the routine. The guy must have had a bladder of prodigious capacity, because it seemed like hours before he finally excused himself and went to the john. I followed him.

It was empty except for us. While the guy did his business at the far end, I busied myself combing my hair at the mirror, gambling that he was fastidious enough to wash up after. He was. I let him get his hands full of soapy lather before I said, "Think we can do some business, pal?"

He hardly glanced at me as he scrubbed. "Buzz off."

I shook my head regretfully. "Not good." I reached into my hip pocket, pulled out the nice, crisp, three-by-five color glossy, and dropped it on the aluminum shelf below the mirror in front of him. "That's what I'm selling," I said softly. "You interested?"

The picture was a tight shot of him and Marybeth, noses inches apart over the rough-hewn booth table in Rushing the Growler. I was quite proud of it. Good focus and composition, sharp and clear, with only available light yet.

He stopped scrubbing and studied the picture as the water rinsed his hands clean. He was a young fellow, younger than Marybeth—she's about my age—dark-haired with deep eyes and a thickly muscled, symmetrical, almost handsome face, the skin of which showed five o'clock shadow. He wore a light gray jacket, open-necked white shirt, and dark slacks. His tan could have come from the sun or a lamp, you just can't tell anymore. He shut off the water and flicked the wet off his hands and straightened to face me. He did not look happy.

I said: "For shame. See that ring on your finger? No, not the pinky ring, the one on the *next* finger there. That means you're married, remember? And so's she."

"What's your interest?" His voice was a toneless, husky whisper.

"Not financial, for once. It's just this. Get off her and stay off, and this goes no further."

He nodded, lips pressed tight over his good white teeth. Then he said, "Now I'd like to show *you* something, friend. I'm going into my inside jacket pocket, real slowly, fingers only. All right?"

I was unarmed and had made no threats of violence, but I nodded. He reached inside his jacket, came out with a small black wallet, and opened it. The badge gleamed, an embossed picture-ID next to it. Donald Boltz, special agent, Michigan Bureau of Investigation. I said, with more assurance than I felt right then, "That supposed to mean something important?"

"You know," he said, "there's a thing called obstruction of justice. There's another called interfering with an official investigation. I could mangle you lots of ways, ways you haven't even heard of yet. You follow?"

"I'm scared to death here. Really I am. So humor me."

"I'm on police business," he answered, closing the wallet and putting it away. "There's no funny stuff between her and me. Now, if you don't mind my asking, who in the hell are you?"

For some deep instinctive reason, probably because he would have died laughing, I did not show him my private detective license. I answered, "Ben Perkins. I'm her brother-in-law."

Boltz stared at me. Then he dumped his head back and laughed at the ceiling, even white teeth gleaming in the fluorescent light. I stood impassively, hands folded in front of me, wanting badly for some reason to hit him very hard. When he recovered, he mused, "Isn't that a riot? Out-of-the-way place like this . . . no suspicious eyes . . . her brother-in-law!"

"Yeah. Real thigh-slapper. What I'd like to know is, why is the MBI interested in Marybeth?"

He still smiled, but the humor had fled his eyes. "I don't have to waste my time explaining anything to you. She's your brother's wife, so fine, I've explained there's nothing personal going on and that's all you need to know." Boltz's jaw tightened. "Don't cross my path again. I get upset really easily."

He walked past me, brushing intentionally close, to the door and then out without looking back. I stared at the space he'd left, remembering his casual yet high-quality and expensively tailored suit, his six-hundred-dollar lizard-skin shoes, the gold pinky ring with diamond chips. For a policeman, Special Agent Donald Boltz seemed to pull down an abundance of disposable income.

DICK DENNEHY studied the picture through his aviator glasses. He snorted. "So. One of the glamour boys."

"How's that?" I asked.

Dennehy stared at me bleakly. He's a big, somewhat out of shape, grayish blond, wound tight with the cheerful malevolence of the career cop. He wore a gray suit—I believe he buys them by the gross at K-Mart—and the inevitable Lucky straight-end smoldered from the fingers of the hand in which he held the picture. We sat in a booth in Pringle's, the Novi saloon where we met once a week to straighten out the world.

Dennehy, eyes still on me, dropped the picture. "Glamour boys," he repeated. "I'm with the state police, remember? We're the ones who get called in on cases *after* these glamour-boy clowns with the 'Michigan Bureau of Investigation'"—he snarled the name—"screw them up."

"I get the picture." The barmaid expertly dropped another Signature and rum-and-Coke on our table. "Thanks, Cindy," I said absently. "So," I said to Dick as he took a pull from his drink, "since apparently you state police boys don't get along with the MBI, can I assume there's no way you can find out what—or if—Boltz is investigating that involves Marybeth?"

Dick made a gleeful, crooked smile. "O ye of little faith! Sure I can, my spies are everywhere. Be glad to." He slipped the picture into his jacket pocket, fired up another weed, leaned forward on his elbows, and asked quietly, "You think he's doing the dirty deed to her?"

"Hell, I don't know, Dick."

"What'll you do if it turns out he is?"

"Don't know that, either."

"Huh. Now that we're clear on what you don't know, tell me: what *do* you know, Ben?"

"I know what I feel. I feel like Boltz is a bad act. I got a real bad smell from him. I don't trust him—I don't trust much of anything anymore—but I trust that feeling." I stared over his shoulder at the window that fronted the place. "I feel like I have to watch out for Marybeth at this point."

"You don't mind my saying so, I didn't think you and your family were particularly close."

"We're not." I met his eyes. "But you still watch out for them."

THE NEXT MORNING I waited at the curb in front of the City of Frederick police department. At ten sharp, Marybeth Perkins came out the big revolving glass door, stopped on the steps, and scanned the street looking for me. She didn't spot me right away, because I was right there in plain sight. Then she grinned, waved, and walked toward me. She passed a tall, gray-haired, hump-shouldered uniformed man headed into the building and said cheerfully, "Good morning, Chief Harran." He nodded. I got a good look at him before he disappeared into the building. It isn't every day you get a good look at a chief of police, even of a small burg like Frederick. I was impressed.

It was a brilliantly clear hot day, and I had the Mustang's top down. Marybeth swung into the passenger seat with the agility of a dancer, slammed the door, and said, "I'm on break, I've got ten minutes. Drive." I fired up the motor and rolled away slowly.

Marybeth lighted an Eve cigarette from the dashboard lighter, hung her right elbow out the gunwale of the car, and looked at me. She was tan and freckled, thin and supple, whip-like, energized, and just Bill's height, which explains why she wore shoes like the flat brown dress sandals she had on today. Above that she wore pink snug slacks, and a ruffly white-on-white blouse with a gold pin inserted over her left breast. Her brown hair was a series of waves that ended neatly just above her shoulders. She had a keen mind and, sometimes, a sharp mouth, and I braced myself a little, wondering why she'd asked me to meet her here.

As I swung right on the Milan road, she said, "Don Boltz told me about your conversation with him."

"Look, it was strictly by accident I saw you two there—"

She interrupted with an edge in her voice. "You thought I was stepping out on Bill."

"The thought crossed my mind. But—"

She waved her hand. "Never mind. I'm going to tell you what Don told me not to tell anybody." She breathed deeply. "I'm helping the MBI investigate our department. On deep background."

I glanced at her. "Funny stuff going on?"

She drew on her cigarette and said quietly, "Worse than that, Ben. It's the chief. He's dirty. Dirty as can be. I've been there eight years, I've seen a lot, and it starts right at the top. Kickbacks, protection, grease, you name it. I looked the other way for a long, long time. Finally it got to be too much. So I contacted the MBI."

"Does Bill know?"

She stared at me, composing her thoughts, and said, "No. Don said not to tell *anybody*. Besides . . . well, you know Bill."

"Sure I do. But go on."

She took a last offhand hit from her half-smoked cigarette and flicked it away from the car as I made a right into an old residential neighborhood and circled a big block, headed back toward the police station. "Bill's very . . . traditional. He's a quiet man. He absolutely detests confrontations. He avoids trouble. He's very dutiful, a good husband, Ben, but underneath he's scared. He worries and frets. He doesn't understand trouble, and he doesn't understand people who get into it. You know what I mean?"

It rang true. It explained part of the narrowness of my relationship with my own brother, the tight groove of conversation limited to cars and tools and baseball and the old neighborhood. Bill had really liked Charlotte, my first serious girlfriend, and never understood why I didn't marry her, had never married anybody. He'd never understood why I left my assembly line job to be a gofer for a union boss. During the endless federal investigation of my boss's racketeering and tax-evasion activities, in which I was a notorious and uncooperative material witness, Bill had refused to speak to me. He found my private detective work incomprehensible and never asked about it. For two guys who'd slept in the same room for better than ten years, we'd grown about as far apart as two people can get.

I right-turned on red onto a major street. The police station loomed ahead on the right, and I threaded through traffic toward it. Marybeth said pensively, "I don't make a habit of keeping secrets from Bill. But this time I have to, at least till it's over. And I'm asking you not to tell him, either, ever; you let me do it when the time is right. He's your brother, but I'm his wife, and I'm calling the shots. You've got to help me."

I stopped in front of the station and turned to her. "Of course I'll help you. Anytime, anywhere, anyhow."

She had her door half open when she froze, turned, leaned over, and kissed me. I gave her a squeeze and patted her back. She was warm and smelled good, but it was brother-sister stuff, no more. I eased her away and said, "Just one thing. I know the street, I know this work. Something doesn't feel right about this thing, this Boltz fellow. You take real good care, Marybeth. Stay in touch." I grinned. "*I* don't mind trouble. It's what I do."

She smiled, nodded, got out, and walked across the sidewalk toward the door. "I'll be watching out for you," I called.

I HELD THE tester up and examined the colors. The pH was right on, the chlorine a tad down. I threw three concentrated chlorine eggs into the skimmer, screwed down the lid, and headed back to

Building One of Norwegian Wood as a battalion of kids carrying towels and flotation devices screamed out the side door toward the pool. The phone in the maintenance office was ringing when I got there. It was Dick Dennehy.

"You hollered?" he asked.

"I got the story already. MBI's investigating the Frederick P.D. It's dirty, top to bottom, the chief included. Right?"

"Wrong," he answered equably.

"No, I'm not. Marybeth told me all about it." I drew up short as Dick's meaning sunk in. "No word of it out there?"

"Nope. Nothing like that. Boltz is a soldier, nothing more. His thing is chop shops, bad-check artists, stuff like that. Listen, Ben, Boltz isn't senior enough to be doing something like a background inquiry into a police department. Even if he were, he wouldn't be doing it alone. There'd be a task force. And the state police would probably be doing it, not the MBI." Static whirred in the line for a second. "This smells like leftover fish, pal."

The phone receiver felt very warm and damp in my hand. I struggled to sound certain, and failed. "Maybe your contacts are uninformed."

"Don't underestimate me. My contacts are top-aiders. They'd know, no matter how quiet it was. Whatever Boltz is up to, he's in business for himself."

"I don't like the sound of it."

"You'll like *this* even less. Boltz is thought of as an operator. A little fast, a little flashy, they think he's been off the reservation more than once, if you catch my drift, only they've never gotten the goods on him. No idea what his game is right now, but if I were you, it being the sister-in-law involved, I'd be extra careful."

"I'll do that, Dick. Thanks."

"Chalk up one to that instinct of yours."

"I'll take a bow later, if it's all right with you. You, uh, you want a piece of this, maybe?"

"Thought you'd never ask. Hell, I'd like nothing better than to find dirty hands on an MBI guy. Tell you what. In this deal, the Michigan State Police is at your service. You just let me know, and we'll, like, charge over the hill to the sound of bugles, flags streaming."

FORTUNATELY, IT was a weekend. Everything was under control at Norwegian Wood, and my corporate client didn't expect progress on his applicants till Monday. So I had plenty of time for real excitement: following Donald Boltz around.

He worked at the MBI substation in Adrian. He lived in a swanky lakefront condo near there. He drove thirty-plus Gs worth of loaded Audi 5000. I literally took up residence in my Mustang. I lived on drive-through Wendy's and Macs, washed up in gas station johns, slept stiff and cramped across the bucket seats, and tailed Boltz real smooth, real careful.

Problem was, he didn't go anywhere, or do anything, suspicious.

By Sunday evening I was a wrinkle-clothed, sore-muscled, aromatic, exhausted mess. And for it I had to show exactly nothing. And though he'd gotten in his car in the late afternoon and set off northeast, in the general direction of Detroit, my initially rising excitement dimmed considerably when he ended up at the K-Mart in Westland. K-Mart, for God's sake.

He knew what I looked like, so I hung way back from him in the crowded store as he strolled back to the men's clothes area and began browsing. I kept several rows of clothes between us, engaged with him in a long-distance, surreptitious dance of surveillance, while he leafed in a casual, almost bored fashion through racks of trousers and shirts and jackets. Suddenly—a little *too* suddenly, considering how lackadaisical he'd been operating till then—he selected a snappy green blazer and a pair of green-checked slacks and walked swiftly to a pair of freestanding dressing closets. The one on the left was closed and occupied; the other one was open, and he locked himself inside.

Crowds swirled around me. Muzak blared from loudspeakers, interrupted by an announcer pitching blue-light specials. Moms herded gaggles of kids. Teenage girls in cutoffs and tank tops floated along in a daze of nubile youth. I watched the closets for what seemed like a long time. Then the door on the left opened and a man stepped out. Tall, gray-haired, hump-shouldered, dressed casually in civilian clothes. Carl Harran, chief of police, City of Frederick.

He looked around quickly, then walked away into the crowd while I stared at him, frozen.

After a minute, the right-hand door opened and Donald Boltz came out. His hands were empty except for a business-sized envelope, which he tucked into his inside jacket pocket as he strutted toward the front of the store and away.

The single pay phone at the entrance to the store was being used by a skinny teenage kid in a whacked-off T-shirt and jogging shorts, grinning and whispering into the receiver as he leaned against the glass wall. I took the receiver away from him with one hand, handed him a quarter with the other, growled, "Call her back in a minute," then broke the connection and began to dial as he stared incredulously at me. The phone rang in my ear as the kid started to say something, but one look from me stifled him. Finally the ringing stopped and Marybeth said, "Hello?"

Thank God.

WE SLOGGED ankle-deep up the steep incline of an enormous sand mountain. Beyond us sprawled the dunes and rubble piles and the cratered landscape of the abandoned sand and gravel quarry. The rusted snout of a huge crane reached high into the black sky. A couple of tin buildings, roofs sagging, stood sentry at opposite ends of the flat, sandy yard far, far below us. There was no one there. We stopped at the bluff and steppped back, panting from the exertion, Dick Dennehy most of all.

Jerry Mooney, Dennehy's squat, short, bull-shouldered partner (the term "brick outhouse" was coined with him in mind), adjusted the strap of his walkie-talkie, checked his watch, and said in a hoarse whisper, "Ten minutes to three. Ten minutes to three A.M., on the Fourth of July. Jesus Christ." He looked at me in the darkness. "Your theory better hold up, Perkins."

I retorted, "All I know is, Marybeth told me that Boltz told her to meet him here tonight. Something real fishy's going on, believe me. Anyhow, if I'm right, for you state police guys it'll be a dream come true. You'll catch an MBI guy engaged in a criminal act."

"He's right, Jerry," Dennehy said.

"Don't worry," I added. "If this works out, I don't want any credit for it, hear? It's your collar."

"*Our* collar?" Dennehy snorted. "Hear that, Jer?"

"I heard that. Hee-hee. *Our* collar. Right."

Dennehy checked the time. "Everybody in place?"

"Oughtta be," Mooney answered. He slogged through the sand to the bluff, peered over, and said tensely, "Whoa. Here she comes."

Dennehy and I crawled to the bluff, flanking Mooney, and looked down. Marybeth's light-blue Escort sedan, lights off, rolled down the narrow, weedy, sandy lane from our right and parked next to one of the tin buildings.

Jerry Mooney whispered into his walkie-talkie. Dennehy kept his eyes on the woman, who wore a light poplin raincoat, as she got out of the Escort and stood alongside it, and got out his gleaming Colt Python. My heart was thumping as I pulled my .45 automatic from the waistband against my spine and cocked it. There was no need to work the action; I carried a live round under the hammer.

The woman leaned against the door of the Escort, face indistinct in the half moonlight, layered brown hair flowing down to her shoulders. An engine hummed from our right, and a black Mercury sedan approached the tin building and stopped near the Escort. Its engine kept running as the driver's door opened and a man got out.

The moonlight caught the man's features and I said, "That's not Boltz! It's Harran!"

Chief Carl Harran wheeled, raised a .38 revolver over the roof of the Mercury, and shot the woman five times. The flares from the snout of the revolver flashed well in advance of the boom of the shots. The woman went down.

"Let's do it!" Mooney shouted into the walkie-talkie. As the three of us charged over the bluff and down the sandy slope, a siren wailed to our right, and two state police cars roared up the lane toward the chief, headlights illuminating him as he jerked his head around wildly. From our left, another police car swerved on the sandy lane toward him, cutting off that escape route. He hurled his empty revolver away and ran diagonally to our right. I skidded to a halt, dropped to a crouch, and fired three times. Even in the hands of a marksman, which I am not, the .45 auto is ineffective at that range, but the plumes of sand from the heavy slugs bursting around him were convincing, and he skidded to a halt and sprawled into the weedy sand. The cars stopped, the doors flung open, and the policemen converged on him, weapons extended warily.

Breathing hard, I dropped my gun hand to my side and walked over to the Escort. Up this close, the woman looked little like Marybeth. She was on her feet, the bullet-riddled raincoat open, showing the heavy pleated armored vest. I grinned at her and she grinned back and gave me the thumb's up. Behind me, a woman's voice called, "Ben?" and I turned and Marybeth Perkins, who'd been in the back of one of the state police cars, waved and ran into my arms so hard she nearly knocked me down. I held her and she held me and we said nothing, but when she finally stepped back, my cheeks were wet from her tears.

Dick Dennehy came up to us as Jerry Mooney directed the loading of the chief into one of the cars by the other officers. "Harran's singing like a bird," he told us grimly. "Boltz sold Marybeth out to Harran as an informant in return for ten big ones. Jerry 'n' I are going to pick Boltz up now. Fun, *fun!* Wanna come along?"

"I do," Marybeth said.

I checked my watch. "Not me, thanks. I got a date."

"At four in the morning?" Dick demanded.

"Fishing," I grinned. "See y'all."

IT WAS FIVE after six and the sky was brightening fast when I arrived at the landing on Stapfer Lake. Bill's green seventeen-footer with its Chrysler outboard bobbed in the water at the end of the landing. His blue Ford Econoline van dragging the empty trailer was parked in a V on the gravel lot. Bill Perkins himself sat patiently on the rear bumper of the van, wearing a narrow-brimmed canvas hat, chambray shirt, dark blue slacks, and knee-length rubber boots. He looked at me calmly as I walked up to him. "You're late," he said.

"Sorry."

He rose and we walked down to his boat. It was fully equipped with two sets of tackle, a full bait buckle, nets and anchors, and extra gas and oil, and all the rest. Good old thorough Bill. As he made ready to cast off the boat, I said, "Reckon Uncle Dan's not coming, huh?"

"Reckon not."

I climbed clumsily into the boat. "One of these days, Bill."

He gripped the transom, dug his boots into the wet sand, shoved the boat out into the water, and climbed nimbly in. "Yeah, bro. One of these fine days."

We fished all day, didn't catch much, and talked about cars, tools, baseball, and the old neighborhood. Back at his house, we devoured Marybeth's terrific steak dinner, and I got home early. I don't know if she ever told Bill the Harran/Boltz story or not. I've never asked. It's none of my business.

DOUG ALLYN

FINAL RITES

December 1985

THIS STORY WAS Doug Allyn's first publication, and it won him the Robert L. Fish Award for Best First Short Story. It introduced Lupe Garcia, a Detroit policeman who would go on to be featured in *The Cheerio Killings* and *Motown Underground*. Allyn has written over two dozen stories for *AHMM* and is a reader favorite. In addition to his writing career, Allyn plays in a rock band called The Devil's Triangle, along with his wife.

■

He didn't look much like the law. In his grubby sweatsuit and sneakers he looked more like a Class C high school coach during a losing season. Snoring softly, feet on his cluttered desk, a Detroit Tigers baseball cap tipped forward over his eyes—Norman Rockwell would have loved it. I rapped on the desk.

"Sheriff LeClair? I'm Sergeant Garcia. Lupe Garcia."

One eye blinked open, briefly. "They're not here."

"I haven't told you what I want yet." I eased cautiously down on a battered office chair upholstered in argyle blanket, wondering why I'd bothered to wear my good suit.

"Algoma's a small town. . . . Garcia, is it? I found a note when I came in this morning said a guy from the Organized Crime Task Force was flying up from Detroit to see me. I take it you're him. I also take it you're here about Roland Costa and his son, since the only thing anybody from Motown wants to talk to me about is them. If I need help on a hot car or a runaway, nobody gives me the time of day. Anyway, they're not here. They were in town a couple of weeks ago to bury Charlie, I haven't seen 'em since."

"I'm not surprised. Neither has anyone else."

He tipped his baseball cap back and looked at me for the first time. We were of an age, but he had more miles on him. A lot more. His eyes were red-rimmed and he looked exhausted.

"Are you saying they've disappeared?"

"They had Charlie brought to Algoma for the funeral," I said, "and that's the last time anybody saw them."

"So they've disappeared," he shrugged. "That's not uncommon for people in their line of work, is it?"

"Did you see them when they were here?"

"Difficult to miss 'em. They were driving a Lincoln limo that must've been a block long. We don't see many cars like that up here in the boondocks."

"Was a woman traveling with them?"

"No woman. Just Roland Costa and Rol Junior. They had a room at the Dewdrop Inn the day of the funeral, and they were alone. Why?"

"Charlie Costa had a girlfriend, Cindy Kessel. She's been talking to the DA's office about buying immunity for herself with information about Charlie's operations. She's missing, too."

He grunted, massaging his stubbled face with work-roughened paws. I noticed the single gold strand around his right wrist. "Look, I'm afraid I'm not really awake yet," he said. "A little retarded kid wandered away from Camp Algoma yesterday. Found her at sunup this morning, in good shape considering, but I haven't been to bed, and I've gotta wait on a call from the National Guard commander to tell him we won't need any troops for the search. Tell you what, why don't you grab breakfast across the street at Tubby's, and I'll be along as soon as I can."

"If they stayed at a local motel, I could . . ."

"Look, Garcia, this isn't Detroit. This is my town. I said they're not here and they're not. Now maybe we can get a line on 'em, but you're a stranger here, so nobody's gonna tell you squat and they might just forget what they do know. So get yourself a cuppa coffee and wait for me, okay? Please?"

"All right, I'll wait a bit. Don't be too long."

"You get homesick you can sit in the supermarket parking lot and sniff the exhaust fumes. I'll be over as soon as I can." He tipped his cap back down and was asleep before I was out the door.

He was right about one thing at least. Algoma was definitely a small town. A single paved street lined with tacky little shops, supermarket at one end, self-service gas station at the other. Like most northern Michigan towns it had probably been a lumber camp once; God only knew what kept its economy afloat now.

Tubby's had no yogurt, no fresh granola, and no air conditioning. The pale August sunlight beating through the smeared windows made the room considerably warmer than my toast, which wasn't very, and I shed my tie and sportcoat. Passed the time trying to decide whether the place was named after the waitress or the cook. It was a tossup. LeClair came in just as my third glass of iced tea arrived. He'd pinned his badge on his cap.

"Christ," he said, sliding into the red vinyl booth. "My call didn't get through, so about four o'clock I got sixteen National Guardsmen arriving on a wild goose chase, or I should say, *another* wild goose chase, counting yours. Okay, so you wanna fill me in?" The waitress brought him coffee in a mug with a chip out of it, and he nodded his thanks.

"I already have," I said. "They came here. They apparently never came back. That's really all we know."

"So what brings you all the way up here? You got a warrant for 'em or anything?"

"No, but if I can find the girl, we may just get a shot at them. We know they're into shylocking and narcotics, but they're very cautious people. Without the girl . . . anyway, it's fairly basic police procedure to keep track of the bad guys."

"No kidding? Gosh, I wish I had something to take notes on. You see, I usually wait till folks do something illegal, and then I arrest 'em. Pretty unsophisticated, I guess."

"Why did they bring Charlie all the way up here to be buried?"

"Roland and Charlie grew up here. Their old man was a bootlegger back in the thirties, or so I'm told. After Prohibition he moved on to bigger things in Detroit, but the family still has a good-sized cottage on the river. They come up for a month or so in the summer, and sometimes during hunting season."

"You know them then? Personally, I mean."

"Yeah," he said, sipping his coffee, "I've known 'em since I was a kid, and everybody else in this town, too. So?"

"So nothing. I was just asking. Look, have you got some kind of a complex about being from the sticks? Or don't you like Chicanos, or what?"

He carefully placed his coffee cup on the table between us and took a deep breath. "Garcia, I'm tired. I've been up for over thirty hours now. I know nothing happened to those clowns in Algoma, because if a chipmunk craps in the woods around here, I hear about it. I'd like to go home, go to bed, maybe say hello to my wife so she remembers who I am, but instead I'm gonna nursemaid you around until you're satisfied there's nothing here, because it's part of my job and because I noticed your Vietnam bracelet. Okay? But don't expect me to be cheery about it. I haven't got the energy."

"Terrific," I said. "So why don't we get on with it, and I can be on my way. Where do you suggest we start?"

"We see Faye at the Dewdrop," he said, rising, gulping the last of his coffee. I noticed he didn't bother to pay for it. I paid for mine.

FAYE AND THE Dewdrop Inn were like a couple who'd been married too long. They resembled each other, and both had seen better days. Her red hair was carelessly rinsed, matching the blush of surface capillaries in her cheeks, and both she and the ramshackle motel needed tidying up. If she was pleased to see us, she managed to conceal it.

"Morning, Faye. I need a look at your slips, if you don't mind."

"Wouldn't matter if I did, would it? Here, help yourself." She pushed a battered recipe file box across the counter.

"Roland Costa and Junior stayed here the day of Charlie's funeral, is that right?"

"If that's what it says there. No law against it, is there? They add a little class to this town, you ask me." Her diction had the forced precision of a serious drinker.

"There's no checkout time on the card. When did they leave?"

"Hell, Ira, there's no times for half the people that stay here. I can't be at the desk every minute. Folks pay in advance and that's what I'm in business for, not to . . ."

"What time do you *think* they left?" LeClair interrupted.

"I already told you I don't know," she said sullenly. "Now if you don't mind, I got things to do."

He stared at her for a moment, frowning. She traced a gouge in the scarred countertop as though she'd never seen it before.

"All right, Faye," he nodded, flipping the box lid shut. "I guess that'll do it. For now."

"GEE," I SAID, "it's a good thing you came along, LeClair. She might not have told me a thing."

"She seems a bit . . . edgy," he conceded, keeping his eyes on the dirt road ahead as he skillfully piloted my rented sedan through the potholes on the road north from the village. Except for an occasional farmhouse, the countryside was as empty of people as the back of the moon.

"Faye's been known to be a bit light-fingered with her guests' belongings," he added. "That's probably all it was."

"I'll keep that in mind."

"No need to," he said curtly. "With luck you won't be in town long enough to need a room. We'll visit the cemetery and talk to the groundskeeper, Hec Michaud, and that should do it. You can get back to Motown, and maybe I can get to bed."

He slowed as we approached a line of elderly houses huddled beside a clapboard church and turned in. The cemetery covered most of a hill behind the church, an island in a sea of cornfields. The tombstones were a hodgepodge of styles and sizes, but the lanes were swept, the grass neatly trimmed, and not everyone in it was dead.

Two men were working on a plot about halfway up the hillside, or to be precise, one man was working, digging mechanically in a waist-deep grave, while the other sat with his back against a weathered headstone sipping from a can of generic beer. He was fortyish, barrel-shaped, with a stubbled moonface and wispy spikes of steel-gray hair poking out from beneath his greasy engineer's cap. He lumbered to his feet as we climbed up, smiling with beery good fellowship. "Welcome to Lovedale, gents. It ain't much as cemeteries go, but it's home. Hey, Paulie, quit diggin' for a minute. We got comp'ny."

The digger was younger, mid-thirties, lanky, an open apple-pie face and sandy hair. A deep welt of a scar ran from his left temple to the nape of his neck, the hair bordering it bone white. Despite the heat of the day, his sweatstained denim work shirt was buttoned at the cuffs and throat. He clambered eagerly out of the hole with a grin like an April morning.

"Hey, Ira, good to see you."

"Good to see you too, Paulie. Looks like Hec's got you doing most of the work, as usual."

"Ahh, Paulie don't mind," the beer drinker said. "Strong as an ox and twice as smart. Right, Paulie?"

"Sure, Hec. You want me to keep shovelin'?"

"Take a break, Paulie," LeClair said. "I've got some questions for you both." Hec's smile remained fixed, but his grip tightened on the beer can.

"You want a beer, sheriff? Paulie, run up to the toolshed and get Ira a cold one."

"I don't want a beer, Hector, and Paulie isn't paid to be your errand boy. I want to know . . ."

"Who's this guy?" Hec asked, nodding warily toward me. "Maybe we don't wanna answer no questions with him here."

"This is Sergeant Garcia from Detroit. We're working together."

"What kinda work you gonna be doin?" Hec sneered. "Bean pickin' season's over."

LeClair pushed two fingers into the heavier man's chest, backing him up. Michaud lost his footing in the loose earth and sat down hard in the open grave. Without spilling his beer. He stared up at LeClair more in surprise than anger, and a momentary flicker of satisfaction showed in his eyes.

"You had no call to do that, Ira," he said slowly, "none at all."

"Maybe not, Hec," LeClair said, kneeling at the edge of the grave, "but there are a few things I've been meaning to discuss with you for a while, and today's as good a day as any. If I were you, I'd just stay in that hole for a bit while we have our little talk. Paulie, you take Sergeant Garcia up to the toolshed and get him a beer. He'll have some questions for you, and you answer 'em. Okay?"

"Do what he says, Paulie," Hec said from the grave. "Maybe he'll wanna talk to Billy, too, while you're up there."

I WAS PUFFING when we reached the toolshed. The climb hadn't affected Paulie at all. He took two beers from a cheap foam cooler and handed me one. "You in Vietnam?" he asked. I nodded.

"I thought so. I seen your bracelet. Ira's got one, too. I been meaning to get one, but . . . hey, you know, I had a friend there who was Mexican. I think he had a lotta names. You got a lotta names, too?"

"Sure," I said. "Lupe Jose Andrew Mardo Flores Garcia." My saints' names rolled off my tongue with surprising ease. I hadn't spoken them in years.

"Flores," he exclaimed eagerly, "hey, that was my friend's name. It means 'flower,' right?" I nodded, and I couldn't help smiling. His mood was contagious.

"Well, okay, Flower, why don't we pick out a comfortable hunk o' dirt here and we can sit and drink our beers. Ira said you wanted to ask me something?"

"Maybe you should ask Billy to come over," I said, glancing around uncertainly. "That way I won't have to ask the questions twice."

"You can ask him from here if you talk loud enough," he said. "He's buried over there by the fence next to Major Gault."

I took a long, thoughtful pull at my beer before glancing over at him. He was watching my reaction out of the corner of his eye, deadpan. "Gotcha," he said softly, the smile finally breaking through. "Don't worry, Flower, I'm not bananas. I talk to Billy sometimes, but only to get a rise out of Hec. I know he's dead. I damn near died with him. We was friends in high school, got drafted together, same outfit in 'Nam. We was even in the same foxhole when this Cong grenade drops in. We both tried to throw the damn thing out and wound up knocking ourselves cockeyed instead. It would have been pretty funny except then the grenade went off, and Billy came here to Lovedale and I wound up at the vet's facility in Grand Rapids for two years. Believe it or not, it's nicer here at Lovedale."

"How long have you been working here?"

"I'm not really sure," he said, frowning. "Major Gault's been here since 1864 or '62, and Billy's stone says 1973, but I'm not very good at numbers anymore, so I can't say exactly how long I've been here. That's a funny thing about cemeteries. Time doesn't matter much anyway. Like, the major and Billy lived maybe a hundred years apart, but now they're here together, probably swapping war stories and stuff. At least, I hope so." He lapsed into silence, sipping his beer.

"About three weeks ago there was a funeral here. Charles Costa's. Do you remember that?"

"Sure I remember it. It's only numbers I have trouble with, things like that."

"Sorry, I didn't . . . well, anyway, were both you and Hector working that day?"

"Nah, just me. It was on a Saturday, and Hec don't like to work Saturdays. It was a funny one, though."

"What do you mean, funny?"

"It was the biggest send-off I ever seen. See that big ugly hunk of marble with the cedars planted around it, like they were keeping it separate from the riffraff in the rest of the cemetery? That's Costa's. Really something, isn't it. And you shoulda seen his casket. It must've been standard size, but it sure looked bigger, burnished copper with burled walnut inserts. Probably weighed a ton. Maybe that was the problem."

"Problem?"

"After the funeral, the director couldn't get the mechanism that lowers the box to work, but that isn't what I meant about its being funny. The funeral director wasn't a local guy, he was from Detroit, Claudio something or other, and he must've had a dozen assistants with him, dressed like headwaiters and scrambling around here like a school gym on prom night putting out flowers and stuff. Then, after all that, nobody came. Just Rol Costa Jr. and his old man. Just the two of 'em."

"They were here, then? You saw them?"

"Yeah, I know Rol from school, and I've seen his old man around. They showed up in this big Lincoln, stuck old Charlie in the ground, and that was that."

"And no one was here other than the funeral people, you, and Hec?"

"I already told you Hec wasn't here," he said, with a trace of irritation. "Hec don't like working Saturdays."

"It looks like you do most of the work even when he's here."

"Could be," he shrugged. "Look, maybe Hec takes advantage of me a little, but I don't care. I'm just glad to be out of that hospital and doing something, even if it's only digging graves. Besides, sometimes Hec stands up for me, like with old lady Stansfield. She's got a house near the west fence, and she don't like me, you know? When we had a complaint about me working without a shirt, I knew who it was, and I asked Hec to talk to her about it and he did. He don't get many complaints about my work, though. This place looks pretty nice, doesn't it, Flower? Maybe not to move into, but you know what I mean."

"It looks good, Paulie," I agreed. "Anybody can see you work very hard. When did the Costas leave?"

"Right after the funeral, I guess. I'm not sure, 'cause I was asleep behind the toolshed."

"Thanks," I said, "I appreciate your help." Without thinking I slipped the thin gold band from my wrist and handed it to him.

"Hey, Flower," he said, his eyes widening, "you don't have to give me nothing. I mean, I'm just glad to have somebody to talk to, you know?"

"It's all right, Paulie, I . . . I've got another one at home. Take it, please."

"Well, thanks. I've been meaning to get one, but . . . well, thanks a lot." He eased it carefully on his wrist, admiring it as it caught the glint of the morning sun. "I wish I had something I could . . ." He fumbled in the pocket of his faded work shirt. "Here, you want a couple of joints? It's not bad stuff."

I accepted one of the crudely rolled cigarettes and sniffed it. It was pure, uncut. "Where did you get these?"

"You ever do a long boonie recon in 'Nam?" he asked, smiling slyly.

I nodded.

"Well, that's how I got it," he said. "I just lived off the bounty of the land."

I glanced around, and for a moment the cemetery and the fields around it had the scent of danger, like the jungle, but only for a moment. "I think I'd better be going," I said, getting to my feet. "I see the sheriff's helping Hector out of his hole."

WE DROVE MOST of the way back to town in silence, each of us in his own thoughts. "Paulie said they were here, and then they left," I said finally. "You get anything from Hector?"

"Nope, and I don't think he'll vote for me in the next election, either. He said he wasn't here the day of the funeral. That about wrap it up for you? I can't think of anyone else."

"I can't, either. Look, I appreciate your help on this thing."

"No charge," he sighed, "it comes with the territory. You know, if I'd been awake when you came in this morning, I could have saved us some running around. The Costas are a hard lot, all of 'em, and they grew up around here. There's no way anything could have happened to 'em in a place like Algoma."

"You're probably right," I said. "Still, checking things out is part of the job. Paulie mentioned a funeral director named Claudio. Mean anything to you?"

"Rigoni's Funeral Home. They do work out here sometimes, but they're based in Detroit. Legitimate, as far as I know."

"I'll look them up when I get home, but it doesn't sound like much."

He pulled the sedan over to the curb in front of his office. "Well, here we are. Sorry things didn't work out for you, but I told you so. You going straight back?"

"Maybe I'll do a little sightseeing," I said. "I don't get out of the city much, and you've got a nice little town here."

"We like it. If you need anything else, I'll be in my office, at least until those Guardsmen get here. I'll have to thank 'em for coming, I guess, even if it's for nothing. I really oughta find an honest job. Have a good trip, Garcia." He flipped me a mock salute and strode off.

I drove around for a bit, wondering what people found to keep them in a town six blocks long. I pulled in at a storefront office with "Village of Algoma" stenciled crudely on a plywood sign in the window.

The clerk literally dragged himself to the counter, a stroke-shattered old hulk of a man with a paralyzed leg, an arm strapped to his belt, and one side of his weatherbeaten face sagging like so much melted wax. His cheek was further distorted by a huge cud of tobacco. He leaned his good arm on the counter and spat a stream of brown juice in the general direction of the spittoon against the wall. Dead center. "Do somethin' for ya?" he asked.

"I'd like to see a plat book for the county, please."

"Got one right here." He pulled a slim folder from beneath the counter and flipped it open to Algoma County. "Some of these titles ain't current, but I know most of the landholders around here. Any particular parcel in mind?"

I traced the line of Lovedale Road north on the map with a fingertip. "Here, the land around the cemetery."

"Well, there are houses north and south of it, but . . ."

"No, I'm interested in these fields around it to the west. All of that property seems to be owned by . . . somebody named Lund?"

"Max Lund," he nodded, "He don't live in Algoma no more, but he still owns the land."

"It has corn growing on it now."

"He's farming it on shares. I believe Hec Michaud is working some of it. He put in some raggedy-ass corn this spring. Hec ain't much of a farmer."

"I thought he was in charge of the cemetery."

"He is. You from the city?"

I nodded.

"Figured so," he said, and spat another stream toward the spittoon. "You see, in a town like Algoma, a man can't make it with just one job. Most folks do a little of this and that to get by. Hec docs the cemetery, paints houses, and does a little farmin' now and again."

"How about the sheriff?" I asked. "He do a little farming, too?"

"Sometimes," he said, examining me carefully with his good eye, "sometimes he does."

LeClair was sleeping in his office chair, his grubby jogging shoes up on his desk. I let the door slam behind me, and he jerked awake with a start.

"You back again?" he said, groggy and still half asleep. "I thought you'd left. Those Guardsmen here yet?"

"I haven't seen them," I said, sitting on the edge of his desk. "I've got a little time to kill before my plane'll be ready. Thought maybe we could have a good-bye smoke." I took the joint from my shirt pocket and placed it on his desk. "Have one on me. It's bomb weed."

He stared at me blankly.

"Go ahead. You'll feel better and nobody's here but us cops."

A slow flush rose above the collar of his T-shirt. "Garcia," he said tightly, "I noticed Paulie was wearing your bracelet when you came down the hill today. That was a nice thing to do. So, because of that, and since you're a city boy and don't know any better, I'll give you thirty seconds to flip that reefer in the wastebasket and get the hell out of my office, or I'm gonna throw your butt in jail."

"Open it up," I said, "take a look at the weed."

Still scowling, he tore the paper apart, spilling the leaves on his desk. He picked one up and sniffed it. "This is green and it hasn't been cut. I'd guess it's local, right? Where did you get it?"

"From a guy who knows how to live off the land. As an informant, he'll have to remain anonymous, of course."

"Sure," he said dryly. "Gee, I wonder who it could be? Where did he find it?"

"In the cornfields near the cemetery. There's an area to the southwest where maybe every fourth plant is marijuana."

"Hec Michaud!" he said, slamming his fist on the desktop. "I knew something was wrong out there today! I could feel it in my bones, but I thought it had something to do with the Costas. How much do you figure is out there?"

"I don't know, a couple of bales, maybe. Enough."

"And you thought maybe I was in on it, didn't you?"

"Sorry," I shrugged. "Like you said, I'm from out of town."

"*'Sorry'* doesn't quite cover it. Where the hell do you get off assuming I was corrupt? Or don't they have honest cops in the city anymore?"

"You're right, it was stupid of me. I mean, what kind of graft could you get around here anyway? Chickens and ducks?"

"I manage to scrape by on my salary. Dumb, maybe, but . . ."

"Look, I've already apologized, okay? And you might as well accept it, 'cause it's all you get. You'd have wondered, too."

"Yes," he conceded, grudgingly, "I suppose I would have. All right, apology accepted, for now. At least I'll have something for those Guardsmen to do when they get here. You want in on the collar?"

"No, it's not what I came here for, and I haven't had anything to eat all day. I'm gonna pop over to Tubby's for a sandwich. Maybe I'll stop out later to see how it's going."

THE HARVEST WAS in full swing when I pulled into the cemetery. A dozen National Guardsmen in green fatigue uniforms were hacking industriously away in the corn and carrying the marijuana plants to a pile at the edge of the field, where LeClair and two Guard officers were conferring. I noticed Hec Michaud sitting disconsolately in a jeep, handcuffed to the steering wheel. I walked over. "Hey, meester," I said, "ju know where an hombre can find a chob pickin' beans?" He just stared at the dashboard. No sense of humor.

"Hey, Flower, come on up! I got bleacher seats and cold beer!"

Paulie was sitting with his back against the toolshed on the hill, observing the proceedings. I made the long climb and sat next to him. He passed me a can of generic beer. "Quite a show," he said.

"So it is," I said. "Look, I'm sorry if this . . . puts a crimp in your recreation."

"Hell, Flower," he grinned, "I can't smoke that stuff. I have enough trouble keeping track of things as it is. Hec gave me those joints, probably so I'd keep my mouth shut. Maybe I should have. I'm sure gonna hate losing my job here."

"I don't see why you should."

"Maybe you don't," he said quietly, "but you're going to, because if they keep searchin' in the direction they're going now, they're gonna find the car."

I turned slowly and stared. "What car?"

"A silver Lincoln." His voice was a whisper now, and he wouldn't meet my eyes. "Hec was gonna hide it in the field and then get rid of it later, but it got stuck, so we just covered it up."

"The Costas' car?"

He nodded.

"When did this happen?"

"You mean when did we hide it? I'm not sure," he said, frowning. "It was after the casket got stuck . . . but I already told you that, didn't I?"

"You told me it got stuck, but you didn't tell me the rest, did you? Paulie, it's going to come out anyway now. I want you to tell me what happened. All of it. Just take it slow. Now, you said the casket got stuck?"

"Well, I didn't know it was stuck at first. I was sacked out behind the toolshed when this guy Claudio wakes me up. He's havin' a heart attack because his box is jammed in the frame, and everybody's gone but him and Mr. Costa. So I went and took a look at it. It was jammed all right, but we got a crank here in the shed to lower 'em manually if that happens, so I came back up here to get it. On the way back I could hear Claudio and Mr. Costa arguin' clear across the cemetery. Finally, Claudio went stompin' over to his hearse and drove off, which was odd because the director's supposed to see the casket's lowered and the vault lid is in place before he leaves. Mr. Costa was just standin' there lookin' at the coffin when I came up behind him. That's when I noticed it. Charlie's million-dollar box had a little hunk of red cloth sticking out along one seam. Not very neat. Mr. Costa'd noticed it, too, 'cause that's what he was starin' at. He jumped a foot when I walked up. He told me to lower the box, and I said the funeral director was supposed to be there. 'Mr. Rigoni's been called away and I'll take full responsibility,' he says. 'You just lower it, and here's something for your trouble,' and he holds out a hundred-dollar bill. That's a lotta money, right?"

"Yes," I said, "that's a lot of money."

"I thought so, too. I'm not very good at numbers anymore, but I figured there was something wrong, you know? So I said I couldn't lower it by myself, I'd need help. He started to argue, but he noticed me staring at the box. His eyes kind of narrowed, and he just turned and walked down to his car and tore out of the cemetery, spraying gravel all over the place.

"I knelt down and took a closer look at the red cloth. It moved. Just a little, like something was trying to pull it back inside the coffin. So I rapped on the lid. 'Is anybody in there?' I said, feeling really stupid. It was the first time I ever tried talking to a stiff when I wasn't just trying to get a rise out of Hector. Still, it seemed like the cloth had moved."

"What did you do?"

Paulie shrugged. "Well, there wasn't nobody there but me and that box, so I unscrewed the lid dogs and opened it. She sat up and I sat down. Hard. A lady in a red dress, with blood on the side of her head, groggy, and maybe blinded by the light. 'Help me,' she said."

"Cindy Kessel," I said. "Charlie's girlfriend."

"She was mumbling about not saying anything about Charlie's business," he nodded, "but she was just sort of rambling, like she was in a daze. Then she must have come out of it a little, because she looked down at who she was sitting on. Her eyes rolled up and she fell back down on old Charlie. He didn't seem to mind."

"What happened then?"

"Well, I didn't know what she was to Charlie, but I didn't figure she belonged in the same box with him, so I hauled her out and shut the lid. I wasn't sure what to do. She needed help and nobody was around, and I didn't want to just leave her there, so I picked her up and jogged over to Mrs. Stansfield's. The old lady doesn't like me much, but I couldn't think of anyplace else to go.

"I hammered on the door, but nobody came and the damn thing was locked. I was tired from the run, my head was pounding . . ." He took a deep breath. "The girl . . . Cindy? Is that her name?"

I nodded.

"She was still unconscious. I could see the dust of Costa's limo coming back, and I knew I had to do something, so I put my shoulder to the door, got it open, and set the girl inside. Then I ran back to the grave, keeping low. I didn't want Costa to know where I'd been, and it was kind of fun anyway, like being back in the army.

"Mr. Costa had brought his son with him, Rol Junior. Do you know Rol?"

"I know who he is," I said. "He's a . . . rough customer."

"I knew him from school," Paulie said, "mean as a snake. Mr. Costa said he'd brought him along to help with the casket. I said okay, but he musta noticed I was breathing hard or something, because he looked at me kind of funny, and then he checked the box. I hadn't screwed the lid dogs back in. When he looked at me again, his eyes had gone as dead as Charlie's. 'Where is she, boy,' he says, 'what have you done with her?'

"I just played dumb, which ain't too hard for me. 'I don't know what you mean,' I says.

"'We got no time for this,' Rol Junior says. 'He'll tell us when I show him what his guts look like,' and he pulled an eight-inch blade. Man, that thing flicked open in his hands like magic."

"What happened?"

"He wasn't no soldier," Paulie shrugged, "he was just a guy with a knife. My head doesn't work so good since the grenade got me and Billy, but I can still understand a guy with a knife. He came straight at me, which was a big mistake. I snatched his knife wrist and spun him around into a choke hold, keeping him between me and his old man. Mr. Costa pulled this ugly little automatic, and he was circling around trying to get a shot when the girl screamed and he looked away. That was an even bigger mistake." He took a long pull from his beer.

"Where are they now, Paulie?" I asked quietly. "Are they in the car?"

"The car? Nah. I figured that monument stone of Charlie's was too big for one guy anyway, but it's just about right for three, and it says 'Costa' on it, right?"

"And the girl, Paulie? What about the girl?"

"She's still staying at Mrs. Stansfield's. I went over there later to talk to her, but she was pretty weak and couldn't say much. I'll bet she's glad to be out of that box, though."

"I imagine she is," I said, releasing a long, ragged breath I hadn't realized I'd been holding. "Paulie, we're going to have to tell Ira about this, you know."

"I wanted to in the first place, but Hec said I'd get in trouble. I think he just didn't want anybody snooping around here. One good thing at least, Mrs. Stansfield seems to like me a little better now. Maybe she was only grouchy before because she was lonely."

"Maybe so," I said, frowning. Something he'd said was gnawing at the back of my memory. "Paulie, didn't you tell me Mrs. Stansfield's house was west of the cemetery?"

He nodded. I stared across the fields of golden corn that ran unbroken to the pine-covered hills on the horizon. The setting sun was hanging above them like a single fiery eye. "Paulie, there is no house west of the cemetery."

"Sure there is," he said, with a trace of irritation. "That stone one, over by the fence. Mrs. Stansfield's been there even longer than the major, since 1852, I think, or maybe '51. I'm not very good at numbers anymore."

"WHAT DO YOU think will happen to him?" I asked.

"You tell me," LeClair said, slumping back in the seat of my rental sedan. He looked utterly exhausted, but his eyes were bright, almost feverish. He was watching the men in the rear of the jeep ahead of us as we followed the small convoy back to Algoma in the gathering dusk. Paulie was talking animatedly with a couple of Guardsmen, their smiles occasionally visible in the flickering headlights.

"Can you see Paulie on the stand at the coroner's inquest?" he said softly. "They'll tear him apart. He'll go to Ypsilanti for a three-month psycho evaluation, then back to the vet's facility if he's lucky, and maybe prison if he's not."

"That's probably how it'll go down," I conceded. "He killed two people, and at least contributed to the death of a third."

"Actually, I don't know whether he did or not," LeClair said thoughtfully. "I only know what you told me. I'm just a small-town sheriff, and the Costas and Stansfields are rich, influential folks. I might be very reluctant to order an exhumation on the word of some poor, brain-damaged vet."

I glanced over at him. "You can't be serious."

"I don't know," he said. "I'll give it to you straight. I don't give a damn about what happened to the Costas, I'm just sorry it happened here. I feel bad about the girl, but she should have been choosier about her playmates, and there's no helping her now. That only leaves Paulie. He's already been ground up in the machinery once, and I really hate to see him fed back into the hopper again."

"Three people are dead."

"You're wrong, sport, a lot more people are dead than that. They got their tails shot off while Roland Costa's son was using his draft exemption to learn the family rackets, and Paulie Croft was getting his head rearranged so he could be a grave digger instead of a trucker like his old man. So I'll tell you what I'm going to do, Garcia. Nothing. Nada. I'm dumping it on you. You decide who owes who what, and then let me know. Okay?"

"That's not fair," I said flatly.

"No kidding?" he said, stifling a yawn, "Well, we don't have to be fair. We're the law. And don't worry about Hec. I can handle him."

"You've got to be hallucinating from lack of sleep," I snapped, "or maybe all this fresh air's affected your mind. You could never get away with anything like that."

"You're probably right," he admitted, "but at least I'm covered if we get caught. I'll just scuff my toe in the dirt and say I was taken in by a smooth-talking slicker from the big city. I don't know what your excuse could be, but that's your problem."

The faint sound of laughter from the jeep ahead drifted past us on the wind, and I could see the streetlights of the village glowing in the distance. Both of them. "I don't know, either," I said slowly, "but maybe I won't need one. I mean, what could possibly happen to anybody in a hick town like this?"

STEPHEN WASYLYK

THE SEARCH FOR OLGA BATEAU

November 1987

STEPHEN WASYLYK ALSO made his publishing debut in the pages of *AHMM*, with "The Loose End" in 1968; he went on to publish more than a hundred stories in the magazine. When we solicited reader suggestions for stories to include in this anthology, one of the most frequent responses was "anything by Stephen Wasylyk." Here's a story about a newspaper columnist and a decades-old mystery.

■

Scrolling the column he had just written, Conner critically scanned the sentences as they appeared on his CRT screen, a touch of apprehension tightening his stomach.

Something was missing. Even though the words had been strung together smoothly and professionally, whatever magic he'd had was gone, like the faded skills of an athlete. But a mind doesn't weary and slow with age the way muscle does. The ability was still there. He simply had forgotten how to tap it.

He reached for the phone automatically when it rang, his eyes still on the screen.

The voice was thin and gravelly with age.

"Do I have the pleasure of speaking to Whit Conner?"

"You do," said Conner, "but terming it a pleasure may be premature."

"I've been reading your columns for years. I like the way you think."

"Very nice of you to call and tell me," said Conner cautiously. Compliments were always welcome, so long as they weren't stretched out or a prelude to a request for money.

"My name is Hapford. I'd like to discuss something with you. A mystery that occurred many years ago."

Conner suppressed a groan. He didn't need this now.

"Mr. Hapford, as a reader of my column, you know I write about what I see before me today. The puzzles and bittersweet memories of yesterday I leave to others."

"Indulge me for a moment, Mr. Conner. I have always understood that every writer injects something of himself into his work, and if you read enough of it, you can form a conclusion as to his character. If the theory is wrong, I have misinterpreted yours and I am wasting time when I have none to waste. However, if it is even partially correct, you will be at 610 Baysmore Road this afternoon at two. Good day, Mr. Conner. It has been nice talking to you."

The phone went dead.

Conner leaned back. He often thought many of the strange calls and letters were inspired by the photo at the head of his column as much as by what he wrote. The camera had turned his rather ordinary face with a slightly too-big nose into one so thin and bony it was almost fierce, the eyes glowing and holding a challenge.

The owner of that elderly voice hadn't been lying about reading him for years. Anyone who had would know damned well he'd never resist an invitation like that, even if he suspected it was from an irate reader who wanted nothing more than to break his fingers. Almost every column spawned a few of those.

He flipped through the street directory on his desk. Baysmore Road was well out in the affluent suburbs. A pleasant ride, and the way he'd been writing lately, a few broken fingers might be considered a blessing by some of the paper's subscribers. Not to mention Grainger. The editor had been looking at him out of the corner of his eye lately.

BAYSMORE ROAD had been there a great deal longer than many of the small scale palaces along it that could only be glimpsed through the trees. The people who had built these homes originally couldn't have been concerned about the size of the monthly mortgage payments, because they probably owned the banks.

Six ten had a pair of stone columns flanking the driveway entrance, the number and the name "Hapford" showing through the patina of the bronze plaque on one.

Conner turned in and followed winding macadam he thought would never end, a black strip that didn't carry enough traffic to discourage weeds from sprouting through the cracks and edged by an untended forest laced with underbrush and fallen trees.

The driveway climbed. And climbed. And after a sharp turn burst forth onto a carefully trimmed lawn surrounding a peaked and turreted mass of brownstone and brick.

He stepped from the car and looked up. Queen Victoria would have felt right at home. He'd always admired the style, and this was one of the finest he'd ever seen, a little weathered now and showing its age, but still saying exactly what the man who had built it wanted said—he had taste and money.

Weeds might grow in the driveway, but the sweeping lawn and blossoming flower beds were well tended, as though it were a private enclave deliberately hidden.

A waist-high stone wall flanked the driveway, broken by a tier of flagstone steps that led to a wide terrace of grass, another tier of steps beyond it leading up to a columned and arched portico framing double doors of oak.

Conner started climbing. It would take one helluva throw by the paperboy to reach that portico.

Fronted by a bed of flowers, another wall at the rear of the grass terrace sheltered a kneeling man working at the soil with a trowel.

"Afternoon," said Conner when the man looked up. "Are you responsible for all of this?" He waved at the lawn and the flowers.

The man unfolded a gaunt frame until he was upright, boot-camp-short gray hair emphasizing prominent ears. "I am."

"Very beautiful," said Conner. "Would you be Mr. Hapford?"

The man grinned. "You'll find Mr. Hapford inside, but it's always nice to be mistaken for a wealthy man. I'm Ross, the gardener. Are you interested in gardening?"

"Lord no. I wouldn't know a peony from a weed, but I know beauty and tender loving care by someone who knows his business."

Ross placed the backs of his hands on his hips and looked out over the grounds.

Conner hadn't realized how high the driveway had taken him. The house was on top of the highest hill in the vicinity, and he could see for miles over the tops of the trees. Below them, the tended lawn and strategically placed flower beds were confined to a short radius from the house; the balance of the hill was turned over to nature to do with as she pleased. Conner wondered if Hapford was running out of money.

Ross sighed. "You should have seen it when I was a boy. We had ten gardeners then. It was like this to the bottom. I'm alone now and I can only do so much, and J. A. wants it that way. He says to take care of only what he can see and let the rest go, and his eyes get a little worse each year. Which isn't too bad, I suppose, since I'm losing a little range myself."

Conner smiled. "Mr. Ross, when you get down to four roses before the front door, I'm sure they'll be the finest four roses in the county."

Ross grinned and lifted a hand. "I'll drink to that. And listen, when you go inside, don't let Madame Defarge scare you."

Conner chuckled. The trip was worth it already. He'd found a great gardener with a sense of humor who read Dickens.

AN INTRICATE, flowery, etched border in the glass left enough clear to see the large, white-uniformed woman approach out of the shadows inside.

The aged voice on the phone evidently required the services of a nurse. This one was heavy-set, broad-beamed, and middle-aged; the type no one argues with, especially the patient.

"Mr. Hapford is expecting me," said Conner.

She peered over a pair of half spectacles. "You're that writer?"

The tone said she was no fan of his, but then she might have greeted Shakespeare the same way. Some people regard a writer as only a step or two above a used car salesman or a politician.

Conner smiled. "I seldom use dirty words. Does that help?"

She sniffed and beckoned.

In the large center hall, paintings hung side by side on gleaming mahogany paneling and marched up the angled staircase. A crystal chandelier gleamed with light captured and reflected by hundreds of facets, and the parquet floor edged with contrasting oak was as smooth and unworn as the day it was installed. It had seen less traffic than the driveway.

Waiting in the doorway of a large room, the nurse eyed him as though she expected him to walk off with the massive grandfather clock in the corner.

"People pay money for tours through homes like this," he said.

"You're not on tour," she snapped. "Step this way."

The room fulfilled the promise of the hall. One paneled wall held more paintings, hung from eye level to the ceiling. The furniture was dark and massive and art in itself, the fabric coverings rich.

The rug was so soft and deep Conner felt he was floating as he approached the little old man, robe across his lap, seated in an ancient oak wheelchair with a high wicker back.

Almost bald, face deeply lined, shriveled and thin, he had to be at least eighty, but he sat erect, slightly hazed blue eyes peering at Conner. Lap robe and wheelchair notwithstanding, he was clean shaven and wore a starched shirt, tie, and brown tweed jacket. All dressed up and nowhere to go, but a gentleman never received a guest without wearing a coat and tie.

Behind him was a huge fireplace, a grand piano in the corner to his left, and a massive mahogany desk, pedestals curved and inlaid with contrasting burl, placed to take advantage of the light from the french doors to his right. Beyond the doors were a red brick terrace, a wrought-iron railing, and a bulky sculpture that Conner took to be that of a woman, backed by a grove of pines.

The giant-size Florence Nightingale said, "Mr. Conner," as though hoping the man would tell her to throw him out.

He smiled and flicked a set of bony fingers at her in dismissal.

"You are eight minutes late, Mr. Conner."

"Not really. I didn't anticipate such a long driveway, and I spent the rest of the time admiring your home."

"I had an idea you'd appreciate it. After my imminent departure, it will become a museum for others to enjoy." Hapford indicated a chair. "We receive so few visitors I forget my manners. Can we get you some refreshment?"

Conner shook his head. "No, thank you, sir. What I would like is the reason you invited me here. You mentioned a mystery. Since you call it that, I assume it is an incident that has never been explained, and if you tell me it is of an occult nature, I'm leaving."

"You misjudge me. I called you because you write about people, not the spirit world."

"Every newsman does."

"Most prefer only those who make news. You, on the other hand, are interested in people whose lives would otherwise never be noticed."

"You place yourself in that category?"

"Good heavens, no. You may indeed write something about this, but that is a very minor consideration." Hapford waved. "You'll find a book on the desk. While I'd like to sit and discuss it with you, I no longer have the strength to converse for any length of time. I'd like you to take it with you. Go through its contents. Check the material against other sources if you wish. Then return tomorrow at the same time. With the preliminaries disposed of, no long discussion will be necessary. Is that agreeable?"

The tone said take it or leave it.

"Let me examine the book," said Conner.

The polished desktop was bare except for a lamp and a large, flat volume bound in red leather.

He leafed through. Newspaper clippings, notes, typewritten pages, photographs. The clippings were laminated with clear plastic to preserve the newsprint, and the pages were case bound. It certainly wasn't a typical family album. It was more like a collection of memorabilia on which the collector had lavished a great deal of time and money and perhaps, like other projects important only to their creators, of no interest or value to anyone else once they were gone.

The first clipping was dated October 12, 1935, multi-headlined: *Sculptor's Wife Vanishes While Husband Works*. Below that: *House in Disarray; Intruders Suspected*. And below that: *Foul Play Feared; Police Seek Information*.

Hapford was right. He was holding two hours or more of reading.

"The woman was never found?"

Hapford nodded.

"You need a detective, not a writer."

"You'll find the reports of several."

"I'm sure you know there are writers who would jump at the chance to go through this material and discuss it with you. Instead you call someone like me and indicate that telling the story is not your purpose. You've lost me before the dance has begun, Mr. Hapford. Why me?"

Hapford smiled. "All will be clear in time. You have nothing to lose by reading what is in the book. However, the choice is yours. You can leave without it, taking with you only the memory of an enigmatic old man in a beautiful home."

The challenge was in his voice again.

Conner weighed the book in his hand. Even if he didn't know why, going through it would please Hapford and he had no real reason to refuse.

He tucked it under his arm. "I'll be happy to read your book. Now, I suggest you get some rest. I'll see myself out, and tell your large health-care person not to worry. I haven't stolen anything in some time."

Hapford chuckled. "Don't mind Mrs. Smallcross. Her only interest is my welfare. She thinks visitors tire me out. She's correct."

Outside, Conner placed the book on the seat and looked up at the house. Ross had disappeared. Mrs. Smallcross was staring at him through the glass of the door, probably making certain the clock or one of the paintings wasn't projecting from the trunk.

He drove absently, his mind on the small figure in the wheelchair. Assuming that an eighty-year-old man would be up to anything at all, what was Hapford up to?

While his eyes were failing, his brain certainly wasn't. He might forget where he'd placed his false teeth now and then, but Conner wouldn't want to get into a knock-down, drag-out argument with him.

The three columns he wrote each week were about people he met as he walked around the city; human interest with the slight twist and sardonic humor that made him what he was. No one was more aware that what he wrote would probably end up lining the bottom of a bird cage or a kitty litter box the next day, so he tried not to take himself too seriously. Let the reporters looking for the big story, or the political pundits who always knew how the country should be run, scramble for the Pulitzers. He was content to take his paycheck and go home after doing exactly what Hapford had said, spotlighting a few lives that would otherwise never be noticed. Perhaps Hapford would be one of them, but if he were, he could see the old man deliberately tearing the column to shreds. That wasn't what he wanted at all.

The question was—what did he want?

He dropped the car off in the parking garage across from the white-towered newspaper building and, Hapford's book under his arm, took the elevator to the editorial offices.

The cubicle with SOCIETY EDITOR lettered on the door had a card jammed into the slit between the frame and the glass with the name SUSAN FRAMLING inked in as though her occupancy was temporary.

The blonde young woman typing at the computer terminal alongside the desk glanced up, eyebrows arching above blue eyes. She looked like a society page editor. The short hair, glasses, and silk blouse were timeless styles—and expensive.

"Hi, Susan," said Conner.

She frowned. "What happened to your usual, I'm-free-Saturday-afternoon-Susan-let's-get-married routine?"

"After your twenty-fifth refusal, I sensed you might be trying to tell me something. From now on, I'll simply worship your intelligence and beauty silently and from afar, locking deep within me the flames of passion and desire."

"Good Lord," she said thoughtfully, "he's taken to reading romance novels. They're for women, Conner."

"Be cruel. Condemn me simply because I seek solace from this heartless world, my nights wells of torturous darkness where I spend agonizing hours longing for someone like you to make my blood course fiercely through my entire being as we love madly and without restraint and drive each other to heights of soul-throbbing ecstasy never before experienced. Your callousness is enough to make me weep, but before I break into uncontrollable sobbing, does the name Hapford conjure up images of blue blood?"

"So blue, it's almost purple. Why?"

"I just had an interview with the man and am looking for a little background."

"You're lucky. Up until three months ago, I had never heard the name until I attended a party where I learned a great deal. What's the information worth?"

"A sticky bun, a cup of coffee, and my admiring glances."

"No wonder your nights are wells of torturous darkness. Hasn't anyone ever told you that diamonds are a girl's best friend?"

"Next to sticky buns. Admit it."

She smiled. "With those words, she realized he had found the key to her heart, had solved the age-old mystery of unlocking a woman's deepest desires. I'll take a raincheck, Conner. At the party the conversation centered on the days when the society page meant something. With no television, commercial aviation still a novelty, long train rides a complete bore, and every motor trip an expedition, the wealthy and well-to-do stayed home and entertained one another, all duly reported in the paper. Hapford's name was brought up by one of the elderly women there, who was in her teens at the time. Julius Antonius—"

"Julius Antonius?"

"His father was a Latin scholar, but Julius Antonius was majoring in living it up. He was well on his way to graduating with honors when he ran into a beauty named Olga Bateau."

Conner thought of the clipping in the book.

"Who was married to a sculptor and who disappeared."

She frowned. "You know the story?"

"No. I just happened to know that."

"Anyway, Hapford supposedly was having an affair with Olga Bateau, and the night she disappeared, the two lovers told Bateau that she intended to leave the next day and file for divorce. On the way home, Hapford, undoubtedly filled with champagne and jubilance, ran his car into a tree in his own driveway and was in the hospital for weeks. His father died of a heart attack, which was attributed to his accident, and if that weren't enough, Olga Bateau was kidnapped that same night and never seen again. When he recovered, Hapford accused Bateau of faking the abduction and killing her. Bateau, in turn, accused Hapford of being whacko from the head injury he'd received in the accident, or of lying because he felt the sculpture he'd commissioned wasn't worth the money he'd paid for it, or both. Furthermore, a man testified he'd seen a woman answering Mrs. Bateau's description in a car with two men only a few miles away from the house at approximately the time she disappeared, and that the woman had been very pale and appeared frightened."

"Which reinforced the abduction theory."

"And left Hapford standing in the cold after having bared his soul to the delight of the tabloids. He never could prove anything against Bateau. Bateau even denied the two of them had come to him that night and told him his wife intended to divorce him. Hapford couldn't prove that either. After the fuss and accusations died down, Hapford withdrew from society, filling what I understand is a magnificent mansion with priceless art, discouraging all visitors, and labeled as a nut by the people who know he exists."

Her eyes narrowed. "Exactly what are you up to, Conner? People like you don't talk to men like Hapford more than once a century."

"You're right. He must be eighty if a day."

She waggled an index finger at the book under his arm. "What's that?"

"Something he asked me to look over. I guess you'd call it his personal journal of the incident."

Her eyes gleamed. "Let's talk bribery, Conner. I have to see that."

"As much as I'd like to sit and hold hands as we go through it together, I could never concentrate with you so close. How could I keep from staring at the angelic downiness of your delicate white skin, the throbbing pulse in your throat as you struggle to suppress the desire you feel for me, and the delightfully obtuse earlobe that drives me wild? Besides, I'm sure he meant the book for my eyes only."

She shook her head. "I don't suppose I'll ever understand how a nut like you can see into people's souls, much less write about them, but I suspect that underneath the smart-talk exterior is a real nice guy. You should let him out once in a while, Conner. In the meantime—"

She pointed at the door. "Out."

"As your humble slave, I can but obey."

He was at the door when she called.

"What in the hell is an obtuse earlobe anyway?"

He grinned. "The description can only be murmured in the dark confines of a bedroom."

He ran into Grainger in the corridor. The editor held up a hand.

"I read your column, Whit."

"And?"

"Passable, but not the Whit Conner we all know and love. Have some sort of problem I can help with?"

"I wish I did. Let's hope for something better next time."

Grainger looked thoughtful. "I can only say that so many times, Whit."

IT WAS WELL past dinner when he closed the book. With Susan's story as background, it made far more sense than if he'd simply plunged in.

The police, with other things to do, had eventually dropped the investigation. Hapford hadn't.

Over a period of years, he'd had three separate private investigators search for Olga Bateau. They had been no more successful than the police. One had either been very thorough or had enjoyed spending Hapford's money. He turned in a report the length of a short novel that said nothing. All extended the possibility that Bateau had arranged the abduction and the subsequent murder of his wife, but none was willing to declare unequivocally that Olga Bateau was dead.

Hapford must have commissioned someone to save every reference in the papers not only to Mrs. Bateau but to her husband, including the one seven years later when a judge ruled Olga Bateau officially dead and Bateau free to remarry.

Bateau hadn't enjoyed wedded bliss long. His new wife killed him six months later with one of his own mallets. The details of her horrendous marriage must have been pitiful enough to earn her an innocent verdict at a time when juries were still inclined to believe that marriage vows included the right of a man to beat his wife.

Fifty years. Much too long ago to even hazard a guess, but Conner sensed there was an answer somewhere between the lines.

Aside from a few passing sentences in the stories about the accident and his father's death, there was nothing in the book about Hapford himself, which meant a great deal had been left out.

He could get the rest from the newspaper files, but this had always been a conservative, family-style publication. Fifty years ago, five other papers had been competing for readers, each covering the news in its own way.

Six viewpoints. If he couldn't come up with an angle from those, there was none.

Three hours later, he emerged from the public library and stood on the steps, breathing deeply.

The city was dark, the night soft, the boulevard lamps surrounded by misty halos.

Checking all that microfilm had been a waste of time. He'd learned nothing more. If there was an answer, it was still between the lines and couldn't be read without a key, and if there was a key, it was in Hapford's hands.

He'd accommodated Hapford only to be polite, but he'd spent far more time than he'd anticipated. He really didn't give a damn what had happened to Olga Bateau. That had been Hapford's problem. He'd lived with it and should have died with it and left him alone. He'd drop the book off tomorrow and get out of there.

MRS. SMALLCROSS seemed even more unpleasant when she ushered him inside the next afternoon.

If the nurse had undergone no change overnight, Hapford had. The brightness of the day before was replaced by a pale weariness, and his hand trembled when it rose to meet Conner's.

"I assume you went through the book thoroughly, Mr. Conner, and no discussion is necessary. Did you reach any conclusions?"

"Since Olga Bateau's body was never found, doubt will always exist that Bateau killed her. At this late date, there is no answer."

"If a man persists, the truth will always be found." Hapford motioned. "Wheel me out onto the terrace, if you will."

The terrace was wide and long, the wrought-iron railing ending at a set of broad steps. Wearing a blue baseball cap, Ross leaned with folded arms against the railing, a heavy sledge beside him.

Before them, evergreens accented the weathered gray as they curved around the sculpture, high in the center and descending as they swept toward the front, while twin beds of red and white roses completed a circle bisected by a flagstone walk that led to the statue and formed a patio before it, a small concrete bench off to one side.

The grove was obviously a shrine dedicated to the statue.

"Quite lovely, isn't it?" asked Hapford.

With those eyes of his, he had to be speaking from memory.

"That was Bateau's commission?"

Hapford nodded. "Many consider it only an ugly pile of cement. What do you see, Mr. Conner?"

The sculpture was blocky, almost crude, lacking detail, more form than shape and studded with small, polished stones, yet Conner thought he could see the image of a woman there; a sad woman, hands clasped before her, head bowed; as though what he saw was beneath the surface and waiting to be released by the sculptor's chisels.

He felt ice ripple down his spine. "I'm not quite sure."

"I've felt the same way for fifty years," said Hapford quietly.

The ice spread into Conner's stomach. "How did Bateau work?"

"He spent a great deal of time building his forms. Then he mixed and poured the concrete himself. Once he began, he couldn't stop until it was finished, since the concrete had to be of the same texture and consistency throughout. That was the point he made, you see. Busy mixing and pouring, he was aware of nothing else, so that it was quite possible for his house to be ransacked and his wife abducted while he worked in utter concentration. More than one person testified that it was not unusual for him to work through the night, completely unaware of what went on around him. If forced to stop, he would tear the form apart and reduce the work to rubble with a sledge."

"I think that if I had been you, I would have reduced this one to powder," said Conner slowly.

"Don't be so certain."

"Dammit, you had no choice!" Conner snapped.

Hapford's voice was thin and tired. "Think fifty years ago, Mr. Conner."

Conner's anger faded. The old man was right. He was thinking now, not then.

The sculpture had been commissioned, completed, and delivered. What happened to it was up to Hapford. If he smashed it and didn't find the body of Olga Bateau inside, he had nothing but his memories of the woman he loved to sustain him, and finding nothing would prove nothing—she could be dead and buried elsewhere, or she might even still be alive.

If he did find her body, he would have the satisfaction of seeing Bateau convicted, but the sweetness of revenge couldn't last forever, the statue of the woman he loved would be gone, and worse—whatever slight hope he was clinging to that she was still alive would also be gone.

Either way, he'd lose.

"I apologize," said Conner. "On second thought, I'm not sure I would have done differently."

Hapford nodded. "I knew you'd understand. You see, I know you, Mr. Conner. I've admired your insight and depth and warmth for years, but lately the tenor of your columns has changed. I think I know why. You no longer seek the truth. You pursue the truth as you see it."

Conner suppressed the touch of irritation that criticism always brings.

"Maybe we should postpone this discussion to another day."

Mrs. Smallcross appeared and took up a position behind Hapford's chair, her eyes concerned.

The old man's voice was tired. "There are no more days left. I have traveled the road as far as medication and the tender care of Mrs. Smallcross can take me, but I wished to make a point. The statue stands before you. So does the truth. With the sledge, you can destroy the sculpture in moments if that is where you believe the truth is. Mr. Ross will help you. Or you can walk away, certain that the truth is as you see it."

"Is this your way of getting me to smash the statue for your benefit?"

Hapford smiled. "Not mine. Yours. I already know the truth. It took me fifty years to discover it, because I did what you have been doing. Certain that I was right, I looked no further."

His voice faded along with the smile as he leaned back against the yellowed wicker.

Suddenly aware of his stillness, Mrs. Smallcross touched his throat, held her fingers there for a moment, and looked at Ross, tears in her eyes. Ross slowly removed the blue baseball cap.

The nurse tucked the lap robe around Hapford tenderly as if it still mattered and wheeled him inside.

Shaken, Conner stared after her. It was as though Hapford had willed himself to stay alive until he talked to him.

No one else had known what was wrong with his columns, and he'd been unable to put a finger on it himself, but the old man had. "You pursue the truth as you see it," he'd said, which meant he'd been injecting into those columns what he wished he saw, rather than what was actually there, and they had become contrived and flat.

He stepped from the terrace and studied the statue, painted by the sun with light and shadow. He was certain Olga Bateau was inside. Bateau had committed a perfect murder, sat back, and laughed at Hapford because he had known Hapford wouldn't have the nerve to destroy it. It was a perfectly reasonable explanation of why her body had never been found, but without smashing the sculpture, there would always be a slight doubt, and Hapford had used that doubt to make him take a look at himself. He had, and was grateful.

He waved at Ross, took two steps toward his car, and stopped. Hapford hadn't said it had taken him fifty years to *realize* the truth. It had taken him fifty years to *discover* it. And Hapford had not been the sort of man who ignores the precise meaning of words.

He walked slowly around the semicircle of flowers and back again. The beds were two embracing arms held apart by the flagstone walk, the stones set precisely, filling the circular area before the sculpture with a fan-like pattern that radiated from a rectangle in the center.

Conner stepped back. There was no logic in the rectangle.

In keeping with the circular pattern, the center should have been square so that it was equidistant from all edges.

He studied the shrine. If the centerpiece was not the sculpture but the rectangle, then the sculpture was positioned like—

A headstone.

Ice rippled down his spine again.

He turned to Ross. "He never knew?"

"Not until last week. He asked me to wheel him out. Mrs. Smallcross usually did that, but she had to run into town. You see, no one else knew, so they would walk on the flagstones in the center. I could never do that. Walk on a grave. I steered him around them. He noticed. He sort of looked at them and then up at me and asked very quietly, 'What happened, Ross?'"

"What did happen?"

An errant blade of grass at the edge of a flower bed had escaped the shears. Ross replaced his cap, knelt, broke off the blade, and chewed it thoughtfully.

"What took place before the accident, I have no idea, but he hadn't been alone, as everyone thought. She was with him. He liked to drive fast, it was a rainy fall night, and the driveway was covered with wet leaves. He skidded off the curve. She was killed, he was knocked unconscious. The only people here were his father and me, a kid of fifteen. My dad was the gardener then. The crash brought both of us running. Real nightmare for a kid. For anyone, when it comes to that. His father sent me to the house to phone for an ambulance, but I knew, and I guess he did, too, that it would take an hour to get here. When I came running back, he said, 'We have to bury her, Ross.'"

Ross spat out the remnants of the blade. "Understand, I was fifteen, and old Mr. Hapford was a sort of god to everyone who worked here. That was the height of the Depression, and if you had a job, you had to keep it because there were no others, and plenty of men would be happy to take my place making seven dollars a week helping my father on the estate. He said we have to bury her, and I said sure, Mr. Hapford. If there were any questions about what we were doing, he'd have to answer, not me. We carried her here. My father had already started a flower bed, so the earth was soft and loose, and no one can dig faster than a scared kid. By the time the ambulance came, she had been buried."

Conner stared at him. "What in the hell could his father have been thinking?"

Ross shrugged. "Family name, that sort of thing, I suppose. Name splashed all over the newspapers. Scandal. Drunken son out with married woman. Kills her. He was real straight-laced. We'll never know. There we were, covered with mud and standing in the rain, but the ambulance men never looked at us, and I was wondering what the old man could say to his son if he didn't die, when he sort of coughs and keels over and they took him along. I couldn't tell if J. A. was dead, but I was sure the old man was, so if there was any explaining to do, it was going to be me."

"You should have said something right then," said Conner slowly.

Ross smiled. "Remarkable how good hindsight is. I should have, but I didn't. No one ever asked and I never volunteered. After all, what could a kid know? The statue was delivered while he was in the hospital. I told my father that J. A. had told me he wanted it here, with the trees and the flower beds and the flagstone, making it all up as I went along. J. A. was in a coma for a few days, and when he came out of it, he couldn't remember a thing about that night. It always did remain a blank. I'm sure you've heard of cases like that. Guilt blockage or something, they call it."

Conner nodded.

"Well, hell, I didn't know that at the time. I thought he'd surely remember and then I'd tell him, but he never did and I kept my mouth shut. I think he and Mrs. Bateau must have talked about telling her husband, and to fill in that gap in his memory, he told himself it actually happened. That's why he accused Bateau. You can understand why a fifteen-year-old kid in my position wasn't going to stand up and tell him he was wrong. Four years later the war came along. I went to Canada and joined the Royal Canadian Air Force. I sometimes wondered if I were killed would the secret die with me, or would someone stumble across it someday, but I wasn't, and when I came back, he'd accepted it and lived with it, so there was no point to putting him through it all again. Maybe somehow he knew, which was why he shut himself off. When I told him last week, he said, 'Thank you, Ross,' as though I'd done him a favor."

"Maybe you did," said Conner.

"Only we two know now. Have anything in mind?"

Conner looked at the shrine. "I think not."

Ross stooped, snipped off a rose, and held it out. It was a deep purplish red, blue toward the bottom.

"Developed it myself. I call it a Bateau Blue. J. A. liked that."

Conner turned the rose over in his fingers. "So do I."

SUSAN LOOKED up and smiled.

"Find out what Hapford wanted?"

"To give me a lesson in humility. He called it looking for the truth, which was his gentlemanly way of telling me I'd become a fat-headed bore."

"Three very loud cheers for Hapford."

"He'll never know of your approval. He died at approximately two thirty, and I regret that very much. I'd have liked to have known him better."

He placed the rose on her desk. "For you. It's called a Bateau Blue."

She breathed its fragrance with closed eyes. "It's beautiful. Thank you, Conner. But what about Olga—"

"Care to trade in that sticky bun raincheck for a dinner?"

She studied him for a moment. "I have the feeling that it won't be necessary to bring my mace."

"All we'll do is talk like two sensible adults."

She smiled. "Sounds like a dull evening, but I'll be pleased to accept, Mr. Conner."

He met Grainger in the corridor again and held up a hand before the editor could speak.

"Don't derail my train of thought." In his office, he slid behind his keyboard.

All of the people who had searched for Olga Bateau through the years had never thought to ask a gangly, fifteen-year-old kid if he knew anything. If they had, the kid would have made news.

He didn't write about people who made news. He wrote about people who would otherwise never be noticed.

Like a gaunt genius of a gardener with prominent ears and a blue baseball cap who grew blue roses, whose work few people had ever seen because it was on top of a hill where time had stood still for fifty years.

CONNIE HOLT

HAWKS

June 1989

THIS STORY, PUBLISHED in 1989, won for its author the Robert L. Fish Award for the Best First Short Story. In a genre where the subject matter is violence and the realism is often "gritty," this story is a small jewel of understatement and implication, but no less disturbing for that. We like the way the little details accumulate to create a subtle but powerful ending.

■

The mourners gathered in small groups on the hillside, some under the red-leafed oak and others before the monuments to their own dead in the overgrown Irish cemetery. Aunt Hattie was back home in the kitchen seeing to supper for the "hungry folks after a funeral." Aunt Sue, Uncle Joe's wife, stayed down to help her. So did Miss Tatum Harris, the telephone operator for Arkansas Bell in Republican. Miss Tatum had brought two of her lemon layer cakes to do for dessert. Her neighbor, Mrs. Loder Smith, the wife of the general store proprietor, went over to Miss Tatum's house to take the switchboard whenever trouble called the good lady away. Aunt Sue seemed low as she rolled and cut biscuits, but Aunt Hattie and the telephone operator kept up an effort to jolly her out of it.

The children—nieces and nephews of the dead man, Preacher's five young ones, and a few second cousins from Gilbert—were charged to be on their best behavior and to stay among the older graves at the top of the hill. Soon they were running through tall grass that tapped the spines of Irishmen one hundred years dead. Shrieks of happy laughter bounced off crumbling stone, and a game of marbles got under way on the bare, packed earth above Baby McDonough, 1865.

Sarah and Donald sat side by side in quiet dignity upon the granite slab of Lough MacDougal, the one stubborn old Scot to lie up in that Celtic hillock. They spoke in somber tones to honor their uncle's funeral day, and to impress their maturity on the younger children.

"Preacher says Elmo ain't goin' to heaven 'cause he's a pagan," said Donald. At thirteen a deep furrow already showed between his brows.

"What's a pagan?" asked Sarah.

"Save they don't go to church and they're sinners, I'm not real sure," he replied.

"Daddy said Aunt Hattie says he ain't goin' too, 'cept 'cause they cain't find him," Sarah said.

"Uncle Abe ain't goin' to heaven neither?" asked Donald.

"No, silly, not Daddy," she laughed, "Uncle Elmo. 'Cause they cain't find his body is how come he cain't get into heaven."

"What difference does that make?" Donald asked.

Sarah mused the point and decided. "I guess you got to have your body with you when your soul goes."

"'At don't sound right," said Donald with a knowing nod. "People don't use their bodies in heaven. Only your soul goes to Jesus. Nobody'd drag along to heaven somethin' that's been in a hole."

"All the same," she replied, "Aunt Hattie says there cain't be no Christian burial, so he cain't go."

"Maybe so," Donald said, "but it don't matter none. If he was a pagan it ain't like he could of gone anyhow."

Just then Preacher's son, Lavon, yanked Sarah's long hair. She cried out in more surprise than pain, but Donald had to beat him smartly for it anyway.

The sun was high and hot when Sarah's mother came up to get them. Marble players had to dust off the knees of their good dark britches, and Lavon had to tuck in the tail of his white shirt.

"Quieten down now," said Mrs. Knox sternly, "and listen good." There was a deal of drawer tugging and grimacing . . . and here and there a shove. "This ain't no play-party. Y'all are goin' to go down there an' stan' with your mommas. Don't stan' with Abe ner Joe, you hear? You stan' with your mommas. All a' Joe's children, you stan' with me.

"There won't be no flibbity-jibs in the prayin', neither. I plan to pray with one open eye, an' I see anybody actin' flighty, I'll pray right then an' there they get their bottoms blistered. There ain't a grave, but it's a funeral just the same." She surveyed the group with the cold blue eye she'd probably chosen to keep open. "Anybody here wunder anythin'?" All small heads wagged no. If anyone was nursing a question, it wasn't likely to be about a point of etiquette. "Then you'll be walkin' down this hill behin' me."

The people stood in a loose circle with Preacher at the southern end to keep the sun out of his eyes. Abe and Joe Knox were on his right, a space carefully reserved between their dark presences and the rest of the bereaved. Across the circle Donald watched them. He watched his father's jaw muscles work. He watched something still and fierce lying back in his eyes. He saw Uncle Abe pick a spot in the weeds and stare at it stolidly, standing as still as a graven man. The children switched and twisted, and had their eyes all over, only accidentally including heavenward.

Preacher dropped his chin into his bow tie and clutched the Bible in both hands up to his wheezy chest. The circle grew silent waiting for him to call Jesus to the meeting. Only the brush rustle at the edge of the woods sounded until God came loud and sudden, like near thunder. All the children and a few grown men started visibly.

"Lord!" Preacher boomed out sharply. "Hear your children callin' your precious name in a wilderness of sorrow. Help this poor sinner to find the words that will open their hearts to you, so they can feel your healing power today. Show mercy to the soul of Elmo Knox. I pray, Lord Jesus, that when he was layin' out in that ditch somewhere, he had time to repent and ask you to come into his life. I pray that any wrong he ever did is forgiven . . ."

Sarah listened at first, just like Sunday. The litany of Uncle Elmo's sins rolled out with the same cadence as mankind's from the pulpit, the sins written down in dark letters in Peter's book, the one he'll read from on the last day. Elmo Knox didn't go to church. He feared God so little that he didn't care who heard him blaspheme. He said God lived in trees and mountains and spoke in birdsong. He said river water was God's own blood. He said he was, himself, an animal no finer than a wood duck or worse than a bobcat. When he died off in the woods last summer, he lacked the foresight to make his remains available to box in fragrant Arkansas pine against the day of judgment. After a while Sarah ignored Preacher, just like Sunday, and dwelled in her mind on the dead man. She remembered the clear June day when she'd seen him last. . . .

THEY SAT IN the shade with their backs against an outcrop of stone halfway down Sugarloaf. Sarah appreciated the many colors of sunlighted green and blue before her, though she formed no thoughts about it. Elmo watched a redtailed hawk make wide circles above a bend in Latter's Run, and he thought about the hawk as he watched it.

"Hawks are patient birds," he said aloud. "They'll lay on the wind all day just waitin' for their best chance." Sarah began to watch the hawk, too. "They don't kill very often," he continued absently, "'cause it's hard. Try to kill somethin' with sharp eyes an' quick feet." In a while the hawk drifted off his circle and headed east, away from the sun. Uncle Elmo spoke very pointedly then, and seemed to Sarah to be talking to the bird. "But sooner or later he'll kill. You can be sure of that. He has to."

He turned suddenly to the girl. "Good hunters are patient. You remember that. Your daddy an' Uncle Joe an' me are all good hunters. It's patience makes it so. You gotta watch hawks."

"I don't wanna kill animals," Sarah spoke solemnly. "I wanna catch 'um like you do. Just catch 'um to look at, see 'um up close, an' turn 'um loose."

"That's a good way," he agreed. "It gives all the fun of huntin' without hurtin' anybody. Seems like you hurt ever'thin' if you hurt one thin'. Now an' again I don't even like to walk on grass. Did you ever try to figger how many little grubs an' bugs are under your feet when you tramp aroun'? Or that the grass itself could maybe holler, only you cain't hear?" He shook his head and looked out to where the hawk had been, but Sarah was sure he was seeing inside his own head. "You gotta be real careful, though," he murmured. "Some animals ain't proper to catch."

"We oughta get on, Uncle Elmo," Sarah said half an hour later. "Momma'll have dinner on time we get there."

They walked together down Sugarloaf and out the dirt road toward home. Elmo showed her a nuthatch. "Any time you see a little bird headin' nose down a tree trunk like a fly, you know it's a nuthatch." He told her about the soft, pink pockets to be found in the pale belly fur of mother 'possums, and about their fearsome teeth and claws.

"You know, we could sure catch us a 'possum an' have a look," he said. "A box trap's all we'd need if we get real familiar with a partic'lar 'possum."

"We could fix up that ol' 'coon cage while we're waitin' to get to know a 'possum," Sarah suggested brightly, already able to see the small gray creature snug behind chicken wire.

"Knoxes start learnin' patience an' thinkin' ahead when they're little-biddy baby birds . . ." said Uncle Elmo. His mouth smiled but his eyes didn't.

It was the next day that he walked alone into the woods. Even when her father and Uncle Joe had searched and come back without him, Sarah set about collecting a vegetable crate, heavy cord, and a stout stick to make a box trap for a mother 'possum.

PREACHER WAS making his closing salvos on the flown spirit of Elmo Knox while the assembled mourners "amened" and praised God. The child, Sarah, was the only crier on the hillside.

After the funeral everyone drove back down the hill to Republican. Aunt Hattie had dinner waiting: fried chicken and frog legs, baked bass and biscuits, rice and gravy, greens . . . everything steaming in crockery bowls on the big kitchen table. There were sliced tomatoes, fruit salad, and cold milk in a tall pitcher.

The women and babies ate in the kitchen. The men ate outside, some sitting on their running boards and others hunkered down nearby. The children sat on the gray, planked porch cross-legged like Indians or dangling skinny ankles off the sides. Sarah and Donald had the north end of the porch to themselves.

"I been thinkin'," Sarah mused aloud between bites of chicken leg. "I figger Uncle Elmo ain't dead."

"'Course he's dead," Donald returned flatly. "We were just to his funeral."

"Yeah, but we didn't bury nobody, now did we?" she said with her little pointed chin tilted smugly. "We didn't have no box 'cause we didn't have no body, an' we didn't have no body 'cause he ain't dead."

Donald considered this new thought carefully as his jaws worked over his plate.

"Looky here," continued Sarah reasonably. "Uncle Elmo never could of got lost in the woods on account of him knowing woods so good. And he'd have to of got bad lost for my daddy not to find him, on account of him bein' such a good tracker. Hey, even your daddy'd of found him 'cept he was bad lost, an' he cain't get lost! You see! It's just simple that he ain't dead."

"Well, where is he then?" asked Donald after a few moments to clear his mouth.

"New Orleans, I reckon," she said with an airy shrug. "He always said how he'd like to see that big causeway over Lake Ponchetrain."

The boy's eyebrows puckered and his lips pinched as he concentrated on Sarah's argument. At last he shook his head, slowly at first and then with violence.

"'At's stupid. 'At's just real stupid!"

"No, it ain't!" she cried indignantly.

"He ain't a bird that just flies off," Donald sputtered, feeling angry without knowing why. "He ain't in New Orleans, neither! He's dead, you hear me?" He leaped sideways off the porch and ran around the side of the house.

Twilight was deep before Sarah went looking for her cousin. The air was cooling quickly with the sunset these autumn days, and the purple colors of evening added to the child's sense of summer's end. She found the boy behind the house, sitting on the "step box" beside the rain barrel.

"Hey, Donald," Sarah spoke gently into the shadows. "You wanna play checkers?" No answer came. "I got my checkers in the house. You wanna play?"

In that instant purple turned to black. It was that moment when day stops. If you see it happen, night seems very sudden.

"You mad at me?" she asked. But the boy was silent. "You're actin' mad, but if we play checkers or somethin' you'll cheer up." Still no words came from the shadows by the rain barrel.

"Donald!" she snapped, finally in a huff. "You're about the sorriest thing I ever saw!"

"You're the sorriest thing in the whole world," said the boy at last. "Sayin' dead men ain't dead, they're only fishin' in Lake Ponchetrain. That's purely stupid. 'I'm at the funeral but I ain't sad,'" he mimicked her, "''cause Elmo ain't dead, he's in Paris, France.'" His voice was hard and angry. Sarah began to cry.

"You're so meanhearted," she whimpered, "I don't want even to mess with you."

"Aw, hush," he said, softening. "I ain't mad at you. 'At threw me how you said Elmo ran off. I think I wisht he had run off. I think I wisht he'd run off more'n anythin'. You understand?"

"Well, how come you're so dang sure he didn't?" she sniffed.

"Okay, listen an' use your head . . ."

"Huh!" she pouted.

"What did Uncle Elmo take with him when he left?" he asked.

"A cane pole and a bag of cold biscuits," she replied. It was common knowledge. Everybody knew that.

"If he was goin' off travelin', would he of took that?"

"No," she nodded doubtfully. "I reckon he'd not of tooken off half cocked."

"'Course not," said Donald. "He always was careful what he took on a Sunday drive. If he had a pole an' a bite to eat, he was goin' to the river an' no place else. Right?"

"I guess so," Sarah agreed sadly. "I just don't see how he could of got dead between here an' there, an' my daddy couldn't find him."

"I cain't either," he said through tight lips, "an' that's just what's botherin' me. Since our daddies are as good in the woods as Uncle Elmo, how come they cain't find their own brother on a gravel road? It don't make sense to me. Do you see what I'm drivin' at?"

"Not percisely, no," she answered.

"Ain't you seen Momma cryin'?" he asked.

"Gosh, yes," she said. "She's awful sad about Uncle Elmo. They was good friends, wasn't they?"

Donald was silent again. After a while Sarah knew he wasn't going to play checkers at all. She went into the house where all the adult funeral-goers were gathered over Miss Tatum Harris's lemon cakes. They were in a deep discussion of the quarter horse auction in Fayetteville.

JEFFRY SCOTT

UNBEARABLE TEMPTATIONS

August 1990

JEFFRY SCOTT is the pseudonym of a British journalist who made his fiction debut in *AHMM* in 1976 and who has gone on to publish more than a score of stories in the magazine. This story, from 1990, concerns two journalists who meet in an unlikely spot on England's south coast and recall their days together in war-torn Beirut.

■

He swears that it's never his fault and may even believe that. Manganelle, with his autopsy-conducting gaze and face the color of rare steak, is my least likeable and most worrying friend. Ancient Norsemen would have shunned him as an ill-bringer. He's a lightning conductor for scandal and worse; lumbers through such storms without so much as a scorch mark, leaving charred victims in his path. This makes him uneasy though interesting company.

Eric Manganelle is a journalist, so he has been everywhere and seen everything. Par for the course, except that he probably *caused* most of everything as well.

We ran into each other at Palmcastle on England's soft and seemly south coast recently. Palmcastle is where mildly affluent, strongly elderly Britons wait for death. They crave dignity and are confident of their passing's arousing minimal fuss, because hardly anyone will be able to tell the difference. Even the waves break in an undertone there, and thunder neither rolls nor rumbles overhead. It clears its throat—diffidently at that.

Nothing ever happens at Palmcastle, that's what Palmcastle is for. When I laid this insight on Eric Manganelle, he sneered like a silent movie heavy, as if to say, "Much *you* know." But what he did say over the first of many scotches, none going on his bill, was: "I'll tell you something funny about Beirut."

"Nothing's funny about Beirut." We'd spent too long there, starting with the Israeli invasion of Lebanon and siege of Beirut, on through the PLO's departure and beyond.

"Shut up," he remarked, "I'm telling this. The funny thing about Beirut, seeing that it was the capital of a country where anarchy had been the norm for a decade or so *before* our impulsive friends from Jerusalem kicked the front door down and started smashing the china, is that it was such a terribly safe place."

He took my breath away. Finally I said feebly, "Sorry to bother you with the facts, but I was there, remember. Safe place? The Four Horsemen of the Apocalypse have been using Beirut for their stable, years on end."

"Oh, that," he grunted, dismissing air raids, sniping, shelling, rockets, and seventy different factions of the PLO alone. "Yes, there was fighting and so forth—"

"Ever the trained observer, Mangy. Nothing escapes your attention, born reporter."

"But apart from that," Manganelle persisted, "it *was* a very safe place. Think about it, if you're capable. S-a-f-e, providing you were a genuine civilian or a hack, a journo, with the right accreditation documents. Keep a civil tongue in your head, lie low when it got noisy, and none of the citizenry or warriors would look at you crosswise. This was before the hostage-taking lunacy, mark you. Can you deny it?"

"Well, maybe . . ."

"No maybe about it. Remember how we'd blunder about at night, feeling no pain, wandering down the most appalling dark alleys and getting thoroughly lost? There was always a crone or a thug with an assault rifle and a checked tea towel on his head who'd pop up to show the way back to the Commodore. Dozens of us, bouncing about after dark, loaded with cash, expensive cameras, and tape recorders. Answer me this: did you ever get mugged? Did you ever hear of *anybody* getting mugged, rolled, having their pocket picked?"

"No," I conceded, "now you mention it. They must have been too busy with their war to waste time on that kind of thing."

"Just so. Israel was hammering the PLO, the Christians were hammering the Muslims and vice versa, and most of them had a bash at the Druse when otherwise unoccupied," Manganelle recalled. "Yet foreign civilians could get away with things they'd never risk in London, New York, Paris. Indulge in conduct rightly regarded as hazardous in civilized cities, such as braving those aforementioned dark alleys, asking total strangers for directions—really reckless, provocative stuff of that persuasion."

"I was there," I repeated; "stop lecturing me."

"Reminding, old boy, reminding. It was a few years ago, fine detail soon blurs into mush at your time of life." Only Manganelle can drink on your tab without a word of thanks, let alone acknowledgment, before implying senility in his benefactor.

Driven to waspishness, I said, "Talking of getting old, when somebody keeps hanging on and on with the same remark, it's a sure sign he's over the hill."

Either Manganelle had been hit by the hideous possibility of buying his liquor, or he was treating me to a look of hurt dignity. "I'm establishing the context, you blockhead. Setting the stage for the last untold drama of Beirut in '82, the strange affair of Lancelot Pasover."

"Never heard of him," I scoffed. "Fine old Middle Eastern name, though. Skipper of a trading dhow, was he?"

"That's the way, glory in your ignorance." He snapped his fingers and grinned balefully. "Ah yes, you never met Pasover. You'd sneaked away to loll about in Cyprus when the going got tough, leaving stauncher colleagues to face shot and shell."

I had sneaked away on a stretcher and been absent for all of two weeks, before returning with an ankle in plaster but raring to go, sort of. Perhaps I forgot to mention Eric Manganelle's compassion and his obsessive concern to show professional rivals' conduct in the best possible light.

Once we'd sorted that out, unprintable on my side, he complained, "D'you want to wrangle like a nasty little guttersnipe or hear about Pasover?"

"Is there a choice?"

Deliberately dense, Manganelle agreed, "It's a choice story, certainly, the . . . the . . ." My heart sank, for Manganelle adores excruciating puns. "The passing over of Lancelot Pasover," he boomed, sizzling with satisfaction.

He wagged a fat finger, tip beveled flat from striking sundry million typewriter keys. "Pasover died in a far land, a foreign field, but he was a Palmcastle man born and bred. Which is why I'm here—in at the death, all over again."

ERIC MANGANELLE is a good reporter, but even a bad one would have done well in Beirut during the early years of the eighties. You couldn't very well miss the story, for instance.

There was too much story, if anything. Or rather, too many of them, all squeezed between the city's Green Line frontier, held by the Israeli army with its Lebanese Christian onlookers, and the sea a mile or so away, to which the PLO and Muslim militias of East Beirut had their backs.

It was an extraordinary time and matching place, not at all what outsiders could expect from words such as "siege." Bombs fell, shells slammed home, Israeli missiles lanced in from their gunboats, making savage echoes chatter among the tower blocks. Assault rifles were fired in the air as a gesture of defiance or simply to clear traffic for an ambulance. Sometimes all these incidents took place within the same few minutes, which was hard on the nerves.

Yet between whiles, and occasionally *during* whiles, West Beirut's life went on, dinners were served, people strolled, business was done. And there were a lot of people: TV and print journalists and their entourages by the scores, volunteer doctors and nurses, United Nations officials, representatives of international charities, questing executives impatient for the shooting to stop so they could start dealing.

Some of them, Manganelle reasoned, had to be spooks— intelligence men under cover. His paper loves that sort of thing, so Manganelle set about locating an agent. He never did, not provably, but he did meet Lancelot Pasover.

Incredibly, considering that Lebanon had been a killing ground for so long, there remained a sizable expatriate community. This included French nationals who'd been around Beirut since its pre-war days as a colony, Americans connected with the university, and Britons who taught English for a living, served in bars, or generally hung out.

Lancelot Pasover's reason for being there was so odd that Manganelle felt sure he must be a spook. Then he looked again, sighed, and scrapped the idea.

MANGANELLE NOTICED Pasover in the lobby of the Commodore hotel one morning. Pasover caught his bloodshot eye and smiled goofily, a balding young fellow in sandals over tartan socks, baggy lightweight suit, and a hand-knitted tie, lopsided and full of dropped stitches.

"Hello," Pasover beamed, "are you British by any chance, sir?" Which was such a bloody silly question, nearly an insult, that Manganelle harrumphed at him in fury.

But he was bored and at a loose end until Arafat's daily press briefing, so Manganelle bought Lancelot Pasover breakfast— putting it on the bill of an unwary new chum from the *Washington Post,* naturally.

"What am I doing here? Sometimes I ask myself that," Pasover answered the obvious question.

"Never mind the epigrams," Manganelle entreated sourly.

Young Pasover nodded, still smiling. He was too dim to have hurt feelings. "Well, sir, I'm just settling up Auntie's estate. Soon as that's done, and I'm confident of success within days, I shall be back to Palmcastle like an arrow. Anne's missing me dreadfully. Anne is my wife. You know how women are, they need a strong, protective male at hand."

"I hope she finds one," Manganelle grunted.

Oblivious, Pasover prattled on. "I have been here five weeks, imagine! My first time out of England." This intrigued his listener; Beirut seemed a decidedly rum place to launch one's overseas vacations.

Lancelot Pasover was surprised. "It's not a holiday, Mr. Manganelle. I told you, my aunt died and left me her business. I'm just selling it, fixtures, fittings, and goodwill. Er, would you like to see the place?"

The upshot was that they agreed to meet at Auntie's place that afternoon. Given the address, Manganelle's driver shook his head. "Nothing there, all gone," was his laconic verdict.

"Rubbish," Manganelle boomed. "You're idle, Abu Droopydrawers, you want to sleep in your motor all day, eating your head off at my expense. Here's the street and the number, that little twit wrote them as plain as day. Take me there, instantly."

Soon he saw what the driver was getting at. They went down to the port area past what had been the Middle East's largest, most modern Holiday Inn, by then the world's largest, most modern disused Holiday Inn. But that was in terrific shape compared to the streets down which the battered Merc began rolling. Civil war had turned whole blocks into something uncommonly like Hiroshima or Dresden after the bombing; derelict, abandoned cliff dwellings, blurred holes where windows, doors, or projectiles had been.

After two or three sharp arguments, the driver spotted an unsuspected alleyway, backed up, and there at the far end of the cul-de-sac was Lancelot Pasover's inheritance. The driver grumbled in liquid Arabic and curled up on the bench front seat; Manganelle waddled off for a closer look.

The closer he got, the more intense was his unkind amusement, so that by the time he reached the doorstep, Manganelle was wheezing and quivering helplessly.

The little building was only two floors high, facade tinted a defeated, long-faded amber from what had once been brave red. Over the door a signboard bore the ghost of block letters: SOPHIE'S CAFF***TEA LIKE MOTHER MAKES***REAL FISH AND CHIPS***CLEAN BEDS UPSTAIRS. Obviously it hadn't been active in years.

The door creaked open, a bell jangled pathetically. Lancelot Pasover, defensive at Manganelle's cruel mirth, mumbled, "Well, it's the off-season," which made the reporter bray with laughter.

"It's not funny," Pasover said reproachfully. Then he brightened. "Come on in, sir. I've been thinking, maybe you could put a bit in your paper about my looking for a buyer—"

"Do leave off," Manganelle pleaded, "you'll do me a mischief. Lance, you must be short of a full deck, lights on but nobody in, that class of behavior. Nobody's going to buy your auntie's caff."

"Don't say that." Alarmingly, Pasover's eyes filled with tears. "I've come all this way, it's got to work out!" And he explained about his Aunt Sophie, who in 1945 had married a Lebanese entrepreneur who turned out to be a Lebanese hotel porter. The new Mrs. Sophie Habib had come to terms with the disaster, worked hard and saved harder, and set up her cafe.

No doubt it did well enough before Lebanon's nightmare began, when cruise ships still called and British crewmen and package tourists were in the market for a taste and sound of home, within sight of the quays. "It was doing very well," Aunt Sophie's nephew kept saying, "and she always promised it would come to me when she, um, left us. Which she did, her heart, she was well into her eighties. I came straight here, war or no war. It's my birthright, Mr. Manganelle!"

Manganelle couldn't decide whether to giggle or weep when Lancelot patted the rusted urn, fount of Tea Like Mother Made, or declared that this was a prime site and must have value. Beirut was full of prime sites, primer by far. Walk in under the right flag or bearing a big enough gun, and the lease was yours. . . .

"I'm sure it will work out, Lance," Manganelle lied, and fled to his car. He considered writing an ironic little feature piece on Lancelot Pasover and his doomed enterprise, but it would take too much explaining and the vision of an innocent dunce peddling a teashop went right against the grain of all the "I See Hell In World's Most Dangerous City" copy that Manganelle was filing.

Still, it was a cracker of an anecdote, something to dine out on—in his case, booze out on. He told it well, funny voice for Lancelot, vivid description, until Manganelle had only to show his hideous face in the Commodore's bar for somebody to groan, "No more caff, Mangy, okay?"

Probably Lancelot Pasover overheard one such recital, since he stopped his wistful patrols of the hotel lobby and dropped out of sight.

Manganelle resumed the half-serious quest for spooks. Harry Lamburn seemed promising. Lamburn wasn't staying at the Commodore; nobody seemed sure where he was based or exactly what he did. Harry Lamburn was one of those men who always knows first names, even before introduction, and who is good company without saying anything memorable.

"Business," he replied vaguely, when Manganelle asked. "Passing through, bit of a hitch because of this siege nonsense, all be sorted out in a day or two. Between ourselves, I think the deal's cooked. Rightly, I should be in Abu Dhabi, selling some tugs. But you know how things can be. . . ." His gesture was equally vague.

Not a spook, Manganelle sensed, but Harry Lamburn was a touch bogus somehow. A crook, then? More than likely. Lebanon's national products being mayhem and drugs, the latter a thriving rural industry, it would figure.

Harry Lamburn knew of Palmcastle, hardly surprising since he was English and Palmcastle is both premier resort and a synonym for sedate retirement. So Manganelle tried the Lancelot Pasover tale on him, the saga of Palmcastle's wandering dabbler in real estate. Lamburn was flatteringly amused and attentive.

Too attentive, Manganelle considered, and was ready to snap, "Oi, this is *my* story!" before assuring himself that Lamburn was no journalist and therefore it didn't matter, he would not pinch the piece and pass it off under his byline.

Manganelle had met Lancelot Pasover on a Wednesday, and exactly eight days later was drowsing in the Commodore lobby when his driver scurried in and sleeve-twitched him awake. "What?" Manganelle exploded. "How d'you know, Abu Droopydrawers?"

The driver spread his hands in amused contempt at such naivete. Everyone in West Beirut knew everything as soon as it occurred—often before, since bustling streets like Hamra had a trick of clearing a minute or so before shelling or air raids.

"Take me there," Manganelle ordered. Sophie's Caff was locked, there was no sign of Lancelot Pasover's body, and the local police in their smart, milky-coffee uniforms, were staying firmly on the southern side of the Green Line and out of the city's besieged half.

But with the driver translating, Manganelle got a story of sorts from neighbors—there were neighbors even in that wasteland, several refugee families sheltering in a gutted warehouse round the corner from the cafe—and men of a militia checkpoint in the main street.

That morning Lancelot Pasover had been found dead in the alley leading to Sophie's Caff. He had been bludgeoned, his pocket linings pulled out, his watch was missing. Eerily, civilians and militiamen alike were indignant over the crime and faintly suspicious and accusing as they answered the driver while staring at Manganelle. The victim was foreign, Inglesi, the fat man was foreign, Inglesi; no local could have done this, and a non-local had returned to the scene . . .

"We go now, I think," the driver murmured, from inside the Merc. "'Nough said," his master agreed, and they got the hell out of there. Manganelle found his original notes on the meet with Pasover, neatly filed on the back of an envelope screwed up and discarded under the bed in his shared room. That reminded him how the name was spelled and gave Pasover's age.

Manganelle phoned the story to his foreign desk, but it ended up as a single sentence, because on that day Arafat left Beirut and Fleet Street was intent on larger matters than a single violent robbery in a place notorious for sudden death in large amounts.

Months later, the following year in fact, Manganelle was back in London, and among mail awaiting him was a letter from a Foreign Office functionary, asking for details of Lancelot Pasover's demise. Also a letter from a firm of Palmcastle solicitors, seeking much the same information. He dictated one answer for both parties, telling everything as far as he knew. Mainly hearsay, Manganelle warned, though just before leaving Lebanon for good, he had been called to police headquarters in East Beirut, then taken to a mortuary where he'd identified Pasover's corpse.

Rather belated that, Manganelle felt. But the authorities were anxious to show law and order, or a semblance, returning to both sides of the Green Line. Motions had been gone through and that was that.

He wondered whether he might write to the widow—Anne, he remembered the name—but what he did was let the matter slide into the trinket box of memoirs, boasts, and tall stories at the back of his mind.

NOW WE REACH Eric Manganelle's role as catalyst and card-carrying ill-bringer.

Banish carping doubts that it all depended on a whacking great coincidence, for the overt element of chance is delusive. He was a journalist, and many Fleet Street men go to Palmcastle in the conference season sooner or later. He liked women, and Mrs. Lamburn was a woman, no mistake. The Lamburns were invited to most civic receptions—he wealthy, she decorative—while Manganelle went to receptions regardless of official invitation, on the principle of receptions being where the booze was.

All that being so, the outcome was as near inevitable as makes no odds.

Manganelle fell out with his editor, no great challenge. The editor made him cover an ecology conference at Palmcastle by way of punishment. It wasn't so bad. Manganelle took a suite at the four-star Royal Courier Hotel and improved idle hours by ringing cronies in Australia, Africa, Malaysia to ask what the weather was like there. Bills went direct to his paper, no sordid money would be demanded from him. Punishment can cut both ways.

He even attended conference sessions, slumbering benignly if noisily before lounging back to tear the Press Association report from the machine in the Royal Courier's lobby and phone it in, not a word altered. Nothing was printed, he did not expect it to appear; the whole thing was a bit of a joke. Though the *Intelligencer*'s shareholders might have missed the cream of the jest.

Gratifyingly, Palmcastle's city fathers threw a party on the final day. Manganelle trundled along on the promenade from his hotel to a yet larger, more opulent one, a seasoned campaigner marching toward the sound of the guns—champagne corks, anyway.

This was his sort of occasion. The Splendide's ballroom was a human sea dotted with white linen islands where waiters toiled to keep the alcohol flowing. And there was, in Eric Mariganelle's dewily romantic phrase, A Lot of Crumpet About. Women in the plural, delightfully diverse, birds of every species and plumage or lack of it.

Manganelle confesses to being a closet heterosexual. He guzzled champagne, he grew gently amorous, he feasted on flashes of rounded knee and bobbing bosom, he ogled and leered and his furry eyebrows bounced in yo-yo mode. Success with women, he believes, is akin to selling vacuum cleaners during the Great Depression. Prospects may be bleak, but knock at a hundred doors and you're bound to make one sale. . . .

Maybe it only works with vacuum cleaners. Manganelle had to settle for a toothy, gaunt maiden with a squint and a motormouth who knew everybody. It was her job, as social columnist for the weekly rag, the Palmcastle *Herald*. Ms. Potter, for it was she, was thrilled to hobnob with one of Fleet Street's finest.

Fresh from being snubbed, teased, or laughingly rejected by many of Palmcastle's pretty ladies, he was willing to settle for Mandy

Potter's company. Her running commentary was fitfully witty, unless that was the champagne. Manganelle had been pumping her in an abstracted way when glancing up . . .

A magnificent creature, just his type: plenty of miles on the clock but bodywork in splendid condition, and a classic never ages. (Take the sexism up with Manganelle, please; he's the one telling it.) "I think," he purred, "I have just fallen in love."

"Anne Lamburn, Mr. Lamburn's wife," Mandy whispered, making "Mr. Lamburn" sound a name that mattered. Adding cattily, "She's attractive if you like a blast from the past, all Hollywood B-pictures and Spirit of the Forties." In truth, Anne Lamburn was wearing a strapless dress and black gloves to the elbow, auburn hair falling over one eye to foam on her ivory shoulders. Only the long cigarette holder was missing, and perhaps a few bars of Glenn Miller in the background.

Fair-mindedly, Mandy conceded, "It's ever so romantic about the Lamburns, a real fairy tale. They were sweethearts at school but somebody else cut him out, and Mr. Lamburn—a teenager at the time, wild—made terrible scenes and got in trouble and Lord knows what. But then he made his fortune and they found each other again in the twilight of their lives, so to speak."

Manganelle choked on his drink. Mrs. Lamburn was forty years old, maximum, and thus a mere slip of a girl in his estimation.

"Enough frivolity," he hissed, "duty calls," and jostled away through thickets of guests. Mrs. Lamburn appeared to be without an escort for the moment, and he'd devised a thin yet just about tolerable pretext to pester her. Planting himself before Anne Lamburn, he took her hand (she started, focused on him out of a daydream, and was palpably displeased by the view) and made a fairly revolting kissing sound half an inch above her captive fingers. The slight bow involved in this courtliness enabled him to peer earnestly into her cleavage. "Eric Manganelle, *Daily Intelligencer.*"

"How nice for you." Hand snatched back, she turned a shoulder, searching for rescue.

"You were pointed out to me, Mrs. Lamburn, and the name struck a friendly chord. Good ol' Harry spent hours eulogizing his lovely wife, and I wondered . . . Harry Lamburn, we were out in Lebanon together, a relation of yours by any chance?"

He was agreeably surprised when she swung round, lips parted. "Lebanon . . . Harry?" She was puzzled. "How strange."

"Sorry?"

Touching his arm, Anne Lamburn said, "You must wonder what on earth I'm talking about. My present husband's never been to Lebanon, you see, but my first . . . died there." Her tone hardened as she corrected herself. "He was killed in Beirut."

Appalled, he stammered, "Awfully sorry, never dreamed that—"

"Please don't worry about it. That was in 1982, I'm used to it." Mrs. Lamburn's smile was not happy. "Complete adjustment: it must be, I have remarried."

He was aware of sharp interest in her glance, and not so fuddled that he mistook it for flirtation. Further, the significance of what she'd been saying had just started to sink in.

Both Anne Lamburn and he glimpsed patent-leather hair and a brace of glasses held aloft as their bearer edged through the throng. Manganelle's visual memory was exceptional: he'd last seen that shiny-topped head with rulered parting poolside at the Commodore hotel.

Mrs. Lamburn lowered her voice, hurried and almost conspiratorial. "You were in Beirut. Maybe you met my husband, my rea—first husband? His name was Lancelot Pasover?"

"NATURALLY I AGREED to meet her next morning," Eric Manganelle told me. "Spare me the dying codfish look. I wasn't planning to make a pass, any fool could tell our Annie was a one-man woman; one at a time, leastways.

"But I wanted her side of the story, for my own satisfaction. I was getting a grip on the original story for the first time, come to that. I beat it before Harry Lamburn saw us together. Oh yes, it was the same Harry, my chap in Beirut, the good listener.

"It was all rather silly, I hired a car after breakfast and drove out to Hardpath Heights, the cliffs beyond Palmcastle. Local beauty spot, see all the way to France on a clear day, though why one should make the effort is a mystery to me, bloody Frogs doing Froggy things at extreme range. . . ."

I sighed stagily, and Manganelle glowered. "Anne Lamburn was waiting for me there, in a Bentley if you please, this year's model. I decided I'd been right about her old man, Harry *was* a crook. And a murderer, of course."

"Of course. Sticks out a mile."

Manganelle gave me a pitying look. "Don't act stupid, old lad, you have a head start in that department as it is. Come on, Harry Lamburn is besotted with Anne, but she married Supertwit, little Lancelot Pasover instead. Harry throws a tremendous wobbly, vows revenge, camps on her family's doorstep saying he'll never give her up. Local scandal, police called, finally her parents go to court and get an order against Harry, forbidding him to approach their daughter.

"Harry storms off to seek his fortune in foreign climes, Anne is wed to Lancelot. Time passes, Pasover goes on his fool's errand to Beirut, I—all unwittingly, mind—zero Harry Lamburn in on him. Lo and behold, Pasover is murdered and suddenly Harry is nowhere to be seen. I never noticed at the time, but Lamburn made himself scarce directly after Lancelot Pasover was killed. Shot off to Cyprus, then a flight to Anywhere. It was happening all the time. The Israelis controlled PLO movements, but Brits could come and go as they liked, we were flitting back and forth like swallows."

"Granted, Lamburn could have done it. So could a quarter of a million other likely suspects—anyone within a few square miles of him," I objected.

"Twaddle! He had the motive, means, and opportunity, isn't that the standard litany? And there's more. . . .

"Anne Lamburn apologized for our cloak-and-dagger date but said it had to be that way because her husband was neurotically jealous and possessive, always checking on her. She often came out to the Heights so if anyone mentioned seeing the Bentley, Harry Lamburn wouldn't find it suspicious.

"'Harry lost me once and he isn't rational about it, he cannot believe it will not happen again,' Anne told me. That was when she filled me in on the teenage melodrama when Lancelot Pasover swept her off her feet. Hard to picture Lance sweeping the floor, even, but women are funny.

"Before she could ask me about meeting Lancelot in Beirut, I pretended to forget our conversation the previous evening and asked her if Harry Lamburn had ever been there. No, she said, definitely not, he'd made his pile in Africa and never set foot anywhere in the Middle East. Harry had made a sentimental journey back to Palmcastle, heard of her bereavement through mutual friends, and was astonished to learn that his teenage obsession had been widowed for six months . . ."

"Aha!"

"Well put," Manganelle approved. "My very thought at the time. That's when I *knew* Lamburn had polished off his rival. Why lie? Because if he told Anne that he'd been to Beirut all right, and her husband happened to be rubbed out during Harry's brief visit . . . you follow? She had to put two and two together, and the answer wouldn't come out orange blossom and Wedding March.

"Meanwhile, Anne Lamburn was getting a trifle restive with me. Had I or had I not met Lancelot?" Manganelle indulged in one of his patented, shifty grins. "I blarneyed her, said we'd spoken briefly, Lancelot and me, he'd been a typical British gent, tragic end, probably mistaken identity, and he was tragic victim of terrorism."

Staring at him, I said, "You covered up for Harry Lamburn?"

Shrugging moodily, Manganelle countered, "I couldn't prove anything beyond a strong smell. Why get the wretched woman worked up? It was painfully obvious that, twit or no, she'd thought the world of Lancelot Pasover, and I saw no good in presenting her with the nightmare that she was living with his killer—who had killed for her, into the bargain."

Manganelle sniggered bitterly. "Too late, old boy. Always engage brain before operating mouth . . . but what with the champange and everything, I'd had to chat her up, and the goose was cooked."

"How d'you mean?"

"Something in her eyes," he said, pulling a face. "A glint putting me in mind of a cat at a mousehole, very strongly in mind of that. Disagreeably so, old boy. And the minute I ran out of soothing lies to make her feel better, she gave me a real sergeant major's look, a cut-the-crap look. Know what she said? 'Why did you ask if Harry had ever been to Beirut?' And then, no time for me to stick my oar in, she said, statement not question, '*You met him there.*'"

"Awkward," I suggested.

"You spat a bootful. Let's take a stroll, breath of fresh air on the prom." Not Eric Manganelle's style at all, leaving an unemptied glass.

It was a gorgeous night, black velvet sky, pumpkin moon, air like warm milk, and fairy lights twinkling their reflections across the placid sea. From the shadow came the singing of cicadas: in reality the scrape of alloy on asphalt as geriatric strollers deployed their walking frames.

"Women have bouts of ESP," Manganelle argued. "I never said a word about seeing her husband, both of them in fact, present and future tenses as it were, in the same place at the same time. But she . . . she picked up that thought and drew it out of my head like pulling silk from a silkworm."

I had to laugh. "She wouldn't need ESP! You're tactful as a bull elephant and transparent as cellophane, two minutes of your so-called soothing lies and Mrs. Lamburn was bound to smell a rat."

Out of character, he took that passively. "Possibly, possibly; 'pon my word, though, I tried to act for the best." He sounded so subdued that I nagged.

"You're keeping something back."

Manganelle gave me a sideways look blending shame, pride, and sheer mischief. "Um, well, there's a *bit* more," he admitted coyly.

A suspicion was growing. "Hang on, exactly when was this conference where you met the lady?"

"Months back, half a year or more."

"So why are you here now?"

Eric Manganelle tried to look solemn, regretful. "I came down for the inquest, actually. Open-and-shut thing, over in minutes. Sad case, feller is up there on Hardpath Heights, sudden attack of vertigo, loving wife makes futile attempt to yank him back by the collar, just misses, and is left holding his toupee, rest of hubby three hundred feet below on the rocks.

"Verdict: misadventure. You could tell the coroner was quite smitten by the widow—but then there's nothing like designer mourning to complement a mature redhead."

We paused by mutual consent and watched serene Palmcastle, where nothing happens because that is what Palmcastle is for. "She killed him, *executed* him, and you are letting her get away with it," I accused.

Manganelle simpered and pursed his lips. "Two wrongs can make a right is the way I prefer to see it. Impulse, old boy: the moment of unbearable temptation. We all know about that, generally from standing outside a pub, sixty seconds before opening time."

"What are you talking about?"

"Harry Lamburn found himself in Beirut with Lancelot Pasover, whom he saw—correctly, as events proved—as the only barrier between himself and the love of his life. What's more, Pasover was ripe for the zapping, in the world capital of random violence. Where d'you hide a leaf but the forest? Where d'you hide a murder but jolly old downtown West Beirut? Unbearable temptation.

"Same thing goes for Anne Lamburn. I blurted something out, and she made inquiries and was morally certain that she'd married a murderer. The Lamburns liked going to that cliff-top, she told me so. Unbearable temptation Part Two, Mr. Lamburn tries parachuteless skydiving." Manganelle drew himself up, or at least puffed harder and pushed his paunch out. "Don't go preaching at me—if you think I had no proof about Lamburn giving poor Lance the chop, there's even less against the repetitive widow, Mrs. L. I was at the inquest, heard the witnesses. Graphic evidence that onlookers can't tell the difference between a grab and a shove."

"All the same, you should go to the police, get the investigation reopened, the inquest verdict set aside. I'm sure there is a procedure for that."

Eric Manganelle drew himself up to his full five-three or thereabouts, toadly countenance florid with righteous indignation. "Bite your tongue! *Me*, make trouble for a poor, lone, widow-woman? I never make trouble for anyone!"

GEORGE C. CHESBRO
PRIESTS

September 1991

GEORGE C. CHESBRO is probably best known for his creation Dr. Robert Frederickson, P.I., criminologist, karate black belt, and a dwarf who, as "Mongo the Magnificent," was once a world-class circus performer. The Mongo stories often featured elements of fantasy or the supernatural, and though "Priests" is not a Mongo story, it shares their concern with fundamental forces such as evil.

■

Symbols **that had** once given him comfort and a sense of belonging to a community of infinite continuity now evoked in him opposite emotions, reminding him of his loss and his isolation from all the people, places, and things that had permeated his soul and defined his being until five years ago, when he had been banished from this world.

Flanked by the plastic statuary of the Stations of the Cross in their shadowy alcoves, feeling like a naked, vulnerable runner in a gauntlet set up to test his spirit, Brendan Furie, his footsteps muffled by thick maroon carpeting, strode quickly down the center aisle of the dimly lighted cathedral. He had not been inside a church in the five years since his excommunication, the amputation of his soul from the body of the church engineered by the figure in black who was kneeling, head bowed in prayer, at the railing before the white-draped altar at the front of the sanctuary.

Brendan had the distinct feeling that he was being watched, and he wondered if this might not be a kind of vestigial sense of the eyes of God, a psychological reaction to this return after a long absence to physical surroundings that had once meant everything to him but now seemed only a distant memory from another life, perhaps one only dreamed.

He reached the front of the sanctuary, but the frail, kneeling figure remained still, and Brendan was not certain the other man was even aware of his presence. For a moment he felt the old, virtually instinctive urge to genuflect before the altar, but he knew he no longer had either the obligation or the right, and so he simply sat down at the end of the first pew and waited for Henry Cardinal Farrell to finish his prayers.

Almost five minutes went by before the old man, without raising his head or unclasping his hands, said in a low voice, "Thank you for coming, father."

"I'm here because you asked me to come, eminence," Brendan replied evenly. He swallowed, added softly, "I would appreciate it if you wouldn't call me 'father.' Frankly, it sounds rather odd when you say it. You, of all people, know that I'm no longer a priest."

There was a prolonged silence, and Brendan began to wonder if the cardinal had heard him. But then the kneeling figure said, "Other people still call you that."

"No."

"You've become famous."

"Have I?"

"I've seen it in the newspapers. They call you 'the priest,' or sometimes just 'priest.'"

"It's not the same thing, eminence."

"No," the old man replied, and then shuddered slightly, as if he had suddenly experienced a chill. "And I'd prefer you not to address me as 'eminence.' It's been some time since I felt eminent. I appreciate your courtesy, but it isn't necessary."

"As you wish, sir."

"Brendan, are you . . . carrying a gun?"

It seemed a decidedly odd question in this stone house of worship, and Brendan stared at the old man's back for a few moments. But the kneeling figure remained inscrutable, old bones and flesh draped in black. Finally he replied, "No."

"I thought you might be. The stories . . ."

"Sometimes I carry a gun, but not often. In my business, a gun doesn't do much good. I've yet to meet the superstition, ignorance, obsession, or hatred that I could kill with a bullet."

Now the cardinal raised his head, unclasped his bony hands, straightened his back. He put both hands on the rail in front of him and struggled to rise. Brendan got to his feet and started forward to assist the other man, stopped when the cardinal vigorously shook his head in protest. Brendan resumed his seat, waited. Finally the cardinal managed to stand. He turned, walked unsteadily to the pew across from Brendan, eased himself down. Brendan gazed into the eyes of the man sitting across the maroon-carpeted aisle and was shocked by the stark gauntness of the features, the parchment-colored flesh that seemed almost translucent, the dark rings around the eyes. Henry Cardinal Farrell looked, Brendan thought, like a piece of fruit that had shriveled, or been cored.

The old man's lips drew back in a kind of bemused smile, and emotions Brendan could not decipher moved like moon shadows in the watery gray eyes. "Danger, the world, and good works seem to have served you well, priest. You look very well."

"You do not."

"I shall die . . . shortly."

"I'm sorry."

The frail Prince of the Church made a dismissive gesture with a trembling hand, and once again he smiled. "God really does work in mysterious ways, doesn't He?"

"I've heard it said, father."

"I suppose it could be said that in a certain way I created you."

"How so, father?"

"I created this 'priest' that you've become, this man of such fame—or notoriety, as some would have it—who is now a private investigator, of all things, specializing in religious and spiritual matters, a fierce defender of children and their rights. Before, you were just a . . . priest. I have heard it argued again and again that you are a far more effective avatar for Christ in your state of disgrace than you ever were before your . . . career change. The implications of this for the church are a subject of some heated debate among certain theologians. My name is almost never mentioned. I actually believe my role in it all has been forgotten."

Brendan said nothing. He felt oddly distanced, separated from this old enemy and the institution he represented by an unbreachable wall of betrayal, loss, pain, and death.

"You were never a good priest, Brendan," the cardinal continued in a voice that seemed to be growing stronger with a passion born of either anger or regret. "You were always a rebel, never at ease with the church. You were always questioning things you had no right to question."

"I questioned things you didn't want me to question, eminence, but I always obeyed you, didn't I?" Brendan paused as he felt waves of his old resentment and anger rise in him, waiting for them to recede. When they were gone, he continued, "I went into retreat to do penance when you ordered me to, and I came out to do your errand when you ordered me to. It was not the church that made me ill at ease."

The cardinal stiffened. "Errand?"

"That's what I said."

"It was God's business."

"It was your business."

"The reason you were sent to retreat in the first place was to teach you that it wasn't your place to make such judgments."

Brendan suppressed a sigh. "Why did you ask me to come here, father?"

The old man looked away from Brendan, toward the altar and beyond at the huge, painted wood figure of Christ nailed to a cross. "I've told you I shall die shortly. I have my secular affairs in order, and now I am trying to do the same for my soul."

"What is it you want from me, father?" Brendan asked in a neutral tone.

"I want you to hear my confession."

Brendan could not believe he had heard the other man correctly; if he had, it could only mean that his being asked to come here was the sad joke of a dying old man, or that the mind of that dying old man was deteriorating. Brendan said nothing.

"You would refuse the request of a man who is so close to death?"

"I don't understand the request."

"I don't ask you to understand it, only to grant it."

"I'm not exactly qualified to hear your confession, am I? Why should you wish to participate in a heretical act? Some of your more conservative colleagues might say you've committed heresy merely by making the request—that's assuming you're serious."

The old man opened his mouth and made a strange, rasping sound. It took Brendan a few moments to realize that the other man was laughing. "Since when have you concerned yourself with what the church did or did not consider heresy? I don't think you much cared even before they defrocked you."

"What concerns me is my business, father," Brendan replied evenly. "Forgive me for saying that you've played games with me before, and I can't help but wonder if this isn't just part of some other game."

The cardinal abruptly looked away; when he looked back at Brendan, his pale, watery eyes seemed unnaturally bright. "This is not a game, Brendan," he said forcefully.

"Your sins have nothing to do with me."

"You know that isn't so." He paused, leaned forward in the pew, added: "Some sins have a way of coming back to punish you in this life. Listen to me."

"I won't hear your confession."

The cardinal sighed, leaned back in the pew. "Why do you accuse me of having played games with you? You were asked to perform an exorcism. As a result of your miscalculations, the mother of the young girl in question committed a mortal sin by killing herself. Church authorities determined that the suicide of this woman was a direct result of your malfeasance—your lack of proper preparation and perhaps even your lack of faith and purpose; the sin, it was decided, was yours, not hers, and the punishment was your excommunication. That judgment may have been harsh, but it was influenced by your past attitudes and writings and your reputation and actions as a dissident priest. You were consistently involved with organizations, social and political causes that the Holy See deemed inappropriate. You were warned more than once. Those are the facts. Do you dispute them?"

"I do not. Those are the facts. But the truth lies someplace else."

"Oh? Just what is the truth?"

"You sent me out to perform a rite for which you knew I wasn't prepared and in which you suspected I didn't believe."

"You don't believe in demonic possession?"

"I believe in obsession founded on greed, lust, hatred, or a dozen other human evils. But it's hard enough to get people to take responsibility for their actions without providing them with the potential excuse that the devil made them do it."

"It's not like you to be flippant or disrespectful of ideas other people take very seriously, Brendan."

"I'm telling you the truth you claimed to want to hear. If you think I'm being flippant, you still don't understand me and you can never understand what happened. Lisa Vanderklaven wasn't possessed by demons; her erratic behavior was, under the circumstances, rational and healthy. She had a very good reason for defying her father and continually running away from home, namely that she was being persistently and brutally abused by the same man who had made her mother his mistress and who was her father's close business associate. When Lisa told her father about the abuse, he refused to believe her. Henry Vanderklaven preferred to believe that his daughter was possessed by demons, for to accept that she was being molested by Werner Pale would have interfered with his business interests and cast considerable doubt on his ability to judge character. Lisa Vanderklaven needed protection, not exorcism.

"In my initial interview with Lisa, she broke down; she couldn't believe that her father could actually believe she was possessed. That was when she told me that Pale had not only been molesting her, but had been involved in a sexual relationship with her mother for some time; Pale had bragged about it to her. At the time, I didn't feel I had any choice but to talk with Olga Vanderklaven, not only to try to confirm Lisa's story but to offer the mother my help, if she wanted it. *That* was my mistake. Faced with the fact that Lisa and I knew about her lover, and that the lover was molesting her daughter, she committed suicide.

"If anybody in that family could have been described as possessed, it was Lisa's father, and he'd created his own hell out of a deadly combination of greed and self-righteousness. Vanderklaven's greed was what led him to employ a man like Werner Pale in the first place. Vanderklaven was an arms dealer, as you well know. What you might not have known was that Werner Pale was a murderous soldier of fortune whom Vanderklaven employed to train *provocateurs*. Those *provocateurs* were kept busy whipping up brush wars in various parts of the world in order to keep up the volume of sales of the arms Vanderklaven manufactured.

He saw nothing wrong with what he did; he was an impossibly self-righteous man who could not see the evil around him that he'd created. He was a zealous Catholic with powerful friends in Rome, a church benefactor who gave millions to various church causes. He was so assured of his reservations in heaven that he could destroy his family and be blissfully unaware of the cause— the evil he had brought home with him, the man he considered a friend as well as a business associate. When Lisa told him that his friend was raping her, Vanderklaven demanded that she see a psychiatrist; when she ran away, he sent Werner Pale to find her and bring her back. When she ran away again, he went to his golf buddy—you, eminence—and asked you to arrange for an exorcism to free his daughter from her demons. Demonic possession was the only explanation he could think of for her behavior.

"I believe, eminence, that when you heard the story, you knew it would not withstand the scrutiny and investigation Rome requires before declaring officially that someone is demonically possessed, and that it was highly unlikely you would be able to get a trained exorcist to intervene in the affairs of this very troubled family. But you were afraid to offend Henry Vanderklaven by telling him the truth; you were afraid he might tighten his purse strings to the detriment of the church's interest, perhaps even afraid he might complain to his friends in the Vatican about your lack of sensitivity. And so you looked around for another solution to the problem he'd handed you, and I was it. You would send this young priest you were trying to break to go through the motions of performing an exorcism; once again you would force me to submit to your will while at the same time making Vanderklaven happy. I failed, father, yes, and because of my failure as a human being to fully perceive and deal with Olga Vanderklaven's torment, she committed suicide as a direct result of my inquiries. Well, Rome was not about to declare that the soul of the wife of this important lay pillar of the church would burn in hell; in their view, and perhaps yours, it was preferable to consign *my* soul to burn in hell, and I was subsequently excommunicated. I didn't disagree with their action then, and I don't now. I was responsible for the woman's death, because I should have ignored your machinations, scrapped the whole idea of an exorcism, and referred the case to social workers. Olga Vanderklaven died because of my failure as a priest, eminence, but she also died because you sent someone you knew to be spiritually unequipped for the task of performing a rite that wasn't even called for to meddle in an incredibly raw emotional situation. *That,* eminence, is the truth."

Brendan waited, anticipating defense or denial. Instead, the cardinal simply said, "You are right, priest. That is the truth."

"If you understand that, it seems to me that you have confessed all you need to."

The old man slowly turned to face Brendan, and his pale eyes went wide. "Understand this, Brendan," he said in a trembling voice. "Satan himself was there. It was Satan himself you were battling against."

Brendan studied the other man's face, saw real fear there—as well as something else he could not read. "I assume you're speaking metaphorically, father." He paused, frowned when the cardinal responded by shaking his head. "Werner Pale?"

Now the cardinal nodded. Brendan ran his hands back through his black shoulder-length hair, looked down at the floor as he resisted the impulse to say something flippant or sarcastic that he knew he would regret. Finally he looked up, said, "No, father. Pale was a murderous psychotic and a totally useless human being, not Satan. Believing that is just your way of avoiding taking personal responsibility for what happened. That's what Henry Vanderklaven did, and it's what killed his wife."

The cardinal's eyes went even wider, and his hands began to shake along with his voice. "But what if I'm right, Brendan? What if it was Satan?"

"What you believe is none of my business, eminence," Brendan replied evenly. "Believe what makes you at peace, but don't then ask me to help resolve the conflicts that remain."

The old man took a deep breath, slowly exhaled. His trembling eased, and he sank back wearily in the pew. "I would very much like to know what happened afterward," he said in a voice so low Brendan could barely make out the words.

"Didn't Vanderklaven tell you?"

The old man sighed, producing an odd rattling sound in his lungs. "Henry Vanderklaven put a bullet in his brain soon after returning here from Europe, which was about three months after the events we have been discussing transpired. I believe it was because of something you said or did to him."

Brendan searched inside himself for some feeling of pity for Henry Vanderklaven, a man who, according to his belief system, had sentenced himself to eternal damnation. He felt nothing. He believed the man had done nothing to himself except end his life. He found he no longer believed in hells or heavens, save for those created by living human consciousness and deeds, and perhaps never had. His faith had always been about living each day as a human trying to live up to the example set by Christ, not eternal rewards or punishments. What he did believe, what he knew, was that Henry Vanderklaven had created a hell for others that still tormented them, and he was glad the man was no longer alive.

"Brendan?" the cardinal continued softly. "What happened?"

"After Lisa ran away for the second time and came to the children's shelter, I promised her she would be protected from any kind of demons—human or otherwise—until I had investigated to try to determine the truth," Brendan said in an even tone that belied the turmoil once again building inside him. "I failed her. Not only did her mother commit suicide as a result of my bungling questions, but Werner Pale—acting on the father's orders—kidnapped her a second time while I was otherwise occupied trying to defend myself against excommunication. Then father, daughter, and Werner Pale left for Europe. As far as law enforcement and social welfare agencies here were concerned, the matter was out of their jurisdiction. But it wasn't a situation I could live with. I'd promised Lisa she wouldn't be harmed. I searched for them, and I found them. The details aren't important. What matters is that I finally found a way to make Henry Vanderklaven face up to the fact that the friend he relied on to stir up his business of death had cuckolded him and raped his daughter repeatedly. He saw, finally, how his own greed had blinded him, destroyed his wife, and caused his daughter to hate him. I didn't know he'd killed himself. For all his outward zealotry, he apparently didn't believe in forgiveness, not even for himself, and he certainly must not have believed in redemption."

"And where . . . is the girl now?"

"In New York. She's happily married, with a child. She works for a private children's social service agency."

Now the old man again slowly turned to look at Brendan, studied his face for some time. Finally he said, "Ah, yes. It's the same agency, I presume, for which you have done such good work, the one operated by the former nun with whom you are rumored to have a . . . relationship?"

"I don't think that's really a part of this story, eminence, is it? The point is that Lisa is safe now, with her own life to lead. She still has nightmares, but those will pass with time."

The cardinal nodded slightly. "And . . . Werner Pale?"

"He's dead. I killed him."

Brendan watched the other man react with what could have been surprise, but also with something else Brendan could not quite determine. "You, priest, killed this professional soldier?"

"He was trying to kill me. We fought, and I was lucky. He'd planned to burn me to death, but he was the one who fell into the fire."

Once again the old cardinal, apparently lost in his own thoughts, was silent for some time. At last, he said, "I've heard it said that you've killed a number of men since you left us. Can you have changed so much, priest?"

"How much I have changed is not for me to say, eminence. I've harmed no one who was not trying to harm me, or sometimes a child. I've told you what you wanted to know. Are you satisfied?"

"Would you care to hear what has happened to me over the past five years?"

"If you feel the need to tell me, I will listen."

"God has turned his face from me, Brendan. I wronged you, and I've been punished. While it's true that the decision to excommunicate you came from Rome, the same people ultimately blamed me, for they knew the truth you spoke of. I often feel as if I have been excommunicated along with you. There has been no peace for me during the past five years."

"It sounds to me as if you've been busy punishing yourself, eminence. You made a mistake, and God will forgive you. Where is your faith?"

The cardinal shook his head impatiently, with renewed vigor. "It was more than just a mistake. It's true that I never believed the girl was possessed, and yet I sent you to perform a sacred ritual simply to mollify her father. That is blasphemy, sacrilege. I need not only God's forgiveness, but yours, Brendan."

"You have it."

"Hear my confession."

"I believe I already have."

"In the confessional. Please."

"I don't think so, eminence. This is the second time you have asked me to perform a sacred rite under inappropriate circumstances. The—"

"Precisely!"

"—first time neither of us believed in what we were doing, and death and my excommunication were the results; now that I have been excommunicated, church authorities would not recognize the sanctity of any confession you made to me. I don't understand what it is you really want, but I do know that it can't be the sacrament of confession."

The old cardinal slowly rose to his feet, turned to face Brendan, drew himself up very straight. Suddenly his eyes were very bright. "If you do not understand, priest, then you have not been listening to my words carefully, as I asked you to. I need to confess to you so that I can hear you say the Hail Marys."

Suddenly Brendan felt the hairs rise on the back of his neck, and he resisted the impulse to make any sudden movement. "As you wish, eminence," he replied in an even tone, bowing his head slightly.

"The confessor will come to you," the cardinal said in the same strong voice, and then turned away.

Brendan forced himself to remain still, to breathe evenly, as he watched the old man hobble across the sanctuary and disappear through a door to the right of the altar. He waited a few seconds, then rose and walked toward the ornately carved wood confessional stalls to his left. He hesitated just a moment before entering the priest's section of the confessional and sitting down.

Sins have a way of coming back to punish you in this life. Listen to me.

Almost five minutes passed, and then Brendan heard the door in the section on the other side of the wood screen open. Brendan glanced through the screen and watched as a stooped figure wearing a white robe with a cowl entered.

Even without the cardinal's cryptic request to hear him speak Hail Marys, which was a reversal of the rite and all wrong, he would have sensed danger now, for this robed and hooded figure wore the white sash, the alb, around his neck, and that was wrong; a priest wore the alb to receive confession, not to enter the box as a penitent.

His earlier sensation of being watched had not been a fantasy, Brendan thought, but the eyes watching him had definitely not been those of God.

. . . Are you carrying a gun?

Brendan stood and hurled himself at the screen, hitting the wood with his right shoulder and placing his left forearm across his face to protect his eyes from splinters. He hurtled through the fragile latticework, landing against the robed figure, and they both fell to the floor of the stall. Brendan used his left hand to grab the wrist of the man's right hand, which had emerged from the robe holding a .22-caliber pistol, while he drove his right fist into the man's midsection.

The cowl slipped back, revealing a face that was a nightmare mass of milk-colored, puckered scar tissue and lines of pink scars that could only have been the results of a series of failed operations. Werner Pale writhed beneath Brendan with the strength born of bottomless hatred and rage, swung at his head with the steel hook that had been used to replace his left hand. Brendan ducked under the blow but felt the sharp tip against his back as the steel began to dig its way through his leather jacket toward his flesh. He reached out with his free hand, found a shard of wood from the shattered screen, wrapped his fingers around it. As the steel tip sliced through his jacket and touched skin, he raised the stake in the air, then drove the tip down into Werner Pale's throat.

Blood spurted from the pierced jugular. The scarred O of the man's mouth opened in a silent scream, but almost immediately the one seeing eye began to glaze over. The body beneath Brendan twitched violently for a few moments, then was still.

Brendan rose from the corpse, threw open the door to the confessional, and, wiping blood from his face, ran through a labyrinth of narrow stone and wood corridors toward the cardinal's private chambers.

He found the old man, looking even paler and with pain clearly evident in the watery eyes, sitting at the desk in his study, seemingly holding himself upright with his palms on the polished oak surface before him.

"Brendan," Henry Cardinal Farrell breathed as Brendan came through the door, stopped. "Thank God. My prayers have been answered." He paused and squinted, as if he were having trouble seeing. "You're hurt . . . ?"

"The blood is Werner Pale's, eminence, not mine."

"Thank God."

"Thank you for your warning. It saved my life."

"I couldn't warn you outright, priest. He was listening."

"I understand," Brendan said and again started forward. He stopped a few feet from the desk when the cardinal raised one trembling hand with the palm outward, as if to push him back.

"He came to me . . . to kill me, of course, since I was responsible for sending you into his life. He wanted to know where to find you and the girl, and he said that he would kill me quickly if I told him. There is nothing he could have done to make me tell him, Brendan. Believe me."

"I do, eminence. You don't have to explain."

"But I want to," the old man said in a voice that was growing progressively weaker.

"I believe he spent most of the past five years in hospitals, or he would have known how famous you've become. He would have had no trouble finding you, and you would have had no warning. He might also have traced the girl, Lisa. I decided to gamble for your life and the girl's; you had defeated him once before, and perhaps you could do it again. I sensed that he was afraid of you. But I also sensed that he badly wanted to make you suffer, and that shooting you down from some rooftop would not be satisfying for him. I acted well, Brendan. I got down on my knees before him and begged him for my life. I told him I would bring you to him and extract the information he wanted, if only he would spare my life. I also told him I would help trap you in a closed space, where you would be at his mercy. He was very pleased with the idea of killing you in the confessional booth, positively delighted when I suggested that he could pretend to be me. He said he was going to shoot you in the belly or kneecaps first, and then carve you up. He couldn't stop laughing when I showed him the robe and sash he could wear. He loved the idea of dressing up like a priest to kill you." The old man paused, and the broad smile that suddenly appeared on his face seemed to belong to a much younger and less troubled man. "That's when I knew we had a chance, priest, for you, of all people, would find it rather odd that I, of all people, would ask you to join me in an act of heresy."

Then the cardinal coughed blood and pitched forward on the desk. Brendan rushed forward, lifted the old man by the shoulders, saw the blood, and the handle of the stiletto that was protruding from the other man's stomach. He also saw that it was too late.

"Pray for me, priest. God listens to you. Pray for me. Help my soul find its way to heaven."

"I will."

"Do you . . . understand what I . . . mean?"

"Yes. I will."

And then the old man was gone. Brendan walked to the wardrobe in a corner of the office, removed a robe, and put it on. He removed the crucifix from the cardinal's neck, put it around his own. Then he knelt beside the old man's body and began performing the last rites, his last rite. For the first time in five years he prayed in the old way, as if it mattered.

MARTIN LIMÓN

PUSAN NIGHTS

May 1991

MARTIN LIMÓN made his publishing debut in *AHMM* in 1990 with the historical mystery "A Coffin of Rice," and a few months later he introduced his best-known characters, George Sueño and Ernie Bascom, in our pages in "The Blackmarket Detail." Sueño and Bascom are military police officers stationed in Seoul, South Korea, and Limón has subsequently featured them in both novels and short stories. Limón himself spent ten years in South Korea when he was in the army; unlike many of his fellow soldiers, he learned the language and took every opportunity to soak up Korean history and culture. That experience infuses his stories with a rich sense of authenticity.

■

"**The last time** the USS *Kitty Hawk* pulled into the Port of Pusan, the shore patrol had to break up a total of thirty-three barroom brawls in the Texas Street area. Routine. What we didn't expect was the fourteen sailors who were assaulted and robbed in the street. Six of them had to be hospitalized.

"From eyewitness accounts, the local provost marshal's office ascertained that the muggings appeared to have been perpetrated by Americans, probably the shipmates of the victims. However, no one was caught or charged with a crime."

We were in the big drafty headquarters building of the 8th Army's Criminal Investigation Division in Seoul, two hundred miles up the Korean Peninsula from Pusan. When the first sergeant had called me and my partner, Ernie Bascom, into his office, we expected the usual tirade for not having made enough black-market arrests. What we got was a new assignment. The first sergeant kept it simple.

"First, make sure you get on the right flight out of Kimpo. Then, when you get to Pusan, infiltrate the waterfront area and find out who's been pulling off these muggings."

Ernie adjusted his glasses and tugged on his tie.

"Maybe the gang who did it has left the navy and gone on to better things."

"Not hardly. The *Kitty Hawk* was here only six months ago. The tour in the navy is four years, minimum. Not enough time to break up the old gang."

Ernie got quiet. I knew him. He didn't want to seem too anxious to get this assignment, an all-expenses-paid trip to the wildest port in Northeast Asia, and he was cagey enough to put up some objections. To put some concern in the first sergeant's mind about how difficult it would be to catch these guys. That way, if we felt like it, we could goof off the whole time and come up with zilch, and the groundwork for our excuse was already laid.

I had to admire him. Always thinking.

"And you, Sueño." The first sergeant turned his cold gray eyes on me. "I don't want you running off and getting involved in some grandiose schemes that don't concern you."

"You mean, stay away from the navy brass."

"I mean catch these guys who are doing the muggings. That's what you're being paid for. Some of those sailors were hurt badly the last time they were here, and I don't want it to happen again."

I nodded, keeping my face straight. Neither one of us was going to mouth off now and lose a chance to go to Pusan. To Texas Street.

The first sergeant handed me a brown envelope stuffed with copies of the blotter reports from the last time the *Kitty Hawk* had paid a visit to the Land of the Morning Calm. He stood up and, for once, shook both our hands.

"I hate to let you guys out of my sight. But nobody can infiltrate a village full of bars and whores and drunken sailors better than you two." His face changed from sunshine to clouds. "If, however, you don't bring me back some results, I guarantee you'll have my highly polished size twelve combat boot placed firmly on your respective posteriors. You got that?"

Ernie grinned, a little weasel-toothed, half-moon grin. I concentrated on keeping my facial muscles steady. I'm not sure it worked.

We clattered down the long hallway and bounded down the steps to Ernie's jeep. When he started it up, he shouted, "Three days in Texas Street!"

I was happy. So was he.

But I had the uneasy twisting in my bowels that happens whenever I smell murder.

BY THE TIME we landed in Pusan I had read over the blotter reports. They were inconclusive, based mainly on hearsay from Korean bystanders. The assailants were Americans, they said, dressed in bluejeans and nylon jackets, like their victims and like all the sailors on liberty who prowled the portside alleys of Texas Street. The navy shore patrol had stopped some fights in barrooms and on the streets, but they were unable to apprehend even one of the muggers.

By interservice agreement, the army's military police increased their patrols near the dock areas when a huge naval presence moved into the port of Pusan. The aircraft carrier *Kitty Hawk,* with its accompanying flotilla and its over five thousand sailors, more than qualified as a huge naval presence.

The MPs were stationed, for the most part, on the inland army base of Hialeah Compound. They played on Texas Street, knew the alleys, the girls, the Mama-sans. But somehow they had been unable to make one arrest.

Sailors and soldiers don't often hit it off. Especially when the sailors are only in town for three days and manage to jack up all the prices by trying to spend two months' pay in a few hours. It seemed as if the MPs would be happy to arrest a few squids.

Something told me they weren't trying.

WE CAUGHT A cab at the airport outside of Pusan and arrived at Hialeah Compound in the early afternoon. We got a room at the billeting office, and the first thing we did was nothing. Ernie took a nap. I kept thumbing through the blotter reports, worrying them to death.

There was a not very detailed road map of the city of Pusan in a tourist brochure in the rickety little desk provided to us by billeting. Hialeah Compound was about three miles inland from the main port and had got its name because prior to the end of World War II the Japanese occupation forces had used its flat plains as a track for horse racing. The U.S. Army had turned it into a base to provide security and logistical support for all the goods pouring into the harbor. Pusan was a large city, and its downtown area sprawled between Hialeah Compound and the port. Pushed up along the docks, like a long, slender barnacle, was Texas Street. Merchant sailors from all over the world passed through this port, but it was only the U.S. Navy that came here in such force.

Using a thick-leaded pencil I plotted the locations of the muggings on the little map. The dots defined the district known as Texas Street. Not one was more than half a mile from where the *Kitty Hawk* was docked.

ERNIE AND I approached the big MP desk.

"Bascom and Sueño," Ernie said. "Reporting in from Seoul."

The desk sergeant looked down at us over the rim of his comic book.

"Oh, yeah. Heard you guys were coming. Hold on. The duty officer wants to talk to you."

After a few minutes, a little man with his chest stuck out and a face like a yapping Chihuahua came out. He seemed lost in his highly starched fatigues. Little gold butter bars flapped from his collar.

"The commanding officer told me to give you guys a message."

We waited.

The lieutenant tried to expand his chest. The starched green material barely moved.

"Don't mess with our people. We got a good MP company down here; any muggings that happen, we'll take care of them; and we don't need you two sending phony reports up to Seoul, trying to make us look bad."

His chest deflated slightly. He seemed exhausted and out of breath.

"Is that it?"

"Yeah."

Ernie walked around him and looked back up at the desk sergeant.

"How many patrols are you going to have out at Texas Street tonight?"

"Four. Three MPs per jeep."

"Three?"

The desk sergeant shrugged. "We'd have four per jeep if we could. The advance party of the *Kitty Hawk*'s arriving tonight."

"All patrols roving?"

"No. One in the center of the strip, two more on either end, and one patrol roving."

"You must put your studs in the center."

"You got that right."

"Who performs your liaison with the shore patrol?"

The desk sergeant shrugged again. "The lieutenant here, such as it is. Mainly they run their own show, out of the port officer's headquarters, down by the docks."

"Thanks. If we find out anything—and there's time—we'll let your MPs make the arrest."

"Don't do us any favors. Those squids can kill each other for all I care."

The lieutenant shot him a look. The desk sergeant glanced at the lieutenant and then back down at the comic book on his desk.

We turned to walk out. Ernie winked at the lieutenant, who glared after us until we faded into the thickening fog of the Pusan night.

TEXAS STREET was long and bursting with music and brightly flashing neon. The colors and the songs changed as we walked down the street, and the scantily clad girls waved at us through beaded curtains, trying to draw us in. Young American sailors in bluejeans and nylon jackets with embroidered dragons on the back bounced from bar to bar enjoying the embraces of the "business girls," who still outnumbered them. The main force of their shipmates had not arrived yet, and the *Kitty Hawk* would not dock until dawn. But Texas Street was ready for them.

We saw the MPs. The jeep in the center of Texas Street was parked unobtrusively next to a brick wall, its radio crackling. The three MPs smoked and talked, big brutes, all. We stayed away from them and concentrated on blending into the crowd.

Ernie was having no trouble at all. In bar after bar we toyed with the girls, bought drinks only for ourselves, and kept from answering their questions about which ship we were on by constantly changing the subject.

One of the girls caught on that we were in the army by our unwillingness to spend too much money and by the few Korean words that we let slip out.

"Don't let the Mama-san hear you speaking Korean," she said. "If she does, she will know that you're in the army, and she will not let me talk to you."

"What's wrong with GIs?"

I could answer that question with volumes, but I wanted to hear her version.

"All GIs Cheap Charlie. Sailors are here for only a short time. They spend a lot of money."

We filed the economics lesson, finished our beers, and staggered to the next bar.

Periodically we hung around near one of the MP patrols, within earshot of their radio, waiting for a report of a fight or a mugging. So far it was a quiet night.

Later, a group of white-uniformed sailors on shore patrol duty ran past us, holding on to their revolvers and their hats, their nightsticks flapping at their sides. We followed and watched while they broke up a fight in one of the bars. A gray navy van pulled up, and the disheveled revelers were loaded aboard.

We found a noodle stand and ate, giving ourselves away as GIs to the wizened old proprietor by knowing what to order. Ernie sipped on the hot broth and then took a sip of a cold bottle of Oriental beer.

"Quiet night."

"No revelations yet."

"Maybe tomorrow, when the entire flotilla arrives."

"Flotilla. Sounds like the damn Spanish Armada."

"Yeah. Except a lot more powerful."

Just before the midnight curfew the shore patrol got busy again chasing the sailors back to the ship or off the streets.

We had taken a cab all the way back to Hialeah Compound before we heard about the mugging.

"One sailor," the desk sergeant said. "Beat up pretty bad. The navy medical personnel are taking care of him now."

"Any witnesses?"

"None. Happened right before curfew. Apparently he was trying to make it back to the ship."

In the morning, before our eggs and coffee, we found out that the sailor was dead.

THE BUILDINGS that housed the port officer's headquarters were metal Quonset huts differentiated from the Army Corps of Engineers' Quonset huts only by the fact that they were painted battleship gray, while the army's buildings were painted olive drab. Slightly less colorful than Texas Street.

The brass buttons on the old chief's coat bulged under the expanding pressure of his belly. We showed our identification.

"Who was the sailor who got killed in the mugging last night?"

The chief shuffled through some paperwork. "Petty Officer Third Class Lockworth, Gerald R."

"What ship was he on?"

"The USS *Swann*. One of the tenders for the *Kitty Hawk*. They say he was carrying a couple months' pay."

"Nothing left on him?"

"No."

"Maybe the girls got to it first."

"Maybe. But I doubt it. He was a three-year veteran of the Pacific Fleet."

"What was the cause of death?"

"Massive hemorrhage of the brain."

"Have you got your eyes on any particular group of sailors that might be preying on their shipmates?"

"Not really. The brass tends to think that it's some Korean gangs working the streets. Maybe they've developed a taste for the 7th Fleet payroll. That would explain why there haven't been any arrests made."

"The police here want to protect the sailors. There's a lot of pressure from the ROK government to make the U.S. Navy feel welcome."

"Maybe. But at a lower level, policies have a habit of being changed."

"Do you buy all that, chief?"

"Could be. I keep an open mind. But in general I tend to go with the scuttlebutt."

"What's that?"

"That it's some of your local GIs that got a taste for the 7th Fleet payroll."

"If the average sailor starts to believe either one of those viewpoints, it could cause a lot of trouble down here on Texas Street."

"Yeah. I wouldn't want to be a dogface on liberty in this town tonight."

"Thanks for the encouragement."

"You're welcome."

The *Kitty Hawk* finally pulled in at noon, and standing by the dock were the mayor and the provincial governor and the U.S. Navy's 7th Fleet band. The sailors lined the deck of the huge floating edifice, their bellbottoms and kerchiefs flapping in the breeze. The ship's captain and his staff, in their dazzling white uniforms, bounced down the gangplank to the tune of "Anchors Aweigh" and were greeted by a row of beautiful young Korean maidens in traditional dresses who placed leis over their necks and bowed to them in greeting.

The governor made a speech of welcome, and the captain answered with a long, rambling dissertation on the awesome firepower of the *Kitty Hawk*. Greater, he said, than the entire defense establishments of some countries.

"I thought he wasn't supposed to confirm or deny that they have nuclear capability," I said.

Ernie smirked. "He's also not supposed to confirm or deny that he's a jerk."

After the tedious ceremony was over, the sailors—free at last—poured like a great white sea into the crevices and alleys of Texas Street.

THE NIGHT WAS mad. The shore patrol ran back and forth, unable to keep up with all the explosions being ignited by the half-crazed sailors. Even the MPs had to keep on the move. They were tense. Alert.

I saw different faces in the jeeps tonight and asked one of the MPs about it.

"We're on twenty-four-hour alert while the *Kitty Hawk* is here, but we have to get some rest sometime."

"Twelve-hour shifts?"

"Or more, if needed."

Ernie and I wandered away from the bright lights, checking the outskirts of the bar district. Like all beasts of prey, the muggers would look for stragglers, strays who'd wandered from the main herd.

It was mostly residential areas back there, high walls of brick or stone and securely boarded gates.

There were a few bars, however, and a few neighborhood eateries. Some sailors were wandering around, those who wanted to get away from the hubbub.

A couple of big Americans about a block in front of us turned a corner. They looked familiar to me somehow. We trotted after them, but by the time we got to the dimly lit intersection they were gone.

"Who was it?"

"I'm not sure."

We walked into a bar closer to Texas Street proper and ignored the girls until they left us alone with only two cold beers for company.

"We're not getting anywhere," Ernie said.

"Something's got to break soon."

"It better. It's not just muggings anymore. It's murder."

I felt my innards sliding slowly into knots.

"We got to stay out tonight. Through curfew if we have to."

"Yeah."

I looked at Ernie. "Could it be the Koreans?"

"It could. But if the Korean National Police really believed it, they'd be cracking down on every local hoodlum hard, trying to squeeze the truth out of them."

"What if the local police are in on it?"

"Then we're in trouble. But I don't believe it. Too much pressure from up top. The Koreans need us to ensure that their Communist brothers to the north don't pour down here like they did more than two decades ago. And maybe more important nowadays is that they need the foreign exchange the fleet brings in."

"And if the navy seriously believes that the Koreans aren't doing everything they can to stop the assaults on their sailors, they could stop coming into port here."

"They'd lose dock fees and resupply money . . ."

"Not to mention tourism."

We both laughed.

"Somebody in the navy then. In the advance party?"

"Could be that, since the *Kitty Hawk* was still at sea last night."

I thought about the map I had made and the blotter reports. "The last time the *Kitty Hawk* was here, there were no muggings until they had docked."

"So?"

"We've been assuming that it's probably a gang of sailors aboard the *Kitty Hawk* that have been preying on their own shipmates."

"Yeah, but maybe there's more than one group. Ideas like this are catching."

"That's possible. But maybe it is somebody in the advance party, or maybe it's somebody who's here all the time. Somebody who knows the terrain, the lie of the land, the ins and outs of all the back alleys.

"And if it's not Koreans . . ."

"That's right. GIs. GIs who spend a lot of time down here."

"Village rats."

"All the GI village rats have gone into hiding until the fleet leaves."

"So it seems."

I took a sip of my beer. I didn't like what I was going to say. "That leaves the MPs."

Ernie thought about it for a minute. "That would also explain why there were no arrests made in the past."

"It sure would."

He looked at me. "But why do the muggings only occur when the *Kitty Hawk* is here? And not other navy ships?"

"That I don't know yet." I looked around. "Let's find a phone."

"A phone?"

"Yeah. I got a call I want to make."

The desk sergeant didn't want to answer any of my questions at first, because he could see what I was getting at, but I reminded him that this was an official investigation and he would be obstructing that investigation if he didn't cooperate in every reasonable way.

I borrowed paper and a pencil from the Mama-san and wrote furiously, trying at the same time to keep one finger in my ear to drown out the insane rock music. I seriously considered asking Ernie to hold his finger in my ear, but he was busy flirting with a couple of the girls.

Besides, there are limits to a partnership, even for crime busters.

I had what I needed. Ernie looked at the sheet. A bunch of names, ranks, and times scribbled across the wrinkled paper.

"What's that?"

"No time to explain. Let's go."

The girls pouted on our way out.

The MP jeep that held the central position on Texas Street was cruising slowly down the crowded block. I waved them down, and they came to a halt. I looked at my notes and read off three names to them.

"Have you seen any of those guys? Tonight? In civilian clothes?"

I'm not too good a judge of whether someone is telling the truth or lying, but this time I had an edge. The young buck sergeant on the passenger side let the muscles beneath his cheek flutter a couple of times. Then he blinked his eyes and said, "No."

I thanked him for the information. He'd given me more than he knew.

We walked off into the darkness away from the men, heading from the center of Texas Street toward the place a few blocks away where I had seen the two big Americans turn down a dark alley and disappear. We wandered around for a while, and in order to cover more ground we split up, agreeing on our routes and where to meet in fifteen minutes.

A couple of blocks later I saw the big guy I had seen before, standing at the mouth of an alley. He looked into the alley at something and then back at me, as if undecided what to do.

I shouted, "Hey!" And I started running toward him.

He hesitated for a second and then ran. I let him go and turned down the alley he had been protecting. It was dark. I could see nothing. Then I tripped, sprawled, and something hit me from behind.

WHEN I CAME to, Ernie was looking down at me, surrounded by some sailors in their dress whites and shore patrol armbands. I was never so happy to see squids.

They got me into their van and took me somewhere. Ernie told me, but it didn't register. Nothing much did. On the way there, I passed out again.

THE NEXT MORNING when I woke up I waited for a while and then asked the medic when he walked into the room.

"Where am I?"

"The dispensary. On Hialeah Compound. Had a pretty nasty bump on the noggin last night."

"What's my condition?"

"Hold on."

The medic left the room, and after a few minutes a doctor came in. He looked at my head, checked some X-rays up against a light-board, and then pronounced me fit for duty.

No shirkers in this man's army. I could've used a few days off.

While I was getting dressed, Ernie showed up. He consoled me by reminding me about the happy hour at the Hialeah NCO Club tonight.

"Exotic dancers, too," he said.

I smiled, but it hurt the back of my head.

THE BRIGHT SUN of southern Korea was out. In force.

"Personnel? Why personnel?"

"I want to check something out. On Leonard Budusky."

"Who?"

"An MP who I think is an acquaintance of mine."

After we showed him our identification, the personnel clerk got Budusky's folder. "He came to Korea over six months ago," I said.

The bespectacled clerk ran his finger down a column of typed entries.

"Seven," he said.

"What state is he from?"

"Virginia."

I held up my hand. "Wait a minute. Let me guess. Norfolk."

The clerk looked up at me, his eyes almost as wide as his mouth.

"How the hell did you know that?"

Ernie tried to pretend that he was in on the whole thing, but when we got to the Main Post Snack Bar, he bought me some coffee and threatened me with disembowelment if I didn't tell him what was going on.

Considering the pain I was in, I probably wouldn't have noticed it much if I'd let him go through with it. Instead, to humor him, I explained.

"First of all, to find the culprit, we've got to figure out motive and opportunity."

"I remember that much from C.I.D. school."

"The motive seemed to be money. Now, that narrows our list of suspects down to anybody in the 7th Fleet, any GI stationed near Pusan, or any of the Korean citizens of this wonderful city.

"The next step is figuring out opportunity. That brings us closer, because that narrows it down to the four thousand or so sailors who had liberty during the stopover, the three hundred or so GIs who had passes, and, again, all the Korean citizens of this fair city."

"So it's a tough job. We knew that."

"But the mugger got anxious. On the first night, when only the advance party was in, he attacked. That eliminated all the sailors who were at sea with the *Kitty Hawk*. When Petty Officer Lockworth died, it also eliminated, in my mind, the Korean civilian populace. Because there is no doubt that the Korean authorities would take the mugging of American sailors seriously, but they realize the enormity of the bad public relations they would get back in the States if a Korean were found to have done a killing. The fact that they still didn't launch an all-out manhunt meant to me that they must be confident, through their own sources, that it wasn't the work of one of their local hoodlums.

"That leaves the GIs. When the fleet is in, soldiers tend to be conspicuous. They stick out, by virtue of their stinginess, from their seafaring compatriots, and the girls down in the village can spot them a mile away.

"We wandered all over Texas Street for two nights and didn't see any, did we?"

"Not except for the MPs."

"Exactly, and except for the two big guys we saw in that alley who looked familiar to me. After I called the desk sergeant and got the names of all the MPs who had duty on the first night, it started to click. The three big studs in the central patrol had all stayed on duty past curfew. Of the four patrols, theirs was the only patrol that did. Of the three of them, the desk sergeant told me that the biggest and meanest was Corporal Leonard Budusky. I remembered their faces. Two of them were the guys we saw scurrying down that alley. When the MPs on duty denied having seen them, I knew it had to be a lie. When MPs are in the village having fun, they will seek out the on-duty patrol, to let them know where they're at or just to say hello.

"When that young buck sergeant on duty realized that the notorious out-of-town C.I.D. agents were asking about his partners, his first reaction was to lie and protect them."

"So you know two MPs were on duty the first night, when the guy got killed, and you know they were out the second night, off duty, when you got beaned. You still don't have any proof."

"You're right about that. And they'll know it, too. Probably just go about their work as if nothing happened and if we ask them any questions, deny everything. But the one thing I do have, that the killer doesn't know about, is the motive."

"Money?"

"Partially. But mainly his motive is something that abounds in a city with a big naval base like Norfolk."

"What's that?"

"Hatred." I took a sip of the hot bitter coffee. "Hatred of the U.S. Navy."

IT WAS A lot easier stalking Texas Street now that we knew who we were looking for. The desk sergeant had already told me, but I checked all four MP jeeps just to be sure. Leonard Budusky and his burly partner were not on duty tonight. They had pulled the day shift and got off about two hours ago.

Ernie had been disappointed when we missed happy hour at the NCO Club, and the exotic dancer, but I told him it would be in both our best interests if we remained sober.

The Pusan streets were filling again with fog. It was damp, cold, and dark.

This time we had weapons. A roll of dimes for me. Ernie had a short, brutal club, a wooden mallet, tucked into the lining of his jacket.

We patrolled methodically, keeping to the shadows. The Texas Street area is big, but not that big. Eventually we found them.

They were coming out of a bar, laughing and waving to the smiling girls.

"Spending money like sailors on shore leave," Ernie said.

"Must have come into an inheritance."

Budusky was tall, about six foot four, with squared shoulders and curly blond hair. His partner was the young guy who had enticed me into the mouth of the alley last night. He was tall, almost as tall as Budusky, and just as robust.

I'm pretty big myself, and have had a little experience on the streets of East LA, but Ernie was a lightweight in this crowd. Less than six feet and only about a hundred and seventy pounds.

We followed them carefully, one of us on either side of the street, hiding as we went. They weren't paying much attention, though. Still laughing and talking about the girls.

Finally, when the alleys ran out of street lamps, they stopped. They took up positions, one behind an awning, the other behind a telephone pole, as if they'd been there before. I wished I had brought my little map, to check the positions of the previous muggings. It didn't matter much now, though. The opening to a dark, seemingly pitch-black alley loomed behind them. They had chosen their position well.

Ernie and I remained hidden. We could see each other from across the street, but the two MPs couldn't see us.

It took twenty minutes for three sailors, lost in their drunkenness, to wander down the road. They were little fellows, in uniform, hats tilted at odd angles. Two of them had beer bottles in their hands, and each had his wallet sticking out from beneath his tunic, folded over his waistband.

The navy's into tradition. Even if it's stupid. Or maybe especially if it's stupid. No pockets.

We let the sailors pass us. I was glad Ernie didn't warn them. Of course, he wasn't the type to warn them anyway.

They didn't see us as they passed. They were laughing and joking, and I doubt they would have noticed a jet plane if it had swooped down five feet over their heads.

What did swoop down was Budusky and his partner. Two of the sailors went down before the third even realized what was happening. He swung his beer bottle, but it missed its mark and he was enveloped by the two marauding behemoths.

Ernie and I slid out of our hiding places and floated up the hill, my roll of dimes clenched securely in my right fist. Ernie smashed his mallet into the back of the MP's head, and I knew all our problems were over with him. But just as I launched my first punch at Budusky, he swiveled and caught the blow on his shoulder. I punched again, but I was off balance from having missed the first blow, and he countered and caught me in the ribs. It was hard, but I've had worse, and then we were toe to toe, belting each other, slugging viciously. It could have gone either way, and I was happy to see Ernie looming up behind him. I jabbed with my left and backed off, waiting for it all to end, but then, as if a trapdoor had opened beneath his feet, Ernie disappeared. I realized that one of the sailors had gotten up and, thinking Ernie was one of the enemy, had grabbed him and pulled him down. Another of the sailors came to, and now the three of them were rolling around on the ground, flailing clubs and beer bottles at each other, cursing, spitting, and scratching.

Something blurred my vision, and Budusky was on me. I twisted, slipped a punch, and caught him with a good left hook in the midsection. He took it, punched back, and then we were wrestling. I lost my footing, pulled him down with me, and we rolled down the incline. I threw my weight and kept us rolling, I wasn't sure why. Just to get us into the light, I guess.

Our momentum increased our speed, and finally we jarred to a stop.

Blind chance had determined that it would be Budusky's back that hit the cement pole with the full force of our rolling bodies. I punched him a couple of times on the side of his head before I realized that he was finished. I got up in a crouch and checked his pulse. It was steady. I slapped his face a couple of times. His eyes opened. Before he could pull himself together, I rolled him over on his stomach, pulled my handcuffs out from the back of my belt, and locked his hands securely behind the small of his back.

I heard whistles and then running feet. The shore patrol surrounded me and then a couple of MPs. The MPs stood back, as if they wanted nothing to do with this.

I lifted Budusky by the collar and pushed his face back to the pavement.

"Why? Why'd you kill Lockworth?"

His face was contorted, grimacing in pain. His eyes were clenched. I lifted him and slammed him back again.

"It was your dad, wasn't it? Your dad was a sailor. And he left you, you and your mother."

It was an old story and didn't take a great leap of imagination. An illegitimate kid from Norfolk, growing up to hate the navy, joining the army as an MP, finding his opportunity to take his revenge. A few bumps, a few bruises, a few dollars, and a sailor would get over it. It was the least they owed him for what his dad had done to him and his mother. Until he went too far. And killed.

I heard Budusky talking. It was choking out of his throat.

"He left us, like you said. That's why they owed me."

"And when you last heard from him . . ."

"Yeah." The tears seemed to be squeezed out of his eyes. "When the last letter came, he was on the *Kitty Hawk*."

ERNIE AND I left the next day with the date for Budusky's court-martial set for next month.

Back in Seoul the first sergeant requested that the venue be changed about a hundred miles north, to Camp Henry in Taegu. Ernie and I had to appear in court as witnesses, and it wouldn't be smart to give the MPs in Pusan a chance to get at us.

I could understand their feelings. They saw us as traitors to the Military Police Corps. Maybe we were.

But none of those MPs ever sat down to write a letter to the parents of the late Petty Officer Third Class Gerald R. Lockworth.

I did.

S. J. ROZAN
BODY ENGLISH

December 1992

A FORMER ARCHITECT, S. J. Rozan has won a wide following and garnered numerous awards for her series featuring Chinatown detective Lydia Chin and her sometime partner, Bill Smith. Herself a resident of lower Manhattan, Rozan has also written a stand-alone novel about the attack on the World Trade Center, *Absent Friends*. This early story features her popular series characters Chin and Smith before they made their first appearances in a novel.

■

It was the first case I took that I didn't want. My instincts were right, too, because it also turned out to be the first case that made me wonder whether I wanted to be a private investigator for the rest of my life.

"And she doesn't really even want me, either," I fumed. I was ranting to my sometime partner, Bill Smith, at the Peacock Rice Shop on Mott Street. "Because I don't know Mandarin. She almost stomped out when she found that out. Stuck-up Taiwan lady! And she absolutely refused to speak Cantonese. She insisted we speak English. Can you believe that?"

"I always insist you speak English," Bill pointed out. He lifted sauteed squid from the serving dish into his rice bowl.

"Don't start!" I speared my chopsticks into a mass of deep green watercress in glistening sauce. "You big coarse clumsy foreign characters are exactly what the problem is, anyway."

Bill stopped a piece of squid just short of his mouth. "Foreign?"

I was feeling argumentative and crabby. "I grew up in this country. *Some* people spent their childhoods trotting around the world."

"That was my adolescence, and you grew up in Chinatown, which you've always said is another *planet*. Listen, Lydia, how about we talk about the case before you stab me with a chopstick?"

"Let me eat first," I said sulkily. I tried the squid; it was pungent and tender. It cheered me up a little, and the smoky, jasmine-scented tea cheered me more. Maybe my blood sugar was just low. "Actually," I said aloud, "maybe I was just nervous."

"Mrs. Lee made you nervous?"

I hated to admit it, but it was true. "She's a very powerful woman in Chinatown. She owns four big factories here." "Factory" was Chinatown for "sweatshop," but Bill knew that. "My mother was terrified I'd offend her. It would have humiliated my mother if Mrs. Lee hadn't approved of me."

"But you say she didn't."

"No, but she hired me. She won't criticize me publicly while I'm working for her. That would make her look foolish, you see. Hiring someone as obviously inadequate as I am."

"I think you're adequate. I think you're way beyond adequate. Don't glare at me, tell me about the case. You're hiring me. What are we doing?"

"Following a woman. I figured you'd be good at that."

"Only if she's gorgeous and small and Chinese and furious like you."

He drank some beer, and I glared at him.

"I know why you're mad." He put the bottle down. "You hate this woman for making you nervous. You wanted to turn her down, but you had to take her case so your mother wouldn't lose face, and now you're stuck. Boy, you really hate being told what to do, don't you?"

"You should know." I finished the squid. The stainless steel teapot wasn't empty yet, so I poured another cup.

Bill waited until I'd finished before he took out his cigarettes. "Is it all right?"

I didn't know if he was asking me if he could smoke now, or if I felt better. "Go ahead." Then I sighed, ran my hand through my hair. "I guess you're right."

"Well, that's rare enough." He dropped a match in the white ashtray with the red peacock on it. "Then the case is okay, it's the client who bothers you?"

I shook my head. "I don't like this case."

"Why? What's it about?"

"Mrs. Lee wants us to follow her son's fiancée. A woman named Jill Moore."

"She doesn't sound Chinese."

"That's sort of the point. She's tall and blonde and according to Mrs. Lee completely untrustworthy. Mrs. Lee thinks she's cheating on her son."

"Does her son think so?"

"No, and Mrs. Lee doesn't want him to know what we're doing until we have proof."

"Do you know him? The son?"

I nodded. "Lee Kuan Cheng. Kuan Cheng Lee to you. He's a few years younger than me, but when you grow up around here, you sort of know everybody."

"What's he like?"

"When he was twelve he took on my twin cousins in the schoolyard because they beat him out on a math test. He's very competitive. They fought like weasels in a sack; I had to separate them. I think I still have a scar."

"Can I see it?"

"Not a chance."

"Sounds like your cousins were sort of competitive, too."

"In my family? Don't be ridiculous."

Bill tipped the ash off his cigarette. "So what don't you like about it?"

"She wants it to be true."

"Mrs. Lee does?"

"Yes. She was sitting there with an I-told-you-so smile, as though she'd already proved it. 'Jill Moore like rice,' she said. She looked like—what is it you people say? The cat that ate the canary?"

"That's what we people say. What does that mean, to like rice?"

"Yellow fever. Whites who are attracted to Asians just because we're exotic, or whatever it is your people think we are."

"Paranoid."

"Is that attractive?"

"On you it is. Go on."

I sighed, but I went on. "Jill Moore and Kuan Cheng are both NYU students. Kuan Cheng is getting an MBA so he can go into his mother's business. Jill Moore's in Asian studies."

"That's suspicious."

"Mrs. Lee thinks so. Kuan Cheng took Jill over to Mrs. Lee's apartment about six weeks ago, trying to make a good impression on the future mother-in-law. It was the first and only time they've ever met. She got Jill alone for twenty minutes, and based on that conversation, she's sure Jill Moore is only interested in Kuan Cheng for some perverse white-creature sexual reason."

"Don't knock white-creature sexual perversions until you've tried them."

"Oh, drop it, will you?" Sometimes I'm in the mood for that sort of stuff from Bill, but not always. "Anyhow, when I asked Mrs. Lee what made her suspect that, she gave me this superior look and said, 'Just, mother know. You follow, you see.' I wanted to sock her."

"Sounds to me like she wants to break up what she considers an unsuitable match for her baby. That's not admirable, but it's not unusual."

"Yeah, but I like happy endings. If Jill Moore and Kuan Cheng Lee love each other, what business is it of his mother's? I mean, who *asked* her? But if I can't get proof that he's being cheated on, she won't believe it's because she was wrong. She'll go around telling all of Chinatown what an incompetent detective I am. That would be terrible for my mother."

"So," Bill said, "you can't win either way. If she's right, you'll be disillusioned. If she's wrong, you'll be in trouble."

"That's it," I sighed. "Exactly."

The waiter appeared, smiling shyly. He brought us the check and two glass bowls of quivering maroon gelatin, each crowned with an almond cookie.

"What's that?" Bill eyed his bowl suspiciously.

I looked over to the door where Mr. Han, the proprietor, smiled broadly at me. I called to him in Chinese; he answered.

"It's a bean paste jelly his new chef makes," I told Bill. "He says even white people like it."

"At least he admits I'm a person."

"Well, he didn't exactly say that." He put his cigarette out, and we tried the jelly. It was sweet, tasting delicately of lychee and orange.

"Tell him I like it," Bill said.

I called to Mr. Han again. From his post by the door he smiled and bowed.

"What you're speaking with him," Bill said, "that's Cantonese?"

"Uh-huh. Only spoken by peasants like Uncle Hun-jo and me. I'm sure Mrs. Lee understands it, since she's lived in Chinatown twenty years, but she wouldn't stoop to speak such a harsh, nasty-sounding language."

"Is it nasty-sounding?"

"Of course not."

"I didn't think so."

Out on the crowded sidewalk the November air was cold. High thin clouds diluted the sunlight, and a breeze herded papers this way and that in the gutter, practicing for winter.

Walking north, we maneuvered around old Chinese ladies with short gray hair and padded jackets, picking over vegetables shoulder to shoulder with uptown shoppers who didn't know the names of the greens they were buying. A group of camera-hung tourists peered into guidebooks at the streets I grew up in. Vendors hawked cotton socks and radio-controlled toy cars, calling in broken English, "Three, five dollar!" and, "See it goes!" The street vendors are often the newest immigrants; sometimes those are the only English words they yet know.

"I think Mrs. Lee speaks better English than she lets on, too," I said to Bill as we crossed Canal. "Or at least understands more."

"Her English wasn't good?"

"It was snooty and condescending, but her grammar was terrible. I think she refuses to learn it better, or to speak it as well as she already knows how. It would be giving in."

We single-filed past the sidewalk tables of a cafe in what used to be Little Italy and is still called that, though every other storefront sign now is in Chinese. "So," Bill said, "what now?"

"Now we go lurk outside Jill Moore's afternoon class and see how far we can tail her without getting spotted."

"Together? About a foot and a half."

Bill's thirteen inches taller, eighty pounds heavier, and twelve years older than I am, with big hands and a face that sort of shows he's been a P.I. for twenty years. I'm small, though I'm always saying I'm quicker and he's always saying I'm in better shape than he is. And we both know I'm a better shot, though it was him who taught me to shoot. I practice a lot.

And besides all that, of course, I'm Chinese. And he's not. We do make a weird-looking pair.

"No," I said. "Not together. We lurk in different places."

It's a technique he taught me, and we use it often. It's good to have two people on a tail, because subjects can be surprisingly sneaky about losing you, even when they don't know you're there. The only reason not to do it is if the client can't afford it. When I'd quoted rates to Mrs. Lee, she'd balked— "Too much. Inexperience child. I pay half."—and we'd had to haggle, but I'd expected that, so I'd started high. Now, for what she thought she was paying for me, she was getting both me and Bill.

I considered that a bargain.

Jill Moore's afternoon class met in an old white big-windowed NYU building on the east side of Washington Square. Tracking her down had taken me most of the hour between the time Mrs. Lee had sniffed her disdainful way out of my office and the time I'd met Bill for lunch. I'd had to use two different voices on the phone. For the Student Life office I was a confused clerk from the bursar's office who'd gotten Jill Moore hopelessly mixed up with Joe Moore, or Joan Moore, or God knows who. The other voice, when I'd gotten Jill Moore's address and schedule, was for Asian studies.

"Herro," I'd said, blurring the distinction between L's and R's the way we're all supposed to. "I am Chin Ling Wan-ju—" that was the true part "—ah, guest lecturer in Flowering of Ming Dynasty Art, today. Supposed speak on 'Spirit Scrolls of Ming Emperors.' So foolish, lose all direction. Tell me, please, where to meet?"

They were glad to.

Bill pointed out, when I told him about it, that they might have been glad to if I'd just called up like a regular person and asked. But I always like to try out my moves when I get a chance.

Armed with the photograph Mrs. Lee had given me from the afternoon with her daughter-in-law-elect, Bill settled on a bench at the edge of the park with the other bums. I felt his eyes on me as I crossed the street to the classroom building.

I entered the building along with a group of four NYU women, one in jeans, one in sixties daisy-patterned leggings, two in short skirts. I made three in short skirts. The guard at the security desk, who would have stopped Bill in a second, hardly even looked at me, except to evaluate my legs relative to the other legs sticking out of the skirts.

We all got on the elevator, but I got off first, on the third floor. I went around the corner to the room where someone was lecturing to a hall full of students on the Flowering of Ming Dynasty Art. Not on Spirit Scrolls, presumably, even if there really were such things, which I doubted.

I settled myself on the floor at the other end of the hall where I'd have a good view of the classroom door and took *The Catcher in the Rye* out of my leather knapsack. I'd read it when I was fourteen and it hadn't done a thing for me, but I thought maybe, in this setting, I'd give it another chance.

After fifteen minutes of giving it another chance, a bell clanged and all hell broke loose. Doors burst open everywhere. The advance guard—students whose next class was all the way across campus—charged out of the classrooms and were in the elevator or bouncing down the stairs before the profs had finished giving the reading assignments. Then came the slower ones, juggling books, notebooks, backpacks, and handbags the size of carry-ons. Textbooks thumped closed and zippers zipped and kids called to each other down the hall in exuberant voices and lots of different accents.

I stood, slipped my knapsack on, searched the faces pouring out of the lecture hall for the one in Mrs. Lee's photograph.

Jill Moore was not hard to spot. She wore a white shirt and blue-jeans, dangling brass earrings, and, I noticed, a small diamond ring on her left hand. That encouraged me. A woman who was cheating wouldn't wear her engagement ring while she did it, would she?

Of course, rings are easy to take off.

As Jill Moore made room in her canvas carryall for her notebook, a handsome Asian man worked his way through the throng.

He called her name. She turned, spotted him, smiled playfully. He reached her, seemed to be asking a question, but they were speaking low; I couldn't hear them. Still smiling, she shook her head, then looked around quickly. She leaned close and whispered something. He nodded. Then she squeezed his arm, twinkled her eyes, and was gone down the stairs.

I clumped down after her, thinking damn, damn, damn. I didn't know who that guy was, but he wasn't Kuan Cheng Lee.

I followed Jill Moore for the rest of the afternoon, through Washington Square Park, where the fallen leaves were restless on the asphalt paths, to the NYU library where she studied for two hours, and I decided to give away my copy of *The Catcher in the Rye*. After that we shopped a little along Sixth Avenue, had cappuccino at the Caffee Lucca—she indoors, I out—and then, around seven, we wandered back to an old brick building on MacDougal Street. The whole time I could feel Bill nearby, always down the block or across the street from us, a figure at the corner of my eye who wasn't there when I looked.

The MacDougal Street building was what I'd been given as Jill Moore's address by the helpful secretary at the Student Life office. I watched her go in, and I watched the lights come on in a fourth-floor front apartment a minute later.

Across the street and down a little was another cafe. That's what I love about New York. I don't know how P. I.'s do this in the suburbs.

I settled at a table by the window in time to see Bill stroll around the corner and disappear. If the apartment building had a rear exit into an alley, I wouldn't see him again for a while. He'd plant himself there, waiting until Jill Moore came out that way, or until I found him to say we were knocking off for the evening. This case was mine, so that decision was mine to make.

There must have been no alley, because he was back in a few minutes, lighting a cigarette on the street corner. I stuck my head out the cafe door, waved for him to come in.

He joined me at my round wooden table, ordered espresso and a Napoleon. I got peppermint tea.

"Thanks, chief," Bill grinned when the waiter was gone. "It was getting cold out there."

"Well, she may be in for the evening," I said. "If she's not, we can leave here separately."

But it turned out she was. As we sipped our drinks I told Bill about the man Jill Moore had huddled with outside of class. He said that seemed innocent enough to him, and I said the same thing, but I wasn't so sure, and neither was he, although he didn't say that. After about an hour we ordered an antipasto and shared it, dividing up chewy pepperoni, vinegared hot peppers, creamy rounds of provolone.

"How can you eat this after pastry?" I demanded.

"It's the white trash way of life."

"See," I said glumly. "The fact is we will never understand each other."

"And if we don't," Bill said, unearthing an anchovy and depositing it on my plate, because they're my favorite, "is that necessarily because I'm white and you're Chinese?"

"Yes," I said. "It necessarily is."

When we'd come in, there had been opera in the air, dramatic voices crashing together or lamenting separately in ways I was sure would break my heart if I understood them. After that there had been silence softened by murmured conversations. Now the elegant mahogany-skinned waiter clicked a new tape into the tape deck, and the swift notes of a piano tinkled around us. Bill's face grew distracted, just for a moment; maybe someone else wouldn't have noticed.

"Do you play this?" I asked him.

"Yes."

"What is it?"

"Beethoven. The Waldstein Sonata. I don't play it this well."

"Do you—" I began. Bill put a sudden hand on my arm.

"Look," he said, nodding toward the window. "Is that the guy you saw this afternoon?"

The outer door to Jill Moore's building stood open. As we watched, a young Asian man took the stoop steps two at a time, then unlocked the inner door and let himself in. He was carrying a knapsack and a bag of groceries.

"No," I said. "That's Kuan Cheng Lee."

Nothing else happened that evening. Kuan Cheng, according to his mother, had an apartment on East Ninth Street. "Good for

340 S. J. Rozan

son," she'd informed me. "Live by own self, learn manage household. Later will able treat mother proper way." I didn't know what sort of household Kuan Cheng would learn to manage in a Ninth Street walkup, nor had I been sure that this wasn't just Mrs. Lee saving face by pretending to approve of her son's moving out. What was clear was that she intended, eventually, to establish herself in whatever household he set up. Well, as a Chinese mother, that was her right.

Kuan Cheng didn't come out, and no one else we cared about—meaning no Asian men—went in, and around ten I called it off. I paid the check, took the receipt for Mrs. Lee, and left a big tip. Bill and I walked south on Sixth to Canal in the chilly, blue New York night. Traffic rushed up Sixth in a hurry to get someplace, it wasn't clear where.

At Canal we arranged to meet the next morning and start all over again. We kissed good-night lightly, the way we always do, and I felt a little guilty and confused, the way I always do. Bill wants more than that from me, but he understands how I feel, and though he comes on a lot in a kidding sort of way, he never pushes it. Somehow that makes me feel guilty and confused.

Then we parted. Bill turned right to his Laight Street apartment and I turned left, to Chinatown.

THE MORNING WAS overcast and chillier than the day before had been. Jill Moore had a nine o'clock class; at a quarter to nine Bill and I watched from separate corners as she and Kuan Cheng Lee came out of her building and walked up MacDougal Street. They were smiling and talking, Jill Moore's eyes twinkling as they had the day before, with the other Asian man.

The day was pretty boring, and I began to feel bad for Bill, who spent most of it on park benches. He doesn't like to be cold. I was fine, sitting in the hallway of the white building, in the student cafeteria (which was noisier than I ever remember my college cafeteria being), in the library, and then back in the white building. I had ditched *The Catcher in the Rye* and wrapped *Surveillance and Undercover Operations: A Manual* in brown paper so I had something to read in the long stretches between clanging bells.

Jill Moore's afternoon class let out at three-thirty. I was sitting on the windowsill at the end of the corridor when her lecture hall door opened. She was among the first out, hefting her bag, hurrying to the stairs. She galloped down them, and I followed her in a crowd of rushing people. I didn't get a chance to shove *Surveillance and Undercover Operations* back in my knapsack until we were striding across Washington Square Park. Jill Moore had much longer legs than I do—well, who doesn't?—and I began to wish for my Rollerblades, except that I had no idea where we were going. I also had Bill, who was keeping up with her pretty well, strolling along in a bum sort of way.

My idea about where we were going was right, and as Jill Moore unlocked the door to her building, Bill and I converged on the cafe across the street. The window tables were taken, but it was a small cafe; we could see the old brick building from the table we chose.

"Jesus Christ," Bill said, breathing on his hands to warm them. "I ought to charge you double for freezing."

"You ought to wear silk underwear."

"Will you buy it for me? I'll model it."

The thought of Bill's striking model's poses in silk underwear almost made me spray my peppermint tea all over the table. "Go ahead," he said. "Laugh at me. I—" He stopped. I followed his gaze out the window, and we saw what I'd been hoping we wouldn't.

The handsome young Asian man Jill Moore had twinkled her eyes at yesterday came quickly down MacDougal from the direction of NYU. He looked around, entered her vestibule, rang an apartment bell. He was buzzed in.

"Oh, damn," I said, in a little voice.

We watched; nothing else happened; we drank a little. With a lift of his eyebrows Bill offered me some apricot tart. I turned it down. The guy didn't come out. "Kuan Cheng has an afternoon class," I told Bill. "A seminar. His mother told me. Tuesdays and Thursdays until six."

"Otherwise his schedule coincides pretty much with hers?"

I nodded.

"So this is the only time she can be sure of being alone."

"I guess."

Bill sipped his cocoa. "Listen," he said. "This isn't your problem. You were hired to find out what's going on. Now your job is to take the client proof. How people behave isn't your problem."

"I know," I said. "But I like happy endings."

We discussed the fact that it might not be what it looked like, and of course that was true. We also discussed more practical things, like how to get photographs of whatever it was. This is where investigating in the suburbs has its advantages. You can't slink through the shrubbery and shinny up the drainpipe when the subject's in a fourth-floor walkup on MacDougal Street.

You can, however, climb to the opposite roof.

Bill zipped his jacket and left. I watched Jill Moore's window. The shade, which she had pulled last night after she'd switched on the lights, was still lifted, and the lights were off. We had reached that time of year when it begins to get dark by four-thirty. I was hoping we'd have time to find a place to look into the window before Jill Moore felt she needed lights and drawn shades.

Or, maybe, for what she was doing, she wouldn't need lights at all.

Bill was back in ten minutes. "Okay," he said, sitting down. "The building directly across from her, where the laundromat is. I talked to the super."

"And he just said go ahead?"

"I gave him fifty dollars."

"Fifty?" I was aghast.

"The guy could get in trouble. The guy could lose his job. The guy could smell a quick buck when it came his way."

"Well, I guess it's okay. I guess Mrs. Lee won't mind paying that to get the goods." I knew she wouldn't. I paid the check, went out the door Bill held open for me.

At the laundromat building we rang the super's bell. An unshaven man emerged from a rear apartment, led us word-lessly up slanted stairs to the roof. He unlocked the bulkhead door for us.

"You be sure to close the damn thing tight, you come in," he growled at Bill.

"Sure," Bill said. "Thanks."

The super grunted, looked once at me, turned and shuffled downstairs.

The building was lower than Jill Moore's building across the street; the roof was about half a story higher than her window.

The asphalt roofing slanted up to the top of the cornice at the front.

I lay on my belly on the asphalt and took the binoculars out of my knapsack. Peering through them over the cornice, I had a perfect view into Jill Moore's window.

"What's happening?" Bill was low beside me.

"It's a living room. They're drinking tea and talking." I crawled back down a little and passed him the binoculars.

He peered over the top of the cornice.

"The light's fading. If you're going to take pictures, you'd better do it soon."

"This isn't very juicy stuff to take pictures of," I grumbled, but I got out the camera, attached the telephoto lens, and clicked away. I took half a roll, then waited in case Jill Moore and the unknown Asian did something more dramatic. Instead, Jill Moore got up, turned on a lamp in the living room, and drew the shades.

"Fooey," I said.

"We can come back Thursday if you want," Bill said.

"Personally I don't want. But Mrs. Lee might want."

We went back in the bulkhead door—closing it tight—and down the street. We trudged south on Sixth Avenue; the air was cold and the car horns blared at each other ill-temperedly.

"I don't understand white people," I said. "I really don't. You saw her this morning with Kuan Cheng. She was *happy*. She's enjoying this. She's having a great time. You white people."

"Hey," Bill said. "I didn't do it."

"Yeah, but I'll bet you understand it. Romantic love isn't even a Chinese concept. Your people invented it. How come you mess around with it like this?"

I knew I was being unfair to him, and he knew not to answer.

I called Mrs. Lee as soon as I got back to my office. "I have something I think you'll want to see," I said. "I left some film to be developed. They say I can pick it up at six." I didn't ask her to meet me. That would be too forward, not respectful. If what I said was of interest, she would tell me what she wanted me to do.

"I come your office," Mrs. Lee told me. "Six thirty. You there. On time."

"Yes," I said, controlling my temper. "I'll be there. On time. Thank you, Mrs. Lee." I hung up the phone furious with myself. Thank you? *Thank you?*

I went home, kissed my mother, and told her Mrs. Lee and I were getting along fine. I grabbed my Rollerblades before she could ask me any questions and speedskated through the spookily empty downtown streets to Battery Park. I worked out hard, until it was time to skate back to Chinatown and give Mrs. Lee proof that there are no happy endings.

I called Bill early the next morning. "I gave her the pictures," I said.

"How did she like them?"

"She loved them. She gave me this horrible smile—all hard around the edges, you know?—and said, 'Mother know. Mother always know best for son.' I said they weren't doing anything interesting in the picture, just talking, and that usually in this sort of situation I'd recommend keeping the surveillance going another few days."

"What'd she say?"

"She sort of smirked. 'Oh-ho, greedy girl. Not need, not pay. Plenty here. How much bill?' I worked it out and she paid, right there, in cash."

"So that's it."

"Well," I said, "well, no."

"Oh-ho," Bill said. "Masochist girl. You want follow Jill Moore more."

"That's right." I ignored his phony Chinese accent, which was really pretty good. "I know it's none of my business—"

"I'll meet you in half an hour outside her building."

I hesitated. "I'm not sure I can pay you," I said. "I mean, the case is over."

"There are other ways you could pay me."

"Yes, but I won't."

"I know. But just think of the debt you're racking up."

"Junk bonds," I said.

We followed Jill Moore for the next two days. She was taking her classes: Ming Dynasty Art; Admiral Perry and the Opening of Japan; Topics in South Asian Political History; and Women in Chinese Culture. You'd better study harder in that one, I thought. I hung around all her classrooms, and even sat in on the Ming Dynasty Art lecture. It was pretty interesting, nice slides of glazed bowls and sumptuous silk robes. I tailed her to lunch, to the bookstore, and to the library, where she hauled a thick green book and a spiral notebook out of her bag and was so deep in concentration when I walked by her that she didn't even look up. I walked by the other way, too. I just wanted to see what she was doing.

"That was a little risky," Bill said later that afternoon, in the cafe I'd come to think of as ours. It was Thursday by now, the day Kuan Cheng Lee had a seminar until seven.

"I know," I said. "I shouldn't have. I was bad."

"So what was she doing?"

"Nothing interesting. Translating very, very elementary Mandarin. Filling a notebook full of clumsy characters."

"Like me? Big coarse clumsy foreign characters?"

"Is that still bothering you? I'm sorry I said that. I didn't mean it."

"It doesn't bother me. I just wanted to make you feel guilty."

"It's a cheap shot, making a Chinese daughter feel guilty. Anybody can do it. Oh, Bill. Oh, damn. Look."

Bill turned where I was pointing. Hurrying up MacDougal Street was the handsome Asian fellow. He had three textbooks under his arm, and he was in such a rush to get to Jill Moore's doorbell that he dropped one of them on his toe as he leapt up the stoop.

"Serves him right," I announced, as we watched him hop around for a minute, then scoop up the thick green book and hit the bell. He was buzzed, limping, in.

"That's unworthy," Bill reprimanded me. I didn't listen, because I'd just had a thought. I wanted to tell Bill about it—god, I hoped I was right!—but I didn't get the chance. As I opened my mouth, Kuan Cheng Lee raced down the sidewalk and up the same stoop. He let himself in the vestibule door, but not before his jacket blew open in a gust of wind.

He had a gun.

Bill must have seen it, too, because he jumped from the table at the same time I did. We charged out the cafe door, leaving the elegant waiter open-mouthed.

By the time we got to the vestibule the door was closed, and we lost seconds trying to be buzzed in. You always can in New York and eventually we did, but not before my heart was pounding crazily and I'd caught such an adrenaline rush that I wanted to kick the door in myself.

Bill went first because he can take stairs two at a time. I dashed up straight flights and around landings after him. A baby howled behind a door. Bill's footsteps thumped over my lighter, faster ones: then the sound of his changed as he hit the fourth floor and ran down the hall. He was almost at the front apartment's door when we heard a shot.

If you hadn't known, it could have been carpentry, hammer hitting wood. But he knew. Bill pounded on the door. "Police! Open up!" Crude, but effective. All sound stopped within.

I reached the door. "Lee Kuan Cheng!" I called. "It's Lydia Chin. Let me in. Don't shoot again."

Bill and I flattened ourselves on either side of the door, guns drawn, backs against the wall. Down the hall a door cracked, a face peered out. "Police!" Bill barked. "Get back inside!"

The face retreated hastily.

"Someday you'll get in trouble for that," I whispered.

"I always do."

"Can you break it in?"

He looked at the door, nodded.

"Kuan Cheng!" I called again. "Let me in! Let me talk to you. Don't hurt anyone, Kuan Cheng."

Nothing happened. Bill's eyes met mine. He backed a little, then threw himself against the unsuspecting door. It shuddered; he did it again, harder, and the door flew open, hinges shrieking. Bill went in low with it. I dived in even lower, so that any bullets Kuan Cheng fired would have a chance to miss us in the empty doorway. But he didn't fire any. He stood in the kitchen, maybe eight feet from us, face twisted in anger and fear. His skin was shiny with sweat. He held his elbows locked, his gun gripped in both shaking hands. Bill and I held guns on him, too, which meant if we were lucky, one of us would survive this.

Great.

"Kuan Cheng, don't," I said. "Put it down." I wasn't sure he could hear me over the beating of my heart.

He spoke. "She took a lover!" His voice was loud and hoarse. "Not even married yet, and she took a lover. Humiliated me everywhere! My *mother* knows! I'll kill her. I'll kill them both!"

"No," I said.

"No," a woman's cracked voice came from the shadowed room behind Kuan Cheng. "No!"

I peered down the hallway to the living room. In the fading light from the windows I saw Jill Moore kneeling, her arms wrapped protectively around the other man, the handsome Asian, whose white shirt showed a dark stain at the shoulder. His eyes were wide open with fear.

"Please!" Jill Moore's high, quavering voice was close to hysterical. "Kuan Cheng! It's not what you think!"

"Oh, no?" He whipped the gun in their direction, and his skin flushed darker.

"No," I said, grabbing for his attention. He was close to hysterical, too, and the sight of the other man in Jill Moore's arms wouldn't do him any good. "Kuan Cheng, he's not her lover."

He spun back to me. "Not her lover?" he sneered. "What, her younger brother?"

"No," I said. "He's her Mandarin teacher."

Disbelief, confusion, and anger chased each other across his face.

"Jill!" I yelled. "Am I right?"

"Yes!" she called. Her voice cracked again. "Kuan Cheng, I was going to surprise you. I didn't want you to know until I could speak it well." She made a small sobbing sound.

Kuan Cheng, his gun still trained on me, his body rigid and tense, glanced quickly into the living room, then back to me. He said nothing.

I stood slowly, lowered my gun, and put it in my belt clip. I looked at Bill. Sweat beaded his forehead and the back of his hands as he answered my look. Then he holstered his gun, too, and stood up.

God, I thought, if you shoot now, Kuan Cheng, shoot me, because I couldn't live with the guilt. Kuan Cheng didn't shoot anybody. He didn't put his gun down, either. He didn't move, just stood, paralyzed by indecision and disbelief.

"Kuan Cheng?" Jill's voice was clearer, though soft. "It was for your mother. I wanted her to like me."

Kuan Cheng laughed a short wild laugh. "My mother? That's ridiculous. What makes you think my mother will like you if you speak Mandarin?"

Jill said. "Because she said so."

My blood froze. No one spoke. There was silence everywhere.

Jill hurried on, trying to reach him. "That day at her apartment? She said if I learned to speak her language I'd be showing the proper respect. Then she'd accept me as a daughter-in-law. I mean, she never said she'd like me, but I thought it was a beginning. I wanted it to be as right as I could make it." In the dusk a tear glistened on her cheek.

"My mother said that?" Kuan Cheng whispered.

"Yes. She even found Chyi-Jou to teach me. We started that week."

"My god," I said low, unbelieving. I looked at Bill. Anger shone in his eyes; his jaw was tight. He knew, too. I said it anyway. "We were set up."

He nodded.

In the darkness of Jill Moore's apartment, Kuan Cheng lowered his gun.

We stopped the bleeding from Chyi-Jou Kwong's shoulder, called an ambulance, and concocted a story. Kuan Cheng had bought the gun for Jill, for protection. Neither of them knew how to use it, and it went off. Bill and I were on our way there, just for a visit, because I'm an old friend of Kuan Cheng's. We heard the shot and assumed there was trouble, thus the scene in the hallway.

We pulled it off, though it was sort of a pain, Bill and me at the 6th Precinct for an hour answering the same questions separately until the cops gave up. Kuan Cheng was arrested for gun possession, but Chyi-Jou Kwong wasn't badly hurt and Kuan Cheng was a model of upwardly mobile Asian youth. A good lawyer would be able to wiggle him out of anything serious. I was mad enough to let him figure his own way out of spending the night in jail, but Bill pointed out that it was our licenses on the line if Kuan Cheng, in his perilous emotional state, blew the story.

So I called Mrs. Lee and told her where he was and what had happened, and suggested she send him a lawyer fast.

"How'd she take it?" Bill asked as we left the police station. Tenth Street was carpeted with fallen leaves; streetlights shone gently on brick row-houses. It all seemed lovely and peaceful, but I was cold. And I knew that behind those cozy facades lurked legions of mothers gleefully plotting to double-cross their sons.

"She wailed. She yelled. She called him a stupid boy. She said it was all the white witch's fault. Then she said it was all *my* fault. Then I hung up on her."

"Without telling her where to get off?"

"Well," I admitted, "I told her a little bit where to get off. Because it won't get around and embarrass my mother. From now on, I guarantee Mrs. Lee will pretend she never heard of me."

We stopped at a corner to let a car drift past.

"How did you know?" Bill asked. "That he was teaching her Mandarin."

"The book he dropped on his toe. It was the same one she was translating Mandarin from at the library. She's not taking any Mandarin courses, so I guessed he was her tutor. But I never guessed Mrs. Lee had set us all up."

Bill said nothing, just lit a cigarette and let me go on, thinking sad thoughts out loud. "The thing is," I said, "I can't believe a mother would do that. Do you know what she said, when I called her on it?"

"Tell me."

"'Mother know best for son. White witch bad wife, undutiful daughter-in-law.' That was all she cared about—that Jill Moore wasn't the daughter-in-law of her dreams. What kind of mother is that?"

"Human," Bill said. "Flawed. Too desperate to see past herself."

"Desperate?" I snorted.

"Selfish. Diabolical. Manipulative. A classic Chinese mother."

"Is your mother like that?"

"Of course not! Just because she doesn't like *you*—"

"Will it help if I learn Cantonese?"

I stopped, looked at him, and laughed. Then I hugged him.

When we started forward again, the night wasn't as cold and the houses weren't as hostile.

"Maybe it's not that I don't understand white people," I said. "Maybe I don't understand anybody."

"Who does?"

"You do. Here's this woman who sets up her own son, and he almost kills a whole bunch of people including us, and you just say, 'She's human.'"

"That doesn't mean I understand her. Just that I know not to expect too much."

"Maybe nobody understands anybody." That thought made me cold again.

Bill took my hand. "Come on." We turned up a quiet street. "There's a cafe with a fireplace where they play Vivaldi. I'll buy you a hot apple cider."

I didn't have to say anything, because he was reading my mind.

JAN BURKE

THE MUSE

February 1995

AUTHOR OF THE popular Irene Kelly mysteries, Jan Burke published her first short story in *AHMM*; her first Irene Kelly short story,
"A Fine Set of Teeth," also had its first general publication in *AHMM*
in October 1998 (after an earlier limited edition). "The Muse," with its
integral and cleverly deployed Hitchcock references, was a natural
for *AHMM*.

■

The jet black pantyhose were calling to him. The feet of the pantyhose, to be precise. He knew he shouldn't look. Knew it would
only encourage her. But he folded the edge of the newspaper down,
giving in that much.

"Bee-yoll," her voice was childlike, crooning. Her puppeteer
voice.

"I'm not in the mood for this, Ellie," Bill said.

"Oh, Beeeeee-yoll."

Her hands were all he could see of her, and not really much of
her hands. The makeshift pantyhose puppets were "looking" at
each other.

"He's very angry with you," the right hand admonished the left.

"No, he's not," the left answered, then they both looked at
Bill.

"I'm not angry," Bill said to the hands, giving in a little more.
Addressing the puppets now. "Not really angry. Just tired."

"Quit distracting him. He's on an important deadline, and he
has writer's block," the right said.

"He never has writer's block," the left replied. "He's upset
about Mir."

"The prospect of a visit from Miriam is an unpleasant one," he agreed.

Ellie's head emerged above the edge of the breakfast table. He saw that she had cut the crotch out of the pantyhose, and was wearing them over her head.

"You are the strangest woman I know," he said, causing her to smile. Ellie considered this a grand endearment. Bill knew that.

Her head tilted a little to one side, as if studying him for a portrait. "It's fine now. Not even my evil twin can stop you."

"She is your younger sister, not your twin," he said, but she was leaving the table, pulling the pantyhose off.

Ellie was right, as always. Not about the twin business, of course, but about the novel he was working on. He got up from the table feeling invigorated and went straight to the computer. He had a new slant on a passage he had considered unworkable until a moment ago. This was the effect she had on him. Ellie was his Muse.

He had known she would be from the moment he first saw her. Seven years ago, well past three o'clock in the morning on a hot summer's night, at a gas station on Westwood Boulevard. Bill supposed he would forget his own name before he forgot that night.

He had been uneasy, at loose ends. It wasn't insomnia: it's only insomnia when you're trying to sleep. He had been trying to write. It was his best-kept secret then, his writing. None of his professors at UCLA, who knew him as a recent graduate in mechanical engineering, would have ever guessed it. Well-written papers and a flair for creative problem-solving didn't make him stand out as more than a good student. His friends, although from varied backgrounds and majors, held the same prejudices as the few women he had dated: they assumed that engineers were unlikely to read novels, let alone write them. His father, who expected him to come to work for the family company in September, was also unaware of Bill's literary aspirations.

In those days Bill thought that was for the best. If he was going to fail, he preferred not to advertise it. And while he had faith in the basic idea for his novel, he had to admit it wasn't working out. Frustrated when he stalled in that place in the manuscript where he had stalled no fewer than ten times before—where the boy ought to get the girl back again—he stood up and stretched. He needed some fresh air, he decided. At least, the freshest he could find in LA.

And so he had restlessly made his way down to Westwood Boulevard, head down, his hands shoved down into his pockets, his long-legged gait taking him quickly past record stores and restaurants. He glanced up just to keep from running into parking meters and lampposts, glancing at but not really seeing the boutiques and movie theaters closed for the night. The gas station was closed, too, but the sight that greeted him there made him slow his stride.

A lithe young woman was tugging on one of the water hoses most people use for filling radiators. She was using it to wash a gold Rolls-Royce.

He came to a halt on the wide sidewalk, fascinated. She looked up over the hood, used the back of her hand to move her bowl-cut, thick dark hair away from her eyes. Big brown eyes.

"Want to go for a ride?" she asked him.

He nodded but didn't move forward.

"You'll have to give up hesitating if you're going to ride with me," she said, opening the driver's door. But Bill was distracted from this edict when he saw an elderly man sleeping on the front seat.

"Wake up, Harry," she said, gently nudging the old man, who came awake with a start. "We're taking . . ." She looked over her shoulder. "I'm Ellie. What's your name?"

"William. William Gray."

She turned back to the old man. "We're taking Bill here for a ride on Mulholland Drive. You can sleep in the back."

The old man reached for a cap, rubbed a gnarled hand over his face, and quickly transformed himself into a dignified chauffeur, moving to hold the passenger door open for Bill, waiting patiently as Bill finally moved toward the car. Harry gave a questioning look at Ellie, now behind the wheel.

"No, you need your rest."

Harry nodded and climbed into the back, asleep again before Ellie had started the car.

They had traveled Mulholland and beyond that night, climbing canyon roads that twisted and turned.

She was a good driver, calm and assured, not crazy on the winding roads. At first he was afraid, wondering if he had made the biggest—and perhaps the final—mistake of his life. He started envisioning bold headlines: "Missing UCLA Student Found

Dead," or "Still No Suspects in Topanga Canyon Torture-Murder Case." Perhaps he wouldn't be missed much. Maybe he would only rate a small article on a back page, near a department store ad: "Boy Scout Troop Makes Grisly Discovery in Canyon."

"Either you just had a big fight with your girlfriend or you're a writer," she said, not taking her eyes off the road. "I'm betting you're a writer."

He hesitated, then said, "I'm a writer. Or I want to be one. How did you guess?"

"The time of day, the way you were walking. You looked frustrated, I suppose."

"Anyone can be frustrated. Why would you think I'm a writer?"

She shrugged, then smiled a little. He waited, hoping she would answer, but she startled him by saying, "You're also a bit of a romantic."

He laughed nervously. "That's an odd thing to say."

"I am odd. But there's nothing odd about knowing a romantic when you see one. At three—" she glanced at the clock on the dash. "At approximately three twenty-five in the morning, you agreed to get into a Rolls-Royce with a sleeping old man and a woman you had never met before."

"Perhaps I just needed an adventure."

"Perhaps. Perhaps both. So, what's your favorite movie of all time?"

"*Rear Window,*" he said without hesitation.

"Wonderful!" she said, laughing but still not taking her eyes from the road. "Whose work in it do you admire, Hitchcock's or Woolrich's?"

He smiled. Many people knew that Hitchcock directed *Rear Window.* Fewer knew that it was written by Cornell Woolrich. "Both, really," he answered. "I'm a fan of both. I've seen every Hitchcock film, with the exception of a few of the very early British ones."

Soon they were discussing Hitchcock and Woolrich, and Bill forgot all about Boy Scouts and headlines. She had seen most of the films he had seen, read more Woolrich.

He eased back into the passenger seat, studying her. She didn't make a move toward him, didn't reach across the seat, didn't even look at him much. Every so often, finding a vista she liked,

Ellie would stop the car. The first time she stopped, Bill expected her to turn her attention to him. But she didn't do more than glance at him. "Just look at it," she said, gesturing to the carpet of city lights below. Soon he realized that was all she would ask of him—just to look at it.

At one of these turnouts, she kicked off her shoes and rolled down a window, resting her bare feet on the sill. She drove barefooted the rest of the night.

She asked him questions. He talked more that night than he had ever talked in his life. About his writing, his family, his childhood, his love of Woolrich stories and Hitchcock films and chocolate and on and on, even describing the furniture in his apartment.

"And you?" he asked. "Where do you live?"

"Somewhere in these hills. Perhaps I'll take you there someday."

As many questions as she asked, and as few as she answered, somehow she still managed to make him feel that he was of vital interest to her. Not in the way some questioners might—scientists studying an insect—but as if she had cared about him from before the time she had met him. He was wondering at the trust he had placed in this stranger as dawn was coming up over the hills. She had parked the car on a ridge. Harry was snoring softly. "I'll take you home," she said.

"I'm not sure I want to go home," Bill answered, then quickly added, "Sorry, I don't mean to be pushy. You've been a great listener. You're probably tired and—"

She reached over then and laid a finger to his lips. She shook her head, and he stopped talking, unsure of what she was saying no to.

SHE TOOK HIM back to his apartment, leaving Harry asleep in the car.

"Do you want to come in?" he asked on his doorstep.

She shook her head, an impish smile on her lips. "I know exactly what it looks like—I'm sure you've described it perfectly. Besides, you're very busy. You've got to get a little sleep, and then you'll wake up and write your book. It's going to be terrific, but no one will ever find that out until you write it." She turned and skipped back to the car.

"Will I see you again?" he called out.

"Stop worrying," she called back. "Write!"

And he had. He slept about three hours, woke up feeling like he had slept ten, and wondering if he had dreamed the woman in the Rolls-Royce. But dream or no dream, he suddenly knew how to get around that problem in his story and went to work.

Harry appeared a few hours later, a picnic basket in hand. "Miss Eleanor sends her regards, and provisions so that you need not interrupt your work."

"You can talk!" Bill exclaimed.

"When necessary," Harry said, and left.

Bill searched through the basket and found an assortment of small sandwiches, a salad, a slice of chocolate cake, and several choices of beverages. He also found an old-fashioned calling card:

> *Miss Eleanor Wingate*

On the back she had inscribed her phone number.

"Delicious," Bill said, holding it carefully as if it might skip away, disappear as quickly as she had.

AND SO HE went back to writing. Bill saw little of Ellie during the weeks that followed their ride through the hills, but he called her often. If he found himself staring uselessly at the place where the wall behind his computer screen met the ceiling, unsure how to proceed, a brief chat with Ellie inspired him. They played a game with Hitchcock films and Woolrich stories.

"A jaguar," he would say.

"*Black Alibi*," she would answer. "A name scrawled on a window."

"Easy—*The Lady Vanishes*."

And his writer's block would vanish as well.

When Bill completed his manuscript, Harry took him and the manuscript to her house for the first time. Bill, trying (and failing) not to be overawed by the elegance that surrounded him, handed her the box of pages. She caressed the corners of the box, looking for a moment as if she might cry. But she said nothing, and set it gently aside without opening it. She held out her hand, and he took it. She led him upstairs.

LATER, WAKING in the big bed, he found her watching him. "Did you read it?"

"No," she said, tracing a finger along his collarbone. "I don't want any misunderstandings about why you're here. It's not because of what's in that manuscript box."

He savored the implications of that for a moment before insecurities besieged him, "Maybe you'd hate it anyway."

"I couldn't."

It was the last time they talked about the manuscript for three days. At the end of those three days, he mailed it to an agent, called his father to say he'd found other work, packed up his belongings, and moved in with Ellie.

The agent called back, took him on as a client, and sold the book within a week. Bill was already at work on his second novel. The first one was a critically acclaimed but modest success. The second spent twenty-five weeks on the best-seller list. When Bill got his first royalty check, he asked Ellie to marry him.

She gently but firmly refused. She also refused after books three, four, and five—all best sellers.

Today, as he finished the chapter he was working on, he wondered if she would ever tell him why. Ellie could be very obstinate, he knew. If she didn't want to give him a straight answer, she would make up something so bizarre and absurd that he would know to stop asking.

"There was a clause in my parents' will," she said once. "If I marry before my fiftieth birthday, the house must be turned into an ostrich farm."

"And the courts accepted that?" he played along.

"Absolutely. The trust funds would go to ostriches, and Mir would be very unhappy with you for putting an end to her healthy allowance."

"Your parents would have left Miriam a pauper?"

"She thinks she's a pauper on what I give her now."

"A pauper? On ten thousand dollars a month?"

"Pin money for Mir. We grew up rich, remember?"

"Hard to forget. Why not give it all to Miriam and live on my money instead?"

She frowned. "I'd be dependent on you."

"So what? I was dependent on you when I first lived here."

"For about four months. And you had your own money, you just didn't need any of it. Do you want to be married for more than four months?"

"Of course."

"So now you see why we can't be married at all."

He didn't, but he resigned himself to the situation. She probably would never tell him why she wouldn't marry him, or why she allowed Miriam, who often upset her, to come to the house on a regular basis to plead for more money.

"WHERE'S HARRY?" Miriam demanded when Bill answered the doorbell.

"On the phone," Bill explained as he took her coat. "He's placing ads for a cook and housekeeper."

"Not again," Miriam said.

"The last ones managed to stay on for about six weeks," Bill said easily.

Miriam turned her most charming smile upon him. She was gorgeous, Bill thought, not for the first time. A redhead with china blue eyes and a figure that didn't need all that custom tailoring to show it off. What was she, he wondered? A walking ice sculpture, perhaps? But he discarded that image. After all, sooner or later, ice melted.

"I don't know why you stay with her, Bill," Miriam purred, misreading his attention.

Bill heard a door open in a hallway above them.

"If you're here for a favor," he said in a low voice, "you're not being very kind to your benefactor."

Miriam stood frowning, waiting until she heard the door close again. Still, she whispered when she said, "Even *you* must admit that she drives the entire household to distraction."

"Yes," he said, thinking back to the night he met Ellie. "But distraction isn't always such a bad place to go."

"She's crazy," Miriam said scornfully. "And a liar!"

"She's neither. What brings you by this afternoon?" They were halfway up the stairs now, and although Bill thought Ellie was probably past being injured by Miriam's remarks, he didn't know how much longer his own patience would last.

Miriam pointed one perfectly shaped red fingernail at him. "How can you say she's not a liar? She once told you Harry was her father."

"She knew I wouldn't believe it. She never tells me any lie she thinks I might believe. Come on, she's waiting."

Bill had heard Ellie cross into one of the upstairs staging rooms. This meant, he knew, that she had staged some clues for him, placed objects about the room intended to remind him of specific Hitchcock movies. It was an extension of the old game they played, and one of the reasons that housekeepers didn't last long. The last one left after finding a mannequin, unclad except for Harry's cap, sitting in the bathtub. (*"The Trouble With Harry,"* Bill had said, earning praise from Ellie even as they tried to revive the fainting housekeeper.)

Ellie, knowing Miriam hated the game, always had one ready when her sister came to visit.

Wearing a pair of jeans with holes in the knees, Ellie was sitting cross-legged on top of a large mahogany table, passing a needle and thread through colored miniature marshmallows to make a necklace. She smiled as she moved the needle through a green marshmallow.

"How much this time?" she asked without looking up.

"Ellie darling! So good to see you."

Ellie glanced at Bill. "Too many Bette Davis movies." She chose a pink marshmallow next.

"What on earth are you doing? And why are you wearing those horrid clothes?"

"Shhh!" Ellie said, now reaching for a yellow marshmallow.

Bill was looking around the room. As usual in a game, there were many oddball objects and antiques in the room. The trick was to find the clues among the objects. "How many altogether?"

"Three," Ellie answered.

"Oh! This stupid game. I might have known," Miriam grumbled.

He saw the toy windmill first.

"Foreign Correspondent," he said.

"One down, two to go," Ellie laughed. "How much money this time, Mir?"

"I didn't come here to ask for money," Miriam said, sitting down.

Bill looked over at her in surprise, then went back to the game.

Searching through the bric-a-brac that covered a low set of shelves, he soon found the next clue: three small plaster of Paris sculptures of hands and wrists. A man's hand and a woman's hand were handcuffed together; another male hand, missing part of its little finger, stood next to the handcuffed set. *"The Thirty-Nine Steps."*

"Bravo, Bill. Of course you came here for money, Mir. You always do."

"Not this time."

"What then?" Ellie asked, watching as Bill picked up a music box from a small dressing table.

"I want to move back home."

Ellie stopped stringing marshmallows. Bill set the music box down.

Don't give in, Ellie, he prayed silently.

"No," Ellie said, and went back to work on her necklace. Bill's sigh of relief was audible.

"Ellie, please, I'm your sister."

"I'll buy you a place to live."

"I want to live here."

"Why?"

"It's in the will. I can live here if I want to."

Ellie looked up. "We had an agreement."

Miriam glanced nervously toward Bill, then said, "It's my home, too, you know. You've allowed a perfect stranger to live here. Well, I don't deserve any less."

"Why do you want to come back, Mir? You haven't lived here in years."

"I think it's time we grew closer as sisters, that's all."

Ellie only laughed at that. Bill was heartened by the laughter. Ellie was protective of Miriam, had a soft spot for her despite her abuses. But if that sister plea didn't get through to her, maybe there was a chance . . .

"Look, you've been living up here in grand style," Miriam said petulantly, "and I just want to enjoy a bit of it myself."

Bill saw Ellie's mood shifting, saw her glancing over at him. He felt awkwardness pulling ahead of his curiosity by a nose. He decided to leave this discussion to the sisters. It was Ellie's house, after all. She could do as she liked. He started to edge out of the room, but Ellie said, "This concerns you, too, Bill. Don't leave."

He wasn't put off by what others might have taken to be a commanding tone. In seven years, he had never heard the word "please" come out of her mouth. Although he thought of few things as certain when it came to Ellie, one certainty was that she rarely asked anything of others. Knowing this, he treated any request as if there were an implied "please."

"This isn't his house!" Miriam shouted.

"Lower your voice. He is my guest and welcome here."

Bill turned away, forced himself to look again at the objects on the dressing table.

Ellie went on. "You spent all of your inheritance in less than two years, Mir. Grandfather knew you were like our parents."

Bill knew this part of the story. Their grandfather had raised the girls after their parents—wild, spoiled, and reckless, according to Ellie—were killed in a car wreck. While Miriam received a large inheritance, Ellie's grandfather had left the house and most of his money to Ellie, thinking Miriam too much like his late daughter.

"Don't start speaking ill of the dead," Miriam protested to Ellie.

"All right, I won't. But the fact remains . . ."

"That you've made money and I've lost all of mine. Don't rub it in, Ellie. Now I've even lost the condo."

"I know."

"You know? Then you understand why I want to live here."

"Not really. But this time I'll keep the title so you can't mortgage it endlessly."

"I want to live here. This is my home!"

"Fine. Then you won't get another dime from me."

Bill watched in the dressing table mirror as Miriam swallowed hard, then lifted her chin. "All right, if that's what you want to do. My bags are in the car. Harry can pick up the rest of my things—"

"No!" Ellie interrupted sharply, clenching her hands, smushing part of her marshmallow necklace. She shook her head, then said more calmly, "You won't badger that man. I swear you won't be allowed to live here if you do. I'll sell this place first."

"All right, all right. I won't cause trouble, Ellie. You'll see. I'll even bring my cook and housekeeper with me. That will save Harry a lot of work."

Bill was hardly paying attention by then. He was nettled. So nettled, he didn't offer to help Miriam with her bags as she left the room. He kept his back to Ellie, pretending to be caught up in the game again.

My guest. It was accurate enough, he supposed. Not "my lover." Not "my friend." Not "the man I want to spend my life with." My guest. He picked up the music box again.

"You've got a burr under your saddle, Bill. What is it?"

He ignored her for a moment, lifting the lid of the music box. It played "The Merry Widow Waltz."

He heard Ellie sigh behind him. "I'm not happy about it, either," she said, "but there's nothing I can do. Perhaps having Miriam here won't be so bad."

He closed the lid of the music box. *"Shadow of a Doubt,"* he said, and schooled his features into a smile before turning toward her. "Thank you for all the effort, Ellie. It's always an amusing game."

She looked puzzled. He hadn't fooled her, of course. Belatedly he realized that she must have watched him in the mirror. But if she could be obstinate, well, by damn, so could he. He excused himself and left the room.

As he paid the tab in a bar that evening, Bill had to acknowledge that the slight had escalated into silent warfare, and much of it was probably his fault. He had not yet managed to tell Ellie how she had given offense. In one moment, it seemed of so little importance that he was ashamed of himself for thinking about it at all. In the next moment, it seemed to stand as a perfect symbol for everything that was wrong between them. There were several drinks between moments. But in the end he had firmly resolved to talk to her, not to let one comment ruin all they had shared until then.

Bill looked up to see a familiar figure coming toward him. Not the one he most wanted to see, but close enough. Harry had come to fetch him.

"Did she send you for me, Harry?" Bill asked, allowing Harry to lead him outside.

"No, sir."

"You came on your own?" he asked in surprise. Harry had never indicated approval of Bill, a lack Bill took to mean disapproval.

"No, sir," Harry replied, but Bill noticed that the old man actually seemed a little embarrassed to admit it. Harry gently guided him into the backseat of the Rolls.

Bill waited until Harry got into the car. He felt as if he might be sick, but he fought it off. "Why'd you come after me?"

"Miss Miriam suggested it. She has many suggestions, sir."

Bill signaled him to wait, opened the door, and spared the upholstery.

Harry drove him home, windows down. But even during the long ride, Bill had sobered little. He made it into the house under his own steam and began the climb up the stairs. He swayed a bit as he reached for the bedroom doorknob, twisted it, and found it locked. He stared at it in his hand, as if somehow he were just doing it wrong, this simple act of opening a door.

Harry came in then and, quietly coming up the stairs, asked in a whisper if Bill might need some assistance. Bill was hanging on to the knob, staring dumbly at the door. Harry tried the knob, then murmured, "It's locked, sir. Perhaps . . ." but his voice broke off as they heard another door open.

Miriam, clad in a nightgown that seemed to offer little difference from sleeping in the nude, smiled and called out, "Ellie left some things for you outside the bedroom off your office downstairs. I guess you're in the doghouse tonight, Billy Boy."

"You seem happy to hear it," Bill said, trying to stand up straight. Having this greedy woman in the household would sorely try him. Harry stepped aside as Miriam came closer. Miriam tried to put an arm around Bill, giggling when he clumsily pushed her hand from his waist. She stepped back.

"Why do you two stay together?" she asked. "Ellie doesn't seem interested. I could see why you tried to win her over at first, but now—well, why bother? You've got plenty of money. Most women would consider you quite a catch."

"For your information," Bill said, his drunken state not obscuring her intentions, "I wouldn't make any money without your sister. If I leave her, I can't write. She's my Muse."

Whatever reply Miriam might have made was lost when a loud crash sounded against the other side of the bedroom door.

"Ellie! Are you all right?" Bill called frantically.

"Go to hell!" came Ellie's voice from the other side.

Bill heard Miriam giggle behind him as she closed her bedroom door.

"DON'T DO this, sir."

Bill was so taken aback by Harry's plea that he stopped packing for a moment. But he shook his head and latched the suitcase.

"Sorry, Harry. I can take the silent treatment, and finding out that she threw a portrait of me against the door that night. I can even take the blame for starting this. But I can't stay here if she doesn't trust me."

Until that afternoon Bill hadn't heard a word from Ellie in three days. After that first morning, when Harry brought Bill's clothes into the bedroom adjoining Bill's office, Bill hadn't tried to go back to the room he had shared with her. He had heard her move about in her office, just on the other side of the wall. Each day she had gone from her room to her office and back again, speaking only to Miriam or Harry. Miriam, suddenly the solicitous sister, would take meals to Ellie in her room. Bill tried to ignore it, told himself her temper would cool and he would be able to tell her just how much she meant to him, that she was much more to him than the means to an end. Until then he would keep his distance.

But this morning she had ventured outside the house, asking Harry to take her for a ride. They had been gone for about an hour when Bill heard someone rustling papers in her office and went to investigate. Miriam was bent over some documents on Ellie's desk, pen in hand.

"What are you doing?" he asked, startling her.

"None of your business."

He moved closer, and she snatched one of the pages off the desk and wadded it up in her hand.

"Why are you in Ellie's office?" he asked, glancing at a contract Ellie had signed, the document Miriam had been studying.

"I said, none of your business."

He reached out and grabbed the hand with the paper in it. She clawed at his face, struggling furiously, but he caught both of her wrists and squeezed until she let the paper drop. He bent to pick it up even as Miriam ran crying from the room.

He sat down at the desk, ignoring the sting of the scratches. The contract was nothing unusual, he noted, as he smoothed the paper out. Ellie's signature was on the scrap. But as he studied it closer, he realized it was *almost* Ellie's signature.

A tearful voice took his attention from the paper. "I caught him trying to forge your signature. I grabbed the paper he was practicing on, and he attacked me!"

He looked up to see Ellie staring at him in disbelief. "Ellie . . ." he protested, standing up.

"Did you do this to her?"

She held out Miriam's wrists.

There were dark red marks on them.

"Yes, but Ellie . . ."

"I don't want to hear it!"

She led Miriam from the room, consoling her.

AND SO HE left the house in the hills. He had no trouble finding a house to rent. He told himself he only rented one because he was too busy finishing his manuscript to do serious house hunting. Never mind that he was finished before his deadline. While waiting for his editor's response, he began outlining another work, writing character sketches. He told himself this productivity was a sign that he was readjusting, living a new life.

But he knew that wasn't the truth. The truth was, he wrote because writing was all he had left. He felt closer to her when he wrote, even as he told himself he didn't miss her. But that was the biggest lie of all.

When his editor proclaimed the new manuscript Bill's best work, Bill didn't feel the sense of elation such praise might have once brought. Ellie wasn't his link to writing after all. It wasn't inspiration he missed; it was Ellie herself.

HE FOUND HIMSELF on Westwood Boulevard at three in the morning, staring at the place where the gas station had been. It was gone, transformed into a parking lot. But as he stared, a gold

Rolls-Royce pulled into the empty lot. For a moment, his heart leapt. But then he saw that Harry was driving. Alone.

It wasn't the first time he had seen Harry. Harry kept tabs on him, he knew. In the beginning, he thought she might have asked Harry to do so, then realized that Harry only appeared on his day off. Harry seldom spoke to him and never mentioned Ellie. But it seemed to Bill that Harry was looking older each time he encountered him.

"Evening, sir."

"Hello, Harry." And then, breaking a promise he had made to himself, he asked, "How is she?"

Harry seemed to perk up a bit. He studied Bill's face, then seemed to make up his mind about something. "She's not well, sir."

"Not well?"

"No, sir."

"Nothing serious, I hope?"

Harry was silent.

"Harry, did she put you up to this? Is she trying to get me to come back? Because I'm doing just fine on my own now."

Harry shook his head. "You disappoint me, sir." He stepped back to the car.

"Harry, wait."

Harry waited.

"Does she know you watch over me?"

"No, sir. But for some time now she has . . . I mean to say, sir, that whatever has gone before, at present she may be too ill to contact you herself."

Bill frowned. "I don't like hearing that she's ill."

Harry stayed silent.

"I know she dislikes doctors. Has she been to a doctor about this illness?"

"Miss Miriam has supplied a doctor, sir. He often comes to the house to care for Miss Eleanor."

"Oh." He looked away from Harry's studying gaze for a moment. "Well, I don't suppose . . . that is, if Miriam has found a doctor who will make a house call, I don't suppose Ellie needs me for anything."

Harry hesitated, then said, "Permit me to say, sir, that I'm not certain Miss Eleanor has done well under this physician's care."

"Tell her that you saw me," Bill said. "Tell her that you saw me here. She'll know what that means. Tell her to—to let me know if she needs me."

Bill didn't sleep at all that night. If she were seriously ill . . .

HE HESITATED until late the next afternoon, then called the house. Miriam answered.

"Miriam, this is Bill."

"Bill the caterer? Terrific. About this evening . . ."

"No, no. Bill Gray. Let me talk to Ellie, please."

"Oh, that Bill." After a long pause, Miriam said, "She doesn't want to talk to you."

"Let me hear her say that herself."

"Listen, she has a new man in her life. One who doesn't cause so many problems. We're having a dinner party tonight, and he's the guest of honor. So I really don't think you're someone she wants to talk to."

The line went dead.

A new man. He half believed it. If the wrenching in his gut was any indication, he believed it more than half. But Harry said she was ill, seeing a doctor. Why would she throw a dinner party if she wasn't well? Why would Harry look for him if she was seeing someone else?

Not much later, he heard a car pull into his driveway. Bill looked out the window to see the Rolls. He hurried out the front door when he saw the look of worry on Harry's face.

"Is she all right?" Bill asked.

"Sir, I'm to give you this."

Harry pressed a key into Bill's palm.

"There is a dinner party tonight, sir. I believe the persons in attendance are interested in acquiring the house and surrounding properties."

"Ellie is selling the house?"

"No, sir. But there now exist documents that say Miss Miriam is given power of attorney over the sale of the house, due to her sister's ill health. And indeed, her sister is ill."

Bill looked down at the key.

"She said you could win the game, sir. Do you know what she means?"

"The game? The Hitchcock game. It must be *Notorious*."

"The game is notorious, sir?"

"No, Harry. *Notorious* is a Hitchcock film. Claude Rains plays one of the leaders of a group of Nazi scientists living in Brazil. They're trying to build an atom bomb. Ingrid Bergman has married him, but as he discovers, she's an American spy working with Gary Grant."

"Does the key give you some clue about her health, sir?"

"No," Bill said absently, "but in a Hitchcock film, the story is always larger than the objects that become the focus of the suspense."

"I beg your pardon, sir?"

Bill continued to stare at the key. "The key is to a wine cellar, where an important secret is kept. But the film isn't really about spies and secrets. Gary Grant and Ingrid Bergman are in love, but misunderstandings and mistrust stand between them. It isn't until the end of the film, when he realizes that . . ." Bill suddenly looked up at Harry. "Harry, when you said she was ill . . . oh no. Get me to the house at once! Drive like a bat out of hell!"

HARRY COMPLIED. As they drove, Bill asked him questions that made Harry wonder if the young man had somehow spoken to Miss Eleanor, even though Miss Miriam had taken the phone out of Eleanor's room long ago. Bill asked about Miss Eleanor's symptoms, and every time Harry said, "Yes, sir; she's had terrible stomach cramps," or "Yes, sir, very dizzy," Bill seemed to grow more frantic.

"Keep the motor running," he said as they pulled into the drive. "I'll be out in a minute."

Bill burst through the front door, nearly knocking a startled maid off her feet. He could hear voices in the dining room, but he didn't bother with the dinner party in progress. He ran up the stairs.

"Sir!" the maid called. "You can't go up there!"

He ignored her.

His only moment of hesitation came as he stepped inside Ellie's bedroom and saw her for the first time in a month. He had expected to find her bedroom door locked but quickly realized why it wasn't.

She was too ill to run away.

He forced himself to move again, went quickly to her side. Her skin was jaundiced, and she was so thin, almost skeletal, he thought, then pushed the thought away. Her hair, her beautiful hair, was dull in color and missing in patches. Her breathing was steady but rasping. He put his hands beneath her and lifted her frail body from the bed, keeping the blanket wrapped around her. He told himself that self-recrimination must wait.

Her big brown eyes were open now, watching him.

"Good to see you," she whispered.

"My God, Ellie." He tried to gather his wits. "How long has she been poisoning you?"

"Little at a time," she said, wincing as she spoke.

"Don't talk now, not if it hurts. Has it just been since I left?"

She nodded, the effort seeming to wear her out.

A month. A month of arsenic. "I'm not leaving again, Ellie. Except to take you with me."

She continued to watch him, but now the barest smile came to her lips.

He had started down the stairs when Miriam, dinner party in tow, entered the foyer.

"What are you doing?" Miriam screeched.

"I'm taking her to a hospital. To see a real doctor. You had better pray to God that I'm not too late."

Miriam tried to block his way. "She's too ill to move! You have no business . . ."

"Careful, Miriam," he said in a low voice. "She's awake and lucid. Shall we discuss this in front of your guests, or do you want to wait until after Harry describes your so-called doctor to the gents at the sheriff's office? Ellie's blood work will probably give them all they need to go after both of you."

Miriam paled, then stepped out of the way.

"What's going on here?" one of the guests demanded.

"My sister's . . ."

"*Fiancé,*" Bill supplied as he reached the front door. "Her fiancé is taking her to a hospital."

The group followed him toward the car. He wasn't watching them. He was watching Ellie. She moved her hand, covered his with it. Her skin was cool and paper dry. "You're safe now, Ellie," he told her.

"I'm coming with you!" Miriam said, hearing the guests murmuring behind her.

"No, you aren't, miss," Harry said, helping Bill into the backseat.

"She's her sister!" one of the guests protested.

"Her sister will remain here with you," Bill said. "She wants to tell you about a Hitchcock film."

"What are you talking about?" another man asked.

"*Notorious,*" Bill said, closing the car door.

"You've won, sir, haven't you?" Harry said as they drove off.

"I've had help," Bill replied. "All along, I've had help."

Ellie squeezed his hand.

CAROL CAIL

SINKHOLE

December 1995

THE AUTHOR OF a series of mysteries featuring Maxey Burnell, the owner of a Colorado newspaper, Cail has published poetry and romance novels in addition to mysteries. In this charmingly creepy story, a man finds that what goes down may very well come back up.

■

"**We've got to** stop meeting like this."

He couldn't believe Maudie had actually said that, in all seriousness, less than fifteen minutes ago at the Kentucky Hunker Inn.

"Right," he'd said, pointing his foot to slide on the first sock. "In the future I can just cross the street from my house to yours. Saves a motel bill, too."

Then she had pursed her rosebud mouth and uttered the next cliché. "If you don't tell your wife about us, I will."

"Maudie! Love!" He twisted around to grab and agitate her. It was like shaking his ten-year-old son, all loose, light bones.

"Let go," she squealed. "No more touching me till Karen knows." She brushed his hands off her arms and swatted his chest.

Staring morosely at the flaccid sock caught on his toe, he said, "I'll take care of it tonight."

"You'll tell Karen tonight? You promise?"

"I promise. Tomorrow night latest."

"Arrrrgh!" She flounced off the bed, snatching up clothes, red hair wild as a bonfire. "All right, Craig Richard Longworth. You have exactly two hours from this moment. That's—" she wrenched his arm out of his lap to read his watch "—eight forty-six. If you haven't broken the news to Karen by then, *I'm* telling her at eight forty-seven."

"Jeeze, Maudie—"

The slamming bathroom door chopped off all appeals.

Now on his way home, Craig turned the Camry in at Trudy's Tavern, needing to soothe his nerves and shore up his resolve.

The first beer disappeared as if he had a train to catch. Looking over the sparse early evening crowd, he sipped the second.

"Burger and fries?" Trudy suggested.

What the heck, might as well spoil his supper; Karen wasn't going to feed him tonight after they had their little talk.

Swiveling on his stool, leaning his elbows on the bar behind, he studied faces. Most of them were familiar, including Lionel Eads's, who was nuzzling the pale ear of a buxom blonde boothmate. Craig didn't recognize the lady, but he did know she wasn't skinny, redheaded Mrs. Eads. Torn between being scandalized and being envious, he stared at their blatant billing and cooing till Trudy slammed his hamburger plate onto the counter.

Turning around, he sighed. It was a whole different story for Lionel. He didn't have any children for his wife to take away if he asked for a divorce.

Divorce. The word conjured up horrendous visions of infinite alimony and inequitable division of property. Karen would get the stereo and the boat, and he'd get the Mickey Mouse telephone and the 1970 fake leather encyclopedias.

Craig took a vicious bite of the hamburger, swabbed grease off his chin with the cocktail napkin, and lurched forward under a hearty slap to his back.

"Hi, neighbor," Lionel bellowed. "Whaddya know?"

Squinting over his shoulder, Craig nodded at Lionel and took another look at the blonde waiting for the next round of beer and sweet talk.

"I got a date with your wife in the morning," Lionel said in the same robust volume, hand-signaling an order to Trudy.

Grinning was an effort that made Craig's face ache. "Yeah? Why's that?"

"We're going to plant a half-ton boulder on that sinkhole in your backyard."

"Oh. Oh yeah. Karen did say she'd contracted to have that covered over. We've been afraid one of the kids would twist an ankle in it. Or worse."

"Hey, Trudy honey, how about some service?" Lionel called as she rushed by with empty pitchers.

"Um, who's the young lady with you?" Craig stage-whispered, curiosity overcoming tact.

"My sister." Lionel punched Craig's arm.

"Does your wife know you have a sister?"

"You mean, does my sister know I have a wife!" Reaching across Craig for the mugs Trudy offered, Lionel roared a malty laugh.

A few minutes later Craig watched them leave, holding hands and giggling like teenagers.

He ought to go, too. Checking his watch, he decided to put it off till the last minute, and he stood up to challenge someone to darts.

CRAZY CHESTER GOMPERS was telling another outrageous joke. Guffawing, Craig banged his forehead against his wrist on the bar, and one eye focused on the slime-green digits of his watch. Eight forty-two.

Giving a Cinderella gasp, he slapped bills on the bar and caromed to the front door. In a few panting seconds he was spinning tires for home, thirty minutes away if he didn't break any speed laws.

Driving forty in a twenty-mile zone, he argued with himself. Maudie wouldn't really march across their quiet little dead-end street and blab the whole sordid—

Sure she would. She loved him, wanted him, would do anything—

Realizing his preening had allowed a drop in the miles per hour, Craig shook himself and tramped on the accelerator again. The car clock blinked another minute older.

It said eight fifty-six when he turned through the stone arches of Country View Estates (Your Little Piece of the World). He noticed that Lionel Eads's house loomed black as he passed it, and a minute later he was on Strawberry Lane. In no hurry now that he could see his and Maudie's houses, he rolled quietly along, craning to see which lights were on at either place, searching for female shapes inside or out.

Maudie's ranch style was completely dark. Oh-oh. His own split-level beckoned with one gleaming kitchen window. As his headlights swept the barricade at the end of the street, oak trees in the cow pasture beyond waved colorless leaves at a late summer breeze.

"Karen?" he asked an obviously empty house from the garage/kitchen door.

Hearing a clink of sound, he nipped on the outside flood-light and squinted into the backyard. Karen was by the far fence, wrestling a long-handled shovel that had the weight advantage.

Craig strolled out to face her with a casualness he couldn't have faked without a stomach full of beer. "Digging for gold?"

She wiped her cheek with a limp wrist.

"I saw Lionel Eads today," Craig said with the same false cheerfulness he'd disliked from Lionel. "Says he'll be by to-morrow to cover this up."

Karen grunted.

"So what are you doing?" Craig said.

"Just trying to level it off. Spread some dirt on it. Make it smaller."

He eyed her handiwork critically. The fist-sized sinkhole was now more than a foot across. Considering what else he needed to tell her, he didn't think he'd mention she was doing a lousy job.

Jamming hands in trousers, he twisted to look around the board-fenced yard. "Where is everybody?"

"Everybody?"

"Rick. Where's Rick?"

"Slumber party at Mitchy Best's."

"Uh, I noticed Maude Lamar's house is all dark. Thought she might be over here."

"Nope." She threw a half shovel's worth of dirt on the hole, and it slithered out of sight like flour down a funnel. "She was here awhile ago, though."

"Oh?" Craig cleared his throat and lowered his voice to nor-mal range. "What did our little widow want?"

Karen whacked the hole with the flat of the shovel. "She picked up Rick to take him and her Jimmy to Mitchy Best's slumber party."

"Oh. I guess she was in a hurry and didn't have much to say?"

"Actually, she did say—" She leaned on the shovel and stared at the house.

Craig poised in a tennis player stance, awaiting a tricky serve.

"—her aunt in Cleveland died. Hope you don't mind if we keep Jimmy till Maude gets back from the funeral."

A weak breeze licked his damp forehead. "No problem! What's for supper?"

"Oh, I don't know. How about steak?" She jabbed the shovel at a line of loose gravel and scraped it in a sibilant rivulet down the hole.

"You know that's hopeless," Craig said, buoyed by the reprieve Maudie's aunt had given him. "How many rocks and sticks and junk have we thrown down that hole the last couple of years?"

"And toys," Karen said. "The boys have been dropping in Lincoln Logs and Tinkertoys and other stuff they think they've outgrown. Rick lost his birthday dump truck down here today." She straight-armed the shovel handle at Craig and bent to get the sweater she'd shed on a nearby bush.

"It's probably part of a limestone cave network," he said, jiggling the shovel up and down and from hand to hand. He narrowed beer-bemused eyes at the white stripe of neck between her black hair and T-shirt. "Bottomless."

Eureka, his mind exalted as the inspiration zapped him, as his arms elevated on their own accord, as the shovel descended with the accuracy of a heat-seeking missile, as the blow reverberated up his wrists, elbows, shoulders.

Karen collapsed without a sound, imploding from a woman to a bundle of clothes. Squeamish about touching her, Craig toed her over to the sinkhole. Her head dropped in. Her shoulders were too wide.

Yanking her up and away, he grabbed up the shovel and made panicky jabs at the opening's edges, twisting off chunks of dirt that disappeared silently inside. Whimpering, Craig tried Karen for size again, dragged her out of the way again, stabbed at the hole's perimeters again.

Now he was expecting her to groan and sit up. He imagined her lying there playing dead till he should have the hole big enough and then—wham—she'd shove him between the shoulder blades and he'd fall into the gaping black, his screams echoing off the clammy walls as he fell, eyes bulging in a vain effort to see as he fell, the air whistling past his ears as he fell and fell and fell.

He slammed down the shovel, grasped his wife, and stuffed her through the opening.

No screams. No thumps. No splash. No sound except his breaths sawing in and out.

Craig spent an hour beside the sinkhole, listening to crickets, expecting two bloody hands to reach out of the abyss and grab him by the throat. Then he went to bed and dreamed a rerun of his fears.

IN THE MORNING, as Craig sipped at his fourth cup of black coffee, Lionel Eads and his winched truck and a muscular helper arrived to cover the sinkhole with a granite boulder the color of ashes. Lionel looked as if he could use four cups of black coffee, too; he yawned and stared off into space with red-rimmed eyes.

Two days passed. Because he sold insurance, Craig had a home office. He found excuses to be away from it as much as possible. It overlooked the backyard and Karen's giant grave marker.

Maudie didn't come home. Craig watched her driveway with the eagerness of a child expecting Christmas.

If anyone asked, Karen had gone to visit friends in California. Craig hoped for an earthquake in which she could conveniently go missing.

"DAD, LOOK WHAT Jimmy and me found!" Rick deposited a muddy truck on the kitchen table, just missing Craig's pepperoni pizza supper.

"Where you guys been?" Craig scolded like a mother. "Wash up and get it while it's hot."

"Yeah, but look, Mr. Longworth," Jimmy insisted. "We found Rick's dump truck."

"Right where he left it, right?" Craig ruffled the two heads of hair, one dark, one orange.

"No!" they said together.

Rick's deeper voice won the fight to tell. "We lost it down the sinkhole."

Craig felt for a chair back and eased himself into the seat. "Yeah, I remember now. And where did you find it?"

"In the cow pasture. Over the rise. Down by a little creek."

"We figure there's a underground river right under your yard," Jimmy butted in. "We're going to dig up close to the boulder and see if we can make more stuff disappear and watch for it to come out."

"No!" His own voice gave him a headache. More quietly he added, "It sounds dangerous to me. No, listen. You stay away from both ends of it till I have time to check it out. I mean it, now. No sneaking over to the pasture or I'll tan you both."

CRAIG SNEAKED OVER to the pasture. The moon glowed nearly as bright as his flashlight. The cool night smelled of damp grass and cattle.

Having scaled the wire fence, he hiked up the long, gentle incline, using the shovel as a walking stick, then down the steeper other side. Toward the bottom, the hill deteriorated into a cliff. Dodging scrub oak, Craig skidded on heels and rear, down to the creek and halfway across it.

Cold water seeped into his shoes while cold dread seeped everywhere else. The flashlight glared on a creekbed full of brown pebbles, some shaped exactly like Lincoln Logs.

Aiming the light upstream, Craig waded toward the rock that hung, cavelike, over the water. Resting a hand on the gritty limestone, he leaned to peer at the spot where the creek percolated out of a ground fissure the size of a bathtub.

He groaned and sat down on the nearest half-submerged boulder. The dump truck had been lost just hours before Karen went into the sinkhole. She must be due any moment now. He pointed the light into the bathtub and steeled himself to wait. His chin slipped off his hand, and he jerked up straight. The gurgling creek had begun to gargle. Trying to steady the flashlight, he peered into a growing whirlpool. When the first sneakered foot floated up, he scrubbed at his face, thinking—hoping—he was still asleep.

An ankle, bloodless as the white shoe, drifted into view. Another foot appeared, the shoelaces trailing gracefully. Legs sheathed in dark blue denim. Knees. Thighs.

Unable to stand the suspense a heartbeat longer, Craig waded into the chilly water, grasped the slick ankles, and yanked. No Ahab ever fought harder to subdue his obsession. Floundering for footholds on the slippery rock, his muscles aching with her dead weight, he finally fell backward, the cold body enveloping him like a nightmare.

Rolling out from under, he sat up coughing—and froze, seeing her still radiant red hair.

He doubled over for several moments, hyperventilating. Wiping his eyes and nose with the tail of his shirt, he dragged the shovel over and used it as a crutch to haul himself upright. Still snuffling water, he reached down unwillingly and tipped her over.

It wasn't Maudie.

Surprise dropped him onto his hands and knees, and closer up, he confirmed it. Not Maudie.

Mrs. Lionel Eads.

Where did that son-of-a-bee come off using *his* sinkhole to dispose of *his* dead bodies?

When the first wave of anger sucked away, he indulged in a few tears of relief that this limp, marble-eyed woman wasn't Maudie. Then he stomped off into the flatter pastureland, looking for a suitable place to bury her.

Digging through the grass was like digging through woven cloth, and the earth underneath rang like concrete. Craig worked up a sweat and a strength-endowing fury.

"Doing *his* dirty work," he muttered, jabbing with the shovel. "Kills his *wife* and leaves *me* to clean up the mess. Probably with his *sweetie* pie right now. Not a worry in the *world*. Some people just have no *consideration* for others."

He planted Mrs. Eads about two feet under, and then he returned to the creek to wait for Karen. Every few minutes he felt the need to throw back his head in a mute, face-wrenching scream.

MORNING ARRIVED before his wife's body did. He tried to think what to do, which wasn't easy, his mind being fuddled from lack of sleep.

Finally he hid the flashlight and shovel in a patch of wild raspberries and trudged up the hill to the fence. Crouching behind it, he scouted the peaceful neighborhood before climbing over and striding home.

After the first three cups of coffee, he phoned his sister. Barbara Junior answered.

"Howdy, partner. Let me talk to your mom."

"Uncle Craig, Rick has been taking my stuff and not giving it back."

"Okay, I'll get after him. Let me talk to—"

"He broke the head off my Barbie, and he said he'd fix it, but he never did. And he and Jimmy played keep-away with Fozzie Bear and—"

"Yeah, yeah. I'll talk to him. First I got to talk to Barbara."

Barbara Junior yelled, "Mommaphone'sforyou!" in his ear.

He had time to chew his left thumbnail to the quick before his sister answered.

"Karen's gone to California and Maudie's gone to Cleveland," Craig said in a rush. "I've got the two boys and I'm sick—the flu or something. Okay if I send them over to you for a while?"

"I guess." Barb sounded as thrilled as Barb Junior would be when she got the news.

The boys weren't all that thrilled either.

"Their house smells like cats," Jimmy said.

"And their cats smell like skunks," Rick said.

THE PASTURE SMELLED of skunk, too, when Craig slipped over into it later in the morning. He struggled to carry a sleeping bag, a gallon thermos of coffee, a brown bag full of ham sandwiches, a bottle of insect repellent, a bottle of aspirin, a couple of paperback books, and a pickax.

He had to force himself to walk straight to the head of the stream and look into the natural bathtub, afraid of finding Karen but wanting her to be there so this could be over. The water rippled empty in the dappled shade.

Maybe she had snagged on a rock or something! Maybe she was too big to fit through the underground stream outlet, and she wouldn't reappear until time whittled her down to bones. Maybe she was still alive, clawing her way randomly through the endless dark.

He had to watch for a while.

Craig spread out the sleeping bag, ranged the rest of his property along one side, picked up a book, and sat down. A cloud slid in front of the sun, graying the landscape, making him shiver. The pool coughed softly.

The book was short stories. He opened it at random. Poe. "The Tell-Tale Heart."

The body arrived just after dark.

A mass of clouds had shut down the moon, and lightning exploded on the west horizon, a little closer every blast. Toward the south, the brush crackled, and bass voices murmured, indicating cows on the prowl. Craig wished he'd brought extra batteries for the yellowing flashlight. His life had become a horror movie.

Like Mrs. Eads's, this body came feet first and stomach down. As the legs swam into view, Craig stared, trying to decide whether this would be Karen or Maudie. He no longer believed in Cleveland.

The hips undulated free and then an expanse of pale waist where the shirt had hiked up and ripped. Back. Arms. Ringless hands, unnaturally white and puckered. Craig's eyes burned, unblinking and dry, as he strained for a first glimpse of her hair.

Thunder smashed. Sharp, cold rain began to beat. The neck came into view. There was no head.

Craig sunk down in the pouring rain to cry. It felt as if all the moisture streaming down his face came from inside him, a flood of guilt and grief.

After perhaps five self-indulgent minutes, he moved to haul the body from the stream. Not having the strength to bury it, he squatted on the soggy sleeping bag for another vigil.

AFTER PERHAPS an hour, the dog came out. It was black and sleek, though that was probably because it was wet and dead. In life, it might have been an unsheared brown poodle. Perhaps the one that used to yap at anything that moved, over on Quince Court.

Groaning, Craig waded in to pull him out and lay him beside the headless woman.

"I should have charged my neighbors for the waste disposal service I didn't know I was running," he complained.

Renewed splashing signaled something else being regurgitated from the sink. Craig shuffled to the edge. "You speak, and I obey."

This time boots showed first, heavy combat boots, followed by green and brown blotched pants. Craig blinked rain out of his eyes. Numbed beyond any capability for surprise, he gazed at the muscular arms, the camouflage-shirted chest, the thick neck, the gleaming, piggy eyes.

The soldier gently rocked on his back in the susurrous bathtub. After a moment of studying him, Craig returned to the sleeping bag and sat on its puddled middle.

THE NEXT MORNING, sun sizzled against his eyelids until he opened them.

Like a vision, an angel, Maudie came slip-sliding down the cliff above the creek. She wore white slacks, a yellow blazer, white sneakers, and a shining smile.

"Hey. What are you doing?" she called ahead.

Craig scrambled up and rushed to intercept her.

"Camping out," he said. "Don't look."

"Don't look at what? Phewie. When did you last have a bath?"

"You really were in Cleveland?" He touched her neck reverently, admiring how it securely attached her head to her torso.

"Where are the boys?" She leaned to peer past him, and he jumped sideways to block her view.

"They're at my sister's. Karen's in California. Maybe there'll be an earthquake. How did you know where I was?"

"Mrs. Judd saw you and your gear schlumping over here last night." Maudie laughed uncertainly. "Are you okay? You're as white as a sheet."

"No clichés!" He clapped his hands over his ears.

"You're too weird, Craig. I'm going home and have some breakfast." She patted one of his hands, which still covered his ear, and, turning, struggled provocatively up the hill.

WHO SHOULD SHE call? Maudie labored through the pasture, unmindful of the stick-tights, the poison ivy, the cow pies. She walked hard and fast and planned to climb the fence the same way, all the while expecting Craig to shout for her to stop.

Who should she call? The police? A doctor? Who *do* you call when the man you've slept with a few times sets up camp in the middle of a field to, apparently, play with toys?

She would let Barbara handle it. "Here's the deal, Barbara," she'd say. "I don't know your brother very well, but being a friend of Karen's, I feel I have a duty, you know? Craig is around the bend, flipped his lid, off his rocker. He's hermiting down by the creek with a bunch of Lincoln Logs, a teddy bear, a GI Joe, and a headless Barbie doll, for God's sake."

Thank goodness her relationship with Craig hadn't passed the point of no return. She wasn't worried that he'd told Karen about their fooling around. You can put a man over a barrel, but you can't make him drink.

SATURDAY NIGHT AT THE MIKADO MASSAGE

November 1996

LOREN D. ESTLEMAN'S Detroit P.I. Amos Walker has found a home in seventeen novels to date since 1980s *Motor City Blue*. A second series features the hit man Peter Macklin. But Estleman also writes Westerns, historicals, and even Sherlock Holmes pastiches. Among the many honors he's received are numerous Shamus Awards from the Private Eye Writers of America and Golden Spur Awards from the Western Writers of American. This story exemplifies Estleman at his hard-boiled best.

■

The ironic thing about the night Mr. Ten Fifty-Five died on Iiko's table was that she was supposed to have that Saturday off.

She'd asked for the time three weeks in advance so she could spend the weekend with Uncle Trinh, who was coming to visit from Corpus Christi, Texas, where he worked on a shrimp boat, but the day before his bus left, he slipped on some fish scales and broke his leg. Now he needed money for doctors' bills, and Iiko had volunteered to work.

The Mikado Massage was located on Michigan Avenue in Detroit. On one side was an empty building that had once sheltered a travel agency. The Mystic Arts Bookshop was on the other and shared a common wall with the Mikado. There was a fire door in this wall, which came in handy during election years. When the mayor sent police with warrants, they invariably found the bookshop full of customers and the massage parlor empty. On the third Sunday of every month a man came to collect for the service of keeping the owner informed about these visits. Iiko had seen the man's picture under some printing on the side of a van with a loudspeaker on the roof. Detroit was the same as back home except for no Ho Chi Minh on the billboards.

Although its display in the Yellow Pages advertised an all-Japanese staff, the Mikado's owner, Mr. Shigeta, was the only person in residence not Korean or Vietnamese, and he was never seen by the customers unless one of them became ungallant. He was a short, thick man of fifty-five or seventy with hair exactly like a seal's, who claimed to have stood in for Harold Sakata on the set of *Goldfinger* and had papered his little office with posters and lobby cards from the film. He kept a bottle of Polish vodka and a jar of pickled eggs in a crawlspace behind the radiator.

Iiko had been working there four months. She made less than the other masseuses because she was still on probation after a police visit to the Dragon's Gate in the suburb of Inkster, which had no fire door, and so she gave only massages, no specials. She kept track of the two months remaining on her sentence on a Philgas calendar inside her locker door.

The man she called Mr. Ten Fifty-Five always showed up at that time on Saturday night and always asked for Iiko. Because he reminded her a little of Uncle Trinh, she'd thought to do him a kindness and had explained to him, in her imperfect English, that he could get the same massage for much less at any hotel, but he said he preferred the Mikado. The hotels didn't offer Japanese music or heated floors or scented oils or a pink bulb in a table lamp with a paper kimono shade.

Normally, Saturday was the busiest night of the week, but this was the Saturday after Thanksgiving, when, as Mr. Shigeta explained, the customers remembered they were family men and stayed home. Mr. Ten Fifty-Five, therefore, was the only person she'd seen since early evening when Mr. Shigeta had gone home, leaving her in charge.

Mr. Ten Fifty-Five was duck-shaped and bald, with funny gray tufts that stood out on both sides of his head when he waddled in from the shower in a towel and sprawled facedown on the table. He often fell asleep the moment she began to rub him down and didn't wake up even when she walked on his back, so it wasn't until she asked him to turn over that Iiko found out that this time he'd died.

Iiko recognized death. She'd been only a baby when the last American soldier left her village, but she remembered the marauding gangs that swept through after the Fall of Saigon, claiming to be hunting rebels but forcing themselves upon the women and carrying away tins of food and silver picture frames and setting the buildings on fire when they left. Iiko's brother Nguyen, sixteen years old, had tried to block the door of their parents' home, but one of the visitors stuck a bayonet between his ribs and planted a boot on his face to tug loose the blade. Iiko hung on to her mother's skirt during the walk to the cemetery. The skirt was white, the color of mourning in Vietnam, with a border of faded flowers at the hem.

When Iiko confirmed that Mr. Ten Fifty-Five's heart had stopped, she went through his clothes. This was much easier than picking pockets in Ho Chi Minh City, where one always ran the risk of being caught with one's hand in the pocket of another pickpocket. Iiko found car keys, a little plastic bottle two-thirds full of tiny white pills, a tattered billfold containing fifty-two dollars, and a folding knife with a stag handle and a blade that had been ground down to a quarter-inch wide. She placed it and the money in the pocket of her smock and returned the clothes to the back of the chair. The tail of the shabby coat clunked when it flapped against a chair leg.

Iiko investigated. There was a lump at the bottom where the machine stitch that secured the lining had been replaced by a clumsy crosshatch of thread that didn't match the original. This came loose easily, and she removed a small green cloth sack with a drawstring, whose contents caught the pink light in seven spots of reflected purple. When she switched on the overhead bulb, the stones, irregular ovals the size of the charcoal bits she swept weekly from the brazier in the sauna, turned deep blue.

She found a place for the stones, then went out into the little reception area to call Mr. Shigeta at home. He would want to know that a customer had died so that when the police came they would find nothing of interest except a dead customer. While she was dialing, two men came in.

Both were Americans. One, a large black man with a face that was all jutting bones, wore jeans, a sweatshirt, and a Pistons jacket. He towered over his companion, a white man with small features and sandy hair done up elaborately, wearing a shiny black suit with a pinched waist and jagged lapels. Their eyes continued to move around the room after the men had come to a stop a few feet from the counter.

"Sorry, we close," Iiko said.

She was standing in front of the sign that said OPEN TILL MIDNIGHT.

"You're back open," said the sandy-haired man. "Long enough anyway to tell us where's the fat bald guy that came in here about eleven."

She shook her head, indicating that she didn't understand. It was not entirely a lie. The sandy-haired man, who did almost all the talking, spoke very fast.

"Come on, girlie, we know he's here. His car's outside."

"The stuff ain't in it, neither," said the black man.

"Shut up, Leon."

"Not know," said Iiko.

"Leon."

The black man put a hand inside his jacket and brought out a big silver gun with a twelve inch barrel. He pointed it at her and thumbed back the hammer.

The sandy man said, "Leon's killed three men and a woman, but he's never to my knowledge done a slant. Where's George?"

"Not know George," she said.

"Keep it on her. If she jumps, take off her head." The sandy man came around the counter.

Iiko stood still while the man ran his hands over her smock. She didn't even move when they lingered at her small breasts and crotch. He took the fifty-two dollars and the knife from her pockets. He showed Leon the knife.

"That's George's shank, all right," said the black man. "He carries it open when he has to walk more'n a block to his car. He's almost as scared of muggers as he is of guns."

The sandy man slapped Iiko's face. She remained unmoving. She could feel the hot imprint of his palm on her cheek.

"One more time before we disturb the peace, Dragon Lady. Where's George Myrtle?"

She turned and went through the door behind the counter. The two men followed.

In the massage room the sandy man felt behind Mr. Ten Fifty-Five's ear, then said, "Deader'n Old Yeller."

"I don't see no marks," Leon said.

"Of course not. Look at him. He as good as squiffed himself the day he topped two forty and started taking elevators instead of climbing the stairs. I bet he never said no to a second helping of mashed potatoes in his life. Check out his clothes."

Leon returned the big gun to a holster under his left arm and quickly turned out all the pockets of the coat and trousers, then with a grunt held the coat upside-down and showed his companion the place where the lining had been pulled loose.

The sandy man looked at Iiko. She saw something in his pale eyes that she remembered from the day her brother was killed.

"This ain't turning out the way I figured," the sandy man said. "I was looking forward to watching Leon bat around that tub of guts until he told us what he done with them hot rocks. I sure don't enjoy watching him do that to a woman. Especially not to a pretty little China doll like you. How's about sparing me that and telling me what you did with the merch?"

"Not know merch," she said truthfully.

Leon started toward her. The sandy man stopped him with a hand. He was still looking at Iiko.

"You got more of these rooms?" he asked.

After a moment she nodded and stepped in the direction of the curtain over the doorway. The black man's bulk blocked that path.

"Search the rest of the place, Leon. I'll take care of this."

"Sure?"

"Sure."

Leon went out. Iiko led the sandy man through the curtains and across the narrow hallway. This room was larger, although still small. A forest of bottles containing scented oils stood on a rack beside the massage table. The sandy man seized her arm and spun her around. They were close now, and the light in his eyes had changed. She could smell his aftershave, sticky and sharp.

"You're sure a nice little piece for a slant. I bet old George had some times with you. Especially at the end."

Iiko didn't struggle.

The sandy man said, "I could use a little rub myself. You rub me, I rub you. What do you say? Then we'll talk."

After a moment she nodded. "Take off clothes."

"You first."

He let go of her and stepped back, his small hard fists dangling at his sides. He watched her unbutton and peel off the smock. Without hesitating, she undid her halter top and stepped out of her shorts. She wore no underthings. She knew her body was good, firm and well-proportioned for her small frame. She could see in his eyes he approved.

He took a long breath and let it out. Then he took off his shiny black coat. He hung his suit carefully on the wooden hanger on the wall peg, folded his shirt and put it on the seat of the chair. His ribs showed, but his pale, naked arms and legs were sinewy, the limbs of a runner.

He saw that she saw. "I work out. I ain't going to do you no favor like George and clock out on the table."

She said nothing. He stretched out on his stomach on the padded table. "No oil," he said. "I don't want to ruin my clothes. Just powder."

She reached for the can of talcum. While her back was turned to him, she laid down the folding knife she had removed from the sandy man's pocket while he was holding her, poking it behind a row of bottles.

She sprinkled the powder on his back, set down the can, and worked her hands along his spine and scapula. His muscles jumped and twitched beneath her palms, not at all like the loose, unresisting flesh of Mr. Ten Fifty-Five. She had the impression the sandy man was poised to leap off the table at the first sign of suspicious behavior. She heard glass breaking in another part of the building as Leon continued his search for the blue stones.

Iiko was a good masseuse. Unlike some of her fellow employees, who merely went through the motions until the big moment when they asked the customers to turn over, Iiko had been trained by a licensed massage therapist. She flattered herself that she still managed to give satisfaction even under the strictures of probation. Gradually she felt the sandy man's body relax beneath her expert hands.

To maintain contact, she kept one palm on his lower spine while with the other she retrieved the knife from its hiding place on the rack of bottles, pried it open with her teeth, and with one swift underhand motion jammed the blade into his back as far as it would go and dragged it around his right kidney as if she were coring an apple. The sandy man made very little noise dying.

When the body had ceased to shudder, she dressed and left the room. The sound of a heavy piece of furniture scraping across a wooden floor told her that Leon was moving the desk in Mr. Shigeta's office. The way to the front door and out led directly past that room; she did not want to take the chance of running into the black man as he came out. She let herself into the Mystic Arts Bookshop by way of the fire door in the wall that separated the two establishments.

The shop had been closed for hours. She groped her way through darkness to the front door but found that exit barred by a deadbolt lock that required a key. The same was true of the back door. An ornamental grid sealed the windows. For a moment Iiko stood still and waited for her thoughts to settle. It would not be long before Leon discovered the sandy man's body, and then he would find the fire door. The lock was on the massage parlor side.

She switched on a light. Tall racks of musty-smelling books divided the room into narrow aisles. She removed a heavy dictionary from the reference section, carried it to the common wall, and set the book on the floor in front of the steel door. She repeated the procedure with another large book and then another. At the end of ten minutes she had erected a formidable barrier. Then she sat down to catch her breath and wait.

She did not wait long. She jumped when the thumb latch went down, stood and backed away instinctively when the door moved a fraction of an inch and stopped, impeded by the stacked books. She had already located the telephone on a cluttered counter near the front door of the bookshop; now she lifted the receiver, dialed 911, and, when the operator came on, laid the receiver on its side facing the fire door.

Just then Leon pushed the door hard. Two of the stacks fell, creating an avalanche. Encouraged, the black man gave a lunge.

More books tumbled, but now the pile was wedged tightly between the door and the first rack. It would not budge further.

Iiko switched off the light. A bank of deep shadow appeared on the side of the fire door nearest the latch, and she slipped into it noiselessly. The black man had worked up a sweat searching the Mikado for the missing stones. She could smell the clean sharp sting of it where she crouched.

Nothing stirred in the bookshop. She heard the black man's heavy breathing as he paused to gather his strength, heard the buzzing queries of the 911 operator coming through the earpiece of the telephone a dozen steps away.

With an explosive grunt, Leon threw all his weight against the door. The pile of books crumpled against the base of the rack. The rack teetered, tilted, hung at a twenty-degree angle for an impossible length of time; then it toppled. Books plummeted from its shelves. To the operator listening at police headquarters it must have sounded like an artillery barrage. Leon thrust his arm and shoulder through the widened opening. The big silver gun made the arm look ridiculously long. His entire body seemed to swell with the effort to squeeze past the edge of the door. He grunted again, and the noise turned into a howl of triumph as he stumbled into the bookshop.

But his eyes were not accustomed to the darkness, and he set his foot on a poorly balanced book that turned under his weight. He sprawled headlong across the pile.

The opening into the massage parlor was more than wide enough for Iiko. She darted through, and before Leon could get to his feet, she seized the door handle and yanked it shut behind her, flicking the lock button with her thumb.

In the next minute it didn't matter that the 911 operator could hear the black man pounding the steel door with his fists. The air was shrill with sirens, red and blue strobes throbbed through the windows of the Mikado. Gravel pelted the side of the building as the police cruisers skidded around the corner into the parking lot of the Mystic Arts.

Iiko did not pay much attention to the bullhorn-distorted demands for surrender next door, or even the rattle of gunfire when Leon, exhausted and confused by the turn of events since he and the sandy man had entered the Mikado, burst a lock and plunged out into the searchlights with the big silver gun in his hand. She was busy with the narrow metal dustpan she used to clean out the brazier in the sauna, sifting through the smoldering bits of charcoal in the bottom. The stones were covered with soot and difficult to distinguish from the coals, but when she washed them in the sink they shone with the same icy blueness that had caught her eye in the massage room.

The glowing coals had burned away the green cloth bag as she'd known they would. She wrapped the stones carefully in a flannel facecloth, put the bundle in the side pocket of the cloth coat she drew on over her smock, and started toward the front door. Then she remembered the fifty-two dollars the sandy man had taken from her and put in the pocket of his shiny black suit.

The sandy man was as she'd left him, naked and dead, only paler than before. She thrust the money into her other side pocket and went out.

Waiting at the corner for the bus, Iiko thought she would take the stones to the pawnshop man who bought the jewelry and gold money clips she managed from time to time to take from the clothing of her customers. The pawnshop man knew many people and had always dealt with her honestly. She hoped the stones would sell for enough to settle some of Uncle Trinh's doctors' bills.

GREGORY FALLIS

LORD OF OBSTACLES

January 1997

GREGORY FALLIS is himself a former private investigator, and this, his first short story, became a finalist for the Shamus Award given by the Private Eye Writers of America. He is also the author of the nonfiction books *Be Your Own Detective* and *Just the Facts, Ma'am: A Writer's Guide to Investigators and Investigative Techniques,* among others.

■

I don t have much to do with Protestant ministers, or clergy of any sort if I can help it. I'm Irish and Catholic, as you can tell by my name—Kevin Sweeney. My wife, Mary Margaret, is also Irish and Catholic, and unlike me she takes both seriously, so I can't always avoid contact with priests and nuns. Protestant ministers, though, are another matter altogether. They're outside my usual circle.

Jails *are* part of my usual circle, and it was at the county jail that Joop Wheeler and I first met the Reverend Jason Hobart. A lot of priests and ministers visit jails and prisons during the holiday season. But Hobart wasn't there bringing cheer and the gospel to the inmates. He wasn't visiting at all. Hobart had been arrested for setting fire to his daughter's garage.

The three of us were crowded into a small, stale, interview room—me, Hobart, and my partner, Joop. Hobart had been in jail over the weekend awaiting a bail hearing, and the time had worn at him. You could see he was normally a fastidious man, a man careful about his appearance, but a couple of nights in jail had played merry hell with his grooming. He was dirty and smelled of sweat and fear and worry.

It's never a pleasant place to be holding a conversation, the jail, and it's even worse during the Christmas season. The prisoners are more desperate, and the atmosphere is made more depressing by the unrelentingly cheerful Christmas music piped over the public address system. But Joop and I had to be there. We wanted to talk to Hobart before his bail hearing. Hobart had a good lawyer—Kirby Abbott—and he was certain to be released. A man newly released on bail has needs and interests that take priority over answering questions.

That's why Joop and I were there—to get answers to questions. Kirby Abbott, like I said, is a good lawyer, but even the best lawyer is limited by what his client tells him. Hobart, for some reason, wasn't being cooperative. He denied setting fire to his daughter's garage, but he'd refused to tell Kirby where he was at the time of the fire. That's why Kirby called us in. We're private investigators.

We do a lot of criminal defense work, Joop and I, but we rarely get a client like Jason Hobart. Before he took the cloth— if that's what Protestant ministers do—Hobart had been a successful local businessman; he owned several apartment buildings, two car dealerships, a local radio station, and probably a few other things. It made him an attractive client, for the lawyers and for us. We wouldn't any of us have to worry about collecting our fee.

When Joop and I sat down with Hobart, he repeated the story he'd told Kirby. He was innocent, he said, but he wouldn't say where he'd been when the fire started.

"It's a grand thing to be able to say you're innocent," I said. "Not many can do that. But it's not enough for the police, you know, and it won't be enough for a jury if it goes to trial."

Reverend Hobart nodded, but he didn't seem concerned. He just seemed tired and sad. "A jury would do the right thing. The Lord will look out for me."

I looked at Joop and nodded toward Hobart. Joop's a Protestant—a Southern Baptist, of all things. Maybe he could talk some sense into the man.

"Juries are weird creatures," Joop said. "I suspect a jury would want to know where you were when your daughter's garage was torched. I'm sure a jury would want to know why your daughter, Sarah—your daughter her own self—told the police *you* were the one who chucked a Molotov cocktail through her garage window."

Joop's accent seemed to catch Hobart's attention for a moment. He's from South Carolina, Joop, and he has one of those slow, soft, cultured Southern accents. It seems almost exotic up here on the Massachusetts coast.

Hobart slowly shook his head, and there was real pain in his eyes. "Sarah," he said. "I don't know. I just can't believe she'd . . . Did she say she *saw* me setting fire to her garage? That she actually *saw* me?"

I shook my head. "No. What she told the police is that you'd been threatening to burn down the garage for some time."

"Not the garage," Hobart said. "Not the garage, but what was inside it."

"The statue?" Joop asked.

"It's not just a statue," Hobart said. His eyes teared up. "It's an image of a pagan god. You have to understand, the idea of my daughter, my only child . . . my Sarah, worshiping graven images. Especially now at this time of year. I just couldn't allow . . ." He wiped his eyes and shook his head.

"Graven images?" Joop said. "I though it was an elephant." He flipped quickly through the notes Kirby Abbott had copied for us. "Uh, yeah, right here. Wooden statue of an elephant. Doesn't say a thing about any graven images."

Hobart shook his head. "It had the *head* of an elephant, but the body of a man. A man with four arms. It was a pagan god."

"Really?" Joop asked. "Here it just says elephant."

"Well, I'm afraid it's wrong."

"Elephant or elephant god, it doesn't matter," I said. "What matters is that the police believe you threw a Molotov cocktail through your daughter's garage window, that you deliberately tried to destroy her statue and garage."

"Tried?" Hobart said. "I thought . . . I was under the impression it had been destroyed."

"Nope," Joop said. "Just some minor damage is all. Singed around the edges."

Hobart looked up. "Are you talking about the statue? Or the garage?"

"Neither was badly damaged," I said. "At least that's what we were told. We haven't gone there to look yet."

Hobart shook his head. "I thought it . . . I thought the police said the statue had been destroyed."

"That's the problem with a Molotov cocktail, you know," Joop said. "You got almost no control over the results. If you go chucking Molotov cocktails through garage windows, you can't complain when the job doesn't get done."

"I've said I didn't do it," Hobart said. "I've told that to the police. I've told it to my lawyer, and I've told it to you. I—didn't—do—it."

"Well, there you go," Joop said. He turned to me. "He didn't do it. This is probably all just a simple mistake. Probably if we tell the police, they'll let him go."

It's impossible to keep Joop from joking around, and I've given over trying, but someday the boy is going to get us fired. "It would help us if you'd tell us where you were at the time of the fire," I said to Hobart.

"I can tell you I wasn't at my daughter's house," he said wearily.

I nodded. "Yes, but why can't you tell us where you *were?* We know you weren't at your house. Your neighbors saw you drive away around seven P.M. We know the fire was extinguished around eight thirty, and we know you didn't return home until around eleven fifteen. What we don't know is where you were between seven and eleven fifteen."

"That was really bad timing, by the way," Joop said. "Coming home just when you did. Just as the police are knocking at your door to ask you questions. If you'd stayed away another fifteen, twenty minutes you probably wouldn't have had to spend the weekend in jail."

"Do you think you could find your way clear to tell us where you were?" I asked. "We're trying to help you, remember."

"I've already told Mr. Abbott," Hobart said. "I was doing the Lord's work."

I nodded. "Yes, I'm sure you were—but *where?*"

Hobart shook his head. "I can't tell you without breaking a confidence," he said. "All I can say—and all you need to know—is that I was doing the Lord's work."

"Doing the Lord's work may get your earthly butt tossed in prison," Joop said.

"The Lord will take care of me," Hobart said.

"Well, then the Lord will have to take care of you in jail," Joop said.

Hobart glared at Joop.

"Mr. Hobart, Joop isn't always a tactful as he could be," I said. "But he's basically right. Unless we can show you weren't at your daughter's house that night, there's a good chance you'll be spending a lot more time behind bars."

Hobart sadly shook his head. "I'm sorry," he said. "I can't help you. I can't break a confidence." He looked up at me. "I assume you'll talk to my daughter?"

I nodded. "Probably. If she'll talk to us."

"When you see her, will you give her a message for me?" Hobart said. "Will you tell her I'm worried about her? About her soul? And will you tell her I love her?"

I shook my head. "I'll tell her you're worried about her and that you love her," I said. "But souls aren't our business. Dealing with the flesh is tough enough."

It was a relief to get out of the jail, away from the gloom and the wretched Christmas music. I like *real* Christmas music—the old carols and motets I heard in church when I was a boy. I don't want to be hearing about snowmen and reindeer and mommy kissing Santa Claus.

Joop was cheerful as we drove away from the jail. "I think we ought to go take a peek at this statue thing," he said. "I think it's imperative is what it is." Joop takes an unhealthy pleasure in his work. I sometimes think the only reason he became a P.I. is so he'd have a legitimate reason for nosing around in other people's affairs.

"Okay," I said. "We need to interview the daughter. There's no reason we can't look at the garage and the statue at the same time."

"This is so cool," he said. "Four arms *and* an elephant head. Four arms would have been enough. But an elephant head, that's gravy. We didn't have anything like that at the First Ezekiel Baptist Church down home. We didn't have any statues at all. Hell, we didn't even have any *pictures*. Just plain white walls. Now my Aunt Cooter, she had a picture of . . ."

"You have an aunt named Cooter?"

"Well, her real name is Delma," Joop said. "And she's not really my aunt. But I've called her that all my life. I think she's really just a woman my . . ."

"I don't need to know your family history," I said. Joop has the strangest assortment of relatives, and he's happy to talk about all of them. "I was just curious about her name."

"Right," Joop said. "Aunt Cooter, she's got this habit of pulling her head down between her shoulders, just like a cooter. Which is what we call a turtle down in Carolina. The point is that Cooter, she used to have a picture of Jesus on her living room wall. Maybe still does. At least she claimed it was Jesus. I'm not so sure my own self. He sure didn't look very Jewish. This guy had pale white skin and a lot of long, semicurly blond hair and huge brown eyes. What he looked like, he looked like a spaniel who'd been whacked with a newspaper for wetting on the carpet. It wasn't what you'd call awe-inspiring. But it was one of those pictures where the eyes open and shut when you move. I used to stand there in Cooter's living room, shifting back and forth, making Jesus blink. Sarah Hobart has an elephant-headed god with four arms, and all I got was a cheesy painting of a spaniel-looking, blinking Jesus. What did you have?"

At St. Aloysius we have a statue of the Virgin. Some people say it weeps sometimes, though I've never talked to anybody who's actually seen it. I don't go to mass as often as I should—just now and then to please Mary Margaret. But I was raised Catholic, and that's something that can't be escaped. St. Aloysius is an old stone church built in 1829, a solid and imposing building, set in the ground like it grew there. When you walk inside, it puts you in your place; the stained-glass windows cutting the gloom, the dark pews, the altars, the warped wooden floors, the votive candles flickering off to the side. There's a darkness to it, and a sense of mystery. It's a house of worship, and the very building itself reminds you what worship means. I didn't say all that to Joop, of course—just that we had a statue of Mary that wept.

"You and Hobart's daughter, you got all the cool religious stuff," Joop said.

Sarah Hobart lived in an older part of town, a neighborhood of postwar brick houses, tall maple trees, big yards, and hedges to keep the nosy neighbors away. Not the sort of neighborhood where you'd expect a college student to live.

We arrived to find Sarah hauling a plastic trash bag to the garbage bin near the garage. We were probably lucky to find her at home. Sarah was a graduate student in history at the university, her father had told us, and she spent most of her waking hours on campus. Maybe there was a holiday break, though it was still a couple of weeks until Christmas.

She turned to look at us as we got out of the car. "Are you the insurance guys?" She glanced at her wristwatch, then flashed us a smile that was an orthodontist's dream. "I'm really glad to see you. I didn't expect you so soon."

"I'm afraid we're not the insurance people," I said. "My name is Kevin Sweeney, and this is Joop Wheeler. We've just come from talking to your father at the jail."

Sarah's smile disappeared. "Oh no. Look, I don't want to hear any more Jesus crap." She tossed the trash in the bin and closed the lid with a bang. "Why don't you go bother somebody else. Go on, now. Take off."

Joop laughed. "No, no," he said. "We're not here for that. We're here about the fire. We're private investigators." He handed her a business card.

She took the card and looked us over. "Well, you don't look like my dad's usual missionaries. He's always sending people here, you know. Telling me I'm going to hell, just because I have a Ganesha in the studio."

"A Ganesha?" Joop asked.

"Yeah," Sarah nodded. "You know, the Hindu god? The Lord of Obstacles? The elephant-headed god?"

"Ah," Joop said, smiling. "*That* Ganesha."

"You're *sure* you're not one of my dad's Jesus buddies?" Sarah asked. "You're not going to get on your knees and pray for me? Because I hate that."

"Scout's honor," Joop said, holding up his hand in the Boy Scout pledge. "The last time I was on my knees I was throwing up. We're just here to ask a few questions and look at the damage. With your permission, of course."

Sarah's smile gradually found its way back. "You're from the South," she said.

"Yes, ma'am, I surely am from the South," he said. "Georgetown County, South Carolina. Which is only just a wink away from heaven."

Joop was laying it on thick, and I knew we were in. People in New England are saps for a cultured Southern accent. We've worked this routine many times before, Joop and I. He chats and charms and asks questions while I nose around in the background. It works well for us.

"Tell me about this Ganesha," Joop said. "Can we see it?"

Sarah hesitated for a moment, then shrugged. "Why not?" she said. "It's right over here in the studio."

The "studio" was the garage. The main garage door had been sealed shut, and the small building had been converted into a single large room.

"The original owner used to have a potter's wheel and a kiln out here," Sarah said. "I kept my loom out here for a while, but luckily I moved it inside the house a few days before the fire. It's just too cold to weave out here in the winter."

The fire damage was mainly limited to the west wall, but as with most small fires, the firefighters had done nearly as much damage as the fire itself. The fire had burned some two-by-four studs and joists, but not enough to weaken the wall or ceiling. The floor of the garage was littered with bits of wood, broken glass, and big lumps of sodden pink insulation. The insulation had probably been pulled down by firefighters searching for concealed fire in the roof. Three of the four garage windows were broken. Two of the windows had probably been broken by firefighters to vent the heat and smoke; the third would have been broken by the Molotov cocktail. Everything in the garage was coated with an oily black layer of soot and grime left by the smoke.

On a wooden workbench by the west wall, near one of the broken windows, was the statue that had apparently sparked this whole event. It was about two feet tall, carved out of some dark wood. It was an odd-looking thing—the body of a chubby man with four arms and, just as everybody had said, the head of an elephant. The figure seemed to be swaying as if he were dancing. There was something graceful about the statue, and despite the fire damage it was attractive. Whoever had carved it had managed to make the elephant head look like it was smiling. Aside from a couple of spots at the base of the statue—the parts where the gasoline from the Molotov cocktail had pooled—it wasn't badly damaged at all.

"Cute little bugger, isn't he," Joop said. "Why do you keep him out here in the gara . . . in the studio?"

Sarah gave an embarrassed shrug. "Well, he doesn't really go with my decor."

Joop nodded as though he understood the difficulty of incorporating Hindu gods into the decor. He reached out and touched the statue. "He's only got one tusk. What happened? He get in a fight?"

Sarah smiled. "The legend is that Ganesha broke off his other tusk and threw it at the moon," she said. "He was angry with the moon, but I don't remember why."

"Threw it at the moon," Joop said. "Did he hit it?"

Sarah laughed and said she didn't know.

The wooden workbench on which the statue sat was charred. It was far more damaged from the fire than the statue itself. Bits of bottle glass were scattered across the surface—presumably from the Molotov cocktail. The larger pieces of the broken bottle would have been seized by the fire investigators, who'd test it to find out exactly what sort of fuel was in it.

Joop was still examining the statue. "What's he got in his hands?" he asked.

"That's a radish," Sarah said, pointing at one of the statue's hands. "And there, that's a bowl of sweets. And over there, a lotus blossom. And down there by his feet? That's his rat."

"His *rat?*" Joop asked. "Ganesha has his own personal rat?"

"Yeah," she said, laughing. "He rides it."

"He rides it?" Joop said. "He rides a rat?"

"It's better than most Indian mass transit," Sarah said.

I examined the broken window on the wall nearest the statue. There was broken glass on the floor beneath the window, which made sense if a Molotov cocktail had been thrown through it. I went to look at the other windows.

"You called him the Lord of Obstacles," Joop said. "What does that mean?"

"Hindus believe Ganesha helps them overcome obstacles." Sarah'd learned that academic tone of voice, the one professors use—disinterested and lofty, but oh so enlightened. "Ganesha is worshiped at the beginning of any new undertaking, especially a risky one. He's also the god of foresight and prosperity."

Joop nodded. "Sort of an all-purpose god," he said. "A god for the nineties."

Sarah laughed. "That's right. Works hard, plays hard. Ganesha's also known for his sense of humor and love of dancing."

"Are you . . . have you become a Hindu?" Joop asked. Then he smiled shyly. He has a grand shy smile, Joop, and he uses it with great effect. "I hope you don't mind my asking. It's none of my business. I'm just being nosy."

"I don't mind," Sarah said, smiling back. "My dad, he thinks I've converted. And maybe I let him believe I did. Just to make him mad, you know? No, I'm not a Hindu. But my dad thinks just having Ganesha around puts my soul at risk. Whatever that means. He's so provincial. When he first saw it, I thought he'd have a stroke. He told me to get rid of it or he'd cut me off. Can you believe it?"

There were fewer shards of glass beneath the other two windows. Probably the firefighters had broken them from the inside, so most of the glass would have fallen outside the window. The glass under each of the three windows was covered with the same oily soot that covered the entire interior of the garage. I rummaged through my jacket pockets until I found an old bank deposit envelope. I picked up a piece of broken glass from under each of the three windows and put them all in the envelope.

"It's a lovely piece of work," Joop said, touching Ganesha's soot-covered trunk. "Where did you get it?"

"I got it in India," she said. "I talked my dad into letting me go to India last summer. I'm doing my thesis on the Sepoy Mutiny. While I was doing my research, I found this Ganesha in a market near a town called Cawnpore and just had to buy it. Got it for about sixty-two hundred rupees."

"What is that in American money?"

"About a hundred and eighty dollars," she said. "That's a fortune in some parts of India. People are so poor there. They're so poor their priests sometimes have to sell off religious artifacts to buy food." She nodded toward the Ganesha.

"Your daddy gave you a summer in India?" Joop asked. "Nice guy."

She shrugged. "He can afford it."

"And when you said your daddy was threatening to cut you off," Joop said, "did you mean cut you off financially?"

Sarah made a face. "It's crazy, isn't it? Just because I brought this statue home with me. He's been weird like that ever since Mom died. He was normal up to that point. Well, not *normal,* but more normal than he is now. He used to spend all his time working and we hardly ever saw him, but at least when we did see him he didn't spend all his time talking about Jesus. Then Mom died and Dad found Jesus. And if that weren't bad enough, he went and became a minister. Now he spends all his time doing church stuff. First it was his job, now it's Jesus. It was never Mom, never me."

"Your daddy, did he help you buy this house?" Joop asked.

Sarah shook her head. "No, that was my mom. She grew up in this neighborhood. Just a couple of blocks from here. She left me some money when she died. Not enough to buy the house outright, but it made the payments reasonable."

"I'm going to take a look around outside," I said.

Joop nodded but kept his attention on Sarah—and kept Sarah's attention on him. "Tell me about your thesis," he said. "What's this Sepoy Mutiny business? What's a sepoy? And what about the mutiny? I love a good mutiny."

The outside of the garage told the same story as the inside. A little bit of broken glass under the west window indicating it had broken inward and more broken glass under the other two, indicating they'd been broken outward. It seemed pretty clear what had happened. I went to the car, found another envelope, and put a piece of glass from each of the three windows into it.

Joop and Sarah were still talking about her thesis when I returned.

"Let me see if I understand this," Joop said. "You're saying this whole mutiny business might have been avoided if the British had been more sensitive to their Hindu and Muslim soldiers?"

She nodded. "That's right. There were rumors that the British were using pig and cow fat to grease their rifle cartridges. Those things are forbidden to observant Hindus and Muslims. But rather than try to dispel the rumors—and they *were* only rumors— the British tried to force the soldiers to use the cartridges. It didn't work. The sepoys mutinied instead."

Joop turned to me. "Sweeney, you got to hear this." He turned back to Sarah. "Sweeney's Irish; he hates the British."

"I don't hate Brits," I said. "Just their army. Maybe you can tell me about this mutiny later. We should be going. Have you asked all your questions?"

Joop turned to Sarah. "Have I asked you enough questions?" And he gave her one of those smiles. He's a terrible flirt, Joop.

She beamed back at him. "Oh, I think so."

"Okay, then," Joop said. He shook her hand. "Thanks for . . . Oh, wait. Your daddy. I never asked about your daddy."

Sarah's smile disappeared. "What about him?" she asked.

"You told the police he'd threatened to burn down the garage. The studio, I mean. Now, just when did he say that?"

"Just about every time we talked since I got back from India," she said. "He'd go on about my soul and about graven images, then he'd say if I didn't get rid of the Ganesha, he would. I think he even said something about cleansing by fire."

"Ah," Joop said. "And where were you when the fire started?"

"I was supposed to be on campus," she said. "But I wasn't feeling well, so I cut my class. Lucky for me I did. If I hadn't come home then, the whole studio probably would have burned down."

"Can I give you some advice?" I said to Sarah.

She hesitated a moment. "Sure."

"Don't clean this place up yet. Even if the insurance people tell you it's okay to clean it up, wait a week or two before touching anything. Just to be safe. You wouldn't want anything to screw up your insurance settlement."

Sarah indicated the broken windows. "But what if it snows?"

"Put plastic over the windows," I said. "But I wouldn't touch anything else. They're strange people, insurance types, and you can't be too careful."

"Okay," she said. "Okay, thanks."

As we drove away, Joop started to scribble some notes. He likes to act the fool, but he's a good, thorough investigator. "Smart kid," he said. "Hates her daddy, but basically a nice kid. What did you think?"

I shrugged. "She was nice enough," I said.

"Religion is so weird," Joop said. "Everybody's so certain they are right and everybody else is wrong. Hobart's afraid his daughter will go to hell because she's got a Ganesha stashed in a converted garage, Sarah is pissed at her daddy because she thinks he cares more about Jesus than about her. A hundred and forty years ago a whole bunch of folks in India died on account of the British didn't have any respect for Hindus or Muslims. My Aunt Cooter's Jesus looks more like an Episcopalian than a Jew. And who knows what you Catholics are up to?"

"Joop, take a Prozac," I said. "We can leave religion out of this. We've got something better than religion. We've got evidence."

"Evidence? Of what?"

"Of who set the fire," I said.

"What are you talking about?" Joop asked. Then he started to grin. "Wait a minute. You found something, didn't you?"

"I found something," I said, then concentrated on my driving.

"Well?" Joop asked. "You going to tell me about it?"

I handed him the two envelopes, which he opened gingerly. "It's glass," he said.

"Clever lad yourself."

Joop waited for me to explain. When I didn't, he shook his head. "You're not going to tell me, are you?"

I smiled and kept my eyes on the road.

"Sweeney, did anybody ever tell you that you're a rat bastard?"

"You do," I said. "All the time."

"Well, that proves I *am* a clever lad," he said.

Joop likes to play the redneck at times, but the truth is he's better educated than I am, and probably smarter. So when I get a chance to torment him, I like to take advantage of it. He does the same to me. It's a guy thing.

"I'll tell you when I tell Hobart," I said.

"Is that where we're going now, back to the jail?"

"It is," I said. "I'm just hoping we get there before he's taken to his bail hearing."

Kirby Abbott, Hobart's lawyer, was with his client in the interview room. Kirby looked even more uncomfortable in the jail than Hobart did. Kirby's a good man and a whiz in the courtroom, but he's better when his clients are white-collar criminals. He doesn't do so well with what he calls "the lower criminal classes." Give him a client accused of securities fraud and our Kirby's a happy man. Give him an accused arsonist, even if the arsonist is a rich Protestant minister, and Kirby turns a bit uneasy.

"How long before the bail hearing?" I asked.

Kirby consulted his watch. "We have a little over an hour. Why?"

I put the two envelopes on the table. "You'll want to know about this," I said. "It's glass from the broken windows in the garage. The first envelope has glass from inside the garage, the other has glass found outside the garage."

Kirby glanced in each envelope. "So?"

"So it suggests that Reverend Hobart has been telling us the truth," I said. "He didn't set the fire."

Hobart started, then reached for the envelopes Kirby held in his hand. Kirby, though, didn't hand them over. Instead he cocked his head and looked confused. He gave the contents of both envelopes a second look.

"I don't understand," he said. He looked at Joop, who shrugged.

I took the envelopes and emptied the glass onto the table. "Now compare them," I said.

Kirby, Joop, and Hobart all leaned over the table, looking at the shards of glass.

"I don't see any difference," Kirby said. "Both sets are covered with oily smoke."

"Well, that's not quite right," Joop said, pointing at the shards. "The glass from outside the garage only has that oily smoke stuff on one side. The glass from inside has the smoke on both sides."

"So what?" Kirby said. "What does that mean?"

"Damned if I know," Joop said.

"It means the statue of Ganesha was . . ."

"Ganesha?" Kirby asked.

"Ganesha is your basic four-armed, elephant-headed Lord of Obstacles," Joop informed him. "The Hindu god of foresight and prosperity."

Kirby still looked confused.

"The statue that got itself burnt," Joop said.

"I see," Kirby said. "Right. Ganesha."

"These bits of glass show the statue was on fire before the Molotov cocktail was thrown through the garage window," I said.

Kirby looked at the glass again. "How is that possible?" he asked. "And how can you tell from these bits of glass?"

I pointed to the glass. "If an object is thrown through a window, what happens to the glass? It breaks and falls on the floor, right?"

"I think we all grasp the basic concept of gravity," Kirby said. He can get snotty at times, Kirby.

"And if the object that broke the window starts a fire, we'll get smoke. Right?"

"We understand gravity and combustion," Kirby said.

"And what happens to the glass on the floor?" I asked. "It gets covered with smoke. But it only gets covered on the one side. The side that's up. The side that's against the floor stays clean."

Joop grinned and clapped his hands. "I get it," he said.

Kirby cocked his head like a dog that's heard a sound it doesn't understand. He pointed to the glass shards that had come from inside the garage. "Then why do these pieces of glass have smoke on both sides?"

"There's only one explanation," I said. "The Molotov cocktail didn't start the fire. The fire had to be burning *before* the window was broken. The inner side of the window was covered with oily smoke, then the bottle was thrown through the window, the glass was shattered, and the other side of the glass was covered with smoke."

Kirby was nodding. "Okay. So the fire was going before the Molotov cocktail broke the window. But why does that prove Reverend Hobart didn't do it?" He turned to Hobart. "This is purely a theoretical question, you understand. I'm not doubting you when you say you're innocent." They're marvelous creatures, lawyers, always willing to give their clients the benefit of the doubt.

"It doesn't make any sense," I said. "Hobart's got a motive for tossing a Molotov cocktail through the garage window—he's worried about his daughter's soul. But there isn't any reason for him to break into the garage, set fire to the statue, then go outside and throw a Molotov cocktail through the window."

"But who *would* have a reason to do that?" Hobart asked.

"Your daughter," Joop said.

"Sarah?" Hobart asked. "Why?"

"On account of she's sincerely pissed off at you," Joop said. "She feels you neglected her and her mother. First with your work, then with your church."

"And for the insurance money," I said. "Sarah was expecting the insurance people when Joop and I arrived. I assume the garage was covered in her insurance policy?"

"The garage *and* the statue," Kirby said. He searched through his briefcase and pulled out some notes. "The statue was insured for eight thousand dollars."

"Bingo," Joop said. "Sarah only paid a touch over six thousand rupees for the little guy. That's a hundred and eighty American dollars. With one simple move Sarah gets back at her daddy *and* picks up some serious cash."

"But why would she need money?" Hobart asked. "I've got plenty of money. If she needed something, all she would have had to do is ask."

"You were threatening to cut her off unless she got rid of the statue," I said.

Hobart hung his head.

"She has a thesis to write," Joop said. "You can't study the religious implications of the Sepoy Mutiny when you're worried about making the house payments, you know."

Hobart looked up. "It still doesn't make sense. I thought she worshiped the statue. Why would she burn it?"

Joop shook his head. "Naw, she doesn't worship it. She just thinks it looks cool. Sarah's no Hindu. She's just a kid who's pissed off at her daddy."

"It all fits," I said. "She even moved her loom out of the garage a few days before the fire. I'd call that suspicious."

"The loom," Hobart said. "That was her mother's loom." He looked miserable, poor guy. He was beginning to believe it.

"It would have been easy for her to do," I continued. "The days are short now, so she could do it in the cover of darkness."

"Not that she needed the dark," Joop said. "Her house is surrounded by those big hedges. So there wasn't anybody who could see her in mid-Molotov cocktail toss."

"And isn't it an odd coincidence that she returned home at just the right moment?" I said. "Just in time to call in the fire department? The garage and the statue were probably damaged more than she'd have liked, but even so, the damage was minimal."

Hobart closed his eyes and put his face in his hands. I could see his lips moving. He was praying, I suppose. He had good reason to.

Kirby looked at his watch. "Well, this certainly changes things. We'll need to talk to the district attorney before the bail hearing," he said. "If we turn this information over to the DA, there's a chance he'll dismiss the charges at the bail hearing."

Hobart looked up. "But what will happen to Sarah?"

Kirby stammered for a moment. He seemed to have forgotten that Sarah was Hobart's daughter. "Uh, well, uh, I'm not entirely . . ."

"She could be arrested," I said. Hobart had a right to know. "She could be charged with obstructing justice and filing a false police report, but that's small beans. Sarah's biggest problem is with attempting to defraud the insurance company out of eight thousand dollars. That's a felony."

"But at least she wouldn't be charged with arson," Kirby said. "It's not illegal to burn up something you own."

Hobart shook his head. "No, I won't have my daughter arrested," he said. "I won't have her charged with a crime. I'd . . . I'd rather plead guilty. Can I do that at this bail hearing?"

Kirby seemed stunned. "Plead guilty?"

"If I pled guilty, would I be required to do it under oath?" Hobart asked.

Kirby held up his hands. "Wait, wait. Let's just deal with the bail hearing. We don't have to go to the district attorney with this information immediately. Let's get you out of jail first, then we can figure out what to do."

Hobart started to speak, but there was a sharp knock on the door and one of the corrections officers put his head in. "Sorry," he said. "Mr. Abbott, you have a phone call. And the deputies are here to take your client to court for his bail hearing."

"Damn," Kirby said. "Damn, damn. Sweeney, come with me and explain all this one more time."

I nodded and started to follow Kirby out the door. I held the door open for Joop.

"Go ahead on," Joop said. "I've got something I want to say to the Rev here."

I hesitated. I wasn't sure it was a good idea for Joop to talk to Reverend Hobart alone. As I've said, he's not always as diplomatic as he could be. But he'd already turned toward Hobart and started talking, so I left them alone.

While Kirby and I walked to the telephone, I explained the glass and smoke to him once again. He understood it well enough; he was just being careful, which is why he's a good lawyer.

Joop caught up with us a few minutes later. He was grinning like a lord's bastard. He held out his hand.

"I need to borrow your car," he said. "Kirby can give you a lift back to the office after the bail hearing."

"What's going on?" I asked.

Joop smiled. "I'll tell you when I get back to the office."

"Joop Wheeler, you're a rat bastard." But turnabout is fair play—I'd made him wait for the smoke and glass explanation. I gave him my car keys, but I didn't like it.

We had to wait half an hour for the bail hearing. It was a half hour made miserable by still more tacky Christmas music. A holly, jolly Christmas, indeed. I thought about finding the clerk of court and complaining about the separation of church and state, but nobody could seriously claim *that* music had anything to do with religion.

When we finally got into the courtroom, the hearing only took about ten minutes. The courts don't keep people like Jason Hobart in jail awaiting trial. If you have money, you walk. It's not right, but there it is and the whole world knows it.

After the hearing Hobart borrowed Kirby's cellular telephone and went off to a quiet corner to make a call. He came back a few minutes later, looking somber.

"Chet Wilkins," he said.

"Who is Chet Wilkins?" Kirby asked.

"It's who I was with when Sarah . . . when her garage caught fire," Hobart said. "I was at his house, praying with him. Chet is one of the deacons of my church. He's just tested positive for HIV."

"And you were with him that night?" Kirby asked. "He's willing to testify to that?"

Hobart nodded. "He'd rather not, but he will if it's necessary. You can see why I couldn't tell you where I was. There are some members of our church—maybe most of them—who wouldn't understand. They think AIDS is God's curse. Chet's a good man. He's made some mistakes, but he sincerely wants to get right with God."

Kirby looked at him for a moment. "Come on, let's get out of here," he said. "I'll take you home."

"Could you take me to Sarah's house?" Hobart asked. "I have a lot to make up for. If I'm not too late." He smiled sadly. "But I can't believe I'm too late. I don't think God would do that to me. I think the Lord set all this up, to show me what's important in my life. I told you the Lord would take care of me."

Kirby nodded. He wasn't comfortable with all the talk about God. Nor was I, for that matter. Catholics don't talk about God like He's the neighbor down the street. "Yeah, sure," he said. "Let's go."

Rather than tag along to Hobart's reunion with his daughter, I took a cab back to the office. The cabbie had Christmas music on his radio, so I was nearly murderous by the time I got there.

I'd been there just long enough for the teapot to come to a boil when Joop came in. He was carrying the scorched Hindu statue from Sarah Hobart's studio/garage.

"What's that?" I asked.

"Ganesha," Joop said, "You remember. The Lord of Obstacles."

"Yes, but what are you doing with it?"

"I bought it," he said.

"You what?"

"Bought it. Which word didn't you understand?"

"You bought it? How much?"

"Eight thousand American dollars," he said. "That's what it was insured for."

I stared at him. "Are you *mad?* Where did you get eight thousand dollars?"

"From Hobart," he said. "He said we could bill him."

"So that's what you cooked up with Hobart," I said. "Am I right in thinking Sarah will now cancel her insurance claim?"

Joop nodded. "It was the only logical solution," he said. "Hobart didn't want his little Sarah to lose her soul. And he didn't want her to commit insurance fraud. And Sarah wanted the cash to finish her thesis. This way everybody's happy."

He was awfully full of himself. But I had to admit, it was a neat solution.

"What are you going to do with it?" I asked.

"I'm going to clean the little booger up," Joop said. "He's not that badly damaged."

"And then what?"

"Then I'm going to put him in that corner," he said, pointing. "Sweeney, bud, if there's any folks in the world who need a god to clear away obstacles, it's us private detectives."

JAMES LINCOLN WARREN
BLACK SPARTACUS

May 1999

JAMES LINCOLN WARREN debuted his Eighteenth-century sleuth Alan Treviscoe in the pages of *AHMM* in March of 1998 with "The Dioscuri Deception." A habitué of Lloyd's Coffee-house, Treviscoe is an "indagator" for the maritime insurance firm—a position that didn't exist at the time. Warren created the position for this character in this scrupulously researched series.

■

Lord Mansfield, resplendent in his scarlet robe and long white wig, stared at the man in the dock. The accused was a large black African dressed in what had once been very fine livery, and his tiewig, although indifferently powdered, was of the highest quality. The learned judge's gaze shifted to Sir Richard Pelles for the defense, and he wondered again how a slave had managed to engage one of the finest barristers in England.

Sir Richard was questioning the young man with the somnolent eyes from Lloyd's, whose testimony was evidently to be of prime importance to the defense.

"Mr. Treviscoe, where did you make the acquaintance of the accused?"

"At a prizefight in Hyde Park, sir. Hero was one of the combatants . . ."

A POWDERED Frenchman collided with Alan Treviscoe in the milling crowd and nearly knocked off his tricorn. Steadying himself, Treviscoe put his right hand on the hat and his left on the hilt of his smallsword to keep it from swinging out and striking somebody's shin. Monsieur's right hand went likewise to his own sword, his black eyes flashing above his rouged cheeks, anticipating a challenge. Recognizing that Treviscoe had no obvious intention to draw, he relaxed and ceremoniously bowed in apology. Treviscoe returned the bow, careful not to let his hat fall from his head, and he and Captain Magnus Gunn of the Royal Navy continued threading their way through the throng.

"Gunn!"

Gunn stopped and touched his hat to a richly dressed man in his forties whose face was a map of dissipation. "Sir Beaumont Clevis," he said, his Scottish accent failing to hide his dislike. "Allow me to introduce Mr. Alan Treviscoe of Lloyd's."

Sir Beaumont looked at Treviscoe as if he were a horse for sale at a country fair.

"Your servant, sir," said Treviscoe, bowing.

"Now is the time to change your mind," Sir Beaumont said to Gunn.

"My wager has been laid, Sir Beaumont."

"Then you'll stand to lose it all! Strong bastards, these blacks, but boxing is an art that requires more than strength. Oh, I warrant they have low cunning enough, but Muldaur's buck can be no match for a white man, especially not an Englishman."

"I'm afraid it were not in my power to agree, Sir Beaumont, having seen Hero fight, and low cunning's no' in it. But if ye'll excuse us, we must pay our respects to Captain Muldaur."

"Respects," Sir Beaumont snorted sarcastically. "Well, you can't say I didn't warn ye."

They parted with a mutual display of unfelt respect by bowing, and Gunn and Treviscoe flung themselves back into the crowd.

"There he is now," said Gunn, gesturing toward a knot of people ahead of them. He boldly advanced, and Treviscoe followed.

"Captain Muldaur! This is my particular friend, Mr. Alan Treviscoe of Lloyd's."

The stout Irishman sported a trim military mustache and was armed with an ear trumpet. Treviscoe wondered at its necessity, since Gunn was roaring away in his quarterdeck voice.

"Alan Treviscoe, allow me to introduce Captain Ragnall Muldaur, formerly of the Royal Marines. He owns the boxing slave we came to watch."

"What was that name again?" asked Muldaur, staring fixedly at Treviscoe's lips.

"*My* name, sir?" Treviscoe asked.

"Of course *your* name! What other person would I be asking the name of?" Muldaur stepped forward, a short step that drew Treviscoe's attention to the stout peg the man had in lieu of a right leg below the knee. He rotated the ear trumpet so that the bell hovered in Treviscoe's face.

"My name is Treviscoe, sir—Alan Treviscoe, at your service."

"Treviscoe? Did you say Treviscoe?"

"That is correct, sir."

"Then you are a relation to the late Captain Charles Treviscoe?"

"That was my father's name, sir. Did you know him, sir?"

"Was your father a naval man?" asked Gunn. "I never knew that."

"For a time he was purser to Boscawen," replied Treviscoe, "but he held no royal commission, and later in life he was a merchant captain who tried to find his fortune in the West Indies trade."

"Charlie ne'er mentioned any whelps," exclaimed Muldaur. "But 'tis no matter. Aye! Knew him! Fine man, he was, young—Alan, is it?"

"Yes, sir."

Muldaur nodded again, his short and battered scratch wig bobbing as he did so. "Come to see me Hero, have ye?"

"We have, Captain Muldaur," interjected Gunn. "I reckon 'twill be a bonny fight."

"Ye've never seen the like," Muldaur said smugly. "Hope ye've placed your wagers anon."

"Oh aye," replied Gunn. He turned to Treviscoe and spoke in a lower tone of voice. "Our money's on Muldaur's black—learned the art in Barbados, I'm told. An old Irish hallion Muldaur may be, but he's never the man to sell his pride. 'Twill be an honest battering, I promise."

Treviscoe nodded. Since Jack Broughton had lost the championship to Jack Slack twenty-one years before in 1750, boxing had fallen into some disrepute without losing any of its popularity among the gaming set. In these corrupt times the usual trick in betting on a boxing match was to know who was being paid to lose.

Muldaur took Treviscoe by the sleeve and spoke with a conspiratorial earnestness.

"Not to worry, my boy. Always pay me debts—more dear than blood is the honor of a Muldaur—as soon as the Malian's debt is discharged, but Ragnall Muldaur is no breakvow."

"This is a fine wager, Alan," said Gunn gleefully. "I got five to two. Who among these bluidy Sassenachs—present company excluded, mind ye—who among 'em will admit that some poor black savage can best a brawny Englishman at fisticuffs, eh? But win he will, I am certain of it."

A clamorous cheer erupted from the carousing multitude, and Treviscoe's attention was drawn to the center of the green, where an area had been roped off.

The combatants had taken their places.

The Englishman, Butcher Bill Blankett, was a beefy youth of near eighteen stone, his balding forehead a stark contrast to the ursine mat on his chest. The slave Hero, who like Blankett was stripped to his breeches, was as different from his opponent as a man of roughly the same age could possibly be. Treviscoe's first impression was of an ebon Apollo. His head was completely shaved, reflecting the sun like a polished cannonball, and the curves of his muscles shone like black marble. He was tall, taller even than Magnus Gunn, and whereas Blankett was built like a broad ship of the line, Hero was constructed like a sleek frigate, all lines for speed.

The two men faced off.

The referee hoarsely called out, "May the best man win!"

There was another rousing cheer and the contest began. Treviscoe would never recall the exact details of the fight—his knowledge of the pugilistic art was too poor. His first impression was of a succession of violent images: heads snapping back, sweat and blood being flung onto the rowdy onlookers, the boxers grappling and wrestling each other desperately, like Titans, and an endless and merciless shower of pummeling to face and torso. He began to sense a little of the rough science of it, not unlike fencing—the parries and ripostes, the maneuvering for position and room—and finally it seemed to him that he was watching a kind of chess match, witnessing the headlong race to checkmate between two masters, and all the blows and grapples were nothing more than pieces advancing and colliding.

Each time a man was forced to the ground, a round was called. In the early stages of the combat Treviscoe's inexpert eye judged that the fighters were evenly matched, and he began to worry about his ten-guinea wager. But as the contest drew on, it became increasingly clear that Hero was getting the better of his opponent. Cheers became less frequent, and boos and catcalls increased.

Finally, inevitably, Butcher Bill collapsed like a shack in a hurricane, smearing the grass with the freely flowing blood from the cuts on his face. He failed to rise. The referee declared Hero the winner.

Hero seemed insensible of his victory. He gasped for air, made difficult by his swollen face. His dark skin was mottled with crimson.

The outcome was not popular. The crowd growled with anger and disappointment. Treviscoe glanced around with worry, his normally half-lidded eyes wide open in apprehension.

"The mob is close to riot," he whispered urgently to Gunn.

Gunn laughed ebulliently. "Nonsense, Alan. They're sore that they have had to pay for their sport is all. Now to collect our winnings!"

Sir Beaumont, fuming with wrath, pushed his way through the crowd, filling the air with oaths and deprecations, until at last he approached Captain Muldaur, whose gap-toothed grin displayed a vicious glee. "Laugh, will you, Muldaur?" cried the gentleman. "We will see about that!"

"Remember Othello's words, Sir Beaumont: 'They laugh that win,'" replied the Irishman, his mirth unchecked.

Sir Beaumont glared at the panting Hero with undisguised malice. "'Twould be well for *you* to remember the blackamoor's fate, Muldaur."

Muldaur's joy transformed instantly into a snarl of contempt. "Thou Iago! Nay, not even, art naught but Iago's creature!"

Sir Beaumont raised his hand back still clutching his walking stick and with an effort controlled his temper.

"I have no need to demand satisfaction from a one-legged deaf Irish son of a bitch," he said acidly, "most especially when I observe that his wretched body has already been compensated for the nature of his character. Good day!"

Muldaur's barking laughter followed him.

Captain Muldaur turned next to Treviscoe. "If you would pursue your own interests, I beg that you call on me at my lodgings: Number 5, Red Rose Alley, off White Cross Street, the day after tomorrow. We have somewhat to discuss."

"AND DID YOU accept the invitation?"

"I did," said Treviscoe, "and went to keep the appointment at the designated hour. It had thundered furiously during the night, and the rain was still considerable that morning . . ."

TREVISCOE MADE HIS way under a recent investment he had made to protect his large and expensive tricorn: a fine black umbrella. They were becoming something of a fad in the city. He addressed the problem of muddy streets by wearing boots as if he were a soldier on campaign. Although they were not fashionable, he did not expect Muldaur to care.

Muldaur's habitation was in the warren of tenements that catered to London's impoverished Irish. The captain's presence there was somewhat incongruous: as a king's officer he was at least nominally a Protestant, and the exclusively Catholic populace would view him with suspicion. But he must have had his reasons.

Murky puddles had collected in holes where the dismal street was missing cobblestones. Some of the displaced stones were scattered around the door to Muldaur's domicile.

A worn and harried woman whose wide and darting eyes reminded Treviscoe of a field mouse watching for an owl answered the door and told him timorously that the captain lived on the second story and that his slave lodged in the attic. The stair was narrow and decrepit. It could not have been an easy climb for a man with a wooden leg.

The door to the room was ajar. He placed his hand on the door, and it swayed gently back.

Muldaur was face up on the floor. His head and open nightshirt were horribly bloody, and his face was swollen almost beyond recognition. Treviscoe knelt and knew from the coldness of the flesh that there would be no pulse. He quickly examined the body.

The most obvious injuries were to his face and arms, but his left leg, the whole one, was bent unnaturally. His chest and abdomen were pale and unmarked except for a fresh, thin bruise across his chest stretching from armpit to armpit. The palms of his hands were raw, red, and chapped, and some of the skin had been scraped away. The knuckles were unmarked. His nightshirt was damp, but the floor around him was dry.

Rain gusted in from the open window, falling short of where the body lay.

Treviscoe went to the window to pull it shut. Hanging from the eave of the roof was a black iron hook from which depended a wooden naval block, but there was no rope reeved through it. It had obviously been installed so that something might be lifted to the window directly from the street.

He pulled the window shut and surveyed the room. He remembered how, at the prizefight, blood had freely spattered the observers. But there were no bloodstains anywhere except in the immediate vicinity of the body, where small pools of blood had dripped off the face. Under the bed he found a cleat, such as were used to belay lines aboard ships, affixed to the floor. He looked back to the window, at the image of the block through the closed window swinging in the wet wind, smeared by the cheap glass and spattering raindrops.

Where was the rope?

"WHAT SIGNIFICANCE did you attach to your observations, Mr. Treviscoe?" Sir Richard asked.

"Objection, m'lord!" The crown prosecutor stood. "Of what conceivable relevance can the speculations of Mr. Treviscoe be to the court? May I remind my learned colleague that the jury and the jury alone are the triers of fact."

"Perhaps the distinguished advocate for the crown has forgotten Mr. Treviscoe's particular profession as an investigator of fraudulent claims against the insurance underwriters of Lloyd's. I am sure it is not necessary to remind the court that many times ere now, and in this very room, his testimony has served the cause of justice, although he has not previously been before Your Lordship. A man's very life is on trial, and to deprive the jury of Mr. Treviscoe's expertise were to flaunt the purpose of this assembly."

"Just so," said Lord Mansfield after a considered pause. "You may continue."

"Mr. Treviscoe?"

"The only conclusion I drew with certainty was that Captain Muldaur had not been murdered in his room, but that his corpus had been transported thither after the commission of the crime. Otherwise blood would have been spattered on the walls or on the bed."

"But there were no clues as to the identity of the murderer, were there?"

Treviscoe paused. "There were none to identify anyone positively, that is true, but by scientific reasoning some parties could easily be ruled out. His wounds were not consistent with those sustained by fisticuffs. I should say his assailant, or more precisely his assailants, were not boxers."

"He was beaten senseless. Is not that consistent with being struck repeatedly by a powerful fighter?"

"He was never once struck 'tween belt and shoulder, judging from the entire absence of bruising on his torso save the thin line I mentioned, and he never returned a blow with his own hands, which though obviously distressed were unmarked on the obverse. A man striking back would surely have marked his knuckles. The wounds to his forearms showed he had tried, with a lamentable lack of success, to protect his face. It were a strange boxer who insists on pummeling a man's head when his midriff is exposed."

"Objection, m'lord! Mr. Treviscoe is pleased to say who the murderer cannot have been solely on the basis of what was *not* done. We are not to imagine, I hope, that should a baker commit murder he should always make of his victim a pie."

"Your objection is sustained, Mr. Juddson, even if your metaphor exceeds the proper decorum expected in this court," said Mansfield coldly. "The witness will confine himself to only those positive observations that may be derived from the evidence of his own eyes, and the jury will disregard speculative testimony that the murderer cannot have been a boxer."

"Very good, m'lord," said Sir Richard, satisfied, knowing that what is said cannot be unsaid. "Mr. Treviscoe, were there any other clues as the identity, or identities, of Captain Muldaur's assailant or assailants?"

"As noted, not at the scene . . ." replied Treviscoe, pausing.

Looking directly at the judge, his tentative manner suggesting that he delicately weighed whether or not he might be silenced for exceeding His Lordship's instructions, he continued, "But that is not to say there were no clues. There was his unusual history, and his strange words at the prizefight . . ."

"HAVE YOU SEEN this, Alan?" Gunn waved a broadsheet in Treviscoe's face. "Hero is caught! He has confessed!"

"What do you mean?" Treviscoe put his clay pipe in his mouth and accepted the newspaper. The common room at Lloyd's buzzed with the usual flurry of activity beneath a thick pall of smoke. "'The Black Spartacus Captured.'"

"He was heard to say, 'Then my actions have killed him.' That's the end of the mystery, I would say."

"Confessed?" Treviscoe's forehead furrowed. "I would never've imagined it. But 'tis a strange confession. 'Then my actions have killed him.' What actions?"

"Murder, surely," said Gunn.

"My dear Magnus, on infrequent occasions I have observed that people actually choose the words that express most precisely what they mean. Hero certainly did not actually say he had *murdered* the captain; contrariwise, his diction seems to indicate he did not know of the consequences of his actions till he was informed of the crime upon his arrest."

Gunn frowned. "Well, 'tis clear that Captain Muldaur and Hero quarreled the night of the murder. The landlady, Mrs. O'Reilly, heard Hero shouting from two floors above."

"What of it? Muldaur was deaf, and his ear trumpet was not in his room when I discovered his body, else I have lost any capacity to effect a thorough search."

"Do you then perversely insist that Hero is innocent?"

"Innocent? Of murder, perhaps, but of what else I can only guess. There are too many strange little facts in this case, Magnus, for me to be satisfied that the most obvious culprit is the true culprit, although I concur as to the matter appearing—I almost said black, but this is no matter for levity; bleak is mayhap more apposite—for the slave. Consider: why were there no blows to the captain's ribs and abdomen? Is that consistent with being beaten to death by a boxer? I think not, and neither would you think so if it were not convenient to so do. Remember also that Captain Muldaur had other enemies beyond any disputation if his relationship with Sir Beaumont Clevis is to be judged at face value. It would be instructive to know more of his history, to glean who those enemies were. I wish I knew, for example, how he came to lose his right leg, and his deafness seemed unusually pronounced for a man of such hearty middle age."

"Why, 'tis no mystery there. Both the debilitations followed the explosion of HMS *Leonidas* in Belfast Lough in the year '60."

"Was that the year the French occupied the castle at Carrickfergus?"

"Aye, the very same. 'Tis not an event generally known, but *Leonidas,* a fourth rate of fifty guns, was dispatched under secret orders to defend Carrickfergus whilst frigates harassed the French commodore, whose name was Thurot, at sea. The officer in command of *Leonidas*'s marines was none other than Captain Ragnall Muldaur.

"The ship anchored off the north shore of the Lough to meet the French and do some damage before they could land. But a party of Frenchmen were led overland, and reaching the shore, they launched a boat in the early morning darkness so they might detach the ship from her cable, whereupon she ran hard aground on the morning flood-tide. In the confusion there was a fire belowdecks, and the powder magazine blew, killing near every soul on board. Of three hundred sailors and marines only Muldaur lived to tell the tale, minus his leg and his hearing lost to the blast."

"You said the French soldiers were led but not by whom."

"Scuttlebutt said 'twere some paddy Judas paid his thirty pieces out of Commodore Thurot's own pocket."

Treviscoe's pipe had gone out, but he didn't notice. His concentration was interrupted by the sound of a man clearing his throat.

"In the absence of someone to introduce us formally I must needs introduce myself, Mr. Treviscoe," the man said in a harsh Ulster accent. He was dressed well but not richly, his sole concession to vanity being silk stockings that showed off his well-rounded calves to good advantage.

"Michael Flynn, solicitor, at your service. I had the honor to represent the late Captain Ragnall Muldaur and have come to inform you as to the provision in his will by which, under the normal turn of events, you would have benefited had circumstances not dictated otherwise."

"You astonish me, Mr. Flynn," replied Treviscoe. "What can you mean? I hardly knew the captain."

"Two days ago Captain Muldaur altered his will to favor you, Mr. Treviscoe, by making you his sole heir. I have the document here. As I understand it, he was moved to this gesture out of gratitude to your father, who had succored him in his recovery after serious injury and sponsored him in a business venture in the Barbados. Alas, the sole remnant of what by his description must have been a once respectable fortune is now manifested solely in the person of his slave Hero, whom the newspapers have pleased to fashion the Black Spartacus. I presume you have heard of the affair, and of how the captain made a gladiator of the poor black and how Hero avenged himself."

Treviscoe was thunderstruck. "I have no want of a slave."

"Then 'tis just as well, for your inheritance now amounts to nothing, there being no power on earth that can stand between Hero and the gallows," said Flynn. "Your slave sits now in Newgate Prison awaiting trial for the murder of his master."

Treviscoe stood up in agitation.

"My slave! My slave! What ill-sounding words. Am I some Carolina indigo plantationer? But you are wrong in assuming that there is nothing to be done, as Hero has become my personal responsibility. It cannot now suffice merely to be unconvinced of his guilt; instead I must do everything in my power to steer him clear of Tyburn hill. There is no power like the truth, and it has become imperative that it now be wholly discovered. Magnus!"

"Yes, Alan?"

"There was a considerable purse for the fight, was there not?"

"Five hundred pounds."

"What has become of it?"

"What was it Muldaur said at the contest? That he owed someone and that the debt should be paid. Perhaps he discharged it."

"The *Malian's* debt, he said. Mark the words, Magnus. I remember them well, though I did not then fully perceive their import. In light of what you have told me about his career, I would scarce imagine that five hundred pounds would cover such a debt as to the *Median*. No, the money went elsewhere, stolen most like by the perpetrators of the murder. It will not stand—but you are better acquainted with the sporting world than I, and I would consider it a personal favor if you were to look into the matter of who put the purse forward and at the same time find out if there were any other wagerers whose loss was, to express it with moderation, *inconveniently* large. I can think of no likelier person with whom to begin, in the absence of more information, than Sir Beaumont. He is not, I believe, our quarry, but he may know who is. The man we seek must be an Irishman, middle-aged, of brutal temperament and mercenary reputation."

"How can you know that, Alan?"

Treviscoe looked at him in surprise. "Why, from your own lips."

Gunn opened his mouth and shut it again. Then he asked in a low voice, "Where shall we meet after I have discharged this—this *quest?*"

"Call upon me at my lodgings this evening. Now, Mr. Flynn, I shall require your professional services, for though I am in no position to grant him liberty forthwith, yet if Hero is to meet his Maker he shall not do it in bondage as a slave. Be so kind as to prepare the document of manumission, and thence to Newgate!"

"AND WAS YOUR interview with the prisoner fruitful?"

"It was, sir."

"Describe the meeting."

THE SQUALOR AND filth of Newgate Prison was the worst Treviscoe had seen in England. Hero was confined to a cell that would not have suited a beast. The room was so dark that his clothing seemed disembodied, so that it was like looking at an invisible spirit in a white shirt above which hovered two points of light, his eyes. He said nothing when the turnkey admitted Treviscoe to the cell.

"My name is Alan Treviscoe."

There was no reply.

"I have brought some things for your comfort. Can you read?"

"Yes, I can read." The voice was deep and resonant.

"Then I have brought something to bring you hope withal."

"Hope?" It was a cry of despair and incredulity. "Are you not my new master? I am already in chains. There is no further debasement you can subject me to except to pretend to offer hope."

"I have brought you a Bible and some twist and a pipe," said Treviscoe, proffering the gifts, "and I have brought you this—it is a document of manumission with your name affixed. I am not your new master nor shall any man ever be again."

Hero took them. "I see you mean well," he said at last, "but the gift comes too late. I shall only truly be free in the bosom of the Lord, after I have been condemned."

"As to that, I should remind you that despair is a sin," replied Treviscoe. "Deliverance oft arrives unbidden. Pray but answer one question I shall put to you and I shall trouble you no further. Who is the man who was known to your late master as Ephialtes?"

There was a tense silence. Finally Hero sighed and answered. "I did not think anyone would believe me. But I perceive you know everything."

"Not yet everything, Hero, and until this very moment I had only suspicions. But we have very little time, for the murderer may even now have taken flight. Who is this Ephialtes?"

"I do not know his name, only that he was the traitor, sir, the traitor of Belfast Lough."

"Then it is as I thought, even to the name that Captain Muldaur assigned to him, for I had heretofore heard of Ephialtes only as the Malian. But this is good news, Hero, and it means there is yet a glimmer of hope. I have pledged myself to deliver you from the threat of Tyburn. You have not, I assume, an alibi."

"Would that I had, sir. But it is of little moment, for 'twas my own anger that killed Captain Muldaur as surely as he who committed the actual deed."

"What do you mean?"

"We had a proper shout at each other that evening, Mr. Treviscoe. It cannot have escaped your observation that the captain had little power to cause me to remain in bondage to him if I had chosen to remove myself."

"That is a common enough eventuality in England, as you must know. Sir John Fielding has written on the subject, expressing his view that to bring a slave to Britain is unwise—it encourages the slave to seek his freedom by whatever means available, lawful or no, and can only lead to unrest."

"Then you should know that Captain Muldaur had promised me my freedom in exchange for my skill in the ring and my participation in his plan, whatever it was, to mete vengeance upon Ephialtes. I knew him for a man of his word, and as long as I knew him, he never failed to live up to what his honor demanded until that night. He told me I was not to be free after all."

Treviscoe frowned. "I fear the cause of his renegation was the discovery of my own existence."

Hero looked at him in surprise. "And so it was. The money Captain Muldaur had used to make my purchase in Barbados had been lent him by Captain Treviscoe, who was, as I understood him, your father. He therefore believed you had the prior claim upon his honor, and upon me as the property purchased with your father's money. So he told me that he could not grant me my liberty as he had promised but had arranged that I should become your own slave."

"My father?" said Treviscoe. "I had no knowledge that my father had any interest in the slave traffic."

"I do not believe the money was given Captain Muldaur for that purpose, sir, as he claimed he was sent ahead to Barbados to act as Captain Treviscoe's agent in the sugar trade. But trading in sugar or molasses or indigo and tobacco, sir—it is all the same, for the goods are the fruit of the labor of slaves, and the money to pay for these goods will be invested in yet more slaves. But when the report came of the loss of your father's ship, the captain chose instead to buy me from my master in furtherance of his revenge."

"I cannot begin to imagine the horror of being a slave."

"You cannot, nor can any man who has not lived through it. But I was grateful to the captain for his intervention, sir, because by purchasing me whole, he saved me from certain dismemberment and death. Goaded beyond endurance by the cruelty of my previous master, I had at last thrashed him to within an inch of his life. I was in shackles, due to be executed even as I am now, when Captain Muldaur appealed to the greed of my former master and was given the bill of sale on condition that I was not to remain on the island."

"So you were a willing confederate in Captain Muldaur's intention to avenge himself on Ephialtes. But what was his plan?"

"As to that I cannot say except that it must have had something to do with the boxing ring."

"But you must have apprehended that Captain Muldaur was placing his own life in danger and mayhap your own by crossing Ephialtes."

Hero nodded. "Aye, I knew it as well as he knew it, sir. But a danger postponed is less terrible than a certain death. As I said, I was grateful to him, and had I not left him in anger, I would have been there to protect him. Thus does the responsibility for his death fall upon my shoulders."

"I have but one last question, Hero: were you meant to lose the fight against Bill Blankett?"

"Never in this life, sir, would I deliberately allow a man to beat me, in the ring or out of it," said Hero with a hint of resentment in his voice, "and Captain Muldaur would never have countenanced such a compromise of his honor."

"AND WHY DO you believe that Captain Muldaur called this traitor by the peculiar appellation of Ephialtes the Malian?" asked Sir Richard.

"It was in direct reference to the betrayal of HMS *Leonidas* in Belfast Lough in 1760," said Treviscoe. "Remember that the French had a native guide to lead them to where the ship lay at anchor, and as a result of the guide's treachery, three hundred men died. So at the Battle of Thermopylae, Herodotus tells us, did Ephialtes of Malis betray King Leonidas of Sparta and his three hundred warriors by leading a Persian war party through a secret pass behind the Spartan lines.

"Somehow Captain Muldaur learnt the identity of the Irish Ephialtes—by what arts we are forever unlikely to discover—and that he was in London, and so he came hither with Hero to exact his revenge. The sequence of those events will probably remain hidden from us, as I said, but in the meantime I pursued other enquiries . . ."

MAGNUS GUNN CALLED at White's Chocolate-house, where Sir Beaumont Clevis was sure to be at a gambling table. Gunn's taste in games of chance tended to backgammon and dice rather than to cards, but he felt certain that Sir Beaumont would be more fashionably inclined. He was right: Sir Beaumont sat at a faro table, and his luck had not improved since the day of the fight. He was losing so immoderately and acting so belligerent that Gunn intervened.

"Sir Beaumont! I ken we've had enough of these amusements. It should be home for us, I reckon."

"Home! No, my good captain, home will never do unless you'd care to wager at billiards? My damn'd luck will change ere dawn, mark you."

Gunn's profession as a seaman had imbued him with a considerable skill in geometry, and billiards was a game for which he had an unusually strong affinity. He readily agreed, and they departed for the baronet's house on Soho Square.

Sir Beaumont's table was one of the new English billiard tables, ten feet long with pockets in the corners and on each side. The familiar three balls were there, but any interrogation would have to wait until Gunn learned the new rules: winning and losing hazards, two points off a white ball and three off the red. Caroms were still allowed and earned a single point each.

They took their stances for the fade, Sir Beaumont on the right and Gunn on the left, then drew back their sticks and struck.

The faint clicks as the flat wooden tips of their cues hit the ivory balls were nearly simultaneous. Gunn won the honors, and the game began in earnest. Talk flowed freely, abetted by the equally free-flowing port, absent from Sir Beaumont's grasp only when it was his shot.

"That damn'd paddy and his buck," Sir Beaumont snarled, "winning at five to two, damn his eyes. I can hardly credit it. And for what? A mere five hundred more?"

"That exceeds a year's income for some gentlemen. To a man in Muldaur's reduced circumstances, it were seemingly a considerable inducement to victory."

Sir Beaumont gave Gunn a canny look. "Now, there must've been more than another five hundred pounds in it," he said archly, "else why did you bet on the black?"

"That is the second time ye've said there was more than one payment of five hundred pounds. For myself, I bet as I did because I expected Hero to win," said Gunn bluntly, "just as clearly as you expected him to lose."

"Blast it all to hell!" exclaimed Sir Beaumont, his cue ball sinking into a side pocket after having struck the red ball. "The devil take it and you, too. Aye, you expected him to win, I daresay. I wonder how you knew he meant not to give in."

"I was unaware of any arrangement to the contrary," said Gunn, trying to keep the ice out of his voice. "Had ye been led to believe that Hero was to throw the fight?"

Sir Beaumont snorted.

"D'ye think I would have wagered two thousand guineas on a fair fight? You'd see me in Bedlam ere that."

"Who was it who put you onto it, then?"

Sir Beaumont gave him a look bristling with suspicion.

"I wouldna care ever to place a bet with an unreliable agent," Gunn hastily explained, "and so 'twould be only prudent to know whether a man can be trusted or no. Bold action is very well in war, but in uncharted waters prudence is the mariner's watchword."

"There's sense in that," said Sir Beaumont, "although I swear the agent, as you put it, was as taken for a fool as the rest of the syndicate he convinced to put up the sop to Cerberus—and Muldaur was a dog at that. I call it dishonor when you take a five-hundred-pound bribe and fail to deliver. And as to our agent, I cannot see how he shall cover all his bets in the event."

Gunn shot a perfect winning hazard, the red ball flying into a corner pocket. He regretted it when he saw Sir Beaumont scowl.

"Dr. Stephen Synge is the man's name, not a better man for being a paddy like Muldaur, for all his education and fine airs," said Sir Beaumont angrily. "Where he's to come find the money is any man's guess."

Gunn sighed inwardly with relief and contrived to lose the game but not by so much as would seriously inhibit his purse.

"YE WERE RIGHT, Alan," Gunn said, removing his hat. "Sir Beaumont suffered a significant loss on a wager he felt certain of winning."

"How certain?"

"The fight was not intended to be a fair one. Sir Beaumont said that Captain Muldaur had been paid to see that Hero should lose, and paid handsomely by a consortium of gentlemen led by a certain party whose business it was to arrange such matters, a Dr. Synge by name. By curious coincidence, that party is—"

"An Irishman of middle age, of brutal temperament and mercenary reputation," finished Treviscoe. "Furthermore, he was awarded the degree of Philosophiae Doctor at the Sorbonne, and he has been suspected of being a spy for Versailles."

"How did ye learn all that?"

"He is not unknown in the city, where he enjoys a particularly equivocal reputation. I might have known it was he who is Ephialtes.

"You must have deduced, Magnus, that Muldaur never meant for Hero to lose that fight, but to win against tall odds so that the fortune of his enemy should be totally sacrificed. Harken now, Magnus, for I believe I've reconstructed all the details of the crime and there merely remains the simple matter of proving Hero not guilty."

"How d'ye propose to do that?"

"There must have been witnesses. At the very least it defies reason that Mrs. O'Reilly should not have seen the encounter."

"Mrs. O'Reilly? She's the besom who testified *against* Hero."

"Precisely. If she heard Hero shouting from two stories above, she could hardly have escaped seeing what happened afterward."

"But you said that he was not murdered at the house."

"Not *inside* the house, Magnus. Consider: his hands were raw and chapped, the very indicia of a severe rope burn, which you as a nautical man should recognize. That means that Captain Muldaur must have been holding on to a rope with all his strength whilst it slipped painfully from his grasp. Why? Remember the block outside the window, and the cleat on the floor under the bed, surely installed for the express purpose of leading a rope out the window and down to the street. Such a machine was no doubt intended to lift something up to the second story that could not be accommodated by the stairs, but it could also serve the reverse process of allowing something out of the window and down to the street. In short, it is precisely the device with which a man might inflict rope burns upon his hands were he to attempt to use it as an avenue of escape."

"Then how did he get outside the window?"

"Imagine the scene: it is late at night. Captain Muldaur has quarreled with Hero on the subject of the slave's freedom, which had been promised him but withdrawn when Muldaur learnt that a scion of Charles Treviscoe still lived. In anger Hero departs, knowing the captain is in danger from the Ephialtes of Belfast Lough and in his rage not caring, knowing also that the captain has no power to stop him if he chooses to go.

"Muldaur, however, is not insensitive to his circumstances, so before he retires, he hitches a line to the cleat, reeves it through the block, and coils the remaining length on the floor beneath the window so that he may defenestrate it given a moment's warning, thus giving him a means to withdraw from the confines of the room without having to force his way through the door and down the stairs.

"As he fears, the danger comes. He tosses out the line and swings into space, hoping to climb down the rope to a chance at safety. It is raining, and within minutes his nightshirt is drenched; that is why it was damp when I discovered the body.

"There must have been two, probably three, of the murderous scoundrels come into the chamber and one to stand lookout on the street below. They would not want to face Captain Muldaur—protected as they believe by the redoubtable Hero—without a substantial superiority of force. But Hero has gone out. And so they have a greater advantage than they expected. Once in the room they see that Muldaur is not there, nor Hero, but the window is open, rain is flinging itself inside, and a rope trails out into space. They go to the window and find Muldaur dangling like a spider, not halfway to the street.

"They pull the rope up as if to draw him in, but at the last moment, perhaps out of a sportive cruelty, they let it go, letting his weight pull it back down toward earth.

"No doubt they expected the shock of the impact to send him falling off when the rope reached its full length and strained against the cleat. But they've underestimated his strength and, though he slips several feet, he manages to hold on, but not without corresponding wounds to his hands. They pull him up again, enough so that the bitter end of the rope is too far above the street for Muldaur to safely descend. Then one of them gets an idea and calls to the lookout below to collect cobblestones and bring them up. The lookout runs up the stairs bearing the missiles. They pelt the captain's head with the stones, which attack he tries to fend off with one arm, then t'other, which tells how he received wounds to his head and arms but not to his body. Finally, exhausted by the struggle, wounded beyond endurance, and quite literally at the end of his rope, he loses his grip and falls, his leg breaking on the hard ground.

"The murderers do not want to leave his senseless body in the street, where it may attract the attention of a charlie on his rounds, so they tie the rope under his shoulders, haul him up, bruising his chest in the execution, and then remove and take away the rope to make it seem as if he had been attacked in his room. If he still lived then, it was not for long, as his wounds were too severe. That is how it was done."

"But surely the scene you describe is fantastic, Alan."

"How is it fantastic? It reconciles the facts, Magnus. It explains the burnt hands, the wet nightshirt, the bruising on the body's chest, the peculiar placement of the wounds on his head and arms, even the scattering of cobblestones at the threshold of the house. What *is* fantastic is that there is not a single soul in all that crowded alley who can recall such a spectacle. Such a failure of the senses is impossible.

"Tell me, Magnus, for you knew him: was Captain Muldaur the kind of man who would suffer such abuse in silence? He must have screamed with the fury of demons. And what about the clamor of the stones striking the side of the house and clattering on the street below, pounding like drums and thunder? How could Mrs. O'Reilly have slept through all that? It surpasses the imagination. She must have seen enough to know that Hero is innocent, or why else would she maintain such a stubborn silence about the details of the crime? Why else? Because on the way out the bravos let her know how it will be for her if she talks."

"How can you get Mrs. O'Reilly to testify?"

Treviscoe frowned. "As much as it disgusts me, if Hero is to avoid the gallows, there is no other way. I must somehow get the permission of Dr. Synge."

THE ROOM WAS dim. The man in a chair opposite Treviscoe looked like nothing so much as a fat hawk and wore a coat so long and wide it might have passed for a justaucorps from the days of the Stuarts. He wore an ornate ticwig powdered gray. Spectacles perched on his beaklike nose. He smiled gently.

"Mr. Treviscoe, I am honored by your request for this interview, but I hardly see how I can be of any assistance." The voice was soft, mellifluous, with more than a hint of Irish charm.

"Dr. Synge, I come on behalf of the prisoner Hero, late the property of Captain Ragnall Muldaur, deceased, and now awaiting trial for murder. I believe it is in your power to retrieve him from the gibbet."

"You have a flatteringly high opinion of a mere scholar, Mr. Treviscoe, if you think I can perform such a feat of legerdemain," replied Dr. Synge.

"And you must have a correspondingly low opinion of my perspicacity, doctor, if you expect me to believe it is not in your power to acquiesce in this matter. All that is required is that Mrs. O'Reilly be allowed to testify as to what she saw the night of Captain Muldaur's death. There are no names that need be mentioned and no prisoners besides Hero who are to be identified. Her testimony can in no way compromise your activities."

"You mystify me, Mr. Treviscoe."

"I think not, Dr. Synge. I beg you to recall my profession, which, to my knowledge, is unique in London if not the world. I expose frauds to the world for the benefit of compensation by assurance men who would otherwise lose fortunes. As you may be aware, I have met with considerable success in my endeavors. Normally, my fee is ten percent of the value of the insurance. In this case, however, I am prepared to perform the same service on my own behalf, and forgo remuneration, should Hero be hanged."

"I do not understand you."

"I believe you do."

There was silence.

Dr. Synge cleared his throat. "Am I correct in apprehending that you are threatening blackmail to some lawless personage? Blackmail is a crime itself, Mr. Treviscoe."

"I prefer to think of my words as a pledge of vengeance, Dr. Synge, even aware as I am that this entire episode is the result of reciprocal pledges of vengeance."

At length Dr. Synge sighed. "You are obviously a man of some courage, Mr. Treviscoe, to take upon yourself such a dangerous course of action. But as I understand your proposal, it would seem to me, speaking entirely as a philosopher, mind you, that Mrs. O'Reilly has no need for a commensurate courage simply to tell the truth in court, which is the duty of every loyal subject. Providing, as you assert, she cannot make any identifications of the miscreants you seem to believe she observed."

"There is also the matter of five hundred pounds' prize money, though some make it nearer a thousand—and a missing ear trumpet," said Treviscoe. "You may be unaware, Dr. Synge, that I am Captain Muldaur's heir, so that money and the ear trumpet are rightfully mine. I can understand why the murderers would steal the money, but the collection of the ear trumpet can only be attributed to someone wanting a most peculiar trophy."

"A trophy? Of what?" There was a smug amusement in Dr. Synge's voice.

"First, of the fell deed of murder," replied Treviscoe, "and second, perhaps to remind him of his satisfaction in doing an earlier injury to Muldaur many years ago in Belfast Lough. But I reckon these things—the money and the trumpet, I mean—are beyond recovery."

"No doubt," said Synge, his eyes narrowing.

"Then accept my gratitude, Dr. Synge. I am, of course, your servant." Treviscoe bowed with punctilious formality.

"Your servant, Mr. Treviscoe," Synge said stiffly, failing to rise. "Good afternoon."

"THE DEFENSE CALLS Mrs. Frances O'Reilly."

She was all nerves. Sir Richard questioned her gently, and bit by bit the description of the murder that Treviscoe had given

Captain Gunn was confirmed. As she gave her testimony, she became progressively agitated. Sensing she would not long continue to give helpful evidence, Sir Richard ended his questioning after she described how Muldaur's body was hoisted back to his room.

It was now the turn of Mr. Juddson.

"Mrs. O'Reilly, can you explain to the court why you did not come forward with this amazing and incredible story whilst the prisoner, whom you describe as an innocent man, languished in prison?"

"Which I was afraid to, sir," she responded, gripping the rail before her as though to let go would send her plummeting to death like Muldaur.

"Afraid? Afraid of what, or of whom?"

"I can't say, sir, don't ask me to say. I am not allowed, sir. He said I could tell the truth as I saw it, but there was to be no names, sir."

"Do you then refuse to answer?"

"I can't, sir, I can't—"

"Are you aware of the penalty for perjury, Mrs. O'Reilly?" Juddson thundered.

"Objection! The witness cannot have perjured herself by refusing to answer."

"Perjury?" Mrs. O'Reilly laughed, on the edge of hysteria. "What's perjury to a creature like himself? The very devil's own spawn is Dr. Synge."

Sir Richard engaged in a loud debate with his learned colleague, and Mrs. O'Reilly collapsed, howling and weeping, and had to be led off the stand by the bailiff. Hidden in the gallery a bespectacled man of raptorial aspect frowned deeply. Drawing his enormous and richly decorated coat around his broad girth and pulling his fine beaver tricorn over his eyes, he made a quiet exit.

"HAVE THE JURY reached a verdict?"

"We have, m'lord. We find the prisoner, Hero the African, not guilty of the crime of murder."

"The prisoner is free to go. This court is adjourned."

The gavel smacked down.

ON FLEET STREET Treviscoe and Hero walked together away from the Old Bailey. "You are a free man, now, Hero, in every sense of the word. What do you intend to do with your liberty?"

"'Tis a condition so long dreamt of that I hardly can believe it is a reality, Mr. Treviscoe. I suppose I shall enter service, for in Barbados I was a house slave before Captain Muldaur bought me away from my master. Aside from the ring it is the only trade I know."

"Then take my hand, Hero, and with it my best wishes."

"My thanks to you, sir," said Hero, seizing Treviscoe's hand with both his own. Powerful emotions played across his face, but before another word could be said, he turned and walked swiftly away.

IT WAS LATE in the evening when Alan Treviscoe went home. The street lamps on the houses were well lit. But there were shadows enough to hide the three men who lay in wait for him.

They were large enough to be chair-men by day but at night they had less honest employment. They bore no weapons but their fists, which were curled tight into cudgels of flesh and bone. They bore down upon their victim in a rush.

Treviscoe was reaching for his smallsword when he was grabbed by a fourth man from behind. The sword was pulled from its sheath by one of the bravos and clattered on the pavement.

"'Ere's summat to remember us by—remembering there was to be no *names*—" sneered the leader, swinging his massive fist into Treviscoe's stomach.

Treviscoe doubled with pain, only to be struck in the face. Colors obscured his vision, and his ears rang as he was slammed again.

He dropped to the pavement, and then he heard cursing. He lifted his head and saw a blurred figure strike his assailant with the suddenness of a blacksmith's hammer, then swiftly withdraw and engage the next tough with the same powerful stroke.

Heads snapped back, and Treviscoe imagined he was back at the boxing match, watching Hero demolish Butcher Bill. He vaguely heard the crack of yielding bones and cries of pain. The altercation was short-lived, however, and he next heard running footsteps fading away.

He felt hands under his shoulders, and he was lifted to his feet. Hero picked up the smallsword from the ground and presented it to him hilt first. "Let's be going now, sir," said Hero urgently, leading him up the stairs.

"Thank you, Hero—"

"'Tis only just, sir," said Hero.

They struggled to the door of Treviscoe's room. Hero sat him on the bed and helped him lie down.

"I'll just fetch the apothecary, sir."

"I will be all right—"

"That is God's truth, Mr. Treviscoe. I'll see to that."

Treviscoe shook his head. Waves of pain surged through him. "I cannot afford a manservant, Hero."

Hero laughed. "I think you can't afford otherwise, in your line of work, sir. And 'tis certain you won't find a better man than me for this kind of task."

"Perhaps so. My head!"

"I'll be off then, sir. Not to worry, won't be but a moment."

"Yes, all right. I will lie here quietly till you fetch the apothecary."

"That's as it should be, sir." Hero noiselessly shut the door behind him.

And things were as they should be, reflected Treviscoe. Things were exactly as they should be, except for Dr. Synge. But Dr. Synge was sure to have fled London, dodging his debts and the law alike, before daybreak.

Magnus Gunn came to attend Treviscoe the next morning.

"I have often thought that there is never so dangerous a course as to injure a proud man's honor," said Gunn. "I am fair amazed at the lengths Captain Muldaur resorted to so that he might reclaim his own."

"But it cannot have been honor, Magnus," said Treviscoe. "'Twas pride and hatred. It were to satisfy honor if Captain Muldaur had challenged Dr. Synge to a duel and kept the combat between them. Instead he saw fit to involve a slave, a man without recourse to his own will, and submit him to the indignities of bondage and the boxing ring, and even to renege on a promise of manumission so his pride might be salved through an act of vengeance. I cannot call that honorable behavior."

"But Hero is free at last."

Treviscoe nodded.

"Yes, there is that. I do not think that a man of his parts will long be satisfied to submit to a life of service, having so recently gained his liberty. Yet he is old to 'prentice to any trade."

"He has skills you may find useful in your profession, Alan. It may be just the calling for him."

At that moment Hero entered the room. "I have just been to Lloyd's, sir, to collect your correspondence," he said. "When it became known I was acting on your behalf, a gentleman made so bold as to ask if you might entertain a proposal for a commission."

"Indeed?"

"Yes, sir. It seems there may be some question as to the confidentiality of maritime reports arriving on the Plymouth post coach."

Treviscoe exchanged a meaningful glance with Captain Gunn. He sat up and said quietly, "Tell me more, Hero. There may be work for us here."

STEVE HOCKENSMITH

ERIE'S LAST DAY

May 2000

"ERIE'S LAST DAY" was Steve Hockensmith's entry into the mystery field, and the start of a series of stories featuring the depressive ex-cop Larry Erie and his more upbeat pal Bass. A former editor of *The X-Files Official Magazine* and *Cinescape*, Hockensmith created a column for *AHMM* devoted to crime television and movies called "Reel Crime." In 2006 he published his first novel, *Holmes on the Range*, about a couple of ranch hands who share an addiction to Sherlock Holmes stories in *Harper's Weekly*.

■

7:00 A.M.

The radio alarm by Larry Erie's queen-sized bed turned itself on. A deep-voiced announcer began telling Erie about the morning's top stories. Erie didn't really care what the morning's top stories might be, but he lay there for a while and let the announcer ramble.

There was nobody there to give him a playful kick and tell him to shut that noise off. There was nobody there to make breakfast for. There was nobody there to fetch pills for. It was just him and the announcer.

7:19 A.M.

ERIE FINALLY PULLED himself out of bed and went out to the porch in his pajamas and robe to pick up the morning paper. It was cool outside, just like the cheerful people on the radio said it would be. A storm passing through in the night had left puddles on the pavement.

He scanned the yard for the little black shape that sometimes came bounding up to him from behind shrubs or garbage cans, meowing greetings at him as if he were a long-lost relative. But the cat wasn't there. Erie went back inside.

He ate breakfast sitting on the edge of the bed. It was a habit he couldn't drop even though there was no longer anyone there to keep company.

7:42 A.M.

ERIE SHOWERED, shaved, flossed, brushed, gargled, rinsed, and repeated. Then he carefully picked out his clothes. He pulled on his best white shirt, his best suit, his favorite tie. He shined his shoes before putting them on. He looked at himself in the mirror, straightened his tie, smoothed a few errant hairs into place. Then he pulled his gun off the bureau and clipped it onto his belt.

Some cops started to get a little sloppy years before they retired. Others waited till just a few months or weeks before their last day to start letting themselves go. Erie remembered one cop, a fellow detective, who came in for his last day in a Hawaiian shirt and bermuda shorts. It gave everybody a good laugh.

But that wasn't Erie's way. He was determined to make every day of his time on the force count. Even his last.

8:07 A.M.

ERIE WAS REACHING out to open his car door when he heard the cat. She was hurrying up the driveway toward him, meowing loudly. He knelt and stretched out his right arm. As always, the cat rubbed her face on his hand several times before flopping over on her back and stretching out her legs. He rubbed her stomach. Her fur was long and matted.

"How do you like that, buddy? How do you like that?" Erie asked the cat.

The cat purred.

Erie had never owned a cat, never really known a cat, never been interested in them. He had no idea how old the little black cat was. She'd been hanging around the neighborhood about a month. She had grown noticeably bigger since he'd first seen her. She had also become friendlier. She wore no collar or tags.

Occasionally Erie had found himself worrying about the cat. Where was she sleeping? What was she eating? He'd seen her once over by Green River Road, and the thought of her trying to cross busy streets had haunted him for hours.

But Erie always reminded himself that he wasn't a cat person. And he had bigger things to worry about than dumb animals.

"That's enough for today," he told the cat as he stood up. She rolled over on her stomach and looked up at him expectantly. "Nope. No more. So long."

He climbed into his car and started the engine. He backed out of the driveway slowly, keeping an eye on the cat lest she jump up and dart under the tires. But she stayed where she was, watching him, seemingly puzzled by his desire to leave this perfectly wonderful driveway and this perfectly wonderful cat.

8:33 A.M.

ON HIS WAY into police headquarters from the parking lot, Erie was stopped by three cops. They were all men he hadn't seen or spoken to in the last week. Each one stopped him separately and said the same thing.

"I'm sorry about your wife."

Erie said the only thing he could: "Thanks."

On his way past the human resources office a female coworker called out, "Look who's early! Hey, Larry, don't you know you're not supposed to come in before noon on your last day!"

"The early bird catches the worm," Erie said.

A uniformed officer stopped as she passed. "You don't have to worry about catching worms anymore, Detective Erie. You just head down to Arizona and catch some sun. Leave the worms to us."

8:45 A.M.

ERIE HAD ALREADY cleaned out his office, for the most part. The walls were bare, his desktop was free of clutter, the drawers were practically empty aside from a few stray pens and paper clips and leftover forms. So it was impossible to miss the yellow Post-it note stuck to the exact center of his desktop. It was from Hal Allen, director of Detective Services/Homicide—his boss. The note read, "See me in my office ASAP." Erie hoped it was a special assignment, a favor he could do for Allen or the department, something that would draw on his decades of experience, something that would make his last eight hours as a police officer count.

8:48 A.M.

ERIE KNEW he was in trouble the second he stepped into the office of May Davis, Allen's administrative assistant and official gatekeeper. He'd walked into a trap, and there was no way out.

Twenty people were crammed behind Davis's desk. Behind them was a banner reading WE'LL MISS YOU, BIG GUY! On it were dozens of signatures surrounded by drawings of handcuffs and police badges and men in striped prison uniforms. The people waiting for him, the entire Homicide Division reinforced by a couple of evidence technicians and some of his old buddies from other departments, began singing "For He's a Jolly Good Fellow."

Erie stood there, smiling dutifully, and took it like a man.

9:09 A.M.

ERIE ENDURED THE song and the hugs and the slaps on the back and the vanilla cake with the outline of Arizona in orange frosting. He endured Allen's speech about thirty-three years of service and one hundred twelve murderers behind bars. He endured it all without ever saying, "What about those twenty-nine *unsolved* murders?" or "Why would I move to Arizona without Nancy?"

And after the ordeal was over and the revelers had all drifted away, it became clear that he was supposed to drift away, too. There were forms to fill out and drawers to empty, right? Instead, he asked Hal Allen if they could step into his office.

"What's on your mind, Larry?"

Allen was a different breed of cop. He was younger than Erie. He worked out every day. His walls weren't covered with pictures of his kids or newspaper articles about his big busts. He had his degrees—a BA in criminal justice, a master's in psychology—and inspirational posters about Leadership and Goals. For him, being a cop wasn't a calling, it was a career choice. But Erie liked him and hoped he would understand.

"I was wondering if I could take back one of my cases."

"Come on, Larry," Allen said. "You're going to have to let go."

"Just for today, Hal. I just want to make some inquiries, see if I can get the ball rolling again. At the end of the day I'll turn it back over to Dave Rogers with a full briefing."

Allen shook his head, grinning. "I've heard of this condition. It's called dedication to duty. We're going to have to cure you of it. I prescribe a day playing computer solitaire followed by a much-deserved early retirement in beautiful, sunny Arizona."

"Nancy liked Arizona, Hal. We were moving there for her."

"Oh." The smile melted off Allen's face. "So you're not—"

"I don't know. We hadn't signed anything yet when Nancy took that last turn for the worse. I'm not sure I want to leave Indiana. I've lived here all my life." Erie shifted nervously in his seat. "But that's neither here nor there. I'm just asking for one more day to protect and serve."

Allen leaned forward in his swivel chair and gave Erie a long, thoughtful look as if really seeing him for the first time. "You're not going to solve your one hundred thirteenth homicide today, Larry. You're just going to end up chasing around stone-cold leads and getting nowhere."

"I love days like that."

Allen nodded. "Okay. Do what you have to do. But drop by my office before you go home tonight. I want to talk to you again."

Erie practically jumped up from his chair. For the first time that day he actually felt awake.

"Yes, sir," he said. "Anything you say."

9:31 A.M.

DETECTIVE DAVID ROGERS was on the phone when Erie appeared in the doorway to his office. Rogers waved him in, said, "No problem," and hung up. "The boss says you want to catch a bad guy today," he said.

"I just want to borrow back one of my cases. Is that okay with you?"

Rogers smiled and pointed at a stack of bound folders on one corner of his desk. "Pick your poison," he said. "If you insist on working your last day, I'm not going to stop you."

Erie shuffled through the case files. Did he want the fifteen-year-old crack dealer, four months dead? The unidentified, twenty-something woman found in the woods of Lloyd Park, six months dead? Or the middle-aged insurance salesman, ten months dead?

Lifeless eyes stared up at him from Polaroids paper-clipped to Xeroxed autopsy reports. They looked inside him, told him, "Do something. Avenge me. Avenge *me.*"

But justice isn't for the dead. That was one of the things he had learned in his years working homicide. It's no use fighting a crusade for a corpse. It will still be a corpse even if somebody turns its killer into a corpse, too. But the family, the loved ones, *the living*—they can be helped.

He chose a file and left.

10:07 A.M.

UNLIKE MOST OF the older, lower-middle-class neighborhoods around town, Pine Hills actually lived up to its name. It had both pines and hills, though not many of either. It also had a reputation among Erie's fellow cops for producing wild kids. On Halloween night, patrol cars cruised through the neighborhood as if it were Compton or Watts, and EMT crews waited on stand-by for the inevitable wounds from bottle rockets, M-80s, broken glass, and exploding mailboxes.

O'Hara Drive was a short, crooked, sloping street in the heart of the neighborhood. It was all of one block long, bracketed on each side by longer streets that curved up to the neighborhood's highest hills. From the top of one you could see the airport just a mile away. From the other you could see the county dump.

The house at 1701 O'Hara Drive wasn't just where Joel Korfmann, insurance salesman, had lived. It was where he had died, too. There were two vehicles in the driveway when Erie arrived—a silver, mid-'90s model Ford Taurus and a newer Ford pickup, red. The Taurus he remembered.

He parked at the curb and walked toward the house. All the curtains had been drawn shut. A big plastic trash can lay on its side near the foot of the driveway.

He rang the doorbell. And waited. He knocked on the rickety metal of the screen door. The curtains in the front window fluttered, and a woman's face hovered in the shadows beyond. Erie tried to smile reassuringly. He pulled out his badge.

"It's Detective Erie, Mrs. Korfmann."

The face disappeared. Erie waited again. Finally the front door opened. The screen door in front of it remained closed.

All the lights of the house were off. Candace Korfmann stood back from the door, away from the sunlight. "Hello."

"Hello, Mrs. Korfmann. I'm just dropping by this morning to ask a few followup questions. Is now a good time to talk?"

"Sure," she replied lifelessly. She was dressed in a bathrobe. Erie recalled that she was what people used to call a housewife or homemaker. She didn't have a job to give her life focus again after her husband died. And she didn't have any children to keep her busy, keep her mind from dwelling on the past, on what had happened in her own kitchen. He pictured her brooding in the darkness of the little white house all day every day, alone.

"Good," Erie said. "First off, I'm afraid I have to tell you that we haven't uncovered any new leads. But we're putting a new investigator on the case next week, Detective David Rogers. So don't lose hope, Mrs. Korfmann. He's a good man."

After a moment's pause she nodded. "Okay, I won't."

"Good. Now, second, I was wondering if there was anything new you could tell me—any new memories or thoughts you've had that might help our investigation."

Mrs. Korfmann stared at him impassively. Standing in the shadows, perfectly still, she looked flat, one-dimensional, like the mere outline of a woman. Her shape—the slumped shoulders and tousled hair and slightly tilted head—reminded him of Nancy toward the end, when she was so weak she could barely stand.

"It could be anything, even just a rumor going around the neighborhood," he prompted. "Every little bit helps, Mrs. Korfmann."

She shook her head slowly. "I don't know what to tell you. I haven't heard a thing."

"That's okay. No reason you should do our job for us. I have just one more thing to talk to you about." He pulled a card from his jacket pocket. "I'd like to give you this. It's the number of a woman I know. She runs a group for . . . those who've been left behind. A survivor support group. You might want to give her a call."

Mrs. Korfmann didn't move for a long moment. Then she opened the door and reached out to take the card. As she leaned into the light, Erie could see that her skin was pale, her eyes hollow. He noticed a slight swelling in her lower lip and a dark, bluish smudge of bruised flesh under her left eye.

"Thanks," she said.

"Sure. You take care now, Mrs. Korfmann."

She nodded, then closed the door.

10:24 A.M.

ERIE STARTED his car. The digital clock on the dashboard came to life. Not even an hour back on the Korfmann case, and already he was done. He had driven across town just to stir up painful memories for a sad and lonely woman. There was nothing to do now but head back to the office and shoot the breeze with whoever he could find lounging around. Reminisce about the good old days, trot out old stories and legends, do nothing. Then go home.

He shut off the ignition and got out of the car. He walked to the house across from 1701 O'Hara Drive and rang the doorbell. An old man opened the door. He was wearing glasses so thick Erie couldn't see his eyes, just big, shimmering ovals of pale blue.

"Yes?"

Erie took out his badge. "Good morning, Mr. Wallender. I'm Detective Erie. You and I spoke about ten months ago."

The old man bent forward to peer at the badge. "Of course I remember you, detective. Come on in." He shuffled ahead of Erie into the next room. "You have a seat there and I'll get some coffee." He disappeared around a corner. "I've got some on the stove. Every day I make a pot of coffee and drink two cups. I don't know why I keep doing that. I pour more coffee down the drain in a morning than most people drink in a week." Erie could hear cabinet doors and drawers opening and closing, porcelain sliding over countertops, the hum of an open refrigerator.

"I'll just take mine black, Mr. Wallender," he called.

"Have you arrested Joel Korfmann's killer yet?"

"Not yet. That's why I'm here. I'm making a few followup inquiries."

Wallender shuffled into the living room with a mug in each hand. He gave one to Erie. The liquid in it had the telltale hue of coffee with skim milk. Erie didn't take a sip.

"I was wondering if you'd heard or seen anything else that might have a bearing on the case."

Wallender lowered himself slowly into a recliner. "I've been keeping my eye on the neighborhood kids. They're always planning some kind of prank. I called the police a couple of months ago. Thought I saw a boy with some dynamite. A policeman came out. Do you know an Officer Pyke?"

"Yes, I do." The old man's vision and hearing might be shaky, but his memory was fine. "Have you spoken to Mrs. Korfmann at all? Do you know how she's doing?"

Wallender brought his mug to his lips, his hands trembling badly.

"She kind of dropped out of sight for a while there. I figured she went to be with her family or some such," the old man said. "She was gone maybe two months. When she came back, she seemed to be doing fine. I took it upon myself to drop in and chat with her from time to time."

"And her state of mind seemed good?"

Wallender shrugged. "Far as I could tell. They were always standoffish people, her and her husband both. She seemed a little friendlier for a while there, but then her young man began hanging around and she was the same old Candace again."

"Her young man? You mean she has a boyfriend?"

"I guess you could call him that, seeing as how his truck's there most nights."

"And how long has this been going on?"

"Maybe two months, maybe a little longer." Wallender's thin, trembling lips curled into a sly smile.

"Now, don't go thinking evil thoughts, Detective Erie. She needed a man around, so she found one. It's understandable. People get lonely. I know a little something about that. It's not easy living alone."

Erie tried to smile back but found he couldn't. His mouth, his whole face, felt stiff, dead. "I'm not thinking evil thoughts, Mr. Wallender. I'm just curious. That's my job."

"Sure, sure. I understand. I guess I'm curious, too. Except when it's a neighbor being curious, people call it nosy."

"Have you ever spoken to Mrs. Korfmann's young man?"

"Well, I've tried. He's not a very talkative fella. I've been over to chat once or twice when I noticed him out working on his truck. He didn't have a lot to say. Actually, he reminds me a lot of Joel—Mr. Korfmann."

"Did you happen to catch his name?"

"Ray. He didn't mention his last name. He works over at DeRogatis Ford as a mechanic." The old man grinned again. "That's all I got out of him, chief. If you want me to try again, maybe I could get his Social Security number for you."

Erie finally found himself able to smile back. "You're a real character, Mr. Wallender."

"I certainly am," the old man said with obvious pride. "I just wish more people knew it."

10:43 A.M.

ERIE WAS BACK in his car, faced again with the drive to the station, spending the afternoon killing time, the evening killing time, the weekend killing time, the years killing time until time finally killed him.

He thought about Candace Korfmann. Her dead-eyed stare, the way she had stayed away from the light, the black eye. He tried not to think evil thoughts about Ray. But he couldn't stop himself. Good cops and social workers can smell abuse a mile away, and Erie had caught a whiff of something in the air around 1701 O'Hara Drive. Maybe he couldn't catch a killer in one day, but he sure as hell could sniff out a woman-beater. What he would do about it, he wasn't sure.

He started his car and put it in gear. As he pulled away from the curb, he noticed movement in one of the windows of the Korfmann house—a dark shape quickly replaced by the swaying of a blind. Someone had been watching him.

He drove to the intersection of Oak Hill Road and Highway 41, home of DeRogatis Ford.

11:10 A.M.

A SALESMAN SWOOPED down on Erie before he could step out of his car.

"Good afternoon there! What can I help you with today?"

Erie flipped out his badge. "I'd like to have a word with whoever runs your mechanics shop."

Sweat instantly materialized on the salesman's forehead.

"Don't worry. I'm just making a routine inquiry."

The salesman still looked panic-stricken.

"It has nothing to do with DeRogatis Ford," Erie added. "I'm trying to locate someone who may be an employee. He's not in any trouble. Like I said, it's very routine."

The salesman nodded and gave Erie an unconvincing smile. "Sure, officer. We're always happy to help River City's finest. Right this way."

The salesman led him through the showroom to a bustling garage. About eight cars were being worked on, some with their hoods up, some on hydraulic lifts. Off to the side customers lounged in a waiting room watching *The Jerry Springer Show.* The salesman pointed out a short, middle-aged Asian man leaning over an Escort's engine.

"That's Frank Takarada. He runs things back here." The salesman slipped a business card out of his shirt pocket. "If you ever want to talk cars, I'm your man. I'm here Tuesday through Saturday." He shook Erie's hand and hustled away.

Erie pocketed the card and headed toward Takarada. The mechanic noticed his approach and eyed him warily.

"Mr. Takarada, could I have a word with you, please?"

"I'm very busy. Maybe later."

Sometimes the badge-flash routine got quick results, sometimes—especially in public places when plenty of people were around—it just irritated or embarrassed people. Takarada looked like the irritable type. Erie leaned close and lowered his voice. "I'm a police detective, Mr. Takarada. I promise that I only need five minutes of your time. Do you have an office where we can speak?"

Takarada pulled a greasy rag out of one pocket and began wiping off his hands. "Come on," he grunted. He led Erie to a back corner of the garage. Auto parts in plastic bags hung from pegs on a large partition. Takarada stepped around it. Erie followed, finding a makeshift office complete with desk, computer terminal, fan, and filing cabinets covered with crinkled paperwork. A large board studded with pegs hung on the wall. Car keys dangled from the pegs.

"So what do you want?" Takarada said.

"I'd like to know if you have a mechanic here by the name of Ray or Raymond."

"Nope."

Erie felt foolish. He had followed up a blind hunch, something that had nothing to do with his job, based on the memory of a doddering old recluse. He was about to apologize and leave when Takarada spoke again.

"Not anymore. Had one a few months ago, though. Ray Long."

"What happened?"

"We had to let him go," Takarada said with mock gentility. He didn't volunteer anything further.

"This is off the record, Mr. Takarada. Just between you and me. You can be plainspoken."

"Okay," said Takarada, who seemed glad to have permission to be blunt. "He's an ass. Always was. I put up with him for two years and then—" He mimed dropping a ball and punting it.

"When was this?"

"Six weeks, maybe two months ago, something like that."

"What happened?"

"Instead of being late once or twice a week, he was late every day. Instead of being hungover some of the time, he was hungover all of the time."

"How did he react when you fired him?"

Takarada laughed bitterly. "Typical macho b.s." His voice suddenly took on a Southern Indiana twang. "'Oh yeah, man? Well, I don't need this stupid job, anyway! I'm set up, man! So screw you!'"

Erie's fingers and toes began to tingle the way they always did when he sensed a break. He forced himself to relax before he spoke again. "He said, 'I'm set up'?"

"Something like that, yeah."

"Can you tell me if a Candace Korfmann had her car serviced in this shop in the last few months? She drives a silver Taurus, looks like a '95 or '96."

The mechanic looked annoyed. "I'd have to look that up."

"I would appreciate that, Mr. Takarada. It's very important."

Takarada sighed heavily. "How do you spell that?" He walked back to the computer terminal and took a seat.

Erie's mind was racing ahead of Takarada as he typed. The dealership's records would show that Candace Korfmann had brought her car in about two months ago, maybe three. Raymond Long had worked on the car. He had noticed her waiting—she wasn't an unattractive woman. He took her over to show her something, began flirting. He could sense that she was vulnerable. He got her to agree to a date. He found out she was a widow. Her husband had been an insurance agent. She had received a large amount of money upon his death. Raymond Long saw an opportunity. He wormed his way into her heart, then her home. Now he thought he ran the show. Erie would figure out a way to prove him wrong.

"Yeah, we've got a Candace Korfmann in here. Drives a 1995 Taurus, like you said."

"Does it show who worked on her car last?"

"Sure. Got the initials right here. 'R. L.'"

Erie nodded with satisfaction. "Raymond Long. This was around June or July?"

"Not even close."

"What?"

Takarada turned away from the computer. "Try May—of last year."

Erie stared at the mechanic blankly, his mind racing. His pet theory was blown.

Within seconds another one started to take its place.

He gestured at the key rack on the wall. "These are for the cars you're working on?"

"And the ones waiting out back, yeah."

"You ever work on vans here?"

Takarada shrugged. "Sure, every now and then."

Erie mulled that over for a moment. "Anything else?" Takarada was obviously anxious to get back to work.

"If you could print that out for me, I'd appreciate it." Before Takarada could groan or sigh or roll his eyes, Erie added, "Then I'll be leaving. You've been a big help. Thanks."

Takarada started to swivel back to the keyboard, then stopped himself. "So, can you tell me? Is Long in some kind of trouble?"

Erie gave the safe cop answer: "No, this is just a routine inquiry." But he knew trouble was headed Raymond Long's way. Erie hoped to deliver it himself before the day was over.

11:44 A.M.

ERIE ATE LUNCH at a Denny's across the street from the Ford dealership. A few too many people were probably expecting him to drop by Peppy's, the diner around the corner from police headquarters. But he wanted a chance to think.

His turkey club and fries went down untasted. The file on Joel Korfmann's murder was spread across the table before him.

Erie was pleased to see that the report was neat, thorough, precise. He'd put it together himself months before.

On New Year's Eve, at approximately nine fifteen P.M., Joel Korfmann had been bludgeoned to death in his home. The victim, age forty-one, was a Lutheran Family Insurance representative who had spent the day making calls on potential customers. In the evening he had been at the office doing paperwork. (In parentheses after this information were the words "Indicative of victim's character?" Those were code words. What they meant was, "What kind of jerk makes cold calls selling insurance on New Year's Eve? Then spends the evening doing paperwork when he could be with family and friends?") Security surveillance tapes showed that he left work at eight forty-three P.M. It would have taken him about half an hour to drive home.

The victim's wife, Candace Lane Korfmann, age thirty-eight, spent the evening with her sister, Carol Lane Biggs, and brother-in-law, Rudy Biggs. Witnesses placed them at the Dew Drop Inn on Division Street from eight thirty P.M. until approximately twelve thirty A.M.

Carol and Rudy Biggs drove Candace Korfmann home, arriving at twelve fifty-five. All three entered the house. Mrs. Korfmann immediately noticed that several items—a GoldStar television, a Sony VCR, a Sony stereo—were missing. In the kitchen Rudy Biggs discovered the body of Joel Korfmann. He had been hit from behind by a large, heavy object. Forensics later concluded that he had been hit five times with the butt of his own shotgun, which was also reported missing.

Most of the Korfmanns' neighbors had been away for the evening celebrating the holiday. But a James Wallender, an elderly man who lived by himself across the street, reported seeing a dark van parked on the street near the house at approximately eight thirty P.M. Later, Wallender said, he saw it in the Korfmanns' driveway. (In parentheses here: "Witness seems anxious to help investigation." That was Erie's way of hinting that the old man might not be the most reliable witness. Sometimes lonely people were so eager to please they would "remember" things they'd never seen.)

The report concluded that the victim had surprised someone in the house—an individual or individuals in the process of burglarizing it. Seeing the house dark on a holiday, the perpetrators must have assumed the residents were out of town or would be out all night partying. It was a common scenario.

There had been no evidence when Erie had written his report. There were no fingerprints, no hairs, no tire tracks that could be linked to the crime, and the stolen items had never surfaced. And that hadn't changed. Erie still had no evidence. But he did have something new—a hunch.

Driving back to headquarters after lunch, his mind dwelled on Raymond Long. He pictured him as a young long-haired redneck with muscular arms and fiery eyes. He pictured him killing Joel Korfmann. He pictured him beating Candace Korfmann, finally killing her in a rage—or just because it suited him.

He saw it all, crystal clear in his mind. Long the manipulator, Long the killer. Joel and Candace Korfmann, the victims.

The only thing that interrupted these thoughts was a stray one that crept in from another part of his brain as he maneuvered through afternoon traffic. It was the image of cars and trucks whipping up and down Green River Road, leaving roadkill behind them on the asphalt, on the side of the road, tumbling into ditches. He hoped the little black cat was safe.

1:10 P.M.

AT HEADQUARTERS ERIE checked to see if "Long, Raymond" had a criminal record. He wasn't disappointed. There were three charges of disturbing the peace, two charges of battery, two disorderly conducts, one assault, and the inevitable DWI and resisting arrest. Over the years he had served a grand total of fifteen months in the Vanderburgh County lockup.

The pictures came as a surprise, though. Long was thirty-seven, and he looked every day of it. He was balding, pug-nosed, and jowly. He didn't look like the kind of handsome young devil who could charm a vulnerable widow—or widow-to-be. Erie assumed he was one hell of a talker.

Erie went back to his office (accepting a number of hand-shakes and pats on the back on the way) and began calling all the U-Stor-Its and Storage Lands in town. The people he spoke with knew him, knew what he was looking for, knew the drill, but they couldn't help. No, they hadn't rented space to a Raymond Long in the last year. Yes, they'd give him a call if a Raymond Long came in.

After saying "Thanks, have a good one" for the eighth time, Erie hung up the phone and left his office. It was time to have a talk with Raymond Long.

2:17 P.M.

THERE WAS SOMETHING different at 1701 O'Hara Drive when Erie pulled up. He walked toward the house slowly, trying to pin down what it was.

The curtains were still drawn shut. The Taurus and the pickup were still parked out front. The trash can still lay on its side in the yard.

He was walking up the driveway past the pickup when he realized what it was. The truck was splattered with mud—mud that hadn't been there that morning. Erie crossed the street and rang James Wallender's doorbell.

"Hello there, chief," the old man said as he opened the door. "I was wondering if you'd come back again. Why don't you come in?"

"I'm sorry, Mr. Wallender, I don't have time to visit right now. I just wanted to ask if you'd seen any activity at the Korfmann house today."

"Well, I might have peeked out the window a time or two since you were here." Wallender winked. "Hold on a minute." He shuf-fled away, then returned a moment later with a small notepad clutched in one trembling hand. "You left here at approximately ten forty-five A.M. Around eleven that fella Ray pulled his truck into the garage and brought the garage door down. At eleven twenty he drove out again and was gone for a while."

"Was there anything in the pickup when he left?"

"Yeah. Something big and green."

"Green?"

Wallender checked his notepad. "Yes, green. At least that's what it looked like to me." He tapped his eyeglasses. "I have to look at everything through these Coke bottles."

"Could it have been a tarp thrown over something in the back of the truck?"

Wallender nodded. "Sure, it could have been."

"And how long was Ray gone?"

Wallender looked at his notepad again. "Forty-five minutes."

Erie extended a hand. Wallender shook it. "Mr. Wallender, by the power vested in me by the state of Indiana, I hereby declare you a junior G-man."

Wallender smiled. "I always said I wanted to be a detective when I grew up."

3:10 P.M.

THE SHOES ERIE had shined so carefully that morning were now covered with mud, coffee grounds, and mysterious flecks of filth. His trousers were similarly splattered, and there was a new rip where a piece of jagged metal had snagged his pants leg. Even his tie was beginning to smell bad.

Early on, there had been two other scavengers, a heavyset couple with prodigious guts spilling out from under their dirty T-shirts. They'd seen him—a well-dressed, middle-aged man picking through piles of garbage at the county dump—and stared as if he were some exotic, dangerous animal pacing back and forth in a cage at the zoo. They kept their distance, eventually driving off in a beat-up station wagon loaded with discarded toys and clothes and broken appliances.

Erie told himself he'd only look for another half hour. If he couldn't find anything, he'd head back down to Pine Hills and have that talk with Raymond Long. Not that he was going to make much of an impression in his current condition. Maybe after another thirty minutes wading through garbage he would smell so putrid Long would confess just to get away from him.

The ridiculousness of it made him long for Nancy. He wanted to go home and tell her everything that had happened. He couldn't even tell if his last day had been sad, funny, triumphant, or disastrous without her face to gauge it by.

From off in the distance came the popping and clicking of tires rolling over gravel. More scavengers were headed up the winding back road to the dump. Erie was going to be on exhibit again. He thought about abandoning his crazy theory and just going home for a nice long bath.

And then he found it. It was underneath a big flattened-out cardboard box, the kind washing machines are delivered in. A GoldStar TV. The screen had been broken in and the plastic cracked on top, but it was relatively free of mud and grime. Erie checked the back. Even though someone had made a halfhearted effort to bust up the television and make it look old, they hadn't bothered scratching off the serial number.

Erie tore into the nearest pile of garbage, tossing trash bags and boxes aside with manic energy. At the bottom he found a Sony VCR, the top crushed as if someone had jumped on top of it. He picked it up and looked at the back. Again, the serial number was still there.

It only took him another minute of digging to find the stereo. It was nearby, underneath a pile of newspapers. It had hardly been damaged at all. There was still a serial number on the back.

That left just one item—the most important of all. Once he found that, he could call in the evidence techs to dust everything for prints and look for tracks that matched the tires on Raymond Long's truck. The tracks would have to be nearby. Erie turned around to look.

Raymond Long was walking toward him. "Is this what you're looking for?" he said.

He was holding a shotgun. It was pointed at Erie. His finger was on the trigger.

In the time it took Long to take two more steps Erie had considered five different options: dive and roll and draw his gun; charge Long and go for the shotgun; put up his hands and feign ignorance; put up his hands and try to talk Long into surrendering; run like crazy. Those few seconds were all Erie needed to realize that all his options stank. But he picked one anyway. He put up his hands and started talking.

"Don't do anything dumb, Ray. A lot of people know where I am. If anything happens to me, they're going to know exactly who to point the finger at."

Long stopped about seven yards from Erie. At that range there was little doubt what outcome a shotgun blast would have.

"Yeah, well, maybe by the time they're pointing fingers, I'll be hundreds of miles away." His voice was full of spiteful good ol' boy bravado. But Erie could see the sweat shining on his face, the damp rings that were spreading under the armpits of his T-shirt.

Erie shook his head. "You won't make it. Wherever you try to go. Cop killers never get away. Other cops take it too personally. You'll end up right back in Indiana facing a capital murder charge."

"Don't you mean *two* capital murder charges?" Long sneered. He had a good face for sneering. It looked like he'd done a lot of practicing over the years.

"You should stop talking, Ray. You should put down the shotgun and let me take you in. That's what a lawyer would tell you to do. You haven't crossed the line yet—you haven't doomed yourself. If you put the gun down now, this could all still work out for you and Candace."

Erie knew instantly that he'd made a mistake. As soon as he'd said Candace, Long's sneer had turned into a scowl of rage. Erie had pushed the wrong button. Now he had to get out of the way.

Erie threw himself to the left, twisting in mid-flight so he'd take most of the buckshot in the back, buttocks, or legs instead of the face and chest. There was a boom, and a searing pain lanced his side. But it wasn't bad enough to stop him. He rolled over and came up with his gun pointing toward Long.

But Long wasn't standing there anymore. He was lying on the ground. Erie watched him for a second, stunned. Long wasn't moving.

Erie stood up and winced as a bolt of agony struck in a familiar place: his gymnastics had strained his cranky lower back. He limped toward Long, each step sending pain shooting up his spine.

Long was a mess. And he was dead.

Erie guessed that he'd bent the shotgun's barrel or jammed the chamber when he bludgeoned Joel Korfmann. He might even have used the stock to bust up the TV, VCR, and stereo. So when he tried to shoot Erie, the shotgun had exploded, sending shards of metal and wood out in all directions—but mostly into Long's body.

Erie checked the right side of his abdomen where he'd felt the sting a moment before. He'd been wounded but not by buckshot or shrapnel. His shirt was torn, and a short, shallow gash was bleeding onto the white cotton. When he'd jumped, he'd landed on something sharp.

He began walking very, very slowly to his car, trying to remember the last time he'd had a tetanus shot.

3:55 P.M.

A PATROL CAR was waiting for him at 1701 O'Hara Drive when he arrived as he had requested from the dispatcher.

"Geez, Larry, where did the tornado touch down?" one of the officers asked as he limped to their car.

"Right on top of me. Can't you tell?"

"What's the story?" the other cop asked.

"I need to pick somebody up for questioning. I'm not expecting any trouble, but I wanted a little backup just in case. You two just hang back and observe."

"Hang back and observe," the first cop said, giving Erie a salute. "That's what I do best."

Erie walked up to the house and rang the doorbell. Candace Korfmann opened the door almost immediately.

"I've been waiting for you," she said. She was wearing jeans and a River City Community College sweatshirt. "I'm ready to go."

She stepped outside, closed the front door, and brushed past Erie.

"That's you, right?" she said, pointing at Erie's car.

"Yes."

She walked to the car quickly. Erie followed her.

"Do you want me in the front or the back?" she asked.

"The front is fine."

Mrs. Korfmann opened the door and climbed in. Erie eased himself gingerly into the driver's seat and started the engine. He gave the cops watching from their patrol car an "everything's under control" wave.

"I hope you weren't hurt," Mrs. Korfmann said as Erie pulled away from the curb.

"You're not under arrest, Mrs. Korfmann. I'm taking you in for an interview, that's all. You don't have to say anything if you don't want to."

"Is he dead?"

Erie took his eyes off the road for a moment to watch her. "Yes, Raymond Long is dead. He was killed about half an hour ago."

She grunted. A long stretch of road rolled by in silence.

"It was his own fault," she suddenly announced. "He killed himself when he pulled that trigger." She didn't look at Erie as she spoke. She stared straight ahead, unblinking.

"What do you mean?"

"I filled the barrel with caulk last week." She was still staring at nothing, but tears had begun to trickle down her cheeks. "I was afraid he was going to use it on me."

"He was abusive?"

"Yes."

Erie stole another glance at her. The tears were still flowing, but her face was impassive, blank. "He was your lover," he said.

"Yes."

"He killed your husband."

"Yes," she replied without hesitating.

"He used a van from DeRogatis Ford to fake a burglary."

"Yes."

"He kept the things he took from your house and brought them with him when he moved in with you."

"Yes." She spat out the word this time. "That idiot."

"Will you repeat all this when we reach police headquarters? In a formal statement?"

"Yes."

Another mile rolled under the wheels before Erie spoke again. "Why did you go along with it?" he said. "Did you love him?"

Mrs. Korfmann finally turned to face him. That morning she had reminded him, just a bit, of Nancy. But whatever resemblance he had seen in her then was gone now, crushed with the rest of her spirit.

"Joel used to beat me, too," she said. "Ray said he would protect me."

5:25 P.M.

SHE REPEATED EVERYTHING on the record, just as she said she would. Erie stayed in the interrogation room only long enough to make sure it was all on tape. But he left Dave Rogers to prepare her statement and get a signature. He simply stood up and said, "I'm tired, Dave," and walked out.

Hal Allen was waiting for him outside. "I'd never have guessed it," Allen said. "You've been holding out on us all these years. If I'd known you could wrap up a murder case every day, I never would have let you retire."

"Too late now, boss," Erie replied. "All right if I go home?"

"In a second. I wanted to see you at the end of the day, remember?"

"Oh, right. I guess you need this." Erie slipped his badge-clip off his belt and handed it to Allen. "And this." He unholstered his revolver and handed that over, too.

"Well, yeah, we need those." Allen slipped the items into his jacket pocket. "But that's not what I wanted to see you about. Do you still carry cards for Julie Rhodes, the grief counselor?"

"Um-hmm."

"Could I see one?" Erie pulled out one of the cards. He handed it to Allen, who looked at it for a moment before handing it back.

"Here," Allen said. "I think you should use this."

5:50 P.M.

ERIE STOPPED AT a grocery store on the way home. He found the cheapest red wine in stock and put four bottles in his cart.

But on the way to the register he changed his mind.

He found the aisle marked Pet Supplies and threw a bag of kitty litter and a dozen cans of cat food into his cart. He left three bottles of wine on the shelf next to the "cat treats."

When he got home, he opened one of the cans of cat food and dumped its contents onto a small plate. He took the plate out to the front porch along with his wine, a glass, and a bottle opener. He placed the plate on the walk that led to the driveway, then eased himself down on the first step of his porch.

He opened the wine and waited.

JANICE LAW

TABLOID PRESS

February 2000

IN A CAREER that has spanned nearly thirty years, Janice Law has written nine novels in an award-nominated mystery series, beginning with *The Big Payoff* in 1977. She's also written a historical novel that takes place in Versailles during the reign of Louis XIV, *All the King's Ladies*, and most recently, the literary novel *Voices*, which explores the connection between memory and identity. In this story, a naïve convenience store employee gets caught in a multilayered cat-and-mouse game.

■

Kim is standing there between Princess Diana—tiara, white satin, eyes blue as window spray—and Monica Lewinsky—dark suit, lots of curves, mega-lipstick. Though not as nice as Diana's, Monica's eyes are on the blue side, too, which doesn't surprise Kim. She's had a weakness along those lines herself, named Chris. When she was sixteen and three quarters and bored with school, Chris seemed exciting. Besides the blazing blue eyes he had a truck, a trailer, independence, a job. Now she knows he's got a six-pack-a-day beer habit and a lousy temper from inhaling spray paint at the body shop.

Well, everyone has problems. There's the princess dead with that fat Egyptian: "Diana a Year Later" is the *People* headline, and though Monica looks pretty good in most pictures, today's tabloid screams "Monica on Suicide Watch."

"What a shame," one old geezer had told Kim just that morning, though another one didn't buy the usual and said she'd get more than she wanted on the Internet.

Now the woman off pump four in the dark green Jetta wants to give Kim exact change and can't come up with the final thirty cents. She's got her crap all over the counter—pennies, a pen, car keys, Kleenex. "I know I've got it somewhere," she says with this loopy, idiotic smile.

And pump two is screwed up as it's been all week. Some guy in a big Suburban is yelling over the intercom that he's got five seventy in the tank; and the pump's froze on him. "Yeah, yeah, I'll get it started for you," Kim's saying when Joe, fat and fortyish but agile, hustles behind the counter to stand in her back pocket. He's wearing the baggy gray suit and beige shirt plus, today, the Tweety Bird tie that he claims gives the customers a laugh. Kim can smell his cologne.

Joe says, "I need some help in the storeroom, Kim. Let Michael handle the front."

Automatically Kim looks at her watch; that's what she always does when Joe wants something, she checks the time: twelve thirty-five. Lunch is at one, after the trades guys have come in for sand-wiches, beer, and sodas, after the high school kids have bought ice cream and Tabs, and after the elderly morning shoppers have stopped for gas and papers. Twelve thirty-five: time for her to hump a few dozen cartons and for Joe to try to get his hands down her jeans.

"Michael's gotta leave early today for an exam," she says, thinking quickly because between Joe hitting on her and Chris wanting beer money, Kim doesn't want to stay and can't afford to quit. "Michael's got early class this semester, so I gotta be up front. And pump two's jamming again."

That distracts Joe for a minute because he likes to have everything running just right—pumps fast, counter manned, sand-wiches fresh, coffee made every couple of hours. He's got an eagle eye for the register, too. You have to move fast to get away with anything. He'll count every damn pack of cigarettes himself if he has to.

With this Quick Mart, one in Putnam, another two in Norwich, Joe Gleb should be a rich man, and sometimes Kim tries to imag-ine what if he were handsome. Maybe bald like he is but attractive, even passable, not so fat, nicer manners. Or maybe elegant with fancy suits, gold jewelry, and a convertible like the rich, wrin-kled geezers who pose with blonde girlfriends in the tabloids and who set up love nests and get themselves into expensive divorces.

What then? Would that be a way out? An escape from Chris and misery?

But Rakesh has told her Joe isn't really rich. Rakesh is the other college student, not at the community but at the state college, and he does some of the books cut-rate for Joe. What Rakesh told her was that it's Joe's wife who has the cash. Kim tends to believe that, because Joe is always bitching about money. It's a lousy day at the store after he's been to the casino, and sometimes there are odd phone calls that get Joe upset good.

Twelve fifty: pump two's running again; Michael, who doesn't really have an exam, is on the counter; Kim's back shifting cartons of motor oil with Joe, who really should get one of the guys to do the heavy work. Joe's told her he likes her jeans and likes her tank top, and next she's expecting he'll try to get her onto the night shift, when he says, out of left field, like, "Chris still picking you up?"

"You see me with a car?" Kim asks. One of the few smart things she's done with Joe is to impress him with Chris's temper, jealousy, and strength.

"I wanna talk to him next time he comes by."

"Yeah? I'm not working the night shift," Kim says quickly. "I don't care if you talk him into it, I'm not working any night shift."

"Who said I want you working the night shift?" asks Joe. "I thought you said Chris is outa full-time work. Didn't you tell me that?"

Kim nods.

"So I'm maybe looking for workers."

That's an idea Kim will have to digest on her break. One o'clock sharp, she takes a cigarette from the pack she keeps in the counter drawer, buys a bottle of juice and a brownie, and crosses the road, because lunch choice between the storeroom or the cemetery is a no-brainer. Kim walks through the tall iron gates and down the deeply grooved dirt and gravel road. There are graves on either side, neat rows of gray, brown, and white stones, trees, too, and farther back, the big monuments of the formerly rich, still looking impressive *fifty, eighty, one hundred years after.*

If it's a hot day, Kim likes to pick one of the ones that look like Greek temples, where she can sit in the shade with her back against

the cool stones and have lunch and smoke in peace. But since today
the sun will feel good, she picks a brown mottled obelisk that
supervises a mess of little individual markers. The obelisk's got
KIERNAN cut in the base in letters big enough for a highway road
sign, and Kim's leaning up against it, drinking her o.j. straight from
the bottle, when someone coughs. Kim jumps so quick she slops
juice down her top. "Christ!" she says, and a few other things,
because her new tank top is white and the stain'll be a bitch.

"Excuse me," says this voice. "You're standing on my grave."

WHEN WORK'S OFFERED, Chris is cautious. He's reckless and
wild with every other thing, but he approaches work like it's a
rabid cat. He wants to know exactly what Joe said and how he
said it, and when Kim says, "Why don't you ask him yourself,
he's still there," Chris gets all mad and unreasonable. He smacks
her one and sulks through dinner, though he does make a call
after Kim goes outside with the garbage. Coming back, standing
on the step with one hand on the screen door, she hears him saying, "Yeah, we'll see about it, man. Long's you're talking serious
money."

Of course he tells Kim nothing, though she goes so far as to
ask if Joe Gleb has a job for him. She risks that much. Chris says
it's none of her business and his eyes get mean, so Kim shuts her
mouth and figures she'll find out soon enough.

DULL DAY, MIST so heavy it feels like rain, or rain so light it
feels like mist. Kim goes across to the cemetery anyway; she never
misses a day now, though she always says she has an errand to
run at the supermarket, that she's got to stop by the pharmacy,
whatever. Through the parking lot, dodging cars, carts, delivery
trucks, across the street, three lanes, always jammed, then into
the cemetery, into what she thinks of as real life, but Kim isn't into
irony. She's fallen for happiness.

First they visit the grave, which is in Maureen's family's plot.
Her name was once Maureen Kiernan, which has a nice ring to
it, not like Gleb, which sounds to Kim like something nasty. The
Kiernan plot is a generous square of lawn with the obelisk at the
back and granite blocks on each corner. There are a lot of dead
Kiernans under the grass, including the real money man, Joseph

Patrick Kiernan, who founded the textile mill that's now a high-tech fish farm.

The Kiernan plot is impressive but high maintenance. There's always something to be done, especially around Joey's grave, which has to be kept weedless and perfect with every dead flower and faded plant removed, with each of the little boxwood shrubs perfectly pruned.

"Did he like flowers?" Kim asks once.

"He liked basketball," Eileen says, "but you can't plant basketballs."

Which makes sense to Kim.

After tending the grave, they walk around the cemetery. Maureen always brings a picnic: nice deli sandwiches, cheese pies, or slices of meat bits in jelly with fancy French names; pretty cookies and little square cakes with icing all over; grapes or peaches or strawberries big as ping-pong balls. There's a thermos of coffee if it's cool; a half bottle of wine or cider if it's warm. Kim and Maureen sit on the porch of one of the Greek temples, which are properly called mausoleums, Kim learns, and talk. They talk about Joey and the grave first, and then about themselves and their situations, and finally about their need for different lives, for freedom, for escape.

THIS ONE NIGHT, lights sweep across the trailer windows, the neighbor's coon dogs go wild, and, surprise of surprises, Joe's white Cadillac bounces over the ruts in the yard. Joe hops out, his heavy face sweaty. He's got a cigar in his hand and a big charge of nervous energy on his back.

"Hey, Kimmie," he says. Joe never calls her Kimmie at work, and she takes this to mean he's trying to be chummy and friendly. She assumes he wants something. "Your man at home?"

Kim looks over her shoulder. Chris is sitting in front of the TV in the crowded main room. He's got a NASCAR show on, and the racing motors produce a steady, whining drone that seems to mellow him out as much as anything can. When she nods her head, Joe squeezes past her into the trailer.

"So Chris," he says, and something about the way Chris lifts his head, all alert and interested, tells Kim this is trouble.

"Take a walk," he says.

"In the dark?"

"Go sit in the Caddy," Joe says, tossing her the keys. "Play with the stereo. Check out those dynamite graphic equalizers."

The Caddy has leather seats the color of caramel and nearly as soft, a fancy wood-faced dash, and a stereo with enough lights and dials for four, five ordinary boom boxes. Kim finds copies of *Penthouse* and *Convenience Store Decisions* under the front seat, along with a few old newspapers and an empty bag from the doughnut shop. The glove compartment has maps, a flashlight, aspirin, Tums, an inhaler, and an envelope of photos, mostly showing a boy of ten or eleven, a chubby, round-faced little kid.

In several, he's smiling in a red and white basketball uniform with shorts that come down below his knees and a baseball cap on his head. In others, he's all Sunday-dressed in shirt and slacks and bareheaded, so she can see the dark wavy hair. The boy waves to the camera from the white Cadillac, kneels on the grass to play with a beagle, cocks his arm to throw a football. Kim can see Joe in the fat cheeks and stocky form, but the child's eyes are blue, startlingly blue. Kim flips through the rest of the snaps, quickly and not really paying attention, until the final picture, a family grouping, stops her cold. She's looking at the child, the dog, and a tall blonde woman with the boy's blue eyes. Kim looks at the picture and hears a voice saying, "You're standing on my grave."

"I SHOULDN'T BE here," Kim says the next day. Just after one P.M., break time, a cloudy day with fall in the air. They're eating these really nice ham and cheese sandwiches with fine crunchy green pickles.

"Why not?"

"I'm working for your husband."

"I knew that." Unconcerned. That's one of the things that fascinates Kim about Maureen, that unconcern, that lack of fear. "I think these should have more onion. I like red onion on a sandwich. Don't you think these need more onion?"

"I never guessed," says Kim, who doesn't have unconcern but would like to acquire it. "What if he shows up? What if he comes to visit Joey's grave?"

Maureen's face changes then, and her eyes get dark and hard as if all the grief and anger within are set to come flooding out.

"He never comes to the grave. Never, the bastard. He wanted cremation. He wanted to forget." There's a pause. "Joe believes in moving on, in getting on with his life." The words are dipped in acid, coated in bile as thick as chocolate. Kim imagines each syllable being lowered into some internal vat and coming up dripping. "He thinks I'm crazy," Maureen says. "Crazy in general, crazy because of Joey, crazy about the grave."

Kim protests Maureen isn't crazy. Though she is unusual in a wonderful way.

"He'd like to see me in therapy, which would give him leverage, you see, leverage for the divorce. Or, maybe, if I'm in therapy, he'll fight the divorce and try to get me into treatment. That's what Joe would really like. He'd like me in a little clinic somewhere, and then he'd have his hands on the business, on everything. He's always sniffing around and saving ammunition for the divorce."

Maureen always talks about the divorce as a kind of object, as a real thing, though it doesn't exist yet; no papers have been filed. But Maureen sees life as a series of separate events and things: the accident, the divorce, the meeting, the grave. She's not like Kim, for whom life slides from one thing to another so that working for Joe Gleb somehow leads to this thing with his wife.

"I could maybe be something for the divorce," remarks Kim.

Maureen puts her arm around her. "So you could," she says. "But he never comes here. Never, ever. He couldn't face Joey's death, and he thinks I'm crazy because I can't forget. He thinks he can spend his way back to happiness; he thinks he can gamble and forget. Well, not with my money he can't. I can't forget, and I'll see that he won't, either."

Kim is uncomfortable with all this talk about Maureen's husband, especially since he's Joe Gleb and someone she knows. She's just as glad when Maureen asks, "How did you find out?" Her voice is casual, but there's interest underneath.

Kim explains about Joe's visit, about the snaps in the car. "He wants Chris to do a job for him."

Maureen's eyes register the fact of the snaps, a kind of visual snarl, then, "What kind of job?"

"I don't know. He hasn't come back again."

"Best find out," says Maureen.

BUT KIM DOESN'T worry about the job. She thinks some hot merchandise that Joe wants Chris to haul for him like cigarettes up from the South, where there's less tax. Or else a little damage to one of the lower volume convenience stores for the insurance money. Maybe just to hang around looking ferocious and unpredictable when Joe expects bad company. Those are the sorts of things Chris is good at, so she's surprised when he comes into the kitchenette one night and starts to clean a gun. Not a shotgun or a rifle, like what everyone has in their neighborhood, but a stubby black thing with a textured grip.

"Get your eyes back in your head," he says.

Kim shrugs. Since meeting Maureen, she doesn't get all nervous and upset about Chris anymore. Kim's figuring to stay out of his way until she manages to be rid of him, so she doesn't ask nosy questions, she doesn't bother him when he's drinking or when he's picked up some good stuff. She puts her check on the table and fixes dinner, which makes her, far as Chris is concerned, a together chick. He's starting to tell her so, to let her know that this is for keeps, that she shouldn't think of leaving him.

He twirls the cylinder and takes out a roll of hundred-dollar bills to impress her. "I've got a job worth doing," he says. "And I'll need you to drive the truck."

Kim looks at the money and then at him. "What do we have to do, kill somebody?"

She's joking, but Chris kinda nods his head. "We're going to kidnap somebody and hold him for ransom." He says this like guns and kidnapping and ransom's all part of their normal routine. Then he laughs. "And the best part is he's going to cooperate with us all the way."

"Who is?"

Chris doesn't tell her. He pretends he's said enough already, but Kim can guess, and when she tells Maureen the next day, Maureen can, too.

"That dumb bastard," she says.

KIM'S MAIN THOUGHT is to clear the area, and she thinks Maureen may agree, given her own past history. "Chris is crazy," Kim tells her. "He'll be crazier with a gun." Kim sees Florida or maybe even California, somewhere warm with sand and palms and big hotels looking glassy-eyed at white beaches. But of course they can't do that. Kim knows without asking that they can't leave the grave, Joey, remembrance.

"You could dump Chris," Maureen says. This is the other alternative, their other fantasy. "You could get an apartment. I'd help you. You could get a really nice apartment."

"He'd come after me," Kim says. "And there's the divorce."

"Yes," says Maureen with this funny smile. "There's the divorce."

"I DON'T SEE what you need the gun for," Kim tells Chris. "Not if he's cooperating."

"Don't be dumb. It's got to look realistic."

"A knife would do," Kim says. It's in her mind that the gun is a bad idea, that Chris is too impulsive to be trusted, that he will screw up in some spectacular way.

"There might be trouble," he says. "You get less trouble with a gun."

"They'll question me," says Kim. "They'll question everyone who works at the stores. They'll figure an inside job."

"We get the money and we're out of here." Chris sounds so decisive and confident that, despite her indifference, Kim feels her heart clench. She foresees separation and despair; she sees the truck, the highway, exile from real life.

"All you got to do is to drop me off," he says so enthusiastically she understands that he is enjoying this, the excitement and importance of it. "I take him and his car. He calls the wife. She gets the money and drops it off. We're all home free."

"Where do you leave the car?" asks Kim. "Where do you leave him?"

"Maybe here. You're at work. You don't have to know nothing."

"I take the truck for the first time ever to work, someone's going to notice."

He doesn't like that. He looks like he might want to make an issue of it, make her agree to what's a purely dumb idea. But he surprises her. "Maybe you start driving the truck to work," he says. "I'm thinking of getting a bike, anyway. I saw this Harley I'd like, and I can afford it." He picks his head up like she's going to give him an argument.

"All right," she says, thinking maybe he'll get a bike and break his damn neck. "I'll start taking the truck. But Joe'll want me working the night shift if I have a ride."

"What do you care when you work?"

Kim hesitates, feeling how events can slide one way or the other, life's a teeterboard, and you can slip off either end. "I don't want to be there alone at night. Joe comes by. I gotta watch him, he's always . . ."

"See you don't give him any reason," Chris says. "But if he tries anything, I'll break his face."

CHRYSANTHEMUM SEASON. Maureen has two big pots in the back of her car and four smaller ones. The big ones are the size of bushel baskets and have mauve flowers. The smaller ones have white flowers and should stand the winter, Maureen says. Kim helps her pull out the begonias though they're still pretty, pretty enough so she regrets not being able to take them home. She's getting an appreciation for flowers and sees how the begonias would brighten up the trailer. She thinks about having them on the kitchenette table so she could look at flowers instead of at Chris all the time.

Maureen digs in the new plants, and Kim brings some water from the faucet down the dirt track.

"So you're driving to work now," says Maureen.

"Chris has this bike he bought."

"Used?" Maureen asks, like she's really interested in Chris and his purchases.

"New," says Kim. And Maureen stops tidying up around the plants and looks at her.

"New." Maureen doesn't say anything else, so an idea Kim had put aside comes crashing back: mega cash for a phony kidnapping. Maureen frowns and shakes her head. She's quiet all through lunch, thinking this over, and when she finally speaks, she says, "Would Chris shoot somebody? In cold blood, would he shoot someone?"

Kim doesn't like to say she has no idea, but she doesn't, though she's lived with Chris for two years. "Why do you ask that?" she says. "What do you mean?"

"I can raise maybe fifty thousand," Maureen says. "In an absolute emergency, life and death; with bridge loans, twice that much. Subtract a new Harley-Davidson and probably money afterward, and how much is left?"

"Chris wouldn't know that," says Kim, but she's already hoping maybe they've been wrong. Maybe Chris has another job, maybe Joe Gleb isn't involved at all.

"Joe knows to the penny. He knows our money isn't liquid." Maureen has to explain this to Kim, how money can be liquid or not, how it can be tied up.

"So why is he doing it? Why is he doing this thing with Chris?" Kim asks.

"This is going to be Joe's version of the divorce," Maureen says. "I think he wants to get his hands on everything; I think he doesn't care about the ransom at all."

"You have to tell the police," Kim says.

"And what would happen to you? They'd guess how I found out."

"I could leave," Kim says. "I could get out of town."

"If that's what you want," says Maureen. "But I have a better idea."

CHRIS GOES OUT on the bike the next night, and soon as he clears the yard, Kim begins looking for the gun. She told Maureen "no problem," but after she searches under the bed, the bedside table, Chris's footlocker, the shelf above their coats, the medicine cabinet, even the cupboard by the door where they put canned goods, Kim starts getting nervous. Outside, she checks the truck over like a sniffer dog but can't find a thing.

Back inside, the phone rings.

"Find it?" Maureen asks.

"Not yet. I thought you didn't want to call."

"I'm at the gas station. Would he keep it in the bike?"

"He might. He's got those carrier things. They probably lock."

"You'll have to check," says Maureen.

So there's Kim with bullets rattling in her jeans pocket and the whole trailer turned upside down when Chris roars into the yard.

"Cleaning," she says.

"Don't be crazy. We'll be outa this dump soon."

"How soon?"

"What you don't know won't hurt you," he says and laughs, as if he thinks he's pretty funny.

Within minutes, the phone rings again. Kim knows it's Maureen, she just knows it is, but Chris picks it up, listens a minute, then swears and says he doesn't have time for any damn opinion poll. Kim lets out her breath.

After dinner, when she carries out the garbage, Kim tries the catches on the motorbike's carriers. She tries again later on the excuse that she's left a sweater in the truck, but what she finally has to do is to get up a half hour earlier than usual the next morning. Chris is still asleep when Kim gets the bike keys out of his pocket and goes outside barefoot, half frozen, and shaking with nerves to unlock the carrier. There's the gun, black and ugly and serious looking.

Kim thinks of Joey's accident and freezes.

In her mind she hears Maureen saying, "I always kept the gun locked up, always, always locked up, but Joe wanted it handy. 'What good's a gun you can't get to,' he'd say. Safety, that was his thing, but it wasn't very safe for a little boy, was it?" Kim remembers how Maureen's eyes went wild and dark, how she wept and said, "There were bits of bone on the wall, bits of bone."

So Kim is reluctant to touch the gun, though Maureen went over the whole process with her two, three times. Kim stands there dithering until there's a sound—a car somewhere—and she breaks open the chamber revealing neat, shiny bullets with round brass ends. Out they come and in go the ones Maureen brought her. Close up the gun, wipe it, and put it back quick with the oily rag on top.

The carrier latch snaps loud enough to stop Kim's heart, but there's nothing, no reaction, no door opening, no face at the window, and all she's got left to do is to slide the keys back into Chris's tumbled, greasy jeans and fix herself an early breakfast.

Two days, three days, nothing happens. Kim's beginning to think that maybe there's another deal, that maybe Chris has pulled a fast one, that maybe they'll be okay after all.

Maureen wants to know if she's sure she changed all the bullets, and when Kim says yes, Maureen tells her, "Wait and see."

But Kim's still jumpy, wired with nerves, so Maureen says, "Don't worry; we've defanged them." Maureen seems pleased about that and confident. "There's not a damn thing they can do to us now."

A YELLOW WASH from the neighbor's security light and Chris shaking her shoulder. "Get up," he says.

"What is it? What time is it?" Kim's thinking fire, flood, or a raccoon in the trailer.

"Let's go," he says. "This is the day."

She gets up and dresses, her hands shaking though Chris has been defanged, though the gun is harmless, though no matter what Maureen does—calls the police or raises the cash—nobody gets hurt.

The kitchenette clock reads five thirty A.M. "You're way too early," Kim says. "Joe won't be at the store before seven thirty."

"Who said we were going to get him at the store?" Chris asks.

"You said I just needed to drop you off. You said . . ."

"Listen, I trust you," Chris says with this awful, heavy certainty. "We're in this together."

He puts his arm around her shoulder, and they go outside. She expects him to drive, but he motions her behind the wheel and gives her the keys.

"I'll tell you where to go," he says. "Keep the lights off until we hit the road."

The sky's beginning to gray, but Kim nearly hits the boulder at the driveway end and has to put on the low beams. It's a relief to get onto the main road and have light. Chris sits beside her, giving orders without any real direction, until they reach a country road, all winding and stone walls. After a mile or so he has her pull in at a drive with fancy carriage lamps on either side.

"Cut the lights," he says. Kim has to wait a few seconds until she can see to ease the truck along the circular drive to a three-car garage. An attached breezeway with long windows and a glass door connects it to the house. Chris pulls on a ski mask and takes the gun out of his jacket pocket. "Keep the motor running," he says.

None of this is quite real to Kim, though she can feel her hands, which are freezing, and the clammy coldness of the shirt against her back and a stiffness in her feet. She's really in need of sun and heat and someplace different, but the situation itself is like something on TV, like a film, a drama, a still picture in the tabloids: "Celebrity Home Invaded by Masked Intruder," something like that.

When Kim hears the tinkle of breaking glass, she wants to push on the horn and alert the house. She also wants to put the truck in reverse and get the hell out. Instead, she hangs on to the wheel with both hands and tells herself that everything will be all right: crazy at the moment, but without permanent damage. Kim's still telling herself this when the shots start, one, then two, three, four, close together. She piles out of the truck, stumbles across the gravel drive, and races to the house, where lights are coming on and there's this indescribably bad, scary atmosphere.

"Chris," she shouts and then, "Maureen! Joe!" Though that's careless, not prudent, dangerous, as is running down the hall toward the light, toward the master bedroom, toward Maureen, who, gun in hand, is shrugging her way into a bathrobe. Maureen has a rigid, unfamiliar expression on her face as if the darkness that used to live behind her eyes has come out into the light for good.

"What's happened?"

Maureen recognizes her then, recognizes the voice, the face. "Don't go in there," she says, meaning the bedroom, where Kim can now see objects, bundles like, lying on the floor. Bundles she somehow knows are Chris and Joe. Kim starts to cry.

"Don't do that," says Maureen, touching her shoulder like the old Maureen, the real Maureen, glimpsed for that second, then disappearing. "You don't have time. Go down the field track to the highway and hitch a ride to work."

"I'll be late," wails Kim as if this is all that matters.

"Tell them Chris went out early with the truck," says Maureen. "You don't have to know anything else. But get out of here. You've got to get out of here now."

KIM WALKS OUT the glass doors and takes a moment to see the palms and the crowded strip of sand at the edge of the water. Outside the hotel air conditioning it's really too warm for her nice receptionist's blazer, but green's her best color, and it only takes a few minutes to run to the coffee shop, crowded with delivery guys and workers and other hotel staff on breaks. Kim returns greetings, friendly waves; she's been around long enough to know people.

Coffees, one with, one without, plus a bagel, a doughnut, extra sugar. Kim's already collected her order when she checks the magazine rack and feels time stop for a moment: Princess Diana on the cover again, midnight blue silk, a jeweled necklace broad as your hand, eyes as blue as Maureen's when she stood on the edge of the grave with all the mauve and white mums and handed over the envelope.

"You'll need," Maureen said, "to get started."

Kim took it; there wasn't anything else to do, not if she wanted to leave, to start again, to get away from scary bundles and awkward questions and Maureen's wild eyes.

"Maybe you'll come back," Maureen said.

And though Kim said, "Maybe," at the time, she knows she never can, she never will, because Maureen's crazy; Joe Gleb was right about that. Just the same, standing in her green hotel blazer just across from the sand, Kim can't help feeling grateful, and nostalgic, too, about the cemetery and picnics and real life.

THE O-BON CAT

February 2003

MS. PARKER'S PRIVATE investigator, Sugawara Akitada, an impoverished nobleman in ancient Japan, was first introduced in the pages of *AHMM* with her first fiction publication in 1997. Then her 1999 story "Akitada's First Case" garnered her a Shamus Award for Best P.I. Short Story. The first of her critically acclaimed novels in this series is *Dragon Scroll*. Here is one of Akitada's more recent adventures.

■

Otsu, Lake Biwa, eleventh-century Japan, during the O-bon festival.

The First Day: Welcoming the Dead

He was on his homeward journey when he found the boy. At the time, caught in the depths of hopelessness and grief, he did not understand the significance of their meeting.

Sugawara Akitada, not yet in the middle of his life, was already sick of it. A man may counter hardship, humiliation, even imminent death with resources carefully accumulated in his past and draw fresh zest for new obstacles from his achievements, but Akitada, though one of the privileged and moderately successful in the service of the emperor, had found no spiritual anchor in his soul when his young son had died during that spring's smallpox epidemic. He went through the motions of daily life as if he were no part of them, as if the man he once was had departed with the smoke from his son's funeral pyre, leaving behind an empty shell now inhabited by a stranger.

Having completed an assignment in Hikone two days earlier, Akitada rode along the southern shore of Lake Biwa in a steady drizzle. The air was saturated with moisture, his clothes clung uncomfortably, and both rider and horse were sore from the wooden saddle. This was the fifteenth day of the watery month, in the rainy season. The road had long since become a muddy track where puddles hid deep pits in which a horse could break its leg. It became clear that he could not reach his home in the capital but would have to spend the night in Otsu.

Otsu was the legendary place of parting, a symbol of grief and yearning in poetry and prose. In Otsu, wives or parents would bid farewell, perhaps forever, to their husbands or sons when they left the capital to begin their service in distant provinces of the country. Akitada himself used to feel uneasy about his return on such occasions. But those days seemed in a distant past now. He cared little what lay ahead.

At dusk he entered a dense forest, and darkness closed in about him, falling with the misting rain from the branches above and creeping from the dank shadows of the woods. When he could no longer see the road clearly, he dismounted. Leading his tired horse, he trudged onward in squelching boots and sodden straw rain cape and thought of death.

He was still in the forest when a child's whimpering roused him from his grief. But when he stopped and called out, there was no answer, and all was still again except for the dripping rain. He was almost certain the sound had been human, but the eeriness of a child's pitiful weeping in this lonely, dark place on his lonely, dark journey seemed too cruel a coincidence. This was the first night of the three-day O-bon festival, the night when the spirits of the dead return to their homes to visit before departing for another year.

If his own son's soul was seeking its way home also, Yori would not find his father there. Would he cry for him out of the darkness? Akitada shivered and shook off his sick fancies. Such superstitions were for simpler, more trusting minds. How far was Otsu?

Then he heard it again.

"Who is that? Come out where I can see you!" he bellowed angrily into the darkness. His horse twitched its ears and shook its head.

Something pale detached itself from one of the tree trunks and crept closer. A boy of about five or six. He caught his breath. "Yori?"

Foolishness! This was no ghost. It was a ragged child with huge, frightened eyes in a pale face, a boy nothing at all like Yori. Yori had been handsome, well-nourished, and sturdy. This boy in his filthy torn shirt had sticks for arms and legs. He looked permanently hungry, a living ghost.

"Are you lost, child?" asked Akitada, more gently, wishing he had food in his saddle bags. The boy remained silent and kept his distance.

"What is your name?"

No answer.

"Where do you live?"

Silence.

The child probably knew his way around these woods better than Akitada. With a farewell wave, Akitada resumed his journey. Soon the trees thinned and the darkness receded slightly. Gray dusk filtered through the branches, and ahead lay a pale sliver that was the lake and—thank heaven—many small golden points of light, like a gathering of fireflies, that were the dwellings of Otsu. He glanced back at the dark forest, and there, not ten feet behind, waited the child.

"Do you want to come with me, then?" Akitada asked. The boy said nothing, but he edged closer until he stood beside the horse. Akitada saw that his ragged shirt was soaked and clung to the ribs of his small chest. A deaf-mute? Oh well, perhaps someone in Otsu would know the boy.

Bending down, Akitada lifted him into the saddle. He weighed so little, poor little sprite, that he would hardly trouble the horse. For the rest of their journey Akitada looked back from time to time to make sure the boy had not fallen off. Now and then he asked him a question or made a comment, but the child did not respond in any way. He sat quietly, almost expectantly in the saddle as they approached Otsu.

Ahead beckoned the bonfires welcoming the spirits of the dead. Most people believed that spirits got lost, like this child, and also that they felt hunger. Otsu's cemetery was filled with tiny lights that marked a trail to town, and in the doorway of every home offerings of food and water awaited the returning souls, those hungry ghosts depicted in temple painting, skeletal creatures with distended bellies, condemned to eat excrement or suffer unending hunger and thirst in punishment for their wasteful lives.

In the market people were still shopping for the three-day festival. The doors of houses stood wide open, and inside Akitada could see spirit altars erected before the family shrines, heaped with more fine things to eat and drink. So much good food wasted on ghosts!

They passed a rice cake vendor with his trays of fragrant white cakes. Yori had loved rice cakes filled with sweet bean jam. Akitada dug two coppers from his sash and bought one for the boy. The child received it with solemn dignity and bowed his thanks before gobbling it down. As miserable and hungry as this urchin was, he had not forgotten his manners. Akitada was intrigued and decided to do his best for the child.

He asked if anyone knew the boy or his family, but he soon grew weary of the disclaimers and stopped at an inn. The boy had looked around curiously but given no sign of recognition. Akitada lifted him from the saddle and, with a sigh, took the small hand in his as they entered.

"A room," Akitada told the innkeeper, slipping off the sodden straw cape and his wet boots. "And a bath. Then some hot food and wine."

The man was staring at the ragged child. "Is he with you, sir?"

"Unless you know where he lives, he's with me!" Akitada snapped irritably. "Oh, I suppose you'd better send someone out for new clothes for him. He looks to be about five." He fished silver from his sash, ignoring the stunned look on the man's face.

After inspecting the room, he took the child to the bath.

Helping a small boy with his bath again was unexpectedly painful, and tears filled Akitada's eyes. He blinked them away, blaming such emotion on fatigue and pity for the child. The shirt had done little to conceal his thinness, but naked he was a far more shocking sight. Not only was every bone clearly visible under the sun-darkened skin, but the protruding belly spoke of malnutrition, and there were bruises from beatings.

Judging from the state of his long, matted hair and his filthy feet and hands, the bath was a novel experience for him. Akitada borrowed scissors and a comb from the bath attendant and tended to his hair and nails, trying to be as gentle as he could. The boy submitted bravely. Afterward, soaking in the large tub as he had done so many times with Yori, he fought tears again.

They returned to the room in the cotton robes provided by the inn. Their bedding had been spread out, and a hot meal of rice and vegetables awaited them. At the sight of the food, the boy smiled for the first time. They ate, and when the boy's eyes began to close and the bowl slipped from his hands, Akitada tucked him into the bedding and went to sleep himself.

The Second Day: Ghostly Phenomena

HE AWOKE TO the boy's earnest scrutiny. In daylight and after the bath and night's rest, the child looked almost handsome. His hair was soft; he had thick, straight brows, a well-shaped nose, and a good chin; and his eyes were almost as large and luminous as Yori's. Akitada smiled and said, "Good morning."

Stretching out a small hand, the boy tweaked Akitada's nose gently and gave a little gurgle of laughter.

But there were no miracles. The boy did not find his voice or hearing, and his poor body had not filled out overnight. He still looked more like a hungry ghost than a child.

And he was not Yori.

Yet in that moment of intimacy Akitada decided that for however long they would have each other's company he would surrender to emotions he had buried with the ashes of his firstborn. He would be a father again.

Someone had brought in Akitada's saddlebags and the boy's new clothes. They dressed and went for a walk about town. Because of the holiday, the vendors were setting out their wares early in the market.

Near the Temple of the War God they breakfasted on a bowl of noodles. Then Akitada had himself shaved by a barber while the boy sat on the temple steps and watched an old storyteller who regaled a small group of children and their mothers with the tale of how the rabbit got into the moon.

On the hillside behind the temple, a complex of elegantly curving tiled roofs rose above the trees. Akitada idly asked the barber about its owner.

"Oh, that would be the Masudas. Very rich but unlucky."

"Unlucky?"

"All the men have died." The barber finished and wiped Akitada's face with a hot towel. "There's only the old lord now, and he's mad. That family's ruled by women. Pshaw!" He spat in disgust.

There was no shortage of death in the world.

Akitada paid and they strolled on. The way the boy clung to his hand as they passed among the stands and vendors of the market filled Akitada's heart with half-forgotten gentleness. He watched his delight in the sights of the market and wondered where his parents were. Perhaps he had become separated from them while traveling along the highway. Or they had abandoned him in the forest because he was not perfect. The irony that a living child might be discarded, while Yori, so beloved and treasured by his parents, had been snatched away by death was not lost on Akitada, and he spoiled the silent boy with treats—a pair of red slippers for his bare feet, a top to play with, and sweets.

No one recognized the child; neither did the boy show interest in anyone. But one odd thing happened. After having clung to Akitada's hand all day, the boy suddenly tore himself loose and dashed into the crowd. Akitada panicked, desperately afraid he had lost him forever. But the boy had not gone far. Akitada glimpsed his bright red shoes between the legs of passersby, and there he was, sitting in a doorway, clutching a filthy brown and white cat in his arms. Akitada's relief was as instant as his irritation. The animal was thin, covered with dirt and scars, and looked half wild. When Akitada reached for it, it hissed and jumped from the boy's arms.

The child gave a choking cry, too garbled to be called speech. He struggled wildly in Akitada's arms, sobbing and repeating the same strangled sounds, his hands stretching after the cat. Akitada felt the wild heartbeat in the small chest against his own and soothed the choking sobs by murmuring softly to him. After a long time, the boy calmed down, but even after Akitada bought him a toy drum, he still looked about for the stray cat.

When night fell, they followed the crowd back to the temple, where the O-bon dancers gyrated in the light of colored lanterns. Akitada had to lift the boy so he could see over the heads of people.

His eyes were wide with wonder at the sight of the fearful masks and bright silk costumes. Once, when a great lion-headed creature came close to them, its glaring eyes and lolling tongue swinging his way, he gave a small cry and burrowed his face in Akitada's shoulder.

It was shameful for a grown man to weep in public. Akitada brushed the tears away and knew that he could not part with this child.

He lost the boy only moments later.

Someone in the watching crowd shouted, "There he is!" and a sharp-faced, poorly dressed woman pushed to his side. "What are you doing with our boy?" she demanded shrilly. "Give him back!"

Akitada could not answer immediately, because the child's thin arms had wrapped around his neck with a stranglehold.

A rough character in the shirt and loincloth of a peasant appeared behind the woman and glared at Akitada. "Hey!" he cried. "That's our boy! Let go of him." When Akitada did not, he bellowed at the bystanders, "He's stolen our boy! Call the constables!"

Akitada loosened the boy's grip and saw sheer terror on his face.

But it was over all too quickly. A couple of constables appeared and talked to the couple, whose name was Mimura. The man was a fisherman on the lake about a mile north from Otsu near the forest where Akitada had found the boy. They handed the weeping child over to his parents with a warning to keep a better eye on him in the future.

Even though Akitada knew he had been foolish to give his affection to a strange child, his heart ached when the parents dragged the whimpering boy off. He suspected that they had abused him and would do so again, but he had no right to interfere between a parent and his child. This did not stop him from wandering gloomily about town, trying to think of ways to rescue the boy.

Then he saw the cat again.

Perhaps it was due to the festival's peculiar atmosphere or his confused emotions, but he was suddenly convinced that the cat was his link to the boy. This time he knew better than to rush the animal. He kept his distance, waiting as it investigated gutters and alleyways for bits of food. At one point it paused to consume a large fish head, and Akitada hurriedly purchased a lantern. Eventually the animal stopped scavenging and moved on more purposefully. The streets got darker, there were fewer people, and the sounds of the market receded until they were alone on a residential street, the cat a pale patch in the distance—until it disappeared into a garden wall with the suddenness of a ghost.

Akitada was still staring at the spot when the soft flapping of straw sandals sounded behind him. An old man approached. A night watchman with his wooden clappers. In the distance sounded a faint temple bell, and the watchman paused to listen, then used his clappers vigorously, calling out the hour in a reedy voice. The middle of the night already.

When the old man had finished, Akitada asked, "Do you happen to know who owns a brown and white cat hereabouts?"

"You mean Patch, sir? She lives in the dead courtesan's house." He pointed up the street.

Patch? Of course. The cat was spotted. And that must be what the boy had tried to say. "The dead courtesan's house?" Akitada asked.

"Nobody lives there anymore," the watchman said. "It's a sad ruin. The cat belonged to her."

"Really? Do you happen to know who owns the property now? I might want to buy it."

The watchman shook his head. "Dear me, not that place, sir. The courtesan killed herself because her lover deserted her, and now her angry ghost roams about the garden in hopes of catching unwary men to have her revenge on. I always cross to the other side when I pass."

Akitada looked at the watchman doubtfully. It was the middle of the O-bon festival and the man was superstitious. "How did she die?"

"Drowned herself in the lake."

"Were there any children?"

"If so, they're long gone. The house belongs to the Masudas now."

Akitada thanked the man and watched him make a wide detour up ahead before following more slowly.

When he reached the spot where the cat had disappeared, he saw that a section of the wall had collapsed, and he could see into an overgrown garden hiding all but the elegant curved roof of a small villa. The night watchman turned the corner, and Akitada scrambled over the rubble, aware that he was trespassing and feeling foolish, but more than ever convinced that he must find the cat.

A clammy heat rose from the dense vegetation. Everywhere vines, brambles, and creepers covered shrubs and trees. His feeble lantern picked out a stone Buddha, half hidden beneath a blanket of ivy. Strange rustlings, squeaks, and creaks were everywhere, and clouds of insects hovered in the beam of his lantern. The atmosphere was oppressive and vaguely threatening. When he felt a tug at his sleeve, he swung around, but it was only the branch of a gaunt cedar.

There was no sign of the cat, just dense, towering shrubs and weirdly stirring curtains of leafy vines and wisteria suspended from the trees. He would have turned back had he not heard a door or shutter slamming somewhere ahead.

When he reached the house, he was covered with scratches and itching from insect bites, and his topknot was askew. But there, on the veranda, sat the cat, waiting.

The small villa was dark and empty, its shutters broken, the paper covering its windows hanging in shreds, and its roof tiles shattered on the ground. The balustrade of the veranda leaned at a crazy angle, and where once there had been doors, black cavernous spaces gaped in the walls. But once it must have been charming, poised just above the lake with its lush gardens, perhaps a nobleman's retreat from official affairs in the capital.

The lake stretched still and black to the distant string of tiny lights on the far shore, where people were celebrating the return of their dead. No one had lit candles or set up an altar in this dark place, but Akitada suddenly felt a presence, which sent shivers down his back. He looked about carefully, then walked to the villa. The cat watched his approach with unblinking eyes, motionless until he was close enough to touch it, then it slipped away and disappeared into the house. He called to it, the way he had heard young women and children call to their pets, but the animal did not reappear.

The veranda steps were missing, as was most of the floor. The house, vandalized for useful building materials, had become inaccessible to all but cats. He was turning away when he heard a faint sound. It might almost have been a wail and was definitely not made by a cat. He swung around and caught a movement inside the house.

A tall pale shape—a woman trailing some diaphanous garment?—had moved across the opening to one of the rooms and disappeared. For a moment Akitada blinked, the hair bristling on his head. Then he called out, "Who is there?" There was no answer.

Running around the corner of the house, he climbed one of the supports and held up his lantern, directing its beam into the room where he had seen the woman. The room was empty. Dead leaves lay in the corners, and rainwater had gathered in puddles on the floor. In spite of the warm and humid night, Akitada felt suddenly cold.

When he stepped down from his perch, his foot landed on something that broke with a sharp crack. In the light of the lantern, he saw a shimmer of black lacquer and mother-of-pearl, a wooden toy sword, proof that a small boy had once lived here. He picked up the hilt and saw that it was just like one he had bought Yori during the last winter of his life. It had been an expensive toy, its handle lacquered and ornamented to resemble the weapon of an adult, but Yori's pleasure in it as father and son had practiced their swordplay in the courtyard of their home had been well worth it. A sudden irrational fear gripped Akitada. He felt as if he had intruded in a strange and forbidden world. When he reached the broken wall again, his heart was pounding and he was out of breath.

Dejected, he returned to the inn. He was no closer to finding the boy or making sense of what was troubling him. A courtesan's ghost, a cat, and an expensive toy? What did it all matter? He was too weary to bother.

The Third Day: The Ghosts Depart

IN SPITE OF his exhaustion he slept poorly. The encounter with the child had brought back all of the old grief and added new fears, for he lay awake a long time, thinking that he had abandoned the boy to his fate without lifting a finger to help him. When he finally did fall asleep, his dreams were filled with snarling cats and hungry ghosts. The ghosts all had the face of the boy and followed him about, their thin arms stretched out in entreaty.

Toward dawn he woke drenched in sweat, certain that he had heard Yori cry out for him from the next room. For a single moment of joy he thought his son's death part of the dream, but then the dark and lonely room of the inn closed around him and he plunged back into despair. Waking was always the hardest.

The last day of the O-bon festival dawned clear and dry. If the weather held, Akitada would reach Heian-Kyo in a few hours' ride, but he decided to chance it and spend the morning trying to find out more about the boy, the cat, and the dead courtesan. He thought, half guiltily and half resentfully, of his wife, but women seemed to draw on inner strengths when it came to losing a child. In the months since Yori's death, Tamako had quietly resumed her daily routines, while he had been sunk into utter despair.

The curving roofs of the Masuda mansion rose behind a high wall, its large gate closed in spite of the festival. Did the Masudas lock in their ghosts? Akitada rapped sharply and gave his name to an ancient male servant, adding, "I am calling on Lord Masuda."

"My master is not well. He sees no one," wheezed the old man.

"Then perhaps one of the ladies?"

The gate opened a little wider and Akitada was admitted. The elegance of the mansion amazed him. No money had been spared on these halls and galleries. Blue tile gleamed on the roofs, red and black lacquer covered doors and pillars, and everywhere he saw carvings, gilded ornaments, and glazed terra cotta figures. They walked up the wide stairs of the main building and passed through it. Akitada caught glimpses of a painted ceiling supported by ornamented pillars, of thick grass mats and silk cushions, and of large, dim scroll paintings. Then they descended into a private garden. A covered gallery led to a second, slightly smaller hall. Here the old servant asked him to wait while he announced his visit to the ladies.

From the garden came the shouts and laughter of children. An artificial stream babbled softly past the veranda, disappeared behind an artificial hill, and reappeared, spanned by an elegant red-lacquered bridge. Its clear, pebble-strewn water was quite deep. A frog, disturbed by Akitada's shadow, jumped in and sent several fat old koi into a mild frenzy.

Suddenly two little girls skipped across the bridge, as colorful as butterflies in their embroidered gowns, their voices as high and clear as birdsong. An old nurse in black followed more slowly.

Lucky children, Akitada thought bitterly, turning away. And lucky parents!

The old man returned and took him into a beautiful room. Two ladies were seated on the pale grass mats near open doors. Both wore expensive silk gowns, one the dark gray of mourning, the other a cheerful deep rose. The lady in gray, slender and elegant, was making entries into a ledger; the other, younger lady had the half-opened scroll of an illustrated romance before her. The atmosphere was feminine, the air heavily perfumed with incense.

The lady in gray raised her face to him. No longer in her first youth but very handsome, she regarded him for a moment, then made a slight bow from the waist and said, "You are welcome, my lord. Please forgive the informality, but Father is not well and there was no one else to receive you. I am Lady Masuda and this is my late husband's secondary wife, Kohime."

Kohime had the cheerful, plain face and robust body of a peasant girl. Akitada decided to address the older woman. "I am deeply distressed to disturb your peace," he said, "and regret extremely the ill health of Lord Masuda. Perhaps you would like me to return when he is better?"

"I am afraid Father will not improve," said Lady Masuda. "He is old and . . . his mind wanders. You may speak freely." She gestured at the account book. "I have been forced to take on the burdens of running this family."

Akitada expressed his interest in buying a summer place on the lake within easy reach of the capital and in a beautiful setting. Lady Masuda listened politely until he asked about the abandoned villa. Then she stiffened with distaste. "The Masudas own half of Otsu. I would not know the house you refer to. Perhaps . . ."

But the cheerful Kohime chimed in. "Oh, Hatsuko, that must be the house where our husband's . . ." She gulped and covered her mouth. "Oh!"

Lady Masuda paled. She gave Kohime a look. "My sister is mistaken. I am sorry that I cannot be of more assistance."

Akitada was too old a hand at dealing with suspects in criminal cases not to know that Lady Masuda was lying. Of the two women, Kohime was the simpler, but he could think of no way to speak to her alone. Thanking the ladies, he left.

Outside, the old servant waited. "There's someone hoping to speak to you, my lord. The children's nurse. When I mentioned your name, she begged for a few moments of your time."

Turning, Akitada caught sight of the elderly woman in black peering anxiously over a large shrub and bowing. He returned her bow.

"I don't believe I have met her," he told the old manservant.

"No, my lord. But when her son was a student in the capital, he was accused of murdering his professor. You cleared him and saved his life."

"Good heavens! Don't tell me she is the mother of that . . ." Akitada had been about to call him a rascal, but corrected himself in time, ". . . bright young fellow Ishikawa."

"Yes, Ishikawa." The old man laughed, rubbing his hands, as if Akitada had been very clever to remember. "When the gentleman is ready to leave, I shall be waiting at the gate."

Akitada had no wish to be reminded. It had happened a long time ago, in happier years, when Akitada had been courting Yori's mother, but he sighed and stepped down into the garden.

Mrs. Ishikawa was in her sixties and, it seemed, a much respected member of the Masuda household, having raised both the son and the grandchildren of the old lord. Akitada managed to end her long and passionate expressions of gratitude by asking, "How is your son?"

"He is head steward for Middle Counselor Sadanori and has his own family now," she said proudly. "I am sure he would wish to express his deep sense of obligation for your help in his difficulties."

Akitada doubted it. Ishikawa, a thoroughly selfish young man, had been innocent of murder but deeply implicated in a cheating scandal that had rocked the imperial university, and he had held Akitada responsible for his dismissal. But as Akitada gazed into her lined face with the kind eyes smiling up at him, he was glad he had spared someone the pain of losing a son.

"Perhaps you can help me," he said. "There is an abandoned villa on the lake I was told belongs to the Masudas, but Lady Masuda denies this."

The old lady looked startled. "Peony's house? Lady Masuda would not wish to be reminded of that."

Peony was a professional name often used by courtesans and entertainers. Akitada guessed, "Lady Masuda's husband kept Peony in the villa on the lake?"

Mrs. Ishikawa squirmed. "We are not to speak of this."

"I see. I will not force you then. But perhaps you can tell me about a cat I saw there. It was white with brown spots."

Her face brightened momentarily. "Oh, Patch. Such a dear little kitten, and the boy doted on it. I used to wonder what became of it." Tears suddenly rose to her eyes and she clamped a hand over her mouth, realizing that she had said too much.

Akitada pounced. "There was a little boy then?"

"Oh, the poor child is dead," she cried. "They're both dead. My lady says Peony killed him and then herself." A stunned silence fell. "Oh, sir," she whimpered, "please don't mention that I told you. It was horrible, but there was nothing we could do. It's best forgotten." She was so distressed that Akitada nearly apologized. But his mind churned with questions and, while he respected her loyalty, he saw again the boy's face as he was dragged away from him.

"Mrs. Ishikawa," he said earnestly, "two days ago I found a deaf-mute boy. He was about five years old, and when he saw the cat, he recognized it. I think he tried to say its name."

She stared at him. "He's the right age, but Peony's boy talked and sang all day long. It couldn't be him."

From the garden came the voice of Lady Masuda calling for the nurse. Mrs. Ishikawa flushed guiltily. "Forgive me, my lord, but I must go. Please, forget what I said." And with a deep bow she was gone.

Akitada stared after her. If she was right about Peony's child being dead, then the boy belonged to someone else, perhaps even to the repulsive couple who had dragged him away. But how did Lady Masuda come to tell such things to the nurse? Surely because Mrs. Ishikawa had known Peony and her son and had been fond of them. The elegant lady who had been bent over the account book knew what was in the interest of the Masudas, and the dubious offspring of a former courtesan was best assumed dead.

As he walked back to the gate, the glistening roofs of the Masuda mansion testified to the family's substantial wealth, all of it belonging to an ailing old man without an heir. Akitada wondered about the deaths of the courtesan Peony and her child. Perhaps all the years of solving crimes committed by corrupt, greedy, and vengeful people had made him suspicious. Or perhaps his encounter with the wailing ghost had put him in mind of a restless spirit in search of justice. He was neither religious nor superstitious, but there had been nothing reasonable about the events of the past two days. Or about his own state of mind.

And suddenly, there in the Masuda's courtyard, he realized that the bleak and paralyzing hopelessness that had stifled him like a blanket for many months now had lifted. He was once again pursuing a mystery.

Turning to the old servant who waited patiently beside the gate, he asked, "When did the young lord die?"

"Which one, my lord? The old lord's son died three years ago when his horse threw him, but the first lady's little son drowned last year." He sighed. "Now there are only the two little girls of the second lady, but the old lord cares nothing for them."

Akitada's eyebrows rose. "How did the boy drown?"

"He fell into the stream in the garden. It happened a year ago when Mrs. Ishikawa was away on a pilgrimage and the other servants weren't watching."

So Lady Masuda had also lost a son. And Peony, and possibly her son, had died soon after. Also by drowning. Were all these deaths unrelated accidents?

A picture was beginning to shape in Akitada's mind. To begin with, the story was not unusual. A wealthy young nobleman falls in love with a beautiful courtesan, buys out her contract, and keeps her for his private enjoyment in a place where he can visit her often. Such liaisons could last months or lifetimes. In this case, only the death of the younger Masuda had ended his affair, and there had been a child. What if Lady Masuda, who had lost first her husband and then her only son, had in a grief-maddened state one night wandered to the lake villa and killed both the rival and her child?

Akitada had much to think about. He thanked the old man and left.

Crowds already filled the main streets of Otsu, most in their holiday best and eager to celebrate the departure of their ancestral ghosts. Akitada contemplated wryly that for most people, death loses its more painful attributes as soon as duty has been observed and the souls of those who were once deeply mourned have been duly acknowledged and can, with clear conscience, be sent back to the other world for another year. Tonight people everywhere would gather on the shores of rivers, lakes, and oceans and set afloat tiny straw boats containing a small candle or oil lamp to carry the spirits of the dear departed out into the open water, where, one by one, the lights would grow smaller until they died out completely. But what of those whose lives and families had been taken from them by violence?

Akitada asked for direction to the local warden's office. There he walked into a shouting match among a matron, a poorly dressed man, and a ragged youngster of about fourteen. The warden was looking from one to the other and scratched his head.

As he waited for the matter to be settled, Akitada pieced together what had happened. Someone had knocked the matron to the ground from behind and snatched a package containing a length of silk from under her arm. When she had gathered her wits, she had seen the two villains running away through the crowds. Her screams had brought one of the local constables who had set off after the men and caught them a short distance away. The package was lying in the street, and the two were scuffling with each other.

The trouble was that each blamed the theft on the other and claimed to have been chasing down the culprit.

The ragged boy had tears in his eyes. He kept repeating, "I was only trying to help," and claimed his mother was waiting for some fish he was to have purchased for their holiday meal. The man looked outraged. "Lazy kids! Don't want to work and think they can steal an honest person's goods. Maybe a few good whippings will teach him before it's too late."

The matron, though vocal about her ordeal, was no help at all. "I tell you, I didn't see who did it! He knocked me down and nearly broke my back."

The warden shook his head, apparently at the end of his tether. "You should have brought witnesses," he grumbled to the constable. "Now it's too late, and what'll we do?"

The constable protested, "Oh come on, Warden. The kid did it. Look at his clothes. Look at his face. Guilt's written all over him. Let's take him out back and question him."

Akitada looked at the boy and saw that he was terrified. Interrogation meant the whip, and even innocent people had been known to confess to crimes when beaten. He decided to step in.

"Look here, Constable," he said in his sternest official tone, "whipping a suspect without good cause is against the law. And you do not have good cause without a witness."

They all turned to stare at him. The warden, seeing a person of authority, cheered up. "Perhaps you have some information in this matter, sir?"

"No. But I have a solution for your problem. Take both men outside and make them run the same distance. The loser will be your thief."

"A truly wise decision, sir," cried the matron, folding her hands and bowing to Akitada. "The Buddha helps the innocent."

"No, madam. The thief got caught because his captor was the better runner."

They all adjourned to a large courtyard, where the constables marked off the proper distance, and then sent the two suspects off on their race. As Akitada had known, the thin boy won easily. He thanked Akitada awkwardly and rushed off to purchase his fish, while the thief was taken away.

"Well, sir," cried the delighted warden, "I'm much obliged to you. It might have gone hard with that young fellow otherwise. Now, how can I be of service?"

Having established such unexpectedly friendly relations, Akitada introduced himself and told the story of the mute boy. The warden's face grew serious. When Akitada reached the Masuda family's account of Peony's death, the warden said, "I went there when she was found. There was no child, dead or alive, though there might have been one. Bodies disappear in the lake. The woman Peony had drowned, but there was a large bruise on her temple. The coroner's report states that the bruise was not fatal and that she must have hit a rock when she jumped into the lake. But there were no rocks where she was found, and the water was too shallow for jumping anyway."

"Then why did you not speak up at the time?"

"I did not attend the hearing. Someone told me about the verdict later. I did go and ask the coroner about that bruise. He said she could have bumped her head earlier." The warden added defensively, "It looked like a suicide. The neighbors said she'd been deserted by her lover."

Akitada did not agree. He thought Peony had been struck unconscious and then put into the water to drown, and if the boy was indeed her son, he might have seen her killer. But that boy was mute.

Or was he?

"The boy I found," he said, "was terrified of the people who claimed him. I thought at first it was because he expected another beating. Perhaps so, but I think now that they are not his parents. I believe he has a more than casual connection with the cat and could be Peony's missing son."

"Holy Amida!" breathed the warden. "What a story that would be!" He said eagerly, "They live in a fishing village outside town. I'll ride out now and check into it. If you're right, sir, it may solve the case. But that would really make a person wonder about the Masudas."

"It would indeed. I'll get my horse from the inn and join you."

The weather continued clear. They took the road Akitada had traveled two days before. On the way, the warden told Akitada about the Masuda family.

The old lord had doted on his handsome son and had chosen his son's first wife for both her birth and beauty, but the young lord did not care for his bride and started to visit the courtesans of the capital. His worried father sought to keep him home to produce an heir by presenting him next with a sturdy country girl for a second wife. She proved fertile and gave him two daughters before he lost interest again. It was at this time that the young husband had installed Peony, a beautiful courtesan, in the lake villa, where he stayed with her, turning his back on his two wives. The old lord forced him to return temporarily to his family, and the first lady finally conceived and bore a son, but her husband died soon after.

And, mused Akitada, while all of Otsu took an avid interest in the births and deaths in the Masuda mansion, hardly anyone cared about the fate of a courtesan and her child. In fact, he was surprised they had been allowed to continue living in the villa.

When Akitada and the warden reached the fishing village, they found the man Mimura leaning against the wall of a dilapidated shack, watching the boy sweep up a smelly mess of fish entrails, fins, and vegetable peelings. Dressed in rags again, the child now sported a large black eye.

"Hey, Mimura?" shouted the warden. The boy raised his head and stared at them. Then he dropped his broom and ran to Akitada, who jumped from his horse and caught him in his arms. The child was filthy and stank of rotten fish, and he clung to Akitada for dear life.

Mimura walked up, glowering. "If it's about the boy, we settled all that," he told the warden. "I should've asked for more than the bits and pieces he gave the kid, and that's the truth." He turned with a sneer to Akitada. "You had him a whole day and night. That ought to be worth at least two pieces of silver."

The warden reddened to the roots of his hair, and Akitada realized belatedly that he was being accused of an unnatural fondness for boys. A cold fury took hold of him. "That child is not yours," he thundered. "And stealing children is a crime."

Mimura lost some of his bravado, and the warden quickly added, "Yes. This boy's not registered to you, yet you claimed him as your own. I'm afraid I'll have to arrest you."

Mimura's jaw dropped. "We didn't steal him, Warden. Honest. He's got no family. We took him in, the wife and I."

"Really? Out of the goodness of your heart? Then where are his papers? Where was he born and who were his people?"

"I'm just a poor working man, Warden. This woman gave him to my wife, and she paid her a bit of money to look after him." He turned to call his slatternly spouse from the shack.

She approached nervously and confirmed his story. "I was selling fish in the market. It was getting dark when this lady came. She was carrying the boy and said, 'This poor child has just lost his parents. I'll pay you if you'll raise him as your own.' I could see the boy was sickly, but we needed the money, so I said yes."

"Her name?" the warden growled.

"She didn't say."

"You called her a lady. What did she look like?" Akitada asked.

"I couldn't tell. She had on a veil and it was dark. And she was in a hurry. She just passed over the boy and the money and left."

"How much money?" the warden wanted to know.

"A few pieces of silver. And a poor bargain it was," Mimura grumbled. "He's a weakling and deaf and dumb as a stone. Look at him!"

"Did you give him the black eye?" Akitada asked.

"Me? No. He's a clumsy boy. A cripple."

Akitada lifted the boy on his horse. "Come along, Warden," he said over his shoulder. "You can deal with them later. We need to find this child's family."

On the way back, the small, warm, smelly body in his arm, Akitada was filled with new purpose. He outlined his suspicions to the warden, but he spoke cautiously, for he was now certain that the child could hear very well.

"So you see," he said, "we must speak to Lord Masuda himself, for the women are covering up the affair."

The warden, who had been admirably cooperative so far, demurred. "Nobody sees the old lord. They say he's lost his mind."

"Nevertheless, we must try."

The Masuda mansion opened its gates for a second time. If the ancient servant was surprised to see Akitada with a ragged child in his arms and accompanied by the warden, he was too well-mannered to ask. But he shook his head stubbornly when Akitada demanded to see the old lord.

"Look," Akitada finally said, "I think that this boy is Lord Masuda's grandson, the child of the courtesan Peony. Would he not wish to know him before he dies?"

"But," stammered the old man, "that boy is dead. Lady Masuda said so herself."

"She was mistaken."

The old man came closer and peered up at the child. "Amida!" he whispered. "Those eyebrows. Can it be?"

He took them then. They found the old lord in his study. He sat sunken into himself, one gnarled hand pulling at the thin white beard that had grown long with neglect, his hooded eyes looking at nothing.

"My lord," said the servant timidly. "You have visitors." There was no reaction from Lord Masuda. "Lord Sugawara is here with the warden." Still no sign that the master had heard. "They have a small boy with them, my lord. They say . . ."

Akitada stopped him with a gesture. Leading the child to the old man, he said, "Go to your grandfather, boy."

For a moment he clung to his hand, but his eyes were wide with curiosity. Then he made a bow and a small noise in the back of his throat.

Lord Masuda's hand paused its stroking, but he gave no other sign that he had noticed.

The boy crept forward until he was close enough to touch the gnarled fingers with his own small ones. The old hand trembled at his touch, and Lord Masuda looked at the child.

"Yori?" he asked, his voice thin as a thread. "Is it you?"

The boy nodded, and Akitada's heart stopped. He turned to the servant. "Did he call the boy 'Yori'?"

The servant was wiping his eyes. "The master's confused. He thinks he's his dead son, whose name was Tadayori. The child looks like him, you see. We used to call him Yori for short."

It was a common abbreviation—his own Yori had been Yorinaga—but Akitada was shaken. That he should have crossed paths with this child during the O-bon festival when his grief had caused him to mistake the small pale figure for his son's ghost and he had called him "Yori" now seemed like a miracle. Fatefully, the child had come to him, and together they had encountered the extraordinary cat that had led him to Peony's villa and the Masudas.

The old lord was still looking searchingly at the child. Finally he turned his head and regarded them. "Who are these men?" he asked the servant. "And why is the boy dressed in these stinking rags?"

Akitada stepped forward and introduced himself and the warden. Lord Masuda looked merely baffled.

"My lord, were you aware of your son's liaison with the courtesan Peony?"

A faint flicker in the filmy eyes. "Peony?"

"They had a child, a boy, born five years ago. Your son continued his visits to the lady and acknowledged the boy as his." There was just a broken sword for proof, but a nobleman buys such a sword only for his own son.

The old lord looked from him to the boy and then back again. "He resembles my son." The gnarled hand stretched out and traced the child's straight eyebrows. "You hurt yourself," he murmured, touching the bruised eye. "What is your name, boy?"

The child struggled to speak, when there was an interruption.

Lady Masuda swept in, followed closely by Kohime. "What is going on here?" she demanded, her eyes on her father-in-law. "He is not well . . ."

Akitada's eyes flew to the child. He had hoped for a confrontation between the boy and Lady Masuda, and now he prayed for another miracle. He saw him turn toward the women and his face transform into a mask of terror and fury. Then he catapulted himself forward, his voice bursting into gurgling speech. "I'll kill you, I'll kill you," he screeched. But he rushed past Lady Masuda and threw himself on Kohime, fists flying.

Kohime shrieked, gave the child a violent push, and ran from the room.

Akitada bent to help the boy up. He had guessed wrong, but his heart was filled with joy. "So you found your voice at last, little one," he said, hugging him. "All will be well now."

"She hurt her. She hurt my mother," sobbed the child.

"Shh," Akitada said. "Your grandfather and the warden will take care of her."

Lady Masuda was very pale, but her eyes devoured the child. "Oh, I am so glad he is alive," she cried. "How did you find him? I've been searching everywhere, terrified by what I had done."

The old lord looked at her. "Are you responsible then?" he asked, almost conversationally. "He resembles your son, don't you think? Both inherited their father's eyebrows."

She smiled through tears. "Yes, Father. But he's so thin now, poor child. And I gave that woman all the money we had."

The warden cleared his throat. "Er, what happened just then, sir?" he whispered to Akitada.

"I think Lady Masuda knows," Akitada said. "It would be best if she explained, but perhaps the child . . ." He turned to the boy. "What is your name?"

"You know. Yori. Like my father," he replied, as if the question were foolish.

Lord Masuda's face softened. "Yes. That was my son's name when he was small. But you were about to suggest something, Lord Sugawara?"

"Perhaps Yori might be given into the care of your servant for a bath and clean clothes while we discuss this matter."

"Oh, please let me take him," pleaded Lady Masuda.

"No," said Lord Masuda. "You will stay here and make a clean breast of this." She hung her head and nodded. Her father-in-law looked at the old servant. "Send for my other daughter and bring the child back to me later." When they had left, he sat up a little straighter. "Now, Daughter. Why was I not informed about my grandson and his mother?"

She knelt before him. "Forgive me, Father. I wished to spare you. You were so ill after my husband died."

"You were not well yourself after you lost your child," he said, his voice a little gentler.

"No. I had known all along where my husband had been spending his time. Women always know. I was jealous, especially when I heard she had given him a son while I was childless. But then my husband returned to me, and after my own son was born, I no longer minded so much that my husband went back to her."

Lord Masuda nodded. "My son told me that he wished to live with this woman and her child. As he had given me an heir, I permitted it."

Lady Masuda hung her head a little lower. "But then he died. And when my son also passed from this world . . ." Her voice broke, and she whispered, "Losing a child is the most terrible loss of all." For a moment she trembled with grief, then she squared her shoulders and continued. "I became obsessed with my husband's mistress and her boy. I wanted to see them. Kohime was very understanding. She came with me. It was . . . an awkward meeting. She was very beautiful. I could see they were poor and I was glad. We watched the boy play with his kitten in the garden, and suddenly I thought if we could buy the child from her, I could raise him. He was my husband's son, and . . ." She hesitated and looked up fearfully at Lord Masuda.

He grunted. "I should have taken care of them. If you had brought him to me, no doubt I would have agreed to an adoption."

"I went home and gathered up all the gold I could find, and Kohime added what she had saved, and we went back to her. But when we told her what we wanted, she became upset and cried she would rather die than sell her son. She snatched up the boy and ran out into the garden. We were afraid she would do something desperate. Kohime ran after her and tried to take the child. They fought . . ."

Lord Masuda stopped her. "Here is Kohime now. Let her speak for herself."

Kohime had been weeping. Her round face was splotched and her hair disheveled. She threw herself on the floor before her father-in-law. "I didn't mean to kill her," she wailed. "I thought she was going into the lake with the child, so I grabbed for her. When we fell down, the boy ran away. She bit and kicked me. I don't know how it happened, but suddenly I was bleeding and afraid. My hand found a loose stone on the path and I hit her with it. I didn't mean to kill her." She burst into violent tears.

Lord Masuda sighed deeply.

Lady Masuda moved beside Kohime and stroked her hair. "It was an accident, Father. The boy came back," she said, her voice toneless. "He had a wooden sword and he cut Kohime with it. I saw it all from the veranda of the villa. When Kohime came running back to me, she was covered with blood. I took her into the house to stop the bleeding. She said she had killed the woman." She brushed away tears.

A heavy silence fell. Then Akitada asked gently, "Did you go back to make sure Peony was dead, Lady Masuda?"

She nodded. "We were terrified, but after a while we both crept out. She was still lying there, quite still. The boy was holding her hand and crying. Kohime said, 'We must hide the body.' But there was the boy. Of course, we could not take him back with us after what had happened. We thought perhaps we could make it look as if she had fallen into the water by accident. We decided that I would take away the boy, and Kohime would hide the body because she is the stronger. I tried to talk to the child, but it was as if his spirit had fled. His eyes were open, but that was all. He let me take him, and I carried him away from the house. I did not know what to do, but when I saw a woman in the market packing up to return to her village, I gave her the money and the child."

The warden muttered, "All that gold, and the Mimuras beat and starved him."

"And you, Kohime?" asked Lord Masuda.

Kohime, the plain peasant girl in the fine silks of a noblewoman, said with childlike simplicity, "I put Peony in the lake. It wasn't far, and people thought she'd drowned herself."

"Dear heaven!" muttered the warden. He looked sick.

"You have both behaved very badly," said Lord Masuda to his daughters-in-law. "What will happen to you is up to the authorities now."

After a glance at the warden, who shook his head helplessly, Akitada said, "Peony's death was a tragic accident. No good can come from a public disclosure now. It is her son's future we must consider."

The warden was still staring at Kohime. "It was getting dark," he muttered. "You can see how two hysterical women could make such a mistake."

"You are very generous." Lord Masuda bowed. "In that case, I shall decide their punishment. My grandson will be raised as my heir by my son's first lady. It will be her opportunity to atone to him. Kohime and her daughters will leave this house and reside in the lake villa, where she will pray daily for the soul of the poor woman she killed." He looked sternly at his daughters-in-law. "Will you agree to this?"

They bowed. Lady Masuda said, "Yes. Thank you, Father. We are both deeply grateful."

Akitada looked after the women as they left, Lady Masuda with her arm around Kohime, and thought of how she had said, "Losing a child is the most terrible loss of all."

When they were gone, the old lord clapped his hands. "Where is my grandson?"

The boy came, clean and resplendently dressed, and sat beside his grandfather. "Well, Yori," the old man asked, "shall you like it here, do you think?"

The boy looked around and nodded. "Yes, Grandfather, but I would like Patch to live here, too."

THEY PUT DOWN their offering of fish. The cat was watching them from the broken veranda. It waited until they had withdrawn a good distance before strolling up and sniffing the food. With another disdainful glance in their direction, it settled down to its meal, and Akitada threw the net. But the animal shied away at the last moment and, only partially caught, streaked into the house, dragging the net behind. A gruesome series of yowls followed.

"Patch got hurt," cried the boy. "Please go help her."

Akitada had to climb into the villa. He used the same post from which he had looked for the ghost, but this time he swung himself across the veranda and into the empty room. Walking gingerly across the broken boards, he found the cat in the next room, rolling about completely entangled in the netting. Carefully scooping up the growling and spitting bundle in his arms, he returned the same way. He had one leg over the window frame when he heard the mournful sound of the ghost again. Passing the furious cat down to the boy, he looked back over his shoulder.

One of the long strips of oil paper covering a window had come loose and was sliding across the opening as a breeze from the lake caught it. When its edge brushed the floor, it made the queer sound he had heard.

So much for ghosts!

Outside, Patch, a very real cat, began to purr in Yori's arms.

IT WAS ALMOST dark before Akitada returned to the inn to collect his belongings and pay his bill. He would not reach home until late, but he wanted to be with his wife on this final night of the festival. They would mourn their son together, sharing their grief as they had shared their love.

When he rode out of Otsu, people were lighting the bonfires to guide the dead on their way back to the other world. Soon they would gather on the shore to send off the spirit boats, and the tiny points of light would bob on the waves until it looked as if the stars had fallen into the water.

Someday he would return to visit this other Yori, the child who had come into his life to remind him that life places obligations on a man that cannot be denied.

ED McBAIN

LEAVING NAIROBI

June 2003

THIS WAS THE final story by the late Ed McBain/Evan Hunter to appear in *AHMM*. Typical of this remarkably versatile writer, though best known for his 87th Precinct police procedurals, this story skillfully builds suspense amid the beautifully evoked backdrop of the Kenyan countryside.

■

On the jumbo jet from Nairobi to New York, Jeremy is trying to explain to his wife why he feels . . . well . . . somewhat guilty about Davey Ladd's suicide.

Everywhere around them, passengers are wearing earphones and watching the movie.

Jeremy is whispering all this.

"But why should you feel guilty at *all?*" Therese asks.

She is whispering, too. They have spent the last two days in a courtroom on Taifa Road, where a panel of magistrates ruled that David Lawrence Ladd had taken his own life. It rained during the entire inquest. It was still raining when the plane took off from Jomo Kenyatta International this morning.

"Well, you know," Jeremy says. "Because of the problem we had with him."

"The problem was of his own making," Therese says.

"Even so."

"He was a very troubled individual," she says.

Therese is thirty-two years old, lean and supple, and almost as tall as Jeremy; a startlingly beautiful brunette with large brown eyes and long black hair. On safari, she wore her hair coiled into a bun at the back of her neck. She wore khaki shorts she bought at the Gap and a khaki jacket with huge flap pockets. For the long plane ride home, she is wearing jeans and a baggy white cotton sweater.

Therese is twenty years younger than Jeremy.

He never expected the difference in their ages would become a problem, especially not so soon after their marriage. He knows he is not a spectacularly handsome man, but he considers himself reasonably good-looking in a somewhat distinguished way, with graying sideburns and a tall . . . well, almost stately . . . bearing. He considers himself a modest man, and he's not at all sure he agrees with *New York Magazine*'s evaluation of him as one of the best internists in the city. He recognizes that he is a very good doctor . . . but one of the best? All he knows for certain is that he has tried to live both his personal and professional lives by the credo "Do no harm."

But now Davey Ladd is dead, isn't he?

"By his own hand," Therese reminds him.

"Yes."

"So why should you be feeling guilty?"

"You should have seen him."

"You see dead people all the time."

"Not that many."

"Enough. You're in the hospital every day . . ."

"Yes, but . . ."

"There are dead people in the hospital."

"They don't look the way he did."

Davey Ladd lying naked on his back with his own 9-millimeter pistol in his mouth, blood all over the pillow and the bed . . .

"This was uncontrolled bleeding, Therese. This was . . . wanton. The back of his skull was gone, the force of the explosion burst his eyeballs. It was gruesome."

"I can imagine."

They are silent for several moments. The man sitting on Jeremy's left, on the aisle, has fallen asleep with his earphones half on, half off. He is snoring loudly, and the muted sound of actors shouting at each other comes from the one earphone hanging loose on his cheek.

"I just hope it wasn't anything . . ."

"It wasn't," Therese says.

". . . I said or did."

"How could it have been?"

"I don't know."

"It was getting out of hand, Jere."

"I know."

"He was a very troubled person."

"I know."

"From the very start," Therese says.

"WELL, WELL, WELL," Davey says. "What have we here!"

These are his very first words to them.

They are standing with Frank Dobbs just outside the tent that will be theirs for the next eight days. It was Frank who appeared like a savior out of the maelstrom of baggage and travelers at the Nairobi airport the night before. It was Frank who drove them to their overnight lodgings in Nairobi, Frank who picked them up again early this morning for their charter flight to the Masai Mara. Frank Dobbs, in his early forties, Jeremy guesses, looking ruddy and robust and sporting a handlebar mustache that gives him the appearance of a London pub keeper.

Their campsite is on the banks of the Mara River, which bisects the huge game preserve. Bordered by a patchy forest on one side, the muddy river meanders through the vast plain, hippos lazing in its waters, crocodiles sunbathing on its scrubby banks. The proximity of the crocs is not reassuring to Jeremy; the camp cannot be more than fifty yards from where they tilt their gaping jaws to the sun.

"This will be home till the twentieth," Frank says.

He is showing them a thirty-foot-long sleeping tent with twin cots, a wardrobe, two folding camp chairs, and a low round table. There is a separate toilet enclosure some five feet behind the tent. There is a small shower stall to the left of that. Everything under canvas. This is not the royal palace. Nor does it even seem like the "luxurious accommodations" promised in the Dobbs-Ladd Safaris brochure.

"Well, well, well. What have we here!"

They all turn when they hear the voice.

Davey Ladd is wearing very short, tight khaki shorts that bulge with his masculinity. He is wearing as well high-topped shoes and moss-colored socks, a short-sleeved khaki shirt that exposes muscular arms. A shooting vest over that, with loops for shotgun cartridges. He is perhaps a shade under six feet tall, bronzed from constant exposure to the sun. He is hatless, his hair blond, his eyes a greenish-gray. A 9-millimeter pistol is bolstered on his right hip.

"Well, well, well. What have we here!"

Jeremy might accept these welcoming words as boyish enthusiasm—Davey is perhaps twenty-seven years old—were they not so blatantly directed to Therese.

"Davey," Frank says, "please meet Dr. and Mrs. Palmer. My partner, Davey Ladd."

"How do you do?" Jeremy says, and extends his hand.

Davey takes Therese's hand instead. Looking into her eyes, holding her hand, he says, "My pleasure, Mrs. Palmer."

And holds her hand a fraction of an instant too long.

Flustered, Therese withdraws it.

THE OTHER COUPLE on the safari is from Minnesota.

They introduce themselves at dinner that night as Lou and Helen Cantori. Lou is a building contractor. Helen works at the public library in Minneapolis. They are both in their mid-forties, Jeremy guesses, both a trifle overweight. Helen is eager to take notes and photographs she can use for a talk at the library when she gets home. Lou tells them he would have preferred going to Vegas, but he always goes instead to all these exotic places Helen keeps pulling out of a hat. Last year they went to Papua New Guinea. God knows where they'll end up next year.

They sit around a huge campfire after dinner, looking out over the boundless plain, sparks flying into the darkness beyond. A huge star-filled sky spreads endlessly above them. On the perimeter of the camp they can see the Masai guards patrolling, their spears at the ready.

"Where do all the animals go at night?" Helen wonders out loud.

Davey takes a huge torchlight from where it is resting beside his camp chair. Rising languidly, he snaps on the torch and begins moving its beam in a slow semicircle along the outer reaches of the compound.

Eyes.

There are eyes out there.

Pairs of eyes gleaming in the darkness.

Watching the fire.

Watching the camp.

"Oh my God!" Therese says.

It suddenly occurs to Jeremy that their safety and their well-being—indeed their very lives—are entirely dependent on two strangers their travel agent recommended.

Grinning, Davey snaps out the torch.

"Don't worry, Terry," he says. "I'm here to take care of you."

"JEREMY?" SHE whispers.

"Yes?"

"Are you awake?"

"Yes, darling."

Beyond the canvas walls of their sleeping tent, Jeremy can hear the cries and calls and rumbles of the night, some very distant, some sounding too terribly close.

"What's wrong with him?" she whispers.

"Who, darling?"

"The Great White Hunter."

"He's just trying to be friendly."

"I don't need a friend," she says. "What does he mean he'll take *care* of me? Let him take care of Helen Cantori if he wants to take care of someone."

Something makes a low rumbling sound just outside the tent.

"Did you hear that?" she asks.

"Yes."

"What was it?"

"Maybe the Masai guard."

They lie still on their separate cots, listening.

"I feel very exposed," Therese says.

"Yes."

"Do you?"

"Yes."

"Frightened. I feel frightened."

"Yes, I do, too."

They have been married for only three months now. When Alicia died, Jeremy thought he could never be close to another woman again. But then, two years ago, he met Therese at a medical convention in the Caribbean, staying alone at the same hotel where the assembled internists held their daily meetings under umbrellas on the beach.

"Shall I come to your bed?" she asks.

"Please."

He hears her rustling in the dark. Hears her footfalls on the groundsheet. He throws back the light blanket for her, and she crawls into the narrow cot beside him. She huddles close in his arms. He can hear her gentle breathing beside him. And then the low rumbling just outside again.

"There it is again," she whispers.

They listen.

In the dark, every sound seems amplified.

The rumbling again, just outside the tent flaps now.

"Some honeymoon," Therese says, and they both laugh in the darkness, like terrified children.

THERE ARE TWO Land Rovers.

Frank will be driving one of them, Davey the other. The Cantoris, suspecting that Frank is the more experienced of the two Great White Hunters, if only because he is the older, are already waiting in his car after breakfast, innocent smiles on their faces.

"Ready for a little excitement?" Davey asks Therese.

She and Jeremy climb into the backseat of the vehicle. The top is open. Jeremy wonders aloud if this is safe. "Won't animals be able to jump inside?"

"Don't worry, Doc," Davey says. "You're in good hands."

The lead car is pulling out of the campsite. The native workers are carrying buckets of water up from the river to the cook tent, where they will heat it for the canvas sacks above the shower stalls. As Jeremy understands this, they will shower only in the evenings, before dinner and after the day's game drives. For their morning ablutions, their two tent boys will carry steaming water to the sink just outside the sleeping tent.

All of the sleeping tents—those for the two safari owners, those for the safari guests—are set up in one corner of the camp, not five yards away from each other. The mess tent is in the center of the camp, the cook tent on the far end, closest to the river. There is another small tent Frank calls the "library," full of literature about

Africa. As they drive out of camp, two men in the cook tent are busily stripping some sort of animal.

"Impala for dinner tonight," Davey says, swinging in behind Frank's car. "Ever taste impala, Terry?"

"No," she says.

"Delicious. Bet there are lots of delicious things you've never tasted," he says, turning from the wheel to look back at her and smile.

"You know," she says, "I'm sorry, but nobody ever calls me Terry."

"Hey, *I'm* sorry," he says. "Thought that was your name."

"My wife's name is Therese," Jeremy says.

"Therese—got it, Doc," Davey says, and winks at him in the rearview mirror.

"And I wish you wouldn't call me Doc. That was for med school."

"Sorry, guys," Davey says. "Let's just have some fun here, okay?"

IN ALL HIS years as a physician, Jeremy has delivered only one baby, and that while he was still interning at Beth Israel in New York City. Today, on the endless plain of the Masai Mara, where sudden death is a minute-by-minute possibility, an impala gives birth before their very eyes.

The Land Rover is not five feet from her as she squeezes the newborn from her loins and licks it clean. She raises her head. Her long ears begin twitching. Her nostrils twitch as well. They are close enough to see her wet nose, her nostrils. And then, to their immense surprise, she moves off, leaving the newborn lying in the tall grass, as still as any rock, unable to see or to walk, seemingly helpless.

"There are probably cheetah out hunting," Davey explains. "The mother will be back for her tomorrow. Better and safer not to draw attention to her now."

AT DINNER THAT night, Therese can't stop worrying about the baby impala.

"Will the mother know where to find her?" she asks.

"Oh, sure," Frank says. "Besides, she won't have any scent for maybe two, three months. The predators won't be able to . . ."

"Oh, please," Therese says, "don't even suggest it!"

"She'll be all right, don't worry, hon," Helen says reassuringly and pats Therese's hand.

"She was so adorable," Therese says. "I'd like to take her home with me."

"Take me home instead," Davey says.

There is a silence at the table.

"I'd make a lovely pet," he adds, and this time Helen and Lou laugh at what they realize is a joke.

Davey grins like an adolescent boy.

Shrugs.

Lifts his wineglass in a silent toast to everyone at the table.

"Do you have any children at home?" Frank asks, possibly trying to change the subject; Jeremy can't be certain.

"We've only been married since September," he says.

"Really?" Helen says. "Lou, do you hear this? They're newlyweds."

"In fact, this is a delayed honeymoon," Jeremy explains. "I couldn't get away in the fall."

Therese takes his hand on the table top, squeezes it.

"Oh, how sweet," Davey says.

THERESE IS AFRAID to go to the toilet in the middle of the night, because she will have to cross five feet of open space to get to the primitive hole in the ground, and she is fearful wild animals may be marching around the camp, despite the Masai guards with their spears. Jeremy accompanies her to the toilet before they turn in for the night, waiting outside the small canvas enclosure for her, and then escorting her back to the sleeping tent again.

In the dark, in the personal privacy of their own tent, they begin whispering again. This is only their second night out, but they have come to realize that the sole privacy they will ever have is here in this tent, and in the shower stall behind it, and in the little toilet hut alongside that.

"He makes me uncomfortable," Therese whispers.

"Yes, me, too."

"His remarks are so inappropriate."

"Yes."

"Is it something I'm doing?"

"Don't be ridiculous."

"Maybe I should stop wearing shorts."

"Honey, you can wear whatever you like, whenever . . ."

"I don't *want* his attentions, Jere. I don't *want* his goddamn innuendoes . . ."

"Shhh, shhh."

The canvas walls are terribly thin. Whenever they rustle with the slightest vagrant wind, Jeremy is sure it's a lion rubbing against them.

"I feel so helpless," Therese says.

"Yes."

"I mean, we're in the middle of the jungle . . ."

"The plain."

". . . and they're supposed to be here protecting us and making sure . . ."

"Yes."

"But instead, he keeps hitting on me!"

They are silent for a very long time.

"Do you want to go home?" Jeremy asks at last.

"How can we do that?"

"I'll just tell Frank we want to leave."

"He won't return our money, you know."

"I know."

"There's a 'no-refund' clause . . ."

"I know. But it's only money, Therese."

She nods, says nothing for several moments.

"All this way for nothing," she says at last.

"All this way."

"Jere, am I imagining all this? I mean, he really *is* . . ."

"Yes, he really is."

He hears her sigh heavily in the darkness.

"Let's see how it goes tomorrow," she says.

Far out on the plain, they hear the sound of some poor creature being torn to shreds, its shrieks sundering the night.

THE TWO LAND Rovers are parked side by side.

In the near distance, a pair of cheetah are stalking a herd of wildebeest.

Frank has set up camp chairs for the entire party, and they are observing the hunt through binoculars.

"We'll have wildebeest one night this week," Davey says to Therese. "I'll ask the chef to prepare it specially for you." When she does not answer, he says, as if answering himself, "Thank you, Davey, that's very kind of you."

"Why can't we get closer to them?" Helen asks.

"Scare off the herd," Frank explains. "We're not here to disturb the daily ebb and flow of life."

"I don't know about you," Helen says, "but *I'm* here on vacation."

"Sorry, no can do," Frank says.

And at that moment, a Land Rover from another safari pulls up not twenty feet from where the stalking cheetah sit silently watchful.

"How come *they* can do it?" Helen asks, pouting.

"Doesn't make it right," Frank says.

"I agree with her," Therese says. "We should move up closer."

"If you want to get close to some predators," Davey says, leaning in toward her, virtually whispering in her ear, "I'll take you out early one morning."

Therese does not answer.

BEFORE DINNER THAT night, they sit ranged behind the roaring fire, facing the starry plain and the unseen eyes out there, drinking what Davey and Frank call "Sundowners." Davey takes a poke at the fire, tosses the branch onto the flaming pyramid, and walks back to where Jeremy and Therese are sitting side by side, holding hands, looking out past the fire to the plain. He takes the camp chair on Therese's right. He is silent for a moment, and then he leans in close to her.

"When would you like to see those predators?" he whispers.

"I wouldn't," Therese says.

Davey shrugs.

"The offer stands open, sweetheart," he says, and smiles knowingly.

"TOMORROW NIGHT we'll be having fresh fish for dinner," Frank announces.

"Best fish in the world," Davey says.

"World's largest freshwater fish," Frank says.

"The Nile perch."

"Chris should be here bright and early . . ."

"Chris?" Helen says.

"Our charter pilot," Frank says. "The one who flew us here."

"Bald guy, blue eyes?" Lou asks.

"That's Chris. We should be in Lake Victoria and on the water by nine, nine thirty. A break for lunch at the hotel on Rusinga Island, then out on the water again, and back home in the afternoon."

"To cook up the fish," Davey says, and licks his lips. "Yummy, yummy, yummy," he says to Therese.

IN THE DEAD of night, Jeremy and Therese pack their bags. They have not brought much luggage to the Masai Mara, a single bag each, and so packing is an easy task.

Their plan is a simple one.

At breakfast tomorrow morning, they will tell Frank and his partner that they are leaving the safari. Frank will undoubtedly protest that they've only been out three days, and even so they've seen a plentiful amount of game, it's rare that anyone spots the Big Three in so short a time, but they've already seen cheetah, leopard, and lion—lion in abundance, in fact, so what's the great hurry? Give Africa a chance.

Jeremy will explain that they're not used to roughing it this way. He will explain that what they'd like to do is check into the hotel on Rusinga, stay there for a few days, make their leisurely way back to Nairobi on their own . . .

Frank will undoubtedly remind them that the price of the safari is nonrefundable . . .

Yes, Jeremy will say, we realize that. But we've made up our minds.

By the light of their single flickering kerosene lamp, Jeremy rehearses what he will say tomorrow morning. When he finishes, Therese claps her hands.

Like giddy midnight conspirators, they begin giggling, and then fall into bed together.

THE NEXT MORNING, Therese takes one look at her husband and says, "My God, what happened to you?"

In the mirror, Jeremy's left eye is swollen to the size of a golf ball. He suspects some insect, most likely a spider, has bitten him during the night, and he goes immediately to his traveling medical kit. There, among the Tylenol and the Seconal, there among the pills for nausea or diarrhea or constipation, there among the adhesive bandages and the sterile gauze pads, he finds some alcohol swabs, and cleans the swollen eye, and then dabs it with Neosporin ointment.

Looking at himself in the mirror again, he thinks, I don't even look like myself anymore.

But their bags are packed, and in a little while the plane will be here, and they'll be out of here, they'll be leaving the Masai Mara, leaving Nairobi, leaving Kenya, leaving Africa.

He smiles at his own image, and then winces because the damn eye hurts.

"WE WON'T BE going to Lake Victoria today," Frank announces at breakfast. "Nor any other day this week."

"But it's part of the itinerary," Helen reminds him.

"Yes, I know, and we'll make an adjustment in the tour price. But I just spoke to Chris on the radio . . ."

"I had my heart set on fishing," Lou says.

"It's part of the itinerary," Helen says again.

"I'm sorry, but there's something wrong with the fuel lines on his plane, and he's had to take it into the shop. He doesn't think it'll be fixed till the end of the week, when it's time for you to go back to Nairobi. I'm sorry."

"Then get another plane," Jeremy says.

"No, I can't do that," Frank says.

"Why not?"

"These charter planes are expensive. They're all figured into the price. I have an arrangement with Chris. I can't just go to another company . . ."

"You said you'd make an adjustment," Helen reminds him.

"Yes, but . . ."

"So use the adjustment to charter another plane," Jeremy says.

"No, that would be prohibitive, I'm sorry. No can do."

"Looks like we're stuck right here for the next little while," Davey says, and grins impishly. Shrugging, he picks up his fork and stabs it into the eggs on his plate. Yellow spreads like a stain.

"We'll just have to make our own fun," he says.

A PAIR OF giraffe are eating from thorn trees.

Three giant secretary birds lope across the plain.

A tiny baby elephant rushes from behind the protective cover of his mother's thick legs to charge their Land Rover, trumpeting like a bull, and then hurries back to hide behind his mother again.

Elegant crested cranes spread their wings, glide to a stop just feet from where a herd of Cape buffalo scowl in seeming disapproval.

But always there is the incessant, insinuating, intimidating presence of David Lawrence Ladd.

THE LAND ROVER is parked some fifty feet from where a pair of lions are mating. Everywhere on the plain, there are mating lions. They couple, they collapse to the ground to rest, they couple again.

"That's the life, huh?" Davey says, and turns to grin at Therese.

On this fourth day of the safari, Therese ignores him completely.

Like the Masai women who walk across the Mara to market in neighboring villages, their heads high, their shoulders back, seemingly impervious to the threat of stalking predators, Therese simply ignores him—until it becomes completely impossible to do so.

THAT AFTERNOON, they make a point of placing themselves in the Land Rover Frank will be driving. The Cantoris don't seem to appreciate this too much, but their day brightens considerably when they spot, up close, two sleeping leopards in a tree, and—not ten minutes later—witness six hunting lionesses stalking and killing a huge Cape buffalo.

"A kill!" Lou trumpets. "We actually witnessed a kill!"

As evening approaches, they are all walking along a narrow trail beside a deep pond where earlier this morning they watched hippos splashing and romping in the water. They are following the track of what Frank tells them is a cheetah. Jeremy asks if it's wise for them to be walking around in the open. But Frank assures them they will be perfectly safe. He himself is carrying a high-powered rifle with a telescopic sight, and Davey, of course, has his trusty Glock.

They are walking single file.

Frank in the lead, his rifle at the ready.

Then Helen.

Then Therese.

Then Davey.

And Lou.

And last in line, Jeremy, who is anxiously watching both sides of the trail, alert to every sound.

Up ahead, Therese suddenly stops dead in her tracks.

She turns to look sharply at Davey, and then immediately walks back past him, and past Lou, to where Jeremy is bringing up the rear of the line.

"What is it?" he says.

She shakes her head.

SHE DOES NOT tell him what happened until they are alone later in their tent. Outside, the sky has already begun to surrender to the brilliance of another African sunset.

"He touched me," she whispers. "He ran his hand up the inside of my leg."

"I'll go talk to him," Jeremy says.

"Be careful," she warns, but he has already stormed out of the tent.

THE TWO MEN are silhouetted against the changing sky.

Lou Cantori has a very tall, very dark drink in his right hand. He still can't get over having witnessed an actual kill. He can't wait to show his friends back home the movie he took. Davey seems to be listening intently, smiling as he piles tinder and logs onto what will become their nightly fire. As Jeremy purposefully approaches, there is a sudden caterwauling out on the plain.

"What the hell is *that?*" Lou asks.

Davey throws another log onto the heap. Seemingly addressing Lou, he says, "Probably some young lion trying to take a female from the pride. The patriarch is letting him know he won't let it happen." He kicks the log into place with his booted foot. "But it will, eventually. He can roar all he wants out there, but the young lion'll take over the pride anyway, sooner or later." He stoops before the heap of stacked logs, strikes a match, touches it to the tinder. The fire leaps into flame. He looks up from it, directly into Jeremy's eyes. "That's the way it is out here, Dr. Palmer," he says.

There is an unmistakable challenge in his eyes.

I have touched your wife, those eyes say.

And I will touch her again.

Jeremy stares back into those eyes.

He is thinking, You're twenty-five years younger than I am, my friend.

And you're in great physical shape.

And you carry a 9-millimeter Glock in a holster on your hip. But . . .

"Better check on my bride. See you guys at dinner," Lou says, and ambles off toward his tent.

The flames leap higher, seeming to ignite the sky itself with unimaginable reds, yellows, and oranges.

Without preamble, Jeremy says, "Stay away from my wife."

"What?" Davey says, and turns from the fire, a surprised look on his face.

"Your attentions are unwanted and unsolicited. You are making both of us extremely uncomfortable . . ."

"Hey, Doc, back off a minute, okay?" Davey says, and holds up his hands as if to fend off an imminent blow. "What attentions?"

"Davey, I'm not interested in any of your bullshit, truly," Jeremy says. "If you ever touch her again . . ."

"Touch her? Are you . . . ?"

"Stay away from her, Davey! Don't sit near her, don't talk to her, don't make any more sexual remarks to her . . ."

"Sexual, *Jesus!*"

"Just keep the hell away from her!"

He is talking louder than he realized. Across the compound, he sees Lou Cantori stop before his tent and turn to look at them.

"Do you think you have that?" Jeremy whispers.

Davey says nothing.

"Have I made myself clear?" Jeremy whispers.

"Why, sure, Doc," Davey says, and grins.

JEREMY IS SITTING outside the tent on their so-called veranda, thoughtfully silent, when Therese comes to him. She is wearing a white robe and carrying a white bar of soap. Her feet are bare.

"Did you talk to him?" she asks.

"Yes."

"Did he understand?"

"I think so. I hope so."

She shakes her head.

"I wish this weren't happening to us," she says.

"It'll be over soon," he says.

"Worst week in my life. Ever."

"Yes," he says.

She bends to him, kisses him on the cheek.

"I love you so much," she says.

"I love you, too, darling."

She kisses him again. "I'm going to shower," she says. "Make a drink for me, will you?"

"Do you want me to come with you?"

"No, I'll be okay, it's still light." She turns to go, comes back to him, brushes her hand across his cheek. "Are you all right?" she asks.

"Yes," he says. "I'm fine."

She nods.

"I hate him for this," she says.

"I do, too."

"But it'll be over soon," she says, repeating his words.

"Yes, soon, darling."

He eases himself out of the camp chair.

"Gin and tonic?" he asks.

"Please."

He starts up for the mess tent. The fire is crackling and hissing. Davey is nowhere in sight now. The evening sky is a symphony in brass.

Therese walks through their sleeping tent to the back flaps, and then crosses the five feet or so to the shower stall. Inside the stall, she takes off her robe and reaches through the flap to hang it on a peg outside.

The water from the Mara River is thick and brown. The safari boys lug it in buckets to the cook tent, where they heat it in huge cauldrons and then carry it to the separate shower stalls clustered behind each of the sleeping tents. There, they pour the water into the canvas sacks above each of the stalls. Inside the shower, you pull a chain to unleash a flow of warm water, soaking yourself. You release the chain, and it cuts off the downpour. You soap yourself clean, and pull the chain again to rinse yourself.

Standing on the narrow wooden planking underfoot, Therese pulls the chain now, and lets loose a splash of water. Releasing the chain to stop the flow, she begins soaping herself. Her long hair wet, her body wet and covered now with suds, she is reaching for the chain again, when the flap to the shower stall is suddenly thrown back.

"Well, well, well," Davey says. "What have we here!"

"Get away from me," she says.

"Sorry, I thought the stall was empty."

"Get *away* from me," she says again.

"Sure you don't want me to join you?" he says, and reaches in to touch her breast. She is too startled to scream. She throws the bar of soap at him, full into his face, hitting him over the eye with it. Grinning, he backs away. "See you at dinner," he says. "Nice tits, by the way." Still grinning, he lets the flap fall free of his hand.

Therese stands naked and glistening, covered with soap, gulping in huge breaths of air. At last, she pulls the chain to rinse herself in muddy river water.

When she tells Jeremy what just happened, he merely nods.

That is all.

FOR DINNER THAT night, the chef serves wildebeest.

"There are people all over the world who prefer it to beef," Davey says. "I asked the chef to prepare it specially for you, Therese." When she makes no reply, he goes through his routine again, saying to himself, "Why, thank you, Davey, that was very kind of you." Therese is deliberately sitting very far away from him, on the opposite side of the mess tent table, between Lou and Frank.

Helen proposes a game.

The idea is to describe yourself by attaching an adjective to your first name.

Frank picks up on it at once.

He's had a bit too much to drink.

"Fearless Frank," he says.

"Lucky Lou," Lou says.

"Happy Helen."

Therese hesitates.

"Tired Therese," she says at last.

Davey, too, has been drinking.

"Dominant Dave," he says, and raises his wineglass in a silent toast to Therese, and then turns his head and his smile toward Jeremy.

Jeremy is cold sober.

His eyes meet Davey's.

"Jugular Jere," he says, and everyone bursts out laughing, because they don't know what he can possibly mean.

"Come on, partner," Frank says. "Let's put you to bed before you fall on your face."

AT TWO IN the morning, one of the Masai guards sounds the alarm. Jeremy is already awake when Frank rushes into the tent and yells, "Dr. Palmer, come quick! Something terrible has happened!"

What has happened is that Dominant Dave has put his own 9-millimeter Glock in his mouth and blown off the back of his head.

THE MOVIE HAS ended. The cabin of the jumbo jet is temporarily dim. In the darkness, Jeremy and his wife continue whispering, their heads close together.

"Frank thinks he may have had a drinking problem," Therese says.

"Maybe."

"He certainly drank enough that night."

Jeremy says nothing.

"Maybe he wouldn't have done it otherwise."

"Maybe not," Jeremy says.

"Anyway, it's over," she says. "It's all behind us now."

"Yes," Jeremy says. "It's all behind us now."

He takes her hand in his own. He puts his mouth very close to her ear.

"Therese," he whispers, "he wasn't drunk."

"Yes, he was," she whispers. "Didn't you see him?"

"Therese . . . he was drugged."

"What do you mean?"

"Seconal. Two hundred milligrams."

"What are you saying?"

Her whisper is a sharp hiss in the stillness of the cabin. Beneath it, the jet engines drone incessantly.

"In his wine," Jeremy whispers. "Two big reds. Enough to knock him out completely."

His wife is staring at him now.

"I went to his tent later. I put the gun in his mouth, I put his thumb on the trigger. I blew out his brains, Therese."

Her eyes are wide open in the gloom of the cabin.

"I killed him," Jeremy whispers.

She is silent for merely an instant.

Then she says, "Good," and smiles, and squeezes his hand.

RHYS BOWEN

VOODOO

November 2004

RHYS BOWEN GREW up in Bath, England, but draws on her childhood visits to Wales for her award-winning mystery series featuring Welsh policeman Constable Evan. A second series featuring turn-of-the-century Irish immigrant Molly Murphy as she carves her way in New York City has also garnered awards. Before turning to mysteries, Ms. Bowen was a writer for the BBC in London and a children's book author. Her first story for *AHMM*, "Voodoo" exhibits a keen sense of place and skillfully plays off common misperceptions about Voodoo. Sadly, the New Orleans neighborhoods she captures so beautifully here may have been lost forever in 2005's Hurricane Katrina.

■

Voodoo isn't often the cause of death listed in modern police reports, but that was what Officer Paul Renoir had written on the sheet that reached my desk at the New Orleans Police Department headquarters. Probable cause of death: Voodoo.

I was intrigued enough by this to take on the investigation myself rather than handing it over to one of my juniors. After twenty years in the homicide division of a big city police department, I had had it up to here with gang bangs, drug deals gone wrong, and men who had smashed in their old lady's head simply because they felt like it after a night at the bars.

I called Renoir into my office. He was a serious-looking young man—shorter than cops used to be when I first joined the force, but broad shouldered and with a round, earnest face. He'd only been on homicide duty for a couple of months and was clearly ill at ease in my presence.

"What's this about, Renoir?" I waved the report in his direction. He shifted uncomfortably from one foot to the other. "What is it—some kind of joke?"

"Oh no, sir." His face became even more serious. "I know it sounds really strange, but the widow was so insistent. She said there was no other explanation. And the doctor was equally baffled."

I indicated a steel and vinyl chair opposite my desk. "You'd better take a seat and fill me in on the details."

He perched on the edge of the chair, still clearly nervous. "Officer Roberts and I got a call to go to the Garden District, possible homicide. It was one of those big mansions, sir."

"Mansions are usually big, Renoir. Learn to be brief, okay?"

"Sorry, sir. One of those big—uh—houses on St. Charles. We were met at the door by the distraught wife. She led us upstairs to the master bedroom, and there was this man lying there dead. No sign of struggle, nothing to indicate he hadn't died of natural causes. I asked her when he had died and if she had sent for her doctor, and she said the family doctor had already been there and he'd been as upset as she was. He couldn't find any other explanation for it either."

"Other than what?"

"That's what I asked her, sir. She looked me straight in the eye and said, 'Voodoo.' Then she told me that a month ago he had offended a voodoo priestess. She had cursed him and told him that if he didn't change his mind, he'd be dead within the month."

"I gather he didn't change his mind about whatever it was."

"He didn't, sir, and he started going downhill from that very moment. The wife said it was almost as if he were fading before her eyes." Renoir's own eyes were peering at me earnestly, willing me to believe him. "I really think you ought to go and speak to her yourself, sir. I came out of there feeling really spooky."

"Renoir, police officers are not allowed to feel spooky, even in the presence of a dismembered and partly eaten corpse."

He flinched. "No, sir."

I got up from my chair. "The best thing you can do is go straight back out there."

"Me, sir?"

He tried to keep his expression composed, but the words came out as a croak.

I had to smile. "It's like falling off a horse. You have to get right back on, or you'll be spooked forever. You can drive me."

His face lit up. "You're coming too, sir?"

"Why not? God knows I need a good laugh."

"I don't think you'll be laughing, sir," Renoir said as he left my office.

AN HOUR LATER Renoir drove as we followed the streetcar tracks out along St. Charles Avenue to the upscale Garden District. Here was where New Orleans Old Money was concentrated. We passed an antique streetcar with tourists hanging out of the windows, videotaping the mansions as they passed. They glared at us as we got in their way.

"Here we are, sir." Renoir pulled up outside the home of John Torrance III and his wife, Millie. When Renoir had told me that he liked to be called Trey, the lightbulb went off in my head. Trey Torrance was a familiar name to me, appearing regularly in the newspapers at some charity event or other. I had looked him up in the files before we set out and found out that Mr. Torrance had been fifty-nine years old and still very active in his business life as well as in various philanthropic organizations. He was, for example, a leading sponsor of the Bacchus Carnival Krewe. He had been born to an old plantation family across the river, inherited a sizeable estate of local land, and made himself even richer by putting subdivisions on it and selling it off.

I couldn't fault his taste in houses. Trey Taylor lived in a solid, square brick mansion with white shutters at the windows and an enormous magnolia grandiflora shading it. Nothing too fancy, no Southern-style pillars and porticos. But the gardens were beautifully kept and the place had an air of prosperity about it. We parked under one of the live oaks that draped in a canopy over the street.

"Thank God for trees," I said. "At least the car won't have turned into an oven while we're away."

I had expected the front door to be opened by a maid, but it was Mrs. Torrance herself who stood there, looking quite frail but elegant in a black-and-white-striped dress and pearls. How many women wear pearls at home in the afternoon these days, I wondered. Especially when their husband has just died. I introduced myself.

"I'm so grateful you've come, Lieutenant Patterson," she said. "Do come inside, and you too, Officer Renoir. Can I fix you gentlemen a glass of iced tea or lemonade?" Even the death of her husband had not robbed this lady of her Southern manners.

"Nothing, thank you, ma'am," I said as we stepped into the delightful coolness of a marble-tiled front hall. She led us through to a sitting room that was decorated with understated good taste—good old mahogany furniture and some classy-looking paintings on the walls. One of these was a portrait of a man with a bulldog face of almost Winston Churchillian tenacity. Chin stuck out defiantly, brow set in a perpetual frown. Trey Torrance had clearly been a man who expected to get his own way and dared anybody to cross him.

"You don't have a maid, Mrs. Torrance?" I couldn't help asking.

She was holding a dainty lace handkerchief, and she put it up to her mouth. "She didn't feel comfortable staying here after—after what happened. She said she could still feel the spirits flying around. So I had to let her go home, even though I'm not very comfortable here myself, I can tell you."

I gave her a long, sympathetic look. "Voodoo, Mrs. Torrance?" I asked. "What makes you think it was voodoo that killed your husband?"

"What else could it have been?" She almost snapped at me. "He saw that woman and she cursed him and he died, just like she said he would."

"Whoa—go back a little. What woman are we talking about?"

"Trey owned land across the river. Swampy land. No good for anything. But then he managed to get his hands on some landfill, and he was going to have it brought down in barges from Missouri. He planned to build up that land and put another of his subdivisions on it. Like I said, it was mostly swamp and grass, but there were a few shacks down by the river, and this old woman lived in one of them. She refused to move out, even though she had no right there. Trey owned the title to that land. Trey went to see her and she warned him. She said if he kept on with this, he'd regret it."

"And what did your husband do?"

"He laughed, naturally. He told her he was bulldozing the place and it didn't matter to him whether she was in it or not."

"So your husband didn't take her threat seriously?"

"Of course not. Trey didn't take kindly to threats, and he wasn't the kind of man who would believe in anything as ridiculous as voodoo. He came home and told me about it. 'Silly old bitch,' he said—I'm sorry for the language. Trey was rather outspoken. 'If she thinks she can scare me off with her mumbo jumbo, she can think again.'"

"And then what happened?"

"Then the doll arrived." She looked up at me with hollow, frightened eyes and pressed the handkerchief to her mouth again.

"A voodoo doll?"

She nodded.

"May I see it?"

She disappeared and came back almost immediately with something wrapped in a cloth. Inside was a simple doll, made of coarse unbleached muslin. It was faceless and featureless and might have been some child's toy, except there were red-tipped pins stuck in its heart and stomach and throat. I examined it then handed it on to Renoir, who looked as if he didn't want to touch it.

"I wanted to throw it away, but somehow I couldn't. I thought it might speed up the curse or something," Mrs. Torrance said. "Naturally I didn't show it to Trey."

"This was how long ago?"

"Just under a month. She told him he'd be dead within the month and he was."

"Is the body still upstairs?" I asked.

She nodded, her eyes darting fearfully.

"You'd better take me up to see it."

She led us up a graceful curved staircase to an enormous master bedroom. The drapes were closed, and the room had an aquarium-like quality. I turned on the light. The man lying in the bed looked peaceful enough, but nothing like the fierce bulldog in that portrait. He looked small and shrunken.

"Your husband lost a lot of weight since that portrait was painted," I said.

"Since the curse," she said. "He just shrank before my eyes."

"He didn't eat?"

"He started vomiting the next day, and after that he couldn't keep food down. He'd feel fine, he'd eat something, and the vomiting would start again. He got so weak he couldn't stand."

"You called a doctor?"

"He said it was probably a virus. He didn't take it too seriously."

"I understood it was a heart attack that killed him?"

"That's what the doctor said. The vomiting did stop after a few days, but Trey was as weak as a baby and he found it hard to swallow. Then he started having heart palpitations. He had had previous heart trouble, you know, and he was on medication. The doctor upped his dose of digoxin, but it didn't do any good, did it? I begged him to go to that woman and tell him he'd leave her in peace, but he was so stubborn, he wouldn't do it. Even with his life on the line, he wouldn't do it."

She started to sob quietly.

I stared down at the man lying in the bed and cleared my throat. "Mrs. Torrance, I'm sorry your husband died, but I'm not sure what you think the police can do for you."

She glared at me. "Arrest that woman. Make her pay for what she has done."

I tried not to smile. "Mrs. Torrance, you seem like a sensible woman. I'm sure you'll understand that there is no court in this state that would convict someone of killing via a curse. It would be thrown out before it came to trial."

"But she's just as guilty as if she stabbed him or forced poison down his throat," she said angrily. "You should have seen my husband before. He was a powerful, aggressive man—full of life. The moment her curse struck, he just melted away until his heart gave out. And even if you couldn't prove the voodoo curse, surely harassing him and making threats is against the law, isn't it?"

I shook my head. "If we hauled in folks every time they said 'I could kill you,' the parish jails would be even more crowded than they are now. And sending one doll through the mail doesn't amount to harassing. Did she send anything else?"

"One doll was enough." She looked at me coldly. "It worked, didn't it?"

I started to make my way toward the door. There was something strangely cold and uncomfortable about that dark room with its drawn blinds. I wondered if I was succumbing to the voodoo hysteria myself. "Look, Mrs. Torrance. I'll have the body autopsied to verify the cause of death. If it was a heart attack, I don't think there's anything we can do. I'm really sorry. I'm sure this is most disturbing for you."

"It's even more disturbing to know that people like Maman Boutin can kill at will and nobody is going to stop them," she said.

"Okay," I said with a sigh. "Tell me where I can find this Maman Boutin and I'll go talk to her."

She described where we'd find the shacks. I had Renoir call and arrange for the body to be taken for autopsy, then we paid a call on the family physician.

"I understand that you were uncomfortable about the cause of death," I said to him.

He was a dapper, fussy little man, the kind who wears blazers and has his shirts starched and ironed. He had a gold signet ring on his left pinkie. "The cause of death was a heart attack," he said.

"Brought on by—"

He shook his head. "The man was a walking time bomb. He'd had heart trouble for several years and yet he wouldn't slow down. He loved his beignets and coffee, and his bourbon-and-Seven-Up. Typical type-A personality. Very short fuse. Upset him and he'd explode. The heart attack was only a matter of time."

"So you don't agree with his widow that it was caused by voodoo."

"Is that what she told you?" He looked amused, then shook his head. "She was very upset. She had told me several times that some woman had cursed him, and I agree that he did become sick immediately after the supposed confrontation took place, but as a physician I'm not trained to recognize the symptoms of voodoo. I'd reiterate what I put on the death certificate. He was weakened by a nasty stomach virus and finished off by a heart attack."

"I'm having an autopsy done," I said. "Just in case."

"I don't know what you think you're going to find," he said, "other than a severely damaged heart muscle."

He escorted us to the door and opened it. I paused on the doorstep.

"So in your estimation there was nothing unexpected about this man's death?"

"Only that he went downhill so fast," he said. "He was a big bull of a man, and apart from that heart condition, he was never sick. He caught some little bitty virus and it didn't seem like anything helped."

"You're sure it was a virus?"

"If you mean was it a voodoo curse, all I can tell you is that there is a nasty stomach bug going around this city at the moment, and Trey Torrance's symptoms were consistent with the other cases I've treated. A little more violent and severe, perhaps, but Trey also overindulged in his food and drink. And he probably didn't stick to the bland diet I prescribed for him. He wasn't exactly good at taking directions, as his wife will tell you."

"Thank you, Doctor." I nodded to him and we took our leave.

IT WAS CLOSE to rush hour and it took us awhile to cross the river and get free of the city sprawl. Then we were driving up Highway 18 with water meadows and the occasional horse swishing its tail in the shade of a live oak on one side of us and the great brown expanse of the Mississippi on the other. It was times like this when I asked myself what the hell I was doing shutting myself up in a big city. I was born in Kentucky, came down to New Orleans to attend Tulane, and stayed. But I was still a country boy at heart.

The last mile to the shacks across the river was on a dirt track. It had rained earlier in the week, and the potholes were full of puddles. We splashed, bumped, and slithered our way out to the shacks with Renoir apologizing each time we bottomed out in a particularly big pothole. That boy was going to have to develop some balls if he wanted to survive in the NOPD.

The dirt track ended, and Renoir parked the car under a sorry-looking half-dead tree. We got out and immediately I heard the whine. I barely had time to remember to roll down my shirtsleeves before the mosquitoes descended on us in a cloud. Renoir wasn't so lucky; he was wearing short sleeves. He slapped and waved his arms and cursed under his breath.

"Why would anybody want to live out here, sir?" he muttered. "This is a hellhole if ever I saw one."

"Some people like the peace and quiet, I guess," I said. "And they like to be left alone."

"I'd leave them alone, all right, if I got my blood sucked dry every time I came to visit."

We followed a narrow track through some bushes until it brought us out to a field of saw grass running alongside a bayou. Where the bayou emptied into the river there was a cluster of shacks huddled together in the shade of a tree. The shacks looked as if they had been built in haste by a gang of boys wanting a clubhouse. There were holes in the walls, half-collapsed front porches, and boarded-up windows. A sorrier-looking sight I have never seen.

Renoir echoed my sentiments. "I can't see why this place was worth fighting over. You couldn't pay me enough to stay here."

There was a rustle in the tall grass to our left, and a big old gator slid down the muddy bank and plopped into the bayou. An egret rose from the water and drifted to a safer spot. The mosquitoes kept up their whining symphony. I could feel them biting through my pant legs, but as a senior officer, I was too dignified to slap the way Renoir was doing.

A skinny dog slunk out from beneath the nearest of the shacks and started barking at us. At this signal an old black man poked his head out of the door.

"Good afternoon, sir," I said. "We're looking for Mrs. Boutin?"

"Maman Boutin you's wanting?" he asked in a voice that sounded like a wheel that needed oil. "She don't take kindly to strangers."

"We're policemen. We just need to ask her some questions."

"She don't take kindly to questions," he said.

The mosquitoes and the steamy heat were getting to me. "And the police don't take kindly to being given the runaround," I said. "We can talk to her here or have her hauled in for questioning. It's all the same to me."

The old man shot us a look of alarm. "I wouldn't do that, mister," he said. "It don't pay to mess with Maman Boutin. She give you the eye, and you jus' shrivel up an' die. I seen it for myself."

"I'm willing to chance it," I said, and heard an intake of breath from Renoir standing behind me.

The old man shrugged as if I were a hopeless case. "She in that house over there," he said. "The one beside the tree."

That particular shack was half hidden under the great tree, with curtains of Spanish moss trailing down all over it. It was a pitiful structure of mismatched wood. New boards had been nailed on where old ones had fallen off. The roof had several patches of shingles missing, exposing the tar paper underneath. Being this close to the river I was surprised the place had survived at all. I had seen what spring floods could do.

We made our way between puddles to Maman Boutin's shack. The dog had been joined by another one, and they walked at our heels, growling softly. Not a comfortable feeling. Renoir made sure he stayed as close to me as possible.

"Do I really have to go in there, sir?" he asked.

"You afraid of voodoo, Renoir?"

"It's all right for you, sir," Renoir said. "You weren't born around here. We have it in our blood."

"If she's a real priestess, she'll know you don't mean her any harm. You'll be safe enough," I said.

As I started up the five rickety steps that led to Madam Boutin's front door, there was an unearthly cackling sound. My heart did a flip-flop as several white chickens, who had been sleeping in the shade on the porch, rose up, cackling and flapping around us. The noise produced a face in the darkness behind the doorway.

"I know why you here," a dried-up old voice said. There was a slight twang of French accent.

"Are you Maman Boutin?" I asked.

"That's what they calls me."

"I'm here to ask you some questions about Mr. Torrance. You remember the man who came to visit you?"

"He dead yet?" she asked calmly.

"He died this morning. May we come in?"

"I suppose you can. He can stay on the porch." She indicated Renoir, who looked visibly relieved.

I stepped inside and was enveloped in a darkness so complete that I could only just make out the form of a table and a straight-backed chair. The place stank of a peculiar odor—a mixture of rotting vegetation and sweat mixed with maybe chicken shit and some kind of sweet incense. I coughed and tried not to breathe.

"You can sit there." She pointed at the chair.

I sat. She took up position in an old armchair I hadn't noticed before in the darkness. I could barely make out her face. What I could see was little and wizened like an old dried apple, and so dark that it blended into the darkness of the room. But her eyes were bright enough. As I became accustomed to the darkness, I could see that she had some kind of fabric wrapped around her head and several rows of beads around her neck.

"Mr. Torrance died today," I said.

She nodded as if she'd been expecting it.

"He came to see you a month ago. He told you you'd have to move out because he was going to build on this land. You threatened him."

"I didn't threaten him," she said.

"His widow claims you put a voodoo curse on him."

"I just warned him," she said. "What right did he have coming here and telling me to get off his land? What made him think it was his land, eh? I was born in this place. My mama was born here before me. I tol' him I wasn't goin' nowhere. And you know what he tol' me? He said he gonna bulldoze this place and it don' matter to him none whether I'm in it or not."

"So you put a curse on him?"

She shrugged. "I tell him if he don't change his mind, he's going to be sorry."

"And you sent him a doll."

"I done what?" She leaned forward in her chair.

"A voodoo doll. You sent him a voodoo doll with pins stuck in it."

"I never sent him no doll. That's just mumbo jumbo stuff for tourists. Maman Boutin don't need no dolls to do her work, young man. If I say a man goin' to die, he goin' to die. I got strong magic. The *loa* listen to me."

"So you never sent the doll?"

"I tol' you."

"And you didn't send anything else? Did you give him anything to eat or drink?"

She laughed then, a dry, cackling laugh. "You trying to find out if I give him some kin' of bad medicine? Maman Boutin don' need no bad medicine. You policemen wasting your time here. If my magic made him die, ain't no way you ever goin' to prove it."

She wasn't stupid, I thought as I got to my feet. "I know that," I said. "But this is the United States of America. You can't go around killing people when you feel like it."

"Why not?" she asked. "Don't plenty folk do it in that city of yours? They shoot someone to get his wallet or his shoes or his jacket. That Mr. Torrance was goin' to throw these good folks out of their homes—homes where they was born, homes he had no right to."

"There are courts of law for that kind of thing."

"Everyone know the law don' listen to po' folks," she said. "That's why po' folks need someone like me to look after them." She looked straight at me. In the half light her gaze was intense. "You better go now," she said.

She reached to pick up something. At first I thought it was a stick. Then I saw that it moved. It was a snake. I had read about hair standing on end before, but it had never happened to me until now. I could hear a humming sound that seemed to echo from the rafters above my head as if angry spirits were flying around up there.

"I'm going," I said, and made for the door as fast as I could without appearing to rush.

"And don' come back," she called after me. "You jus' let us live in peace, and we won't bother no one."

I stepped out into the pink glow of a setting sun. Renoir was standing in the shade of the tree, and he looked very relieved to see me. The chickens were nowhere in sight.

"Come on, Renoir. We're going," I said.

He needed no urging. We crossed the compound with giant strides.

"You think she was the real thing, sir?"

"I have no idea, Renoir," I said, not wanting to let him know about the hairs on my neck and the snake.

"Did you notice those chickens were all white?"

"I did notice that."

We crossed the compound. The dogs stood on the track behind us, tails still at the alert. There was no sign of the big gator or the egret. The path was narrow and we had to walk in single file.

"Did she admit to putting a hex on him, sir?" Renoir waited until we were safely through the bushes and beside the car.

"Not exactly. But she wasn't surprised to find he had died, either."

"There's no way we could ever prove a hex, is there?" he asked.

"I wouldn't even attempt to, Renoir."

"So this was really a waste of time coming out here?" He glanced up at me as if he might have gone too far with this question. "Or was it just to satisfy your curiosity?"

"Actually, it wasn't a waste of time at all," I said. "I learned one valuable piece of information. She didn't send the doll."

"She could be lying."

I shook my head. "That old woman might do a lot of things, but lying isn't one of them. If she'd sent the doll, she'd have been pleased to acknowledge it. She told me she didn't need dolls to do her work."

Renoir opened the car door for me. "Then who sent it?"

"That's your job to find out, Renoir."

"Me, sir? How do I go about finding out about voodoo dolls?"

I gave him a long, hard look. "Renoir, you can start to show some spark of initiative or you can end up as a sorry pen pusher. Your choice."

He nodded. "Yes, sir. Okay, I'll find out."

I took pity on the hangdog look. He really was very young. I'd probably been insecure and unwilling to tread on toes when I'd first started in the department, although it was so long ago that I truthfully couldn't remember. I did know that I hadn't wanted to come across as too eager or brash.

"You can start with coming with me to question the maid."

"Oh, the maid." He looked impressed. "Yeah, I'd forgotten about her."

"I'm curious to know why she left in a hurry. Was she really freaked out by the voodoo?"

"Are we going to question her tonight?" Renoir steered around potholes as we bumped down the track.

"Tomorrow morning will do. I'm in serious need of a cold beer right now."

"Good idea, sir." His earnest round face lit up in a grin.

The next morning I put in a call to the pathologist who was performing the autopsy.

"Any news yet?" I asked.

"Cause of death was a massive heart attack. Exactly what the attending physician had said."

"And tissue samples revealed?"

"Initial studies reveal the presence of a digitalis compound, which was to be expected, since it was prescribed medication."

"The expected amount?"

"I don't have details yet. Call us back later."

Then I took Renoir with me to visit the maid. Her name was Ernestine Williams. She was tall, big boned, and dignified looking. The only traces of her Creole ancestry were in her dark eyes and the kink in her hair. She didn't, at first glance, look like a maid, nor like the kind of woman who would have freaked over a voodoo curse. But as Renoir said, I wasn't born in New Orleans. I didn't have that fear in the blood.

"I'm sorry about running out on Miz Torrance like that," she said as she led us into a neat little studio apartment within spitting distance of the Superdome, "but it was just too much for me. Watching that man shrivel up and die—I never saw anything like it. And then that doll with the pins in it. I tell you, I got shivers all over."

"Tell us about the doll," I said, accepting a seat on a vinyl sofa covered in a multicolored crocheted afghan.

"Miz Torrance showed it to me. She said, 'Would you look what she's sent now? I've a good mind to burn it.' She said she certainly wasn't going to show it to him."

"Were you the one who normally brought in the mail?"

She nodded. "Yes, sir. The mailman came at nine o'clock and took the letters through to the master's study."

"So you were the one who took in the package with the doll in it?"

She looked puzzled. "No, sir. I never saw that package until Miz Torrance showed me the doll."

"Wasn't that odd, didn't you think?"

The puzzled look continued. "No, sir. I didn't really think about it until now, but sometimes, if I was out on an errand, Miz Torrance took in the mail herself."

"So you never saw the discarded paper from the package?"

"No, sir. I never did."

I leaned back in the sofa. "So tell me, Ernestine, how long have you been with the Torrances?"

"Going on seven years, sir."

"You must have liked it there."

She wrinkled her nose. "I wouldn't exactly say that I liked it, but they paid me well and the work wasn't too hard. Mind you, Mr. Torrance was a tough one to please. He liked everything just so, and if they were entertaining, then he'd follow me around breathing down my neck. And he'd do a lot of yelling."

"He yelled a lot, did he?"

She had to smile as she shook her head. "Oh yes, sir. He yelled a terrible lot. Anything that wasn't quite to his liking, he'd just stand there and yell for one of us to fix it. Miz Torrance did most of the cooking, because he was so fussy about the way he liked his food."

"And Mrs. Torrance—was she hard to please, too?"

"Only when she was worried that the master wouldn't be satisfied with what I was doing. She went to great lengths to keep him happy."

"And how did he treat her?" I asked.

"Let me put it this way, sir. If my late husband had treated me that way, I'd have clocked him one. Mind you, I think he really cared about her. He could be sweet as sugar to her, when he wanted. If he went too far and made her cry, then he'd show up the next day with a nice piece of jewelry or an armful of flowers."

I looked around the neat little room. "You didn't live in, then?"

"I have a room at their house," she said, "and I stay there part of the week, especially when they want to entertain. But I needed a place of my own to get away to, if you understand me. A bit of peace and quiet."

"I do understand, Ernestine," I said, rising from the sofa and watching Renoir rise from his chair by the door. "So what will you do now? Will you go back now that the body's been removed?"

"That all depends on what Miz Torrance decides to do next, I suppose," she said. "Maybe she don't want to rattle around by herself in that big old house. I can't say I'd be too anxious to sleep there, after this. So I guess I'll just have to wait and see." She opened the front door for us. "I'll do what's best for her. She's been through a lot, bless her heart."

We stepped out into the sticky heat. Even at that early hour the air was so thick and heavy that it was an effort to walk through it.

"So what do you think, Renoir?" I asked him.

"She seemed like a nice enough woman, sir."

"Yes, she did. But sometimes it's the nice ones that surprise you. Check her out when we get back to headquarters. Find out about her late husband. I'll take a peek at Trey Torrance's will."

His eyes opened in surprise. "You don't think, sir . . . ?"

"As of this moment I don't think anything. Maybe the guy caught a virus and died of a heart attack. But somebody sent that doll. Somebody wanted him dead."

THE WILL TURNED out to be simple enough. After several generous bequests to charities, including a large enough sum to his Carnival Krewe to keep them in beads for years, the remainder of his estate was left to his beloved wife. Mrs. Torrance was now a rich widow. I should have left it at that. God knows I had plenty of other, more pressing cases waiting for me—a young kid gunned down outside a dance club last night, a missing mother of four. But I was still intrigued by Maman Boutin. And I still didn't believe in voodoo.

Guys like Trey Torrance make enemies. Had some other developer got his eye on that land? Did Trey have a rival in another business deal? I wondered who else he might have told about the voodoo curse, who had come to see him when he was sick, and who might have sent the doll. I'd set Renoir onto checking into Trey Torrance's business deals and told him to call me the moment he came up with the goods on the doll. I wasn't holding my breath.

In the meantime I paid another visit to Mrs. Torrance. I wanted to inquire about Trey's medication.

"My husband's medication?" She looked perplexed. "What's that got to do with it?"

"Only that traces of digoxin were found in his system, and I need to double-check that the digoxin was what was being prescribed."

"The bottle's in his medicine cabinet," she said, and led me up to a fancy-looking bathroom. Marble tub and crystal fixtures. No expense spared here. She showed me the bottle. "Here it is," she said.

"Was he good about taking his medication?"

"Terrible," she said. "Trey thought he was immortal. He'd never have taken a single pill if Ernestine or I hadn't brought them to him regularly."

"Thanks. That's all I needed." I handed her back the bottle. She held on to it.

"Do you think it's all right to throw it away now?"

"Why don't you hang on to it for a while, just in case," I said, giving her a reassuring smile.

I was good at those. I'd practiced them for twenty years, not letting a single muscle of my face betray what I was really thinking. In this case I had noticed the name of the doctor who prescribed the pills. I had noticed that sixty were prescribed on October first. To be taken three times a day. I had noticed that ten remained. Even if he had started taking them on the date they were prescribed, there should have been at least fifteen left. So either he had lost them or somebody had helped him into the hereafter.

I put in a call to the family physician. "Mrs. Torrance told me that you upped the dosage on his medication after his heart developed abnormal rhythms," I said.

"I did up it slightly."

"To more than three pills a day?"

"No, same number, just an increased strength."

"Thanks." I hung up again. My hunch had been correct.

As I walked in the door at headquarters, I was met by a very excited Renoir. It was the first time I had seen him animated. "I found out who bought the doll," he blurted out so loudly that everyone turned, for the entire length of the tiled hallway.

"Nice going." I patted him on the back. "Who was it?"

"A woman." He looked very pleased with himself.

"Great. That rules out half of the population."

He ignored my sarcasm. "Did you know there are voodoo stores right here in New Orleans? You can actually go to a store and buy gris-gris and *veve* designs and spells!"

"Nothing surprises me about this place," I said. "So you traced the store?"

"I found it on the Internet. You can search for almost anything these days," he said. "I went in and the owner said they usually sell these dolls to tourists, but this lady was definitely a local. Bought it about three weeks ago. So that proves it, doesn't it, sir?"

"Proves what?"

"That she was lying."

"Who was?"

"Maman Boutin. She lied about sending the doll."

"And what makes you think the woman was Maman Boutin?"

"The guy at the store said definitely a local. Maman Boutin looks and sounds like a local, wouldn't you say?"

I put a hand on his shoulder. "Did you get a description of the lady?"

"Well, no sir. I just assumed . . ."

"Rule number one if you want to stay in this job, Renoir. Get all the facts before you open your mouth. Come on—you're taking me back to that store."

Renoir was silent and contrite throughout the drive. He parked outside a row of small shops in what had become a touristy section of town at the edge of the old quarter.

The store clerk looked surprised at seeing Renoir again. Renoir looked mortified.

"I didn't really take in too many details," the clerk said. "But I remembered her because she didn't look like the kind of woman I'd expect to see in the store. She was middle aged. Hair just so. Well dressed. Tourists don't normally wear good clothes and high heels for walking around town."

We got back in the car. "Did you really believe that Maman Boutin would come all the way into town to buy a doll, Renoir?" I said. "If she wanted to send a doll she'd have made one herself and put her own magic in it."

"I guess so," he muttered, still contrite.

"So what are your thoughts?" I asked.

"My thoughts, sir?" He sounded surprised at being asked.

"This is your case as well as mine."

"The maid, sir. She did get out in a hurry, didn't she? And she didn't sound like she was going back."

"What's the first thing they taught you in detective training?"

He frowned. "Who benefits?"

"And who does?"

He kept on frowning. "The maid doesn't. She's just lost her job."

"And she's not mentioned in the will."

"The wife has just lost her husband."

"And has become a rich widow."

"Oh!" His eyes opened wide. "You don't think—his own wife? She seemed to be distraught."

"Let me give you one piece of advice, Renoir. Women are universally good actresses. Any woman I've ever met can cry on demand."

"But why, sir? What would the motive be? She's a little old to have another guy waiting for her, and she was plenty rich before he died."

"Maybe she wanted to be rid of a domineering bully and the voodoo threat suggested an easy way out."

"How do you mean, sir? I thought Torrance didn't believe in voodoo."

"She helped him along with an overdose of his medication. She might even have found a way to weaken him first."

"Will we be able to prove that, sir?"

"The overdose of medication? Probably not. She can say he was forgetful, he was sick with the virus and didn't know if he'd already taken the medication or not. But let's just see what the tissue samples turn up, huh?"

I was right about that hunch, too. They called from the lab the next day. There were traces of arsenic in the tissue. Not enough to kill, but enough to make someone plenty sick. I expect she thought she'd been clever, stopping the arsenic two weeks before he died, not realizing, of course, that arsenic stays around in tissue forever.

I took Renoir with me when we went out to arrest her. He had that perplexed look on his face as he drove.

"What is it, Renoir? You feeling sorry for her? A policeman can never have emotions about a case. You know that."

"I do know it, sir. And I can't say I have any feelings either way. What I can't understand is why she called us in. Her own doctor had signed a death certificate. It would have passed as a heart attack. There never would have been an autopsy. She would have gotten away with it, no questions asked. What reason could she have had?"

"She might have had a personal vendetta against Maman Boutin," I suggested. "She was a New Orleans native. Maybe Maman Boutin's mother had put a hex on her mother. Vendettas tend to linger on around here, don't they?"

Renoir shrugged.

"On the other hand," I said, "maybe she wanted a chance to tell the world what her charming philanthropist husband was really like and what he put her through. She might even have wanted to enjoy the limelight for a change, after always being in his shadow. You never know with women."

Mrs. Torrance never did give away the slightest hint of a motive to us. She remained silent and genteel right up to the day of her court hearing. But she wore a smart, two-piece outfit, with high heels and pearls, to the arraignment, and she actually paused in the doorway and smiled as the flashbulbs went off around her.